INVASION!
"WE HAVE NO TIME FOR DISCUSSION."

Admiral Kirschbaum continued: "A sensor array at the Furies Point has been attacked by five ships of unknown origin. I'm ordering all available ships to the area at top speed."

Captain Jean-Luc Picard's hand tightened on his empty glass mug. He set it down before it could shatter in his grip. "We're on our way, Admiral."

"Good." The admiral's mouth tightened. "I hope I don't have to explain—"

"I understand the urgency, Admiral."

"Captain Picard," Admiral Kirschbaum said heavily, "if those ships are what we believe them to be, then we're at war."

Look for STAR TREK Fiction from Pocket Books

Star Trek: The Original Series

The Return
The Ashes of Eden
Federation
Sarek
Best Destiny
Shadows on the Sun
Probe
Prime Directive
The Lost Years
Star Trek VI: The Undiscovered Country
Star Trek V: The Final Frontier
Star Trek IV: The Voyage Home
Spock's World
Enterprise
Strangers from the Sky
Final Frontier

#1 Star Trek: The Motion Picture
#2 The Entropy Effect
#3 The Klingon Gambit
#4 The Covenant of the Crown
#5 The Prometheus Design
#6 The Abode of Life
#7 Star Trek II: The Wrath of Khan
#8 Black Fire
#9 Triangle
#10 Web of the Romulans
#11 Yesterday's Son
#12 Mutiny on the Enterprise
#13 The Wounded Sky
#14 The Trellisane Confrontation
#15 Corona
#16 The Final Reflection
#17 The Search for Spock
#18 My Enemy, My Ally
#19 The Tears of the Singers
#20 The Vulcan Academy Murders
#21 Uhura's Song
#22 Shadow Lord
#23 Ishmael
#24 Killing Time
#25 Dwellers in the Crucible
#26 Pawns and Symbols
#27 Mindshadow
#28 Crisis on Centaurus
#29 Dreadnought!
#30 Demons
#31 Battlestations!
#32 Chain of Attack

#33 Deep Domain
#34 Dreams of the Raven
#35 The Romulan Way
#36 How Much for Just the Planet?
#37 Bloodthirst
#38 The IDIC Epidemic
#39 Time for Yesterday
#40 Timetrap
#41 The Three-Minute Universe
#42 Memory Prime
#43 The Final Nexus
#44 Vulcan's Glory
#45 Double, Double
#46 The Cry of the Onlies
#47 The Kobayashi Maru
#48 Rules of Engagement
#49 The Pandora Principle
#50 Doctor's Orders
#51 Enemy Unseen
#52 Home Is the Hunter
#53 Ghost Walker
#54 A Flag Full of Stars
#55 Renegade
#56 Legacy
#57 The Rift
#58 Face of Fire
#59 The Disinherited
#60 Ice Trap
#61 Sanctuary
#62 Death Count
#63 Shell Game
#64 The Starship Trap
#65 Windows on a Lost World
#66 From the Depths
#67 The Great Starship Race
#68 Firestorm
#69 The Patrian Transgression
#70 Traitor Winds
#71 Crossroad
#72 The Better Man
#73 Recovery
#74 The Fearful Summons
#75 First Frontier
#76 The Captain's Daughter
#77 Twilight's End
#78 The Rings of Tautee
#79 Invasion 1: First Strike
#80 The Joy Machine
#81 Mudd in Your Eye

Star Trek: The Next Generation

Crossover
Kahless
Star Trek Generations
All Good Things
Q-Squared
Dark Mirror
Descent
The Devil's Heart
Imzadi
Relics
Reunion
Unification
Metamorphosis
Vendetta
Encounter at Farpoint

#1 Ghost Ship
#2 The Peacekeepers
#3 The Children of Hamlin
#4 Survivors
#5 Strike Zone
#6 Power Hungry
#7 Masks
#8 The Captains' Honor
#9 A Call to Darkness
#10 A Rock and a Hard Place
#11 Gulliver's Fugitives
#12 Doomsday World
#13 The Eyes of the Beholders
#14 Exiles
#15 Fortune's Light
#16 Contamination
#17 Boogeymen
#18 Q-in-Law
#19 Perchance to Dream
#20 Spartacus
#21 Chains of Command
#22 Imbalance
#23 War Drums
#24 Nightshade
#25 Grounded
#26 The Romulan Prize
#27 Guises of the Mind
#28 Here There Be Dragons
#29 Sins of Commission
#30 Debtors' Planet
#31 Foreign Foes
#32 Requiem
#33 Balance of Power
#34 Blaze of Glory
#35 Romulan Stratagem
#36 Into the Nebula
#37 The Last Stand
#38 Dragon's Honor
#39 Rogue Saucer
#40 Possession
#41 Invasion 2: The Soldiers of Fear
#42 Infiltrator
#43 A Fury Scorned
#44 The Death of Princes

Star Trek: Deep Space Nine

Trials and Tribble-ations
Warped
The Search
#1 Emissary
#2 The Siege
#3 Bloodletter
#4 The Big Game
#5 Fallen Heroes
#6 Betrayal
#7 Warchild
#8 Antimatter
#9 Proud Helios
#10 Valhalla
#11 Devil in the Sky
#12 The Laertian Gamble
#13 Station Rage
#14 The Long Night
#15 Objective: Bajor
#16 Invasion 3: Time's Enemy
#17 The Heart of the Warrior
#18 Saratoga
#19 The Tempest

Star Trek: Voyager

#1 Caretaker
#2 The Escape
#3 Ragnarok
#4 Violations
#5 Incident at Arbuk
#6 The Murdered Sun
#7 Ghost of a Chance
#8 Cybersong
#9 Invasion 4: The Final Fury
#10 Bless the Beasts

For orders other than by individual consumers, Pocket Books grants a discount on the purchase of **10 or more** copies of single titles for special markets or premium use. For further details, please write to the Vice-President of Special Markets, Pocket Books, 1633 Broadway, New York, NY 10019-6785, 8th Floor.

For information on how individual consumers can place orders, please write to Mail Order Department, Simon & Schuster Inc., 200 Old Tappan Road, Old Tappan, NJ 07675.

BOOK TWO

THE SOLDIERS OF FEAR

DEAN WESLEY SMITH AND KRISTINE KATHRYN RUSCH

INVASION! concept by John J. Ordover and Diane Carey

POCKET BOOKS
New York   London   Toronto   Sydney   Tokyo   Singapore

The sale of this book without its cover is unauthorized. If you purchased this book without a cover, you should be aware that it was reported to the publisher as "unsold and destroyed." Neither the author nor the publisher has received payment for the sale of this "stripped book."

This book is a work of fiction. Names, characters, places and incidents are products of the author's imagination or are used fictitiously. Any resemblance to actual events or locales or persons, living or dead, is entirely coincidental.

An *Original* Publication of POCKET BOOKS

POCKET BOOKS, a division of Simon & Schuster Inc.
1230 Avenue of the Americas, New York, NY 10020

Copyright © 1996 by Paramount Pictures. All Rights Reserved.

STAR TREK is a Registered Trademark of Paramount Pictures.

A VIACOM COMPANY

This book is published by Pocket Books, a division of Simon & Schuster Inc., under exclusive license from Paramount Pictures.

All rights reserved, including the right to reproduce this book or portions thereof in any form whatsoever. For information address Pocket Books, 1230 Avenue of the Americas, New York, NY 10020

ISBN: 0-671-54174-9

First Pocket Books printing July 1996

10 9 8 7

POCKET and colophon are registered trademarks of Simon & Schuster Inc.

Printed in the U.S.A.

For Jerry & Kathy Oltion

THE SOLDIERS OF FEAR

Chapter One

LIEUTENANT ROBERT C. YOUNG, Bobby to everyone who knew him, sat with his feet on the lip of the console before him. He had the stout build of an athlete and blond hair that sometimes got a little longer than Starfleet regulation allowed. He had modified the regulation chair so that it tilted backward easily, comfort being his highest priority. Life on Brundage Station was dull, routine, and his punishment for telling Admiral Kirschbaum that nothing in Starfleet compared with snow skiing down Exhibition in Sun Valley, Idaho. On Earth.

Bobby hadn't realized he was talking with an admiral at the time, only some pompous fool who seemed to believe that every officer aspired to interstellar travel. Bobby had gone to Starfleet Academy at the urgings of his mother, a dear woman who was afraid that Bobby would spend his entire life on the slopes of the sector's snow-covered mountains and therefore never achieve anything of importance. She was afraid he would die broke and without skills; he, on the other hand, believed skiing was skill enough for any man and more than enough to live a full life.

But he loved his mother. He had joined. And because he had been a good cadet who had done well in officer training, he had gone to one too many off-campus parties, and insulted the wrong admiral.

Friends later told him that if he had made the same comment to Admiral Zlitch, she would have laughed, agreed, and then compared the latest in ski-boot technology with him.

Admiral Kirschbaum had merely said, *If you find all of the galaxy boring, young man, I have the assignment for you.*

Brundage Station, armpit of the galaxy. Some wag—another skier, obviously—fifty years before had given the station the Brundage nickname after a famous ski hill in McCall, Idaho, because, rumor had it, Brundage stood on the slippery slope to nowhere.

Brundage was now officially known as Brundage Point Listening Station. Sometimes, in the oldest references to the station, it was called the Furies Point Defensive Listening Station. Over eighty years before, some incredibly powerful beings had come through a point in space near the post, and had eventually declared themselves the enemy. In coming they had destroyed an entire solar system, the remains of which now swirled slowly in the screens. Bobby had seen the old holos, read the old materials, and studied everything he could about the battle that had taken place deep in Klingon space, not because he was interested, but because it was required.

Starfleet believed the Furies would come again.

They hadn't, of course.

Other lieutenants had run Brundage Station, shifting to real duty after three years of service, always swearing they would never watch an empty part of space again.

Bobby had been here two years. After three days, he had been ready to write the admiral an apology. Now he understood what the wily old man had been about. The admiral had given Bobby easy duty to show him that truly active duty was better than sitting on his duff all day, guarding the site where a supposed enemy had appeared the year his grandfather was born.

In most ways, the duty was like any other. The station was small, and sometimes ships stopped. Bobby commanded a team of three others. In addition to the Furies Point, they monitored forty unmanned listening posts, most along the Klingon border. Occasionally they saw something. Usually they didn't.

His evening watch promised to be no different.

He had holographic brochures of several nearby ski resorts in his room, including a low-grav, highly specialized ski center on Regal III. He planned to go through all of them before he slept tonight. His first extended vacation was coming up, and he planned to enjoy every minute of it.

The observation room always seemed big to him, even though it was the size of a shuttlecraft's piloting area. The two viewscreens, opened to the vastness of space, gave an illusion of size. So did the constant emptiness and the inactivity on the control board.

He had some diagnostics to run through, but they could wait. His evening shift had a routine that kept him awake and functioning through the long, lonely hours.

A red light flashed on the control board. The light intermittently illuminated the sole on his black regulation boot. He frowned, sighed, and sat forward.

A malfunction.

At least it would give him something to do.

But the light flashing wasn't the one he expected to see.

Something had triggered the warning devices at one of the listening posts.

His hands shook with excitement, and he had to remind himself that the last time this happened, it had been caused by space debris in the listening post's delicate trigger mechanism.

His fingers flew over the console as he ran a quick systems check.

Everything was in order at both the station and the outpost. But there seemed to be a slight drop in the mass of the outpost. That made no sense at all. How could the mass of an outpost drop?

He tapped his comm badge. "Wong! Airborne! Judy! I got something happening up here."

"On our way," Wong's clear voice came through the comm. "Run the diagnostics."

"Already done," he snapped back. Wong had no right giving orders, even if he was the only one with engineering experience.

But for good measure, Bobby ran a second level of diagnostics. No sense making a mistake when he had time. It would take the others a few moments to get to the control room. They had been in their quarters. Bobby always took the graveyard shift, never liking the concept of artificial night or artificial day.

The second diagnostics checked as well. The mass of the listening post continued to drop slightly, even though that seemed impossible. Something was clearly going on out there. Just what was the question.

He let the air whistle through his teeth. Behind him the door hissed open and Wong, a slender man twice Bobby's age, hurried in.

Wong grabbed the empty chair beside Bobby's, leaned over the console, and ran a third set of diagnostics, his fingers flying over the board almost faster than the eye could follow.

"Mine already checked out," Bobby said. "Both times."

"Hmm," Wong said, apparently unimpressed. When the diagnostic finished, he said, "That makes no sense," and began a series of other tests that Bobby had only heard about. Bobby didn't stop him; better to be careful. Bobby's mouth was dry. He had never thought about what he would do if something real triggered one of the outpost alarms.

Judy hurried in next. Her long silver hair was still down, and she wore a robe over her nonregulation lounging clothes. She was tiny, in her mid-fifties, and the unofficial leader of the group. She had two fully grown children, both in Starfleet, and she liked to cook. Sometimes they even called her "Mom" and she never objected.

"What have we got?" she asked, sliding into the chair to Bobby's left.

"Something triggered one of the posts."

Wong grunted, and started yet another set of diagnostics.

"Have you run tests?"

Bobby glared at her. Did everyone think he was incompetent? "Twice," he told her.

"Hmmm," she said, as unimpressed as Wong had been.

Then Airborne burst in the door, his hair sticking up at all angles. He, like Bobby, had a tendency toward wildness. Airborne liked to jump—out of anything moving, safe or not. His tall, lanky frame had survived more broken bones than Bobby could imagine. Over the past year Bobby had been convincing Airborne that jumping off things while on skis was more fun than anything he'd tried. But Airborne had been reluctant to put in all the time learning how to ski, just to jump off rocks. He said he could do that without skis.

"More space junk in the listening posts?" Airborne asked, rubbing a hand over his sleep-puffy face.

"No," Wong said curtly. "I'm reading a major drop in mass. There's something really strange happening out there."

His tone took the levity out of the room. Bobby forced himself to swallow.

"It's for real, then," he said. He leaned forward.

"I'll get Starfleet Command," Judy said, sliding her chair toward the communications console.

"Yeah," Wong said.

Airborne came up behind him, and placed both

hands on the back of the chair. "Tell us now, Wong. No sense grandstanding."

"He's not," Bobby said. Wong never tried to take advantage of the others. He just usually thought the others were incompetent.

"Something has just destroyed the warning device at Point 473," Wong said.

Judy paused in midpunch, her hand extended over the console. "Destroyed?"

Bobby ignored her. He was pulling all the information he could on the point. "Information on 473 coming up on screen," he said.

"We don't need it," Airborne said, sinking into the only remaining chair.

Bobby glanced at him. Airborne's normally dark skin had turned a sickly shade of gray.

"The Furies Point," Wong said, his voice sounding to Bobby as if he were going to be suddenly sick.

"No," Bobby said. Sure, they'd all been prepped on the Furies battle, that was a condition of serving at the post, but the Furies tale sounded like one of those grandiose stories skiers told when they got off the hill, trying to make a normal run seem like something special.

Judy was punching the console frantically.

Airborne was double-checking Wong's information. Airborne had a thing about the Furies. He liked to goad the others with stories of them when the tour got too routine.

"Damn," he whispered.

Bobby didn't want to know. But he had to. "Did you scan the area?"

Airborne shook his head. "Just confirmed the point

number," he said. "The listening post is gone and we got some strange things happening out there."

Before he lost complete control of the situation, Bobby had to do something. "Well, then, keep scanning it. I want to know exactly what's going on."

"I don't," Airborne whispered. But he bent over the console just the same.

His fingers flew over the console.

"You got Starfleet yet?" Bobby asked Judy.

"No, sir," she said, automatically slipping into protocol. Bless her.

Wong let out a breath. "There seems to be a very large temporal disturbance," he said, "almost as if a black hole has formed where the beacon used to be. Only it's much more than a black hole. More like a tear in space."

"Oh, man," Airborne said. He was hunched over his console. "Bobby—ah, Lieutenant, sir—I've got a reading near there of five ships. They just appeared."

"What?" Bobby hadn't seen any ships a moment before. He stopped the scrolling information, and turned the screen back toward Point 473. Even on full magnification, he still couldn't see anything.

"I've got the same thing, sir," Wong said. "There seem to be five ships surrounding the disturbance, all in stationary positions. And they're huge!"

"Can you identify the ships?" Bobby asked, making sure to keep his voice level.

Wong shook his head. Bobby scooted his chair over and looked at the readings. He'd never seen anything like them before. At least not in all the manuals he'd studied.

THE SOLDIERS OF FEAR

"Two have left position and are headed this way," Wong said.

"How long?" Bobby asked.

Wong glanced at the panel. "Three minutes."

"They've come back," Airborne said, his voice trembling. Bobby watched as Airborne seemed to shake himself, then take a deep breath.

"I've reached Starfleet, sir," Judy said.

Bobby let out breath he hadn't realized he was holding. "Scramble this message," he said.

He waited the two beats until Judy nodded that it was done; then he started. "This is Brundage Point Observation Station. We have a Priority One Emergency."

Wong and Judy both gasped, and Bobby knew why. A Priority One Emergency was the highest there was in Starfleet. But if Airborne was right, then they would need all the help they could get.

"Two minutes," Wong said. His voice was shaking.

Admiral Kirschbaum's face filled the screen. Bobby was actually relieved to see his old nemesis. "Go ahead, Lieutenant."

Bobby squared his shoulders and made himself speak with authority, not panic, even though he could feel the rising tension in the room. "The beacon at the Furies Point was destroyed. Our scans showed a small drop in mass of the beacon before it vanished. Now a large temporal disturbance has formed where the beacon used to be and five very large ships of unknown origin have taken up positions around it. Two are headed this way and will be within firing distance shortly."

Bobby watched as Admiral Kirschbaum's face went pale and he swallowed hard. "Five ships?"

Bobby nodded. "Yes, sir. Five."

Admiral Kirschbaum leaned toward the screen. "Can you evacuate before they arrive?"

Bobby glanced at Wong. He shook his head.

"There's no time, sir," Bobby said. "Those two ships are almost on us."

Kirschbaum straightened and nodded once, the closest thing Bobby would ever get to an apology. "Remember your training, Lieutenant. Anything that comes from Point 473 must be considered a Furies vessel. Consider those ships hostile, and their approach an act of war. Respond accordingly. Understand? Relay everything you are getting through this channel for as long as you can."

"Done," Judy said beside Bobby. "Starfleet is getting it all. And I've downloaded all our logs."

Bobby glanced up at the two black ships growing on the screen beside Admiral Kirschbaum's face. They were like no ships he'd ever seen, not even in the old holos of the first Furies attack. These ships were black with swept-back wings. They looked like a bird in a dive for a kill.

"An act of war," Bobby repeated. He clenched his fists. "Yes, sir."

"Good luck to you all," Kirschbaum said, and cut the picture.

The silence in the room was louder than anything Bobby had ever heard. Then Airborne put his head in his hands.

They didn't have time for despair. Bobby had to act.

"Get those shields up and all weapons at ready," he ordered.

"I'm still feeding all information and telemetry," Judy said.

Bobby reached into the panel below and removed the emergency phasers. He found only three. He would give them to his staff. He was the only one in uniform. He already had a phaser.

"Both ships have stopped," Wong said as Bobby laid a phaser on the panel beside him. "I can't seem to get a scan on them."

Suddenly a red beam shot from what looked like the beak of one ship.

The station's shields flared a bright blue, then red, then white. The station shook and tumbled as if riding a wave. Bobby gripped the console. "Report!" he snapped.

"Screens are down," Judy said as the firing broke off. "They seem to be hailing us."

"On screen."

Judy nodded. The screen cleared. In the second before the image appeared, Bobby felt as if a bolt of sheer terror struck him in the back of the head and shimmered down his spine. His first real command. The feeling had to be because this was his first real command moment.

He forced himself to breathe, but the air caught in his lungs as the terror filled him.

Then the blankness on the screen resolved itself into a large scarlet face, with a black snout, and ram's horns instead of ears. The eyes were long and narrow, and in the corners feeding maggots looked like tears.

Judy gasped, Airborne buried his head in his arms,

and Wong pushed his chair back as if the thing could come out of the screen and attack him.

Bobby's fists were clenched so hard that his nails were digging into his palm. The terror in the room seemed to shimmer and grow as if it were a real thing.

Bobby forced himself to breathe. Again he failed.

The creature on the screen opened its mouth. Silver saliva dripped from sharp, pointed teeth. "Surrender," the creature said in a voice so deep, so powerful, that Bobby could feel it in his toes. "Or be destroyed."

Then the image winked out.

Bobby didn't move. He couldn't. The sheer terror he was feeling had him frozen in place. But he had to move, for the sake of the others.

Judy and Wong were still staring at the screen, their mouths wide. Airborne raised his head. His carefree attitude was completely gone. His eyes were dark holes in his face.

"History is repeating itself," he whispered. "For the second time in a hundred years the devil has opened the gates to hell."

Bobby took two quick breaths, then said, "And for the second time we'll close it." He made his voice sound as firm and confident as he could, as he imagined a perfect Starfleet officer would do. But he didn't believe a word he said.

Chapter Two

A DROP OF SWEAT ran down Will Riker's face. He gripped the control stick of his jet firmly with both hands and pulled into a steep climb away from the bluish green ocean waters below. A stream of bright red laser fire flashed past his cockpit as the force of his climb pinned him into his seat.

He hadn't used these old atmosphere dogfight simulations since his days in the Academy, and his lack of practice was showing. He was ranked as one of the best space pilots in Starfleet and the best on the *Enterprise*, but these old dogfight holodeck simulations used ancient jets at low planet altitudes and kept score with laser hits. Twenty hits and you were considered downed.

The screen in front of him lit up bright red, indicating he'd taken a hit on his port wing. "Damn," he said softly, swinging his plane over into a tight barrel roll before the stream of laser fire could cause more damage. A full-second burst of laser fire in the center of a plane would easily count as more than twenty hits and end the game.

This time he managed to escape with only one hit.

"That's fifteen for me," his opponent, Lieutenant Sam Redbay, said through the headphones, as Redbay's plane streaked past on Riker's starboard. "You're out of shape, Will."

"Out of practice," Riker said, slamming his plane into a sharp turn in an effort to get Redbay back into his sights. "Just out of practice in these old things. Program a space dogfight and we'll see who's out of shape."

"Excuses, excuses," Redbay's voice came back. "We'll try that tomorrow."

Riker laughed as he pulled up behind Redbay's streaking jet and got him in his sights. "That's a deal."

Riker could see his old friend laughing at him right now. Redbay was a tall, thin redheaded man who moved slowly, as if the world around him was in too much of a hurry. He laughed a lot, and his freckle-faced grin was infectious to most people around him, including Riker.

The red light on the board showed he had a computer lock on Redbay's plane. "Now," Riker said, and fired, but he was an instant late. Redbay took his plane down and twisted, moving away from the stream of laser fire from Riker.

No hits. Again he'd missed. He had to admit, his old friend was good. Very good.

THE SOLDIERS OF FEAR

Riker shook his head and attempted to follow the other jet at the steep downward angle. At one time he and Redbay were evenly matched fighters at this holodeck simulation game. In their last year at the Academy, they had rented the holosuites and programmed dogfight after dogfight. And with each fight, not only did their skill and reflexes get better, but the stakes rose, too. It started with bragging rights, then lunches, then escalated to cleaning rooms. Their last match, the day before graduation, Riker had won and promised Redbay a rematch.

But until today, that rematch had not been possible. Now, since Redbay's assignment to the *Enterprise,* it was possible. And Riker had to admit he was enjoying this, even though he was losing badly.

"More excuses, Will?" Redbay's voice came back strong as his plane flashed past. Riker could imagine his friend's red hair and his freckled face grinning. He was probably doing everything in his power to not laugh out loud.

"All right," Riker said, laughing instead. "Excuses, then. But I won't make them for long."

Redbay's choked laugh let his enjoyment come back clearly to Riker. Then Redbay said, "Actually, Will, I wouldn't have expected you to be up on the latest atmosphere-dogfight techniques. I can't imagine how you'd have time, being first officer on a ship like *Enterprise.*"

Riker heard and understood the mixture of envy and admiration in Redbay's tone. They had been on the same career track at the Academy. Their differences were minor: Redbay had taken two more piloting points than Riker; Riker had been evaluated higher in the politics of persuasion. Their classmates had always seen a rivalry between them, but no real rivalry had actually existed, even in these made-up dogfights. They had been best of friends, and would never have gotten as far as fast without each other.

Then they separated, Redbay to years of test-piloting the latest high-speed shuttles for Starfleet, Riker to work on starships. It wasn't until a reunion several years back, when Riker had asked Redbay why he hadn't gone into starships, that Redbay leaned back, frowned, and said, *I was planning to. I just lost track of it.*

You still can, my friend, Riker had said, *but if you wait too much longer, you'll be off the career track.*

Redbay had nodded, and the next thing Riker knew, Redbay was flying his first mission on the *Starship Farragut*. His skills and deportment led to numerous promotions, until he got the plum: a berth on the Federation's flagship, the *Enterprise*.

"With you here, I'll make the time," Riker said. "You never know when it might come in handy. But tomorrow we add in space combat."

"Deal," Redbay's voice said. "But in the meantime, you might want to watch your ass."

Riker slammed his plane hard to the left as a string of red laser fire flashed past. Then, in a quick thrust, he pulled his plane up and into a tight loop. For a moment he wasn't sure if it was going to work; then Redbay's plane dropped into sight and quickly into his scope.

Computer lock. Riker fired.

Redbay moved up and left, but not before Riker caught him with a shot.

"That's ten for me," Will said.

"You were setting me up," Redbay's voice came back. This time the laughter and enjoyment were clear in his voice.

"Excuses, Sam?" Riker asked sweetly.

"You're still behind," Redbay said. "And just wait until tomorrow in a no-grav battle. I'll show you a stunt or two."

Riker laughed. "You may be famous for the Redbay Maneuver, but don't think I don't know about it. And how it's done."

Redbay laughed. "Been studying the books, huh? That's only one of many maneuvers I have up my sleeve. You don't test-pilot for Starfleet for as many years as I did and not learn a few tricks."

"I won't be as easy as you think," Riker said, laughing as he rolled his plane into a tight turn, trying to spot where Redbay had gone. But the other plane was nowhere in sight.

The his comm badge trilled.

He let go of the stick with one hand and tapped it. "Riker."

"Commander." Captain Picard's rich voice sounded strained. "I need you in my ready room. Immediately."

"Yes, sir," Riker said. "I'll be right there. Computer. End simulation."

The blue air, white clouds, and world around Riker vanished, leaving him sitting inside a sphere suspended in midair over the floor of the holodeck. Beside him was another sphere. Inside, Redbay was pulling off his helmet and undoing his seat straps. He glanced over at Riker and then back down to finish the work on his straps. He looked serious. Very serious. He too had caught the captain's tone.

Redbay climbed out and dropped to the floor. He was sweating and his workout suit was sticking to him. Behind him, the sphere dissolved. "We'll have to finish this another time."

Riker grinned as he climbed out of his control sphere. "Have the computer save this game. I can still recover."

"That's what I'm afraid of," Redbay said, patting Riker on the back.

Riker nodded, then exited the holodeck, the game already forgotten.

The air in the corridor was cool, and it made him shiver despite the sweat that coated him. Everything had been fine when he left the bridge a little while ago. He wondered what could have rattled Captain Picard so quickly.

Or for that matter, what could have rattled Captain Picard at all.

The message from Starfleet had been curt. Assemble the senior officers. Prepare for a Priority One Message at 0900. Picard hadn't heard a Security One Message since the Borg were headed for Earth. The highest-level code. Extreme emergency. Override all other protocols. Abandon all previous orders.

Something serious had happened.

He leaned over the replicator. He had only a moment until the senior officers arrived.

"Earl Grey, hot," he said, and the empty space on the replicator shimmered before a clear glass mug filled with steaming tea appeared. He gripped the mug

THE SOLDIERS OF FEAR

by its handle and took a sip, allowing the liquid to calm him.

He had no clue what this might be about, and that worried him. He always kept abreast of activity in the quadrant. He knew the subtlest changes in the political breeze. The Romulans had been quiet of late; the Cardassians had been cooperating with Bajor. No new ships had been sighted in any sector, and no small rebel groups were taking their rebellions into space. Maybe it was the Klingons?

He should have had an inkling.

His door hissed open and Beverly Crusher came in. Geordi La Forge was beside her, and Data followed. The doctor and Geordi looked worried. Data had his usual look of expectant curiosity.

The door hadn't even had a chance to close before Deanna Troi came in. She was in uniform, a habit she had started just recently. Worf saw her and left his post on the bridge, following her to his position in the meeting room.

Only Commander Riker was missing, and he was the one most needed. Picard couldn't access the message without him.

It was 0859.

Then the door hissed a final time and Will Riker came in. His workout clothes were sweat-streaked, his hair damp. He had a towel draped over his shoulder, which he instantly took off and wadded into a ball in his hands.

"Sorry, sir," he said, "but from your voice, I figured I wouldn't have time to change."

"You were right, Will," Picard said. "We're about to get a message from Starfleet Command. They requested all senior officers be in attendance—"

The screen on the desk snapped on with the Federation's symbol, indicating a scrambled communiqué.

"Message sent to Picard, Captain, *U.S.S. Enterprise,* and the senior members of his staff," said the generic female computer voice. "Please confirm identity and status."

Picard placed a hand on the screen on his desk. "Picard, Jean-Luc, Captain, *U.S.S. Enterprise,* Security Code 1-B58A."

When the security protocol ended, the Federation symbol disappeared from the screen, replaced by the battle-scarred face of Admiral Kirschbaum. His features had tightened in that emotionless yet urgent expression the oldest—and best—commanders had in times of emergency.

"Jean-Luc. We have no time for discussion. A sensor array at the Furies Point has been destroyed. Five ships of unknown origin are there now, along with what seems to be a small black hole. Two of the ships attacked the Brundage Station. We lost contact and don't know the outcome as yet. I'm ordering all available ships to the area at top speed."

The Furies Point. Picard needed no more explanation than that. From the serious expressions all around him, he could tell that his staff understood as well.

Picard's hand tightened on the empty glass mug. He set it down before he could shatter it with his grip. "We're on our way, Admiral."

"Good." The admiral's mouth tightened. "I hope I don't have to explain—"

"I understand the urgency, Admiral."

"If those ships are what we believe them to be, we're at war, Jean-Luc."

How quickly it happened. One moment he was on the bridge, preparing for the day's duties. The next, this.

"I will act accordingly, Admiral."

The admiral nodded. "You don't have much time, Jean-Luc. I will contact you in one hour with transmissions from the attack on the Brundage outpost. It will give you and your officers some idea of what you are facing."

"Thank you, Admiral," Picard said.

"Godspeed, Jean-Luc."

"And to you," Picard said, but by the time the words were out, the admiral's image had winked away.

Picard felt as if someone had punched him in the stomach.

The Furies.

The rest of the staff looked as stunned as he felt.

Except for Data. When Picard met his gaze, Data said quietly, "It will take us two-point-three-eight hours at warp nine to reach Brundage Station."

"Then lay in a course, Mr. Data, and engage. We don't have time to waste."

Chapter Three

THE LIGHT SEEMED TO GROW in intensity inside his eyelids as Bobby struggled to wake up. That had been one terrific nightmare. The Brundage Station attacked and overrun by the devil. Wow. He'd have to tell Judy about that.

He was hot.

He pushed at the blankets, but he was uncovered. Then he moaned. He would have to get up now and fix the environmental controls. Someone had probably messed with his room as a joke. The other members of the crew knew that Bobby Young hated temperatures above thirty-two degrees Celsius. He also hated humidity, and the faint smell of sulfur was making his nose itch.

He felt melted to the bed, as if his body made a permanent indentation in the mattress. A band tightened across his chest. Next time he would warn them; his lungs seemed to expand in the heat, and it was not a pleasant sensation. Maybe he would even order them, as their commanding officer, not to play games anymore.

The light grew in intensity, so that the protection of his eyelids felt thin and unimportant.

His bed was softer than this one, and he realized that no one could mess with his environmental controls, not since Wong had made his room a virtual sauna. After that Bobby had put three different levels of security devices on all his personal effects, including room controls.

A chill ran down his spine despite the heat. The feeling of the nightmare returned, thick and heavy.

"What in the—?" He tried to sit up, but the band on his chest turned into a restraint. He tried to grab at it with his hands, and found that his arms were imprisoned across the biceps.

He forced his eyes open. The light was blinding and he couldn't see beyond it. He had never seen a light so bright. His eyes watered, and a stabbing pain shot through his head. He tried to bring an arm up, but the restraints caught him.

He couldn't protect himself.

If this was a practical joke, it had better end quickly.

Although deep down, he knew it wasn't.

He swallowed, took a deep breath, and tried to keep the panic out of his voice. "Judy? Airborne? Wong? What's going on?"

No one answered. His shiver grew. He took a deep

breath of air that tasted of sulfur and was so humid that it burned his lungs. It hadn't been that bad a moment before. He coughed, jerking against the restraints, feeling bruises form on his chest. The heat grew more intense, and he almost thought he felt the lick of flames on his legs.

"Wong?" Bobby tried again, only this time his voice wobbled.

Laughter startled him. Deep, throaty laughter that made him want to back away, only he couldn't. He was strapped in place.

"I am afraid your friends can no longer hear you."

The voice sounded mechanical and forced. Suddenly the bright light shut off, and Bobby slowly opened his eyes. Green, red, and black spots danced in front of him. Behind the spots, he could see a figure. He squinted, and his eyes adjusted.

A face came into view.

A red, smiling face.

A face covered with maggots that crawled in and out of its long slanted eyes.

A face with a black snout.

A face with ram's horns in place of ears.

Bobby screamed.

A red hand the texture of leather covered his mouth. Long yellow fingernails scratched his skin.

The hand smelled of rotted flesh. Bobby tried to twist away, but he couldn't.

"You may scream only when I allow you to," the creature said. "I enjoy screaming—in its proper place. Now is not the time. You will be quiet, won't you?"

Bobby swallowed, trying to keep his gorge from rising.

"Won't you?"

Bobby nodded.

"Good. When I release your mouth, we will have a civil discussion." The creature's voice was deep and cultured, at odds with its appearance, and somehow more menacing because of it. This was no monster that Bobby was facing. This was something evil. Intelligent and evil. And it knew how to get at him, like some nightmare loosed by his own mind.

"Won't we?"

Bobby nodded again. The creature's breath was as foul as its skin. The creature removed its hand. Bobby's skin crawled where the creature had touched him. Despite his best efforts not to, Bobby wiped his mouth against his shoulder.

The creature laughed. Heat from its mouth touched him like tiny flames.

Bobby shuddered. He tried to hold his body still, but he had never felt such an urge to run in his entire life. The creature's mouth was full of long sharp teeth, and threads of saliva showed each time it parted its lips.

The saliva shimmered green.

"What do you want from me?" Bobby asked. He needed to gain control of this situation. If he could get the creature to tell him what it needed, maybe he could leave then.

That was the only solution he could think of. All his Starfleet training had abandoned him except for a last, tenuous grasp on the panic building within.

Somehow this thing had breached all of his internal defenses and made him feel like a frightened child again instead of an officer.

"Such an original question." The creature grinned at him, revealing those awful pointed teeth and that green-tinged saliva. Bobby tried to suppress his recoil. "Isn't it?"

"We were told we should always expect it of humans," another voice answered. A face appeared behind the creature's. An almost human face, but not quite. She had stunning features: oval eyes, a narrow nose, and high cheekbones. But Bobby barely noticed them.

His gaze was on her hair. Or what should have been her hair. Instead the strands moved on their own. It took only a moment for him to realize that he wasn't seeing hair, but small, writhing snakes that hissed and snapped at him.

Poisonous snakes.

Rattlers, cobras, copperheads.

She smiled. She knew what he was looking at. She touched the snakes almost as if trying to make sure they were in place and perfect.

"What do we want from you?" she asked as she leaned closer to him. The creature leaned with her. "Simple. We want to know your fear. You see, we like your fear. We enjoy it. And we want to use it." She laughed and the snakes surrounding her head moved even faster.

A maggot fell from the creature's eyes onto Bobby's face.

Bobby screamed, trying to shake it off. The creature

laughed as it bent over and pulled the intense bright light back over Bobby's face.

"Now," the voice said. "Tell us what we want to know. Give us all your fear."

And into the bright, intense white light, Bobby screamed again.

And again.

Chapter Four

AT 1000, PICARD'S SENIOR STAFF had reassembled in the conference room. In the last hour, Data had ingested all the historical information he could find on the Furies. Riker had prepared the crew for the possibility of war. Troi had advised families on how to protect the children from the difficulties the starship would face.

The list went on. Picard knew that each task had just begun when he needed the staff in the conference room again. La Forge had managed to get the engineering crew to double-check the engines and weaponry; Dr. Crusher had revamped sickbay into an emergency center; and Worf had prepared his security team. But none of those jobs could be finished in an hour. To prepare for battle of this scale took days, sometimes weeks.

THE SOLDIERS OF FEAR

During the last hour Picard had studied Captain Kirk's personal logs from the first *Starship Enterprise,* and the information he found unnerved him. Kirk had been called in by a panicked Klingon admiral who felt he needed one devil to fight another. As it turned out, the Klingon had been right. Kirk and the original *Enterprise* had defeated the huge Fury ship. But just one Fury ship destroyed much of a Klingon fleet before Kirk managed to win.

Picard glanced around. His officers all sat at the conference table. His seat at the head was empty, because he couldn't sit. He had to pace.

The transmission from Brundage Station had just played on the screen. Protocol had obviously been lax on Brundage—not unusual on a distant outpost—but the four station members had worked with professionalism once the crisis became apparent.

Except for the fear they had all displayed when that horrible visage appeared on their screen. Picard had understood their fear. That face, vaguely similar to the demons portrayed in European artwork and sculpture, had sent a shiver through him. But he had held that feeling back. He had seen worse things in his time.

How the crew of the Brundage station reacted bothered him at a deep level. Those reactions were not normal for trained Starfleet officers.

The view of the Furies' descent on the station, and of the subsequent attack, had left him with a restless energy—one he wouldn't have time to vent, since he knew the admiral would appear on screen at any moment.

The conference room was silent. That in itself was

unusual. His staff would normally have taken the time afforded by the delay in transmission to discuss what they had just seen.

Then the screen filled with the admiral's face. His skin was ashen, his eyes hollow points. That tape had unnerved Picard after one viewing. He didn't know how he would have felt after several.

His gaze met the admiral's, and an understanding carried across the light-years.

"Even though the ships you saw are radically different in design and shape from the first Fury ship, we have no doubt that we are facing the Furies," Admiral Kirschbaum said without preamble. "I don't need to tell you what this means."

Picard nodded. He was turned away from his staff, but he heard nothing from them.

The admiral's lips tightened. His skin seemed to have lines where it hadn't had any earlier in the day. "The *Enterprise* will be the first ship on the scene, Captain. We need information about the Furies. We need to know how many ships they have sent through the Furies Point. And if the point is a wormhole, as James T. Kirk and the first crew of the *Enterprise* suspected, then we need to know all we can about that anomaly. It seems to interact only with the Furies, which isn't like any wormhole we know."

"Either that, or they know when it will open," Picard said. "And they were waiting for it."

The admiral nodded. "The *Starships Madison* and *Idaho* are six hours away. They will arrive as quickly as they can. There are two smaller Federation ships that will join you, but they will be hours behind the starships. Don't count on them."

THE SOLDIERS OF FEAR

Three starships against five Fury ships. From what Picard had read in Kirk's logs, that would not be anywhere near enough if it came down to a fight.

"For the moment," the admiral said, "that's all we can spare. We will be setting up fallback lines of defense in case you have no success."

"I understand," Picard said. And he did understand. The *Enterprise*'s proximity to the Furies Point was the luck of the draw. It meant, though, that Picard's ship and his crew would be the first line of defense in a war that would be difficult to win.

Cannon fodder was what his ancestors called that position.

The admiral knew it too. "Captain, do your best to negotiate, discover what they want. Kirk had some success with that the first time around. His personal logs report he felt that Vergo Zennor of the Fury ship *Rath* was his friend."

"I have read Kirk's reports and logs."

The admiral nodded. "Good, but I must be clear on one point. If there's a way to close that wormhole, take it. No matter what the cost."

The chill Picard had felt on viewing that tape grew. He always knew commanding the *Enterprise* might come to this. He was willing to take those risks, but like any commander he always hoped he would never have to.

No matter what the cost.

And only three starships against all the power of the Furies.

"We will do everything we can, sir," Picard said. "The Klingons are nearby. Have they been contacted?"

The admiral grimaced. "They have, but after their first run-in with these monsters, I doubt—"

"The Klingons will fight." Worf growled the words. "I guarantee it."

"Mr. Worf," Picard said. His officers knew better than to speak out of turn.

"It's all right, Captain," Admiral Kirshbaum said. "I understand that Klingon honor is at stake here. We are counting on that. We are hoping that they will be able to overcome their memories of that first battle, and their fears. Indeed, we are hoping for help from a number of quarters. But I am afraid, Jean-Luc, that this will not change the fact that you will be on the scene first. Whatever you do will affect the future of this sector."

"I understand, Admiral," Picard said. "But there is one more matter."

The admiral nodded, as if he knew what Picard was going to say.

"Where is the Furies' lifepod containing the poppets?"

Around the room Picard could hear his staff moving, stirring, wondering just what he was talking about. But the admiral knew about the poppets from the first Fury ship. The Furies, it seemed, carried poppets, images of themselves stuffed full of pieces of their lives. Vergo Zennor had filled a lifepod with all the poppets of the crew of the first Fury ship and, right before the ship exploded, sent the lifepod into space. Kirk picked the poppets up and had them stored, waiting for just this time.

"They are being picked up from storage by the *Starship Idaho*. Use them as you see fit."

THE SOLDIERS OF FEAR

"Understood," Picard said.

"Good luck, Jean-Luc," the admiral said.

"Thank you, sir."

The admiral's image winked out.

Picard tugged on his shirt and turned to face his staff. Worf was glowering. "Captain, I apologize—"

"You were out of line, Mr. Worf," Picard said. "But the admiral understood, as did I. We may be heading into one of the most difficult battles we have ever faced."

Picard paced back and forth, talking. "One Fury ship nearly defeated the entire Klingon fleet the first time. It was only through the ingenuity of the original *Enterprise* crew that that ship was defeated. Captain Kirk's logs warn that the Furies are extremely intelligent and very powerful. He said, quite explicitly, that he believed the tactics he used eighty years ago cannot be used in any future attack. He believed that if the Furies returned, they would return stronger, smarter, and even more prepared than they had been before."

Picard took a deep breath and went on. "It is thought that complete information about our cultures and capabilities was sent back to the Furies' homeworld before their first ship, *Rath,* was destroyed. They know as much about us as we do about them."

He went on. "Federation tacticians have speculated that when or if the Furies returned, their technology would be equal to or greater than our own. We must be prepared for this. We are going against an enemy that is both cunning and advanced. We must be careful never to underestimate them."

Deanna Troi's hands were folded tightly. Geordi La Forge was toying nervously with his VISOR. Riker was tapping his fingers on the conference table. They all stared at him.

Only Data seemed calm.

"We only have another hour," Picard said. "In that time, I want you to remind your staff about the Furies' effect. The way they look can stir buried fears. Unlike the first *Enterprise,* we are prepared. The Furies may try to use our fear of them against us, but they will not succeed."

His officers stared at him, their gazes intense and focused.

"I want you all to use the files. Mr. La Forge, I want you to analyze the Kirk-Furies battle from an engineering perspective. Their first ship had the ability to use energy from weapons fired at it. I want to know how to counteract that if these new ships can do the same."

La Forge nodded.

Picard turned to Data. "Mr. Data, review the myths from every culture represented on this ship. Deanna, work with Data."

"Yes, sir," Data said. Deanna only nodded.

"Mr. Worf, you and Commander Riker will study the original battle from a tactical standpoint. No use repeating the same mistakes. And watch how the *Rath* responded. They may have a tactic we can use against them."

"Yes, sir," both Worf and Riker said at the same time.

"Very well, people," Picard said, moving over behind his chair. "Let's get to our stations. We have a great deal of work to do in a very short time."

The officers stood as a unit and filed out the door.

No conversation, no joviality, no conviviality. Only a determination to survive the next few hours.

They would need all the determination they had. If the research done since the first ship appeared was correct, the Furies had once ruled all of this sector of space. They had somehow been pushed out and only luck and Captain Kirk had kept them from returning the first time.

Now they were trying again.

As he watched his senior officers leave, he silently wished he could talk to Captain Kirk. Somehow Kirk had defeated hell itself and closed the door. Now that door had opened again. And unless it was slammed shut, the old term "hell on earth" would take on an entirely new meaning.

Or a very old one.

Chapter Five

RIKER'S BACK ITCHED. Even though he grabbed a moment to change into his uniform, he hadn't been able to shower off the sweat from his mock dogfight with Redbay since the crisis began. He felt as if he had been on the bridge for days instead of hours.

Deanna would say it was easier to concentrate on the minor discomfort than the problems ahead.

She would probably be right.

He had been on edge ever since he saw that tape from Brundage Station.

The others had too. Captain Picard was unusually silent. Worf was even more taciturn than usual. But it was Deanna that Riker worried about. As she had left the conference room, she had had a preoccupied look, as if she were concentrating on voices within instead of events without.

She and Data were working in the science officer's station, and occasionally Riker glanced over from his chair beside the captain.

"Brundage Station is within scanner range," Worf said, his deep voice booming from the security station behind Riker. "The station appears to be undamaged."

The captain sat up straighter. The news had obviously surprised him. It had surprised Riker too. From what he had seen on the transmission from the Brundage Station, the Furies attacked first. Riker assumed that when the transmission to Starfleet had been cut off, the station had been destroyed. Obviously the captain had thought the same thing.

"Put it on screen, Mr. Worf."

The captain stood and took two steps toward the screen as if he were going to have a conversation with whatever appeared. He had been filled with an odd energy that Riker had never seen before. It almost seemed as if he were nervous, his movements as out of character as Deanna's.

"Magnify," the captain said.

Riker turned his attention to the screen. Brundage Station looked normal. He had expected to see signs of the Furies' presence, but the station looked as it always had: a cylinder hanging in space. The surface of the station was covered with antennas and sensor dishes. Riker saw nothing unusual. No laser blasts. No holes.

And yet . . .

Something was wrong. He could feel it. It was a cursed place, a place where people had died, a place where evil had happened.

He forced those thoughts to the back, then glanced over his shoulder at Deanna. Her wide eyes were filled with apprehension. She felt it too—

Or was she picking up his mood? His fears. He had to control his mind and focus.

He got up abruptly and walked to Captain Picard's side.

"Captain," Data said, his voice seeming almost unreasonably calm, "the station is still functioning normally. The environmental controls are operational, the weapons systems are on-line, and the computer array seems to be intact."

"Could this be an illusion?" Riker asked.

"No, sir," Data said. He paused. "The scans also show one life-form is still aboard the station."

"A Fury?" The captain asked.

"No, sir. According to the readings, this life-form is human."

"It is a trick," Worf said. "The Havoc are doing what they can to get us aboard that station."

"Are you getting different readings, Mr. Worf?" the captain asked.

"No, sir." Worf crossed his arms over his massive chest. "It would be logical, after the attack we saw, to assume that the Havoc—what humans call the Furies—have left the station intact to lure us aboard. It is a very old trick of combat."

It seemed likely to Riker too. "Perhaps we should beam the life-form aboard the *Enterprise*," he said.

"But if we follow Mr. Worf's logic, we don't know what we're beaming aboard, do we, Number One?" The captain asked the question in a tone that required no answer. He walked up the steps to the security station. "The admiral reported five Fury ships. Where are they now?"

"The five ships of unknown design are surrounding the Furies Point, sir," Data said. "While this design of the ship matches the one seen by the Brundage Station crew, it matches nothing we have in our records, including the original Fury ship, the *Rath*. We are only assuming these are Fury ships."

"Thank you, Data." Picard nodded, and glanced at Worf's relay himself. Then he looked at the helmsman. "Mr. Filer, take us to a position between the station and those ships."

Riker felt his mouth go dry. He knew the drill. The captain was following a very clear protocol. Riker knew what the next order would be.

"Number One, take an away team onto Brundage Station. Gather as much information as you can, and find that life-form. Be prepared for anything, as Mr. Worf so clearly reminded us. We will keep a lock on you at all times. Use the emergency beam-out at the first sign of trouble."

Riker strode up the stairs toward the turbolift. "Aye, sir," he said. He could only take a handful of people. This would be a risky away mission. But he had to take people who could absorb a lot of information in a short period of time. "Data, you're with me."

Data stood from his seat at the science station, and hurried toward the turbolift. Riker tapped his comm badge. "Mr. La Forge, meet me in transporter room three."

The turbolift's doors closed around them. Riker wiped his damp palms on his pants legs. "Transporter room three," he said.

The faint reassuring whir of the lift filled the room.

"I do not understand the level of anxiety the crew seems to be feeling," Data said. "Captain Picard assured us that we would have no trouble facing the Furies as just another life-form, yet his actions seem to say otherwise. Is it a fear of how they look?"

"No," Riker said, more harshly than he intended. "We don't fear looks."

"Yet the crew seems on edge. Or am I perceiving this incorrectly?"

"Data, we've all been trained for the return of the Furies from the beginnings of our careers."

Data nodded, looking solemn. "I would think that would reduce the anxiety instead of raise it. Or am I again misinterpreting the response?"

"It's a little more complicated than that, Data," Riker said, and stopped as the lift's doors opened onto the transporter room. Anderson, the transporter chief, was already in position, hands on the controls.

"The captain says I'm to monitor your every movement," Anderson said.

"See that you do," Riker said.

Data shot him a puzzled look.

Riker realized he *was* on edge. He usually had more finesse than that.

Geordi entered from the hallway. "Forgive me, Commander, but I'm not sure I should be away from engineering."

"I don't anticipate being on the station very long, Geordi," Riker said as he stepped onto the transporter pad. "And what you see there might be able to help us on the *Enterprise*."

Geordi climbed onto the pad.

Riker glanced over his shoulder. Data was in place. "Energize."

His body dissolved into multicolored light. Then, almost instantly, he was rematerializing on Brundage Station. The air felt hot and sticky.

It smelled of sulfur.

A shiver ran down Riker's spine.

The lights were on, but a thin haze of smoke and mist floated in the air, reminiscent of the smoke in the holodeck nightclubs where Data had once practiced his awful comedy routines.

The anxiety Riker had felt since that morning rose, catching in his throat like a bone. The hair on the back of his neck rose. Yet, except for the smell and the smoke, nothing looked out of place.

He pulled out his phaser. "Data, analyze the air for me. What am I smelling?"

Data sniffed, not even needing his tricorder. "The air has a sulfuric component that is slowly fading. The humidity is at ninety-seven percent, and the temperature is ten degrees above normal. I do not detect any trace of fire. The smoke mixed with the humid mist seems to be from some sort of heat weapon."

Riker nodded. Data's matter-of-fact answer enabled Riker to put some of the anxiety aside. Alongside Riker, Geordi also had his phaser out. He then removed his tricorder. It hummed as it ran through its routine.

"If I didn't know better," Geordi said, "I would think we were in the steam baths of Risa. But I couldn't tell you what's causing the effect. My readings show the environmental controls are working normally."

"Risa smells better than this," Riker said. "Draw your weapon, Data."

"Aye, sir," Data said, his tone puzzled. He obviously saw no threat.

They stepped off the transporter pad as one unit, but moving in three slightly different directions.

"The life-sign readings are coming from that corridor," Geordi said, indicating the door with his phaser. "They're faint."

"Are you getting anything else?" Riker asked as he made his way to the door.

Geordi shook his head.

Data moved quicker than they did. The door opened automatically. Riker stopped, but Data went on as if nothing were wrong. Riker hadn't felt this tentative since he was a cadet at the academy.

He glanced at Geordi, who also hadn't moved. "You feel it too," Riker said softly.

Geordi nodded. "Something terrible happened here. And I don't much like it."

"Over here!" Data said from outside the door.

Riker took a deep breath of the oppressive air, and hurried toward the door. There a young officer—the same officer who had faced the Furies on the transmission—leaned against the wall like a broken toy soldier. His head lolled to the side.

Data was running his tricorder over the boy. "I see no obvious wounds," Data said, "but his life signs are very weak."

Riker knelt beside the boy and saw that his eyes

THE SOLDIERS OF FEAR

were open. "Lieutenant," Riker said. "Lieutenant Young?"

"I don't think he can see you," Geordi said. He crouched beside them, observing Young's eyes.

"Is he blind?" Data asked.

Geordi shook his head. "Probably catatonic."

Riker slapped his comm badge. "Riker to *Enterprise.*"

Lieutenant Young jerked away from Riker's voice and covered his head. Only a croaking came from his throat as he tried to scream.

Young's action made Riker shiver.

"Enterprise here. Go ahead, Number One."

"We found Lieutenant Young. He appears to be in shock. I suggest we beam him directly to sickbay."

"Acknowledged, Number One." As Captain Picard's voice faded, multicolored light enveloped Young. Young cringed even more as he disappeared.

"He was not injured," Data said again.

"Yes, he was, Data," Geordi said softly. He stood and went to the computer access panel near the door.

Riker took out his own tricorder, and checked its readings. With Young gone, the three men were alone on the station.

Or so it seemed.

The hair still standing on the back of Riker's neck told him otherwise.

"Geordi, how long will it take you to download the station's records?"

"Only a minute," Geordi said.

"Data, come with me," Riker said. "Let's see what else we can find."

The smoke and the damp, warm mist grew thicker

the deeper they went into the corridor. The carpet was burned in several places as if this part of the station had been on fire.

Writing covered one wall, red writing, as if it had been done in blood.

"Can you read that, Data?" Riker asked.

Data frowned at it. "I believe it is ancient Hebrew. However, it is written in reverse, as if the writer either did not know the proper sequence of letters or—"

"It might have been intentional. What does it say?"

"It is not a message or a warning."

"Then what's its purpose?" Riker asked.

"I believe," Data said, "it is a statement of the powerlessness of Yahweh. It would have horrified the ancient Hebrews. But these words have not been considered blasphemous for at least two, almost three, millennia. I find it curious that they think this will frighten our crew."

"Some ancient imagery terrified some of the old *Enterprise* crew," Riker said. "Kirk theorized these images trigger buried memories—"

"I am familiar with the theory, Commander, although I do not understand why imagery would have an effect and words would not."

"Neither do I," Riker said. The crawly feeling from the back of his neck had worked its way down his spine. He continued down the hall, stepping over the burned patches.

Around a shallow corner was a sight that made him freeze. A red pitchfork-like instrument stood upside down, stuck on a pile of bones. Riker swallowed. "Data?"

Data scanned the bones with his tricorder. "These

bones are real, Commander. They belong to two human males. The red pitchfork has no nondecorative function that I can ascertain."

Riker closed his eyes. He didn't want to think about how these men had died.

"I will run a DNA scan?" Data asked.

Riker nodded. "Be careful. I think we should avoid touching the display. We need to be as careful as we can."

He wiped a hand on his forehead. The corridor had grown hotter and the mist thicker.

He pulled out his own tricorder and scanned, but no life-forms registered. He stepped around the pile of bones and moved on.

Ahead was another corner in the hall. He was almost afraid to move forward, but somehow managed to push himself around the corner—

—and there he stopped, his gaze locked on the eyes of the station's only female crew member.

She was standing in a circle of flame. Her hair had burned away long since, but her flesh was intact—at least the flesh that was visible. The flames rose around her like an inverted waterfall. The glimpses it gave of her face revealed chapped lips, a slightly reddish cast to her skin, and empty eyes.

"Data?" Riker said.

Data stepped past Riker instantly and approached the burning woman. He stopped near her, just outside the ring of flame. "She is dead, Commander, but I do not believe the flames killed her. Like Lieutenant Young, she has no life-threatening injuries."

Riker nodded, his feet rooted to the spot.

Data did not seem to notice his commander's

distress. "The flames seem to be shooting from the floor, but there is no mechanism creating this illusion. I could get closer—"

"No!" Riker said. He cleared his throat, forced the overwhelming anxiety down. "This might be the trap Worf suspected."

"I rather doubt that, sir," Data said. "My study this morning leads me to conclude that this is the eternal hellfire and damnation that Earth's Judeo-Christian ethic speaks of. It would make sense, since this officer was raised within that tradition."

"And she was literally scared to death," Riker said. He tapped his comm badge. The sooner they left this place, the happier he would be. "Are you finished, Geordi?"

"Almost," Geordi said. "I'll have everything in a moment."

"Excellent." Riker whirled and moved back down the corridor, heading toward Geordi's position as quickly as he could.

"Commander—" Data said, hurrying to catch up. "Commander, we have yet to explore the entire station."

"I don't think we should stay here any longer, Data," Riker said. He wasn't sure he could stay here much longer.

"But, sir, our duty—"

"Are there other life signs?"

"No, sir."

"Then I don't think it's our duty to go any farther into this station. Captain Picard made it clear that we would get the information and then leave."

"Aye, sir. I had thought that—"

THE SOLDIERS OF FEAR

"Save it, Mr. Data," Riker said, more harshly than he intended. He passed the bones and didn't look at them. His instincts had been right; this was a hall of death. And the Furies were cunning. They knew that by creating a mystery around the deaths, they would engage the imagination.

His nerves were frayed by the time he reached Geordi. Before Geordi could say anything, Riker hit his comm badge. "Three to beam up."

And as the beam took them, he didn't feel relief. He felt as if he had gazed into the Pit, and saw a small corner of the future.

His future.

Chapter Six

THE SHIPS HADN'T MOVED. But they knew the *Enterprise* was at Brundage Station.

They had to.

The Furies were not insanely violent. Kirk had recorded that. History proved that. He had talked to them, reasoned with them.

Unless they had changed over the decades.

Picard felt as if he were being set up.

But that was his mission. His was the first ship on site. He glanced at Ensign Eckley at the helm this shift. She was a good pilot. Not the best, but one of the best. Good enough to allow his other crew members to fill different roles.

Deanna had left the bridge. Worf glowered at the screen from his position at the security console. Picard was pacing.

He couldn't seem to stop pacing.

Each second the away team had been on Brundage Station had been an eternity. Even now, for Riker to return to the bridge and report seemed as if it were taking forever.

Finally the turbolift opened and Riker strode onto the bridge. His face was white and sweat streaks marred his skin. Not the streaks from healthy exercise that Picard had seen earlier. No. This had been caused by something else entirely. And his passage left a faint odor behind it. Something familiar and yet odd.

Sulfur?

Sulfur.

And the creature who had spoken to Lieutenant Young had looked like a medieval devil.

So that was what the Furies were about this time. Devils and hell. Picard's European past. He was prepared. He would be able to handle that.

Geordi La Forge had already returned to engineering. Data followed Riker off the turbolift. Data's uniform had dark smudges on it, as if he had rubbed against soot.

The mission clearly had not gone as planned. Something about Riker's behavior warned Picard that this discussion should not be held before an audience.

"In my ready room," Picard said. He crossed the bridge and entered his room. Riker followed, eyes averted. Data slipped in just as the door closed.

Picard crossed behind his desk. "What so disturbed you, Will?"

Riker brought his head up, startled at the question. He glanced at Data, who was regarding him as if

Riker were an unfamiliar life-form. "I—ah—those deaths were gruesome, sir."

"Tell me about them," Picard said.

Riker opened his mouth, closed it, and then turned away. Data tilted his head. His gaze met Picard's.

"Mr. Data?"

"As you suspected, sir, the Furies are using ancient religions and mythologies to base a psychological attack. In this case they mixed medieval Earth ideas of hell with even older damnation imagery. Liberal use of fire, smells, and—"

"She was burned alive, sir," Riker said, his voice unsteady. "Only her flesh hadn't charred. I think she died of fright. The others were bones. Just bones."

"And the survivor?"

"Didn't have a mark on him, sir. We sent him to sickbay."

"Geordi has the logs in engineering. Someone might want to view them." Riker's voice broke slightly. "But I won't."

"No need for you to, Number One." Picard tented his fingers on his desk and leaned forward. "But we only have a moment and I need you tell me what unnerved you so badly."

Riker shook his head. "I don't know, sir." Picard recognized the underlying anxiety in Riker's tone. No officer liked losing control, even a small portion of control, and losing that control for no reason at all was even worse. "The station just felt bad, as if it were an evil place."

He shook his head and wiped a hand through his dark hair. "I've been trying to figure it out since I've returned. I've seen worse, Captain. Much worse. But nothing has ever *felt* like this before. It was as if, just by breathing the air, I was taking evil inside me."

"Mr. Data?" Picard needed a clear perspective.

"Commander Riker is correct, sir. We have seen much worse. The loss of life, tragic though it was, seemed stylized and deliberate rather than calculated to horrify and disgust. Yet from the moment we materialized, both the commander and Geordi appeared to be on edge. I am at a loss for an explanation."

Riker squared his shoulders at that description and clasped his hands behind his back. Data's analysis of the station seemed to calm Riker. "My best guess, sir," Riker said, "is that Geordi and I were both raised in the culture that produced those images of hell. I think humans like us were the intended targets, and I think we felt that as an underlying unease."

"What do you think, Mr. Data?"

"It would fit with what I observed, sir. I must note that both the commander and Geordi were able to perform their duties despite their"—Data glanced at Riker as he chose the next word—"their, ah, discomfort."

"Thank you," Picard said. "Data, return to the bridge. I want you to scan the records that Mr. La Forge brought back from Brundage Station. See how the Furies accomplished their attack, and also keep an eye open for anything that we can use."

"Aye, sir," Data said. He started toward the door. Riker followed.

"Number One, stay for a moment."

Riker paused, his eyes down. Picard had never seen his first officer so off-balance before. He needed Riker.

Riker had to be on his feet and thinking clearly before they faced the Furies.

"Will," Picard said softly. "You performed your duties."

"But that fear—it shouldn't have happened at all, Captain," Riker said. "I was prepared. I shouldn't have felt anything."

Picard smiled. "If only it were that easy, Will. You cannot stop the feelings. You must keep them from overwhelming you. The information that you gave me is critical, and your emotional reaction even more so. The Furies may use many tools against us, from appearance to smell. I would have been uncomfortable there. The fact that you completed your mission despite your feelings gives me hope for all of us."

He rounded the desk and clasped Riker on the shoulder. Riker started, then gave Picard a shocked look.

"Good work, Number One. Return to the bridge. I'll join you momentarily."

Riker nodded, then left.

Picard took a deep breath. The descriptions of the station were horrible, but not terrifying. He had seen worse—suffered worse—himself. Yet he could not discount his first officer's reaction. Riker had also gone through a lot in his tenure at Starfleet. Smells, and death, should not have unnerved him this badly. They never had in the past.

Kirk's description of the Furies was right.

But Kirk had kept his emotions in check, and so would Picard.

Admiral Kirschbaum had told him to negotiate.

Kirk's records placed the Furies as a threat even though he had negotiated and even considered the captain of the Fury ship a friend. But this time the Furies had come through the wormhole with five ships. More than one, but clearly not an entire fleet. They still wanted conquest. The attack on the station was only a reminder of what they could do. A warning.

A calling card.

Picard hoped beyond hope that was the way it was, but his heart told him he was wrong.

He strode back onto the bridge.

Data had returned to his post at the science station. Material was flowing rapidly across the screen before him. Commander Riker had taken his seat near the captain's chair. He looked calmer.

"Ensign Eckley," Picard said to the helmsman as he made his way to his command post. "Take us within communications range of those ships."

"Aye, sir," Eckley said.

Picard noticed Riker's fist tighten. The tension on the bridge grew. Picard sat and leaned back in his seat, not allowing himself to move with the mood shift.

Perhaps all the study of the Furies at the Academy had been wrong. Perhaps Starfleet crew members would approach the attack with a more open mind if they hadn't been told that the Furies were so powerful. Despite generations of study, no one completely understood the human mind. Perhaps the warnings had intensified the feelings of danger instead of alleviating them.

"We're within range, sir."

"All stop." Picard stood and tugged on his shirt front. "Hail them."

He had seen the images from Brundage Station. He had seen his own trusted first officer's reaction to the mess the Furies left behind them. He knew what he was in for.

"Sir," Worf said, his deep voice booming across the bridge. "We have a response to our hail."

"On screen."

The bridge seemed abnormally silent, as if the bridge crew were holding their breath. Picard felt as if he had contained his emotions in a small bottle buried deep within his stomach.

He was as ready as he could ever be.

The screen flickered to life. Picard had to fight an involuntary urge to step backward. The creature facing him was both familiar and unfamiliar. It had ram's horns and a long snout. Its scarlet skin and piggy eyes matched portraits of the devil made on Earth, matching illuminated manuscript drawings he had seen as a boy in Paris museums. If he had time to lay a wager, he would bet that the creature before him had the body of a goat yet stood on its hind legs, had cloven hooves instead of feet, and had no tail at all.

His stomach felt as if it were about to burst.

"I am Captain Jean-Luc Picard of the *Starship Enterprise.*"

The creature laughed. Maggots swarmed out of its open mouth. Its teeth were long and sharp. Saliva dripped from them. "Captain," it said, its voice a warm caress that was somehow more hideous than the voice he had expected. "I know who you are. I even know of your Federation of Planets. But you do not know who I am. You have faced my people, but not my kind."

Picard took a deep breath. He would not play this guessing game, but suddenly he couldn't think of any other response. Everything he had planned to say had fled from his mind. The emotions he had bottled away were straining at their prison.

"I," the creature said, its bass tones reverberating all the way down to Picard's toes, "am fear."

Its words echoed in the silent bridge as the screen went dark.

Already they were seeping through: images of himself . . .

. . . locked alone in a room near the vineyard, the smell of fresh grapes and sunshine taunting him . . .

. . . alone on Casius II, his shuttlecraft in pieces around him, night with its poisonous chill approaching; and naked in the Borg hive, imprisoned in one of their devices, a needle longer than his finger heading straight for his temple . . .

He wrenched himself out of the memory.

He was here.

On the *Enterprise*.

Safe.

The seeping fear was still there, but slowly, as if a spider had dropped a web over his emotions, his control returned. He knew the control was as flimsy as a spider's web and would break just as easily. But it gave him something else to work with.

He blinked, turned, and finally saw the bridge before him.

The sight shocked him.

Riker sat in his chair, his elbows braced on his knees, his head buried in his hands. He was shivering.

Ensign Eckley had her arms wrapped around her head. She had fallen to the floor and she appeared to have passed out.

Ensign Wilcox was sobbing, the harsh guttural sobs of a man who had never cried before.

Ensign Ikel was pounding on the turbolift door as if he were trying to escape the room.

The big surprise, though, was Lieutenant Worf. The devil had no place in his tradition, yet he stared at the empty screen, his dark, foreboding features the color of Ferengi grub worms. He seemed frozen in place.

"Captain, I have finished the analysis. . . ." Data swiveled his chair, and stopped speaking as he saw the condition of the bridge crew. A tiny frown furrowed his normally wrinkleless face.

"It seems," he said, his gaze meeting Picard's, "that I have missed something."

Picard took another deep breath and let the fine web of his self-control strengthen just a little bit more. "I think we may be lucky that you did," he said.

Data frowned, and for some reason Picard found that very reassuring.

Deanna Troi sat on the bed in her quarters, her door locked. Her comm badge rested on the table in the main room. She could hear it, but had chosen not to respond. Already she had gotten calls from fifteen crew members, no doubt wanting to discuss the anxiety they had been feeling since the *Enterprise* had come to this area near the Brundage Station.

The anxiety she was feeling was threatening to overwhelm her.

A Betazoid, her mind said with the voice of her mother, *knows how to control the impact of the emotions of others.*

"I know, Mother," Deanna said. She gripped her knees and went through a calming ritual that had helped her in times past. Usually she handled these overwhelming crew emotions better than she was now. She suspected her reaction was due to the strength of the emotions.

And they would only get stronger, magnified within her own self.

Unless you get control, Deanna. I don't recognize this lack of control anywhere in my family. It must come from your father.

Deanna never heard the voice of her mother in her own head. Unless, of course, her mother was nearby.

"Computer, is my mother on board the *Enterprise?*"

"Lwaxana Troi is not aboard this ship."

"Computer please check again."

"Lwaxana Troi is not aboard this ship."

Deanna nodded. Her anxiety level was high. She hadn't made up her mother's voice since she was a very young girl. Then that had been normal. A child always heard voices where there were none. It was the task of the Betazoid to learn the difference between a projected voice and an imagined one.

Deanna stood, her skirts falling about her legs. Her mother's voice—real or imagined—was right. Deanna needed control.

She left the bedroom, grabbed her comm badge, and put it on. Her research with Data showed that the Furies had not encountered Betazoids. The Furies would have no knowledge of Betazed mythology. Only her human side would be affected, and she could control that much.

The problem she would have in any encounter with the Furies would be the shipboard reaction. But she suspected, and Data hypothesized, that the Furies had come through this sector long before the original *Enterprise* encountered them.

Her mother's planet had no history of them.

None.

That would give her strength.

If you can keep everyone else out of your mind, her mother's voice said.

"You leave first, Mother," Deanna snapped. She didn't need this distraction. Her mother always made her nervous. . . .

She paused. *Her mother made her nervous.* Deanna sighed. So even when she was trying to block the low-level anxiety from the ship, it appeared in the form of her mother.

Deanna would go to her counseling offices. She had practiced control there more than she had in her own rooms. She was amazed she hadn't thought of that immediately.

"Computer," she said, "please block all non-emergency calls. I will set appointments after this crisis has ended."

"Affirmative," the computer said.

There. That part at least was settled. No one on the

ship had the luxury to discuss their emotional difficulties. They simply had to live through them.

Just as she would.

She felt better now. The control she had been seeking had returned. She started for the door.

And fell forward as a wave of cold hit her as hard as a physical blow. The cold was full of voices—screaming, shouting, babbling—and imagery:

A woman whose head was covered with snakes.

A creature with maggots for eyes.

A giant Klingon, his teeth covered with blood.

Mixed in with those were a hundred others, less prominent, but as forceful.

And behind it all, her mother's voice.

Deanna, you need control. Deanna—

But she had no control. Her mother would have had no control. There was too much. Too much for anyone to handle all at once.

Deanna fought the cold back, the voices back, but the images kept coming— A great dragon, spitting fire.

A Romulan, poised over her with a disruptor.

A Craxithesus, screaming its blood cry.

More and more and more.

—She couldn't stop them, and as she fought, she grew weaker, and weaker.

The images crowded in on her until her senses overloaded.

She could fight no more.

Chapter Seven

LIEUTENANT SAM REDBAY straddled a chair in engineering. He held a laser under his arm as he pulled apart the panel before him. Just his luck to be in engineering instead of on the bridge during what promised to be the biggest event of his career. But he had told personnel that if they assigned him to a starship he would work in any department at any time, and he had always had an aptitude for engineering.

And, to be fair, he liked the work. Although he liked working the helm better.

But Lieutenant Tam was down with the Xotic flu, a deadly (and fortunately not very communicable) virus that damaged the internal organs if not monitored properly. And Dr. Crusher had ordered complete bed rest.

Tam had contacted La Forge when the crisis started, and he gave her some sort of mental puzzle to work on from her sickbed. If it had been Redbay, he would have crawled to his battle station, virus be damned.

Still, if he had to be somewhere outside of the action, he would rather be in engineering than anywhere else. Geordi La Forge ran a tight section. The equipment was always in top condition. The *Enterprise* functioned at maximum capacity, and everything the crew did only made it better.

Like the work Redbay was doing now. La Forge believed, based on the things he had read and some things he had noticed in his trip to Brundage Station, that some of the Furies' powers over human fears might be artificial and therefore could be effectively blocked. Redbay had already worked on a shield oscillator so that unusual frequencies would be scrambled. Now he was modifying the viewscreens to minimize intentional distortions.

The job should theoretically take two people eight hours.

He had an hour to finish it.

Alone.

The rest of the engineering staff were working on similar tasks. A few were modifying the warp engines—for what he did not know—and La Forge himself was in a Jeffries tube, adjusting the internal sensors.

They would be ready when the Furies struck.

If they struck.

Redbay had his doubts about that. His own personal opinion, based on some historical study, was that

Captain James T. Kirk was a bit of an exaggerator. No one, no matter what his position and no matter what the tenor of his times, could have been involved in so many important events in the history of the sector.

Redbay's history professor at the Academy had ridiculed that conclusion, pointing out that the history records clearly showed Kirk's involvement.

This, of course, would be the test. Kirk and his crew were the only ones who left a record of the Furies' visit. The Klingons had been suspiciously silent about the entire encounter. And from the punishment they took, Redbay could understand why.

His hand was getting tired from holding the laser in place. He still had some tweaking to do. With luck, he would be able to get the task done in the time allotted. If it hadn't been for the prime condition of the *Enterprise*'s systems, the job really would have taken him the full eight hours.

Then, suddenly, his heart rate increased, his hands started shaking, and his fingers lost their grip on the laser. It slipped from his mouth and clattered on the console, denting the surface.

He dropped his tools and grabbed for the laser, knowing that the monsters under his bed were going to get him, they were going to kill him, like they had killed his father and his mother and the entire colony.

He had to hide now.

Now!

Hide! Right now!

He slid under the console and drew his knees up to his chest, but that didn't drive the feeling away. The monsters were made of light, multicolored light, and they burned everything they touched. He had seen his

THE SOLDIERS OF FEAR

father die that way, and his mother had made him run—

A man was on his back, phaser clutched in both hands, pushing, pushing, pushing his way toward Redbay using his heels as propulsion, eyes focused on a point near the ceiling. The man was wearing a Starfleet uniform (Starfleet? how did they get here?), and he was moaning as he moved.

A long drawn-out scream echoed from a Jeffries tube (a what?), and two ensigns were lying on the floor, each a shivering mass of flesh.

They had to hide. Didn't they know they had to hide? If they were in the open, the light would get them and—

and—

Starfleet didn't belong on Nyo Colony. The colony had broken with the Federation. That's why so many people died. Because they had no one to turn to for help. That's why Redbay joined Starfleet, so that he could help people who needed it.

Redbay joined.

He was in Starfleet.

His parents had died a long, long time ago.

He peered out from under the console. The man in the Starfleet uniform (Transporter Chief Anderson) was still pushing himself with his legs, moving on his back, aiming his phaser at shadows.

Redbay was in engineering on the *Starship Enterprise*. Getting ready to face the Furies.

Who terrified their opponents by manipulating their emotions.

Terror.

He had only felt this kind of terror once in his life.

The day his parents died.

Only once.

His parents had died thirty years ago.

Thirty.

Years.

Thirty.

He kept repeating that inside his head, over and over.

He had been modulating the ship's screens. He had no reason to be so frightened.

None.

But his limbs were shaking.

He eased out from under the console, the terror still a part of him, but slowly coming under control. If he kept his mind focused the terror would always be under control

He had learned that at age six, living alone for a month on Nyo before a passing freighter had picked up the automated distress signal.

Redbay kept his gaze on Chief Anderson—no sense in startling a panicked man—and slowly stood, his legs trembling.

The surface of the console was dented where the laser initially hit, but *again,* none of the important sensors were damaged.

The damage all seemed to be internal—within the engineering staff.

Then La Forge rolled out of the Jeffries tube, slapping himself as though he were on fire. He landed on his back, and gasped as the air left his lungs. His hands slapped their way up to his face. When they reached his VISOR, he stopped.

Anderson hit his head against the console, yelped, and aimed his phaser at the wall.

Redbay didn't move. He wasn't going to move until Anderson put the phaser down.

La Forge removed the VISOR and sat up, leaning against the opening of the tube. He was breathing hard, but he seemed to be calmer.

Anderson put his phaser away.

Redbay let out breath he hadn't even realized he was holding. Slowly he made his way to La Forge. La Forge's face looked odd without the VISOR. Redbay had never seen his eyes before, didn't realize that they were a milky white. The eyes didn't focus on him.

"M-Mr. La Forge?" Redbay's voice sounded strangled. He cleared his throat. "Sir?"

With a hand not yet completely steady, La Forge put his VISOR back on. "Lieutenant."

He sounded calm. If Redbay hadn't seen him fall out of the Jeffries tube in a panic, he would have thought that La Forge had felt nothing.

"I can see two crew members who still haven't controlled themselves," Redbay said, letting La Forge know that his panic was not unique. "Anderson seems to be coming out of it. I haven't been able to get to the warp drive to see what's happening there."

"Great," La Forge said, and he didn't have to explain what he meant by that. If La Forge had panicked and fallen out of a Jeffries tube, and Redbay had panicked and allowed a laser to damage a console, then what kind of damage happened to the warp core?

La Forge pulled himself to his feet. "Engineering to bridge," he said as he stood.

"Go ahead, Mr. La Forge."

Redbay found the captain's normal response unusually reassuring. But La Forge frowned. He had worked with Picard a long time. He might have heard something in the captain's voice that Redbay hadn't.

"Captain." La Forge paused and glanced around, then took a deep breath and continued. "Something pretty strange just happened down here. I don't know how to describe it. We all seemed to panic for no reason at all. Two of my ensigns are still huddled in terror on the floor, and I don't know what's going on near the warp core. There might be some systems damage. I'll need help from the bridge in running a systems check."

"That isn't possible at the moment, Mr. La Forge."

Now Redbay heard it too. There seemed to be an abnormal amount of caution in the captain's tone, as if he were choosing his words too carefully.

"Then, sir, give us five minutes before attempting to use any major system. I need to check—"

"Mr. La Forge," the captain interrupted as if he hadn't heard La Forge at all. "Did you have the screens on during the last transmission?"

La Forge glanced at Redbay. Redbay shook his head. He had been working on the screens, not watching them.

"No, sir," La Forge said.

"Fascinating." The captain's comment was soft, as if he were mulling that piece of information.

The silence seem to stretch too long. Finally La Forge said, "Captain?"

"Mr. La Forge." Picard's voice seemed somewhat stronger. "We have a problem that extends beyond engineering and the bridge. We must assume that the entire ship has felt this wave of terror. Repair what you can, Mr. La Forge, but remain at your posts."

"Yes, sir," La Forge said.

"Geordi," Picard said, his voice lower, almost as if he were asking a favor. "Get your crew on their feet again, if you can. We need to discover where this feeling is coming from, as quickly as possible."

"Lieutenant Redbay and I are already on our feet," La Forge said, "and Anderson seems to have regained control as well. Between the three of us, we should be able to get the rest of engineering in order."

"Good," Picard said. "I need a report as soon as you can get it to me."

"Aye, sir," La Forge said.

Redbay swallowed convulsively. It was taking most of his strength to stand beside La Forge and look calm.

La Forge's hand went to his VISOR again, then dropped to his side. "I suspect we don't have much time."

"I suspect you're right," Redbay said. "I think those of us who can work should. If we find a way to block whatever is causing this, the others will come around immediately."

La Forge glanced at his crew members. One ensign was still huddled in a fetal position, but the other one was sitting up, his skin green, his eyes glazed. He was tracking, though. Redbay suspected he had looked like that only moments before.

"I'll scan," La Forge said. "You run diagnostics. Let's see how fast we can find the source of this."

Redbay nodded. He liked being busy. Being busy

kept his mind off that feeling of terror gnawing at the lining of his stomach. He went back to the console and picked up his tools. Beneath the control, beyond the terror, he had the awful feeling that something was missing.

Something that should have guided them all.

He bent over another console and started the diagnostics.

Then he realized what was wrong.

No one had ordered a red alert.

If Picard was right, then the entire crew had been hit with a bolt of fear, a literal assault on the senses.

A clear attack and Picard had not called a red alert.

He had probably been too shaken to think of it.

And that worried Redbay even more.

Chapter Eight

SICKBAY GLEAMED.

The extra beds were lined against the wall, the emergency equipment was out on tables, and extra medical tricorders hung from pegs near the door. Beverly Crusher had even ordered her assistants to place the research tubes into medical storage so that they could use the experiment area during any emergency that might arise. The handful of patients, three sick with the Xotic flu, were in the farthest wing of sickbay, tended by one nurse who was instructed to watch the monitors for any fluctuations.

Beverly tucked a strand of red hair behind her ear and looked at the readings on the diagnostic bed one more time. She had prepared her trauma team, not her research team. After working on Lieutenant

Young, however, she wondered if she had made the right decision.

Lieutenant Young was still wrapped in the diagnostic bed, only his head and feet visible above the equipment. Aside from an odd series of bruises across his chest, arms, and ankles, he had suffered no obvious physical wounds. Yet he was nearly comatose.

She had thought, when he first beamed up, that he had had serious internal injuries, or some type of head wound. But as she examined him, then stabilized him, she discovered his lack of physical injury.

Obvious physical injury. She had to keep reminding herself that the key word here was "obvious." Lieutenant Young—who looked, in some ways, younger than her son Wesley—was dying.

And she could do nothing about it until she determined the cause.

Two of her assistants were running double-check scans on his blood and urine. She was also having them run DNA tests and tests for obscure viral infections: for anything that would cause Young's abnormally high blood pressure, his increased adrenaline and endorphin readings, and his extra white-blood-cell count.

The thing she didn't tell her assistants was that she was afraid she knew the cause.

One of her hobbies was the history of medicine throughout the known worlds. It fascinated her that Vulcan developed the art of acupuncture during roughly the same developmental period Earth did— even though the planets were not in communication at that time and the cultures were in different states of growth.

Terminology also interested her: the phrase "in good humor" once meant "in good health" because Terrans once believed that the body was filled with "humors" and that if those humors were in balance, then a person was healthy. She didn't believe in humors any more than she believed in using leeches to bleed a cancer patient, but she did know that some ancient diagnoses held a basis in fact.

She ran a cool hand over Young's forehead. No fever, yet his skin was damp and clammy to the touch. His eyes were open, but they didn't see her. Instead they focused on the ceiling. Occasionally he would moan and cringe. And when he did, his heart rate increased, his breath stopped in his throat, and his blood pressure rose.

She could bring the levels down, but she couldn't predict when the situation would repeat.

And she knew, as clearly as she knew her own name, that Lieutenant Young's ill health was being caused by something within his own mind.

In the terms of the medieval physicians of Earth, Lieutenant Robert Young was being frightened to death.

Literally.

And search as she might for a physical cause—an implanted chip, a stimulant in the brain stem, a chemical trigger in his bloodstream—she could find nothing.

She suspected that he had seen something he could not live with, and his conscious mind, overloaded, was trying to cope in the only way it could. It was overloading his body, trying to force it to shut down.

And it was up to her to stop that.

She dabbed sweat off Young's forehead. Sometimes she felt no better than those medieval physicians who believed that humors governed the body. There were parts of the body—human, Vulcan, Klingon, it didn't matter—that no one understood.

This was one of them.

She needed Deanna. If anyone could help this boy, Deanna could.

Beverly reached for her comm badge when suddenly a wave of terror filled her. The feeling was so intense that it knocked her to her knees. She banged her head on the diagnostic table as she fell.

The boy was going to die.

They all were going to die.

And she could do nothing. She was perfectly helpless. As helpless as she had been the day Jean-Luc arrived with the news that her husband was dead.

That she would raise Wesley alone.

The ship would be filled with a mental plague, causing everyone to die of fright, and she, a trained physician, would have to stand by.

Helplessly.

Her head hurt.

The beginning of the plague.

She knew it.

Bobby Young was only the beginning, and now it had passed to her. Soon she would lie on a diagnostic table while her assistants fluttered over her. Then they would fall, one by one, victim to this unnamed terror—

Someone behind her screamed.

The plague was spreading.

She put a hand to her head, near the source of the pain, and felt—

A lump.

It hurt to the touch, hurt even worse when she pressed on it, making the headache increase.

Something crashed behind her.

She whirled.

One of her assistants—she couldn't see who—had made a white flag out of God knows what, and was waving it from below one of the examining tables.

A white flag.

She frowned. Then giggled, despite her terror. A white flag. No one recognized a white flag anymore. It once meant surrender. Save the bearer from harm.

Save the bearer from harm.

Cautiously, she peered above the diagnostic table. Young was writhing within his confines, his eyes rolling in his head.

Young.

Save the bearer from harm.

She glanced around the room.

Except for her assistants, she was alone.

The flag waved, slowly, like a metronome.

Tick.

Save the

Tick.

bearer from

Tick.

harm.

Her throat was dry. She had never felt such terror in her life. Something was wrong. Something was—

Lieutenant Young choked.

She rose by instinct, opened his mouth, and cleared

the passageway. Her fingers were shaking. She couldn't concentrate. She forgot what she was trying to do.

Save the bearer from harm.

That was her duty. Her oath.

I swear by Apollo the physician, by Aesculapius, Hygeia, and Panacea

His throat was clear.

and I take to witness all the gods, all the goddesses, to keep according to my ability and my judgment the following Oath:

But his tongue was bleeding.

I will prescribe regimen for the good of my patients

She cleansed his tongue, moved it aside, and propped up his head.

according to my ability and my judgment and never do harm to anyone.

He was breathing regularly again.

His eyelashes were fluttering.

And her terror was subsiding. Or more accurately, she had it under control.

Never do harm to anyone.

And it was the oath, the Hippocratic oath, that had saved her. Hippocrates, Father of Medicine, a Greek physician who came from a famous family of priest physicians, and who wrote more than seventy treatises on medicine . . .

Knowledge.

It was knowledge that was keeping her calm. Her mind could overcome anything. Hadn't Dr. Quince told her that during her internship on Delos IV? Her mind was more powerful than any drug. More powerful than anything.

Even fear.

She was standing without assistance. Even in the middle of that terror, she had managed to help Lieutenant Young.

Now she had to help her assistants because she needed them.

She peered over the examining table. Ensign Cassidy was sitting below, both hands clutching the white flag, which was still waving back and forth.

Beverly swallowed. "Etta," she said. "Etta, it's Beverly. You're in sickbay. Put down the flag. You're safe."

Ensign Cassidy looked up, her round face pale with fear. "Don't let them get me, Doctor," she whispered.

"They won't, Ensign. No one is here. Captain Picard warned us this would happen. There are Furies outside. Remember the Furies?"

Ensign Cassidy nodded.

"Use your mind, Ensign. Overcome the fear. Put it aside. Remember your medical training. Your fears don't matter. Your actions do."

In every house where I come I will enter only for the good of my patients. Beverly shivered. The fear was there, below the surface. But she could control it.

Ensign Cassidy lowered the flag. "What's causing this?" she whispered.

"Something from outside us." Beverly took a deep breath. "I need you to focus the others. Remind them of their tasks as medical personnel. Even Lieutenant Young can feel this, and he doesn't seem to feel anything else."

She stopped, the fear caught in her throat. A real fear this time.

Deanna!

"Computer," she said, not caring that the fear filled her voice. "Locate Counselor Troi."

"She is in her quarters."

Deanna. Who was sensitive to everyone's mood. Who could feel what the entire ship was feeling.

Terror like this overloaded a human. Lieutenant Bobby Young was dying from it. Imagine what it would do to Deanna.

Beverly turned to Cassidy. "Keep an eye on our patient. Contact me if there's any problem."

Ensign Cassidy blinked. Her expression was clearer. "I'll be all right," she said.

"Good," Beverly said. That made it easier for her to leave.

And she had to. She had to get to Deanna.

Beverly headed out the door at a run, spurred on by fear. But not the fear sent by the Furies. This fear was for her friend's life.

Chapter Nine

"I SIMPLY DO NOT understand, sir," Data said. "Did I miss some subtle message in your contact with the Furies?"

His head jerked as it turned, looking at the bridge crew. Lieutenant Worf still stared at the screen. Riker brought his head up, an expression of grim determination on his face. Ensign Iket had stopped pounding on the turbolift door and was holding one hand as if it hurt.

Picard nodded. His fear was still there, but the control he had placed over it grew with each passing moment. "Perhaps, Data, but what you missed was not subtle. It affected the crew's emotions deeply."

"What was it, sir?"

"If we knew that, Mr. Data, we would be able to fight it."

"But you seem unaffected, sir."

Picard smiled. Sometimes Data's innocence on matters emotional was just what Picard needed. Still, he could feel the fear trapped within him, under his control, but only barely. "It affected me, Mr. Data, and I fear—" He paused on the word, checked it, and made sure it was accurate. It was. "I fear that this first attack might be a mild one. For a moment, I felt like Ensign Eckley; and in that extreme terror, no human can think clearly."

Picard looked at Data.

Data was watching him carefully, ignoring the emotional chaos around them.

Picard went on. "There may come a time in our dealings with the Furies when you and you alone will be able to think rationally. I will be counting on you to make the correct decisions. Am I making myself clear, Mr. Data?"

"Yes, sir," Data said in his most solemn voice.

Picard nodded. Having Data aboard—and unaffected by this inexplicable fear—took some of the tension out of Picard's back. Data was a good officer. If the survival of the *Enterprise* and her crew landed on his shoulders, he would make the right choice.

Data's presence, and the guarantee of levelheadedness, also made the next few decisions easier.

"Open a shipwide channel, Mr. Worf."

Worf did not break his gaze from the screen. Data watched him, head tilting in puzzlement.

"Mr. Worf," Picard said in his most commanding voice.

Worf snapped to attention. His gaze, when he

turned it on Picard, was fierce. But Picard knew that fierceness was a Klingon cover for embarrassment.

"Sir?"

"Open a shipwide channel."

"Yes, sir," Worf said.

Picard glanced at the bridge. Riker was watching him now, and several other members of the bridge crew were taking deep breaths. Ensign Eckley was unconscious, though, and Ensign Iket had sunken to the floor, hand swelling to twice its normal size.

"Channel open, sir."

Picard nodded. He cleared his mind, pushed the fear even farther down, and met Data's gaze. It was essential that Picard sound calm and collected for this announcement. Since Data was the only calm member of the bridge crew, Picard would use him as an anchor.

"To the crew of the *Enterprise,* this is Captain Jean-Luc Picard. We have made contact with the Furies, and in that contact, they have somehow tapped emotions buried deep within us. As we suspected, they hope to prey upon our fears."

He took a deep breath, keeping his gaze on Data's calm face, and went on. "Many of you are in the grip of that fear now. You must master it—and you can master it. Remember that what you are feeling is not coming from within you, but from without. Your fear is artificial. Use that knowledge to subdue the terrors."

Data nodded, understanding what Picard was saying. That calmed Picard even more as he went on. "Return to your stations. I shall be contacting the

Furies again, and this time, they shall see that we are made of much sterner stuff."

Picard signed off. Riker was staring at him. Data stood, and opened his mouth as if to speak. But Worf spoke first.

"With all due respect, sir, it was your contact with the Furies that precipitated the attack. Do you believe that another contact is wise considering we do not even know the nature or the power of their weapon?"

"It is the Klingon way to face one's fear, is it not, Mr. Worf?"

"Klingons believe, sir, that one must respect one's fears. Occasionally a fear is justified."

"I agree. Fear is the most protective of all of our emotions. But it cannot govern our lives or our deeds. It is the strongest Klingons, those who can go beyond their fears, who become great leaders."

Picard had to choose his words carefully here, given the Klingon history with the Furies. Worf probably hadn't yet realized that he was in danger of repeating it.

"It is my belief, Mr. Worf," Picard continued, "that you are one of your people's great leaders. I have seen you face events that would have destroyed lesser Klingons."

Worf's lips thinned. He clearly understood Picard's implications. "Thank you, sir."

Picard nodded. He turned away from Worf, hoping that his own strength would hold for this next, most crucial action. "Hail the Furies' ship, Mr. Worf."

"Aye, sir."

Riker had stood too. He stayed just out of range of the viewscreen, but he appeared stronger. Perhaps

THE SOLDIERS OF FEAR

Picard's conversation with Worf had helped Riker as well.

"They have acknowledged our hail, sir," Worf said.

Picard straightened his shoulders. He had survived torture by the Cardassians. He could survive anything.

"On screen," Picard said.

The devil—the Fury captain—appeared on the screen again.

Picard shuddered, but he kept himself steady. He had to concentrate for the good of the ship. "When we spoke earlier, you said you were familiar with our Federation. That means you know our mission is a peaceful one. We do not believe in war."

"Our records show that you fight it well enough." The creature's voice swept through Picard.

"Of course we do," Picard said. He held himself rigidly, not wanting any sign of fear to show. "We must defend ourselves. But we believe war is a failure of communication."

"War is more than that," the creature said. "War is glory. It is the only way to achieve heaven."

"Heaven" was the term the first Fury's captain had used for this area of space when he spoke to Kirk.

Tiny shivers were running up and down Picard's back. He forced himself to ignore them. "I was sent to negotiate with you. If you want to settle in this area, we will help you."

The creature tilted its head. Its eyes changed color as it moved, and a bit of smoke or mist curled around its horns. "Negotiate? You believe you can negotiate with us?"

The question was a stall. Even through his fear, Picard could sense that. Kirk had tried to negotiate with them. And he had failed in the end.

"Negotiate," Picard repeated. "Our diplomats will meet with yours, we will establish a truce, and then we will see if we can work out some sort of amenable coexistence."

The creature threw its head back and laughed. Maggots flew from its mouth, and fell against its chin, held there by thin strands of green saliva. "Diplomats? We have no diplomats, Picard. We do not believe in them."

The shivers were growing stronger. Picard swallowed them back. He made himself stare at the screen, even though the maggots disgusted him almost as much as the creature terrified him. "Our leaders will speak with yours. If you tell us your purpose in coming to this sector, we will see what we can do to help—"

"You, the Unclean, offering to help us?" The creature's laughter died, and Picard took an involuntary step backward as the Fury captain's eyes seemed to glow red. "Just as you helped our last ship that arrived here? We ruled heaven once and we are returning to rule it again. Then you will do as we want. No negotiating. No diplomats. It is easier our way."

Picard didn't let his mind dwell on what the creature had said. He didn't dare. "In this quadrant," Picard said, "we work together. We are willing to work with you if you let us."

"Be assured you will work with us." The creature raised its hand, revealing long curling fingernails with razor-sharp tips. "Like little puppets on a string. We shall control your every movement. Your every feeling."

The fear increased so that Picard had to grit his teeth to prevent them from chattering.

The creature leaned forward, as if they were the only two beings in the universe. Its red eyes seemed to glow across the distance, cutting at Picard's insides. "And Picard, we will enjoy your every scream."

The screen went dark. Picard staggered backward, stopping just before he reached his chair. He felt as if someone had taken his insides, squeezed them, and then stretched them. His muscles ached, and he longed to close his eyes and never open them again.

Instead, he slumped into his chair. Sweat soaked the back of his shirt. The bridge crew had not dissolved into anxiety. They still controlled themselves. He wondered if that last blast of terror had been directed at him alone.

"Sir?" Riker said, concern evident in his voice.

Picard took a few measured, deep breaths. "Number One, they know how to tap our deepest fears."

"I know, sir," Riker said.

"But it is artificial." Picard was speaking as much for himself as for his first officer, fighting to wrap that band of control around his thoughts again.

He took a deep, measured breath and let it out slowly. "According to my reading of Kirk's logs, the original *Enterprise* had no problem with this level of fear. That crew's fears came only from the ways the creatures looked."

Picard glanced around the bridge. "Yet everyone on

our ship seems to have fallen prey to these overpowering emotions. Most of have not seen the imagery on the screen."

"A weapon," Worf said. "It is a weapon."

Picard nodded. "I agree. They are using some sort of device now. It is—" Picard took a breath as a wave of shuddering ran through him. Riker's eyes grew wide. Picard bit his lower lip and forced the shuddering to stop.

"It is," he began again, "only logical. We defeated them before. They would come back stronger, using the knowledge they gained about us the first time to fight us now."

Riker nodded. "Just as we are doing against them."

Picard nodded. "Number One, with this in mind, I want you to go to engineering. Several of La Forge's people were overwhelmed by the first wave. I am certain he needs assistance. Provide him with some, and make certain that the entire staff is working on a way to shield us from the Furies' power, whatever this is. Do it as quickly as you can, Number One."

"Aye, sir." Riker actually looked relieved to have something to do. He pushed himself out of his chair as though anxious to be away from Picard, and hurried to the turbolift. As he passed Ensign Iket, Riker paused, spoke softly, and then continued on his way. Even in the middle of his own fear, Riker had comfort to spare for others.

Picard was lucky that Riker had turned down his own command. At moments like this, Picard needed someone solid to rely on. Fortunately, he also had Data.

"Mr. Data," Picard said, "observations."

Data pushed away from the console. "The Fury is justifiably certain of its own power. Ancient history from many different societies shows that they were able to enslave peoples in this sector for thousands of years. Earth, Vulcan, and Klingon cultures all show records of their influence or domination."

Picard nodded. "Go on."

Data looked puzzled for a moment before he continued. "It seemed to me, however, that the captain of the Fury vessel did not anticipate your response to its message. Your offer to negotiate confused it, and your mention of diplomats made it pause for a moment."

"In consideration?" Picard asked. He had been so involved in controlling his emotions that he wasn't able to read the emotions in the Fury captain.

"No, sir. If I had to speculate, I would say that it was not familiar with the term. I do not believe that the Furies have negotiated in their recent history. I doubt they even understood what Captain Kirk was trying to do their first time here. The records show that Kirk delayed the battle and was able to talk to them only because they were looking for proof that this area was their home area. Once they found that proof, they attacked."

Picard steepled his fingers and tapped them against his chin. "Speculate more for me, Mr. Data. If they aren't here to negotiate, why did they arrive with only five ships?"

"There could be several explanations, Captain. If your hypothesis is correct and they have developed a device to incapacitate us with fear, five ships might be all they think they need. It would seem, though, based on historic precedent and standard military tactics, that these five ships are an advance point. Scout ships, for lack of a better way of putting it."

Picard felt himself shudder, but he hoped it didn't show.

Data went on. "With that in mind, I looked at strategy. Those five ships appear to be guarding the Furies' entry point. We think the point is a kind of wormhole, but nearly eighty years of observation have shown us that it is not available to our ships, the way the wormhole near Bajor is. However, this wormhole seems to open at the whim of the Furies. Either they have knowledge of when it will open or the wormhole is artificially created."

Data's analysis was calming Picard. It was good to hear someone speaking rationally.

"What do you believe?"

"The evidence points to an artificial creation," Data said. "If the Furies had to time their arrival in the Alpha Quadrant with the opening of the wormhole, they would have sent in their entire invasion force. If these five ships are indeed an advance team, then the hole is artificially created, and we will see other ships arrive through the wormhole shortly."

Picard swallowed. More Furies. It made sense. But it didn't give them much time.

"Sir," Data said. "While you were speaking with the Fury, I took the liberty of running several tests. I hoped to find a source for the emotional distress the Furies' visage seems to cause the crew."

Relief flooded through Picard. "Good thinking."

"Unfortunately, I was unable to find any obvious cause of the distress. The communication seemed like a straightforward intership exchange. The Fury ships were not using any weaponry that our systems can detect."

But that didn't mean the weapons weren't there. For decades, the Federation could not detect a cloaked Romulan warbird even if the bird were within hailing distance.

"I also ran several experiments on this sector of space, thinking perhaps we had run into some sort of field that generated unease within the crew."

Picard felt startled. He hadn't thought of that, even though it was obvious. Too much of his energy was focused on remaining calm.

"And?" he asked.

"Nothing, sir. We seem to be in a normal sector of space."

For some reason, the news did not discourage Picard. It made him realize that there were answers, and answers beyond the Furies' control of the subconscious.

The key was to find those answers before the Furies' attack began in earnest.

"Excellent, Mr. Data," Picard said. "Keep working along those lines. If you need additional resources, let me know."

"Aye, sir." Data turned back to his console.

Picard resisted the urge to cross his fingers. If they could find a way to block the fear the Furies caused, they would have half the battle won. Perhaps more than that. The fact that Data had come up with ideas Picard had not thought of disturbed Picard, and showed, only too clearly, the advantage that fear gave the Furies.

Picard needed to take that advantage away.

And he needed to do it soon.

Chapter Ten

RIKER KEPT HIS HEAD DOWN as he moved through the ship. He had tried, when he first got on the turbolift, to pretend nothing was wrong, but he couldn't. Seeing fear in the other crew members made fear increase within him. And he needed to bring the fear down. Captain Picard felt the same terror, yet he seemed to continually face it. Somehow it weakened Riker's defenses, made him seem less than he was.

He finally understood how the Klingons felt disgraced in battle with the Furies. Riker had survived on a Klingon ship, against the betrayal, the constant danger, the tests made on his human capabilities, and he had seen that as a challenge. Nothing had brought this kind of deep emotion out in him before.

The same things had probably happened to the Klingons in that first fight. They were used to being tough. They knew how to master difficult circumstances. They never suffered from unreasonable fears. Every fear they faced, and faced down, was justified.

A Klingon always weighed the risks and entered into battle knowing the odds. But that time a Klingon general had panicked and turned to the Federation for help. No wonder they never talked about that battle, even in legends.

Now Riker didn't even know what he was fighting. He suspected he was fighting himself.

Throughout the ship, crew members were down. Some had passed out. Others were moaning. A few were running as if the hounds of hell were behind them—and perhaps they were.

An even larger number of crew were getting back on their feet, surveying their surroundings, mastering their feelings, and helping those around them. Their eyes had a haunted look that probably mirrored the look in Riker's eyes. He knew if he survived this he would never again view his own capabilities the same way.

So, coming into engineering seemed like walking into a haven. Three crew members were unconscious, and someone had propped them near the door. Pale, shaking engineers were examining the warp core. Two ensigns were repairing a sensor pad on top of the screen grid.

Geordi was milling through all of it, appearing busy and concerned. The only thing that gave away his own terror was the speed with which he moved. Geordi always hurried when he felt he could do nothing else. He was hurrying now.

The surprise was Redbay. Someone else had made

out the duty rosters this week, and they had placed Redbay in engineering. He now leaned over a console, his forehead propped against the plastic edge of a screen, his lanky frame hunched forward.

"Sam," Riker said.

Redbay snapped to attention, something he never usually did. Redbay's normal movements were languorous, even in battle. He always moved as if he couldn't be bothered, as if the latest threat were a mere inconvenience. This time was different. This time, he gripped the laser pen in one hand and nodded at Riker.

Redbay's eyes were haunted too.

Their gazes met. Two old friends who knew, without saying, what the other had been through.

"The captain sent me down here. He thinks we can block these waves of emotion."

"I do too," Geordi said from behind him, words clipped and businesslike. "I think there's a link between the fear we felt on the station, and the fear felt shipwide here. Most people paralyzed by terror on the *Enterprise* hadn't seen the Fury. And a significant number aren't human and don't have the same subconscious fears. If I were making a hypothesis, I would say that only select Terrans would be frightened by the imagery we saw on the station, yet it affected me. My parents were in Starfleet, and I didn't hear about the more colorful versions of hell until we studied the Furies at the Academy."

"We can rule out smell," Redbay said. "Our noses aren't detecting anything, and the computer says that nothing has changed in the chemical component of the air."

"I don't want to rule anything out yet," Riker said. "Some gases are odorless, and we can still suffer their effects."

"But the computer should be able to read them."

Riker shook his head. "Our systems are good, but they're not perfect. The Furies are clearly sending something our way, and our sensors aren't picking up a beam or a weapon or anything. They've been in this quadrant before, eighty years ago. They've had plenty of time to develop a weapon that will affect us, but one that we can't detect."

"It would help," Geordi said, "if we could determine the nature of the weapon."

"If there is a weapon," Riker said. But he knew he was being too careful. The *Enterprise* had been attacked, he knew that for certain.

"There is," Redbay said. "There has to be."

Riker grinned at his friend. There had to be not because it was logical, but so that they could save face, within themselves. One of the major tests for Academy admission was the ability to subdue fear. A cadet had to be able to face any situation with strength. That way he could negotiate with creatures that terrified him, or keep a cool head in the middle of an attack.

As the captain had.

As Riker attempted to do, and had, if he were being honest with himself. It just hadn't *felt* that way.

It still didn't. His greatest fear was that he would lose control of himself.

He shoved the fear aside.

"I have some ideas, Will," Redbay said. "I've been

thinking about them since"—he paused, grinned, and shrugged—"well, since I got my brain back. Let's assume that the Furies have developed some sort of weapon that does this to us. If so, it must be something that can be projected across distances. To send a gas through a vacuum would require some kind of containment field, and that would be very difficult to hide."

"We don't know the limits of their technology," Geordi said. "They might be able to hide such a field from us."

"Perhaps," Redbay said. "The reactions you had on the station argue for some sort of assault on the senses. Smell is the most logical. But Lieutenant, we were all hit with this wave, as Will calls it, at the same time. You were in a Jeffries tube. One of the ensigns still out cold over there was in the containment field around the warp core."

"And it has a separate air-filtration system," Geordi said.

"So does the Jeffries tube," Riker said, beginning to follow Redbay's argument. "Anything airborne would have taken longer to hit people in these separate areas, and it seemed that we all got hit at once."

"So we can fairly safely rule out smell," La Forge said.

Riker nodded.

"Sound could have reached all of us at the same time," Redbay said, "but unless I miss my guess, Captain Picard was not broadcasting his talk with the Fury shipwide."

"No, he wasn't," Riker said. He frowned. "For the

Furies to be using sound, they would have to broadcast on some sort of wavelength that was carried along on the transmission. And when the conversation was cut the effect should have stopped."

"True," Geordi said. "It would either have to piggyback on the communication with the captain or it would have to travel long distances and somehow pierce the hull and affect all of us at the same time. Again, a containment field would be needed."

"Not likely," Redbay said, "at least not without detection. I was modulating the screens when that first attack hit. I should have noticed something."

"Data was actually monitoring the Furies' vessels," Riker said, "and he found nothing."

"So they are using something subtler, something not quite as obvious, and something that can affect all of us at exactly the same time."

"It would need to be a beam of some kind, but of a kind we don't recognize right off." Geordi's voice was rising with his excitement. "We would have to test for everything."

"Not everything." Riker believed he knew where Redbay was going. "Only physical things, things which would induce an involuntary fear reaction."

"Smell, sound, sight, what else?" Geordi asked.

"No," Redbay said. "Maybe just the reaction to sight, smell, and sound. What does the body produce in reaction to those outside stimuli? Pheromones? I'm not real strong in that area."

"But doesn't that fall under smell?" Riker asked. He didn't know either. But he knew who to ask.

Geordi shrugged. "It's outside my area of expertise,

too. I suggest we consult with Dr. Crusher. I also think we might want to test you, me, and Data to see if we brought anything back from the station. Maybe the Furies baited a trap for us, lured us over there, and had us bring back the trigger. The trigger might be some sort of virus, airborne, and then they pull the switch on their ship, and voilà, we all get scared."

"It's one theory," Redbay said.

Riker agreed. His logical mind said there needed to be a reason why the Furies did what they did on the Brundage Station. They couldn't have done such a thing just in spite.

"Follow that idea, too," Riker said. "The captain did say that the Furies would be stronger this time."

"Did the first run-in with them have this weapon?" Redbay asked.

"Not that the records show," Riker said. "The reaction back then seemed to be more out of fear of what they looked like, what they represented. Kirk and the rest of that crew never mention that the Furies used such fear as a weapon."

"Except," Geordi said slowly, "those old reports were of cultural demons and devils, figures of myth returned. The Klingons put a high store in that sort of thing, even now. It caused their extreme reaction, that ended up bringing in the original *Enterprise*. Remember Worf's reaction when Kahless returned?"

Riker nodded.

"This is different," Geordi went on. "When I got hit in the Jeffries tube, I was flashing back on that fire when I was five. I could have sworn everything on the ship was burning up."

Redbay nodded. "I was back reliving the horror of the day my parents died."

And Riker, who had never allowed himself real terror, hadn't had anything to pin his fear on. Somehow that bothered him even more. "What's your point, Geordi?" he asked, wanting to move his own thinking away from the terror and his ability or lack of ability to control it.

"This fear hit us, and instead of finding an external cause, our minds searched for the last time we had felt this kind of terror and made up the rest. This wasn't cultural. This is sophisticated."

"A weapon," Redbay agreed. "We're back to that again. But a weapon that somehow triggers fear reactions normally caused by sights, smells, and sounds."

Geordi grinned. "If it's a weapon, we can find it. And we can block it."

Riker grinned too. Even though the fear was still present, like the hum of a machine in the background, it suddenly became tolerable. "Then we need to find a systematic way of searching for it."

"Yes," Redbay started.

Then Picard's voice cut over the comm system. "Senior staff to the conference room."

The order made Riker shudder. He didn't want to know what emergency had broken now.

But that was his fear talking.

He took a deep breath. Geordi clapped him on the shoulder and turned to Redbay. "Lieutenant," Geordi said, "go ahead and begin a search. I'll be back as soon as I can."

Redbay nodded and bent over the consoles. Riker and Geordi left engineering at full run.

"Sam's creative," Riker said as they got on the turbolift. "If anyone can find out what's going on, Sam can."

"I hope so," Geordi said. "Because I have the feeling we don't have a lot of time."

Chapter Eleven

BEVERLY CRUSHER STOPPED outside the door to Deanna Troi's quarters. Fear made her heart race, and because she wasn't sure if the fear was entirely real or a product of her fevered imagination, she actually knocked.

And received no response.

"What am I doing?" she whispered. Around her the corridor was filled with dazed crew members. At an intersection a short distance away a crew member lay unconscious, her arms covering her face as if something had been hitting her when she passed out.

Beverly hesitated, wanting to go to the woman, then forced her mind back on her goal. She took a deep breath, brushed aside a strand of loose red hair, and then said, "Computer, emergency medical override."

The door hissed open, and there was Deanna on the

floor, her face pressed against the carpet, one hand raised and the other bent awkwardly beneath her.

It looked as if she'd been trying to crawl to the door to escape something terrible behind her.

Beverly's fears had been real.

She knelt beside Deanna, and as she pulled out her medical tricorder, she smoothed Deanna's hair away from her face. Deanna's eyes were rolled back in their sockets, lashes fluttered. Her mouth was partially open, and her skin was clammy.

Beverly flipped open the tricorder and ran it over Deanna. Her pulse was too rapid, her blood pressure was high, and the levels of adrenaline in her system were off the charts. Yet she wasn't moving. These readings matched the readings from Lieutenant Young, and the result appeared to be the same:

Deanna was dying.

Beverly grabbed a needle from her kit, and then paused. To wake Deanna would be to put her through hell. According to the tricorder readings, Deanna was still conscious, but her system was overloaded. To stimulate her, to make her mind deal with all of the input it was getting, would probably push her over the edge into total insanity.

No. A sedative would be better, and something to block the psychic transfers. There were a number of drugs that would do the trick. The problem was that they were all in sickbay.

"Computer," Beverly said, "download all information on Betazoid empathic powers and blocks into my sickbay computers."

"Download complete."

"Step one," Beverly said to herself. She found the

sedative she was looking for in her bag, and gave it to Deanna. Deanna's eyes slowly closed and she seemed to breathe a little smoother.

"Computer, is anyone in the transporter rooms?"

"The transporter rooms are empty."

Just what she needed. Beverly bit back a retort.

"Find Transporter Chief Anderson."

"Transporter Chief Anderson is in engineering."

Beverly hit her comm badge. "Anderson," she said. "This is Dr. Crusher. I need an emergency beam-across to sickbay."

"I'm sorry, Doctor," Anderson said. "Someone accidentally blasted the transporter controls here. Have you checked with the transporter rooms?"

"Yes, I have, Chief, and no one is in any of them."

"I could go—"

"Do so, and if I'm not in sickbay when you get to the transporter room, beam me directly there."

"Aye, sir."

Beverly slung her kit over her left shoulder, then picked up Deanna, one arm under her back and the other under her knees. Beverly staggered forward for a moment, then straightened her back, letting Deanna's weight settle more firmly in her arms.

"I can do this," she said to herself. "Just one step at a time and I'll make it."

Slowly, she headed for the door, and by the time she was outside Deanna's quarters she was gaining confidence. And speed. It had been a long time since she had carried dead weight for some distance. Certainly not since she had been on the *Enterprise*.

But she could do it. The key was to breathe deeply and move at a constant pace.

Then Captain Picard's voice echoed through the small corridor. "Senior officers to the conference room."

"Excellent timing, Jean-Luc," Beverly muttered.

Lieutenant Worf was the last to arrive in the conference room. He had stopped by his quarters to touch the *bat'leth* that Kahless had given him, a sign to Worf of his own courage.

He was appalled at his initial reaction to the Furies. He had studied the Klingon response to the original Fury attack all those years ago, and had thought it impossible for a modern Klingon to act in a panicked way.

Then he had argued with the captain about the value of fear.

Argued.

As if he needed to justify his own fears.

Cowards justified their fears.

And Worf was no coward.

He strode into the conference room as if nothing were wrong. Riker and La Forge had entered just before him. As Worf suspected, he had lost no time in stopping at his quarters.

In fact, he had probably gained them all time. He had to remind himself of Klingon honor, not Klingon shame.

Captain Picard was standing beside his chair. The others were sitting. But two chairs were empty.

Dr. Crusher's chair, and Counselor Troi's.

Deanna's empty chair seemed to scream at him, call him a fool and a coward all at once.

Worf glanced at the door. He should have thought

of the effect this overwhelming emotion would have had on Deanna. The fear had caught them all off guard. Deanna would have handled things well if she had been prepared, but she hadn't. None of them had.

Riker was also staring at the empty chair. He must have forgotten, also. That thought gave Worf no comfort.

As a unit, both men started for the door.

"I called a meeting, gentlemen," Picard said softly.

"But Deanna—" Worf said.

Picard nodded once. He understood too. "She will be here if she can."

"But shouldn't someone check on her?" Riker asked.

"Sickbay informs me that Dr. Crusher has already done so." The captain clasped his hands behind his back. Worf recognized the gesture. The captain would say no more. But he just couldn't let it go at that.

"Begging the captain's pardon," Worf said, "but I believe we should check on her condition."

"I understand your concern, Lieutenant, but Dr. Crusher will see to Deanna's needs. Right now, I require your presence here."

Worf took a deep breath. He knew his duty. But he also knew how valuable Deanna was to the ship.

And to him.

He turned and came back to his chair, sitting heavily. Commander Riker was still by the door, looking indecisive. He never looked that indecisive.

"You too, Will," Picard said softly. "We're all concerned for Deanna, but I'm afraid that right now we have other matters to attend to. I just received a scrambled communication from Admiral Kirschbaum. The *Starships Madison* and *Idaho*—"

The door hissed open and Beverly Crusher hurried in. Her long red hair was plastered to her face, and a line of sweat ran down the side of her uniform.

"Forgive me for being late, Captain," she said, and slumped into the nearest chair.

The terror Worf had been feeling all day rose. He had to clench his massive fists to contain it. "The counselor?" he asked.

Dr. Crusher glanced at him, her mouth a thin line. "I don't know, Worf. I got her to sickbay, and put her under sedation. I also used some blockers, hoping to stop the empathic response. But when I found her, her system was overloading."

"Like Lieutenant Young's?" Riker asked.

"It's similar," Dr. Crusher said, "but not the same. The terror we've all been feeling has amplified in Deanna. I don't believe she saw anything or did anything to trigger this. She calmed noticeably once we administered the block."

"Do you believe that she'll be conscious any time soon?" the captain asked.

"I don't know if it's a good idea for us to let her to be conscious until we settle this," Dr. Crusher said. "I'm not sure how much she can take."

"It is only going to get worse," Worf said. "We have not yet faced the Furies directly. We have only contacted them from a distance."

"Do you expect us to face them directly, Mr. Worf?" the captain asked.

"I believe, Captain, given what we found on

Brundage Station, and given the past history of the Furies, that we will face them directly in a fight."

"If they board the ship or come into contact directly with Deanna," Dr. Crusher said, "I cannot vouch for her sanity. In fact, I can't vouch for any of our sanity. I had hoped to get her help with Lieutenant Young, since he was the first. I believe all of his trouble is psychological, not physical."

"Hmm," the captain said, obviously seeing the implications in what Dr. Crusher was saying.

Worf agreed with the doctor. He had thought he might be immune, yet he had felt the terror of the Furies. He had thought he would react differently from his ancestors. But he hadn't. He had been just as terrified from the contact.

The key, though, as the captain had pointed out, was to overcome that fear.

And he would, for his own sake as well as Deanna's.

"Well," the captain said, "we must leave Deanna and Lieutenant Young in your capable care, Beverly."

He unclasped his hands, then clasped them as if he didn't know what to do with them. "Admiral Kirschbaum contacted me again. The *Starships Madison* and *Idaho* will arrive in three hours. The Klingons and Vulcans will assist us as well. Two of the Klingons' closest Birds-of-Prey will be here at the same time as the starships. The Vulcan ship *T'Pau* will arrive within four hours."

"Only two ships?" Worf asked. The fear he had been trying to suppress rose again. The Klingons would not shame themselves. Not again.

"I am told, Mr. Worf, that the Klingon Homeworld

is massing two lines of defense. One is here, and the other, the main one, is farther inside the border to Klingon space. The Federation is doing the same. We are simply the front line, the first battle of what may turn out to be a very long and costly war."

It was uncharacteristic of Klingons to have a backup line of defense. Worf crossed his arms and leaned back, forcing himself into silence. His people had acted so impulsively during the first encounter with the Furies, it made sense for them to act more conservatively this time.

"So no one believes we'll survive this," Commander Riker said without a trace of bitterness.

"Starfleet is operating under the assumptions posited by Captain Kirk, Number One. The first *Enterprise* barely managed to beat one Fury ship. Granted, it was a very different ship from the five we are facing out there, but the thought is that the Furies will arrive stronger this time. Five ships would tend to back up that line of thinking."

"We're stronger now, too," Geordi said.

"We are, Mr. La Forge, and we have to hope that the Furies do not know that. But we cannot rely on their ignorance as a source of defense. Starfleet has had a Furies scenario for eighty years. The first ship on the scene is to negotiate with the Furies, and should that fail, the ship is to consider a breach of the Furies Point an act of war."

"But they attacked the Brundage Station," Worf said.

Picard nodded. "With the Furies' attack on the station, the wartime analysis is assured. We are to do our best to defeat them here, but Starfleet believes that the Furies will sweep through our defenses and move into the quadrant. Hence the backup forces, both on our side and on the Klingon side."

"They could give us a chance before they give up on us," Geordi mumbled.

Worf agreed, but said nothing. Sometimes it was the place of a warrior to die, and to do so on the front lines of battle would be a great honor.

"They have not given up on us, Mr. La Forge," the captain said. "If they had, they would not be sending so many ships here. But we learned in our first encounter with the Furies to be careful. We are not facing another space-traveling race with equal or lesser powers. Instead we are facing a race that ruled this entire quadrant for possibly over two millennia and want to do so again. We must respond accordingly."

Worf moved forward slightly. "What other forces will join in the larger battle?"

"We don't know." The captain took a deep breath, as if he had been hesitating about sharing this next information. "The Romulans have refused to come to our aid. The Cardassians have decided to wait until they know the outcome of this first battle. They claim their concerns are not simply for this sector of space, but for the quadrant itself."

Riker snorted, but said nothing.

"And the wormhole near *Deep Space Nine*. Have the people there been warned?" La Forge asked.

"The entire quadrant now knows and is preparing at this point. Admiral Kirschbaum hopes to have more support as time goes on. Some planets simply do not have strong defensive capabilities. It is up to us to make certain, if possible, that the Furies do not go beyond this area."

Worf found himself nodding in agreement. The most important fight was here. The Federation and the Empire would lose the advantage if the fight spread out over the neighboring star systems and into the quadrant.

"That presents a problem, Captain," Dr. Crusher said. "Even with this limited contact, the crew is not responding well. I have twenty-seven people in sickbay under heavy sedation. Those who can function are picking up the slack and encouraging those who are marginal. But our biggest problem is with the families. We are managing, but certainly we aren't performing anywhere near capacity. I don't know how many personnel would be able to hold their posts during an attack."

The captain smiled tightly. "I am aware of that, Doctor. It is ourselves and our reactions that we must conquer first before moving on to the Furies. To that end, Mr. La Forge, what have you discovered in engineering?"

"Nothing yet, sir," Geordi said, "but we are working on several theories. Lieutenant Redbay believes that this fear response is artificially created and carried on a beam of some sort. In theory I agree with him. He's working right now to discover the source of the reaction and to see if he can block it."

"How long do you estimate this will take?" the captain asked.

Geordi shook his head. "I wish I could tell you, Captain. But right now, we're working on supposition and logic. No definitive proof at all. And since we don't know what we're looking for, we don't know how to block it or what it will take to do so."

"Lieutenant Redbay's supposition would seem to be a correct one," Data said. "The fear response in this ship is, according to my analysis of the old records, far stronger than the reaction the original *Enterprise* crew had. It also does not follow the same pattern that theirs did."

Picard nodded. "Well, if we cannot block the attack from without, we must stop it from within."

Worf knew of the battle within. Klingons fought it most of their lives. "Klingons have a technique called KloqPoq that might serve us well."

"I'm not sure this is the time, Mr. Worf," Riker said.

"KloqPoq does not always entail a ritual," Worf said. "The shortened version requires only the touch of oil upon the forehead combined with words of strength." There had been many times over the years that he had used the ritual, and it had worked every time to calm him.

"Right now," the captain said, "I am willing to try anything that will help the crew. Number One, I want you to issue a statement to the crew about cultural rituals such as the one Mr. Worf described. Some of these might have been invented in response to prehistoric contact with the Furies. We cannot rule any of these rituals out. But do stress, Number One, that these rituals cannot take time away from duty. The shorter the better."

Picard turned and looked at him. "Mr. Worf, you

may perform the short version on any crew member who desires it."

Worf nodded. "Thank you, sir." He was pleased that the captain allowed him to help.

"In the meantime, Dr. Crusher, is there any physical way to block the fear response?"

She frowned and pushed a strand of red hair aside, smearing the dirt and sweat coating her forehead. "There are several in humans, Captain, but I wouldn't want to use any of these before a battle. They also inhibit other responses as well."

"Is there any way to isolate the fear response and block only it?"

"I have several theories," she said, "but I have had no time to focus on them."

"How long would it take to bring one of your theories to fruition?"

"Give me an hour."

The captain nodded. "Then make it so, Beverly. Blocking our own fears would be the best line of defense against this first attack by the Furies."

"I agree," she said.

The captain turned from her to face all his officers. His decisive movements led Worf to believe that the captain had a plan. Whether he did or not was immaterial. The fact that he *acted* as if he did mattered most. It engendered hope in the officers, which would then inspire the crew.

"There is one more potential problem," the captain said. "While we might assume that these five ships are the only ships we will face, we cannot believe that assumption. These ships might be the advance guard for an invasion force. If that is the case, the Starfleet vessels, the Klingon Birds-of-Prey, and the *T'Pau* will not be enough to keep the force from sweeping into the quadrant."

A chill ran through Worf. "Have you evidence of this, Captain?"

"It is only a theory at this point, Mr. Worf."

"I believe this theory to be accurate," Data said. "The evidence suggests that the five ships are waiting for something. Most likely a second, larger force."

Worf nodded. That would be simply good tactics. A small advance force before risking a larger one.

Picard focused his intense gaze on all of them, and Worf straightened his shoulders.

"I do not want an invasion force to come through that wormhole," Picard said, his voice firm. "In fact, I do not want any more Fury ships to come into this quadrant. Therefore, in addition to finding ways to prevent the Furies from attacking us, we must find a way to close the wormhole."

The silence in the room was palpable.

Until now, it seemed, no one had really thought about what all-out war with the Furies would mean. But the thought of an invasion force seemed suddenly very real to Worf. These ships needed to be stopped now and the wormhole closed. Worf understood and he felt ready for the fight.

The captain walked around the table and stopped behind Data. "Mr. Data, I want you to make that wormhole your primary source of study. I need to know the most effective method to close it. And I need it fast."

"Aye, sir," Data said.

The captain made eye contact with each of his officers. When his gaze rested on Worf, Worf nodded back. The captain's confidence was restoring Worf's confidence. He could feel it giving him strength as each minute went by.

"I don't think I need to impress upon you all the importance of what we do here," the captain said. "We are the Federation's flagship, and I have never worked with a stronger, more capable crew in my entire career. The *Enterprise* defeated the Furies once. She shall do so again."

And somehow, for that moment in time, Worf believed that what the captain said was true.

Chapter Twelve

THE SHIP WAS GROWING COLD, the air thin, and the food scarce. Some minor functionary was not doing his job.

Again.

Vergo Vedil unfolded his body from the command chair and groaned as he did so. The bridge of the *Erinyes* had been designed by Ak'lins. Web-footed and secure, they had never thought that a leader might be a Zebub. He had to struggle to keep his hoofed feet from sliding out from underneath him.

It was not dignified for the Vergo of the *Erinyes* to slip and fall on his spiny backside. He scratched behind one of his horns, nearly breaking a nail, and then sucked at the air, catching sweetmeats in the thin strands of saliva that coated his mouth. He glanced around and could almost see the entire distance across the bridge. The atmosphere was far too thin. In a moment he would see that fixed, and someone would pay for the oversight.

He slowly stretched his muscles. This bout of waiting seemed interminable. He had thought the advance guard would have all the pleasure of the invasion. He had not realized that the hours between his first attack and the arrival of the fleet would be long, and filled with emptiness.

Ythion had argued against keeping the live one, and Vedil had had too much fun killing the others. The presents he left for the Unclean should have frightened them beyond their capacity for reason. And if they had had their souls with them, he would have scattered them to air, cutting them open.

He lightly brushed the doll likeness of himself hanging on his side. It felt thick and full, as his life had been to this point. His soul was safe, but it reassured him to check it at times.

He faced the front viewscreen and stared at the Unclean ship hanging in space. They had contacted him again. Perhaps his approach had been too narrow. He had used what the Unclean captive had thought of as a Terran attack. He should have noted that a sweep of the Unclean's mind informed him that many races from heaven filled the ships now. Perhaps Vedil should have allowed one of the Sakill, with their ridged foreheads and long braided hair, to accompany him. Or even a Jequat, a one-eyed stone giant, to squint at the puny captain of the Unclean.

That would have silenced him forever.

The Unclean ship had not attacked yet. Perhaps it never would. Perhaps he would remain, guardian of the Entrance to Heaven, leader of a battle that would never occur.

"Vergo, they have received another transmission." His first assistant bowed before him, the snakes in her hair floating around her, their mouths opening and closing in the ever-thinning air.

He scooped a maggot from his cheek, watched the creature climb in the curve of his longest nail, and then scraped the nail against his left fang. The maggot was sweet and juicy, cool against his tongue.

The rest of his staff watched him, knowing that when he ate so obviously in front of them he was breaking etiquette and showing his displeasure. Hands, claws, and flippers rested against controls, waiting for his next command, or his next outburst.

"And of course we know, Dea, what that transmission said." He swiveled his head until the tip of one horn brushed against the nearest snake.

She jumped away as if burned. "No, Vergo, but we are working on it."

"Working on it. Such an old-fashioned, out-of-date term. These communications are not sophisticated. We have their ancient codes from the ship of Kirk. We should be able to understand what they are saying."

She swallowed, and all the snakes floating about her head closed their mouths, as if in sympathy. "Yes, Vergo."

"I am glad we understand each other," he said, and used his horn to decapitate the snake he had been toying with. Green goo billowed in the atmosphere along with tiny bugs, half a dozen or more. He sucked them in through his teeth.

She blinked in obvious pain. "I will do better, Vergo."

"You will have to," he said. "Since I am now removing your badge of power. You shall go to the food tanks below, see what is thinning the air, and double the level of edibles in the atmosphere."

She nodded. The snakes all watched him, as wary as she was. "Below, then, Vergo." She pivoted on one small, Unclean-like foot, and crossed the bridge. As she stepped into the mobile stairs, the snakes on her head dove at the single snake carcass. They ripped and shredded it in their haste to devour the remains.

Much like his people when they sensed weakness.

"B'el," Vedil said. "You shall monitor the Unclean ship."

B'el bobbed the center of his three heads. The others were already too busy watching the screens. "Vergo," said the first head, "the Unclean are trying to communicate with us again."

Vedil snorted. "Do these creatures do nothing other than talk?"

This was the third attempt at communication. It disturbed him. After their discovery of the outpost and its dead crew, and especially after his first transmission, this Unclean ship should have been his.

"O'pZ," he said to the Ak'lin at the science console. "Has our beam shut off?"

"No, Veeerrrgo." Her beaklike mouth often got stuck on sibilants. He had almost given her a position where she need not talk in the heat of battle. But Ak'lins had a gift for engineering, architecture, and science. O'pZ was the most talented scientist he knew.

And therefore extremely valuable.

"What evidence have you of the beam's effect?"

She lowered her scaly head and hunched her ridged back forward, as if protecting her soft underbelly. "None, Vergo. It is as if the beam is having no effect."

"We should destroy the Unclean ship," her lover, Prote, said. His useless wings unfurled at the thought, nearly hitting B'el.

"And if we do that, we lose all the precious knowledge they hold in their minds and in their electronic systems." Vedil steadied himself against his chair. His feet slid against the slick floor, and he had to struggle for a moment to keep his balance.

He glanced around, then decided. "Increase the beam's intensity. We have ten hours to conquer them without destroying their ship. I would prefer to give this vessel to the fleet as a prize when they come through, rather than have them fly through a ring of debris."

"Vergo, the debris from one puny vessel will not make a difference to two hundred of our ships," Prote said.

Vedil lowered his gaze and glared at Prote. "And the loss of one navigation officer will not make a difference in our return to heaven."

Prote's wings curled and he bowed his head. "Yes, Vergo."

"I thought the beam would work quicker than it has," the Ak'lin said. "I thought it would be easier to enslave them."

"It will be easy to enslave them," Vedil said. "You forget the ease with which we captured their outpost.

Once they see us face-to-face, they will be unable to resist our dominance."

He grinned at his crew. They watched him warily.

"We shall toy with the Unclean for another hour or so, and then we shall make them ours. But I would like to remind them how powerless they are against us, and an hour or two of futile struggle is all we need."

"When the fleet comes through, the Unclean will know we are conquerors," Prote said, obviously trying to make up for his earlier mistakes.

"They will know it before the fleet comes through," Vedil said. "By the time the fleet joins us, this tiny Unclean vessel shall lead us into the promised land, its crew eager to share its enslavement with its companions in the stars beyond."

Chapter Thirteen

REDBAY FOCUSED on the screens in front of him. If he concentrated on work, his fears—the memories of that horrid year when he lost his family and scavenged through the remains of Nyo colony alone—didn't overwhelm him. Sometimes they caught him in the throat or the gut. Sometimes he felt shivers running through him, and once he thought of asking Ensign Moest for a hug. Well, not really. She was beautiful, and he wouldn't mind a bit of female comfort at the moment, but he had learned his lesson early: never start a shipboard romance. If the thing went sour, there was nowhere to hide.

He grinned to himself. Thinking about women was a lot easier than thinking about the past.

But he needed to focus on the task at hand. The

quicker they blocked whatever the Furies were doing to them, the better things would get.

Or so he kept telling himself.

He was doing tests on types of subspace carrier waves, hoping to stumble on something. To him, subspace or interspace seemed the only two logical ways the Furies could send some sort of fear trigger. If the captain's supposition was right, the Furies had the capability to form wormholes. They clearly understood more about the physics of subspace and interspace than the Federation did.

The tests appeared as multicolored light on his screens. Those light patterns sent shivers through him. Multicolored light used to send him screaming from his safe room for years after his parents died. The Federation investigated the deaths on Nyo, but never found evidence of the light creatures. Some counselors believed that Redbay had made them up to cope with the trauma. Those counselors believed that everyone had died of disease or some undetectable cause.

Not genocide.

But he hadn't made it up. His memories were still clear. He had seen those creatures and he had hidden from them, and he had been the sole survivor.

But he was here now. On the *Enterprise*.

Looking at multicolored light patterns *he* had made.

And then he squinted. The effort it took him to block his fears delayed his own understanding of the pink cone he saw on the screen before him.

"Geordi," he said, his voice shaking with awe. "I found it."

La Forge left his seat and hurried to Redbay's side, leaning over his shoulder.

"Look. Right here."

Redbay put a finger on the screen. In his search, he had changed the look of the screen to a variety of different computer models. This one looked like a two-dimensional representation used long before computer imaging came into play. He had only called it up after exhausting the other options.

On it, the Furies' ships showed up as black dots near the yellow, glowing Furies Point. Brundage Station was another black square with a bit of silver light trickling off it, as if it had been raining in space, and now the rain was dripping dry. He had his theories about that, but they weren't important just yet. What was important were the multicolored light waves that ran across the screen, representing the *Enterprise*'s search for the source of the fear.

And, as the light passed over the main Fury ship, a cone of pink light appeared, enveloping the *Enterprise*.

"Wow," La Forge said when the cone became visible. "Can you freeze that? Can we study it as it is?"

Redbay pushed a few buttons. His multicolored light waves disappeared and only the pink cone remained

"At our position," he said, "the radius of that cone is over a thousand kilometers and it extends beyond our sensor range."

"But what are they projecting?" La Forge asked more to himself than to Redbay. He bent over the nearest panel, running his own checks.

THE SOLDIERS OF FEAR

Redbay matched it, fingers shaking. "I don't have a reading yet on the content of that beam, but this is clearly how they're manipulating our emotions. At this frequency in interspace, the beam goes through everything, including our heads."

La Forge glanced at Redbay. A shiver ran down Redbay's spine. The fear rose, as if someone had turned up the volume.

Maybe someone had.

"If they can project something that makes us feel fear," La Forge said softly, "we can block it." Then he paused. "You said interspace?"

Redbay nodded. "That's how they're projecting whatever it is they're projecting. Through interspace."

La Forge paced for a moment, then came back and stood over the cone image. "Interspace. The original *Enterprise* stumbled into interspace during the first meetings with the Tholians? I wonder . . ." La Forge seemed to be talking only to himself.

Redbay suddenly remembered that part of his history class. It had again been the original *Enterprise* and their encounter with the Tholians. But beyond the successful outcome, and the fact that interspace almost took Captain Kirk, he couldn't remember more. But it was clear La Forge did.

La Forge turned to Redbay. "What if the beam they send out is harmless in this universe—but opens a conduit into interspace in the area affected by the beam? Interspace can have a devastating effect on the human nervous system, leading to paranoia and insanity. What if they've managed to control and amplify that effect?"

Redbay grinned. "You might be on to something there. I'll run the checks."

Suddenly, beneath his fear was an elation. La Forge was right. Redbay felt lot better.

He could concentrate now on the task at hand.

"That's it. We've got it," he told La Forge.

La Forge nodded. "I'll tell the captain. I bet this will make his day."

"And Dr. Crusher," Redbay said.

La Forge stopped, and then nodded. "The doctor on the original *Enterprise* came up with something to block the effects, didn't he." He patted Redbay on the shoulder. "On my way."

Redbay turned back to his panel, his fingers flying over the keys. He had work to do, and now he at least knew he was making progress.

She felt as if she were the only physician working on a plague.

Beverly Crusher sighed and ran her fingers through her hair, pushing it back from her forehead. Her eyes were gritty, as if she had gone too long without sleep. She leaned her head against the computer display and gulped the fear down.

Patience, Beverly, she thought. *Take your time.*

Over the years, she had learned that taking her time was the only way to really hurry. Any other method caused her to make mistakes.

She took a sip of the Bajoran root tea that was supposed to calm fears. It was warm and bitter. Then she sat up and peered through the glass of her research area into the sickbay.

Her flu patients were under heavy sedation. They

had awakened earlier, convinced they were dying. She had been unable to calm them; instead she had put them under and hoped that the drug blocked the emotions as well as consciousness. They didn't appear to be having any more bad dreams, so her guess was probably right.

Deanna lay very still on her bed as well. When Beverly had returned to sickbay, she had taken Deanna's pulse just to double-check the machines. Deanna had looked still as death.

Perhaps that was Beverly's fear: losing her friend to an unnecessary cause.

A few other beds were filled with crew members injured in that first wave of fear that swept the station. The medical staff had had a run on the station just after Beverly had left to find Deanna: a series of scrapes, scratches, and burns, all minor—and blown entirely out of proportion because of the fears.

The cases that remained were people brought in by others, people who had been too terrified to notice that they were hurt. Beverly had made a note of their names; when and if they got through this crisis, she wanted Deanna to make a full report on their psychological states.

If Deanna recovered.

Beverly sighed and took another sip of the tea, wincing at its taste.

Then she paused, rolled the tea around on her tongue, and swallowed.

Her tongue was numb. Not completely without sensation, but she had lost enough sensation to get a prickly feeling around the edges.

She had used the root tea before, often on long stressful nights, and had never found that her judgment was impaired.

But it always reduced her stress.

Just like it had calmed her fears now.

She wasn't shaking anymore. She hadn't shaken since she had her first cup.

Then she smiled, pulled out a test tube, and poured the tea in it. The liquid stained the sides of the tube orange. She put the tube in the compositor and had it analyze the contents. While it mixed and remixed the chemicals, Beverly got up and went into sickbay proper. She passed the fear patients and went directly to the flu patients. They were still on the diagnostic beds. She flipped on the overhead screens, and watched as she read the levels.

The flu was running its course. They would be on their feet again in a day or so. But she wasn't interested in their virus. She was interested in brain waves or any indication of REM sleep.

The patients appeared to be sleeping soundly, dreamlessly, and their physical symptoms confirmed it. Heartbeat, respiration, and blood pressure readings had returned to normal—or as near to normal as it was physically possible with the Xotic Flu.

She called up their readings from the past few hours, ever since she had given them the sedative.

No dreams.

None.

The fears were buried, for now.

She went back into her research station. The chemical component of the Bajoran root tea blinked on her screen. As she had thought, the tea had a mild sedative. Very mild, a kind, the computer told her (and her own experience confirmed), that did not impair thoughts or cause drowsiness. It took the edge off certain emotions by blocking the chemical components of those emotions within the body. It did not affect motor skills or judgment.

"Dr. Crusher?" Chief Engineer La Forge's voice came over the comm.

"Go ahead," she said.

"Doctor," La Forge said, "we think the beam hitting us controls and amplifies the effects of interspace."

"Interspace?" She let the word sink in. Why hadn't she thought of that possibility?

"Yes, Doctor," La Forge said.

"Damn," she said softly to herself.

"Excuse me, Doctor?" La Forge said.

"Sorry, Geordi," she said, half laughing. "I'll get right on it. I think I may be able to come up with a block."

"Good," La Forge said. "Out."

She turned her attention back to her screen. With a few keystrokes she had the Theragen formula up on the screen, along with the history of its development and use. For the next few minutes she read, letting the exact details of the drug back into her mind. Its first use was as a nerve gas, developed by the Klingons. But Dr. McCoy on the first *Enterprise* had diluted the drug to stop the effects of interspace on the crew. His diluted form was called the Theragen derivative.

She studied McCoy's work. McCoy had diluted the Theragen with alcohol, but she thought it would make a better mix with the Bajoran tea—that way it would not only block the fear, but have a calming effect on the crew.

She asked the computer to confirm that analysis, and the computer did. Replication possible in both liquid and gaseous form.

Beverly smiled. With a lot of help from Geordi, she had come up with a solution much faster than she had expected.

But barely within the captain's deadline.

She hit her comm badge. "Captain?"

"Picard here." His voice sounded firm and steady. She wondered how he managed that when she knew how he felt. The fears sent by the Furies had affected him too.

"I have found a way to help block the fears within the crew."

"Excellent. If you believe it will work, begin treatment immediately."

He was on edge. She could hear it in his tone.

"Captain, I do have to tell you that what I have come up with is partially a mild sedative."

"Sedative?" His voice rose. "Doctor, we may be about to face the most dangerous enemy known to the Federation, and you want to sedate my crew?"

"Yes, sir." She smiled. She had known he would react like that to the word. Better to get it out of the way now. "The sedative will calm the emotions only. It will not affect judgment or impair motor skills. Since I was unable to test it fully, however, I do not know how long its effects will last." She took a deep breath. "I need to also add small quantities of Theragen derivative to the sedative, to help block the effects of interspace."

The captain did not answer immediately. Perhaps

she shouldn't have worried about impaired judgment from the drug. The fear was doing that all by itself. Captain Picard usually made decisions much quicker than this.

"How long will it take you to inoculate the entire crew?"

"I won't have to inoculate them," she said. "I can make this sedative mixed with the Theragen derivative into a gas and flood the air filtration systems. I'll have to let Geordi know so that the systems won't automatically purify it. Other than that, no one will even notice except that their fears will have eased. They won't abate completely, but everyone will be calmer."

"Proceed," Picard said, and signed off.

Beverly took another sip of her root tea and smiled at the mug. Then she turned and punched in the sequence to begin synthesizing the tea and mixing it with Theragen derivative. This just might be the complete answer. She hoped so.

Commander Riker took a deep breath and uncrossed his arms. Somehow, just sitting beside Captain Picard on the bridge calmed him. Everything was calming him. He was regaining control, even without Dr. Crusher's help. When the gas filled the ship, he would be prepared, and maybe feel like his own self again.

On the screen before them, the entire bridge crew was studying Redbay's discovery: the wave of emotion they had all felt was actually sent in the form of a cone-shaped wave that created an interspace conduit.

And the *Enterprise* was stuck in the middle of it. The wave picked up and amplified—or maybe twisted would be a better way of putting it—the adverse effects of interspace on the human mind. The more he studied the data Redbay and La Forge had come up with, the prouder he felt of the crew of the *Enterprise*. They had withstood a very vicious attack and kept their sanity.

"At least we know that our unusual feelings have been manufactured," Picard said.

"That eased the mind of everyone on the engineering staff," Riker said.

"Yes, I can see how it would." Picard stood and tugged on his shirt. "I hope we have as much success in blocking the effects of the wave."

"Lieutenant Redbay believes we will," Riker said. "He and La Forge are researching the incident that occurred with the original *Enterprise*. It should give them some help."

Picard only nodded his agreement.

"Captain," Worf said, "I have received a short, encrypted message from the *Madison*. They will arrive within the hour."

"Did they say anything about the *Idaho*?"

"The ships are traveling in tandem, sir."

Picard nodded. He stared at the screen another moment, frowning at the data about the interspace beam.

"Captain, those ships will fly straight into that beam," Riker said.

"They will encounter it sooner than we did," Data added. "The strength of the cone-shaped beam at its outer edge might be weaker, but the closer they come the more they will feel its effects."

"Without warning," Riker said, "they will go through the same feelings we did."

"I understand that, Number One," Picard said. "I am trying to figure out a way to communicate to them without letting the Furies know that we have ameliorated the effects of their transmission."

"Oh, I know how to do that, sir," Riker said. "Captain Kiser is quite a poker player. I met him on Rigel in a galaxy-wide tournament."

Picard nodded and seemed to take a deep, almost relaxing breath.

Riker suddenly felt as if he wanted to smile. Dr. McCoy's Theragen derivative and Dr. Crusher's sedative gas must be working. The feeling of fear was clearly reduced. It wasn't completely gone, but it was better.

"Kiser and I," Riker said, "were the only humans left in the contest. We worked out a series of signals that allowed us to eliminate the others—"

"You cheated, Number One?"

"Not exactly," Riker said. "It became clear early on that it wasn't a clean tournament, and that the Ferengi sponsors had set up their own people to win. We just . . . how should I say this . . . made sure that wouldn't happen."

"I do not see how a game of chance will enable you to communicate with Captain Kiser," Data said. "It could not carry the needed information."

"It means, Mr. Data, that Commander Riker and Captain Kiser have already developed a method for saying one thing and meaning another," Picard said. "You will need to bury Dr. Crusher's formula for the sedative in the message as well as the theory of the

Furies' fear wave being sent via interspace. The poker signals will only alert him to the fact the information is there."

Data nodded, understanding.

"Yes, sir," Riker said. "I will tell him that this is a view of the Brundage Station and they need to review it immediately. Since they've already seen Brundage Station, Kiser will know that we have new or different information buried in there."

"I would suggest," Worf said, "that you let the Klingon and Vulcan vessels know this information as well."

"I'll ask Captain Kiser to forward it," Riker said. "The Furies are less likely to be monitoring his communications."

"Do you think they're monitoring ours?" Ensign Eckley asked. She was back at her post, looking shaky but calmer.

"We're monitoring theirs, aren't we?" Riker asked.

Picard smiled. "Go to it, Number One. Record the message and encrypt it. Ask for an encrypted message in return. Use my ready room."

Riker nodded and started across the bridge.

"And, Number One," Picard added, "give Captain Kiser my regards as well. Warn him that the house has the advantage so far."

"I will," Riker said. Then he stopped. "But I will also say that I believe we can turn the tables and use the house's advantage to our own. Kiser always did like a long shot."

"Well," Picard said, returning to his command chair. "I hope he likes long shots not just for the challenge."

"Kiser likes a challenge," Riker said, remembering the ironic, contained man he had played cards with a few years before. "But he likes winning even more."

"Good," Picard said, turning back to the screen showing the Furies' ships. "Because that's the only attitude that will get us out of here alive."

Chapter Fourteen

TEN-FORWARD WAS EMPTY. The entire crew was on duty. Families huddled together in their quarters or the specially assigned safe areas that Beverly had set up.

Picard stood at the door. He had forgotten the room was so vast. Behind the bar Guinan worked over something, then turned around and smiled a full smile at him. She had on a purple robe and flowing purple hat that somehow seemed to blend with her dark skin, making her eyes seem intense. Many times Picard had looked into those clear, knowledgeable eyes for help and gotten it. In many ways he considered Guinan one of his best friends, even though he knew very little about her. He just knew that he trusted her completely and over the years she had never let him down. Not once.

"You'd better come sit down," Guinan said, indicating the barstool in front of her. "I don't have table side service anymore." She set a steaming mug of Earl Grey tea on the bar. Hers was real, not replicated. The drink's delicate perfume drifted through the empty room.

"I don't have much time, Guinan," Picard said.

"I know, but you came here for a reason." She slid the tea forward. "Now sit."

He stepped into the room, feeling vaguely guilty. He should be preparing more for the approaching attack, but he had delegated the duties to people with greater expertise in their areas. He had nothing to do but wait.

And worry.

The job of a commander.

"You are preparing for the attack," Guinan said as he approached. "Stop feeling so guilty."

"Is it that obvious?" He climbed onto the barstool. The scent of the tea tickled his nose. He took the mug, felt its warmth against his fingers, and sipped. The bouquet was delicate, as fine as that of any tea he had ever had.

"I doubt it's obvious to anyone else, but I've known you a long time."

"That you have," Picard said. "And you well know I've never faced a situation like this one."

"But you have," she said, the look on her face clearly showing her disagreement. "Every day when you venture into new territory, you face the same decisions you face here."

He shook his head. "No," he said. "This is different. We came into the sector as the advance troop in a war, Guinan. I've dedicated my entire life, my entire career to peace."

"Yet you serve in Starfleet," she said softly.

"Successful Starfleet officers wage peace," he said.

"Sometimes waging peace is preventing universal destruction." She pulled up a chair, pushed her purple hat back, and leaned her elbows on the bar, as if she were the supplicant.

"Sometimes," he said. "I agree. But I can't help the feeling that we are missing something here. The Furies come through the Furies Point and instantly we're at war. Admiral Kirschbaum told me to negotiate, but that felt perfunctory, Guinan. It is as if we have been expecting a battle for eighty years, and a battle is what we're going to get."

"The Furies have terrified this sector for a long time," Guinan said. Her eyes were hooded, her gaze unreadable. He hated it when she was being inscrutable.

"You think we're wrong, don't you?"

"I didn't say that," she said, "but I do think that terror leads to fuzzy decision-making."

"As do I," Picard said. "Yet I have tried to negotiate with them. They will not talk. They are intent on intimidation. They're even sending a beam filled with fake intimidation, forcing our nervous systems into a state of fear."

"Brundage Station was deliberate provocation," Guinan said.

Picard nodded. "But I learned long ago that even given such attempts to start a war, parties can come to peaceful terms."

Guinan lifted her head, her eyebrows together in a

frown. "You're afraid of them," she said as if it were a revelation. "Aren't you?"

"I felt the fear they sent," he said.

She shook her head. "No. I mean, you're really afraid of them. Underneath." She patted her stomach inside her robe. "Down in here afraid."

He licked his lips. It was a question he had been asking himself, and he had been afraid of the answer. Such irony. And it was probably the question that had led him to Guinan in the first place.

"These creatures," he said, "formed the nightmares of my childhood. Paris is full of their images. They grace buildings in the form of gargoyles, fill the Louvre in medieval paintings, are shown being vanquished in the stained glass of ancient churches. We would return home after a visit to that city, and I would dream of gargoyles climbing off buildings, swarming the streets, and coming to get me. When I saw the leader of the Furies, I saw my nightmare come to life."

Guinan took his nearly empty mug and refilled it. But she didn't give it back to him right away. She held it as if considering serving him at all.

He had seen this look before. Guinan had a lot of knowledge about the universe, and while she shared it, she did so judiciously. Always cautious about offending others, always cautious about revealing more than the listener needed to know, she recognized her knowledge as the potential weapon it was.

"Your childhood nightmares confused the evils, Jean-Luc," she said. She wasn't looking at him; she was looking in the mug. "What do you know of gargoyles?"

"Aside from their architectural uses?"

She smiled then, and set the mug before him. The steam rose, coating his hand. "I'm not going to waste our time talking about decorative water spouts."

"I know that they were common on medieval stone structures, and were often imitated as late as the twentieth century."

"That's still architectural," she said. "Gargoyles were placed on buildings to keep the demons out. Jean-Luc, you're confusing your protectors with your enslavers."

He wrapped his hand around the mug, needing the comfort of the warmth. "What do you mean, Guinan?"

"The hatred you feel deep inside is genetic, Jean-Luc." She was looking at him now, her dark eyes filled with compassion. He wasn't certain he wanted to see that. "The Furies terrorized your people thousands of years ago. And not just your people. The Vulcans, the Klingons, even the Ferengi fell prey to them."

Picard nodded. "I know."

Guinan went on. "But do you really, Jean-Luc?" She gave him a look and he wondered if he really did have any understanding.

"After a millennium of rule in this sector, something arrived and overthrew the Furies. The Klingons called them the Havoc."

She stood upright, looking into his eyes. "The Vulcans wrote only of the terror that ensued in the battle. Humans, on the other hand, had several reactions to their protectors. The ancient Greeks made them into gods, Moors and the ancient pagans agreed with the Klingons. Their graphic representations of these 'saviors' was grotesque. Over time they became stylized in garden statuary."

She paused, then said softly, "And gargoyles."

"But if gargoyles were supposed to protect us, then why did I fear them?" Picard asked. "Was that genetic too?"

"Perhaps," Guinan said. "The wrong kind of protection can also be devastating."

He smiled at her. "You say that for a reason."

She smiled back, like a small child caught in a forbidden act. "You know me too well, Jean-Luc. Yes, I say that for a reason."

"This war talk bothers you as well."

She nodded. "Make certain you're going into this properly. Don't fight them just because they terrify you. And don't make up the purpose of their mission here. You don't know yet why they're here."

"I've tried to negotiate," Picard said.

"Really?" Guinan asked.

"Guinan, I've spoken to them twice. I've told them who we are."

"They know that, Jean-Luc. They terrorized your people once. They learned about the Federation the last time they came through here. Telling them who you are is not negotiating."

He took a sip of the tea. "You're right," he said, "we need to speak from a position of strength."

She shook her head. "That's not what I'm saying at all. You need to make a good faith effort with them. You need to find a peaceful compromise, and offer it—with your whole heart."

"My heart hates them, Guinan. You've just said that's bred into me."

"So is battle lust, Jean-Luc. I have never seen that overtake you."

"A rational man overcomes his heritage?" Picard said, with only a bit of irony.

"In a word." Guinan was not smiling. She meant it. She meant it all.

Then Riker's voice broke the silence in Ten-Forward. "Captain Picard to the bridge."

"Acknowledged." Picard looked at Guinan. Then he reached out a hand and clasped hers. "I value your wisdom, old friend," he said, and left.

As Picard entered the bridge, he saw Riker and Data leaning over the science console.

"Sir," Riker said, coming to attention. "The wormhole has changed."

Data hadn't stopped monitoring the screen. Picard's stomach clenched. The light lingering taste of the Earl Grey tea turned sour in his mouth. He wasn't ready for this, not so soon after the discussion with Guinan. He wanted time to think about what she had said.

Time was the only commodity he lacked.

"Analysis, Mr. Data."

"The size of the wormhole has increased by fifty centimeters. It is expanding at a rate of one centimeter every thirty seconds."

Picard couldn't see the change in the wormhole, but he knew that Data's statistics were always accurate.

"I am afraid, sir," Data said, "that the energy output is also increasing, and at a much more rapid rate. Also, the area around the wormhole shows a slight drop in mass."

"Are you getting other readings?" Picard asked. "Do we have any indication that more ships are coming through?"

"No direct indications, sir," Data said. "But these readings match the readings recorded by Brundage Station in the hours before the first ships arrived."

"The five Furies ships," Riker said, "have moved a slight distance away from the mouth of the wormhole to be out of range of the dropping mass."

"That makes sense," Picard said.

"If the pattern follows the one observed earlier," Riker said, "a Furies ship will be able to pass through within six hours."

A ship. Or a fleet of ships?

Picard held himself rigidly, unwilling to let any emotion show. Six hours. Six hours to control his own fears, his own heritage, and the future of his galaxy.

"Have we had word from Mr. La Forge?" Picard asked.

"Yes, sir," Riker said. "He believes that if we alter our shields on the subspace level, we might be able to block the Furies' interspace beam completely."

"Did he give you a timetable?"

"He hoped to have it finished by now, sir."

Picard turned. "Engineering?"

"Go ahead, Captain," La Forge's voice came back strong.

"Are you ready to test your block?"

"Yes, sir. We are implementing it now."

"Good work," Picard said.

As he spoke he could feel the deeper level of fear easing and flowing away, like water down a drain. The relief was almost measurable. He glanced around. He could see that the other members of the bridge were feeling the same way.

He turned to Data. "See that Mr. La Forge's schematics for blocking the Furies' beam are sent to the incoming starships."

"Aye, sir," Data said.

"Sir." Worf's voice was filled with that deep control he had only when a situation was dire. "Two of the Furies ships are breaking away from the others and heading this way."

"Red alert." Picard swiveled on one foot and gazed at the large screen. Three ships remained in position while two others streaked across the darkness toward the *Enterprise*. He didn't want to face the Furies. Not now, not ever. But at least for the moment he was facing them with his fear controlled and his crew alert. At least now they had a fighting chance.

"All hands, battle stations."

He turned and sat down, staring at the screen as the two ships approached. So they were going to try to knock them out before the rest of the help got here. Well, let them try.

"Hail them, Mr. Worf."

"Sir, they are going into attack position."

"*Hail them,* Mr. Worf."

"Aye, sir."

The ships continued forward at their steady pace. The other three ships did not move.

Picard licked his lips. They tasted faintly of Guinan's tea. He had promised her he would try. He was trying now.

"Sir, they are not responding," Worf said.

"Captain, they're emitting their own interspace

fear beams," Riker's voice said calmly. "Almost as if they are trying to increase the intensity of their main beam.

"I do believe," Data said, his gaze on the screen, "that such beams count as an attack in accordance with Starfleet Regulation Four dash—"

"I am aware of the regulations, Mr. Data," Picard said. He gripped the arms of his chair. "Mr. Worf. Have you finished your study of the original Furies ships' ability to take energy from an opponent's weapons?" Picard knew the answer to the question, but he wanted to run through the drill just to clear the final doubts from his mind.

"Yes, sir," Worf said. "Adjustments have been made to all our phasers and photon torpedoes using the records of the original battle. The energy bursts from both weapons will be phased to not allow their absorption."

"So they will not be helped by our firing on them?" Picard asked, not taking his gaze away from the quickly approaching ships on the screen.

Worf grunted, then said, "They will not, sir."

"Then, Mr. Worf," Picard said, staring at the screen, "target phasers. Full spread. Fire when you are ready."

"Yes, sir," Worf said.

And the *Enterprise* rocked from the first impact of the Furies' weapons.

Chapter Fifteen

THE AIR WAS WAY TOO HOT. Deanna had to breathe through her mouth in order to get any air at all. Things coated her tongue and slid down her throat.

Small, slimy things.

Living things.

She tried to spit them out, but couldn't. Part of her craved them, needed them, like she needed the air.

Concentrate, Deanna, her mother said.

Go away, Mother, I'm sleeping.

One should never cling to sleep, dear, when one is having a nightmare.

Deanna peered at the screen in front of her. The *Enterprise* was a small disk in the distance, its main section a thin line beneath the saucer. It seemed insignificant.

Easy to conquer.

She hoped.

Deanna.

Leave me alone, Mother.

I will not, darling. You know I hate to see you upset.

Mother, you never even notice when I'm upset.

I feel your pain as if it were my own, my child. Wake up, now.

A bead of sweat ran down her cheek, and onto her lips. She licked it away, and something small with legs climbed down her throat.

She choked.

Coughed.

Opened her eyes.

Into Beverly Crusher's.

She felt the thread of worry pass through her even as Beverly covered the feeling with a smile.

"Glad to see you awake."

"Mm," Deanna said, not quite willing to say anything yet. The dream still felt close, too close, as if it weren't a dream at all. If she concentrated on it for a moment, she would know what she had missed. Something, something important . . .

"Nightmare?"

Deanna nodded. Beneath Beverly's worry, Deanna felt other emotions swirling, both nearby and far. Fear. Terror. Deep, deep horror. Red hot, burning, able to dissolve her if she let it.

The dream dissipated. "What happened?" she asked, breathless with the emotions swirling inside.

"The Furies sent an interspace beam at the ship—"

"'Carrying terror on its wings,'" Deanna said.

"What?"

Deanna shook her head. "Just something I dreamed."

"No dream," Beverly said. "An attack through interspace. It overwhelmed you. I found you just in time."

Deanna remembered removing her comm badge, making instructions to the computer, heading toward the bridge—and nothing else.

Except her mother's voice.

"My mother's not here, is she?"

"No," Beverly said. "Why?"

Deanna shook her head. An old terror, that of her mother knowing everything. "These fears people are feeling, they're deep, aren't they?"

"Too deep," Beverly said. "I've managed to block the worst of it, and Geordi has developed a screen to block the beam, but we don't know how long that will last." She looked up, checking the medical panel over Deanna's head.

Deanna wanted to ask her what she saw, but her mouth was dry. The emotions swirling underneath were growing. She could feel them below a haze, as if someone had laid a gauze blanket over them.

"Your levels are rising again. I'm going to have to sedate you, Deanna."

"But you woke me, didn't you?"

Beverly nodded. "As things eased. I needed to ask you a question. Then I'll put you back under, deep enough to block the empathic response until you can gain a little more strength. You just need the time."

Deanna could isolate the fears now. Lieutenant Kobe was nearly paralyzed with fear. Ensign Mael was barely containing his deep horror. And someone nearby was losing his mind to terror. She glanced over her shoulder at a man she didn't recognize, unconscious on the next bed.

"He's dying," she said.

"I know," Beverly said. "Sedating him doesn't seem to help. The dreams keep coming to him. Waking him is worse."

Deanna clenched her fists. Even with this blocked level of emotion, she could feel the tide rising, feel it slowly sweep over her. "What's your question?" She had to know before she was unable to think clearly.

"I don't know how to help him, Deanna. He's dying, and there's no physical cause."

"Who is he?" she whispered.

"Lieutenant Young."

"The man who saw the Furies firsthand?"

Beverly nodded.

He was drowning in terror. She could feel it. He had nothing to hold, nothing to keep him from sliding deeper. "Wake him," she said, her voice shaking with the power of his emotion.

"But waking him makes it worse."

Deanna shook her head. "He has to know he's safe. You have to make him feel safe. If you don't, you'll lose him for sure. Do anything you can, but make him feel safe."

Beverly's concern was clearly growing. She obviously knew that Deanna was losing control. "What about you, Deanna? Is that how I help you?"

Deanna shook her head. "My world is different from his. Dreams can be deadly for him; he's subject to the images within his mind. I can't block his emotions—anyone's emotions—in this conscious state. That's why I passed out."

Beverly reached to the small table beside her. She removed a hypospray. "I'll sedate you again, if that's what you want."

Deanna nodded. "Wake me if you need more help. I think I will get stronger quickly."

"I'll do what I can," Beverly said.

She placed the hypo near Deanna's neck, and paused as Riker's voice echoed throughout sickbay: "Battle stations. All hands to battle stations."

After a moment the ship rocked from an impact. Beverly lost her balance, clutched the table, and stayed upright. Deanna clung to the side of the diagnostic table. Waves of fear flooded through her, but she fought to stay conscious.

She had to. Just for a moment.

She remembered what she had learned in her dream.

"Beverly, tell the captain—" The fear levels were growing within her. She could no longer separate out who felt what emotion. She frowned, losing her train of thought.

"Tell him what, Deanna?"

Tell him. Ah, yes. She made herself concentrate on her own words. "Tell him that the Furies are as afraid of us as we are of them. They fear us because they think we're the ones who condemned them to hell."

Beverly looked surprised, but Deanna didn't have time to say any more. The black wave was coming over the top of her. She brought a hand up, reaching for the hypospray.

THE SOLDIERS OF FEAR

Beverly understood and gave her the shot as terror flooded through Deanna.

Then the silent, peaceful blackness took her. And this time she welcomed it.

The Fury ships streamed toward the *Enterprise*. Dr. Crusher's potion and Geordi's screens must have worked, because Riker felt the usual adrenaline rush that he always felt before a battle, and nothing else.

No terror.

He knew the *Enterprise* was a match for at least one of those ships, and if they were expecting the crew to be frightened, it would be a match for both ships.

The photon torpedoes soared toward the Fury ships. The ships split, one going above and one going below the *Enterprise,* firing as they went. Riker grabbed the edge of his chair, bracing for impact.

The ship rocked, and the lights flickered for just a moment. Picard stood as if the shot had made him angry.

The photon torpedoes hit one of the ships and missed the other. The bright red flash left a black scar on the ship's front.

"Status, Mr. Data," Picard snapped.

"The shields are holding," he said.

"But they are fluctuating, sir," Ensign Eckley said.

"The ensign is correct," Data said. "Their weapons are apparently designed to disrupt the frequency of our shields. This is something new."

The ships were circling around, as if they were animals stalking their quarry. Riker watched them closely, looking for any detail that would help them win this battle.

"Can you modify the shields, Mr. Data?" Picard asked.

"No, sir," Data said. "I believe this type of work must happen in engineering."

Picard hit his comm badge. "Mr. La Forge—"

"I'm on it, sir," La Forge said.

The ships had turned. "Captain, they're coming around for another attack run," Riker said, his voice firm.

"Mr. Worf—"

"Photon torpedoes locked on target, sir," Worf said.

"Fire!" Picard said.

This time, the torpedoes streaked toward the ships, maintaining their locks. They hit with such impact that both Fury ships rocked and went off course. None of the energy of the strikes was absorbed. In fact, it seemed just the opposite, as if the Fury ships were somehow increasing the impact of the weapons against their sides.

"Bull's-eye," Riker said. He felt almost an extra sense of joy.

"Excellent, Mr. Worf," Picard said. "This time, lock on to the tail section. That appears to be their engines."

"It is, sir," Data said.

"Locked," Worf said.

"Fire!"

The torpedoes shot across space toward the still-recovering ships.

"Sir," Data said, "our shields are at fifty percent. They're failing on decks six and seven."

"Mr. La Forge?"

"I know, sir. Give me ten seconds."

"You have five," Picard said.

"Aye, sir."

The torpedoes hit their marks again, but for a moment nothing happened. Riker held his breath, hoping. Then a bright red glow mushroomed off the first ship's engines.

It was like watching an electrical storm over the surface of the ship. The flashes and red glow kept feeding back and forth, from the front of the ship, then to the back.

Faster and faster, the flashes across the face of the Fury ship increased until finally the ship spun for a moment like a top, completely out of control; then it exploded.

The explosion caught the other ship, and it spun away, firing as it went. The shots flew wild, scattering into space.

Worf grunted. The sound was full of Klingon satisfaction. Riker felt like grunting as well. But he kept his gaze on the other ship. Picard was watching too, an unreadable expression on his face. It was as if he was warring with himself; partly pleased, partly dismayed at the turn of events.

Riker felt only pleasure at the victory.

"Mr. Worf," Picard said, his voice displaying none of the conflict that reigned in his face. "Lock photon torpedoes on the remaining ship."

"Locked, sir."

Riker smiled. Worf had responded so quickly he must have had the lock on before Picard told him to.

"The ship is moving away from us," Data said.

Riker clenched his fists. *Shoot them anyway,* he

wanted to say, but the words went against all his training. They were coming from deep within, from a part of himself he had never met before. From the part the Furies had tapped with their fear weapon.

"Captain," Data said, as if the captain hadn't heard. "The ship is heading back to the other ships near the Furies Point."

Picard said nothing. He watched the screen.

"Shall I fire, sir?"

Again, Picard did not respond. His face, which earlier had been a mix of emotions, held none now.

"Do you think this a ploy, sir?" Riker asked.

Picard let out his breath. He had obviously been holding it.

"We've lost shields on decks four, five, and six," Data said.

That seemed to snap Picard to attention. The ship continued to head toward the Furies Point.

"Shall I fire, sir?" Worf's voice held a barely contained disdain. If he were alone, Worf clearly would have finished off the second Fury ship.

"No, Mr. Worf." Picard returned to his seat. "Unlock torpedoes and resume our previous position."

He did not take his gaze from the screen. Riker glanced at it again. The Fury ship took its place in front of the third ship. Somehow it seemed out of place there, as if the formation were incomplete.

Which, Riker supposed, it was.

"We surprised them, Number One," Picard said. "We won't be able to do that again."

Riker swallowed. The fear returned, if only for a moment. "I know," he said. But the surprise had gotten them this far.

"Mr. Data," Picard said, "how long until the *Madison* and *Idaho* arrive?"

"Fifty-two minutes, sir," Data said.

The attack had taken less than ten minutes. Riker returned to his chair. Somehow it felt as if it had taken longer than that.

"The Klingon ships will arrive at the same time," Worf said.

"Thank you," Picard said. "Mr. Data, have you an estimate on how long it will take until that wormhole is large enough to let more Fury ships into the sector?"

"According to my calculations, sir, the wormhole will allow a Fury ship to pass through within eighty-one minutes. I do not know, however, what the status of the wormhole is on the other end."

Eighty-one minutes. Riker glanced at the screen. The four ships hung in space, the wormhole invisible near them. It was growing rapidly, and once it reached the right size, an invasion force of unparalleled proportions just might come through to enslave the sector.

And at the moment, the *Enterprise* was the only thing that stood in its way.

He finally understood how the Klingons felt all those centuries ago, facing the invading Herq. Insignificant.

Doomed to failure without a lucky break.

"I hope your estimates are right, Mr. Data."

Data swiveled in his chair. "Why would I report incorrect estimates, sir?"

Riker shook his head. The others on the bridge knew what Picard had meant. If the timing was somehow off, if the wormhole was growing geometrically instead of arithmetically, then the Furies would arrive before the reinforcements. The rout would be ugly.

It would make the attack on Brundage Station look like an evening on Risa.

Chapter Sixteen

"THAT WAS CLOSE," La Forge said. He closed the panel he had been working on, and collapsed in a chair beside it.

Redbay used the laser driver to lock the panel closed. His shirt was plastered to his back. La Forge was right. That had been close. Too close.

When Picard gave them only five seconds to modify the shields, Redbay had thought it impossible. La Forge hadn't even blinked. Two seconds later, five levels of shields had failed, and La Forge was still working. Four seconds after that, La Forge had effected most of the changes.

"I thought you said you needed ten seconds," Redbay had said.

"Captains always shave time off estimates," La

Forge said. "Build a bit of shave into your estimates and you look like a miracle worker."

"I never would have thought of that," Redbay had said.

"Neither would I," La Forge said, moving to a new panel, "but an expert once assured me it would work. And believe me, it has. Every time."

Now La Forge was staring at the main console. Redbay slipped into a nearby chair and called up schematics on his console. Something about the Furies' attack worried him. The shield failures should not have happened, at least not so rapidly. The Furies had somehow interfered with the shield harmonics. Even with the shield failures, though, the block that he and La Forge had set up continued to work. But he doubted it would work much longer.

He glanced over his shoulder at the rest of engineering. Three crew members were rebuilding the damaged portion of the shields. Several others were still working on the warp core. They had lost four members of their staff to the initial terror, not counting the folks who were already out sick.

He turned his attention back to the console before him. "It amazes me that they weren't able to demolish all our shields," he said.

"I'll wager they didn't think they needed to," La Forge said. He looked preoccupied, his fingers dancing across the console as he worked. "They thought we were terrified of them. One blast should have convinced us to surrender."

Redbay nodded. That made sense, but it still didn't get at what was eating him. He was missing something.

"But if they come back any time soon, they'll get us," La Forge said. "Our emotion block is eroding. I think it'll deteriorate within ten minutes."

That was what he had been missing. Redbay glanced over at La Forge's console. La Forge was right. They would lose their main protection soon.

"Fixing it shouldn't be hard," Redbay said. On his console he sketched a plan for repair that would leave both the shields and their emotional protection in place.

"Good idea," La Forge said, "but you want to tell me how we're going to do that without shutting down the shields while we repair them?"

Redbay's mouth instantly went dry. The terror had eased for him; he now only felt a slight undercurrent of anxiety, less than he had felt as a cadet in the Academy. But he never wanted to feel that kind of terror again.

Ever.

"It's not possible," Redbay said.

"I know," La Forge said. He took a deep breath, then tapped his comm badge.

"La Forge to bridge."

"Picard here."

"Captain," La Forge said. "We're going to lose our shields in the next ten minutes. I can repair them, but I'll have to shut them off while we're working on them."

"We can't do that, Mr. La Forge."

Redbay could almost believe he heard a slight note of panic in the captain's voice. Picard had understood at once that if they lowered their shields, the wave of terror would again hit the crew full force.

"We can, sir," La Forge said, "if we move away from the Furies Point."

Redbay felt some of the tension in his back ease. La Forge was right. Moving them would help.

"Mr. La Forge," Picard said, "I'm given to understand that the beam the Furies have leveled on us expands at greater distances. We would have to go well into the sector to outfly it. We don't have the time."

"The beam weakens as it stretches, sir," La Forge said.

Redbay was punching numbers into his console as fast as he could. They could survive the pressure if it remained the same as it was here.

"I am not convinced, Mr. La Forge."

Within seconds Redbay found that spot and pointed it out to La Forge on the screen.

La Forge nodded and gave Redbay the thumbs-up. "Sir, we don't have to go far. If we travel seven minutes at warp eight directly away from the Furies Point, we'll arrive at a place where the beam is the same level of intensity as what we're feeling now with the shields up. It won't take us long to fix the shields. I think we'd be back here within half an hour."

There was silence on the other end. La Forge glanced at Redbay.

"Why isn't he answering?" Redbay whispered. He could feel his stomach clamping up at the thought of dropping the terror shield this close to the Fury ships.

"He's checking to see what the reinforcements are doing," La Forge whispered back.

"All right, Mr. La Forge," Picard said. "We will

leave this site for exactly one half hour. No more. Is that understood?"

"Clearly, sir."

"You are making new modifications on the shields, is that correct?"

Yes, sir."

"Then send the changes, encoded, to the incoming starships. We want them to be as protected as they can be when they meet the Furies."

"Aye, sir," La Forge said.

Picard signed off.

"Mr. Anderson," La Forge said, "you will monitor our changes over here, and encode them for the other starships."

Anderson left his post near the warp core. "But sir, the core still needs repair."

"This is top priority, Anderson," La Forge said.

"Aye, sir." Anderson pulled over one more chair, took the remaining console, and waited.

At that moment, the engines wailed, like wind through a cave, as the ship went to warp speed and headed away from the Furies Point.

"I don't like the sound of that," Redbay said. He'd heard warp drives sound a thousand times better on freighters.

"It'll be all right," La Forge said. "She's a good ship."

Redbay frowned at La Forge. "She might be a good ship, but that doesn't mean I trust my life to her when she's damaged."

La Forge grinned. "Neither would I," he said. "But I inspected the warp core. The damage is superficial and very noisy. Our concern is these shields. We have to make these modifications rapidly and precisely in order for the work to be completed in that short timeline."

Anderson glanced at La Forge. He obviously heard the undertone in La Forge's voice. If the repairs weren't made and made correctly, not only would the crew of the *Enterprise* suffer, but so would the crews of the *Idaho* and the *Madison*.

"Nothing like a little pressure," Redbay said, "to keep the job interesting."

La Forge slapped him on the back. "Glad you're enjoying it."

Redbay shook his head. He was doing anything but enjoying it. How had Will managed this all these years? Flying test models of new shuttles suddenly looked very relaxing. His old friend was a very strong person.

The air was thick and teemed with food. Dea had done her job, much to Vedil's surprise, but if she thought that would give her a command position again, she was sadly mistaken. The interior lights were dim, blocked by thick air. The humidity felt good on his scarlet hide.

He sat in his command chair, hooves extended.

Something about the Unclean was bothering him.

He tapped his nails against the arm of the chair, staring at the screen before him. He had called up a screen on the chair arm itself—in this murky atmosphere, seeing beyond the navigator's array was nearly impossible—and was staring at the debris, all that remained of Sse's ship.

Sse had not been the best commander. Most of the

core could not see beyond her fluffy pink fur and wide blue eyes. Not all the Furies were monsters.

Still, he could not blame the destruction of her ship on a commander's error. It had taken thought.

Thought which, his experiments with the young Terran's mind on their guard station had assured him, would have been impossible under the circumstances. The Unclean on that ship should be frozen in fear by now. Not fighting back.

"I want a reading on that ship," Vedil said.

"Vergo, Your Eminence, sir," Prote said, "the shields were disrupted before the *Kalyb* pulled away."

"And the significance of that is?" Vedil asked.

"They should be feeling our power tenfold. I personally have checked our weapon's beam and increased the intensity as by your orders."

Vedil continued tapping his fingernails, the sound dying in the thick mist and damp air. "Should be," he said. "They should be feeling our power. But I see no evidence of this, do you?"

"Vergo, sir," B'el's second head said, "they have released two more communications."

"What do those communications say?" Vedil asked, knowing the answer already.

"We haven't broken their code, Vergo," B'el's second head said. "They are, apparently, changing base language on us with each transmission."

"We have superior intellects," Vedil said. "We should be able to break any and all codes quickly."

"We broke the first, Vergo," B'el's third head said.

"You did not report this."

"Because the communication was insignificant. Simply a report on the status of Brundage Station."

Vedil tapped so hard his nails left tiny dents in the metal. Must he lead them all by their cilia? "If such a communication was insignificant," he said, "why did they encode it?"

"I do not know, Vergo," B'el's first head said.

"Of course you do not know because you do not think! Examine the message again. See if there was a code embedded in the communiqué."

"Yes, Vergo."

"And tell me why those creatures are not terrified of us."

"We do not know how you have come to thisssss conclussssssion," O'pZ said.

"They attacked in a reasonable manner. They are sending encoded communications. They—"

"They are leaving, Vergo," Prote said. His wings unfurled with surprise, catching tiny maggots on the sticky tips.

Vedil returned his gaze to his screen. The ship had turned. Within seconds, it winked out in a flash of colored light.

"See?" Prote said. "We did terrify them."

"It sssseemsss very long to wait after an attack to flee," O'pZ said.

Vedil frowned at the screen, his hide pulling along his forehead. It did seem long. "Examine those communiqués," he said. "The Unclean were prepared for us this time. They waited at the Entrance to Heaven, and they sent this ship which destroyed one of ours. Perhaps this is a ploy."

"Perhaps they are going for more ships," B'el's second head said.

"Perhaps they are fleeing," Prote said.

"Perhaps," Vedil said. Then he leaned back. Unlike most of his crew, he had studied the Unclean. He had studied all the information sent back through the Path to Heaven after the *Rath* had failed in its mission. And since he took their puny guard station, he had continued his study. What he knew was this: Individual Unclean could be broken. The Unclean could be enslaved. But as a group, the Unclean had amazing recuperative powers.

The defeat at the Entrance to Heaven a generation before was another example of Unclean determination.

The Unclean could be fleeing. But Vedil doubted it. They were planning something. And he would have to determine what that something was before the fleet came through the Path to Heaven.

Chapter Seventeen

DESPITE HIMSELF, Picard felt relief as the *Enterprise* moved away from the Furies Point. He had thought the fear was buried thanks to his efforts, Dr. Crusher's, and Mr. La Forge's. Yet the distance was making a huge real—and psychological—difference.

Guinan had been right. This hatred and fear went very very deep.

He sat in his command chair, the restless feeling gone. The bridge crew had focused on the work before them while he had double-checked La Forge's engineering plan and found it sound. Then he had checked on the status of the crew. Most were doing well despite the overwhelming feelings. Most were recovering, and only a few had completely lost control and not yet regained it.

Deanna was one of those. Understandable, of

course, but he needed her. He felt blind without her council. He hadn't realized quite how much he relied on it in situations when his own emotions were untrustworthy.

"We've reached the target point, sir," Ensign Eckley said.

"All stop," Picard said. "Mr. Data, what is the intensity of the Furies' beam at this distance?"

Data hadn't left the science console since the last meeting. The Furies' beam, their wormhole, and their powers were his focus at the moment, in accordance with his orders. And as always, he brought to bear his full and considerable powers.

"It is exactly one-tenth of the strength that it had been in our previous position."

"Excellent," Picard said. Mr. La Forge had been right, as always.

The bridge crew were watching him expectantly at this point. They knew what was going to happen next. Eckley had braced herself, her fingers white on the console.

Picard glanced around. Worf maintained a stoic fierceness. Riker sat beside Picard, hands folded loosely in his lap. They all seemed back to normal. But that would change in a few moments. Even at one-tenth power, that beam was still strong. And was still very capable of undermining the confidence of even the strongest person.

Picard hit his comm badge. "Mr. La Forge, are you ready?"

"As ready as we'll ever be, sir," La Forge said.

"Stand by," Picard said. "Open a channel to the entire ship, Mr. Worf."

Worf gazed down at the console without moving his head. Just a slight flicker of the eyes. Worf was in Klingon battle mode.

"Done, sir."

Picard nodded to him. Then he leaned back in the command chair. He didn't want to sound in any way stressed or alarmed. "This is a general announcement to the *Enterprise* crew and passengers. As most of you are aware, our proximity to the Furies' weapon increases the level of fear on board the ship. Mr. La Forge has made changes in the shields which protected us from most of that fear. Now, however, we will have to drop the shields in order to repair them."

He took a deep silent breath and went on. "We have moved several light-years away from the Furies Point. The level of terror you will feel will be considerably less than the terror you felt earlier. However, the terror will return. Those of you guarding small children will need to explain this as best you can. As for the rest of you, please remember that this increase in the levels of anxiety will be short-lived. I expect you to continue your duties. Picard out."

Riker nodded to him. "Well done, sir."

Picard smiled a smile he didn't feel. "Mr. La Forge," he said. "You have ten minutes."

"We'll be done in eight," La Forge said.

Picard stood. "Ensign," he said to Eckley, "drop our shields."

"Aye, sir," she said.

He took a deep breath.

The fear returned instantly, but he had been right; it wasn't as bad as it had been before. It was a low level of terror, merely an anxiety—although, if he hadn't been prepared, it would have slowly built into a full-fledged panic.

Eckley was pale, but continued at her post.

Riker had stood and gone over to the science station.

Worf stared at the screen ahead of him, as if he could see all the way to the Furies Point.

Picard let out the breath he'd been holding and crossed to the science station too. He still had a lot to do while La Forge worked on the shields.

He stopped behind Data. Somehow it was soothing to see Data checking figures, the screen scrolling before him at a rate too rapid to read.

"Mr. Data," Picard said. "You have been studying this wormhole for some time now. Tell me about it."

Data pushed his chair back from his console. He reminded Picard of a professor Picard had at the Academy, a man who loved to expound on things he knew, a man who was full of more knowledge than Picard could amass in a lifetime.

"The wormhole is clearly artificial, sir," Data said. His long pale fingers still flew across the console. Riker leaned against it, blocking his way, reminding him to place his full attention on the captain and the discussion. "Its movements are too precise to be a natural phenomenon. It is also perfectly oblong, a form in such proportions that does not occur in nature. And it opens at regular, predictable intervals. Also, the energy it gives off contains particles that are refined."

Data glanced back at his screen, then up at Picard. "Despite decades of study, we have been unable to discover why a drop in mass in objects surrounding the Furies' wormhole occurs. But it does so as the hole opens."

"Could it controlled from this side as well as the other?" Picard asked.

"No, sir," Data said, "unless the devices are on the ships themselves. I believe if that were the case, the wormhole would have fluctuated when we destroyed one of their ships."

"I did some tests on this too, sir," Riker said, "when I was looking for the source of the fear beam. The Fury ships are as trapped here as we are. The wormhole is being controlled on the other side.'

"How do you know?" Picard asked.

"The wormhole is maintained by a carrier signal that enabled me to scan through it," Data said. "It appears to be controlled by a device on the other side. From what I can tell, the device is located quite near the wormhole entrance. It is quite large, but its projection antenna is small enough that it could be destroyed with a photon torpedo."

Picard spoke quickly. "A photon torpedo could disable this device?"

"I believe so, sir."

"So all we have to do is get close enough to do some precision firing through the wormhole?" Riker asked.

"No, Commander," Data said. "I ran the schematics for that. The particle fluctuations within the wormhole, while they are predictable, would either render the photon torpedo useless in the worst case or, in the best case, throw it off course. The device must be destroyed at an exact point on the other side of the wormhole by a weapon fired from that side."

Picard bent over the science console so that his two

officers could not see his face. He had told Guinan that he wanted a peaceful solution, a solution that would enable them to turn the Furies away without war. She had suggested negotiation. He had tried that, and would again. But if negotiation failed, then he had this.

Destruction of the wormhole.

A suicide mission.

"Do you think we can get the *Enterprise* through there?" Picard asked.

"The odds are six hundred and fifty-six thousand to one, sir," Data said.

"Assuming, of course, that more Fury ships wait on the other side."

"I did not run any other scenario," Data said. "We made that determination."

Picard was cold. He felt better sending in the entire *Enterprise* than doing what he was about to suggest. "And the odds on a single vessel? A shuttlecraft, perhaps?"

"There are too many variables," Data said. "A shuttle, once inside, could make it through the wormhole undetected, but the same particle fluctuations that affect the photon torpedo's trajectory will interfere with the shuttlecraft's. Also its hull structure is weaker than a larger ship's."

"So you're saying that a shuttlecraft has no chance of success," Picard said, almost relieved at the thought.

"No, sir. I am saying that I cannot give you exact odds. But all the scenarios I ran with the shuttlecraft gave odds anywhere between one hundred to one and two to one."

"What was the difference?" Riker asked.

"The pilot," Data said. "I believe that a talented pilot, able to compensate for all the variables, would be able to make it through the wormhole and fire the shot."

"I am the most accurate at target destruction done manually," Worf said. He had turned around, his right fist clenched, the only sign of his increased anxiety. "I would like to go on this mission, sir."

"And I am ranked as one of the best pilots in the fleet," Riker said. "And the best on this ship."

Picard looked at his two officers. If he sent them, they would not return. He would have to run the *Enterprise* without them.

"Sir," Data said, "Allow me to add that my abilities in manipulating data, my imperviousness to the Furies' emotion device, and my proven talent at precision flying within one-billionth of an inch would make me the best choice for this mission."

"There is no mission yet," Picard said. "At the moment, this is all speculation. We need to see how Mr. La Forge's device works, whether Dr. Crusher's drugs can keep us calm, and if the Furies are willing yet to negotiate. We still do not know for certain what they want in this sector."

"They say they want total and complete domination of this area of space," Riker said.

Picard nodded. "But you forget the old tool of negotiation. Ask for everything, settle for less."

"I doubt they'll settle for less," Riker mumbled.

"Engineering to bridge." La Forge's voice echoed over the monitor.

"Seven minutes," Eckley whispered in awe.

Picard smiled. Mr. La Forge was quite reliable. "Go ahead, Mr. La Forge."

"We've finished, sir. We're about to bring the shields back on-line."

"Will they block the Furies' terror beam?"

"Absolutely," La Forge said, his voice bouncing with confidence. "On the way over here we also studied the effect that weapon had on our shields. We think we can withstand anything they throw at us, whether it's a terror beam or a modified shield fluctuation shot."

"Or a photon torpedo?" Eckley mumbled. The fear was showing in her increasing disregard for protocol.

Apparently she mumbled loud enough for La Forge to hear. "Anything," he said.

"Excellent, Mr. La Forge." Picard decided to ignore Eckley's comments. He would have to be somewhat lenient after the Furies' beam pummeled them. "Have you sent your schematics to our reinforcements?"

"Yes, sir. In code."

"Good." Picard swallowed. He had been waiting too long to give this next order. "Then turn on the shields. We have work to do."

"Yes, sir," La Forge said.

Picard left the science console and returned to his command chair. He sat down, and as he did he felt stronger, as if he could face anything. Amazing. This must be how he felt most of the time. He only noted it in its absence.

"Mr. Data," Picard said. "When will the other ships arrive at the Furies Point?"

"In twelve minutes, sir," Data said.

Picard smiled. "Ensign Eckley, time our arrival

back there exactly thirty seconds ahead of the other ships."

"Course laid in, sir."

"Engage," he said.

As the ship moved forward, Riker joined Picard in the command area. "This is quite a force that will appear right in front of the Furies."

"That it is, Number One," Picard said. "And unbeknownst to them, we will be protected against their emotion manipulation and their weapons."

"We'll have the advantage."

"And they will know it." Picard stared grimly at the stars streaking across the screen. "This time the Furies will talk to us."

They had to. Picard was not willing to sacrifice his best officers, his ship, or the Federation.

This time, he would make the Furies listen.

Chapter Eighteen

GEORDI'S SHIELD MODIFICATIONS must have worked. Beverly was calm even though the *Enterprise* was approaching the Furies Point.

Beverly glanced at the screen in her research facility. She had it focused not on sickbay but on the stars themselves. She wanted to monitor the proximity of the Furies Point.

Her sedative had worked. She felt good about that and kept repeating it to herself. But it worked best in combination with the shield modifications.

The problem was that the effect of the gas was going to wear off soon. She was trying to modify the gas slightly so that it would last longer. She had downloaded information from Geordi and was working to match the amount of Theragen derivative in the gas to the interspace field they were surrounded by. At best it was a guessing game. But she had to guess right, because she knew the crew needed it during the battle.

They had to have some protection if the shields failed.

Then her assistant Ensign Orne peeked through the doorway. "Dr. Crusher," he said, "you need to see this."

She set the test tube in its tray and stood. Probably Lieutenant Young. She had awakened him, as Deanna suggested, and he had taken one look at Beverly and screamed. Certainly not the reaction any physician wanted.

But it turned out he was terrified of her hair. She called over her assistant Restin, who kept his skull neatly shaved, and Young calmed. Restin had been spending the last hour talking with the boy, and even though his vitals were unchanged, he seemed calmer.

At least he wasn't screaming.

Restin was still talking, slowly and quietly, to Young. Young's readings were the same as they had been when he slept—a good sign, since when he was conscious before his readings had been elevated. He wasn't out of danger, but his odds were improving by the minute.

But Ensign Orne wasn't leading Beverly to Young. She was leading her to Deanna.

Her eyelashes were fluttering, but no REM sleep was recording on the overhead board. She was near consciousness, though, and she shouldn't have been. That sedative Beverly gave her should have lasted much longer.

Beverly took her hand. "Deanna, are you all right?"

Deanna's large eyes opened. They focused instantly, and were clearer than Beverly had expected them to be. "Something changed," Deanna said.

The shields. So part of Deanna's sleep had been instinctive protection against too much emotion.

"I lightly sedated the crew a while back, and Geordi has modified the shields again to more completely block the Furies' beam."

"People are still frightened," Deanna said, "but not like they were."

"They shouldn't be frightened anymore," Beverly said.

Deanna shook her head just a little. The movement was almost imperceptible. "It's normal," she said. "'Frightened' is too big a word. People are worried. As they always are when the *Enterprise* is in danger."

And Deanna was obviously used to that level of worry. Beverly felt herself relax.

"Except." Deanna looked over her shoulder. "That boy. He's still terrified."

"We're doing all we can," Beverly said.

"It may not be enough." Deanna closed her eyes and sighed. "Is the *Enterprise* in danger?"

"We're heading back to the Furies Point—to take them on, I suspect. But knowing Jean-Luc, he will try to talk with them again."

"Again?" Deanna opened her eyes and pushed herself up on her elbows. "He shouldn't negotiate without me."

"You were hardly in any condition to help him, Deanna."

"But I can help him now," she said.

Beverly shook her head. "I can't let you. Only an

hour ago, you weren't in much better shape than that boy."

Deanna looked at him, her face filled with compassion. "If I stay here, I will have to help him. And I'm not sure I can delve into that level of emotion just yet. Besides, the Furies are complex beings. I've been dreaming of them."

"Dreaming?" Beverly asked. She was always amazed at the twists and turns Deanna's abilities took when she encountered a new race.

She nodded. "They're in my subconscious like a pattern. It must be the human part. But that opens the Betazoid part. I have dreamed about being on their ship."

"You said they were afraid of us."

"They are," Deanna said. "But it is a different kind of fear than the terror they've been projecting toward us. It is the nagging fear that somehow, over the millennia, we have grown even stronger than we were when, they think, we drove them out of heaven."

Beverly laughed, although she didn't mean to. "You're kidding?"

"Not at all," Deanna said. "And it got worse for them in the last eighty years. The generation since their defeat at the hands of the original *Enterprise* has felt weak. This trip is to prove their strength as well as enable their return to this section of space."

"Rather like a Klingon loss of honor."

"Rather," Deanna said. Her voice held just a trace of irony. "On a grander scale. From what I can tell, their entire culture is based solely on returning here."

She swung her legs off the bed. "I have to go to the bridge."

"I wouldn't recommend it," Beverly said. "If the shields break down, if the gas clears, you will be overwhelmed again. Your system still hasn't completely recovered. It may not be able to take another shock like that, and I might not be able to help you."

Deanna was watching Lieutenant Young. His mouth was open and a thin line of drool ran from his lips to the pillow. He was as close to mindless as a human could be and still feel. Even Beverly knew that, and she was no empath.

"I understand," Deanna said. "But it's better to risk my life and be at the captain's side than risk losing this opportunity with the Furies."

"Deanna," Beverly said, "Jean-Luc is used to diplomatic dealings. He can do this without you."

"I'm not so certain," Deanna said. "He is having the same trouble being calm as the rest of the crew. But you know the captain. He won't show it."

Beverly suppressed a smile. It was so like all of them to believe they were indispensable. That was one of the things she liked about working with this crew. Usually.

"But you are being overwhelmed at the detriment of your own health," Beverly said softly.

"Not right now," Deanna said. "Besides, I am used to thinking through intense emotion brought in from the outside. He is not. If something were to change, he might need my counseling more than ever."

She had a point, much as Beverly hated to admit it. The only person on the ship used to working through a haze of outside imposed emotion was Deanna. And to try to face the Furies without her was foolish. What had Jean-Luc said when he learned that Deanna was in sickbay? Hadn't he mumbled something about needing her?

"All right," Beverly said. "It's against my medical judgment to let you go, but these are extenuating circumstances."

"Thanks," Deanna said. She swung her legs off the bed. "I'll be all right. I promise."

Beverly nodded. She even smiled. But she watched carefully as Deanna left the room, memorizing each step, each movement.

Beverly had a hunch she might never see Deanna alive again.

The bridge crew was calmer. They were going about their business with a rapidity that meant their movements were unencumbered by unfamiliar emotions.

Picard felt the shift inside himself. Instead of dreading the meeting with the Furies, he welcomed it. If he could convince them to negotiate, then all would be solved.

He didn't want to think about Data's other solution.

At least, not yet.

The *Enterprise* dropped out of warp, and took up its previous position, facing the four remaining Fury ships. They looked smaller somehow. The loss of the fifth ship had diminished them. Or maybe it was the loss of the fear. Something a person fears always looks bigger.

"Mr. Data," Picard said. "What is the change in the wormhole's growth?"

"In fifteen minutes," Data said, "it will be large enough for Fury ships to pass through."

That made Picard pause. The growth in the wormhole had gone slightly quicker than Data's earlier estimates. Picard didn't know if the other ships had been in contact with the Furies on the other side of the wormhole; if so, then perhaps they had escalated their arrival once the fifth ship was destroyed.

Or perhaps Data's calculations had been in error. He had warned that some of them were based on speculation.

Like the calculations he made about destroying the wormhole. Nothing was certain.

"Fifteen minutes is all we need," Picard said, sounding more confident than he felt. He hadn't been able to talk with the Furies before, but then, as Guinan pointed out, his whole heart hadn't been in it. This time, with the reinforcements behind him, he might be able to talk with them. He hoped that talking was all he needed.

The turbolift door hissed open. Picard turned. He hadn't ordered anyone onto the bridge.

"Deanna," Worf said, his voice filled with a kind of awe.

She was paler than usual, her eyes taking up most of her face. Picard would have thought that she was recovering from a long illness if he hadn't known that she had been fine just the day before.

She smiled at Worf, the expression filling her face with radiance. That smile put not just Worf but Picard at ease. He hadn't really realized how much he counted on her in situations like this one.

"Worf," she said. She went down the two steps toward her seat, and touched Riker's hand as she did so. He looked relieved that she had returned. No, "relieved" was too small a word. He looked as if a well-loved member of his family had just returned from a long voyage.

"Welcome, Counselor," Picard said. "I trust Dr. Crusher gave you a full bill of health."

Troi's smile had a touch of the imp to it. "She let me out of sickbay," Troi said, "does that count?"

"Enough for now," Picard said.

Riker glanced at the screen and then at her. "Deanna, do you think it wise—?"

"Will," she said, and he stopped.

"The *Madison* and *Idaho* have arrived," Worf said. "They have taken positions behind us on either side."

More tension left Picard's shoulders. Part of him, the worried part that the Furies' beam had dislodged, had wondered if the other two starships would arrive on time.

Their arrival took the attention off Counselor Troi.

"I thought the Klingons would be with them," Riker said.

"They are," Worf said, his voice controlled but his annoyance somehow clear anyway. "They have just decloaked. One ship is above us. The other below. It is the Vulcan ship that is delayed."

"Two Klingon ships," Picard said. "Good."

"The Klingons clearly believe this too important to trust to one vessel," Worf said, subtly reminding them all about the honor still at stake.

"So much the better." Picard uncrossed his leg and put his hands on the arm of his chair. He was about to stand when Troi's fingers brushed his sleeve.

"When you speak to them," she said softly, "remember that they are frightened."

At first he thought she was talking about the other ships that had just arrived. Then he realized she meant the Furies.

"This is very important to them," she said, by way of explanation.

"It is to all of us," Picard said.

She shook her head. "No, they believe our remote ancestors were the ones who kicked them out of this area of space."

Picard stared at her for a moment, letting what she said sink in. If he needed it, he would use it. But now that the *Idaho* had arrived, he had another weapon, too. He had the poppets from the Fury ship *Rath*.

He patted Troi's hand as a way of thanks and stood. He adjusted his shirt, and stepped before the screens. "Hail the Fury vessels, Mr. Worf, and when you do make certain all our ships hear this message as well."

"Aye, sir."

Picard hesitated a moment. He needed to add one more element into this equation. "And Mr. Worf, send this all subspace Priority One to Starfleet. I want the entire sector listening in."

"Done, sir," Worf said. "The main Fury ship is answering your hail."

"On screen." As Picard said the words, Riker stood and stopped a half-step behind him. Troi did the same on the other side. He was flanked by two officers. That, combined with the reinforcements, would make this a united front.

The Furies would know that the Federation was no small primitive planet, to be awed and enslaved by beings who thought themselves more powerful.

The screen blinked on, and the creature he had

spoken to before reappeared. Its hide was a duller red, and the edges of its features seemed hazy.

"That's the best I can do," Worf said. "The haze appears to be something aboard their ship."

"Bugs," Troi whispered, and as if to confirm her words, a swarm of tiny black gnatlike insects flew out of the curve of the creature's horns.

"I suppose you would like to talk," the creature said, its voice heavy with irony. "I heard this is how you fight your enemies. You talk them into submission."

"We negotiate," Picard said.

"Negotiate." The creature hooked a maggot on its nail and then slid it off with its teeth. Picard suppressed a shudder. Even without their beam, these creatures plugged directly into his subconscious. Although at the moment, he was registering more disgust than fear. This must be the level of fear that the original *Enterprise* crew felt, before the Furies had their fear beam.

"What is there to negotiate?"

At last. A small breakthrough. "You came through that wormhole because you wanted something," Picard said. "Instead of fighting for that something, perhaps we can supply it. Our beliefs ask us to find a peaceful solution first."

"You destroyed our ship," the creature said.

Riker clenched a fist. Picard straightened his shoulders. As if they deserved blame for this situation. The Fury knew that they had provoked the attack.

"You murdered the crew of our research station," Picard said slowly, making sure he had the force he wanted behind his voice.

"Not all of them," the creature said with a leer. Another creature moved across the screen behind it. The creature had three heads, each different. One looked like a Klingon Scarbaraus statue.

"The KdIchpon," Worf said softly, as if in awe.

Picard refused to be goaded. Or terrified. "We destroyed one of your ships, and you attacked our station. We are even. That seems a good place to begin negotiations from."

Troi brushed his sleeve again. Picard glanced at her. She was staring at the screen, her eyes black coals, her skin even paler. He had forgotten about her human side. She had to see the demons that he saw as well as feel the emotions around her.

"What have we to negotiate?" the devil creature asked.

They were at least talking. Picard had to give them that. Talk was always the beginning of diplomacy.

"They're stalling," Troi whispered so softly that he almost didn't hear her.

His mouth went dry. "You came through the wormhole in search of something. Perhaps we can help you with that search, without bloodshed."

"Oh, you will help us with that search," the creature said.

"Captain," Troi whispered. "He is playing with you."

The creature apparently heard her. It grinned, the look revealing nasty, slime-covered teeth. "She is correct, Picard. We toy with you. We came through the Entrance to Heaven in search of former glory. It is not something you can give us. It is something that can only be won."

Picard latched on to the word "won." "And if we lay down our arms, face you peaceably?"

"Captain!" Worf said, clearly appalled.

"Then we gain even more glory," the creature said, "for you consider us too mighty to fight. Will you surrender, Captain Picard?"

Picard lifted his chin. "Never," he said. "You will never achieve glory, former or future. We defeated you once in battle, and we shall do so again."

He took a deep breath. "I have something to offer you in negotiation. We have an escape pod full of the poppets from the *Rath*. I will turn them over to you to assure you of our goodwill."

"What!" the leader of the Furies shouted, jumping toward the camera. "We will take them from you. You will die!"

Picard stepped back. He had not expected such a reaction. He knew this conversation was at an end. He now had the upper hand, and it would stay that way for the moment.

He whirled and motioned Worf to end the communication. Picard was no longer frightened. He was angry. The Furies believed that only the enslavement of the races on this side of the galaxy would enable them to obtain glory? They would quickly learn how impossible glory was going to be.

"Mr. Data, how many minutes until that wormhole opens?"

"Ten, sir. But—" Data paused, leaned over the console. "The energy emissions are increasing." He slid his chair back, looking as stunned as an android could look. "My calculations were inaccurate, sir."

"They're coming through now?" Riker asked.

Data shook his head. "No, sir. But I estimated a single ship would come through the wormhole. According to these new readings, they are sending ships in waves. Hundreds of ships. It is only the first that will arrive in ten minutes."

"They're storming us as if we were a beachhead," Picard muttered.

"What?" Riker asked.

Picard shook his head. "It is an old saying, Will. One that once worked in Earth's favor."

But this time it wouldn't work in Earth's favor. The *Enterprise,* the *Madison,* and the *Idaho,* along with the Klingon ships, could probably destroy the four ships guarding the wormhole. But after that, hundreds—

—maybe thousands—

—of ships would come through.

The five battle-scarred ships, along with more reinforcements, would be no match.

No match at all.

"Captain," Riker said softly. "We need to close that wormhole."

Picard nodded. He knew that. But until this moment he hadn't been willing to face the fact that he was going to have to send one of his people to their death. But now he had to.

The question was, which one?

Chapter Nineteen

WORF STUDIED THE SECURITY CONSOLE before him. The two Klingon ships, *DoHQay* and *HohIj*, were revolving on the schematic before him. The *DoHQay* was captained by Krann, son of Huy', of the House of Thorne. Krann was a good commander, not very daring, but protective of Klingon honor. The *HohIj* was captained by KoPoch, son of Karch, of the House of Kipsk. KoPoch was a strong commander with a gift for risk. They were both good additions to this force.

But the two houses were at war with each other. It was a brilliant ploy on the part of Gowron. Send the leaders of the warring houses here. Have them outdo each other in battle, and probably die. Both houses would retain their honor, and the feud would end. Three problems solved and, if it succeeded and the

Furies were turned back, Gowron would again be a hero.

The man sometimes was a visionary.

Worf frowned.

But if it failed, the two ships would turn on each other instead of the Furies, and Klingon honor would be even further destroyed.

He looked up as Captain Picard ended his communication with the Fury. Worf ended the transmission and wiped the schematics of the ships off his board.

They could not let this go to war.

The Federation was not able to fight as vicious a fight as was needed. Gowron was more concerned with his own problems than with saving the sector from the Furies. He probably believed that his secondary force would do the real fighting.

Commander Riker, with too much fear in his voice, reminded the captain that someone had to destroy the wormhole. Worf did not fear the task. He welcomed it.

The captain looked directly at Worf. Worf straightened, determined to look like a warrior.

"Sir," Data said. "A Fury ship has come through the wormhole."

The captain whirled, Worf apparently forgotten. "On screen."

The ship flying through the wormhole was larger than the ships already guarding it.

"I thought you said fleets would be coming through," Riker said to Data.

"They are," Data said. "They are apparently entering one ship at a time in sixty-five second intervals."

"How many ships are you reading, Data?"

"I count a minimum of one hundred ships, sir," Data said, "and that only covers the ships which my sensors can pick up. At a distance through the wormhole, the readings become hazy."

"Were your readings on the device on the other side hazy?" Riker asked.

"No, sir," Data said. "Those are accurate. I used—"

"We have no time, Mr. Data," Picard said.

Worf agreed. Very soon another ship would come through the wormhole. They would lose their advantage if the captain did not act.

"Sound the red alert, Mr. Worf."

"Aye, sir," Worf said. He tapped in the command, and within seconds the lights all over the ship glowed red. "Captain. We have only a few moments. Send me through the wormhole."

Data stood. "No, sir. I am the logical choice."

"Your analysis said a skilled pilot was needed," Worf said, letting some of his anger lash at Data. "My instincts are superior to your programming. A skilled pilot knows when to use speculation—"

"Mr. Worf," the captain cautioned.

Worf stopped.

"Mr. Worf has a point," Data said, "but I do not feel the emotional effects of the Furies' beam. I would remain rational throughout."

"Thank you, Mr. Data," Picard said, "but I need you here. If we lose our screens, I need someone here who can still think clearly and take control."

"You need all of us here," Riker said. "But you'll have to choose someone, and quickly."

Worf looked at him. Riker was one of the best pilots

in Starfleet. His record was better than Worf's. Everyone knew that. But he didn't have honor to defend. He had less at stake. And a warrior with a blood vengeance was always more powerful than one without.

"Captain, I have honor to avenge," Worf said. "The Klingons were defeated by the first Fury ship. Let me return honor to my people!"

"Another ship is about to come through, sir," Ensign Eckley said.

"Mr. Worf," the captain said, "I want you to take the shuttlecraft *Polo* with a full contingent of armaments. Have Mr. La Forge download the shield modifications into the shuttle's computers."

"Aye, sir." Worf pivoted, and headed for the turbolift.

"You are not dismissed, Mr. Worf."

Worf halted. He had felt at odds with the captain ever since this mission began. His sense of what was needed obviously differed from Picard's. "I am sorry, sir."

"You shall use the shuttle *Polo* as a shield for Commander Riker." Picard's voice softened as he turned to face Riker. "You are the best pilot on the ship, Will."

"Thank you, sir," Riker said.

"I am the better shot," Worf said, unable to remain silent.

The captain nodded. "I know. Which is why you will defend Will's shuttlecraft," Picard said.

"Sir," Riker said, "Lieutenant Sam Redbay from engineering—he's a damn good pilot. He'll be able to fly third cover."

"Good," Picard said, nodding. "Have him provide defense from the shuttle *Lewis*."

"Captain," Worf said, knowing he had only one more chance at convincing Picard, "Klingons are used to dying for honor. Humans are not."

Picard was standing almost at attention. Deanna looked lost beside him. Her face was blank, her eyes distant as if she couldn't bear to watch what was happening in front of her.

Suddenly Worf's words came back to him. A Klingon commander would not think twice about sending one of his men to die in battle. The captain obviously felt burdened by it.

"I know, Mr. Worf," Picard said. "I shall depend on that finely honed sense of honor to get Commander Riker through the wormhole, alive, and his shuttle intact."

Worf raised his head as the realization hit him. Captain Picard did not believe any of the shuttlecraft would return. He was sending out his troops to die with honor. It did not matter who fired the final shot, only that the final shot was made.

"I shall do everything within my power to make certain Commander Riker enters the wormhole," Worf said.

"I'll destroy that device," Riker said. "You can count on it, sir."

"I am counting on it," Picard said, softly. "Dismissed."

Riker joined Worf.

Both of them looked squarely at their captain, and he returned their stare. It lasted only a moment, but it was long enough for Worf to understand that Picard was very proud of both of them.

It was an honor Worf would take to his death. As a warrior he could be no more blessed.

Deanna took a step toward both of them and then stopped. A tear was streaking down her cheek. Beside him, Riker smiled to her.

All Worf could bring himself to do was nod. This was his proudest moment. Deanna was strong. She would survive.

Together they turned and headed for the turbolift.

The door slid open and they entered, turned, and faced the bridge as a unit. All eyes were on them.

Deanna stood beside Picard, her arms hanging at her side. Worf had never seen her look so upset.

"Good luck," Picard said.

"Thank you, sir," Worf said.

Riker glanced up at him and smiled. "It is," he said, giving voice to the traditional Klingon battle cry—and meaning it, "a good day to die."

Chapter Twenty

DOZENS OF PERSONNEL flooded the shuttlebay. Technicians crowded around all three shuttles. Other people were taking notes.

Redbay noted as he glanced around that one woman was putting emergency medical kits on each shuttle. One-man medical kits, the kind that a person could use with one hand on the console. Not very effective. The kits were often used on missions in which the pilot's health was not an issue.

Staying alive was.

Redbay's mouth was dry. Picard had ordered him to report to Commander Riker in shuttlebay, nothing more. Redbay assumed he would get more orders when he arrived.

The conversation, though, usually so high in a

situation like this, was muted. People seemed to be speaking only when necessary.

Another sign of a serious mission.

Of course, how could the mission be anything else? The Furies were out there, waiting, literally growing stronger by the minute. Any mission at this point would be serious.

Will Riker and Lieutenant Worf were standing near the computer tactical display terminal on the interior wall. An ensign beside them sighted Redbay and tapped Riker on the shoulder, pointing his way.

Riker turned. He had a look in his eyes that Redbay had seen before, a steely determination that made Riker seem twice as powerful as usual. No longer the roommate from the Academy, no longer the jet-dogfight partner, no longer the good friend. This was Riker the warrior, ready to do battle.

And when Riker was like this, he was usually very serious and very, very determined.

So Redbay forced himself to grin. If nothing else he could keep the tension of this down to a reasonable level.

Riker motioned for him to join them. Redbay made his way around the technicians, ignoring the argument near the diagnostic computer, an argument he could have settled with few words, and hurried toward Riker. When he reached Riker's side, Riker clapped a hand on his shoulder.

Will had only done that once before.

A dogfight run the cadets had to fly because the Federation base near Chala IV was under attack.

They had thought they were going to die that day.

So Will thinks we are going to die. No wonder he had the look.

"I only have a few minutes to brief you," Riker said. "The longer we wait, the more Fury ships come through that wormhole."

"There are six ships now," Worf said.

Redbay tensed. He glanced at the monitor. Sure enough, six ships hovered near the wormhole opening. "They're coming through, quicker than expected?"

Riker nodded. "About one a minute. We don't know how long they'll wait before they attack."

"That's where we come in, I take it," Redbay said.

"Lieutenant Data has found a way to destroy the wormhole," Worf said. "However, it cannot be done with the *Enterprise*. It must be done by a sure shot from a shuttlecraft."

Redbay swallowed. He'd seen Worf's records. He knew Will's. All three of them were crack shots and top pilots.

"Here's the schematic." Riker tapped the console. A computer simulation of the wormhole appeared. It looked like the horn of plenty Redbay's mother had put on their dining-room table every fall, even in Nyo when fall didn't really exist.

The six ships hovered around the small side of the horn. A small red dot on the other side of the horn flashed.

The target.

"That's the power source," Riker said, pointing at it. "Hit it just right and there will be a feedback loop that will destroy the wormhole, and the Furies will no longer have a path to us. The problem is the shot. I figure we only have one chance at it."

He tapped the console again, and a blue dot appeared. It was near the mouth of the horn.

On the other side.

The shooter would have to go through the wormhole, past all the Furies' ships, into enemy territory. Suddenly he understood the reason for Will's determination.

This made every other mission Redbay had flown look like a cakewalk.

"All right," Riker said. "Data believes that the shuttles can make it through the wormhole without being detected. The Fury ships in there are in a form of stasis field, crowded one right after another. The shuttle won't be. It should make it through in one-hundredth of the time they are taking coming the other way."

Redbay nodded. "Do we have enough firepower?"

"One photon torpedo is all it will take," Riker said. "Each shuttle is equipped with more than that."

"Only one shuttle will go through the wormhole," Worf said. "The other two will provide cover." He brought his head up and met Redbay's gaze. Klingons were naturally fierce; Worf even more so. "You had better be as good a pilot as Commander Riker says you are."

Redbay glanced at Riker, who didn't even grin. "He is, Worf. Trust me."

"So I am taking one of the shuttlecrafts," Redbay said, "and doing what?"

"Providing cover for me," Riker said.

"You're going through?"

Riker nodded. "You and Worf will make sure I get inside. If the wormhole doesn't collapse in four minutes after that, then you'll have to try. But I doubt that will be necessary. The tricky part is getting into the wormhole and through it. The shot is easy."

"After you destroy the power source," Redbay asked, "how long will it take the wormhole to collapse?"

Riker bent over the console and tapped it once more, and the screen went dark. He didn't say any more.

He didn't need to.

A suicide mission.

Picard was sending his second-in-command because he didn't trust anyone else to get the job done.

With ships coming through the wormhole one every minute, the odds of Redbay and Worf surviving were small too.

But not as small as Riker's.

"You are taking the shuttlecraft *Lewis*," Worf said. "I will be in the *Polo*. I shall head for the wormhole at top speed. When the Furies try to intercept me, I shall veer off."

"Then you will do the same, Sam," Riker said. "When they move to intercept, veer off. You'll take at least one of their ships with you. I will be right behind you. Only I'll go in."

It sounded so easy.

It sounded like it might work.

"What about the starships?" Redbay asked.

"They all will be doing variations of the same maneuvers, trying to pull Fury ships away from the wormhole," Riker said. "The Furies won't fall for this very long, which is why we have to move quickly. You'll be on Worf's tail. Questions?"

Redbay shook his head. What was there to question? He and his best friend were going to die in the next few minutes. It was that simple.

"Good," Riker said. "The shuttles are equipped with the diagram of the target. They also have modified shields. I have no idea how well those shields will hold up with the Furies in close range. In case it gets too much, Dr. Crusher has provided us with her calming gas. I suggest that we not use it unless absolutely necessary. She claims it has no effect on motor skills, but I'm not so certain."

"Sometimes fear has an effect on motor skills," Redbay said, remembering La Forge as he fell out of the Jeffries tube.

"Which is why we're equipped with the gas." Riker turned and faced them both. "You both ready?"

"Yes, sir," both Worf and Redbay said at the same time.

Riker nodded. "Let's do it."

Without another word he turned and walked quickly toward the center shuttle. Worf strode toward the left shuttle.

Redbay stood for a moment watching his best friend move toward his certain death. He knew without a doubt he would never see Riker again. But he couldn't leave it like that.

"Will!"

Riker glanced around, but kept walking.

"I want a rematch when you get back. I saved that last dogfight."

Riker grinned. "You got it."

Redbay ran toward the remaining shuttle. He was the best pilot in Starfleet, and one of the best shots. He was going to prove just how good he was by giving Riker the best cover possible.

And helping him close that wormhole forever.

Picard moved his shoulders trying to ease some of the tension. The bridge seemed empty without Will and Worf. Data still manned the science console, and Counselor Troi remained on the bridge. But Data's news about the wormhole was not good—more ships lined up inside, waiting to come through—and Troi was looking more and more strained with each passing moment.

The five-way conversation with the other two starship captains and the captains of the Klingon ships hadn't helped. They all agreed that Mr. La Forge's schematics helped them, and they also agreed on the coded attack plan Picard had sent them, but the agreement had ended there. Both captains Higginbotham and Kiser commended Picard on his negotiation skills. The Klingon captains believed that negotiating had been a waste of time. They seemed amazed that they could agree upon anything.

Privately Picard agreed with the Klingons. If he hadn't tried to negotiate, Will might have had a better chance of getting through that wormhole.

But if Picard hadn't tried to negotiate, then he never would have been able to live with himself. He would have forever wondered if going to war first had been the best choice.

Now he had no doubts.

Seven Fury ships hung in space around the wormhole. Another one was due at any second. He knew that Will knew the importance of speed. He hoped that speed would be possible.

"Sir," Data said. "The lead Fury ship is hailing us."

Picard's stomach clamped up like a vise. Now what were they trying? "On screen. And make sure the other ships are getting this transmission."

"Done, sir."

The face of the leader of the Fury ships filled the screen. The image seemed clearer this time, as if the haze and fog on the other side had lifted. And the horned captain of the Furies didn't seem as self-assured.

"You claimed to have the souls of those from the *Rath?*"

So that what this was all about. Maybe there was a slight hope yet of stopping this without losing good people to the fight. Maybe those poppets Kirk had saved would save the day here.

"We do. They have been kept safe and brought here. We had hoped to have a peaceful exchange."

The horned captain on the other side glanced at someone offscreen, then back at Picard. "Which ship are they on?"

Picard shook his head, then laughed. "No information. You stop your fleet from coming into our sector and we'll talk. Not before."

"Picard." The Furies' captain stood, its face almost red with anger. For the first time Picard saw the poppet doll hanging at its side. It was a replica of the being wearing it. "If those souls are destroyed or harmed, I personally will kill you slowly and very painfully."

"If those souls are destroyed," Picard said, his voice very level and firm, "you will be the one destroying them. Not I."

Picard signaled for the communication to be cut off. All hope of stopping this fight was now gone.

But if it was a fight they wanted, then a fight they would get. He turned and moved back to his command chair and sat down.

"Shuttles are ready and launching," Ensign Eckley said.

"Mr. Data, signal the other ships to move into position," Picard said. "It's imperative that we move those Furies away from the wormhole. Now."

"Aye, sir," Data said.

Troi's hands clutched the arms of her chair.

"Sir," Eckley said, "another ship is coming through the wormhole."

On screen, the eighth Fury ship took a position near the opening to the wormhole. Eight ships against five. The original *Enterprise* had had trouble defeating just one Fury ship. There was no time left.

"Battle stations," Picard said. "Ahead full impulse. Target photon torpedoes and fire on my mark."

On screen the other two starships moved into position. As planned, the Klingon ships turned and flew away from the battle site. Once they had gone a respectable distance, they would cloak. With luck, the Furies would think that the Klingons had retreated, not realizing that the Klingons had cloaking ability. The Klingons would then attack the Fury ships from behind and above, decloaking at the last minute as they fired.

But the main target of the Furies' attack would be the *Enterprise,* and the moment the ship moved forward, the Furies turned toward it, as planned.

Rays of light extended from the Fury ships, green this time, as if the different color marked different weapons.

The *Enterprise* rocked as the first impact of Fury fire hit the shields.

"Damage, Mr. Data."

"None, sir. The shields are holding," Data said.

Picard took a deep breath. The fight had truly begun. He just hoped it would end here and not on Earth.

"Fire," he said.

Chapter Twenty-one

RIKER'S HANDS MOVED on the shuttlecraft controls as if he were piloting any normal shuttle mission. But he wasn't. This was the most important mission of his career.

Of his life.

If he succeeded, he—William T. Riker—would have stopped the Furies from invading his sector. He would have kept thousands, maybe millions from dying. After his own personal glimpse of hell, he thought it almost worth the cost.

He grinned at himself. He had to qualify the thought, because he wasn't Klingon. He believed in dying with honor, but he would rather not die at all. And if he could help it he wouldn't. He didn't know how he'd get back from the other side of that wormhole, but he'd find a way.

The shuttlebay doors opened. He settled into the familiar shuttle pilot's chair, his hands still dancing across the controls. Oddly enough, he wasn't frightened. Geordi had modified the shields, and that had helped, but that wasn't all of it.

This last mission was the right mission. Not even dying scared him. Not even the possibility of dying scared him.

Not anymore.

Some things were worse than death. And living in a galaxy run by the Furies was one of them.

As he cleared the shuttlebay doors, he pulled up a schematic of the entire area around the Furies Point. Eight Fury ships now encircled the wormhole. Worf was moving as planned at an angle slightly away from the Furies. Redbay flew his shuttle on the same line. Riker dropped into line. Their trajectories should convince the Furies that they were trying to escape. Yet all three shuttles would remain close. They would be prepared to fly into that wormhole at a moment's notice.

Now it all depended on how well Picard's plan worked.

It had to work.

For all their sakes.

Riker kept on the line, monitoring the others. Adrenaline started pouring through him. He was ready for a fight. These few seconds before battle were always the hardest.

The *Enterprise* moved directly at the Furies Point. The *Madison* followed. When they got in close the *Enterprise* would turn to port and the *Madison* would go to starboard on attack runs.

The *Idaho* circled high, a lone graceful starship, apparently on her own path. Gradually, the *Idaho* also closed in on the Furies Point.

The Furies had a lot to watch.

The two Klingon ships had also taken a direction that would allow the Furies to think they had been running away. They were now cloaked, and Riker knew that within moments they would reappear firing.

Then the closest Fury ship shot at the *Enterprise*. The burst of light was sudden and startling. Riker felt a welcome tension in his arms and shoulders.

The battle had started.

He kept on his line, a small ship, unnoticed. He tried to be as invisible as possible, as if willing it would help.

The *Enterprise* returned fire on the closest Fury ship. The *Idaho* swooped down and fired also.

The battle had been joined.

Four of the Fury ships took positions against the *Enterprise* and *Idaho*. The *Madison* took on two others, and space was filled with explosions and flashes of light. Phaser fire connected the ships like deadly lifelines.

"Klingons?" Riker whispered. "Where are you?"

A Fury ship in front of the *Enterprise* exploded in a burst of colored light. Debris flew in all directions.

One down, but thousands more in that wormhole to deal with.

Riker glanced at the shuttles in front of him. Worf and Redbay seemed all right.

For the moment.

The *Enterprise* turned its weapons on the nearest

ship, with the *Madison* lending her firepower. From this distance, the starships appeared to have complete control, but Riker knew the *Enterprise* was taking a pounding.

He hoped the shields would hold.

And that Beverly's drug would work if they didn't.

"Come on, Klingons," he whispered. He hoped the shields worked for them too. If they didn't, there might be a disastrous repeat of the first fight at the Furies Point.

He wished he could see Worf. He wondered if Worf was as worried about the Birds-of-Prey as he was.

He hoped not.

Suddenly the two Klingon ships decloaked close to the wormhole. They looked like giant screaming vultures, with their weapons flaring red against the darkness of space. The two Fury ships closest to the wormhole did not return fire right away.

They were surprised.

"Another point for our side," Riker muttered.

He tapped the communications console. This was it. The big moment. Now or never, and all those other clichés.

"Go!" he shouted to Worf and Redbay, feeling absurdly like a soccer coach.

"Aye, sir," Worf said.

"Yes, *sir!*" Redbay said, and Riker could almost see his old friend snap his arm in mock salute. Riker grinned. He might be alone in the shuttle, but he wasn't alone in space. And for some reason having his friend here made him feel more in control.

Worf's shuttle peeled off and headed toward the wormhole.

Redbay followed.

After a moment both opened fire on the two Fury ships, pretending to be making an attack run.

Riker took his ship right in behind him. He forced himself to block out the surrounding fight. His only focus was that wormhole and getting through it.

Nothing else mattered.

Nothing.

"Captain, shields are failing on decks three and ten," Data said.

Picard nodded, then clutched the arm of his chair as the ship rocked from another hit. In front of him a Fury ship exploded, sending an expanding cloud of debris in a circle outward.

"Ensign Eckley, move us closer to the wormhole," he ordered. No matter how much damage, they needed to be close enough to draw the fire away from the shuttles. Worf and Redbay were both making their runs at the Fury ships, adding their firepower to that of the Klingons. Riker's shuttle lagged behind, but was coming in on the same path.

In just seconds, he would be inside the wormhole.

The ship rocked again. The Furies' weapons concentrated on the shields, as they had before. Picard had a feeling that they had encountered this type of protection from some other group. But he bet they were getting a surprise now that the shields were holding.

"The lead ship has sustained serious damage from our torpedoes," Lieutenant Dreod said. She stood in Worf's place at security.

It felt odd not to have his usual bridge complement.

Counselor Troi sat beside him, her face a mask, yet he could feel the tension radiate from her.

No support from that quarter.

Picard stood.

"The damage on decks three and ten has stabilized," Data said. "The shields on the rest of the ship are holding."

The lead Fury ship still stood between them and the wormhole, far too close for Riker's safety.

"Take that lead ship out of there," Picard said.

A barrage of photon torpedoes streaked from the *Enterprise*. They exploded against the shields of the Fury ship. If nothing else, it would get their attention.

Maybe just long enough for Riker to get through.

Worf leaned into his console. His ship weaved through the fire from the Fury ships. He returned the shots with a vigor he hadn't felt in a long, long time.

Worf, son of Mogh, would die with honors. He would die defending his people from the Furies, and serving his ship with pride.

He would give the Furies a fight they would never forget.

The modified shuttlecraft had a great deal of firepower for its size. He used all of it, dodging and weaving, and shooting, all the time making the Furies think he was the most important enemy, diverting their attention from Commander Riker.

The *DoHQay* made a pass at the Fury ship closest to the wormhole. It was circling above, and about to come in for another shot. Worf saw an opening underneath. He swung the shuttle upward, firing continuously as he went.

The Fury ship's shields were failing. Worf focused his fire on where his computer told him their screens were the weakest. The bright red phasers deflected off the shield, leaving a slightly pink glow. Worf was about to use one of his precious photon torpedoes when the Fury ship spun away out of control and exploded.

The explosion was so close that it rocked the shuttle.

Worf clutched the console as he fought for control. He still had fight in him. But the shuttle was swerving dangerously close to the other Fury ship. If Worf didn't get his shuttle turned, he would hit the Fury ship. It would destroy both vessels, but it wouldn't help Commander Riker. He might get caught in the explosion himself.

Worf swerved and barely missed the ship's hull. Sweat dripped off his ridged forehead. But they didn't let him get away that easily.

A phaser blast at close range destroyed his shields.

The shuttle spun away, and Worf had to grip the console to keep from losing his seat.

The screens went dead. The cabin filled with dark smoke, foul-smelling smoke, smoke that came not from an electrical fire, because he knew that smell. No, from something less familiar.

The warp core.

He struggled to regain his shields.

He struggled to regain any vision he could of the fight.

He struggled to bring his weapons on-line.

The air was disappearing from the cabin. Sweat soaked his uniform.

THE SOLDIERS OF FEAR

Then he brought the computer on-line.

"Engine failure in ten seconds." The familiar voice started her countdown.

Worf pounded on the console, but nothing else responded.

"Seven . . ."

He couldn't breathe. His chest felt heavy.

"Six . . ."

He ignored it, pushing emergency relays, trying to regain any control at all.

"Five . . ."

The voice sounded so calm. Not even a Klingon would sound that calm in this situation.

"Four . . ."

The smoke was now so thick that he couldn't even see his hands.

"Three . . ."

One glimpse of the battle. Just one. To know if Riker made it.

"Two . . ."

But he would never know. All that he would know was that he had done his best. Mentally he saluted the commander and wished him well.

"One . . ."

Riker had been right. It was a good day to die.

Chapter Twenty-two

THE SHUTTLE WAS ON COURSE. The shuttle *was* on course.

Riker stared at the screen and the console, keeping the wormhole firmly in his vision, ignoring the chaos as best he could.

Eight seconds.

In eight seconds he would be there.

Then Worf's shuttle streaked across space, whipping and spinning like a child's toy thrown by an angry child. Riker glanced at it, feeling suddenly helpless.

Seven seconds.

If he helped Worf, he would jeopardize the entire Federation and his mission.

Six seconds.

Both Klingon ships were firing on the Fury ship

THE SOLDIERS OF FEAR

nearest the wormhole. The firefight was incredible, the laser firepower blinding. Redbay had fired a dozen or more shots and then veered away to stay out of the path of the two Birds-of-Prey.

Five seconds.

The *Enterprise* had taken on the main Fury ship in a one-on-one battle. The *Idaho* and the *Madison* were in a three-against-two fight.

Four seconds.

There was no help for Worf. No one could save him. He would die in battle.

"Sorry, old friend," Riker said, wishing Worf could hear him.

But to save Worf would be the worst thing Riker could do. Worf would want to die in battle. It was the best way for a Klingon to die. To make Worf's death meaningful, the mission had to succeed, and it was up to him to make sure it did.

Three seconds. The wormhole suddenly looked huge. The space around it was clear. The other ships had done their jobs.

Two seconds.

Riker glanced at his weapons. The torpedoes were ready. So was he. Worf wouldn't die in vain.

Then, without warning, another Fury ship came out of the mouth of the wormhole directly in front of him.

The ship was huge, and this close, it looked like a demon itself.

He suddenly needed every last ounce of his piloting skill.

He yanked the shuttle hard to port, hoping to flash past the Fury ship before it even had time to react. He was going to be so close that his shuttle would bounce off the Furies' outer screens, he hoped right into the wormhole.

But they saw him.

The ship turned as he did, its larger bulk making the turn shorter. He would make it into the wormhole. They had actually made it easier. . . .

Then a bright flare caught his eye. Point-blank phaser shot.

He didn't even have time to react.

No steering away, no doubling the power of his shields, no time to scream and throw his arms over his head.

One minute he was moving forward, the next his shuttle had turned into a metal fireball, tumbling through space.

"Shields failing," the computer said.

The heat was incredible. The console and chair were both suddenly too hot to touch.

"Environmental controls inoperative," the computer said.

Riker slipped off his tunic jacket, wrapped it around his hand, and hit the stabilizing controls. Somehow he got the shuttle upright, and the screens back on.

Sweat poured from his skin. He had to turn around. He had to get back to that wormhole.

But the Fury ship didn't let up. It followed him, firing as it came.

"Warning. Internal temperature at unsustainable levels," the computer said. "Warning."

"Great," Riker muttered. "Just great."

The heat was even more terrifying considering the

lack of smoke. That meant some sort of severe systems meltdown was imminent.

But it wouldn't take long through that wormhole, if he could just turn around.

"Warning. Systems overload in thirty seconds," the computer said.

He was too far away. He wouldn't make it to the wormhole mouth within a minute, let alone thirty seconds.

Angry, he fired what was left of his phasers at the ship, but it was like firing a water pistol at a three-alarm fire.

He glanced for Worf's shuttle. Maybe, if he couldn't save himself, he could save Worf—but he was too far away.

The Furies hit the shuttle again. The lights flickered on, off, then on again.

"Warning. Shields have failed. Systems overload in fifteen seconds."

He lost his last shields. One more blast and he would be dead.

The console was hot to his wrapped hand. He pounded it with his fist.

"Systems overload in ten seconds."

Ten seconds and no chance of success.

Ten seconds to contemplate the fact that he, William T. Riker, had failed.

The scene on his viewscreens was a nightmare. Redbay had flown thousands of mock space battles while testing ships, but never had he thought he would be a firsthand witness and player in one of the most important battles, with the survival of the Federation and the Klingon Empire at stake.

And the Federation and Klingons were losing.

Worf's shuttle had taken some serious hits and was tumbling out of control. Riker had almost made it when another Fury ship had appeared in front of him, blasting him away from the wormhole like a paper toy in a strong wind.

But luckily, that Fury ship hadn't seen Redbay. Instead it followed Riker, pounding him with shot after shot.

Now Redbay was the only one left.

And the wormhole was there in front of him like a gaping black mouth.

All he had to do was beat any of those Fury ships to it. But Riker's attempt had clued them in. They knew the shuttles weren't escaping, but trying for the wormhole. The Fury ships, fighting with the starships, were actually backing closer to the wormhole.

To guard it.

"Hang in there, buddy," he said aloud as Riker's shuttle took another full blast. "I'll give them something more to think about in just a second."

His hands flew over the controls of the shuttle, keying in a familiar sequence. He'd run a hundred ships through it in test, but never under actual battle circumstances. It was called, among the test pilots, the old "Down and Out" pattern. He had no idea how it got its name, some pilot long before he came along.

The Down and Out consisted of taking a ship at a wide, sweeping, almost lazy arch, then suddenly veering at the target. The theory was that a ship following would be thrown off guard by the move and the ship making the move would gain a slight advantage in distance.

That was the theory, anyway.

He finished the entering the sequence into the computer and engaged.

Around him the battle seemed to flash past as he took the shuttle almost away from the wormhole in a wide arch.

"Three more seconds," he said to himself.

The wormhole was a gaping mouth off his port side. He waited. Waited. Then said "Now!" as he punched the board hard. The shuttle veered sharply to port, increasing speed to its maximum subwarp. The wormhole grew directly in his front screen, now only a few very long seconds away.

"Right on the money." He could feel himself starting to celebrate another successful move, just as he used to do back at the testing area.

Then he was reminded that this was no longer a test as a blast from below hit the shuttle.

"What?"

It took all his skills and strength just to stay in the pilot's seat. The shuttle was knocked away, and its tumbling momentum took it past the mouth of the wormhole, missing by a large enough distance to make no difference.

A miss was a miss.

The shuttle kept tumbling, and he let it as he searched for a bearing on what had hit him. Even with the shuttle spinning, it didn't take him long to find the problem. One of the Fury ships had veered away from its fight with the Klingons to take him out of his run at the hole. But now the Klingon Bird-of-Prey was stalking it, engaging it again. And from the looks of it, the Klingon ship was winning this time.

For the moment he was safe. He quickly stabilized the tumble of the shuttle and turned it around, going in a wide arch over the battle. First things first. He needed to get back to the correct side of the wormhole.

The mouth side.

"Well, that sure didn't work," he said out loud again. "And I got to stop talking to myself so much. Just as soon as this mission is over."

Sweat dripped from his face as he did a quick check of the systems. His screens were at fifty percent, but otherwise the ship was fine. From the looks of it, he was in a lot better shape than Worf. His shuttle seemed to be completely dead in space.

Redbay took the shuttle at full speed back into a position far above and to one side of the wormhole. It seemed to take forever, but in real time it was less than thirty seconds before he was in place.

From here the battle looked like a bunch of toys fighting. But he knew that in those toys real beings were dying, giving their lives for what they believed.

"Looks like I'm still the only shot. Got to make this one work."

He studied the situation carefully. One of the Fury ships had backed almost to the mouth of the wormhole, but the other Klingon ship was giving it a pounding. The oval shape of the hole looked like a small button against the starfields of space.

A very small target.

Very small.

Suddenly he knew how to get in there. "You better

be as good as you've claimed," he said aloud. "Or you're going to be very, very dead."

He punched in a few quick commands, then glanced at the screen. Riker's shuttle was still tumbling out of control. Will had wanted to see the Redbay Maneuver firsthand. "Well, old friend, you finally get your chance," Redbay said, wishing Will were in the shuttle with him. He didn't want to think about his friend on a damaged shuttle, about to die for nothing.

Redbay would make certain they all succeeded.

He never really was starship material. He had always been a pilot. Only now the tests were done. This was real.

Very real.

The Redbay Maneuver was a test-pilot stunt he'd run many a ship through. In essence it was a ninety-degree turn in space. He used impulse drive to move the ship in one direction. Then, with an almost instantaneous firing and shutting down of the warp drive, he would turn the ship ninety degrees while in the forming and collapsing warp bubble. He'd been the first to try it and make it work; thus he got the honor of the name.

He had three problems. The first was simple. He had never run a shuttlecraft through this particular maneuver.

The second was related to the first: The shuttle's stabilizers would be strained beyond the recommended endurance. If they failed he would be nothing more than a large splash of red on the darkness of space. But the stabilizers would hold. They'd have to. He had no other choice if he wanted to live.

And the third was a big problem in and of itself. If he missed the wormhole, he'd be going so fast he'd never make it back into position before the next Fury ship arrived. He'd never have a second chance.

But going fast was a good thing in this situation, because none of the Fury ships would have time to take a shot at him.

So he just wouldn't miss.

It was that simple.

He initiated the procedure, setting the speed at full impulse. Then he aimed the shuttle at a ninety-degree angle across the mouth of the wormhole. It actually would appear that he was heading for the battle between the *Madison,* the *Idaho,* and the three Fury ships. They might even think he was trying to get back to the *Enterprise.*

With only a quick glance at Riker's tumbling ship—it still hadn't righted itself—he focused all his attention on making the turn at exactly the right instant.

"Three."

"Two."

"One."

"Now!" he shouted to the empty shuttle cabin, and triggered the Redbay Maneuver.

The shuttle stabilizers screamed in protest.

But he held on, praying his theories were right.

And all the years of practice would pay off.

Chapter Twenty-three

THE *ENTERPRISE* ROCKED. Picard stood on the bridge, his hands clasped behind his back, presenting, he hoped, a calm in the center of the storm.

Around him, the red-alert lights were flashing. The regular lighting was on three-quarter power, because Mr. La Forge had rerouted the environmental controls to the shields.

So far they were holding.

But Picard didn't know how long they would hold.

The battle raged around the wormhole. He had managed to get the *Enterprise* between the lead Fury ship and the wormhole, providing an opening for the shuttlecrafts.

"Lieutenant Worf's shuttle has been hit," Data said. "It appears to have lost helm control. Life-support is failing."

"Lock on to him, Mr. Data."

"Sir, we cannot beam him out now. We would have to lower our shields."

"I know that, Mr. Data." Picard stared at the screen. The tiny shuttlecraft looked like a bug against the giant Fury ships. "We'll beam him when we can."

"If we wait too long, sir, he—"

"I am aware of the risks, Mr. Data."

Data nodded and swiveled back, facing his console. Troi clasped her hands together. She hadn't gotten out of her chair since the fight started. Picard wasn't sure if she could stand.

She was aware of the risks as well. Most likely neither Worf nor Will Riker would return.

Picard wouldn't lose two good men in a failed mission if he had anything to say about it.

The *Enterprise* rocked again.

"Shields holding," Eckley said.

"Return fire," Picard said.

But as he stared at the screen, he didn't watch his own battle. He watched the shuttlecrafts.

Redbay broke off his run, veering to starboard to give Riker a clear path to the wormhole.

"Another Fury ship is emerging from the wormhole," Data said.

"Warn Commander Riker!" Picard shouted, but it was too late. In horror Picard watched as Riker moved his shuttle in a quick series of moves to a course that would take it speeding past the new Fury ship and into the wormhole.

Only the Fury ship had another plan.

With a phaser burst it sent Riker's shuttle tumbling, then moved after it like a bully chasing a small victim.

"Move to intercept that new ship," Picard ordered.

The deck rocked from the impact of a phaser blast from the one ship they already were fighting.

"Shields failing on decks fifteen through twenty," Data said.

"Mr. La Forge," Picard said to the air in front of him. "Can you give me an uninterrupted phaser blast, sustained for three seconds?"

"Yes, sir." La Forge's voice sounded strong and confident. "But the shot will be a drain."

"Then drain us, Mr. La Forge," Picard ordered.

"Aye, sir."

Picard turned to tactical. "Lieutenant Dreod, target that new ship with a three-second laser shot at full intensity."

The young lieutenant nodded. "Ready."

Picard turned to look at the screen. If the Furies had tried to interrupt the *Enterprise* shields by varying the modulation, then their ships must use the same type of modulating shield. A sustained blast to that type of shield should bring it down.

The new ship was moving slowly after Riker's shuttle. Will might already be dead in there, but those Furies were going to pay the price for killing his first officer. "Fire!"

The laser blast seemed to last for an eternity. And before it had ended, the shields of the Fury ship had gone from blue to a bright red and then disappeared. The ship exploded like a kid's balloon stuck by a pin.

Picard felt no joy. No happiness.

Riker was too far from the wormhole. Even if he turned around, he probably didn't have a chance. Picard could see that without looking at the readings.

The mission had failed.

Picard hoped the other captains had an idea, because he was all out.

The other Fury ship had backed off slightly.

"Sir," Data said. "Lieutenant Redbay's shuttle is moving on an arching course over the wormhole."

Picard turned to the screen. The shuttle was moving at a arching angle almost away from the wormhole.

Why would he do that? He wasn't even close to the target. "What is he doing?" Picard said softly.

"Perhaps he's trying something, sir," Eckley said.

"He is out there. He might see something we don't." Troi sounded tired. She knew it was all lost as well.

Suddenly the shuttle veered sharply and gained speed at the wormhole.

"He is trying a training pilot's stunt called a Down and Out," Data said. "It might work."

But Picard could tell almost instantly that Data had spoken too soon. The Fury ship closest to the wormhole broke away from the Klingon Bird-of-Prey and hit the shuttle with a direct shot.

Redbay went spinning off course and past the wormhole.

The silence on the bridge felt like a smothering blanket. Picard wanted to order the air-filtration system turned up. More than that, he wanted to be anywhere but here. Maybe back in France, sitting on top of a hill with a gentle breeze blowing over his face.

But unless they stopped the Furies here, that might never be possible again. For him or for anyone else.

He turned to Data. "Inform the *Madison* and the

Idaho that they need to launch their shuttles. Make sure they have all the details."

"Yes, sir," Data said, and his fingers danced over his board, sending off his messages.

The *Enterprise* rocked again with the hit of another Fury blast.

"Shields are still holding," Lieutenant Dreod said.

"Good," Picard said, forcing his attention back on the main screen and the battle in front of him. Maybe, just maybe, they could hold on long enough to get one of the other starships' shuttles through. It was possible.

Another Fury ship appeared from the wormhole and moved immediately into the fight with the Klingons.

"Message sent, sir," Data said. "And Lieutenant Redbay has recovered and is moving into a position high above the wormhole."

"What?" Picard said. He turned and stared at the main screen showing the wormhole and the battle. Sure enough, Redbay's shuttle was a large distance above and to the port side of the wormhole.

"He's holding position," Data said.

"Maybe he's injured," Eckley said.

"I show his shields at fifty percent," Data said, "and all other systems on the shuttle functioning normally."

On the screen the shuttle started to move, not at the wormhole, but more in the direction of the *Idaho* and the *Madison*.

Picard made himself stand and stare, not believing that an officer on his ship would not continue to try to carry out his duty. But it looked as if Lieutenant

Redbay was retreating, right at a time when the Federation needed him the most.

Suddenly the shuttle seemed to stop in flight.

The colors of the rainbow flashed, indicating the shuttle had gone into warp. But it was only a flash, and the next instant the shuttle was streaking toward the wormhole.

And then the shuttle was gone.

Into the mouth of the wormhole.

"The Redbay Maneuver!" Eckley shouted in an excited voice. "He pulled off the Redbay Maneuver."

"The shuttle has entered the wormhole," Data said, confirming what Picard had just seen.

One of their shuttles had gone through.

He glanced at Troi. She stood slowly, keeping one hand on the chair for balance. She was weak, but Redbay's action seemed to give her strength.

Picard let out a breath. So Redbay hadn't been running at all. He'd just been outsmarting them all.

Maybe this death wasn't all for nothing.

If the lieutenant knew what to do.

If, if, if.

Redbay felt as if he were sliding down a stair railing in a thick smoke cloud while everyone else was climbing slowly upward. "Weird," he said aloud. "Really weird."

His sensors showed that he was passing over a hundred Fury ships stacked up in the wormhole. The Federation would have no chance if all these ships made it through. It was his job to make sure they didn't.

The inside of the wormhole was nothing like they

described the wormhole at *Deep Space Nine* to be. This one swirled gray and black, with the line of Fury ships being nothing more than hulking shadows streaking past.

Then, almost as quickly as it started, he was back in real space.

He did a quick scan. The power source was right where Will said it would be. It seemed like a small asteroid hanging in the blackness of space, right at the mouth of the wormhole. But it was actually a huge machine, with power flowing at it from twenty different directions.

"Impressive," Redbay said aloud.

A line of Fury ships seemed to stretch off into the distance, slowly making their way into the wormhole. Redbay didn't even think about glancing at how many there were. Just one was more than a match for this shuttle. The rest didn't matter.

For the moment they didn't react to his sudden appearance. But that would last for only a moment. He'd only get one shot, so he better make it quick and right.

He dove the shuttle right at the small asteroid-like machine, quickly finding the spot Will had said was the target.

"Deep breath," Redbay said aloud to the empty cabin. "This is just another test run. Make it happen."

He locked three torpedoes on target and fired them in quick succession at the machine.

The closest Fury ship broke out of line and headed his way, firing as it came. The shields of the shuttle held, but they wouldn't for long.

Redbay took the shuttle into a steep climb away

from the asteroid as the huge machine started to glow red.

Then a tremendous explosion sent the shuttlecraft spinning like a dry leaf in a strong wind.

"Got it," he said, laughing. "I got it!"

He fought to regain control of the shuttle, but without luck. The blast had completely destroyed all his controls.

"Warning. Internal stabilizers failing," the computer voice said.

"Oh, just great," Redbay said as the increasing forces pinned him into his chair.

With a snap the shuttle's internal stabilizers failed, smashing him against the inside wall of the shuttle and sending him into blackness.

Between the *Idaho* and the *Madison*, a Fury ship exploded. Another Fury ship seemed to be nothing more than a dead hulk. The remaining ships turned to the wormhole, but both Klingon ships moved into their paths and began firing.

Another ship appeared at the mouth of the wormhole.

Picard felt his shoulders sink. Redbay's shuttle must have been destroyed going through.

"Sir," Data said. "The wormhole is collapsing."

Picard couldn't see it. The new Fury ship seemed about to come through.

Then it seemed to elongate. He could almost hear the screams of the Furies inside.

The wormhole stretched, then shrank, then winked out as if it had never been, taking the ship with it.

The bridge broke into wild cheering.

"Redbay found his target," Picard said, his voice soft. He wanted to cheer with the others on the bridge, but something inside kept him silent.

He glanced at the ruined shuttles. "Shields down, Mr. Data. Transporter room, beam Lieutenant Worf aboard."

"Sir," Data said. "It is too late—"

"Anderson, beam him directly to sickbay."

"Aye, sir."

"Sir," Data said, his voice soft, "Commander Riker is still alive."

Picard whirled. "Transporter, get a lock on commander Riker and get him out of there. Now."

A moment later Picard heard, "Done, sir. He's here."

"And Lieutenant Worf?"

"We beamed his body into sickbay, sir."

His body. Two officers down. One survived. It was too soon to feel anything.

The battle wasn't done yet.

Picard turned and stared at the screen. "Screens back up. Open a hailing channel to the main Fury ship."

"Done, sir," Lieutenant Dreod said.

On the main monitor, the screen flickered and then the Furies' leader appeared. Its scarlet skin was peeling. The air around it looked clean, but the back of its chair was coated in creatures.

Dead creatures.

Thousands and thousands of tiny bugs.

The mucus around its mouth was white. Its eyes were yellow. Several dead crew appeared on the screen behind it.

"We have closed your wormhole," Picard said. "You are outnumbered and outgunned."

"I am aware of the situation, Picard," the Fury said, its voice raspy as if it were in pain.

"If you surrender, it will be as if we had never fought. We will . . ."

"Talk, talk, talk. I suppose if I turn my ship over to you, you will want to talk about it." The Fury raised a hand. Long ropes of scarlet flesh hung from it, and a black ichor covered the lower part of the palm. "You talk, but you do not listen, Picard."

"I am listening now."

"I told you we do not bargain. We conquer."

"That seems unlikely today," Picard said.

"That it does," the creature said. "So if you would be so kind as to place our souls with those of our brothers from the *Rath,* we will go now. But there will be a tomorrow. On that you can count."

The creature laughed a sour laugh. "But I'm afraid I will not discuss it with you. Sweet dreams."

The creature smiled. The mucus dripped down its chin, and its yellow eyes had a crazed look.

A chill ran through Picard. A chill that had nothing to do with fear rays or heightened senses. Only a race memory generations old.

Picard would see that face in his dreams.

He knew that, and the creature knew that.

And neither one of them would forget it.

Then the screen went black, replaced a moment later by the view of the Fury ship.

It exploded.

As Picard knew it would.

The other two remaining Fury ships did the same almost instantly.

"That makes no sense," Eckley said. "They didn't need to die."

"Yes, they did," Troi said. "They were afraid."

Picard turned to her. She was swaying slightly as she stood. "Of what, Counselor? Us?"

"Captain," she said, "as victorious demons they were all-powerful. As prisoners of war, they were merely creatures from another quadrant defeated."

"They died for an illusion?" he said, not quite able to believe it.

She shook her head. "They died because of the future that one mentioned," she said. "They died because they knew someday, their people will try again."

Picard shuddered, glancing at the debris-filled blackness. And out there he knew were pods full of small dolls. Poppets full of the souls of those in the ships, to be placed with those from the *Rath*, to wait until the next time.

"They'll be back," Troi said.

He nodded. Safe far across the galaxy, they would lick their wounds, and heal. They would be back, stronger than they had been before.

Chapter Twenty-four

LIEUTENANT BOBBY YOUNG still clung to life. His face was yellow with strain, but his eyes were clear. He knew that he was on the *Enterprise* and the ship was fighting a battle with the Furies.

Beverly Crusher believed that if the *Enterprise* lost the battle, Lieutenant Young would lose his mind.

But if the Furies were defeated, Young would recover. He might never serve in Starfleet again, but he would be able to ski. She knew he loved skiing. When she had asked him to name the most important thing in his life, he had finally spoken. One word, whispered like a lover's name.

Skiing.

And now it looked like he would be able to go. The wormhole was destroyed. The Fury ships had exploded, and the Federation was saved.

At great cost.

Commander Riker and Lieutenant Worf. She had shut off the display when she heard that.

"Doctor," one of her assistants cried. "We're going to be getting wounded."

Beverly pulled herself out of the chair beside Lieutenant Young's bed. "Get the beds ready, pronto. Have the standby team ready."

This was what she had prepared for early in the mission, and it was finally happening.

A body made up of particles of light flickered above the main bed. It was long and broad and—

Klingon.

Worf!

His eyes were open, but unseeing. His ridged forehead was covered with black stains, and burns showed through his uniform.

He wasn't breathing.

But he was here.

At least he was here.

She bent over him. She would save him. She had to save him. She would rescue one of their team, even if Riker was gone.

"All right, everyone," she shouted. "Get his heart and lungs working, stat. We don't know how long he's been gone."

She glanced at the diagnostic. His heart wasn't working. He wasn't breathing. The smoke, according to the medical tricorder, had been a deadly mixture of chemicals from the shuttle's engine. His lungs had collapsed.

If she had to estimate how long he was gone, she would guess a good twenty-five minutes. And even if she could bring him back, she might not be able to spare him brain damage.

Behind her the door whooshed open and Deanna came in. She immediately took Worf's hand and held it. Then she looked up at Beverly, who shook her head.

"Anything," Deanna said. "Try anything."

Beverly glanced at the overhead readings. Worf's hearts and lungs seemed to be clear now and his blood had cycled a few times, cleaning out the poisons. But there was no brain activity. The only chance he had was to be shocked back.

She quickly prepared an extra-sized dose of Klaxtal, the strongest stimulant she knew of that would work on Klingons.

She glanced at Deanna, who was staring down at Worf's smudged face. "Stand back," Beverly said. "This might cause some sharp muscle contractions."

Deanna stood back, but didn't release Worf's hand.

Beverly injected the Klaxtal and then moved out of the way. She had seen Klingons break human doctors' limbs while under the influence of this drug.

But Worf didn't move.

Deanna glanced at her. Beverly was about to step in to try again when Worf's powerful body jerked upward, his legs kicking, his arms flailing. Deanna let go and the two of them watched as Worf's body twitched and bucked, then lay still.

Very still.

It hadn't worked. Beverly stepped back up beside Worf. "Worf, damn you," she said. "Come back to—"

THE SOLDIERS OF FEAR

Suddenly the monitor over Worf blinked, and the next instant he took a huge, shuddering breath.

"He's back," Deanna said, moving up beside him and touching his head.

But the question was whether or not he was completely back.

Beverly glanced at the reading. There was brain function, but she couldn't tell if there was damage.

"Worf," she said. "Worf. You need to speak to me."

He still didn't open his eyes.

"Deanna," she said.

Deanna nodded, then bent over him, her hair hiding his face. "Worf," she said. "Please—"

His right hand went to her throat. "I will not talk!" he said.

"Worf," Beverly said. "It's Deanna!"

He let go and she staggered backward, smiling. "Deanna?" he said. "I am on the *Enterprise?*"

"Yes," Beverly said. She glanced at the scan beside the bed. His conscious brain functions gave a better reading. He would be all right.

"The Furies?"

"Are defeated," Deanna said, her voice rasping.

"And Commander Riker?"

"Is fine," Deanna said. "But he insisted on going to the bridge before coming here, even though both his hands are burnt."

Beverly glanced at her. She hadn't heard that Riker lived.

Deanna smiled, never taking her eyes from Worf "The captain should be ordering him here any minute."

231

But something in Deanna's eyes said that wasn't the whole story. Beverly caught the look, but Worf appeared too tired to care. "My head feels as if it has been trampled by a herd of Klingon wildebeests," he said.

Beverly smiled at him, and took her place beside him. "Your head is hard, and that probably saved your life," she said. "But I do need to check the rest of your injuries. And I need to tell the captain that you're all right."

"I will," Deanna said. "He'll be very pleased to hear it."

Several hours later, Picard sank into a chair in Ten-Forward. Commander Will Riker already had a seat at the table. He was staring out the window, at the stars streaking past. His hands were wrapped in light bandages, and his eyes had deep shadows. It looked as if he had lost weight in the last day, and maybe, just maybe, he had.

Guinan came over, a carafe filled with purple liquid in her right hand, two snifters in her left.

"Tea for me, Guinan," Picard said.

She grinned. "I've been saving this Nestafarian brandy for a special occasion. I think defeating the Furies counts, don't you?"

"I don't feel like celebrating," Riker said, his gaze still on the stars.

"I don't think special occasions are always celebrations," Guinan said. She put the brandy down between them, poured a centimeter of purple liquid into the bottom of each glass, and pushed them toward her customers. "Sometimes special occasions are the quiet moments when healing can begin."

She got up, and left them. Picard watched her go. He relied on her wisdom and her strength. She was letting him know that she approved of his action, of the path he had chosen to defeat his fears, and the Furies, all at the same time.

But he didn't approve. He didn't feel as if he'd done enough. He wasn't certain the wormhole was closed forever. And he had lost what promised to be one of Starfleet's top new officers.

Riker held out his bandaged hands. Picard had never seen anything quite like that before.

"Dr. Crusher doesn't trust me not to tear off the new skin," Riker said. "So she bandaged me."

"You're off duty, Number One. You can rest, you know."

Riker nodded. He glanced at the stars. "But I have some practicing to do," he said softly, almost to himself. "Flying old atmospheric jets in a holodeck program. I have a rematch scheduled. Someday."

Picard finally understood. Redbay. They were both thinking of the lieutenant, alone on the other side of the wormhole.

With the Furies.

A sacrifice either one of them would have gladly made in his stead. A sacrifice Riker was supposed to make, but circumstances prevented.

In some ways, it was just as hard on this end, knowing that they would never know how—or if—Redbay survived. They only knew that he had done his job.

Now they had to go on. When they had signed up for Starfleet, they knew the risks.

One of those risks was the loss of their own lives.

The other, harder risk, was losing friends.

Picard picked up his snifter, twirled the brandy, and inhaled. It had a spicy, dark scent. "Tell me about Lieutenant Redbay, Will," Picard said.

Riker stared at Picard for a moment, then took a brandy snifter in one bandaged hand.

"Not the lieutenant I can read about in the records," Picard said. "I want to know the man."

Riker nodded, taking a sip. "Lieutenant Redbay?" He glanced out at the stars for a moment, then went on. "Lieutenant *Sam* Redbay was my friend."

He lifted his brandy snifter in a silent toast.

Picard joined him.

The
Invasion
Continues
In

STAR TREK
DEEP SPACE NINE®
Invasion!

BOOK THREE

Time's Enemy

by

L. A. Graf

"It looks like they're preparing for an invasion," Jadzia Dax said.

Sisko grunted, gazing out at the expanse of dark-crusted cometary ice that formed the natural hull of Starbase 1. Above the curving ice horizon, the blackness of Earth's Oort cloud should have glittered with bright stars and the barely brighter glow of the distant sun. Instead, what it glittered with were the docking lights of a dozen short-range attack ships—older and more angular versions of the *Defiant*—as well as the looming bulk of two Galaxy-class starships, the *Mukaikubo* and the *Breedlove*. One glance had told Sisko that such a gathering of force couldn't have been the random result of ship refittings and shore leaves. Starfleet was preparing for a major encounter with someone. He just wished he knew who.

"I thought we came here to deal with a *non*military emergency." In the sweep of transparent aluminum windows, Sisko could see Julian Bashir's dark reflection glance up from the chair he'd sprawled in after an uninterested glance at the view. Beyond the doctor, the huge conference room was as empty as it had been ten minutes ago when they'd first been escorted into it. "Otherwise, wouldn't Admiral Hayman have asked us to come in the *Defiant* instead of a high-speed courier?"

Sisko snorted. "Admirals never *ask* anything, Doctor. And they never tell you any more than you need to know to carry out their orders efficiently."

"Especially this admiral," Dax added, an unexpected note of humor creeping into her voice. Sisko raised an eyebrow at her, then heard a gravelly snort and the simultaneous hiss of the conference-room door opening. He swung around to see a rangy, long-boned figure in ordinary Starfleet coveralls crossing the room toward them. Dax surprised him by promptly stepping forward, hands outstretched in welcome.

"How have you been, Judith?"

"Promoted." The silver-haired woman's angular face lit with something approaching a sparkle. "It almost makes up for getting this old." She clasped Dax's hands warmly for a moment, then turned her attention to Sisko. "So this is the Benjamin Sisko Curzon told me so much about. It's a pleasure to finally meet you, Captain."

Sisko slanted a wary glance at his science officer. "Um—likewise, I'm sure. Dax?"

The Trill cleared her throat. "Benjamin, allow me to introduce you to Rear Admiral Judith Hayman. She and I—well, she and Curzon, actually—got to know each other on Vulcan during the Klingon peace negotiations several years ago. Judith, this is Captain Benjamin Sisko of *Deep Space Nine,* and our station's chief medical officer, Dr. Julian Bashir."

"Admiral." Bashir nodded crisply.

"Our orders said this was a Priority One Emergency," Sisko reminded his superior officer almost as soon as she released his hand. "I assume that means whatever you brought us here to do is urgent."

Hayman's strong face lost its smile. "Possibly," she said. "Although perhaps not urgent in the way we usually think of it."

Sisko scowled. "Forgive my bluntness, Admiral, but I've been dragged from my command station without explanation, ordered not to use my own ship under any circumstances, brought to the oldest and least useful starbase in the Federation"—he made a gesture of reined-in impatience at the bleak cometary landscape outside the windows—"and you're telling me you're not sure how *urgent* this problem is?"

"No one is sure, Captain. That's part of the reason we brought you here." The admiral's voice chilled into something between grimness and exasperation. "What we *are* sure of is that we could be facing potential disaster." She reached into the front pocket of her coveralls and tossed two ordinary-looking data chips onto the conference table. "The first thing I need you and your medical officer to do is review these data records."

"Data records," Sisko repeated, trying for the noncommittal tone he'd perfected over years of trying to deal with the equally high-handed and inexplicable behavior of Kai Winn.

"Admiral, forgive us, but we assumed this actually *was* an emergency," Julian Bashir explained, in such polite bafflement that Sisko guessed he must be emulating Garak's unctuous demeanor. "If so, we could have reviewed your data records ten hours ago. All you had to do was send them to *Deep Space Nine* through subspace channels."

"Too dangerous, even using our most secure codes." The bleak certainty in Hayman's voice made Sisko blink in surprise. "And if you were listening, young man, you'd have noticed that I said this was the *first* thing I needed you to do. Now, would you please sit down, Captain?"

He took the place she indicated at one of the conference table's inset data stations, then waited while she settled Bashir at the station on the opposite side. He noticed she made no attempt to seat Dax, although there were other empty stations available.

"This review procedure is not a standard one," Hayman said, without further preliminaries. "As a control on the validity of some data we've recently received, we're going to ask you to examine ship's logs and medical records without knowing their origin. We'd like your analysis of them. Computer, start data-review programs Sisko-One and Bashir-One."

Sisko's monitor flashed to life, not with pictures but with a thick ribbon of multilayered symbols and abbreviated words, slowly scrolling from left to right. He stared at it for a long, blank moment before a whisper of memory turned it familiar instead of alien. One of the things Starfleet Academy asked cadets to do was determine the last three days of a starship's voyage when its main computer memory had failed. The solution was to reconstruct computer records from each of the ship's individual system buffers—records that looked exactly like these.

"These are multiple logs of buffer output from individual ship systems, written in standard Starfleet machine code," he said. Dax made an interested noise and came to stand behind him. "It looks like someone downloaded the last commands given to life-support, shields, helm, and phaser-bank control. There's another system here, too, but I can't identify it."

"Photon-torpedo control?" Dax suggested, leaning over his shoulder to scrutinize it.

"I don't think so. It might be a sensor buffer." Sisko scanned the lines of code intently while they scrolled by. He could recognize more of the symbols now, although most of the abbreviations on the fifth line still baffled him. "There's no sign of navigations, either—the command buffers in those systems may have been destroyed by whatever took out the ship's main computer." Sisko grunted as four of the five logs recorded wild fluctuations and then degenerated into solid black lines. "And there goes everything else. Whatever hit this ship crippled it beyond repair."

Dax nodded. "It looks like some kind of EM pulse took out all of the ship's circuits—everything lost power except for life-support, and that had to switch to auxiliary circuits." She glanced up at the admiral. "Is that all the record we have, Admiral? Just those few minutes?"

"It's all the record we *trust*," Hayman said enigmatically. "There are some visual bridge logs that I'll show you in a minute, but those could have been tampered with. We're fairly sure the buffer outputs weren't." She glanced up at Bashir, whose usual restless energy had focused down to a silent intensity of concentration on his own data screen. "The medical logs we found were much more extensive. You have time to review the buffer outputs again, if you'd like."

"Please," Sisko and Dax said in unison.

"Computer, repeat data program Sisko-One."

Machine code crawled across the screen again, and this time Sisko stopped trying to identify the individual symbols in it. He vaguely remembered one of his Academy professors saying that reconstructing a starship's movements from the individual buffer outputs of its systems was a lot like reading a symphony score. The trick was not to analyze each line individually, but to get a sense of how all of them were functioning in tandem.

"This ship was in a battle," he said at last. "But I think it was trying to escape, not fight. The phaser banks all show discharge immediately after power fluctuations are recorded for the shields."

"Defensive action," Dax agreed, and pointed at the screen. "And look at how much power they had to divert from life-support to keep the shields going. Whatever was after them was big."

"They're trying some evasive actions now—" Sisko broke off, seeing something he'd missed the first time in that mysterious fifth line of code. Something that froze his stomach. It was the same Romulan symbol that appeared on his command board every time the cloaking device was engaged on the *Defiant*.

"This was a cloaked Starfleet vessel!" He swung around to fix the admiral with a fierce look. "My understanding was that only the *Defiant* had been sanctioned to carry a Romulan cloaking device!"

Hayman met his stare without a ripple showing in her calm competence. "I can assure you that Starfleet isn't running any unauthorized cloaking devices. Watch the log again, Captain Sisko."

He swung back to his monitor. "Computer, rerun data program Sisko-One at one-quarter speed," he said. The five concurrent logs crawled across the screen in slow motion, and this time Sisko focused on the coordinated interactions between the helm and the phaser banks. If he had any hope of identifying the class and generation of this starship, it would be from the tactical maneuvers it could perform.

"Time the helm changes versus the phaser bursts," Dax suggested from behind him in an unusually quiet voice. Sisko wondered if she was beginning to harbor the same ominous suspicion he was.

"I know." For the past hundred years, the speed of helm shift versus the speed of phaser refocus had been the basic determining factor of battle tactics. Sisko's gaze flickered from top line to third, counting off milliseconds by the ticks along the edge of the data record. The phaser refocus rates he found were startlingly fast, but far more chilling was the almost instantaneous response of this starship's helm in its tactical runs. There was only one ship he knew of that had the kind of overpowered warp engines needed to bring it so dangerously close to the edge of survivable maneuvers. And there was only one commander who had used his spare time to perfect the art of skimming along the edge of that envelope, the way the logs told him this ship's commander had done.

This time when Sisko swung around to confront Judith Hayman, his concern had condensed into cold, sure knowledge. "Where did you find these records, Admiral?"

She shook her head. "Your analysis first, Captain. I need your unbiased opinion before I answer any questions or show you the visual logs. Otherwise, we'll never know for sure if these data can be trusted."

Sisko blew out a breath, trying to find words for conclusions he wasn't even sure he believed. "This ship—it wasn't just cloaked like the *Defiant*. It actually *was* the *Defiant*." He heard Dax's indrawn breath. "And when it was destroyed in battle, the man commanding it was me."

The advantage of having several lifetimes of experience to draw on, Jadzia Dax often thought, was that there wasn't much left in the universe that could surprise you. The disadvantage was that you no longer remembered how to cope with surprise. In particular, she'd forgotten the sensation of facing a reality so improbable that logic insisted it could not exist while all your senses told you it did.

Like finding out that the mechanical death throes you had just seen were those of your very own starship.

"Thank you, Captain Sisko," Admiral Hayman said. "That confirms what we suspected."

"But how can it?" Dax straightened to frown at the older woman. "Admiral, if these records are real and not computer constructs—then they must have somehow come from our future!"

"Or from an alternate reality," Sisko pointed out. He swung the chair of his data station around with the kind of controlled force he usually reserved for the command chair of the *Defiant*. "Just where in space were these transmissions picked up, Admiral?"

Hayman's mouth quirked, an expression Jadzia found unreadable but which Curzon's memories interpreted as rueful. "They weren't—at least not as transmissions. What you're seeing there, Captain, are—"

"—actual records."

It took Dax a moment to realize that those unexpected words had been spoken by Julian Bashir. The elegant human accent was unmistakably his, but the grim tone was not.

"What are you talking about, Doctor?" Sisko demanded.

"These are actual records, taken directly from the *Defiant*." From here, all Dax could see of him was the intent curve of his head and neck as he leaned over his data station. "Medical logs in my own style, made for my own personal use. There's no reason to transmit medical data in this form."

The unfamiliar numbness of surprise was fading at last, and Dax found it replaced by an equally strong curiosity. She skirted the table to join him. "What kind of medical data are they, Julian?"

He threw her a startled upward glance, almost as if he'd forgotten she was there, then scrambled out of his chair to face her. "Confidential patient records," he said, blocking her view of the screen. "I don't think you should see them."

The Dax symbiont might have accepted that explanation, but Jadzia knew the young human doctor too well. The troubled expression on his face wasn't put there by professional ethics. "Are they my records?" she asked, then patted his arm when he winced. "I expected you to find them, Julian. If this was our *Defiant*, then we were probably all on it when it was—I mean, when it *will be*—destroyed."

"What I don't understand," Sisko said with crisp impatience, "is how we can have actual records preserved from an event that hasn't happened yet."

Admiral Hayman snorted. "No one understands that, Captain Sisko—which is why Starfleet Command thought this might be an elaborate forgery." Her piercing gaze slid to Bashir. "Doctor, are you convinced that the man who wrote those medical logs was a *future* you? They're not pastiches put together from bits and pieces of your old records, in order to fool us?"

Bashir shook his head, vehemently. "What these medical logs say that I did—no past records of mine could have been altered enough to mimic that. They have to have been written by a future me." He gave Dax another distressed look. "Although it's a future that I hope to hell never comes true."

"That's a wish the entire Federation is going to share, now that we know these records are genuine."

Hayman thumped herself into the head chair at the conference table, and touched the control panel in front of it. One of the windows on the opposite wall obediently blanked into a viewscreen. "Let me show you why."

The screen flickered blue and then condensed into a familiar wide-screen scan of the *Defiant*'s bridge. It was the viewing angle Dax had gotten used to watching in post-mission analyses, the one recorded by the official logging sensor at the back of the deck. In this frozen still picture, she could see the outline of Sisko's shoulders and head above the back of his chair, and the top of her own head beyond him, at the helm. The *Defiant*'s viewscreen showed darkness spattered with distant fires that looked a little too large and bright to be stars. The edges of the picture were frayed and spangled with blank blue patches, obscuring the figures at the weapons and engineering consoles. Dax thought she could just catch the flash of Kira's earring through the static.

"The record's even worse than it looks here," Hayman said bluntly. "What you're seeing is a computer reconstruction of the scattered bytes we managed to download from the sensor's memory buffer. All we've got is the five-minute run it recorded just before the bridge lost power. Any record it dumped to the main computer before that was lost."

Sisko nodded, acknowledging the warning buried in her dry words. "So we're going to see the *Defiant*'s final battle."

"That's right." Hayman tapped at her control panel again, and the conference room filled with the sound of Kira's tense voice.

"Three alien vessels coming up fast on vector oh-nine-seven. We can't outrun them." The fires on the viewscreen blossomed into the unmistakable red-orange explosions of warp cores breaching under attack. Dax tried to count them, but there were too many, scattered over too wide a sector of space to keep track of. Her stomach roiled in fierce and utter disbelief. How could so many starships be destroyed this quickly? Had all of Starfleet rallied to fight this hopeless future battle?

"They're also moving too fast to track with our quantum torpedoes." The sound of her own voice coming from the image startled her. It sounded impossibly calm to Dax under the circumstances. She saw her future self glance up at the carnage on the viewscreen, but from the back there was no way to tell what she thought of it. "Our course change didn't throw them off. They must be tracking our thermal output."

"Drop cloak." The toneless curtness of Sisko's recorded voice told Dax just how grim the situation must be. "Divert all power to shields and phasers."

The sensor image flickered blue and silent for a moment as a power surge ran through it, then returned to its normal tattered state. Now, however, there were three distinct patches of blue looming closer on the future *Defiant*'s viewscreen.

"What's that?" Bashir asked Hayman, pointing.

The admiral grunted and froze the image while she answered him. "That's the computer's way of saying it couldn't match a known image to the visual bytes it got there."

"The three alien spaceships," Dax guessed. "They're not Klingon or Romulan then."

"Or Cardassian or Jem'Hadar," Bashir added quietly.

"As far as we can tell, they don't match any known spacefaring ship design," Hayman said. "That's what worries us."

Sisko leaned both elbows on the table, frowning at the stilled image intently. "You think we're going be attacked by some unknown force from the Gamma Quadrant?"

"Or worse." The admiral cleared her throat, as if her dramatic words had embarrassed her. "You may have heard rumors about the alien invaders that Captain Picard and the *Enterprise* drove off from Brundage Station. From the spectrum of the energy discharges you're going to see when the alien ships fire their phasers at you, the computer thinks there's more than a slight chance that this could be another invasion force."

Dax repressed a shiver at this casual discussion of their catastrophic future. "You think the *Defiant* is going to be destroyed in a future battle with the Furies?"

"We know they think that this region of space once

belonged to them," Hayman said crisply. "We know they want it back. And we know we didn't destroy their entire fleet in our last encounter, just the artificial wormhole they used to transport themselves to Furies Point. Given the *Defiant*'s posting near the Bajoran wormhole—" She broke off, waving a hand irritably at the screen. "I'm getting ahead of myself. Watch the rest of the visual log first, then I'll answer your questions." Her mouth jerked downward at one corner. "If I can."

She touched the control panel again to resume the log playback. Almost immediately, the viewscreen flashed with a blast of unusually intense phaser fire.

"Damage to forward shield generators," reported O'Brien's tense voice. "Diverting power from rear shield generators to compensate."

"Return fire!" Sisko's computer-reconstructed figure blurred as he leapt from his captain's chair and went to join Dax at the helm. "Starting evasive maneuvers, program delta!"

More flashes screamed across the viewscreen, obscuring the random jerks and wiggles that the stars made during warp-speed maneuvers. The phaser fire washed the *Defiant*'s bridge in such fierce white light that the crew turned into darkly burned silhouettes. An uneasy feeling grew in Dax that she was watching ghosts rather than real people, and she began to understand Starfleet's reluctance to trust that this log was real.

"Evasive maneuvers aren't working!" Kira sounded both fierce and frustrated. "They're firing in all directions, not just at us."

"Their present course vector will take them past us in twelve seconds, point-blank range," Dax warned. "Eleven, ten, nine . . ."

"Forward shields failing!" shouted O'Brien. Behind his voice the ship echoed with the thunderous sound of vacuum breach. "We've lost sectors seventeen and twenty-one—"

"Six, five, four . . ."

"Spin the ship to get maximum coverage from rear shields," Sisko ordered curtly. *"Now!"*

"Two, one . . ."

Another hull breach thundered through the ship, this one louder and closer than before. The sensor image washed blue and silent again with another power surge. Dax held her breath, expecting the black fade of ship destruction to follow it. To her amazement, however, the blue rippled and condensed back into the familiar unbreached contours of the bridge. Emergency lights glowed at each station, making the crew look shadowy and even more unreal.

"Damage reports," Sisko ordered.

"Hull breaches in all sectors below fifteen," O'Brien said grimly. "We've lost the port nacelle, too, Captain."

"Alien ships are veering off at vector five-sixteen point nine." Kira sounded suspicious and surprised in equal measures. Her silhouette turned at the weapons console, earring glittering. "Sensors report they're still firing phasers in all directions. And for some reason, their shields appear to be failing." A distant red starburst lit the viewscreen, followed by two more. "Captain, you're not going to believe this, but it looks like they just blew up!"

Dax saw herself turn to look at Kira, and for the first time caught a dim glimpse of her own features. As far as she could tell, they looked identical to the ones she'd seen in the mirror that morning. Whatever this future was, it wasn't far away.

"Maybe our phasers caused as much damage as theirs did," she suggested hopefully. "Or more."

"I don't think so." O'Brien's voice was even grimmer now. "I've been trying to put our rear shields back on-line, but something's not right. Something's draining them from the outside." His voice scaled upward in disbelief. "Our main core power's being sucked out right through the shield generators!"

"A new kind of weapon?" Sisko demanded. "Something we can neutralize with our phasers?"

The chief engineer made a startled noise. "No, it's not an energy beam at all. It looks more like—"

At that point, with a suddenness that made Dax's stomach clench, the entire viewscreen went dead. She felt her shoulder and hand muscles tense in involuntary protest, and heard Bashir stir uncomfortably beside her. Sisko cursed beneath his breath.

"I know," Admiral Hayman said dryly. "The main circuits picked the worst possible time to give out. That's all the information we have."

"No, it's not." Julian Bashir's voice sounded bleak rather than satisfied, and Dax suspected he would rather not have had the additional information to give them. "I haven't had a chance to read the majority of these medical logs, but I have found the ones that deal with the aftermath of the battle."

Hayman's startled look at him contained a great deal more respect than it had a few moments before, Dax noticed. "There were logs that talked about the battle? No one else noticed that."

"That's because no one else knows my personal abbreviations for the names of the crew," Bashir said simply. "I scanned the records for the ones I thought might have been aboard on this trip. Of the six regular crew, Odo wasn't mentioned anywhere. I'm guessing he stayed back on *Deep Space Nine*. My records for Kira and O'Brien indicate they were lost in some kind of shipboard battle, trying to ward off an invading force. Sisko seems to have been injured then and to have died afterward, but I'm not sure exactly when. And Dax—" He stopped to clear his throat and then resumed. "According to my records, Jadzia suffered so much radiation exposure in the final struggle that she had only a few hours to live. Rather than stay aboard, she took a lifepod and created a diversion for the aliens who were attacking us. That's how the ship finally got away."

"Got away?" Sisko demanded in disbelief. "You mean some of the crew survived the battle we just saw?"

Bashir grimaced. "How do you think those medical logs got written up? I not only survived the battle, Captain, I appear to have lived for a considerable time afterward. There are several years' worth of logs here, if not more."

"Several *years?*" It was Dax's turn to sound incredulous. "You stayed on board the *Defiant* for several years after this battle, Julian? And no one came to rescue you?"

"No."

"That can't be true!" The *Defiant*'s captain vaulted from his chair, as if his churning restlessness couldn't be contained in one place any longer. "Even a totally disabled starship can emit an automatic distress call," he growled. "If no one from Starfleet was alive to respond to it, some other Federation ship should have. *Was our entire civilization destroyed?*"

"No," Hayman said soberly. "The reason's much simpler than that, and much worse. Come with me, and I'll show you."

Cold mist ghosted out at them when the fusion-bay doors opened, making Dax shiver and stop on the threshold. Beside her, she could see Sisko eye the interior with a mixture of foreboding and awe. This immense dark space held a special place in human history, Dax knew. It was the first place where interstellar fusion engines had been fired, the necessary step that eventually led to this solar system's entry into the federation of spacefaring races. She peered through the interior fog of subliming carbon dioxide and water droplets, but aside from a distant tangle of gantry lights, all she could see was the mist.

"Sorry about the condensate," Admiral Hayman said briskly. "We never bothered to seal off the walls, since we usually keep this bay at zero P and T." She palmed open a locker beside the ring doors and handed them belt jets, then launched herself into the mist-filled bay with the graceful arc of a diver. Sisko rolled into the hold with less grace but equal efficiency, followed by the slender sliver of movement that was Bashir. Dax took a deep breath and vaulted after them, feeling the familiar interior lurch of the symbiont in its pouch as their bodies adjusted to the lack of gravitational acceleration.

"This way." The delayed echo of Hayman's voice told Dax that the old fusion bay was widening as they moved farther into the mist, although she could no longer see its ice-carved sides. She fired her belt jets to follow the sound of the admiral's graveled voice, feeling the exposed freckles on her face and neck prickle with cold in the zero-centigrade air. Three silent shadows loomed in the fog ahead of her, backlit by the approaching gantry lights. She jetted into an athletic arc calculated to bring her up beside them.

"So, Admiral, what have you—"

Her voice broke off abruptly, when she saw what filled the space in front of her. The heat of the work lights had driven back the mist, making a halo of clear space around the dark object that was their focus. At first, all she saw was a huge lump of cometary ice, black-crusted over glacial blue gleaming. Then her eye caught a skeletal feathering of old metal buried in that ice, and followed it around an oddly familiar curve until it met another, more definite sweep of metal. Beyond that lay a stubby wing, gashed through with ice-filled fractures. She took in a deep, icy breath as the realization hit her.

"That's the *Defiant!*"

"Or what's left of her." Sisko's voice rang grim echoes off the distant walls of the hold. Now that she had recognized the ship's odd angle in the ice, Dax could see that he was right. The port nacelle was sheared off entirely, and a huge torpedo-impact crater had exploded into most of the starboard hull and decking. Phaser burns streaked the *Defiant*'s flanks, and odd unfamiliar gashes had sliced her to vacuum in several places.

She glanced across at Hayman. "Where was this found, Judith?"

"Right here in Earth's Oort cloud," the admiral said, without taking her eyes from the half-buried starship. "A mining expedition from the Pluto LaGrangian colonies, out prospecting for water-cored comets, found it two days ago after a trial phaser blast. They recognized the Starfleet markings and called us, but it was too fragile to free with phasers out there. We had to bring it in and let the cometary matrix melt around it."

"But if it was that fragile—" Dax frowned, her scientist's brain automatically calculating metal fatigue under deep-space conditions, while her emotions kept insisting that what she was seeing was impossible. "It must have been buried inside that comet for thousands of years!"

"Almost five millennia," Hayman agreed. "According to thermal spectroscopy of the ice around it, and radiometric dating of the—er—the organic contents of the ship."

"You mean, the bodies," Bashir said, breaking his stark silence at last.

"Yes." Hayman jetted toward the far side of the ice-sheathed ship, where a brighter arc of lights was trained on the *Defiant*'s main hatch. "There's a slight discrepancy between the individual radiocarbon ages of the two survivors, apparently as a result of—"

"—differential survival times." The doctor finished the sentence so decisively that Dax suspected he'd already known that from his medical logs. She glanced at him as they followed Hayman toward the ship, puzzled by the sudden urgency in his voice. "How much of a discrepancy in ages was there? More than a hundred years?"

"No, about half that." The admiral glanced over her shoulder, the quizzical look back in her eyes.

"Humans don't generally live long enough to survive each other by more than a hundred years, Doctor."

Dax heard the quick intake of Bashir's breath that told her he was startled. "Both bodies you found were human?"

"Yes." Hayman paused in front of the open hatch, blocking it with one long arm when Sisko would have jetted past her. "I'd better warn you that, aside from microsampling for radiocarbon dates, we've left the remains just as they were found in the medical bay. One was in stasis, but the other—wasn't."

"Understood." Sisko pushed past her into the dim hatchway, the cold control of his voice telling Dax how much he hated seeing the wreckage of the first ship he'd ever commanded. She let Bashir enter next, sensing the doctor's fierce impatience from the way his fingers had whitened around his tricorder. When she would have jetted after him, Hayman touched her shoulder and made her pause.

"I know your new host is a scientist, Dax. Does that mean you've already guessed what happened here?"

Dax gave the older woman a curious look. "It seems fairly self-evident, Admiral. In some future timeline, the *Defiant* is going to be destroyed in a battle so enormous that it will get thrown back in time and halfway across the galaxy. That's why no one could come to rescue Julian."

Hayman nodded, her voice deepening a little. "I

just want you to know before you go in—right now, Starfleet's highest priority is to avoid entering that timeline. At all costs." She gave Dax's shoulder a final squeeze, then released her. "Remember that."

"I will." Although she managed to keep her tone as level as always, somewhere inside Dax a tendril of doubt curled from symbiont to host. Curzon's stored memories told Jadzia that when he knew her, this silver-haired admiral had been one of Starfleet's most pragmatic and imperturbable starship captains. Any future that could put that kind of intensity into Hayman's voice wasn't one Dax wanted to think about.

Now she was going to see it.

Inside the *Defiant*, stasis generators made a trail of red lights up the main turbolift shaft, and Dax suspected the half-visible glimmer of their fields was all that kept its crumbling metal walls intact. It looked as though this part of the ship had suffered one of the hull breaches O'Brien had reported, or some even bigger explosion. The turbolift car was a collapsed cage of oxidized steel resin and ceramic planks. Dax eased herself into the open shaft above it, careful not to touch anything as she jetted upward.

"Captain?" she called up into the echoing darkness.

"On the bridge." Sisko's voice echoed oddly off the muffling silence of the stasis fields. Dax boosted herself to the top of the turbolift shaft and then angled her jets to push through the shattered lift doors. Heat lamps had been set up here to melt away the ice still engulfing the *Defiant*'s navigations and science stations. The powerful buzz of their filaments and the constant drip and sizzle of melting water filled the bridge with noise. Sisko stood alone in the midst of it, his face set in stony lines. She guessed that Bashir had headed immediately for the starship's tiny medical bay.

"It's hard to believe it's really five thousand years old," Dax said, hearing the catch in her own voice. The familiar black panels and data stations of the bridge had suffered less damage than the rest of the ship. Except for the sparkle of condensation off their dead screens, they looked as if all they needed was an influx of power to take up their jobs again. She glanced toward the ice-sheathed science station and shivered. Only two days ago, she'd helped O'Brien install a new sensor array in that console. She could still see the red gleam of its readouts beneath the ice—brand-new sensors that were now far older than her own internal symbiont.

Dax shook off the unreality of it and went to join Sisko at the command chair. Seeing the new sensor array had given her an idea. "Can you tell if there are any unfamiliar modifications on the bridge?" she asked the captain, knowing he had probably memorized the contours of his ship in a way she hadn't. "If so, they may indicate how far in our future this *Defiant* was when it got thrown back in time."

Sisko swung in a slow arc, his jets hissing. "I don't see anything unfamiliar. This could be the exact ship we left back at *Deep Space Nine*. If the Furies are going to invade, I'd guess it's going to be soon."

Hayman grunted from the doorway. "That's exactly the kind of information we needed you to give us, Captain. Now all we need to know is where and when they'll come, so we can be prepared to meet them."

"And this—this ghost from the future." Sisko reached out a hand as if to touch the *Defiant*'s dead helm, then dropped it again when it only stirred up the warning luminescence of a stasis field. "You think this can somehow help us find out—"

The chirp of his comm badge interrupted him. "Bashir to Sisko."

The captain frowned and palmed his badge. "Sisko here. Have you identified the bodies, Doctor?"

"Yes, sir." There was a decidedly odd note in Bashir's voice, Dax thought. Of course, it couldn't be easy examining your own corpse, or those of your closest friends. "The one in the ship's morgue sustained severe trauma before it hit stasis, but it's still recognizable as yours. There wasn't much left of the other, but based on preliminary genetic analysis of some bone fragments, I'll hazard a guess that it used to be me." Dax heard the sound of a slightly unsteady breath. "There's something else down here, Captain. Something I think you and—and Jadzia ought to see."

She exchanged speculative looks with Sisko. For all his youth, there wasn't much that could shatter Julian Bashir's composure when it came to medical matters. "We're on our way," the captain told him. "Sisko out."

Diving back into the shattered darkness of the main turbolift, with the strong lights of the bridge now behind her, Dax could see what she'd missed on the way up—the pale, distant quiver of emergency lights from the *Defiant*'s tiny sickbay on the next deck down. She frowned and followed Sisko down the clammy service corridor toward it. "Is the ship's original power still on down here?" she demanded incredulously.

From the darkness behind her, she could hear Hayman snort. "Thanks to the size of the warp core on this overpowered attack ship of yours, yes. With all the other systems shut down except for life-support, the power drain was reduced to a trickle. Our engineers think the lights and equipment in here could have run for another thousand years." She drifted to a gentle stop beside Dax and Sisko in the doorway of the tiny medical bay. "A tribute to Starfleet engineering. And to you too, apparently, Dr. Bashir."

The young physician looked up with a start from where he leaned over one of his two sickbay stasis units, as if he'd already forgotten that he'd summoned them here. The glow of thin green emergency lighting showed Dax the unaccustomed mixture of helplessness and self-reproach on his face.

"Right now, I'm not sure that's anything to be proud of," he said, sounding almost angry. His gesture indicated the stasis unit below him, which Dax now saw had been remodeled into an odd mass of pumps and power generators topped with a glass box. A fierce shiver of apprehension climbed up the freckles on her spine and made her head ache. "Why haven't you people done anything about this?"

Admiral Hayman's steady glance traveled from him to Dax, and then back again. "Because we were waiting for you."

That was all the confirmation Dax needed. She pushed past Sisko, and was startled to find herself dropped abruptly to the floor when the sickbay's artificial gravity caught her. Just a little under one Earth standard, she guessed from the feel of it—she felt oddly light and off-balance as she joined Bashir on the other side of that carefully remodeled medical station.

"Julian, is it . . . ?"

His clear brown eyes met hers across the misted top of the box. "I'm afraid so," he said softly, and moved his hand. Below where the warmth of his skin had penetrated the stasis-fogged glass, the mist had cleared a little. It was enough to show Dax what Bashir had already seen—the unmistakable gray-white mass of a naked Trill symbiont, immersed in brine that held a frozen glitter of bioelectric activity.

She had to take a deep breath before she located her voice, but this time her symbiont's long years of experience stood her in good stead. "Well," she said slowly, gazing down at the part of herself that was now immeasurably older. "Now I know why I'm here."

YR1,DY6,2340

Patient immobile + unresponsive. Limited contact + manipulation of subject due to fragile physical state and possible radiation damage, no invasive px/tx until vitals, Tokal-Benar's stabilize. Fluid isoboramine values <47%, biospectral scan=cortical activity < prev. observed norm, ion concentration still unstable. (see lab/chem results, atta) No waste products yet; adjusted nutrient mix +10% in hopes of improving uptake. Am beginning to fear I can't really keep it alive after all.

Staring down into the milky shadows of the suspension tank, Julian Bashir blinked away the image of those old medical records and trailed a hand across the invisible barrier separating the two realities. The stasis field pricked at his palm like a swarm of sleepy bees. "I guess I was wrong."

"Does that mean you don't think it's still alive?"

Bashir jerked his head up, embarrassment at being overheard smothering under a flush of guilt as soon as the meaning of Hayman's words sank in. He pulled his hand away from the forcefield, then ended up clenching it at his side when he could find nothing else to do with it. "No, I'm fairly certain it's still living." At least, that's what the readouts frozen beneath the stasis field's glow seemed to indicate. "It was alive when the field was activated five thousand years ago, at any rate. I can't tell anything else about its condition without examining it in real time." Although the thought of holding the orphaned symbiont in his hands made his throat hurt.

Across the table from him, Hayman folded her arms and frowned down at the shimmering box. The watery green of the emergency lights turned her eyes an emotionless bronze, and painted her hair with neon streaks where there should have been silver. "Assuming it's in fairly stable condition, what equipment would you need to transfer this symbiont into a Trill host?"

The question struck him like a blow to the stomach. "You can't be serious!" But he knew she was, knew it the very moment she asked. "Admiral, you can't just change Trill symbionts the way you would a pair of socks! There are enormous risks unless very specific compatibility requirements are met—"

"What rejection?" Hayman freed one hand to wave at Dax, standing silently beside her. "It's the same symbiont she has inside her right now!"

It occurred to Bashir, not for the first time, that he didn't like this woman very much. He couldn't imagine what Curzon Dax had ever seen in her. "It's a genetically identical symbiont that is *five thousand years* out of balance with Jadzia! For all we know, the physiological similarities between the two Daxes could make it even harder for Jadzia to adjust to the psychological differences." Dax herself had withdrawn from the discussion almost from the beginning. She'd turned her attention instead toward the naked symbiont in its stasis-blurred coffin, and Bashir wondered which of her many personalities was responsible for the eerie blend of affection and grief he could read in her expression. He wished he could make Hayman understand the implications of toying with a creature that was truly legion. "These are *lives* we're talking about, Admiral, not inconveniences. Any one of the three could die if we attempt what you're suggesting."

Hayman glared at him with that chill superiority Bashir had learned to recognize as a line officer's way of saying that doctors only earned their MDs because they hadn't the stomach for regular Starfleet. "If we don't find out who carved up the *Defiant* and pitched her back into prehistory," she told him coldly, "millions of people could die."

He clenched his jaw, but said nothing. *That's the difference between us,* he thought with sudden clarity. As regular military, Hayman had the luxury of viewing sentient lives in terms of numbers and abstractions—saving one million mattered more than saving one, and whoever ended the war with the most survivors won. As a doctor, he had only the patient, and even a million patients came down to a single patient, handled over and over again. No amount of arithmetic comparison could make him disregard that duty. And thank God for that.

Hayman made a little noise of annoyance at his silence, and shifted her weight to a more threatening stance. "Do I have to make this an order, Dr. Bashir?"

He lifted his chin defiantly. "As the senior medical officer present, sir, Starfleet regulations allow me to countermand any order you give that I feel is not in the best interests of my patient." He flicked a stiff nod at the stasis chamber. "This is one of those orders."

Surprise and anger flashed scarlet across her cheeks. For one certain, anguished moment, Bashir saw himself slammed into a Starfleet brig for insubordination while Hayman did whatever she damn well pleased with the symbiont. It wasn't how he wanted things to go, but it also wasn't the first time that a clear vision of the consequences came several seconds behind his words. He opened his mouth to recant them—at least in part—just as the admiral turned to scowl at Sisko. "Captain, would you like to speak with your doctor?"

The captain lifted his eyebrows in deceptively mild inquiry. "Why?" He moved a few steps away from the second examining bed, the one that held the delicate tumble of bones that Bashir had scrupulously not dealt with after identifying whose they were. "He seems to be doing just fine to me."

Hayman blew an exasperated breath, and her frustration froze into a cloud of vapor on the air. Like dragon's breath. "Do I have to remind you people that you were brought here so Starfleet could help you avert your own deaths?"

"Not if it means treating Jadzia or either of the Daxes as a sacrifice," Bashir insisted.

Dax stirred at the foot of the examining table. "May I say something?"

Bashir kept his eyes locked on Hayman's, refusing the admiral even that small retreat. "Please do."

"Julian, I appreciate your concern for my welfare, and for everything you must have gone through to keep the symbiont alive all this time..." Dax reached out to spread her cool hand over his, and Bashir realized with a start that he'd slipped his hand onto the stasis field again. "But I don't think this is really your decision to make."

He felt his heart seize into a fist. "Jadzia—"

"Dax." She joggled his wrist gently as though trying to gain his attention. "I'm *Dax,* Julian. *This*—" She patted his hand on the top of the tank, and he looked where she wanted despite himself. *"This* is Dax, too." The pale gray blur was nestled in its bed of liquid like a just-formed infant in its mother's womb. "I trust you enough to be certain you didn't do this as some sort of academic exercise. Preserving the symbiont must have been something you knew for a fact that I wanted—that *Dax* wanted. And the only reason I can think of that I'd be willing to live in a tank like this for so many hundreds of years is the chance to warn us about what happened—to prevent it in any way I can."

Sisko came across the room, stopping behind Dax as though wanting to take her by the shoulders even though he didn't reach out. "We don't know that for certain, old man. And if we lose both you *and* the symbionts testing out a theory . . ." His voice trailed off, and Bashir found he wasn't reassured to know that Sisko was just as afraid of failure as he was.

"We're only talking about a temporary exchange," Dax persisted. "Julian has obviously managed to re-create a symbiont breeding pool well enough to sustain my current symbiont for the hour or two we'll need. And even if we were transplanting a completely incompatible symbiont—" She truned to Bashir again, silently challenging him to say she was wrong. "—Jadzia wouldn't start showing signs of rejection for at least six hours. That should give us plenty of time."

But being correct about the time frame didn't mean she was correct about the procedure. "There's still the psychological aspect," he said softly. "We don't know what the isolation has done to the symbiont's mental stability." His hand stiffened unwillingly on the top of the tank. "Or what that might do to yours."

Dax caught up his gaze with hers, the barest hint of a shared secret coloring her smile as she took his arms to hold him square in front of her, like a mother reassuring her child. "I know for a fact that even six months of exposure to mental instability can't destroy a Trill with seven lifetimes of good foundation. Six hours with some other aspect of myself isn't going to unhinge me." She let her smile widen, and it did nothing to calm the churning in his stomach. "You'll see."

"If you're not willing to perform the procedure, Doctor, I'm sure there are other physicians aboard this starbase who will."

Anger flared in him as though Hayman had thrown gasoline across a spark. Dax's hands tightened on his elbows, startling him into silence as she whirled to snap, "Judith, don't! I won't have him blackmailed into doing this."

The admiral's eyes widened, more surprised than irritated by the outburst, but she crossed her arms without commenting. A more insecure gesture than before, Bashir noticed. He was secretly glad. He didn't like being the only one unsure of himself at a time like this.

"What if there were some other way?" he asked Dax. She opened her mouth to answer, and he pushed on quickly, "Symbionts can communicate with one another without sharing a host, can't they? When they're in the breeding pools back on Trill—when you're in the breeding pools with them?"

The thought had apparently never occurred to her. One elegant eyebrow lifted, and Dax's focus shifted to somewhere invisible while she considered. "It doesn't transfer all the symbiont's knowledge the way a joining does," she acknowledged after a moment. "But, yes, direct communication is possible."

A little pulse of hope pushed at his heart. "And in a true joining, Jadzia wouldn't retain any of the symbiont's memories, anyway, once the symbiont was removed."

Dax nodded thoughtfully. "That's true."

"So what harm is there in trying this first?"

"Trying what first?" Hayman's confidence must not have been too badly damaged, because the impatient edge to her voice returned easily enough. "What are you two talking about?"

Bashir looked over Dax's shoulder at the admiral, schooling the dislike from his voice in an effort to sound more professional. "When they aren't inside a host, Trill symbionts use electrochemical signals to communicate with one another through the liquid they live in. Even a hosted symbiont can make contact with the others, if its host is first submerged in the fluid pool." He glanced aside at the tank while his thoughts raced a dozen steps ahead. "If we can replicate the nutrient mixture that's been supporting the symbiont, and fill a large enough receptacle, I think the Daxes should be able to . . ." He hesitated slightly, then fell back on the easiest word. ". . . talk to each other without having to remove Jadzia's current symbiont."

Hayman chewed the inside of her lip. "We could question this unhosted symbiont that way? It could talk to us through Dax?"

"Through Jadzia," Bashir corrected automatically, then felt heat flash into his cheeks at Hayman's reproving scowl. "Yes, we could."

"Julian's right." Dax saved him from the rest of the admiral's disapproval. "I think this will work."

"And if it doesn't work?" Hayman fixed Bashir with a suspicious glare, as if expecting him to lie to her. "What are our chances of losing the symbiont?"

"I don't know," he admitted. He wished the truth weren't so unhelpful. "I don't know how fragile it is, how much radiation damage it may have sustained back then. It may not live beyond removal of the stasis field, and I don't know what effect physically moving it from one tank to another might have." He looked into Dax's eyes so that she could see he was being absolutely honest, as a doctor and as her friend. "I do know it will be less traumatic than trying to accomplish a joining under these conditions."

Dax nodded her understanding with a little smile, then squeezed his arms once before releasing him to fold her own hands behind her back. "I think this will be our best option."

"All right, then." Hayman flashed Bashir an appreciative grin, all his sins just that quickly forgiven now that she had what she wanted. Bashir wondered if that was supposed to make him feel as guilty as it did.

"Let's give this a try. Lieutenant"—she gathered both Dax and Sisko to her side with a wave of one hand—"you and the captain can tell me how much fluid and what size tank we'll need, then help me get it all down here. Doctor, wake up the symbiont." She leaned across the tank to clap him manfully on the shoulder, and Bashir found he didn't like the contact. "Looks like it's time to finish what you started."

**Look for
Star Trek Deep Space Nine®
Invasion! Book Three
Time's Enemy
Wherever Paperback Books Are Sold
Coming mid-July from
Pocket Books**

1252.01

THE UNIVERSE IS
EXPANDING
STAR TREK
—COMMUNICATOR—
...ENGAGE

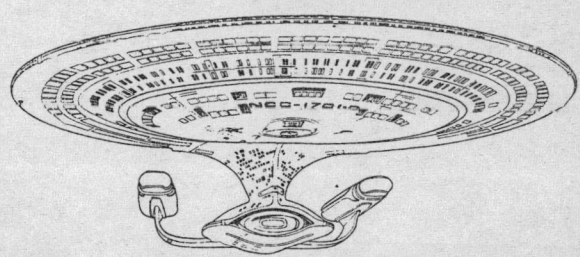

A PUBLICATION OF THE OFFICIAL STAR TREK FAN CLUB ™

NEW

SUBSCRIPTION ONLY $14.95!

Subscribe now and you'll receive:

★ A year's subscription to our full-color official bi-monthly magazine, the *STAR TREK COMMUNICATOR*, packed with information not found anywhere else on the movies and television series, and profiles of celebrities and futurists.

★ A galaxy of *STAR TREK* merchandise and hard to find collectibles, *a premier investment for collectors of all ages.*

★ Our new subscriber kit. It includes a set of 9 highly collectible Skybox Trading Cards and exclusive poster, and discounts on *STAR TREK* events around the U.S. for members only.

TO SUBSCRIBE, USE YOUR VISA OR MASTERCARD AND CALL 1-800-TRUE-FAN (800-878-3326) MONDAY THRU FRIDAY, 8:30am TO 5:00pm mst OR MAIL CHECK OR MONEY ORDER FOR $14.95 TO:

STAR TREK: THE OFFICIAL FAN CLUB
PO BOX 111000, AURORA COLORADO 80042

SUBSCRIPTION FOR ONE YEAR– $14.95 (U.S.)

NAME_____

ADDRESS_____

CITY/STATE_____

ZIP_____

TM, ®&© 1994 Paramount Pictures. All Rights Reserved. STAR TREK and related marks are trademarks of Paramount Pictures. Authorized user.

STVFC

INVASION!
"Drop cloak!"

Captain Benjamin Sisko said as the three alien ships on the viewscreen swung in on the attack. The toneless curtness of Sisko's voice told Dax just how grim the situation must be. "Divert all power to shields and weapons."

"Damage to forward shield generators," O'Brien's voice reported. "Diverting power from rear shields to compensate."

"Return fire!" Sisko leapt from his command chair and went to join Dax at the helm. "Starting evasive manuevers, program delta!"

Alien phaser fire washed the Defiant's bridge in a fierce white light. . . .

Look for STAR TREK Fiction from Pocket Books

Star Trek: The Original Series

The Return
The Ashes of Eden
Federation
Sarek
Best Destiny
Shadows on the Sun
Probe
Prime Directive
The Lost Years
Star Trek VI: The Undiscovered Country
Star Trek V: The Final Frontier
Star Trek IV: The Voyage Home
Spock's World
Enterprise
Strangers from the Sky
Final Frontier

#1 Star Trek: The Motion Picture
#2 The Entropy Effect
#3 The Klingon Gambit
#4 The Covenant of the Crown
#5 The Prometheus Design
#6 The Abode of Life
#7 Star Trek II: The Wrath of Khan
#8 Black Fire
#9 Triangle
#10 Web of the Romulans
#11 Yesterday's Son
#12 Mutiny on the Enterprise
#13 The Wounded Sky
#14 The Trellisane Confrontation
#15 Corona
#16 The Final Reflection
#17 Star Trek III: The Search for Spock
#18 My Enemy, My Ally
#19 The Tears of the Singers
#20 The Vulcan Academy Murders
#21 Uhura's Song
#22 Shadow Lord
#23 Ishmael
#24 Killing Time
#25 Dwellers in the Crucible
#26 Pawns and Symbols
#27 Mindshadow
#28 Crisis on Centaurus
#29 Dreadnought!
#30 Demons
#31 Battlestations!

#32 Chain of Attack
#33 Deep Domain
#34 Dreams of the Raven
#35 The Romulan Way
#36 How Much for Just the Planet?
#37 Bloodthirst
#38 The IDIC Epidemic
#39 Time for Yesterday
#40 Timetrap
#41 The Three-Minute Universe
#42 Memory Prime
#43 The Final Nexus
#44 Vulcan's Glory
#45 Double, Double
#46 The Cry of the Onlies
#47 The Kobayashi Maru
#48 Rules of Engagement
#49 The Pandora Principle
#50 Doctor's Orders
#51 Enemy Unseen
#52 Home Is the Hunter
#53 Ghost Walker
#54 A Flag Full of Stars
#55 Renegade
#56 Legacy
#57 The Rift
#58 Face of Fire
#59 The Disinherited
#60 Ice Trap
#61 Sanctuary
#62 Death Count
#63 Shell Game
#64 The Starship Trap
#65 Windows on a Lost World
#66 From the Depths
#67 The Great Starship Race
#68 Firestorm
#69 The Patrian Transgression
#70 Traitor Winds
#71 Crossroad
#72 The Better Man
#73 Recovery
#74 The Fearful Summons
#75 First Frontier
#76 The Captain's Daughter
#77 Twilight's End
#78 The Rings of Tautee
#79 Invasion 1: The First Strike

Star Trek: The Next Generation

Kahless
Star Trek Generations
All Good Things
Q-Squared
Dark Mirror
Descent
The Devil's Heart
Imzadi
Relics
Reunion
Unification
Metamorphosis
Vendetta
Encounter at Farpoint

#1 Ghost Ship
#2 The Peacekeepers
#3 The Children of Hamlin
#4 Survivors
#5 Strike Zone
#6 Power Hungry
#7 Masks
#8 The Captains' Honor
#9 A Call to Darkness
#10 A Rock and a Hard Place
#11 Gulliver's Fugitives
#12 Doomsday World
#13 The Eyes of the Beholders
#14 Exiles
#15 Fortune's Light
#16 Contamination
#17 Boogeymen
#18 Q-in-Law
#19 Perchance to Dream
#20 Spartacus
#21 Chains of Command
#22 Imbalance
#23 War Drums
#24 Nightshade
#25 Grounded
#26 The Romulan Prize
#27 Guises of the Mind
#28 Here There Be Dragons
#29 Sins of Commission
#30 Debtors' Planet
#31 Foreign Foes
#32 Requiem
#33 Balance of Power
#34 Blaze of Glory
#35 Romulan Stratagem
#36 Into the Nebula
#37 The Last Stand
#38 Dragon's Honor
#39 Rogue Saucer
#40 Possession
#41 Invasion 2: The Soldiers of Fear

Star Trek: Deep Space Nine

Warped
The Search

#1 Emissary
#2 The Siege
#3 Bloodletter
#4 The Big Game
#5 Fallen Heroes
#6 Betrayal
#7 Warchild
#8 Antimatter
#9 Proud Helios
#10 Valhalla
#11 Devil in the Sky
#12 The Laertian Gamble
#13 Station Rage
#14 The Long Night
#15 Objective: Bajor
#16 Invasion 3: Time's Enemy

Star Trek: Voyager

#1 Caretaker
#2 The Escape
#3 Ragnarok
#4 Violations
#5 Incident at Arbuk
#6 The Murdered Sun
#7 Ghost of a Chance
#8 Cybersong

For orders other than by individual consumers, Pocket Books grants a discount on the purchase of **10 or more** copies of single titles for special markets or premium use. For further details, please write to the Vice-President of Special Markets, Pocket Books, 1633 Broadway, New York, NY 10019-6785, 8th Floor.

For information on how individual consumers can place orders, please write to Mail Order Department, Simon & Schuster Inc., 200 Old Tappan Road, Old Tappan, NJ 07675.

TIME'S ENEMY

L.A. GRAF

INVASION! concept by John J. Ordover and Diane Carey

POCKET BOOKS
New York   London   Toronto   Sydney   Tokyo   Singapore

The sale of this book without its cover is unauthorized. If you purchased this book without a cover, you should be aware that it was reported to the publisher as "unsold and destroyed." Neither the author nor the publisher has received payment for the sale of this "stripped book."

This book is a work of fiction. Names, characters, places and incidents are products of the author's imagination or are used fictitiously. Any resemblance to actual events or locales or persons, living or dead, is entirely coincidental.

An *Original* Publication of POCKET BOOKS

POCKET BOOKS, a division of Simon & Schuster Inc.
1230 Avenue of the Americas, New York, NY 10020

Copyright © 1996 by Paramount Pictures. All Rights Reserved.

STAR TREK is a Registered Trademark of Paramount Pictures.

A VIACOM COMPANY

This book is published by Pocket Books, a division of Simon & Schuster Inc., under exclusive license from Paramount Pictures.

All rights reserved, including the right to reproduce this book or portions thereof in any form whatsoever. For information address Pocket Books, 1230 Avenue of the Americas, New York, NY 10020

ISBN: 0-671-54150-1

First Pocket Books printing August 1996

10 9 8 7 6

POCKET and colophon are registered trademarks of Simon & Schuster Inc.

Printed in the U.S.A

Before

Out here where sunlight was a faraway glimmer in the blackness of space, ice lasted a long time. Dark masses of it littered a wide orbital ring, all that remained of the spinning nebula that had birthed this planet-rich system. The cold outer dark sheltered each fragment in safety, unless some chance grazing of neighbors ejected one of them into the unyielding pull of solar gravity. Then the mass of dirty ice would begin its long journey toward the distant sun, past the captured ninth planet, past the four gas giants, past the ring of rocky fragments that memorialized a planet never born. By that point it would have begun to glow, brushed into brilliance by the gathering heat of the sun's nuclear furnace. When it passed the cold red desert planet and approached the cloud-feathered planet that harbored life, it would be brighter than any star. Its flare would pierce that planet's blue sky, stirring brief wonder from the primitive tribes who hunted and gathered and scratched at the earth with sticks to grow their food. In a few days, the comet's borrowed light would fade, and the tumbling ice would start its long journey back to the outer dark.

One fragment had escaped that fate, although it shouldn't have. It carried a burden of steel and empty space, buried just deep enough in its icy heart to send it spinning back into the cloud of fellow comets after its near-collision with another. For centuries afterward, it danced an erratic path through the ice-littered darkness before it settled into a stable orbit in the shadow of the tiny ninth planet. More centuries passed while dim fires glowed on the night side of the bluish globe that harbored life. The fires slowly brightened and spread, leaping across its vast oceans. They brightened faster after that, merging to form huge networks of light that outlined every coast and lake and river. Then the fires leaped into the ocean of space. Out to the planet's single moon at first, then later to its cold, red neighbor, then to the moons of the gas giants, and finally out beyond all of them to the stars. In all those long centuries, nothing disturbed the comet and its anomalous burden. No one saw the tiny, wavering light that lived inside.

Until a fierce blast of phaser fire ripped the icy shroud open, and exposed what lay within.

CHAPTER 1

"It looks like they're preparing for an invasion,' Jadzia Dax said.

Sisko grunted, gazing out at the expanse of dark-crusted cometary ice that formed the natural hull of Starbase One. Above the curving ice horizon, the blackness of Earth's Oort cloud should have glittered with bright stars and the barely brighter glow of the distant sun. Instead, what it glittered with were the docking lights of a dozen short-range attack ships—older and more angular versions of the *Defiant*—as well as the looming bulk of two Galaxy-class starships, the *Mukaikubo* and the *Breedlove*. One glance had told Sisko that such a gathering of force couldn't have been the random result of ship refittings and shore leaves. Starfleet was preparing for a major encounter with someone. He just wished he knew who.

"I thought we came here to deal with a *non*military emergency." In the sweep of transparent aluminum windows, Sisko could see Julian Bashir's dark reflection glance up from the chair he'd sprawled in after a glance at the view. Beyond the doctor, the huge conference room was as empty as it had been ten minutes ago when they'd first been escorted into it. "Otherwise, wouldn't Admiral Hayman have asked us to come in the *Defiant* instead of a high-speed courier?"

Sisko snorted. "Admirals never *ask* anything, Doctor.

3

And they never tell you any more than you need to know to carry out their orders efficiently."

"Especially this admiral," Dax added, an unexpected note of humor creeping into her voice. Sisko raised an eyebrow at her, then heard a gravelly snort and the simultaneous hiss of the conference-room door opening. He swung around to see a rangy, long-boned figure in ordinary Starfleet coveralls crossing the room toward them. Dax surprised her by promptly stepping forward, hands outstretched in welcome.

"How have you been, Judith?"

"Promoted." The silver-haired woman's angular face lit with something approaching a sparkle. "It almost makes up for getting this old." She clasped Dax's hands warmly for a moment, then turned her attention to Sisko. "So this is the Benjamin Sisko Curzon told me so much about. It's a pleasure to finally meet you, Captain."

Sisko slanted a wary glance at his Science Officer. "Um— likewise, I'm sure. Dax?"

The Trill cleared her throat. "Benjamin, allow me to introduce you to Rear Admiral Judith Hayman. She and I— well, she and Curzon, actually—got to know each other on Vulcan during the Klingon peace negotiations several years ago. Judith, this is Captain Benjamin Sisko of *Deep Space Nine,* and our station's chief medical officer, Dr. Julian Bashir."

"Admiral." Bashir nodded crisply.

"Our orders said this was a Priority One Emergency," Sisko said. "I assume that means whatever you brought us here to do is urgent."

Hayman's strong face lost its smile. "Possibly," she said. "Although perhaps not urgent in the way we usually think of it."

Sisko scowled. "Forgive my bluntness, Admiral, but I've been dragged from my command station without explanation, ordered not to use my own ship under any circumstances, brought to the oldest and least useful starbase in the Federation—" He made a gesture of reined-in impatience at the bleak cometary landscape outside the windows. "—and you're telling me you're not sure how *urgent* this problem is?"

"No one is sure, Captain. That's part of the reason we brought you here." The admiral's voice chilled into something between grimness and exasperation. "What we *are* sure of is that we could be facing potential disaster." She reached into the front pocket of her coveralls and tossed two ordinary-looking data chips onto the conference table. "The first thing I need you and your medical officer to do is review these data records."

"Data records," Sisko repeated, trying for the noncommittal tone he'd perfected over years of trying to deal with the equally high-handed and inexplicable behavior of Kai Winn.

"Admiral, forgive us, but we assumed this actually *was* an emergency." Julian Bashir broke in with such polite bafflement that Sisko guessed he must be emulating Garak's unctous demeanor. "If so, we could have reviewed your data records ten hours ago. All you had to do was send them to *Deep Space Nine* through subspace channels."

"Too dangerous, even using our most secure codes." The bleak certainty in Hayman's voice made Sisko blink in surprise. "And if you were listening, young man, you'd have noticed that I said this was the *first* thing I needed you to do. Now, would you please sit down, Captain?"

Sisko took the place she indicated at one of the conference table's inset data stations, then waited while she settled Bashir at the station on the opposite side. He noticed she made no attempt to seat Dax, although there were other empty stations available.

"This review procedure is not a standard one," Hayman said, without further preliminaries. "As a control on the validity of some data we've recently received, we're going to ask you to examine ship's logs and medical records without knowing their origin. We'd like your analysis of them. Computer, start data-review programs Sisko-One and Bashir-One."

Sisko's monitor flashed to life, not with pictures but with a thick ribbon of multilayered symbols and abbreviated words, slowly scrolling from left to right. He stared at it for a long, blank moment before a whisper of memory turned it familiar instead of alien. One of the things Starfleet Acade-

5

my asked cadets to do was determine the last three days of a starship's voyage when its main computer memory had failed. The solution was to reconstruct computer records from each of the ship's individual system buffers—records that looked exactly like these.

"These are multiple logs of buffer output from individual ship systems, written in standard Starfleet machine code," he said. Dax made an interested noise and came to stand behind him. "It looks like someone downloaded the last commands given to life-support, shields, helm, and phaser-bank control. There's another system here, too, but I can't identify it."

"Photon-torpedo control?" Dax suggested, leaning over his shoulder to scrutinize it.

"I don't think so. It might be a sensor buffer." Sisko scanned the lines of code intently while they scrolled by. He could recognize more of the symbols now, although most of the abbreviations on the fifth line still baffled him. "There's no sign of navigations, either—the command buffers in those systems may have been destroyed by whatever took out the ship's main computer." Sisko grunted as four of the five logs recorded wild fluctuations and then degenerated into solid black lines. "And there goes everything else. Whatever hit this ship crippled it beyond repair."

Dax nodded. "It looks like some kind of EM pulse took out all of the ship's circuits—everything lost power except for life-support, and that had to switch to auxiliary circuits." She glanced up at the admiral. "Is that all the record we have, Admiral? Just those few minutes?"

"It's all the record we *trust*," Hayman said enigmatically. "There are some visual bridge logs that I'll show you in a minute, but those could have been tampered with. We're fairly sure the buffer outputs weren't." She glanced up at Bashir, whose usual restless energy had focused down to a silent intensity of concentration on his own data screen. "The medical logs we found were much more extensive. You have time to review the buffer outputs again, if you'd like."

"Please," Sisko and Dax said in unison.

"Computer, repeat data program Sisko-One."

Machine code crawled across the screen again, and this time Sisko stopped trying to identify the individual symbols in it. He vaguely remembered one of his Academy professors saying that reconstructing a starship's movements from the individual buffer outputs of its systems was a lot like reading a symphony score. The trick was not to analyze each line individually, but to get a sense of how all of them were functioning in tandem.

"This ship was in a battle," he said at last. "But I think it was trying to escape, not fight. The phaser banks all show discharge immediately after power fluctuations are recorded for the shields."

"Defensive action," Dax agreed, and pointed at the screen. "And look at how much power they had to divert from life-support to keep the shields going. Whatever was after them was big."

"They're trying some evasive actions now—" Sisko broke off, seeing something he'd missed the first time in that mysterious fifth line of code. Something that froze his stomach. It was the same Romulan symbol that appeared on his command board every time the cloaking device was engaged on the *Defiant*.

"This was a cloaked Starfleet vessel!" He swung around to fix the admiral with a fierce look. "My understanding was that only the *Defiant* had been sanctioned to carry a Romulan cloaking device!"

Hayman met his stare without a ripple showing in her calm competence. "I can assure you that Starfleet isn't running any unauthorized cloaking devices. Watch the log again, Captain Sisko."

He swung back to his monitor. "Computer, rerun data program Sisko-One at one-quarter speed," he said. The five concurrent logs crawled across the screen in slow motion, and this time Sisko focused on the coordinated interactions between the helm and the phaser banks. If he had any hope of identifying the class and generation of this starship, it would be from the tactical maneuvers it could perform.

"Time the helm changes versus the phaser bursts," Dax suggested from behind him in an unusually quiet voice. Sisko wondered if she was beginning to harbor the same ominous suspicion he was.

"I know." For the past hundred years, the speed of helm shift versus the speed of phaser refocus had been the basic determining factor of battle tactics. Sisko's gaze flickered from top line to third, counting off milliseconds by the ticks along the edge of the data record. The phaser refocus rates he found were startlingly fast, but far more chilling was the almost instantaneous response of this starship's helm in its tactical runs. There was only one ship he knew of that had the kind of overpowered warp engines needed to bring it so dangerously close to the edge of survivable maneuvers. And there was only one commander who had used his spare time to perfect the art of skimming along the edge of that envelope, the way the logs told him this ship's commander had done.

This time when Sisko swung around to confront Judith Hayman, his concern had condensed into cold, sure knowledge. "Where did you find these records, Admiral?"

She shook her head. "Your analysis first, Captain. I need your unbiased opinion before I answer any questions or show you the visual logs. Otherwise, we'll never know for sure if this data can be trusted."

Sisko blew out a breath, trying to find words for conclusions he wasn't even sure he believed. "This ship—it wasn't just cloaked like the *Defiant*. It actually *was* the *Defiant*." He heard Dax's indrawn breath. "And when it was destroyed in battle, the man commanding it was me."

"Captain Sisko would let me."

It occurred to Kira that if she had a strip of latinum for every time someone had said that to her in the last forty-eight hours, she could probably buy this station and every slavering Ferengi troll on board. Not that the prospect of owning a dozen wrinkled, bat-eared larcenists filled her with any particular glee. But at least Ferengi were predictable, and they didn't act all affronted every time you refused to jump at their comm calls or told them their problems were trivial. After all, they were Ferengi—any aspect of their lives not directly related to money was trivial, and they did everything in their power to keep things that way.

Humans, on the other hand, thought the galaxy revolved around their wants and worries, and tended to get their fragile little egos bruised when you implied that they might be wrong. With that in mind, Kira had spent the better part of her first day in command—a good two or three hours, at least—placating, compromising, making every sympathetic noise Dax had ever taught her, in the theory that a little stroking (no matter how insincere) was all the crew needed to carry them through the captain's absence. Somewhere around lunchtime, though, she'd elbowed that damned leather sphere off Sisko's desk for the fourth damned time, and the fifth trivial work-schedule dispute let himself into the office while she was under the desk patting about for it, and the sixth subspace call from Bajor—or Starfleet, or some other damned place—started chirping for immediate attention, and it became suddenly, vitally important that she conduct the EV inspection of weapons sail two herself. She fled Ops with the ball still lost in the wilds of Sisko's office furniture, hopeful that shuffling the whining crewman off to Personnel and playing ten minutes of yes-man with a Bajoran minister would buy her enough time to get safely suited up and out into vacuum. O'Brien, bless his soul, only stammered a little with surprise when she plucked the repair order from his hands on her way to the turbolift.

Next time, she'd just have to leave the station without the environmental suit. It would make everything so much easier.

"Well?" Quark hadn't quite progressed to petulance yet, but there was something about having a Ferengi voice whining right in your ear that made even an overlarge radiation hardsuit seem small and strangling. "I'm telling you, this is exactly the sort of thing Sisko would endorse with all his heart."

Kira couldn't help blowing a disgusted snort, although it blasted an irritating film of steam across the inside of her suit's faceplate. She locked the magnetic soles of her boots onto the skin of the sail while she waited for the hardsuit's atmosphere adjusters to clear out the excess humidity. "Quark, Captain Sisko won't even let you in Ops." Which was why he'd wasted no time weaseling onto a comm channel Kira couldn't escape, no doubt. "*I* don't know why he lets you stay on the station at all."

She could just make out his squat Ferengi silhouette scuttling back and forth in the observation port above his bar. "Because the captain has a fine sense of the market, for a hu-man. But not so fine a sense of how to extract profit from opportunity." Kira flexed her feet, breaking contact with the station and letting the momentum of that slight movement swing her around to the front of the sail's arc, out of Quark's line of sight. *I really am out here to do work,* she told herself as she passed a diagnostic scanner slowly down the length of one seam. The fact that she enjoyed a certain cruel satisfaction every time Quark grumbled with frustration and ran down the corridor to the next unobstructed window was really just a perk.

"I'm still picking up some residual leakage," she reported to O'Brien. The rad counter on the far right of her helmet display barely hovered at the bottom of its range, and she scowled around a renewed twist of annoyance. "Not enough to warrant lugging out this twice-damned hardsuit, but . . ."

"Sorry, Major—Starfleet regulations." His blunt Irish brogue managed to sound honestly sympathetic for all that Kira suspected he never much considered resenting Starfleet protocol. "Anytime you send personnel to inspect a first-stage radiation hazard, you've got to send them in ISHA-approved protective gear."

"And in my case, that means a hardsuit built to fit a guy like Sisko."

"Well, they are sort of one-size-fits-all."

Kira stopped herself just before she snorted again and fogged her faceplate. "One size fits all humans over two meters tall."

"Yes, ma'am," O'Brien admitted. "Something like that."

"Major, I really don't think you're giving my proposal the attention that courtesy requires."

Kira pulled herself hand-over-hand down the outside of the sail, dreaming wistfully of pushing off toward the wormhole and letting it whisk her far away from even the slightest whiff of Ferengi. "O'Brien, isn't there some way you can cut Quark out of this channel?"

"Not without cutting you off from the station, too, ma'am. Sorry."

She wondered whether she should tell him how much that concept appealed to her.

"It's just that Captain Sisko doesn't appreciate the *spiritual* importance of recreation the way—"

"No, Quark!"

The squeak of pained indignation in her ear couldn't have been more poignant if someone had gone fishing for the barkeep's nonexistent heart with a spoon. "Major, you have my word that everyone will stay to my back three Dabo rooms."

"That's what you promised the *last* time you organized a gambling tournament." She planted her feet again with a *clang* that she felt through her suit but couldn't hear, and pushed open the access door to the inner sail with as much violence as the microgravity would allow. "Instead, the Bajoran Trade Commission wrote up a four-page complaint about increased shoplifting on the Promenade, and Morn filed sexual-harassment charges against no less than six of your players."

The ragged puffing of another sprint along the Promenade balcony was followed by distinctive slap of Quark plastering himself to yet another window. "But *this* year—" Kira could just imagine the sweet-sour smell of his snaggletoothed grin. "—I've hired an Elasian cohort to serve as exclusive door guards."

"No!" Kira watched her radiation gauge soar to an almost alarming level, and punched one fist against the interior lighting panel to brighten the room. "Now, which word of that didn't you understand?"

"Most likely the declarative negative. It's a recurrent problem with the Ferengi, I'm afraid." Even if Kira hadn't recognized the security officer's gruff sarcasm, the growl of naked animosity in Quark's muttering would have told her it was Odo who had walked in on the Ferengi's noxious attempts at charm. "Apparently the Ferengi don't have a word in their language for 'no.'"

Quark sniffed with what Kira suspected was supposed to be indignation, somehow managing to sound both obsequious and offended at the same time. "That's not true," the Ferengi countered. "We have several, depending on how much negotiation it will take to change your mind."

"Tell me you're taking the whole tournament to the Gamma Quadrant," Kira suggested.

"And never coming back," the constable added.

"—then I might consider giving you permission to use

the station as a jumping-off point. Until then . . ." The diagnostic scanner flashed brilliant white, warning that enough first-stage radiation soaked the weapons sail to light most small cities for a year. Kira barely took the time to fold up the scanner before stepping backward out the door. "Chief, did you see that reading?"

"I saw it." O'Brien sounded more frustrated than upset. Kira suspected he was wishing he were here now instead of her. "I could have sworn we checked all the power units in those phaser batteries on our last external inspection. One of them must have gone bad."

"Should that be throwing off so much first-stage radiation?"

"Not usually," he admitted. "But whatever's gone wrong in there, Major, it's not something you should be tracking down with a handheld scanner and a trouble light. Now that we know where the problem is, I can have my boys start working on it."

"Leaving you more time to consider my proposal," Quark said brightly.

"No, Quark."

She'd never heard a Ferengi hiss like that before. "Fine." Out on the surface of the habitat ring again, Kira saw Quark make a short, frustrated gesture with his arms in the distant window, then pointedly return his hands to his sides with the same finality a Bajoran would have used when dusting herself of someone else's dirt. "Fine! I took you to be a generous, understanding woman with a clear sense of your duties to the people on this station." He angled a petulant glare up at the slim figure towering behind him. "Obviously, I was wrong. So if you'll excuse me, I'll go back to salvaging the economy on my own." He lifted his chin with an indignant sniff, and stalked out of sight beyond the window's frame as though he hadn't been the one trespassing on her comm channel in the first place.

"I don't know how Sisko ever gets any work done around here," she complained—mostly to herself—as she pulled the access door closed behind her.

"By staying in his office, I suspect."

Kira glanced over toward the window as though she could have seen any real expression on Odo's wax-smooth features even if he weren't so far away. She didn't always know how to take the constable's remarks when he wasn't being overtly sarcastic. Did he state the blatantly obvious because he meant some kind of veiled criticism, or just because it was the truth? With Odo, sometimes an answer was just an answer—refreshing after the labyrinthine politics of the Federation and Bajor, but not always any easier to take.

"What can I do for you, Odo?" She turned to push off for the airlock, ready to shed this cumbersome, too-hot carapace and take a private meal in her quarters before falling into bed. "Please tell me Sisko called and said he'd be home for a late dinner."

"Unfortunately, no." And he sounded truly apologetic, as though Kira's lighter teasing were just as heartfelt as anything he ever said. "Although you wouldn't be the only one glad for his return." A data inset sprang to life at the bottom of her suit display, scrolling information past her chin as she walked. Kira glanced a frown toward the window, then chided herself for the uselessness of the gesture and looked away.

"So what's this?" she asked.

"Read it."

Security reports, dating back to seven days ago, all with Odo's blunt, clear signature in the corner. The first three entries looked like a hundred others that had come across Sisko's desk while Kira sat there—the late-night break-in of a store catering to tourists who wanted to backpack their way around Bajor, a discrepancy between goods received and the bill of lading for a shipment of computer components on their way to Andor, the theft of—

Kira paused, cocking her head inside the big helmet as she glanced down at the fourth item on Odo's list, then blinked back up through the other three. "Robberies." She looked ahead, at the station laid out before her, at the wormhole, at the stars. "All of these are robberies of some kind, and all within the last week. A crime syndicate, trying to set up shop on *Deep Space Nine?*" In so many ways, it was the ideal location: The wormhole made for a perfect escape route, and there were no extradition treaties with the Gamma Quadrant.

Odo grunted in his version of grim amusement. "There

really isn't room here for any more organized crime than what Quark already controls. Besides . . ." He must have touched something on his own padd to brightly highlight the item currently on Kira's display. ". . . there isn't much of a black market for household power matrices, much less for portable thermal storage containers." A few flashes of data brought up another report from farther down on the list. "Unfortunately, tactical plasma warheads still bring a healthy profit, no matter where you plan to sell them."

Kira didn't immediately recognize the style of paperwork in front of her, but what it said was clear enough. "Six liters of weapons-grade liquid plasma, missing from a shipment to the starship yards at Okana." A little thrill of almost-panic whispered through her. "That's on Bajor."

"Which is only three hours by shuttle from *Deep Space Nine.*" With only Odo's gravelly voice for company, Kira suddenly felt very vulnerable out here in the open. She made herself start walking again, heading straight for the airlock's neon fluorescent striping. "Anyone with this list of materials," the constable went on, "could spend a few hours in a Federation library and easily construct an explosive device powerful enough to destroy this entire station."

Not to mention vaporize a small starship, or depopulate any province on Bajor. Kira spat an angry curse, and keyed open the airlock on runabout pad F with awkward gloved fingers. "Any guess as to their intended target?" How could the Federation make this kind of information just *available* to any psychotic who asked? Didn't they realize that Bajor wasn't some population of doe-eyed pacifists, but, rather, a roil of scarred soldiers and ex-resistance operatives who had perfected filching the innards for bombs years before the Federation wandered onto the scene?

"That would depend on several factors," Odo said. "We don't even know who 'they' are yet."

"No . . ." Kira drummed one foot impatiently inside its ill-fitting boot, watching the atmosphere readings bloom inside the airlock even as she heard the hiss and rumble of air pressure gathering around her. "But I'll bet we can guess."

She could almost read Odo's thoughts in his grim silence. The constable knew as well as Kira that the paramilitary cells who'd begun shaking their fists in the northern provinces these last few months were little more than old resistance fighters with a new bone to chew. "Oppression is oppression!" was their cry—they claimed little difference between the Cardassians' iron bootheels and the Federation's paternal "control by example" from their lofty space-station pedestal. As far as Kira was concerned, all you had to do was look at their respective medical facilities to appreciate how unrelated their motives toward Bajor were. Still, zealots had a habit of ignoring opinions not directly in support of their cause of the week, and this latest batch seemed just as unyielding as any other; they might not have posted any official threats yet, but Kira knew these sorts of people almost as well as she knew herself. It was really just a matter of time.

"I thought that was supposed to be the difference between democracy and dictatorship," she said aloud, stepping sideways to squeeze through the airlock door as it rolled aside. "You don't have to blow up things just to have your voice heard."

Odo looked up from the other side of the bay, stroking one hand thoughtfully across the nose of an as-yet-unnamed runabout. "The humans say old habits die hard."

Which meant that humans and Bajorans had something in common, although perhaps not the best attributes of either.

A chirp from inside the hardsuit's helmet saved her from having to contemplate the question further. "Ops to Major Kira."

She popped the seals on the helmet anyway, dragging it off her head and tucking it under one arm rather than get trapped inside this suit for any longer than she had to be. "Go ahead, Chief."

"We've just picked up a neutrino flux from the wormhole, Major. It looks like someone's coming through."

Kira glanced a startled look at Odo. "Are there are any ships due back from the Gamma Quadrant?"

Odo shook his head in silent answer even as the human's voice replied, "No, sir. Nobody's due in or out for at least another three days."

She curled one hand over the rim of the helmet to muffle

the comm pickup there as she commented softly to Odo, "I suppose it's too much to ask that our bomb builders chose just this moment to relocate their materials."

He scowled down at her in fatherly disapproval for such a naive suggestion, taking her comment just as seriously as he seemed to take everything. Kira decided it wasn't worth trying to explain her admittedly weary sense of humor right now, and instead withdrew her hand from the helmet and set it on the floor so she could crack the chest on the suit and squirm herself free.

"Chief, I'm still down in Runabout Pad F getting out of this damned suit. Put the station's defense systems on standby, then transfer an outside view to the runabout's viewscreen." Stepping free of the bulky trousers, she motioned Odo to follow as she let herself into the small ship's hatch. "I want to see what's going on."

"Aye-aye, Major."

The inside of this runabout was as identical to every other such craft as a Starfleet shipyard could build it. Oh, the floor plates were too bright and unscuffed, and milky sheets of protective sheeting still draped the four seats and all the stations, but the number of steps from the hatch to the helm were exactly the same, the shadows that fell across her eyes as they walked through the cabin came in exactly the sequence she expected, and the clearance between panel and seat when she slipped into the pilot's chair was so familiar that she barely even noticed the crinkle of sheeting under her hands. She certainly didn't feel any need to pull her eyes away from the newly awakened viewscreen and what it had to show.

Light swirled against the cold backdrop, a spiral blossom of energy and quantum probability far too lovely to deserve its inelegant human name—wormhole. From the moment she'd first seen the gateway twist into being, Kira accepted that this was something more wonderful and significant than merely what the Federation's mathematics justified. That science could touch the tip of this iceberg didn't bother her—understanding the parts of a thing granted you no special insight into its nature, just as a meticulous description of all the biological systems making up a Bajoran gave you no true idea of the person living inside that shell. Four years of watching spaceships come and go through the wormhole's flaming mouth had done nothing to dim her convictions: the phenomenon's very existence proved there was more to life than simply what met the eye.

This time, the wormhole's gift was little more than a twinkle of reflected light, tumbling, spinning, flashing in and out just at the portal's edge, too small to really be seen. When the petals of radiant energy finally folded back in on the singularity and retreated into invisibility, only the tiny glitter of movement remained, drifting lazily, darkly toward Bajor.

"It isn't powered." Odo leaned over the console to peer at the viewscreen, his colorless eyes intent on the tumbling mite. "It's either lost its engine, or it never had one."

Kira nodded with a thoughtful frown, and tapped at her comm badge to reconnect with O'Brien in Ops. "Any idea what that is, Chief?"

He was quiet for a moment, no doubt conferring with his equipment. Kira drummed her fingers on the sheeting covering the panel and willed herself not to hurry him, even when Odo speared her with an intensely irritated glare for the noise she made.

"Iron . . ." O'Brien said at last, his voice distracted and thoughtful. "Nickel . . . traces of duranium and methane ice . . ." He gave a little grunt of surprise that sounded ever so slightly disappointed. "My guess is a cometary nucleus. Maybe an asteroid fragment."

Nothing interesting, in other words. Kira sat back with a satisfied nod and pulled her hands away from the panel. Just as well. She didn't think she could stand much more "interest" around the station just now.

"Major?" O'Brien caught her while only half standing, mere moments before she would have thanked him for his time and gone back to her runabout inventory. "Major, the computer's listing that fragment's course as being right through Bajor's main ore-shipping lanes. We might want to take care of it before it passes out of phaser range."

With the wormhole's location, just about anything that came through under free momentum had to cross a Bajoran shipping lane eventually. "Anything in the fragment that'll react badly to our weapons?"

"No, sir. The minerals are pretty evenly distributed, through and through. It should vaporize nicely."

She straightened the covering on her chair with a flick of her hand, and suppressed a grin when Odo echoed her gesture on the draping he'd disturbed on the console. "Then go ahead, Chief. Minimum burst, though—I don't want—"

Movement shimmered across the still-active viewscreen, and she felt a momentary sting of anger at the thought that O'Brien had opened fire without waiting for her command. Then her brain registered that there'd been no streak of phaser light even as she ducked around the pilot's chair to relocate the newly arrived fragment. The single hard spark of light was gone, replaced by a glittering cloud that drifted away from itself like puff-flower seeds when shattered by a single quick breath. What once was one was now many, and dissipating rapidly.

Kira didn't even get a chance to question O'Brien before his voice volunteered, "So much for weapons practice. It broke up."

"Broke up?" Odo parroted. He frowned a question at Kira that she wasn't sure how to answer while O'Brien confirmed, "Broke up. We've got about ten dozen pieces floating out there right now, none of them bigger than three meters across." Easily small enough to be handled by the screens on any sublight shipping vessel Bajor put out.

The constable didn't look particularly enheartened as he watched the last of the cloud evaporate. "It's deep space on the other side of the wormhole," Kira explained, personally just as glad not to have one more thing to worry about. "The methane ice probably sublimated in the solar wind from Bajor's sun, and it didn't have enough left to hold it together." She reached between the seats to clap him on the shoulder. "It happens all the time."

Odo's face thinned the way it sometimes did when he let his attention get absorbed in something outside himself. "Then why is the wormhole doing that?"

She followed his gaze to where a faint, amber corona misted the void right where the mouth of the wormhole cast its brilliant whirlpool when it appeared. The rippling haze looked like gold dust, floated on a celestial pool.

Pushing aside a corner of the material cloaking the panel,

she woke up the science station and made a brief query back to the Ops computer and its adjacent sensor array. Even if the runabout's sensors were on-line, they couldn't have told her anything from inside the docking pad. What the Ops sensors told her was as elegantly unromantic as all of science's purported truths. "Minor fluctuations in the subspace membrane." She flashed Odo what was meant to be a reassuring smile as she shut down the panel again. "Probably didn't like the taste of that asteroid fragment. It'll settle down in an hour or two, you'll see."

Odo only grunted, his eyes darkened with suspicion even as he let Kira turn him away from the viewscreen and lead him out of the runabout. "Constable," she sighed, "we've got Sisko gone for who knows how many days while the Bajoran Resistance builds a bomb right under our noses, and you're worried about an asteroid fragment that destroyed itself when it entered the star system." She shook her head and switched off the bay's lights. "All of our problems should be so simple."

CHAPTER 2

THE ADVANTAGE OF having several lifetimes of experience to draw on, Jadzia Dax often thought, was that there wasn't much left in the universe that could surprise you. The disadvantage was that you no longer remembered how to cope with surprise. In particular, she'd forgotten the sensation of facing a reality so improbable that logic insisted it could not exist while all your senses told you it did.

Like finding out that the mechanical death throes you had just seen were those of your very own starship.

"Thank you, Captain Sisko," Admiral Hayman said. "That confirms what we suspected."

"But how can it?" Dax straightened to frown at the older woman. "Admiral, if these records are real and not computer constructs—then they must have somehow come from our future!"

"Or from an alternate reality," Sisko pointed out. He swung the chair of his data station around with the kind of controlled force he usually reserved for the command chair of the *Defiant*. "Just where in space were these transmissions picked up, Admiral?"

Hayman's mouth quirked, an expression Jadzia found unreadable but which Curzon's memories interpreted as rueful. "They weren't—at least not as transmissions. What you're seeing there, Captain, are—"

"—actual records."

It took Dax a moment to realize that those unexpected words had been spoken by Julian Bashir. The elegant human accent was unmistakably his, but the grim tone was not.

"What are you talking about, Doctor?" Sisko demanded.

"These are actual records, taken directly from the *Defiant*." From here, all Dax could see of him was the intent curve of his head and neck as he leaned over his data station. "Medical logs in my own style, made for my own personal use. There's no reason to transmit medical data in this form."

The unfamiliar numbness of surprise was fading at last, and Dax found it replaced by an equally strong curiosity. She skirted the table to join him. "What kind of medical data is it, Julian?"

He threw her a startled upward glance, almost as if he'd forgotten she was there, then scrambled out of his chair to face her. "Confidential patient records," he said, blocking her view of the screen. "I don't think you should see them."

The Dax symbiont might have accepted that explanation, but Jadzia knew the young human doctor too well. The troubled expression on his face wasn't put there by professional ethics. "Are they my records?" she asked, then patted his arm when he winced. "I expected you to find them, Julian. If this was our *Defiant*, then we were probably all on it when it was—I mean, when it *will be*—destroyed."

"What I don't understand," Sisko said with crisp impatience, "is how we can have actual records preserved from an event that hasn't happened yet."

Admiral Hayman snorted. "No one understands that, Captain Sisko—which is why Starfleet Command thought this might be an elaborate forgery." Her piercing gaze slid to Bashir. "Doctor, are you convinced that the man who wrote those medical logs was a *future* you? They're not pastiches put together from bits and pieces of your old records, in order to fool us?"

Bashir shook his head, vehemently. "What these medical logs say that I did—no past records of mine could have been altered enough to mimic that. They have to have been written by a future me." He gave Dax another distressed look. "Although it's a future I hope to hell never comes true."

"That's a wish the entire Federation is going to share, now that we know these records are genuine." Hayman thumped herself into the head chair at the conference table, and touched the control panel in front of it. One of the windows on the opposite wall obediently blanked into a viewscreen. "Let me show you why."

The screen flickered blue and then condensed into a familiar wide-screen scan of the *Defiant*'s bridge. It was the viewing angle Dax had gotten used to watching in postmission analyses, the one recorded by the official logging sensor at the back of the deck. In this frozen still picture, she could see the outline of Sisko's shoulders and head above the back of his chair, and the top of her own head beyond him, at the helm. The *Defiant*'s viewscreen showed darkness spattered with distant fires that looked a little too large and bright to be stars. The edges of the picture were frayed and spangled with blank blue patches, obscuring the figures at the weapons and engineering consoles. Dax thought she could just catch the flash of Kira's earring through the static.

"The record's even worse than it looks here," Hayman said bluntly. "What you're seeing is a computer reconstruction of the scattered bytes we managed to download from the sensor's memory buffer. All we've got is the five-minute run it recorded just before the bridge lost power. Any record it dumped to the main computer before that was lost."

Sisko nodded, acknowledging the warning buried in her dry words. "So we're going to see the *Defiant*'s final battle."

"That's right." Hayman tapped at her control panel again, and the conference room filled with the sound of Kira's tense voice.

"Three alien vessels coming up fast on vector oh-nine-seven. We can't outrun them." The fires on the viewscreen blossomed into the unmistakable red-orange explosions of warp cores breaching under attack. Dax tried to count them, but there were too many, scattered over too wide a sector of space to keep track of. Her stomach roiled in fierce and utter disbelief. How could so many starships be destroyed this quickly? Had all of Starfleet rallied to fight this hopeless future battle?

"They're also moving too fast to track with our quantum torpedoes." The sound of her own voice coming from the image startled her. It sounded impossibly calm to Dax under the circumstances. She saw her future self glance up at the carnage on the viewscreen, but from the back there was no way to tell what she thought of it. "Our course change didn't throw them off. They must be tracking our thermal output."

"Drop cloak." The toneless curtness of Sisko's recorded voice told Dax just how grim the situation must be. "Divert all power to shields and phasers."

The sensor image flickered blue and silent for a moment as a power surge ran through it, then returned to its normal tattered state. Now, however, there were three distinct patches of blue looming closer on the future *Defiant*'s viewscreen.

"What's that?" Bashir asked Hayman, pointing.

The admiral grunted and froze the image while she answered him. "That's the computer's way of saying it couldn't match a known image to the visual bytes it got there."

"The three alien spaceships," Dax guessed. "They're not Klingon or Romulan then."

"Or Cardassian or Jem'Hadar," Bashir added quietly.

"As far as we can tell, they don't match any known spacefaring ship design," Hayman said. "That's what worries us."

Sisko leaned both elbows on the table, frowning at the stilled image intently. "You think we're going be attacked by some unknown force from the Gamma Quadrant?"

"Or worse." The admiral cleared her throat, as if her dramatic words had embarrassed her. "You may have heard rumors about the alien invaders Captain Picard and the *Enterprise* drove off from Brundage Station. From the spectrum of the energy discharges you're going to see when the alien ships fire their phasers at you, the computer thinks there's more than a slight chance that this could be another invasion force."

Dax repressed a shiver at this casual discussion of their catastrophic future. "You think the *Defiant* is going to be destroyed in a future battle with the Furies?"

"We know they think this region of space once belonged to them," Hayman said crisply. "We know they want it back. And we know we didn't destroy their entire fleet in our last encounter, just the artificial wormhole they used to transport themselves to Furies Point. Given the *Defiant*'s posting near the Bajoran wormhole—" She broke off, waving a hand irritably at the screen. "I'm getting ahead of myself. Watch the rest of the visual log first; then I'll answer your questions." Her mouth jerked downward at one corner. "If I can."

She touched the control panel again to resume the log playback. Almost immediately, the viewscreen flashed with a blast of unusually intense phaser fire.

"Damage to forward shield generators," reported O'Brien's tense voice. "Diverting power from rear shield generators to compensate."

"Return fire!" Sisko's computer-reconstructed figure blurred as he leapt from his captain's chair and went to join Dax at the helm. "Starting evasive maneuvers, program delta!"

More flashes screamed across the viewscreen, obscuring the random jerks and wiggles the stars made during warp-speed maneuvers. The phaser fire washed the *Defiant*'s bridge in such fierce white light that the crew turned into darkly burned silhouettes. An uneasy feeling grew in Dax that she was watching ghosts rather than real people, and she began to understand Starfleet's reluctance to trust that this log was real.

"Evasive maneuvers aren't working!" Kira sounded both fierce and frustrated. "They're firing in all directions, not just at us."

"Their present course vector will take them past us in twelve seconds, point-blank range," Dax warned. "Eleven, ten, nine . . ."

"Forward shields failing!" shouted O'Brien. Behind his voice the ship echoed with the thunderous sound of vacuum breach. "We've lost sectors seventeen and twenty-one—"

"Six, five, four . . ."

"Spin the ship to get maximum coverage from rear shields," Sisko ordered curtly. *"Now!"*

"Two, one . . ."

Another hull breach thundered through the ship, this one louder and closer than before. The sensor image washed blue and silent again with another power surge. Dax held her breath, expecting the black fade of ship destruction to follow it. To her amazement, however, the blue rippled and condensed back into the familiar unbreached contours of the bridge. Emergency lights glowed at each station, making the crew look shadowy and even more unreal.

"Damage reports," Sisko ordered.

"Hull breaches in all sectors below fifteen," O'Brien said grimly. "We've lost the port nacelle, too, Captain."

"Alien ships are veering off at vector five-sixteen point nine." Kira sounded suspicious and surprised in equal measures. Her silhouette turned at the weapons console, earring glittering. "Sensors report they're still firing phasers in all directions. And for some reason, their shields appear to be failing." A distant red starburst lit the viewscreen, followed by two more. "Captain, you're not going to believe this, but it looks like they just blew up!"

Dax saw herself turn to look at Kira, and for the first time caught a dim glimpse of her own features. As far as she could tell, they looked identical to the ones she'd seen in the mirror that morning. Whatever this future was, it wasn't far away.

"Maybe our phasers caused as much damage as theirs did," she suggested hopefully. "Or more."

"I don't think so." O'Brien's voice was even grimmer now. "I've been trying to put our rear shields back on-line, but something's not right. Something's draining them from the outside." His voice scaled upward in disbelief. "Our main core power's being sucked out right through the shield generators!"

"A new kind of weapon?" Sisko demanded. "Something we can neutralize with our phasers?"

The chief engineer made a startled noise. "No, it's not an energy beam at all. It looks more like—"

At that point, with a suddenness that made Dax's stomach clench, the entire viewscreen went dead. She felt her shoulder and hand muscles tense in involuntary protest, and heard Bashir stir uncomfortably beside her. Sisko cursed beneath his breath.

"I know," Admiral Hayman said dryly. "The main circuits picked the worst possible time to give out. That's all the information we have."

"No, it's not." Julian Bashir's voice sounded bleak rather than satisfied, and Dax suspected he would rather not have had the additional information to give them. "I haven't had a chance to read the majority of these medical logs, but I have found the ones that deal with the aftermath of the battle."

Hayman's startled look at him contained a great deal more respect than it had a few moments before, Dax noticed. "There were logs that talked about the battle? No one else noticed that."

"That's because no one else knows my personal abbreviations for the names of the crew," Bashir said simply. "I scanned the records for the ones I thought might have been aboard on this trip. Of the six regular crew, Odo wasn't mentioned anywhere. I'm guessing he stayed back on *Deep Space Nine*. My records for Kira and O'Brien indicate they were lost in some kind of shipboard battle, trying to ward off an invading force. Sisko seems to have been injured then and to have died afterward, but I'm not sure exactly when. And Dax—" He stopped to clear his throat, then resumed. "According to my records, Jadzia suffered so much radiation exposure in the final struggle that she only had a few hours to live. Rather than stay aboard, she took a lifepod and created a diversion for the aliens who were attacking us. That's how the ship finally got away."

"Got away?" Sisko demanded in disbelief. "You mean some of the crew survived the battle we just saw?"

Bashir grimaced. "How do you think those medical logs got written up? I not only survived the battle, Captain, I appear to have lived for a considerable time afterward. There are several years' worth of logs here, if not more."

"Several *years?*" It was Dax's turn to sound incredulous. "You stayed on board the *Defiant* for several years after this battle, Julian? And no one came to rescue you?"

"No."

"That can't be true!" The *Defiant*'s captain vaulted from his chair, as if his churning restlessness couldn't be contained in one place any longer. "Even a totally disabled starship can emit an automatic distress call," he growled. "If no one from Starfleet was alive to respond to it, some other Federation ship should have. *Was our entire civilization destroyed?*"

"No," Hayman said soberly. "The reason's much simpler than that, and much worse. Come with me, and I'll show you."

Cold mist ghosted out at them when the fusion-bay doors opened, making Dax shiver and stop on the threshold. Beside her, she could see Sisko eye the interior with a mixture of foreboding and awe. This immense dark space held a special place in human history, Dax knew. It was the first place where interstellar fusion engines had been fired, the necessary step that eventually led to this solar system's entry into the federation of spacefaring races. She peered through the interior fog of subliming carbon dioxide and water droplets, but aside from a distant tangle of gantry lights, all she could see was the mist.

"Sorry about the condensate," Admiral Hayman said briskly. "We never bothered to seal off the walls, since we usually keep this bay at zero P and T." She palmed open a locker beside the ring doors and handed them belt jets, then launched herself into the mist-filled bay with the graceful arc of a diver. Sisko rolled into the hold with less grace but equal efficiency, followed by the slender sliver of movement that was Bashir. Dax took a deep breath and vaulted after them, feeling the familiar interior lurch of the symbiont in its pouch as their bodies adjusted to the lack of gravitational acceleration.

"This way." The delayed echo of Hayman's voice told Dax that the old fusion bay was widening as they moved farther into the mist, although she could no longer see its ice-carved sides. She fired her belt jets to follow the sound of the admiral's graveled voice, feeling the exposed freckles on her face and neck prickle with cold in the zero-Centigrade air. Three silent shadows loomed in the fog ahead of her, backlit by the approaching gantry lights. She jetted into an athletic arc calculated to bring her up beside them.

"So, Admiral, what have you—"

Her voice broke off abruptly when she saw what filled the space in front of her. The heat of the work lights had driven back the mist, making a halo of clear space around the dark object that was their focus. At first, all she saw was a huge lump of cometary ice, black-crusted over glacial-blue gleaming. Then her eye caught a skeletal feathering of old metal buried in that ice, and followed it around an oddly familiar curve until it met another, more definite sweep of metal. Beyond that lay a stubby wing, gashed through with ice-filled fractures. She took in a deep, icy breath as the realization hit her.

"That's the *Defiant*!"

"Or what's left of her." Sisko's voice rang grim echoes off the distant walls of the hold. Now that she had recognized the ship's odd angle in the ice, Dax could see that he was right. The port nacelle was sheared off entirely, and a huge torpedo-impact crater had exploded into most of the starboard hull and decking. Phaser burns streaked the *Defiant*'s flanks, and odd, unfamiliar gashes had sliced her to vacuum in several places.

She glanced across at Hayman. "Where was this found, Admiral?"

"Right here in Earth's Oort cloud," the admiral said, without taking her eyes from the half-buried starship. "A mining expedition from the Pluto LaGrangian colonies, out prospecting for water-cored comets, found it two days ago after a trial phaser blast. They recognized the Starfleet markings and called us, but it was too fragile to free with phasers out there. We had to bring it in and let the cometary matrix melt around it."

"But if it was that fragile—" Dax frowned, her scientist's brain automatically calculating metal fatigue under deep-space conditions, while her emotions kept insisting that what she was seeing was impossible. "It must have been buried inside that comet for thousands of years!"

"Almost five millennia," Hayman agreed. "According to thermal spectroscopy of the ice around it, and radiometric dating of the—er—the organic contents of the ship."

"You mean, the bodies," Bashir said, breaking his stark silence at last.

"Yes." Hayman jetted toward the far side of the ice-sheathed ship, where a brighter arc of lights was trained on the *Defiant*'s main hatch. "There's a slight discrepancy between the individual radiocarbon ages of the two survivors, apparently as a result of—"

"—differential survival times." The doctor finished the sentence so decisively that Dax suspected he'd already known that from his medical logs. She glanced at him as they followed Hayman toward the ship, puzzled by the sudden urgency in his voice. "How much of a discrepancy in ages was there? More than a hundred years?"

"No, about half that." The admiral glanced over her shoulder, the quizzical look back in her eyes. "Humans don't generally live long enough to survive each other by more than a hundred years, Doctor."

Dax heard the quick intake of Bashir's breath that told her he was startled. "Both bodies you found were human?"

"Yes." Hayman paused in front of the open hatch, blocking it with one long arm when Sisko would have jetted past her. "I'd better warn you that, aside from microsampling for radiocarbon dates, we've left the remains just as they were found in the medical bay. One was in stasis, but the other—wasn't."

"Understood." Sisko pushed past her into the dim hatchway, the cold control of his voice telling Dax how much he hated seeing the wreckage of the first ship he'd ever commanded. She let Bashir enter next, sensing the doctor's fierce impatience from the way his fingers had whitened around his tricorder. When she would have jetted after him, Hayman touched her shoulder and made her pause.

"I know your new host is a scientist, Dax. Does that mean you've already guessed what happened here?"

Dax gave the older woman a curious look. "It seems fairly self-evident, Admiral. In some future timeline, the *Defiant* is going to be destroyed in a battle so enormous that it will get thrown back in time and halfway across the galaxy. That's why no one could come to rescue Julian."

Hayman nodded, her voice deepening a little. "I just want you to know before you go in—right now, Starfleet's highest priority is to avoid entering that timeline. At all costs." She gave Dax's shoulder a final squeeze, then released her. "Remember that."

"I will." Although she managed to keep her tone as level as always, somewhere inside Dax a tendril of doubt curled from symbiont to host. Curzon's stored memories told

Jadzia that when he knew her, this silver-haired admiral had been one of Starfleet's most pragmatic and imperturbable starship captains. Any future that could put that kind of intensity into Hayman's voice wasn't one Dax wanted to think about.

Now she was going to see it.

Inside the *Defiant,* stasis generators made a trail of red lights up the main turbolift shaft, and Dax suspected the half-visible glimmer of their fields was all that kept its crumbling metal walls intact. It looked as though this part of the ship had suffered one of the hull breaches O'Brien had reported, or some even bigger explosion. The turbolift car was a collapsed cage of oxidized steel resin and ceramic planks. Dax eased herself into the open shaft above it, careful not to touch anything as she jetted upward.

"Captain?" she called up into the echoing darkness.

"On the bridge." Sisko's voice echoed oddly off the muffling silence of the stasis fields. Dax boosted herself to the top of the turbolift shaft and then angled her jets to push through the shattered lift doors. Heat lamps had been set up here to melt away the ice still engulfing the *Defiant*'s navigations and science stations. The powerful buzz of their filaments and the constant drip and sizzle of melting water filled the bridge with noise. Sisko stood alone in the midst of it, his face set in stony lines. She guessed that Bashir had headed immediately for the starship's tiny medical bay.

"It's hard to believe it's really five thousand years old," Dax said, hearing the catch in her own voice. The familiar black panels and data stations of the bridge had suffered less damage than the rest of the ship. Except for the sparkle of condensation off their dead screens, they looked as if all they needed was an influx of power to take up their jobs again. She glanced toward the ice-sheathed science station and shivered. Only two days ago, she'd helped O'Brien install a new sensor array in that console. She could still see the red gleam of its readouts beneath the ice—brand-new sensors that were now far older than her own internal symbiont.

Dax shook off the unreality of it and went to join Sisko at the command chair. Seeing the new sensor array had given her an idea. "Can you tell if there are any unfamiliar modifications on the bridge?" she asked the captain, knowing he had probably memorized the contours of his ship in a way she hadn't. "If so, they may indicate how far in our future this *Defiant* was when it got thrown back in time."

Sisko swung in a slow arc, his jets hissing. "I don't see anything unfamiliar. This could be the exact ship we left back at *Deep Space Nine*. If the Furies are going to invade, I'd guess it's going to be soon."

Hayman grunted from the doorway. "That's exactly the kind of information we needed you to give us, Captain. Now all we need to know is where and when they'll come, so we can be prepared to meet them."

"And this—this ghost from the future." Sisko reached out a hand as if to touch the *Defiant*'s dead helm, then dropped it again when it only stirred up the warning luminescence of a stasis field. "You think this can somehow help us find out—"

The chirp of his comm badge interrupted him. "Bashir to Sisko."

The captain frowned and palmed his badge. "Sisko here. Have you identified the bodies, Doctor?"

"Yes, sir." There was a decidedly odd note in Bashir's voice, Dax thought. Of course, it couldn't be easy examining your own corpse, or those of your closest friends. "The one in the ship's morgue sustained severe trauma before it hit stasis, but it's still recognizable as yours. There wasn't much left of the other, but based on preliminary genetic analysis of some bone fragments, I'll hazard a guess that it used to be me." Dax heard the sound of a slightly unsteady breath. "There's something else down here, Captain. Something I think you and—and Jadzia ought to see."

She exchanged speculative looks with Sisko. For all his youth, there wasn't much that could shatter Julian Bashir's composure when it came to medical matters. "We're on our way," the captain told him. "Sisko out."

Diving back into the shattered darkness of the main turbolift, with the strong lights of the bridge now behind her, Dax could see what she'd missed on the way up—the pale, distant quiver of emergency lights from the *Defiant*'s tiny sickbay on the next deck down. She frowned and followed Sisko down the clammy service corridor toward it.

"Is the ship's original power still on down here?" she demanded incredulously.

From the darkness behind her, she could hear Hayman snort. "Thanks to the size of the warp core on this overpowered attack ship of yours, yes. With all the other systems shut down except for life-support, the power drain was reduced to a trickle. Our engineers think the lights and equipment in here could have run for another thousand years." She drifted to a gentle stop beside Dax and Sisko in the doorway of the tiny medical bay. "A tribute to Starfleet engineering. And to you too, apparently, Doctor Bashir."

The young physician looked up with a start from where he leaned over one of his two sickbay stasis units, as if he'd already forgotten that he'd summoned them here. The glow of thin green emergency lighting showed Dax the unaccustomed mixture of helplessness and self-reproach on his face.

"Right now, I'm not sure that's anything to be proud of," he said, sounding almost angry. His gesture indicated the stasis unit below him, which Dax now saw had been remodeled into an odd mass of pumps and power generators topped with a glass box. A fierce shiver of apprehension climbed up the freckles on her spine and made her head ache. "Why haven't you people done anything about this?"

Admiral Hayman's steady glance traveled from him to Dax, and then back again. "Because we were waiting for you."

That was all the confirmation Dax needed. She pushed past Sisko, and was startled to find herself dropped abruptly to the floor when the sickbay's artificial gravity caught her. Just a little under one Earth standard, she guessed from the feel of it—she felt oddly light and off-balance as she joined Bashir on the other side of that carefully remodeled medical station.

"Julian, is it . . . ?"

His clear brown eyes met hers across the misted top of the box. "I'm afraid so," he said softly, and moved his hand. Below where the warmth of his skin had penetrated the stasis-fogged glass, the mist had cleared a little. It was enough to show Dax what Bashir had already seen—the unmistakable gray-white mass of a naked Trill symbiont, immersed in brine that held a frozen glitter of bioelectric activity.

She had to take a deep breath before she located her voice, but this time her symbiont's long years of experience stood her in good stead. "Well," she said slowly, gazing down at the part of herself that was now immeasurably older. "Now I know why I'm here."

CHAPTER 3

YR1, DY6, 2340
Patient immobile + unresponsive. Limited contact + manipulation of subject due to fragile physical state and possible radiation damage, no invasive px/tx until vitals, Tokal-Benar's stabilize. Fluid isoboramine values <47%, biospectral scan=cortical activity < prev. observed norm, ion concentration still unstable. (see lab/chem results, atta) No waste products yet; adjusted nutrient mix +10% in hopes of improving uptake. Am beginning to fear I can't really keep it alive after all.

Staring down into the milky shadows of the suspension tank, Julian Bashir blinked away the image of those old medical records and trailed a hand across the invisible barrier separating the two realities. The stasis field pricked at his palm like a swarm of sleepy bees. "I guess I was wrong."

"Does that mean you don't think it's still alive?"

Bashir jerked his head up, embarrassment at being overheard smothering under a flush of guilt as soon as the meaning of Hayman's words sank in. He pulled his hand away from the forcefield, then ended up clenching it at his side when he could find nothing else to do with it. "No, I'm fairly certain it's still living." At least, that was what the readouts frozen beneath the stasis field's glow seemed to indicate. "It was alive when the field was activated five thousand years ago, at any rate. I can't tell anything else about its condition without examining it in real time." Although the thought of holding the orphaned symbiont in his hands made his throat hurt.

Across the table from him, Hayman folded her arms and frowned down at the shimmering box. The watery green of the emergency lights turned her eyes an emotionless bronze, and painted her hair with neon streaks where there should have been silver. "Assuming it's in fairly stable condition, what equipment would you need to transfer this symbiont into a Trill host?"

The question struck him like a blow to the stomach. "You can't be serious!" But he knew she was, knew it the very moment she asked. "Admiral, you can't just change Trill symbionts the way you would a pair of socks! There are enormous risks unless very specific compatibility requirements are met—"

"What risks?" Hayman freed one hand to wave at Dax, standing silently beside her. "It's the same symbiont she has inside her right now!"

It occurred to Bashir, not for the first time, that he didn't like this woman very much. He couldn't imagine what Curzon Dax had ever seen in her. "It's a genetically identical symbiont that is *five thousand years* out of balance with Jadzia! For all we know, the physiological similarities between the two Daxes could make it even harder for Jadzia to adjust to the psychological differences." Dax herself had withdrawn from the discussion almost from the beginning. She'd turned her attention instead toward the naked symbiont in its stasis-blurred coffin, and Bashir wondered which of her many personalities was responsible for the eerie blend of affection and grief he could read in her expression. He wished he could make Hayman understand the implications of toying with a creature that was truly legion. "These are *lives* we're talking about, Admiral, not inconveniences. Any one of the three could die if we attempt what you're suggesting."

Hayman glared at him with that chill superiority Bashir had learned to recognize as a line officer's way of saying that doctors only earned their MDs because they hadn't the stomach for regular military. "If we don't find out who carved up the *Defiant* and pitched her back into prehistory," she told him coldly, "millions of people could die."

He clenched his jaw, but said nothing. *That's the difference between us,* he thought with sudden clarity. As regular Starfleet, Hayman had the luxury of viewing sentient lives in terms of numbers and abstractions—saving one million mattered more than saving one, and whoever ended the war with the most survivors won. As a doctor, he had only the patient, and even a million patients came down to a single patient, handled over and over again. No amount of arithmetic comparison could make him disregard that duty. And thank God for that.

Hayman made a little noise of annoyance at his silence, and shifted her weight to a more threatening stance. "Do I have to make this an order, Dr. Bashir?"

He lifted his chin defiantly. "As the senior medical officer present, sir, Starfleet regulations allow me to countermand any order you give that I feel is not in the best interests of my patient." He flicked a stiff nod at the stasis chamber. "This is one of those orders."

Surprise and anger flashed scarlet across her cheeks. For one certain, anguished moment, Bashir saw himself slammed into a Starfleet brig for insubordination while Hayman did whatever she damn well pleased with the symbiont. It wasn't how he wanted things to go, but it also wasn't the first time that a clear vision of the consequences came several seconds behind his words. He opened his mouth to recant them—at least in part—just as the admiral turned to scowl at Sisko. "Captain, would you like to speak with your doctor?"

The captain lifted his eyebrows in deceptively mild inquiry. "Why?" He moved a few steps away from the second examining bed, the one that held the delicate tumble of bones that Bashir had scrupulously not dealt with after identifying whose they were. "He seems to be doing just fine to me."

Hayman blew an exasperated breath, and her frustration froze into a cloud of vapor on the air. Like dragon's breath. "Do I have to remind you people that you were brought here so Starfleet could help you avert your own deaths?"

"Not if it means treating Jadzia or either of the Daxes as a sacrifice," Bashir insisted.

Dax stirred at the foot of the examining table. "May I say something?"

Bashir kept his eyes locked on Hayman's, refusing the admiral even that small retreat. "Please do."

"Julian, I appreciate your concern for my welfare, and for everything you must have gone through to keep the symbiont alive all this time . . ." Dax reached out to spread her cool hand over his, and Bashir realized with a start that he'd slipped his hand onto the stasis field again. "But I don't think this is really your decision to make."

He felt his heart seize into a fist. "Jadzia—"

"Dax." She joggled his wrist gently as though trying to gain his attention. "I'm *Dax,* Julian. *This*—" She patted his hand on the top of the tank, and he looked where she wanted despite himself. *"This* is Dax, too." The pale gray blur was nestled in its bed of liquid like a just-formed infant in its mother's womb. "I trust you enough to be certain you didn't do this as some sort of academic exercise. Preserving the symbiont must have been something you knew for a fact that I wanted—that *Dax* wanted. And the only reason I can think of that I'd be willing to live in a tank like this for so many hundreds of years is the chance to warn us about what happened—to prevent it in any way I can."

Sisko came across the room, stopping behind Dax as though wanting to take her by the shoulders even though he didn't reach out. "We don't know that for certain, old man. And if we lose both you *and* the symbionts testing out a theory . . ." His voice trailed off, and Bashir found he wasn't reassured to know that Sisko was just afraid of failure as he was.

"We're only talking about a temporary exchange," Dax persisted. "Julian has obviously managed to re-create a symbiont breeding pool well enough to sustain my current symbiont for the hour or two we'll need."

But being correct about the time frame didn't mean she was correct about the procedure. "There's still the psychological aspect," Bashir said softly. "We don't know what the isolation has done to the symbiont's mental stability." His hand stiffened unwillingly on the top of the tank. "Or what that might do to yours."

Dax caught up his gaze with hers, the barest hint of a shared secret coloring her smile as she took his arms to hold him square in front of her, like a mother reassuring her child. "I know for a fact that even six months of exposure to mental instability can't destroy a Trill with seven lifetimes of good foundation. Six hours with some other aspect of myself isn't going to unhinge me." She let her smile widen, and it did nothing to calm the churning in his stomach. "You'll see."

"If you're not willing to perform the procedure, Doctor, I'm sure there are other physicians aboard this starbase who will."

Anger flared in him as though Hayman had thrown gasoline across a spark. Dax's hands tightened on his elbows, startling him into silence as she whirled to snap, "Judith, don't! I won't have him blackmailed into doing this."

The admiral's eyes widened, more surprised than irritated by the outburst, but she crossed her arms without commenting. A more insecure gesture than before, Bashir noticed. He was secretly glad. He didn't like being the only one unsure of himself at a time like this.

"What if there were some other way?" he asked Dax. She opened her mouth to answer, and he pushed on quickly, "Symbionts can communicate with one another without sharing a host, can't they? When they're in the breeding pools back on Trill—when you're in the breeding pools with them?"

The thought had apparently never occurred to her. One elegant eyebrow lifted, and Dax's focus shifted to somewhere invisible while she considered. "It doesn't transfer all the symbiont's knowledge the way a joining does," she acknowledged after a moment, "but, yes, direct communication is possible."

A little pulse of hope pushed at his heart. "And in a true joining, Jadzia wouldn't retain any of the symbiont's memories, anyway, once the symbiont was removed."

Dax nodded thoughtfully. "That's true."

"So what harm is there in trying this first?"

"Trying what first?" Hayman's confidence must not have been too badly damaged, because the impatient edge to her voice returned easily enough. "What are you two talking about?"

Bashir looked over Dax's shoulder at the admiral, schooling the dislike from his voice in an effort to sound more professional. "When they aren't inside a host, Trill symbionts use electrochemical signals to communicate with one another through the liquid they live in. Even a hosted symbiont can make contact with the others, if its host is first submerged in the fluid pool." He glanced aside at the tank while his thoughts raced a dozen steps ahead. "If we can replicate the nutrient mixture that's been supporting the symbiont, and fill a large enough receptacle, I think the Daxes should be able to . . ." He hesitated slightly, then fell back on the easiest word. ". . . talk to each other without having to remove Jadzia's current symbiont."

Hayman chewed the inside of her lip. "We could question this unhosted symbiont that way? It could talk to us through Dax?"

"Through Jadzia," Bashir corrected automatically, then felt heat flash into his cheeks at Hayman's reproving scowl. "Yes, we could."

"Julian's right." Dax saved him from the rest of the admiral's disapproval. "I think this will work."

"And if it doesn't work?" Hayman fixed Bashir with a suspicious glare, as if expecting him to lie to her. "What are our chances of losing the symbiont?"

"I don't know," he admitted. He wished the truth weren't so unhelpful. "I don't know how fragile it is, how much radiation damage it may have sustained back then. It may not live beyond removal of the stasis field, and I don't know what effect physically moving it from one tank to another might have." He looked into Dax's eyes so that she could see he was being absolutely honest, as a doctor and as her friend. "I do know it will be less traumatic than trying to accomplish a joining under these conditions."

Dax nodded her understanding with a little smile, then squeezed his arms once before releasing him to fold her own hands behind her back. "I think this will be our best option."

"All right, then." Hayman flashed Bashir an appreciative grin, all his sins just that quickly forgiven now that she had what she wanted. Bashir wondered if that was supposed to make him feel as guilty as it did. "Let's give this a try. Lieutenant—" She gathered both Dax and Sisko to her side with a wave of one hand. "—you and the captain can tell me how much fluid and what size tank we'll need, then help me get it all down here. Doctor, wake up the symbiont." She leaned across the tank to clap him manfully on the shoulder, and Bashir found he didn't like the contact. "Looks like it's time to finish what you started."

"Oh, this is so exciting! My brother has snoopers installed all over his bar, but this is the first time I've ever had a chance to see *legal* surveillance equipment!"

Ferengi. In the last few days, Kira had come to realize that the Prophets had obviously chosen to punish her for all past sins by stranding her on board a space station stuffed to bursting with obsequious Ferengi. It was the only explanation that sat right with her sense of justice, because she just couldn't bear the thought that she'd ended up here by random chance, with no hope of ever changing or avoiding this destiny.

Still, as she stared down into Rom's flat face with its vapid, snaggletoothed grin, all she could think was that she'd never in all her life done anything bad enough to deserve this.

"Move along, Rom," O'Brien suggested from where he lay twisted onto one hip inside the open panel. "The major and I have got work to do."

She was impressed by the chief's casual brush-off, as though they weren't doing anything more unusual than patching a leaky data conduit. She'd almost have thought he'd spent his years in the Resistance, too. Although maybe Starfleet wasn't all that different. It would have been a nearly perfect dodge if Rom possessed any ability to pick up on tone of voice or other such social cues.

"That's an EM snooper, isn't it?" He clutched his little tool kit excitedly against his stomach, squatting to cock his head into O'Brien's workspace. "Who are you monitoring?

Is it on this deck?" Eager grinning gave way to a stunted, breathless laugh. "I guess it would have to be—you'll never home in on a power source from more than a few hundred meters away with that thing."

O'Brien endangered his status as de facto Resistance by angling a questioning look up at Kira. She shrugged behind Rom's back, then spun away from the chief's pursed lips to pace an irritable circle.

She could probably just chase Rom away with threats of physical violence, but that wouldn't do much to preserve their cover as a routine maintenance team. He'd probably go sniveling back to Quark about how Kira was so rude she wouldn't even let him talk to O'Brien about spy devices, and that would land a genuinely intelligent Ferengi on Kira's tail—the last thing she needed. How could something that was supposed to be so simple and discreet swell so rapidly into a quasar-sized pain in the butt?

It had been Kira's idea. She could be honest about that, because she still thought it was a pretty good one. Accepting the assumption that there were militia members on the station trying to construct a plasma device, they sure as hell couldn't be using the station replicators to make their parts. If nothing else, the standard station replicators had governors preventing the manufacture of certain items—like detonators and targeting devices—which meant the militia must have brought their own replicator with them, one that had already had its governing circuits chopped out. Her first thought had been to search for an off-grid power source with the station's sensors. O'Brien, however, had pointed out quite patiently that a scan of that magnitude would probably register on even the cheapest black-market protection box. The militia would have to wonder why Starfleet was scanning its own station. A discussion on what *wouldn't* register had finally led to the palm-sized device O'Brien was struggling so valiantly to install—a hypersensitive sensor shunt that would tingle at the first sign of a nonsystem power flux, letting Kira monitor any off-grid replicator activity from the privacy of Sisko's office. It had seemed like such a perfectly elegant solution by which to locate their would-be terrorists.

At least, right up until Rom came along.

"So can I guess what level EM field you're scanning for?" The Ferengi snorted with an almost endearing humility, admitting, "I may not have good lobes for business, but I've always been good at guessing games."

"Rom . . ." Kira reached down to haul him to his full dwarfish height. "Has it occurred to you that surveillance implies a certain amount of discretion?"

He seemed shocked that she felt the need to remind him. "I won't tell anyone!"

"If we stand here having this discussion much longer, there won't be many people on the station who don't already know!" His shoulders felt thin and without padding, as though stingy Ferengi couldn't tolerate surplus even in regards to the muscles of their own bodies. Kira resisted gripping him too tightly for fear she'd dent his narrow bones. "This is classified Starfleet business, Rom. I could have Odo lock you up until this is all over if I decide you're too much of a security risk. Do you understand?"

Mouth shut, one crooked tooth peeking out past petulant lips, Rom nodded mutely.

"Good. Now go back to work, and don't breathe a *word* of this to Quark unless you want to spend the rest of your fertile years in a jail cell."

"But—"

Kira clapped her hand over his mouth; the skin felt leathery and cool. "Not. A. Word."

The grumble of unhappiness he breathed against her hand almost made her feel sorry for depriving him of what had to be one of his few honest pleasures. It couldn't be easy living under Quark's shadow. Fidgeting as though no longer certain what he was supposed to do with his time, Rom hugged his tool kit even tighter and stepped over O'Brien to scurry back toward the Promenade.

Then he paused, shuffled in nervous indecision, and turned around to scuttle past them again on his way back into the habitat ring.

Kira turned to watch him disappear around the bend. "Rom!"

His lumpy, bat-eared head popped back into view.

"The bar's that way," she said with a jerk of her thumb.

He grinned, nodded, looked abruptly serious again as he pointed back around the corner behind him. "But the job I'm supposed to be doing is that way."

Kira frowned. "That way is the guest quarters."

"I know." He danced forward a few steps, caught up in his own enthusiasm. "I've been doing repair work for guests on the side so that I can send extra money to Nog. He likes to go out with his hu-man friends when he isn't in engineering classes." A look of startled realization cringed across his wrinkled face, and he pleaded suddenly, "But don't tell my brother! If he knew I was using my job at the bar to meet customers, he'd insist on taking half my profit!"

O'Brien pushed himself out of the panel he'd been patiently bugging. "I'm not sure you ought to be doing that."

"It's completely ethical," Rom objected. Then he bobbed uncertainly from foot to foot, grumbling. "Basically. Sort of. Don't hu-mans have a Rule of Acquisition that says 'What your brother doesn't know, he can't keep'?"

"I mean fixing the equipment." O'Brien stooped to lift the access cover back into place, tossing Kira a smooth, expressionless nod as he spoke to Rom. "You're not licensed to do repairs on Starfleet machinery, and I'm not keen on having to follow behind whatever it is you do."

Rom brightened and waved the chief's concerns aside. "Oh, I don't touch the Starfleet equipment. Just the things people bring with them. Data-conversion cubicles, holoplates, portable replicators, gum massagers—"

"Replicators?" The word snapped at Kira's attention like an electric shock. "Somebody on the station brought their own replicator?"

Rom nodded dramatically. "And I don't know *what* they've been making with it, but I've been up here to fix it four times!"

Catching hold of his elbow, Kira shook him impatiently before he could lapse into vivid descriptions of his work. "Can you show us where it is?"

To her surprise, Rom squinted with as much cunning as she'd ever seen him attempt to display, and asked, "Will you show me how your sensing equipment works if I do?"

There was some of Quark's bloodline in there after all.

"Yes," Kira growled, "I'll show you the equipment. Now, where's this portable replicator?"

With the resilience of a springball, he bounced back to cheerfulness and waved for them to follow. "They're very good customers," he explained in a confidential whisper, as though this might help excuse whatever it was they turned out to be doing. "So please try not to look too shocked when you see how they keep their quarters. I never want to offend them, since they pay in cash and all, but I don't understand how Bajorans could live in a place like that. It looks like a bomb went off in there!"

Kira had been thinking a lot about bombs of late, and one look at the cluttered, disarranged stateroom only brought her fears more sharply into focus. Although not for the reasons Rom would credit her for, she was sure.

It was the clothes, more than anything else. The room's inhabitants had shoved everything about—a table over here, the bed lifted up against the wall, the chairs impatiently stacked out of the way in one corner—but nothing was broken, nothing blasted apart into splinters too tiny to see. It was the random, wandering piles of clothes that looked as though they'd just dropped off the people wherever they happened to stand that burned through Kira's conscious thoughts and dragged her back through the decades to when she'd camped with her resistance cell on the edge of Veska Province.

She'd been very young then, not even twenty. Her cell's leader, Shakaar, had volunteered them to help clean up what was left of a farm community after another group of so-called freedom fighters accidentally detonated a fusion bomb in the valley nearby. There hadn't been much left worth salvaging—buildings and trees and fences all lay pushed flat to the ground, as though toppled over by a violent wind; even the blackened ground still felt hot through the soles of her borrowed radiation suit. When they came across bodies, they were blistered and mummy-dry, but it was their nakedness that gnawed at Kira with its insensibility.

"What did they do?" she remembered demanding with

youthful indignation. "Blow up the place, then come through and loot them for their clothes?"

The look of surprised sympathy on Shakaar's face had made her feel immediately foolish and ignorant for having asked. "Nobody looted anything," he said sorrowfully. "The ones who were building this bomb didn't even leave bodies." His eyes lingered painfully on the spread-eagled body of what might have once been a woman, her head burned all bald and shiny. "It was the force of the blast that blew their clothes off. Seams on clothing aren't as strong as skin and bone."

But then where had all the clothing *gone*?

It was an image that had haunted Kira for months after the horrible event, filling her with an aversion to radiation suits that she knew was stupid, but which she'd never been able to completely overcome. The hiss of the air pumps and the inside staleness of breathing her own sweat always took her back to that woman on the street and the maddening question of what had happened to her clothes.

The hardsuit walk this morning had been bad enough. Following it up with Odo's revelation that someone on board the station might be planning to build a plasma bomb had reawakened those old memories with a clarity that nearly made her sick. She almost dreaded going back to her quarters tonight; she had a feeling she wouldn't get much sleeping done.

The clack of O'Brien's fingers on the keyboard of a data terminal drew her back into the moment, and she was shamefully glad for the distraction. Off to one side, Rom wandered nervously around the carnage as though it really were radioactive, picking up things in no discernible order, sorting the pieces into illogical piles in a pointless Ferengi attempt to be helpful. Kira left him to his scavenging to stand beside O'Brien at the terminal. "What have you got?"

"Nothing," he grumped in brusque frustration. He tapped the side of the terminal, where a tangle of technical patchwork marred the casing before bleeding over into the wall. "They used a security bypass to override the lockouts and access the main computer. I thought maybe I could backtrack their work and figure out what they'd been looking at, but they wiped the volatile buffer when they were finished."

A ridiculously haughty snort made Kira turn, and Rom took her shift of attention as some sort of invitation to stump through the piles of litter and join them. "You Bajorans!" he muttered with a shake of his head. "You never listen! I *told* them they'd have to disconnect the bypass, *then* wipe the volatile buffer." He squinted critically at the bypass, clucking with disapproval. "Otherwise, the backwash from the buffer imprints the last few megs of its memory onto the bypass circuit."

Kira fisted her hands behind her back to keep from dragging Rom away by one giant ear as O'Brien leaned around to start disconnecting the bypass. "Anything else about this group you want to tell us?" she asked.

"Uh . . ." Rom's face went slack with thought. "They're irritable about people being in their room when they're not here?"

That sort of went without saying.

"Major . . . ?"

Pushing Rom behind her, Kira moved should-to-shoulder with O'Brien in the hopes she might be able to block at least part of the Ferengi's view with her own body. The chief had patched the bypass through his engineering tricorder, and the little screen now flickered and rolled with the reflection of whatever had last passed through the data terminal. The grim set of the human's jaw told her he wasn't happy with what he'd seen. Taking it from him, Kira turned the little device to face her, and watched a moving schematic of the station tumble by in fading blue and white.

The view stopped, backed up, and froze on a close-up of the station's underbelly. A hand-scrawled circle looped into being around the station's lowermost reactor bays, and the words "Dro—Good location if we want a chain explosion" appeared beside the circle as though penciled in by a ghost.

"Oh, my god . . . !" She lifted her head to meet O'Brien's stark, unhappy eyes. "They're not building it for export," she whispered. "They're planning on using the bomb right here."

CHAPTER 4

REVIVING THE SYMBIONT took longer than replicating the nutrient bath. Bashir crawled under and around every inch of the modified examining bed, tracing circuits, studying connections, wishing he could reach the workings still locked inside the stasis field. He wanted to be sure of what the symbiont's tank was designed to do, wanted to have some vague idea what would happen when he touched *this* switch, irised *that* valve—wanted, more than anything, to reconstruct whatever he was thinking back when this seemed like a good idea five thousand years ago.

They'd hauled in two banks of brilliant floodlights, and suspended them from opposite walls near the ceiling so that they burned every trace of shadows away. The ambient temperature in the medical bay responded by creeping up a handful of degrees. Hands and fingers still felt thin and cold, but words no longer smoked when people talked. It somehow made the room feel even smaller and more fragile than before.

While Sisko guided a grav sled of spun siding into one corner of the tiny bay, Bashir slipped his arm behind the bed's main diagnostic panel and verified that it wasn't included in the stasis field—but it had been deactivated by the simple expedient of a laser scalpel through its primary data conduit. His future/past self must have deemed the power drain not worth leaving the symbiont a panel display it couldn't even read. His current self was forced to agree.

As the first vial of the symbiont's support medium was passed through a tricorder to determine its suitability, he finally realized that what he'd taken as a fluid-drainage shunt was actually part of the coolant system for the tank. The CV pump soldered to the bottom of the table must be how he'd kept the N_2 up to pressure, although he couldn't figure out how it had been tied into the power grid. What could he possibly have planned to use as a replacement if one of those fragile tubes had ruptured?

When Dax finally arrived in an embarrassingly brief hospital gown to confer with Hayman and Sisko, Bashir had just noticed that the symbiont's transparent tank had been built from a single large sheet of hull-grade aluminum. The fourteen-digit part code that had been stamped across its middle was now divided into snippets of three and four, reflecting and re-reflecting each other from all six sides of the container. The last two numbers stared back at Bashir from the bottom of the tank, turned upside down and backward under ninety liters of cloudy fluid. He obviously hadn't thought about the positioning when he fitted that piece into place. He wished he had. Staring at those switched-around numbers every day for more than half a century must have driven him crazy.

"Julian?"

Turning his back on the tank was a little harder than he expected. He clenched the engineering probe he'd been using a bit more tightly in his fist, and tried on a smile for Dax's behalf. Judging from the softening of her already gentle expression, the attempt failed miserably.

"I'm ready whenever you are," she said, patting his arm in reassurance.

He hadn't even heard them fill the pool. "Let's get started, then."

Replacing the probe on the engineering cart, Bashir did his best to push his emotions as far away from him as he could. Now was a time for accuracy, not sentiment; he had a better chance of making Hayman do what he said if she thought he was speaking from the head, not the heart. Still, he'd never been very good at concealing his feelings. This was a hell of a time to have to start.

"I'd prefer to bring the patient out of stasis slowly," he said, moving toward the head of the table so that Sisko and Hayman could join them. Dax stayed close to his shoulder. He was grateful for her nearness. "Judging from my medical logs, the symbiont's condition prior to suspension wasn't good, and I'm afraid of losing it to revival shock."

Hayman scowled down at the waiting tank, drumming her fingers against her leg. "How slowly are we talking?" As though impatience didn't show clearly enough in her stance.

Bashir sighed and shook his head. "I said I'd *like* to bring it out slowly. But I apparently salvaged this stasis field from one of the morgue drawers, and it's strictly binary, either on or off." He meant to look up at Hayman, but found himself facing Dax's cool gray eyes instead. "I just want you to understand that this isn't a simple matter of switching off the field and scooping the symbiont out of the medium. We'll have to proceed very carefully."

Hayman made a face, as though planning to say something cutting, then tossed a sharp glance at Dax—and another at Bashir—before nodding with a half-muffled sigh. "I understand."

Dax answered Bashir's worried look with a smile. "Just do the best you can."

That much had never been in doubt.

The main switch for the stasis field was a small ceramic toggle underneath the lip of the table. When Bashir first examined the tank, he'd found an on-off capacitor patched into a data padd and epoxied to the inside of the tank. For one horrible moment he thought he'd been stupid enough to lock the only controls inside the field with the symbiont. It wasn't until he found the ceramic switch a few minutes later that he realized what he'd left inside for the symbiont: an escape hatch, a way to remove itself from the agonizing centuries of aloneness that must have crawled by between then and now. A kind of temporal euthanasia. As he fingered the switch, poised to catapult the past into the present, he only hoped the creature inside would forgive him both roles he'd played in its long interment.

"Well . . . here goes nothing."

A spark and flash of disruptive energy swept the stasis field away, and the sweet, sharp smell of five-thousand-year-old symbiont billowed out like a sigh.

Bashir had his tricorder open before the field's lingering static charge had faded. Readings leaped into life as though startled, then settled, and sank to an easy throb as they identified the symbiont's biochemistry. A slight climb in cortical activity and a sudden dump of neurotransmitter into the fluid, but otherwise remarkably stable. He breathed a silent prayer of thanks. Inside the tank, a bracelet of ripples patterned the water's surface as the symbiont shuddered, and a weak lightning bolt of energy spattered the side closest to Bashir. He pressed his palm against the tank in unconscious reply.

A thin chill ached against his palm. Bashir blinked his attention downward, suddenly aware of what he'd done. "Dax, how warm is the medium in the pool?"

Retrieving one of the engineering tricorders from the cart behind her, Dax crossed the room to scan the larger fluid bath. Bashir noticed for the first time that it steamed gently, a pale wisp of vapor skating about on its surface. "Thirty-four degrees," she reported.

Steam, he realized. That's what had misled him. A pebblework of condensation studded the underside of the stasis tank's lid, making him assume the interior was warm as well as humid. But his hand on the side registered coolness despite the chilly temperatures in the bay, and his tricorder confirmed that they'd heated the larger pool a good ten degrees warmer than they should have. "We have to bring the fluid temperature down to twenty-one degrees." Then, as another reading leveled out at a different value than he'd detected through the stasis field, "And increase the salinity by another eleven percent." He shook his head in a spasm of self-anger. "God, what was I thinking when I put this together? Why didn't I leave myself notes?"

Correctly assuming that those last two comments didn't require a response, Sisko excused himself with a nod. "I'll get the salination equipment."

Still trailing her hand in the water, Dax looked up at Bashir with a frown. "Julian, the breeding pools on Trill are warmer than this."

Bashir nodded distractedly, keying another request into his tricorder. "But the tank isn't. I don't want to shock the symbiont's system by raising its body temperature too rapidly." Satisfied that the pumps could handle a brief loss of humidity, he felt along the seam between lid and sides for an opening.

"I have to get in this pool, too," Dax grumbled. But she stood to help Sisko lower the salinating infuser into the fluid without questioning the doctor's decision.

Hayman, on the other hand, snorted as Bashir fitted a finger under the edge of the lid and pried it upward. "That tub has almost two thousand cubic liters of liquid in it," she pointed out. "Do you really expect me to wait another twenty-four hours while it cools ten degrees?"

Bashir bit back the first angry words that came to mind and handed Hayman the lid as he eased it out of its fittings. "How you do it is not really my concern," he said stiffly. "I'm telling you that *not* doing it could endanger my patient, and end your precious interrogation before it starts." He snatched a pair of surgical gloves from the kit beside him, pointedly not shying from her distrustful glare. "This is not negotiable, Admiral. If you want me to be your medical officer, you have to do as I say."

Whatever emotion flashed through her pale eyes never really made it to her face, and Dax's hand on her shoulder halted any words before they formed. "Come on, Judith." The Trill cast Bashir a half-amused, half-reproving glance. "I'm sure there must be superconducting coil around here somewhere. We'll work something out."

Hayman startled the doctor with a quick, cryptic smile, then let Dax lead her away toward the exit. Bashir watched them until they disappeared into the unpowered areas of the ship, telling himself he wasn't jealous.

"Antagonizing a Starfleet admiral isn't what most people would consider a wise career move, Doctor."

Bashir shot a quick look toward his captain, surprised to find him already returned to the end of the table. Sisko smiled in response to Bashir's self-conscious blush. "Eleven percent." He gestured back toward the nutrient pool behind him. "Just like the doctor ordered."

Bashir nodded, just as grateful for an excuse to turn his

attention back to business. "I'm not trying to antagonize her," he admitted uncomfortably as he snapped on the skin-hugging gloves. "I just . . ." *Don't like her attitude? Wish she showed more care about a nonhuman species? Didn't sound so willing to sacrifice both Jadzia and Dax to her imaginary time frame?* He set about tugging the gloves up over his sleeves with a great deal more attention than was really necessary. "She's obviously very used to getting what she wants."

"She's a rear admiral," Sisko said dryly. "There aren't many people in Starfleet who can say no to her."

He didn't add "except you," but Bashir heard the words anyway. He felt his face tighten in renewed embarrassment, and bent his head over the symbiont's tank to hide it.

Dax and Hayman returned only a few minutes later with a heat diffusion coil from the *Defiant*'s engine room, and Sisko went to help them wrestle it into place. Balancing his tricorder carefully on the corner of the tank, Bashir busied himself with a hands-on exam of the symbiont while the others unfolded the paper-thin heat deflectors. The fluid in the tank was eerily cold. Not so much so that he lost the feeling in his fingers, but enough to make him sympathize with Jadzia's unhappiness about being immersed in it. He slipped one hand under the symbiont without actually touching it at first, just letting himself adjust to the feel of the medium, letting the symbiont adjust to the presence of his hands. It stirred blindly at the surface of the liquid.

"It's all right . . ." Bashir whispered, wanting to comfort it but not sure what to do. "You know me, Dax, don't you?" He thought again of the bony clutter that was the extent of his organic legacy in this timeline, and smiled wryly. "We spent a lot of time together, you and I."

A snap of chemical lightning lashed out and bit at his hand.

Bashir jerked out of the tank with a startled gasp, sloshing water across the front of his uniform and splashing a milky puddle onto the floor. The symbiont sparked a few more times as it bobbed in the newly turbulent fluid, and Bashir called "It's all right—I'm fine!" before the others could do more than whirl in alarm at the commotion.

"What happened?" Dax's voice had dropped into the

deeper, more serious tone that Bashir always assumed she'd inherited from some previous host.

"Nothing," he assured her, fighting down his embarrassment with a self-deprecating smile. He lifted his hand to show her the small hole burned through his glove by the symbiont's thinking. "It—*you* are just a little more active than I expected, that's all."

Dax smiled back at him, her eyes crinkling with unexpected mischief. "Never underestimate the staying power of a Trill."

"This is a good sign?" Hayman pressed. "Right?"

Bashir peeled off the ruined glove and tossed it back into his kit. "Yes, Admiral Hayman, this is a good sign."

Armed with a fresh glove, he let the others go back to their cooling, and eased his hand back into the fluid. This time the symbiont's electrochemical tendril brushed against his wrist so lightly he couldn't even feel it through the latex.

"That's all right. . . ." It nuzzled into his palm as he came up under it, smaller than he remembered, more wrinkled. "It's my fault—I overreacted. I'm sorry if I startled you." Some odd, detached part of his brain made a mental note to log more clinical hours with Trill symbionts—on his next leave, perhaps, if the Symbiosis Commission on Trill could be convinced. He was the only Starfleet medical doctor within parsecs of *Deep Space Nine*, after all, and he owed it to the station's personnel to be as knowledgeable as possible about all their medical needs. That Jadzia Dax was the only Trill on DS9 didn't absolve him of that duty to her. Besides, he'd have to know a good deal more about unhosted symbionts than he currently did if he was going to take care of Dax for seventy years after—

No. He shook his thoughts back to the present with a scowl. Best not to dwell on that. The whole point of being here was to avoid that timeline, even if their very presence at the starbase said that so far they hadn't. His next leave, then. For no other reason than Jadzia and the present, he would visit the Trill homeworld on his very next leave.

"Twenty-one degrees, Doctor." Hayman's voice jumped suddenly louder, but this time Bashir was careful not to make any sudden moves for fear of upsetting the creature in his hands. "We're ready."

He took a deep breath that still somehow felt not quite deep enough, and lifted the symbiont from the water.

It broke surface with a dainty splash, but didn't spark or struggle. Bashir wasn't sure it could, really. From both his reading and his conversations with Jadzia, he knew that symbionts slipped into a kind of torpor once they bonded with a host, never moving again after their initial nestling for position among the internal organs. He wasn't sure how motile they became after long periods of separation.

—must get to the Trill homeworld—

But, if anything, the symbiont relaxed into his grip as though welcoming the touch. It hung more flaccid than he remembered from the one other time he'd handled it—over five thousand years in its own past—and its skin felt as though the slightest intemperate squeeze would sink fingers right into its vitals. He'd handled brain tissue that felt less fragile. Bashir crossed the tiny medical bay with his eyes on the patient every inch of the way, afraid to do more than cup his hands beneath it, afraid to jar it with the force of his footsteps, afraid the frigid air would sere its delicate tissues beyond any hope of repairing. He only knew he'd reached the pool because Sisko stretched out an arm to stop him before he could bump into the side.

"Please bring me my tricorder." His voice felt dry; he couldn't talk above a whisper. As Sisko obediently retrieved the device, Bashir eased down to one knee to lower the symbiont over the side.

The fluid felt startlingly tepid after the chilly air.

He supported its weight at first, absurdly worried that it would sink to the bottom and drown. But, of course, symbionts didn't breathe, that job being more suited to their hosts or an oxygenated liquid. Still, as Dax stepped carefully into the pool, he glanced up at her and said, "You might have to hold it near the surface. I'm not sure how well it can swim just now."

She nodded seriously, then ruined the image a moment later with a theatrical wince as she slid, chest-deep, into the bath. "Julian, I'm going to cut off your hot-water rations for a *week* for this!"

He smiled despite himself. "I guess I'll just have to shower at your place."

She flicked a handful of water at him, but he was already wet, so he didn't mind.

Dax reached out to accept the symbiont as gently as a mother would receive her newborn child. It stirred spastically at her touch, more a shiver than a movement. Bashir opened his mouth to tell Jadzia to stay still for a moment—just until the ancient Dax had adjusted to her presence—but she was already frozen, her eyes locked on the small gray creature. After a long, silent minute, Bashir gently withdrew his hands from between Jadzia's and the symbiont, and let her cradle its whole eiderdown weight. A smile as odd and fleeting as the symbiont's thoughts ghosted across her face. Bashir wondered what she was thinking as she slowly repositioned her hands, and whether or not the damaged symbiont was thinking it, too.

A crooked platter of lightning flashed across the surface of the water. It dissipated long before it reached the sides, and Bashir realized that it was feeling out its boundaries. It knew it was somewhere different from its stasis tank, but hadn't yet figured out where, or with whom. Bashir sank back on his heels and took the tricorder Sisko silently held in front of his face, quietly unfolding it just as a pale, exploratory tendril brushed against Jadzia's forearm. She twitched with a little gasp.

Bashir glanced up briefly from the first scroll of readings. "Are you all right?"

A snap of energy, strong enough to crackle the water, leapt from symbiont to host. Jadzia stiffened as coils of light flashed up her torso, flickered across her face. Bashir had to quell an urge to drag her out of the pool. Instead, he tightened his grip on his tricorder, and focused grimly on its readings as Jadzia's hands dropped slowly beneath the surface, slipping the symbiont out of sight.

Then, eyes closed and chin bowed almost to her chest, she started to cry.

"What?" Hayman took two urgent steps forward to lean on the side of the tub. "What's the matter? What's happening?"

"Nothing." At least, he hoped it was nothing. Bashir watched the values for both Jadzia and the ancient symbiont as they intersected, overshot each other, then settled fitfully into a parallel rhythm. "I think they're communicating," he said, more to Sisko than Hayman. "I . . ." The symbiont's readings veered upward for a moment, only to slowly rebound and rejoin the others. "What we're seeing is most likely Dax—*old* Dax—and not specifically Jadzia." He turned an apprehensive look up at his captain. "You should be able to talk with it. But be careful."

Sisko's easy nod said the warning was unnecessary, but it had been more for Hayman's sake, anyway.

"Jadzia?" The captain's voice was gentler than Bashir had ever thought it could be. Sisko knelt at the head of the tub as though talking with a child. "Jadzia, can you hear me?"

When her sobbing continued unabated, Bashir suggested, "Talk to Dax," and Sisko nodded again.

"Dax . . ." This time he touched her shoulder lightly. "Old man, it's Benjamin."

The eyes she opened on them seemed darker than before, glossy and opaque. Not Jadzia's eyes, but the time-cracked glass of a much older Dax, one who hadn't seen the world in far too long. When Jadzia turned her head to look around the ruined medical bay, her neck moved in uneven jerks, like a misaligned gear. Those dark doll's eyes never focused on anything. Not really.

". . . same so same and cold stay alive out the back out the first stay alive oh point nine not even that much when surviving all alive stay alive please stay alive not much longer . . ."

"She's rambling." Hayman squatted into Bashir's field of vision on the other side of the pool. "What's she saying?"

Bashir assumed she wanted something more coherent than a direct translation of the Trill's mumbled words. "Give her some time to orient herself . . . itself. . . ." The symbiont's cortical activity jittered like a fibrillating cardiogram at the sound of his voice, and the surface of the medium heaved in response to Jadzia's sudden spastic movement.

"Julian . . . ?"

Her whisper reached straight through him, chilling him to the base of his spine. "I'm here." It was all he could think of to say.

A little ghost glimmer of lightning moved beneath the surface of the fluid, and Jadzia leaned so far forward in the bath that she submerged herself nearly to the chin. ". . . It *is* . . . you . . ." Lifting one unsteady hand from the milky brine, she stopped just short of stroking his face. ". . . so beautiful . . . so *young* . . . Julian, you did it . . . !"

The new flood of tears was too much for him. "We should stop this—"

Sisko clamped a hand firmly on the doctor's shoulder, and bore down hard when Bashir tried to push himself to his feet. "As you were, Doctor."

"But, Captain—" He knew what Sisko would say: Both Dax and Jadzia knew what they were getting into, and neither one would thank Bashir if they failed to avert the temporal disaster because he got cold feet. Clenching his jaw against a new confusion of guilt and anxiety, he shrugged off Sisko's hand and fixed his attention on the tricorder in his hands. "Neurotransmitter levels are up twenty-three percent, and both Jadzia and the medium are exhibiting dangerous isoboromine imbalances."

He didn't have to detail for Sisko what those readings could mean. "We'll pull them out before rejection sets in," the captain assured him with an easy confidence Bashir couldn't share. "Don't worry."

Too late for that.

"Dax . . ." Hayman tugged at the Trill's shoulder from behind. Jadzia responded like a blind man who's heard a distant noise—by lifting her chin attentively into the air, but not moving any other part of her body in response to the admiral's summons. "Dax, it's Judith. You've got to tell us what happened to the *Defiant*. Who attacked you? Where did it happen?"

When did it happen? Bashir thought, but didn't ask. This unorthodox communion was under enough stress already. Cortical activity inside the cloudy pool crept up a stair-step of readings until it froze at a single manic value; the Dax buried inside Jadzia answered its twin only faintly, and the woman caught between them began to shiver. This time when she reached for Bashir across the fluid, he took her hand and held it tightly.

"Tell them," he whispered. *Tell them and get out of there, before we lose you all!*

"Don't go through the wormhole." She spoke the words slowly, with the same careful precision a child might use when reciting something in a language she didn't really understand. Bashir wondered how much of its incarceration the symbiont had spent memorizing this message in order to keep the words even this coherent and clear. "If we don't go through the wormhole, we won't go back in time. If we don't go through, the battle will happen without us. We won't go back in time, and they'll all stay where they were, where they are, back in time."

Hayman scowled. *"They who?"*

Dax didn't seem to hear her. "You have to stop it before it starts. This time can be different. This time I'll be there. Make sure you capture one."

Bashir felt Sisko and Hayman stir uneasily above him, both of them taking breath to ask for details, press for specifics. But he knew it was pointless—this was little more than a recording, and the playback had started. Jadzia's eyes danced across Bashir's face with frantic attentiveness. He recognized with a chill that Dax was telling this to *him*—and only him—after more than five thousand years of painful waiting. For the first time, he wondered precisely who this message was from.

"Capture one. Capture one and talk to it. All you have to do is ask!" She clutched Bashir's hand between both of hers as though desperate to make him understand. "Capture one take it alive *talk to it* . . . !"

"Take what alive?" Hayman grumbled impatiently. "One of the Furies?" Sisko shushed her with a hiss.

". . . capture one talk to it talk to what it's eaten talk to it ask it . . ."

"Jadzia, ask what?" Bashir didn't mean to get drawn into her fugue—didn't want to encourage this to go on any longer than absolutely necessary—but he couldn't turn away from the broken anguish in her plea. "I don't understand!"

". . . the first time they're too many but this time I'll be there and if I just stay alive we can just stay alive it won't be too late because there's no time—" Squeezing her eyes shut against a future-past that only her orphaned symbiont could see, Jadzia bowed her head over the tangle of their fingers, and light flashed scattershot across the surface of the pool. "—too early to leave her to keep it to wait I don't want to I can't help it I never liked the cold—!"

Bashir felt the seizure of her hands around his, and knew what had happened even before his tricorder shrilled its alarm. "Get her out of the pool!"

A single fierce convulsion jerked her upright, almost toppling her back into the fluid as Sisko lunged forward and Bashir clawed at the front of her gown to try and keep her head above water. The captain crashed into the brine, fountaining a great surge of fluid over the sides to splash against the deck. But he had her, one arm across her chest, the other cinched around her middle, heaving himself and Jadzia back over the side and away from the tank while Hayman rushed to intercept them with a too-small towel to serve as a blanket. Bashir registered only that Jadzia was in trusted hands, safe for the moment, then gulped a deep breath and plunged both arms shoulder-deep into the churning bath.

Milky brine splashed against his chest and face, stinging his eyes and making his lips taste like tears. He twisted his head to one side and tried to blink his vision clear, then gave up when some angry instinct reminded him that he couldn't see under the opaque brine anyway. In a strange sense, the sudden darkness helped. The frigid medical bay receded, Sisko's grim, calm voice and Jadzia's ragged gasping both dropping away to some point outside the range of his attention. There was only the pressure of the pool's lip beneath his rib cage, the salty wetness of the fluid soaking the sides and front of his uniform, and the thick, yeasty stench of the turbulent bath. He slid his hands about the bottom of the tank, acutely conscious of how easily he could crush the fragile occupant. Then one wrist bumped something soft and yielding—too much the same temperature as the medium in which it hid to feel entirely real to cold-clumsy human hands—and Bashir rotated awkwardly to cup the slippery mass in both palms, lifting it rapidly to the surface.

The murky liquid shattered under chaotic slashes of

lightning—a symbiont's screams. Bashir felt the electromagnetic seizure through the membrane of his gloves, a prickling itch that made his fingers twitch involuntarily against the symbiont's paper-thin sides. *Don't!* he thought desperately. *I don't want to drop you!* Immediately on the tail of that fear he heard the gentle splash of his footsteps in the puddle ringing the pool, and deliberately focused his attention on walking quickly but carefully across the bay to the empty stasis tank.

It seemed ludicrously still and small after the turmoil at the larger pool. Bashir wondered fleetingly if the symbiont noticed or cared about the size of its confinement, but thrust the thought away as he hunched over to resubmerge it in the five-thousand-year-old liquid. Visible tendrils lashed out to all sides. When he released the symbiont and whisked his hands away, it sank without a struggle, slowly, weakly. The ceramic switch on the bottom of the tank clicked loudly when Bashir slapped it with his hand, and a rainbow meniscus swept across the tank and its occupant. They froze into a silent bubble, the fluid pausing with the waves of Bashir's withdrawal splashing at the lip of the tank, the symbiont haloed by its own outcries like a lightning rod in the center of a storm.

With an almost physical jolt, Bashir's awareness leapt back to the rest of the room. He spun, reaching behind him for the tricorder he remembered leaving on the engineering cart, then flashed on the image of Sisko holding it out to him while he knelt beside the now empty pool. It was easier to find than the symbiont—it lay on the bottom right where he'd dropped it, waiting patiently for him to rush over and scoop it out on his way past. It woke to his touch with a chirp, and was already compiling a report on Jadzia's life signs when he skidded to his knees beside her.

"Ten cc's of diazradol."

A quick clatter of movement, and Sisko pressed the hypospray into Bashir's outstretched hand. Jadzia's skin felt cold and clammy as he felt out the large vein on the side of her throat, but he remembered with a flush of almost-anger that it was his own hands which were wet and chilled, so nothing they told him could be trusted. He delivered half the neurostimulant without pause, then flipped back the towel covering her torso to hike up the hem of her gown and inject the remainder directly into the symbiont's carry pouch. Almost immediately, she took a great breath, stirring groggily, and the tricorder's screen flashed through a series of reports, each glimpse more encouraging than the last. Bashir draped the towel to cover as much of his patient as possible, then sank back on his heels with an unsteady sigh. "We need real blankets, and a warmer place for her to rest until she wakes up." It wasn't until he tried to peel his hands out of his gloves that he realized he was shaking too badly to grab hold. "I'll need a gurney."

Sisko climbed to his feet without needing to be asked, and Hayman reached across Dax to catch at Bashir's wrist when the doctor leaned to retrieve another hypo from the open medikit. "Is Dax going to be okay?"

He'd learned in his first year of medical school never to say "I told you so" to a superior. But, as a result, he'd perfected the precise set of jaw and eyes to say just as much without speaking. "Her vitals have stabilized, although it's too soon to tell what effect this might have on the host-symbiont relationship. I'll know more in the morning."

An expression that was almost amusement wisped across the admiral's face, and her gray eyes flicked toward some point beyond Bashir's shoulder before she released his wrist and sat upright. "Actually, I was asking about *Dax*. The symbiont." She jerked her chin toward the stasis tank again. "Is it going to live?"

He swallowed a surge of anger, and dug once more at the cuff of his gloves. "I don't know." This time, a glove came off with a whiplike snap, and he threw it to one side before starting just as furiously on the other. "We certainly can't risk any more such experiments and expect it to survive."

She grunted unhappily, then settled into a long moment of silence. "Not right now, at least," she finally sighed. He didn't look up at her, afraid he'd see the cold indifference on her face and forget that she outranked him. "You'll let me know when you've got it stabilized and ready to thaw out again?"

"Of course, Admiral." It was easy enough to promise. By the time it became an issue, he hoped to be too far away for Hayman's orders to matter.

CHAPTER 5

LIKE ANY STARFLEET officer in a frontier quadrant, Benjamin Sisko had heard many of his comrades talk about staring death in the face. For all he knew, he might even have used the phrase himself once or twice. He'd just never expected to really do it.

There was no question that the man in the stasis drawer was him—or would be him, Sisko corrected himself grimly, if they found no way to avert this timeline. Despite the explosion that had shattered his left side and leg to stripped bone and ribboned flesh, the coffee-dark face wore the same thinly carved mustache and beard Sisko had seen in his mirror this morning. He craned his head, peering at the slate-gray collar beneath the stasis shimmer. It might have been his imagination, but he thought one of the four captain's pips shone just a little brighter than the rest. Without meaning to, he lifted a hand to his own collar.

"I've been meaning to order all new ones," he murmured.

"Sir?"

Sisko glanced over at Bashir, who'd been standing so quietly on the other side of the drawer that he'd almost forgotten he was there. To his critical eye, the young doctor looked more tired than a night's lost sleep should account for. When neither he nor Dax had shown up for breakfast with the admiral this morning, Sisko had assumed both were still sleeping after the stress of the night before. His early-morning arrival in the *Defiant*'s medical bay, however, had found the doctor still immersed in his old medical logs. Whatever he'd read there, it didn't seem to have made him any happier than he'd been the night before.

"It's nothing, Doctor." Sisko glanced back at his preserved corpse. "Have you determined an exact cause of death?"

Bashir ran his fingers through already ruffled hair, looking a little harried. "Sorry, Captain. I didn't spend much time examining you when I first came down, and after that—"

"Understood," Sisko said quietly. "But I'd like you to take a few moments now and see what you can find out. We need to know as much as we can about what happened—or will happen—to us, if we're going to prevent it."

"True." Bashir went to fetch his tricorder from the data station he'd been sitting at. He came back frowning. "In order to get a complete scan, Captain, I'm going to have to release the stasis field for a few minutes. Is that going to bother you?"

Sisko shook his head. "Not after having survived a Borg attack, Doctor. Go ahead."

Bashir reached out to toggle the stasis control on the front of the drawer. The shimmer withdrew back into its generating unit, releasing the metallic smell of blood and an even stronger smell of scorched circuits and ozone.

"It was a torpedo hit," Sisko said, before Bashir had even finished his tricorder scan. That particular combination of odors was inescapably linked to his memories of the torpedo blasts that had crippled the *Saratoga,* killing Jennifer and half the crew.

The younger man frowned at his readout. "A torpedo *explosion,*" he corrected after a moment. "According to this, the remnant radiation has the frequency you'd expect from one of the *Defiant*'s quantum torpedoes."

"So something triggered a torpedo explosion on board, and I got caught in it." Sisko forced himself to look more closely at the ruin of his left side. "No vacuum damage? This wasn't a hull breach?"

"Apparently not." Bashir frowned and tapped an inquiry into his tricorder, then scanned it across the body again. Whatever it told him made a muscle jerk in his thin face.

"Although there is evidence of partial bone oxidation and secondary trauma to the major blood vessels."

"What does that mean?"

"That you lived at least a short while after the explosion," Bashir said stiffly. "And that I didn't get you into stasis soon enough to save you." He startled Sisko by slamming the morgue stasis field back on with a great deal more force than it required. "I'm starting to wonder just why the hell I did *any* of the things I'm apparently going to do."

Sisko gazed down at his still body with slitted eyes. "If I had to guess, Doctor, I'd say that by the time this happened, we already knew, or guessed, that we'd been thrown too far back in time to be rescued. And that I needed to stay conscious long enough to get the ship to safety."

"But why?" Bashir demanded hotly. "So I could spend the next seventy years making sure Dax stayed alive long enough to go completely around the bend? It would have been better if we'd put you in stasis and lost the ship!"

"No, Julian. Then we'd have had no warning at all that this was going to happen."

Sisko swung around at the sound of that calm voice to see Jadzia Dax levering herself into the sickbay's gravity field. She looked a little pale beneath her spatter of freckles, but her stride was steady when she came to join them.

"Morning, old man," Sisko said, moving aside so she could join him beside the drawer. "How do you feel?"

"Not good enough to be up," Bashir answered before the Trill could. He had angled the tricorder toward her and was watching it with creased brows. "Jadzia, your isoboromine levels are still fluctuating too much. You should be off your feet."

Dax gave him an exasperated glance. "I can't feel any worse than you look," she retorted. "What have you been doing?"

Bashir grimaced in frustration. "Trying to track down any notes I might have made in my medical logs about what happened to us. I can't believe I wrote diary entries for seventy years and never mentioned when or how we got pitched back to prehistoric Earth." He scrubbed a hand through his dark hair again, making it even more disarranged than it already was. "Of course, I also can't believe I never bothered to make an index or catalog of my notes in all that time."

"Knowing you, Julian, you did both of those things, and then put the data chip somewhere for safekeeping," Dax said. "Of course, by the time you got around to doing that—"

"—who knows where I thought the safest place was," he agreed, grimacing again. "In any case, I've found only a few hints so far of what happened to us. It may take me a few weeks to plow through the rest of those records."

"The problem is, we may not have weeks," Sisko said grimly. He gestured at the version of himself that lay inside the stasis drawer. "Dax, how much older do I look to you there?"

She frowned down into the shimmering field. "Not much, Benjamin," she said after a moment. "In fact, I'm not sure you look older at all."

"That's what I thought. That means whatever is going to happen to us could occur anytime between tomorrow and half a year from now." Sisko rubbed a thumb across his captain's pips again, thoughtfully. "Dr. Bashir, is there any way you can narrow down that time estimate?"

"By comparing your current physiology with that of your future self?" Despite the tired lines around his eyes, the doctor hadn't lost any of his keen intelligence. "The trouble is, that will only work if you didn't make any trips through the wormhole between now and then."

"Why is that?"

"Molecular clock reset." Bashir looked up from his tricorder, a trace of his usual mischievous humor returning to his brown eyes. "Don't you remember the paper I submitted to the *Journal of Quantum Medicine* last month, about the submolecular effects of wormhole passage?"

"Uh—vaguely."

Dax gave him a reproving look. "I remember it, Julian. Didn't you conclude that particle-flux effects inside the wormhole introduce small errors into our molecular clocks?"

"Giving rise to apparent time anomalies between our biological and chronological ages," Bashir finished for her. He scanned his tricorder slowly over Sisko, then tapped in an analytical routine. His eyebrows went up abruptly. "According to the random molecular drift of your mitochondrial DNA, Captain, your future self is exactly the same age you are, within the limits of uncertainty imposed by the wormhole."

"And what are those limits, Doctor?"

"Plus or minus about a week, assuming you made at least one trip through the wormhole. Add on two or three days for each additional trip."

"Not good enough," Sisko said bluntly. "If we're going to avoid ending up here, I'll need a better estimate than that."

Bashir shrugged and slid the stasis drawer shut with a definitive clang. "You're not going to get that from medical analysis, I'm afraid."

"But we might get it from the ship's warp core," Dax said. "By looking at the isotopic decay records of the *Defiant*'s dilithium crystals and comparing them with Chief O'Brien's maintenance records back at *Deep Space Nine*."

Sisko lifted an eyebrow at her. "You think Admiral Hayman will let us talk to him?"

The Trill's gray eyes warmed with amusement. "Oh, I think Curzon can talk her into it."

"You want to know *what?*"

Sisko scowled at his chief engineer. Despite parsecs of distance and the slight buzz of the high-security communications link to *Deep Space Nine,* he could still practically hear the gears clicking over in O'Brien's highly logical brain. It had taken Dax almost an hour to convince Admiral Hayman that the information O'Brien could give them was worth the risk of making this call. The last thing he needed was for his too-brilliant station chief to decipher what must be happening here at Starbase 1, right in front of Kira Nerys.

"Don't worry about why we need the information, Chief," he suggested, stiffening his voice just enough to make it clear that was an order, and not idle conversation. "Just tell us what the isotopic ratios are in the dilithium crystals from the *Defiant*'s warp core right now."

O'Brien's eyebrows rose dubiously, but he made no other protest. "Very well, sir," he said in a carefully neutral voice.

"I don't routinely keep that kind of data in my records, but if you give me a few minutes, I'll run a scan and get it for you."

Sisko's mouth twisted slightly, seeing the impatient way Kira hovered over the engineer's shoulder. "I'm sure my second-in-command can keep me occupied until you get back. Get to work, Chief."

O'Brien nodded and disappeared from the viewscreen. To Sisko's relief, Kira made no comment on the oddly trivial request he'd just made through Starfleet's highest-priority channel. Instead, she leaned both hands on the console in front of her and scowled—not at him, Sisko realized after a startled moment, but at the admiral standing silently at his shoulder.

"Does Starfleet have any idea when we can expect you back at *Deep Space Nine*, Captain?" she demanded.

Sisko exchanged glances with the admiral. "We're still not sure about that, Major. I suspect it will be within the next day or two. Why?"

"Because we have a situation shaping up here that I don't like the looks of," Kira reported. "I think a branch of the Bajoran paramilitary forces is using *Deep Space Nine* to build tactical nuclear weapons. There's a chance—a good chance—that they're planning to blow up the station itself."

Sisko frowned. After a day spent trying to figure out how to reroute the course of time itself, it felt almost nostalgic to be dealing with such a typical Bajoran crisis. He'd done this so many times, he didn't even have to think about his response. "Do you have any idea who's behind it?"

That got him only a fluid Bajoran shrug and a frustrated look. "Not yet. Chief O'Brien and I tracked down an unauthorized replicator they were using in the habitat ring and I have Odo staking it out, but so far no one's sprung the trap."

"Then you don't need me there yet, do you?"

Kira scowled again, this time at him. "Captain, have you considered what Kai Winn's going to do if—when!—she finds out about this? She'll accuse us of giving support to the Bajoran Resistance."

"As I recall, Major," Sisko said quietly, "one of my senior officers has already admitted to doing that."

Kira's face tightened in embarrassment, but she didn't back down. "Which is exactly why we can't give Winn another excuse to sever Bajor's ties with the Federation."

"Agreed," he said. "I suggest you contact Bajor's security forces immediately and enlist their assistance in tracking down this paramilitary cell."

Kira gave him a look of wide-eyed incredulity. "With all the sympathizers the paramilitary has in the regular forces? That would be as good as telling the local cell we're on to them!"

"Precisely, Major." Sisko smiled at her baffled look. "With any luck, that will flush your paramilitary targets out of hiding."

"That might work," she admitted, although a glimmer of doubt still lingered in her dark eyes. "I'll get on it."

"Good." There was still no sign of O'Brien in the viewscreen. "Any other problems since I've been gone?"

Kira glanced down at the ops board in front of her, then shook her head. "Nothing major. One unscheduled wormhole opening due to natural causes, and some minor quantum interference with the communications array. Nothing we can't work around."

"Good." Sisko had already seen the familiar stocky figure of his chief engineer appear behind Kira. "Any luck with those isotopic ratios, Chief?"

"I've got them right here." O'Brien plugged a data chip into the Ops communications console, then tapped in the order to transmit. A scroll of numbers, many of them incorporating the symbol i, promptly rolled across the screen. Sisko glanced at Hayman and got the quick nod that meant they'd been recorded. "That look like what you need, sir?"

"I hope so, Chief. If not—" Sisko paused, realizing he wasn't really sure how to end that sentence. "—well, you'll probably be the first to know. Sisko out."

Admiral Hayman snorted, leaning over to unplug the data chip from her private communications console and toss it at him. "Do you really think this is going to tell us how soon the *Defiant* will run into trouble?" she asked bluntly.

"Dax does," he said, swinging around and heading for the door to Starbase 1's operations center.

"*Jadzia* Dax does." Hayman matched him stride for stride across the busy hum of her command center. "A young science officer on her first tour of duty."

"With a very wise old man inside her." Sisko stepped into the turbolift and waited for her to follow him before he spoke to the computer. "Control room, fusion bay one."

The admiral fell silent, letting the swift whine of the turbolift close around them. "I'll give Jadzia this much," she said at last. "I'm not sure Curzon Dax would have argued quite as strongly for accepting back that old symbiont last night." Her lined face creased with an unexpected hint of humor. "Of course, if it *had* been Curzon, maybe that young medical officer of yours wouldn't have argued so strongly against it."

The turbolift doors opened before Sisko could respond to that, this time on a control room that looked as if it had come straight out of a history book on spaceflight. Walls of monitors and optical circuitry lined three sides of the narrow compartment. The fourth side was made of thick glass panels, turned a gossamer shade of antique gold by the hundreds of fusion blasts they'd weathered. Outside, the condensate inside the huge fusion bay had thinned enough to show them the dark smudge of the ancient *Defiant* floating in its halo of work lights.

Dax swung around from the temporary sensor panel she'd leaned against the central window, gray eyes intent. "Did you get the isotopic ratios I needed from O'Brien?"

"I think so." Sisko handed her the data chip, then went to stand at the window. The exhaled breath of the comet still obscured much of what had been his ship, but the ice had melted enough to show him the gaping crater where a quantum torpedo had exploded far too close to unshielded hull. He frowned. "Was there enough left of the warp core for you to examine?"

"It was completely intact, Benjamin." Dax tapped the chip into its slot with impatient fingers. "That's why Julian's medical bay was still running."

"Of course." Sisko shook his head, annoyed at not remembering that. Seeing the amount of damage the *Defiant* had sustained, that fact amazed him more now than it had the night before. "I had no idea the warp core was that well shielded."

"Me either. It took me a while to get the right range for the sensors." Something beeped on Dax's panel, and she tapped back a response, then glanced out the gold-stained window. Out in the fusion bay, a tiny glitter of floating machinery swung itself into a new position above the shattered ship. "One more scan, and I'll have the current isotopic ratios of the dilithium crystals."

Sisko grunted and turned back to join her. "And that will tell us exactly when we got thrown back in time?"

"No," Dax said promptly. "It will tell us exactly how many times the warp drive was engaged between now and when the ship was crippled." She pointed at the complex numbers pulsing across her sensor screen. "Each time we break the speed of light, Pedone's Law of Imaginary Energy Usage says that the ratio of dilithium isotopes will be altered by a factor of i. By measuring the total change in ratios from our current *Defiant* to the ancient one, we'll get an estimate of how many trips we made before the one that took us here."

Sisko grunted. "Not very helpful, old man, considering the *Defiant* only goes out when she's needed. Three trips might be anything from three days to three weeks."

"True," Dax agreed, not sounding flustered in the least. "But when we're back at *Deep Space Nine*, we'll know exactly how many trips we can safely make in the *Defiant*—and we'll know which one will be the trip that destroys us."

"Assuming you make the same decisions in this timeline that you would have if we hadn't found the *Defiant*," Admiral Hayman pointed out from the back of the room.

Dax nodded, her eyes never leaving the screen. The complex numbers on it were almost steady now, only a few of their digits wavering to new values as the dilithium scan neared completion. "Fortunately, we'll have Chief O'Brien and Major Kira back at the station to give us their unbiased input about that. If they both agree with Captain Sisko's decisions—"

She broke off, a frown tightening her face to unaccustomed grimness as she ran a finger down the column of numbers on the screen. A quick toggle of her controls brought a second column of complex numbers up beside it. To Sisko's untrained eye, the jumble of numbers and symbols looked nearly identical.

"Then and now?" he demanded, and saw Dax's confirming nod. "How much difference is there?"

"Exactly one factor of i," his science officer said slowly. Her gaze rose to meet his in mutual awareness of what that meant. "That means the next time we take the *Defiant* to warp speed—"

Sisko nodded grimly, his gaze going back to the mist-shrouded comet and the impossible wreck it sheltered. "—we won't be coming back."

A shriek of coruscant energy burned past Kira's cheek, close enough to blind her and powerful enough to warm the chain on her metal earring. *This is the last time I take Sisko's advice!*

"Major, this may not be the best time to mention this . . ."

She shot a glance at Odo on the other side of the corridor. He'd pressed himself to only a few centimeters thick, all but disappearing behind a narrow wall support.

". . . but I don't think contacting Bajoran security forces was a very wise move."

Kira gritted her teeth and flashed a random shot down the corridor just to remind their quarry that she was still there. "It flushed them out for us, didn't it?"

Odo's only response was a wordless grunt.

"Okay, so I didn't exactly plan for them to go on a shooting spree through the station." Another barrage of phaser fire burned the reek of hot ozone through the middle of the hallway, and Kira used the interruption to turn away from Odo and slap at her comm badge. "Kira to Eddington! Where in hell are you people? We could stand a little backup here."

"This is Eddington." Banging and muffled human curses overlapped behind the Starfleet officer's clipped reply. "I'm trapped at the juncture of corridors eleven and six with

Kirich, Glotfelty, and Robb. I'm afraid—" A certain unprofessional impatience snuck into his otherwise self-possessed tone, and Kira could just picture the prim grimace on his narrow face. "The militia crystallized the hydraulics in the bulkhead controls and caught us between sectors. We don't seem to be able to force the manual override, but we might be able to cut our way out."

Odo grunted disdainfully. "In a few hours."

"Yes, sir." Although it sounded like Eddington had to swallow his own tongue to admit it. "I'm afraid that's probably about right."

Kira sighed and drummed the butt of her phaser against one leg. *It's not his fault,* she told herself firmly. *It's not his fault he's human.* Of course, if he'd been Bajoran, this particular little setback would never have occurred. There probably wasn't a Bajoran working on this station who hadn't spent half her young adulthood luring Cardassians into cul de sacs just like the one Eddington and his Starfleet team were trapped in right now. In fact, any resistance fighter worth her salt could recite the specific intersections on *Deep Space Nine* that were best suited for a convenient bulkhead hydraulic failure. Starfleet didn't share that history, and it was probably unfairly racist to be angry with them for that fact. Still, Kira couldn't just turn off the irritation in her voice, no matter how much her head knew she ought to.

"Don't bother, Eddington. Just have Ops send a technician down to replace the hydraulics on those doors." It would be the quickest way to get them out without actually burning down the entire door. "A *Bajoran* technician." Because that would also make the fast way the safest— Bajor had killed a lot of Cardassians through the years with the booby traps left behind in the hydraulic mess.

"Very well, sir." Then, with a somewhat stiff sincerity, "I'm sorry, sir. Eddington out."

His apology left her feeling strangely guilty for having been angry with him, and that only frustrated her more. "You know what Starfleet's problem is?" she asked Odo with a sigh.

"Their officers aren't devious enough?"

She smiled a little, amused by his insight more than by his candor. "Something like that."

He nodded very seriously. "It's a good thing we have more than enough Bajoran personnel to make up for that failing, then."

Kira wondered if he was referring to the Bajoran security guards who weren't caught up in the bulkhead trap with Eddington, or to her for having thought up the details of this crazy plan in the first place. As a blur of shouts and gunfire roared down the hall from the cornered terrorists, she decided it would probably be better not to ask.

"You've got squads on the edges of the Promenade?" she said instead. Concentrating on business was always a good way to sidestep conversations you would rather avoid.

"Half-squads," Odo admitted. "That should be enough to keep the militia from breaking through to the public areas."

But only if they keep them moving. "Who's watching beta sector?"

"Sergeant Nes."

A memory of the young Bajoran came easily to Kira—bright, coltish, barely old enough to wear an adult's earring. The first generation who, in a very few years, would have lived more of their lives free of Cardassian rule than as slaves to it. Their very existence was something Kira still reacted to as some sort of magnificent dream, and something that made her intensely proud. "Kira to Nes. How are you holding up down there?"

"We've got them stopped well enough," the younger girl answered promptly, "but I don't think we'll be able to push them back very well."

"That's all right—I want to funnel them down your way, away from the Promenade." She motioned for Odo to get ready, and switched her phaser back over to her right hand. "Once we start pushing from our end, fall back and let them drive you toward the habitat ring—"

Nes hesitated only slightly. "But, Major, if they're trying to reach the docking ring—"

"Precisely." Kira smiled wickedly, even though she knew Nes couldn't see it. "Hold out for about one minute, Sergeant, then cave in. Got that?"

"Yes, sir, Major." Her young voice held all the iron of a veteran resistance fighter. "Nes out."

Slipping around the next arching wall support wasn't

nearly as hard as getting the attention of the security team down the side corridor, but Kira resisted calling them up on the comm—she didn't want the sound of her steady chatter to alert the militia that a well-organized maneuver was in the offing. Across from her, Odo extruded himself through a crack in the wall support and neatly recongealed on the other side. "What if the militia doesn't know about the ore-delivery chute?" he asked while still little more than a glossy sheen on the wall. "If they don't think they can escape, you'll be driving them into the habitat ring."

Kira waved frantically in a frustrated effort to catch the other team's eye, then had to throw herself back against the bulkhead with a curse when the militia, who were paying considerably more attention, rewarded her with a new round of phaser fire. At least that made the security squad look around. "Oh, they know about the chute all right," she said as she flashed the Bajoran in charge a series of quick hand signals. "They've been on this station long enough to steal everything but Quark's bar. They probably know about chutes we haven't even found yet."

Odo grunted and swelled up to his usual height. "Let's just hope they all lead to the docking ring."

The squad from the side corridor was larger than Kira expected, and apparently more than the militia had counted on. What started as a grim push on the part of station personnel deteriorated quickly into shouting and cursing and pounding as the militia crumbled under the new onslaught. Kira heard their frantic voices recede down the curve of the corridor, felt the dull rumble of pounding footsteps through the deckplates as both security and militia broke into a run. The next time phasers shrilled in the distance, there was no return fire from Nes's little group.

"Go! Go! Close on them!" She shouted as loudly as she could while running, half wanting the militia to hear the fierceness in her voice, half wanting Nes to know that she had done just right. When she skated around the corner with her phaser thrust in front of her, though, it was a small sea of startled Bajorans in security brown who jostled to a stop two meters away and not the expected militia ragtag.

"Where are they?" Nes turned almost in a full circle, as though half expecting the quarry to be hidden among her own men. "They didn't come past us, sir, I swear they didn't!"

"They damn well better not have...." She'd have no respect for them at all if they did something so common as simply running. Jamming her phaser back into its holster, she waved Nes impatiently aside and felt along the edges of the closest wall panel from top to bottom. Her hands found the sharp gouges in the metal before her eyes did. It popped off with the first bang from her fist, and the scarred, dirty access hatch beyond it looked as though it had been attacked by a dozen manic laser drills. Crowing with triumph, she threw Odo a smug grin as she straightened and slapped at her combadge. "Heads up, Chief! They're on their way to the docks!"

"I'm with you, Major," O'Brien came back briskly. "I've got an engine start-up on sensors. Pylon two, fourth level." He was silent for a moment, and Kira took the opportunity to disperse Nes and the others to their regular positions before heading for the turbolift with Odo. "They're trying to override traffic control and disengage the docking clamps," O'Brien said at last. "Tell me when you want me to release them."

She swung herself into the lift without slowing down. "Play with them a few times, then pop the clamps." She waited for Odo to slip in behind her before punching the controls for the docking ring. "And get that tracer ready."

"Already up and loaded."

"Good work, Chief." She caught at the rail as the lift heaved into motion, already drumming one foot impatiently in her want to be already parked at the docking ring, setting the next stage in motion.

"You know, Major . . ." True to form, Odo reclined against the other wall of the lift with a cool lack of tension only available to the truly boneless. "If they take their ship through the wormhole, the subspace matrix will erase all signature of the trace."

That was a worry so far from her mind that she almost laughed at the suggestion. "They're not going through the wormhole. They stole those bomb components for Bajor." No matter how misguided, they always thought they were doing it for Bajor. "Either they're running back to their buddies for protection, or they're hoping to pass off the components before they get caught. But either way, they're not going through the wormhole."

Odo pulled his face into a grimace Kira could only assume was one of skepticism. "For all our sakes, I hope you're right."

So did she. But it didn't seem a good idea to reinforce the constable's uncertainties right now.

By the time the lift sighed to a stop just outside the runabout bay, Kira had decided that some glitch in the Cardassian computer system must be responsible for slowing down the station's workings whenever speed was most required. Why else would it take the turbolifts four times longer to get anywhere during an emergency than it did all the rest of the time? And what other explanation could there be for O'Brien taking just as long to announce, "Okay, they've pulled free of the station and are bringing warp engines on-line"? Surely the Ops computers weren't responding with their usual alacrity.

Kira threw herself into the *Rio Grande*'s pilot seat without chastising O'Brien for slowness that was obviously none of his fault. "Mark them, Chief!"

He didn't bother verbally responding, not trusting the equally sluggish comm system to relay his words in time, no doubt. Kira heard the deep whine of the weapons sail next door as its phaser batteries built a charge, and ordered *Rio Grande* lifted to its external launching pad while Odo was still fastening himself into the his own chair. At least the phasers seemed to be operating in normal time—the weapons sail loosed its shot with a short, ripping scream just as the runabout broke vacuum, and Kira saw the brilliant flare of light splashing against the militia ship's unshielded hull without even slowing it down. "Bull's-eye!"

O'Brien sounded significantly less impressed with his own shooting as the familiar blur of warp effect swallowed the militia ship and whisked it away. "Now let's just hope it takes."

"It took." Odo flicked colorless eyes across the runabout's sensor controls. "I'm picking up a faint but steady ionic trace, even after they've gone into warp. We should be able to follow them from several light-minutes' distance with no problem."

"And where are they heading?" Kira asked, trying not to sound too pleased with herself as she eased *Rio Grande* up off its launching pad.

Odo slid her a wry look, his lipless mouth curving into just the faintest hint of a smile. "Bearing oh one seven mark three," he acknowledged gracefully. "Away from the wormhole."

"Of course." It was only slightly better than I-told-you-so, but the least Kira could allow herself. "Chief, you get to mind the store while we're gone."

"I'll try to make sure Quark doesn't run off with too much of the merchandise," he said with a smile in his voice. "Good luck, Major. O'Brien out."

Just finding terrorists on board was the best luck I've had all week. The thought startled her, and she hoped Odo wouldn't notice the heat that washed into her face as she swept the runabout between the huge arching pylons and away from the station proper. It's not that she wanted anything bad to happen to the station, or even that she thought the militia consisted of anything more than the cream of an admittedly demented crop. It was just that activity—almost any kind of activity—would always fit her better than the kind of administrative desk duties Sisko seemed to wear with such ease. It probably said something disturbing about her psyche that she would rather chase a shipload of fugitives with an illegal plasma device than figure out how to display Klingon death icons alongside human menorahs in the Promenade without offending anybody's sensibilities. As she eased the ship through warp one and up to a relatively sedate 2.3, she had to admit that leaving the station and its Ferengi, radiation leaks, and death icons far behind calmed her all out of proportion with the situation she was likely rushing into.

"How are we doing?" she asked Odo, just because this *was* supposed to be a business trip, and not a relaxation cruise.

"The trace is holding strong. Judging from the rate of decay, I'd say they're about eighteen light-minutes ahead of us, proceeding at warp five." He glanced aside at her, one hand resting lightly on whatever reading he'd just been checking. "That's probably their maximum speed, given the age of their ship."

Kira nodded, passing a quick look over Odo's sensor panel more from unconscious habit than because she really needed any verification of the constable's statement. She'd already turned her attention back to the viewscreen, to the soft, computer-corrected blur of stars streaming by the runabout's nose, when something she'd only half-noticed tickled at the back of her awareness. Not quite turning away from her own panel, she tossed a nod at Odo's screen with a frown. "What's that?"

He looked at her, then at the sensor readout as though never having studied it before. "What's what?"

"That!" Kira stabbed a finger at the unidentified ship outline. "That's not the militia, is it?"

He answered with a slight, eloquent cock to his head that Kira always secretly labeled an Odo shrug. "It's some sort of sublight transport. This near the asteroid belt, I'd say an ore carrier, most likely."

An ore carrier. She glanced once, twice at the string of readings as the unknown ship all but rushed up on *Rio Grande* on the sensor screen. "If it's an ore carrier," she asked, "why isn't it moving?"

"Because it's stopped?" His voice held the weary resignation he usually reserved for stubborn Federation officials who refused to acknowledge that the world sometimes moved outside the lines of their little designs. "Major," he said, very carefully, as she leaned over to read the coordinates off his screen, "we technically have no authority over civilian spacecraft inside the Bajoran system. If they choose to stop—"

"Nobody chooses to stop in the middle of nowhere, Constable. Look at them!" She waved at the sensor console, forcing him to look down at his own readings. "The closest moon is thirty light-minutes away."

"And Chief O'Brien's tracer will only last for another three hours."

Yes, she had to admit with a swell of irritation, there was that. She hated it when she couldn't do things exactly as she wanted. "We're not going to be here for three hours. Worst-case scenario, we'll just beam the crew to the runabout." Especially if it was a bulk-ore barge—those almost never crewed more than four people. "That'll take, what? Five minutes? We ought to stay a few thousand klicks behind the militia, anyway."

He didn't reach over and stop her from bringing the ship to sublight, but she could tell that he wanted to by the way he stiffened to a good six centimeters taller than normal. "Major, this is precisely the sort of thing the Bajoran interim patrol is supposed to be responsible for. *We,* on the other hand, are responsible . . ."

She didn't even notice at first when his voice fell silent. Her own thoughts had stopped just as dead, and for the longest time nothing seemed able to get past the visual image of the ore transport hanging lifelessly against the veil of stars. It wasn't even the broken darkness of the ship that first slapped into her consciousness and shivered like ice through all her bones. It was the blossom of frozen gases pluming around the ruptured hull, and the glitter of trailing debris as it painted a slow-motion comet's tail behind the drifting bulk.

"Never mind," Odo said quietly. "The militia can wait."

CHAPTER 6

It was a council of Starfleet's highest-ranking admirals, from the venerable Hajime Shoji to the steely Alynna Necheyev. Even in telepresence, the combined focus of so many piercing stares made Sisko feel like a cadet at his final oral exam. Just as he had then, he folded his hands on the table in front of him to keep his unruly fingers still. This time, however, the emotion he was concealing was a drumming impatience, not nervousness.

"I don't see what the problem is," Necheyev said, voicing Sisko's exasperation for him. It was one of the few times Sisko could remember when his sector commander had been in total agreement with him. "We've discovered that the battle which destroyed the *Defiant* happened on the far side of the time warp, right?"

"Yes," Admiral Hayman said, before Sisko could respond. Sisko settled back into his chair, knowing her gruff voice probably carried more conviction than his own neutral tones. "Our contact with the surviving Trill symbiont gave us very clear evidence of that. The *Defiant* went into the wormhole, was thrown back five thousand years into the past, and *then* encountered the aliens who destroyed it."

Necheyev shrugged, although her razor-blade face lost none of its intensity. "Then whoever destroyed the *Defiant* has been dead for as long as the pharaohs have—and they obviously didn't disturb Earth's history, since we're still here. Why don't we just dry-dock the *Defiant* back at *Deep Space Nine* until it disappears from Starbase One? Then we'll know we averted that timeline."

"And we will also have lost the only stable wormhole known to exist in the galaxy." That voice, as elegantly cold as silk, came not from a wall monitor, but from the third person actually present in Starbase One's small conference room. With her usual curtness, Hayman had introduced the middle-aged Vulcan woman just as T'Kreng, letting Sisko deduce from her civilian robe and platinum medallion that she must be a member of the Vulcan Science Academy. A very high-ranking member indeed, if she had the security clearance to attend a meeting both Dax and Bashir had been barred from. "From either a scientific or a diplomatic viewpoint, I believe that is an outcome we would wish to avoid."

A younger admiral whom Sisko didn't recognize leaned forward, dark eyes intent above his steepled fingers. "But is the loss of the wormhole a certain outcome, Professor T'Kreng? Could the *Defiant* simply have been the victim of a freak quantum fluctuation of the wormhole? One perhaps initiated by some action or accident that occurred while they were traveling through it?"

"The equations governing wormhole physics do allow for that possibility," T'Kreng conceded. "And the spacial displacement created by such a fluctuation could certainly reach as far from Bajor as Earth. However, Admiral Kirschbaum, my calculations indicate that the maximum temporal displacement that could be caused by such a spontaneous quantum event is two hundred standard years, plus or minus ten years." She lifted one graceful hand, in a gesture that somehow managed to convey the enormity of the problem with a minimum of expended effort. "Clearly, we have exceeded the time limits imposed by the wormhole's internal energy sources."

Sisko swung around to frown at her. "You're saying the wormhole *couldn't* have thrown us this far back in time?"

T'Kreng graced him with a frosty look, although he couldn't be sure if it was the blunt question or his scientific illiteracy that irritated her. Unusually for a Vulcan, her eyes were the pale gray of moonstones, making her look even more remote than most of her race. "I made no such statement, Captain Sisko. What I said was that such a massive temporal displacement could not be caused by normal quantum fluctuations in the wormhole. It can be achieved, however, by adding a significant amount of external energy to the singularity matrix."

"And it's the addition of external energy that will destroy the Bajoran wormhole?" Kirschbaum demanded.

"Yes." T'Kreng's icy gaze shifted back to her wall monitor. "The amount of energy needed to produce a temporal displacement of five thousand years is more than a starship could produce with anything short of a total warp-core explosion. I conclude that something other than the *Defiant* caused the disruption of the Bajoran wormhole, and that the temporal displacement experienced by the *Defiant* was a symptom and not a cause of the problem."

"And once it's disrupted, the Bajoran wormhole will stay disrupted?" Hayman asked.

The Vulcan sighed. "The explosion will most likely catapult the wormhole into an indefinite succession of chaotic gravitemporal fluctuations. Even if a ship managed to survive the unstable gravity flux inside the singularity matrix, it could emerge from the other side at any time within the past five thousand years. Or within the next five thousand. The singularity would still exist, but it would be essentially useless."

"Let me ask you a different question, Professor." That polite, grasshopper-thin voice came from the oldest of the admirals, the centenarian Hajime Shoji. "Could this disruption of the Bajoran wormhole have been deliberately induced by some entity trying to subvert the wormhole to its own purposes?"

The Vulcan scientist lifted one eyebrow by so small a degree that Sisko wondered if anyone but he and Hayman could see it. "It is highly unlikely that the temporal displacement in the wormhole was deliberately induced. Not even I can work out the equations required to accomplish that."

Kirschbaum cleared his throat. "I think what Admiral Shoji is suggesting, Professor, is that the time rift may have been caused inadvertently by aliens attempting to take control of the wormhole."

T'Kreng frowned, a minuscule tightening of cheek and forehead muscles. "I am not a diplomatic expert, Admiral, but I believe all the known races have acknowledged Bajor's possession of the singularity."

"Not all of them." Hayman rummaged in one pocket of her coveralls and then startled Sisko by hauling out a small, grotesquely realistic effigy of a horned, yellow-eyed figure. She dangled it in front of her screen, letting reflected light wash across its age-stained but still powerful grimace. "And this one in particular sure hasn't."

"Ah." T'Kreng's pale eyes narrowed to slits. "You suspect that the alien coalition we know as the Furies will tamper with the Bajoran wormhole? Why?"

Hayman glanced up at Shoji, who answered in the slow deliberate tones of someone who'd spent a lot of time considering that question. "Our knowledge of Fury history is incomplete, Professor, but we know that they were driven out of our sector in a war with another alien empire millennia ago." His age-faded eyes slid to regard Sisko thoughtfully. "The five-thousand-year-old battle that the *Defiant* witnessed, just prior to its destruction by one or another of the participants, was undoubtedly part of that war."

Sisko nodded, deliberately keeping his gaze away from the tiny horned devil dangling from Hayman's bony hand. "I suspected as much from the logs, Admiral."

"We also know that the Furies have used artifical wormholes to invade our quadrant twice since then, in an attempt to reclaim what they believe to be their territory." Unlike Sisko's, Kirschbaum's dark gaze seemed to have become glued to the Fury effigy in Hayman's viewscreen. "Now that the *Enterprise* has destroyed that technology in the battle at Furies Point, they may want to coopt the Bajoran wormhole and use it in a similar fashion."

"That is possible," T'Kreng said after a considering pause. "Although I find it a less probable cause of the wormhole's temporal displacement than a natural input of energy from a drifting black hole or cosmic string."

Shoji rubbed his hands together, a paper-dry rustle of ancient skin that carried clearly across the parsecs. "In either case, it's clear that our strategy must be to save the wormhole and prevent the *Defiant*'s fatal trip. Is that feasible, Honored Professor?"

The Vulcan scientist's slim eyebrows lifted again, in the barest of detectable motions. "If you are asking in terms of scientific feasibility, Admiral, the answer is yes. Because the addition of external energy is not a natural part of the wormhole's evolution, no law of science bars us from preventing it."

"But how good are our chances of actually doing it?" Necheyev demanded bluntly. "We don't even know where this energy input is going to come from."

Sisko frowned, remembering Kira's newly discovered paramilitary group and their tactical weapons. He opened his mouth to contradict his sector commander, but T'Kreng's smooth voice had already claimed the monitor's video focus.

"The source of energy is irrelevant, Admiral. By examining the wormhole's current resonance state, I can extrapolate to the precise time and place where the energy input will occur. All you need do is send a starship to that point and order it to destroy whatever energy-producing device or cosmic phenomenon it finds there."

Hayman snorted and set her small totem down on the table with a thump that rattled its contents into an odd, jangling sound. "If you can extrapolate to an event that hasn't occurred yet, Professor T'Kreng, why aren't you out playing Dabo instead of writing four-hundred-page grants to fund your fancy research ship?"

This time the censure in those ice-pale eyes was slanted at the silver-haired admiral. "Because the theory of temporal symmetry applies only to objects outside the Einsteinian frame of gravitational reference. And since a Dabo table is neither a black hole, a wormhole, nor a cosmic string, it is not subject to those equations."

Admiral Shoji cleared his throat diplomatically. "I assume you will need to examine the wormhole at first hand to make this extrapolation, Professor?"

She nodded again. "I will need to make several runs through the singularity matrix itself, to obtain the necessary precision."

"How soon can you leave for Bajor?" Kirschbaum demanded.

T'Kreng made another small gesture, this time one of gracious accommodation. "My research vessel is fully staffed and ready to depart Starbase One within the hour. We can make the run to Bajor in approximately eleven standard hours."

Shoji exchanged consulting looks with his fellow admirals, and got back silent, confirming nods. "Then consider yourself funded at priority research levels for the next week, Professor. You will be working directly under Admiral Nechayev, with onboard liaison provided by Captain Sisko. Are these conditions acceptable?"

"I find them so." T'Kreng gave Sisko a long, measuring glance. "But are you willing to travel on my ship in that limited capacity, Captain?"

Considering that the alternative was to take the *Defiant* on a short trip to a foregone conclusion, Sisko wasn't sure how much choice he had in the matter. Aloud, all he said was "So long as I can bring along my science officer, yes."

T'Kreng's elegant shoulders lifted in the barest of shrugs. "That hardly seems necessary, Captain. Half my shipboard staff hold degrees in either singularity physics or quantum chronodynamics."

Sisko didn't bother arguing with her, since he knew she wasn't the one he had to convince. Instead, he glanced up toward the viewscreen that held the age-crinkled but alert face of Hajime Shoji. "My science officer, Jadzia Dax, is the Trill whose symbiont survived all this time in the *Defiant*," he said quietly. "They communicated at some length this morning. We're not sure yet exactly how much she learned, but she might provide some additional clues that we couldn't get any other way."

Shoji nodded. "In that case, I'm sure Professor T'Kreng will be happy to accommodate both of you." The Vulcan scientist didn't look happy, Sisko thought wryly, but then he wasn't sure she had ever looked that way in her life. "And I suggest you both prepare for an immediate departure. After viewing the visual logs from the *Defiant*, I find myself most troubled by the aspect of this problem that Admiral Nechayev has pointed out."

Necheyev looked puzzled, and for once even T'Kreng's moonstone eyes reflected back incomprehension rather than Vulcan certainty. It was Judith Hayman, however, who had the gruff courage to demand, "What aspect are you talking about, sir?"

Shoji's ruffled white eyebrows rose. "Why, the fact that the aliens who destroyed the *Defiant* five thousand years ago—whether they were the Furies or the unknown conquerors they accuse us of being—had no effect on the ancient Earth. Surely it has occurred to you all why that may be so?"

Sisko took in a deep breath, feeling several disconnected fragments of his daylong uneasiness suddenly congeal to an unwanted conclusion. "Because they didn't stay in that timeline?"

"Precisely, Captain." The rear admiral might be elderly, but he'd been both a tactical and engineering genius in his day. He gave T'Kreng an ironic glance. "I may not hold a degree in quantum chronodynamics, but I've studied the basic equations governing time travel, and there's one thing I'm sure of. Any mechanism that can transport matter backward through time also has the ability to transport it forward."

"Wait! Let me ease it around the replicator—that's it.... Now bring it back, straight back—Back! Back! Jadzia, what are you *doing?*"

"Trying to think of a good reason not to hit you."

And she said it through clenched teeth, in the voice Bashir had learned to think of as her "Joran voice." It was the one that showed up right about the time you suspected another sentence or two of argument would get you murdered. She hadn't killed anyone yet—at least so far as he knew—but Bashir had learned long ago not to take anything for granted with an alien life-form, even one that looked so young and lovely. Waving her away from the end of the brine tank, he squeezed himself between the stasis field and the wall to wrestle it into the corner without her. "I'm sorry," he sighed as he leaned his weight into the unit and shoved. "Between sorting through my medical records and pulling together a temporary battery for moving the unit, I didn't get much sleep last night." Actually, he hadn't gotten any sleep at all. But that was a whole other potential conflict that he really didn't want to get into right now. "I guess it's just made me a little cranky."

"Don't apologize." Jadzia crouched to thread the tank's power cable through its tangled workings and under the room's only bunk. "I should have known this would make me edgy." She flushed a little as she handed him the cable at the other end of the bed. "I've never done anything like this before."

Bashir smiled, but accepted the cable and its implied exoneration. "You've never kidnapped yourself?"

"Never done *anything* like this!" She hiked herself up onto the edge of the bunk to give him room to pry open a small access panel on the wall. "Stolen Starfleet equipment, let myself into a science ship's cargo bay, slipped through all sorts of security checkpoints—"

Bashir caught the panel before it clattered against the floor and slipped it up onto the bed beside Jadzia. "Oh, come on! I find it hard to believe Curzon didn't borrow a Starfleet runabout or two in his day."

"Oh, *Curzon* once stole an entire *grakh'rahad* during trade negotiations with the Klingons," she admitted with a smile that wasn't quite memory, and wasn't quite hers. "And *Torias*—" She broke off abruptly, and Bashir wondered if Trill had some code of ethics that discouraged one host from revealing a previous host's indiscretions. Before he could ask, she busied herself handing him a tool he could reach perfectly well by himself. "*Jadzia*'s the one who's never done anything like this." And then, in case this hadn't ever occurred to him before, "She's actually rather proper and dull compared to most of Dax's other hosts."

"Proper, maybe," Bashir allowed, surprised to feel his own face warming, "but never dull." He fitted the tank's power cable against one of the conduit junctions leading to the replicator, and spliced it neatly into the circuit with a few strokes of the welder. "Try thinking of it as an interstellar Academy prank. Instead of moving the Cochran Memorial to the top of Brin Planetarium, we're moving it to Trill." He glanced at the tank as its subliminal purr rose to an audible rumbling with the influx of steady power. "In a five-thousand-year-old stasis tank that weighs only slightly less than the Brin Planetarium."

Dax smiled and rubbed him briskly between the shoulders in motherly support as he rose to sit beside her on the bunk. "How are you going to hide the power draw from ship's sensors?" Apparently, he hadn't been the only one to notice the step-up in the tank's functions.

"It doesn't use as much as you might think," he told her, studying the frozen turbulence of its occupant without quite realizing he did so. "Still, I entered a request for extra replicator time when the captain first told me we'd be taking the *Sreba*. T'Kreng thinks I'm running the tissue reconstruction and cloning experiments Admiral Hayman ordered for the symbiont. The extra mass, of course, is my incredibly sensitive and extensive medical equipment." He pulled his eyes away from one Dax only to face the other with a wry, tired grin. "As long as they only do periodic spot checks on power usage, they shouldn't notice any pattern to my consumption."

Dax returned his smile gently. "You hope."

"Yes," Bashir admitted, sighing. "I hope."

The brisk knock at the cabin door jerked through Bashir like a phaser blast, and he whirled on the bed with a stab of guilt so sharp it almost startled a cry out of him. *I'm not well suited to this,* he thought as he stood, hesitated over what to do about a visitor, and abruptly sat again. He had a tendency to blush and stammer when he knew he'd done something he oughtn't; it had been an unfortunate trait when trying to get away with anything as a child, and it hadn't become any more helpful now that he was an adult. It had a lot to do with why *he'd* never done anything like this during his Academy days, either.

Another knock banged against the door, louder this time, and Bashir looked helplessly at Dax in search of a suggestion.

"It's *your* room!" she hissed, swatting his shoulder on the way toward waving at the door.

Yes, it was. Which probably meant someone was waiting for him to answer before going on their merry way. "Uh . . ." He took a deep breath, straightening himself as though whoever waited on the other side could actually see him. "I'm sorry, but I'm rather busy at the moment. Could you come back later?" Not bad on such short notice. Polite, professional, and appropriately vague. He flashed Dax a relieved grin, pleased to have averted disaster, however temporarily.

"Doctor," Sisko's voice said ominously from the hall, "open this door."

For one suicidal moment, it occurred to Bashir that he could actually refuse—assert his inalienable right to privacy and tell the captain to go away. Then the likely repercussions of that madness cascaded into his rational mind even as Dax was shoving him off the bed to stumble toward the door. He didn't even have time to construct a plausible explanation for what they were doing here before he found himself confronting a handsbreadth view of Sisko's grim, dark face through the barely opened hatchway. "Captain, I'm afraid I'm right in the middle of—"

"Is Dax here?"

Bashir tried not to steal a glance over his shoulder, but it was hard to maintain eye contact with Sisko when he was angry. "I'm here, Benjamin," she called, saving Bashir from having to decide whether or not he should implicate her in his dealings.

The dark burn of Sisko's glare never left Bashir's face as he said, very plainly, "Not you."

The doctor felt as though his stomach would fall straight through into the floor. "Captain—I can explain—"

"I'm sure you can." Sisko reached past with a quick efficiency that startled Bashir into pulling away from the doorway as though expecting the captain to catch him by the collar. Instead, Sisko slapped at the inside door control and keyed the hatch all the way open. "May I?"

Bashir knew a rhetorical question when he heard one. Stepping aside, he granted Sisko access to the rest of the room without trying to stammer any further explanations. On the bunk, Dax returned the captain's scowl with an indignantly raised eyebrow as he stalked past her to glare down at the stasis tank and the frozen creature within.

"Do you two realize that what you've done could get you both court-martialed?" he asked without turning around.

Actually, the thought hadn't occurred to Bashir at all—any concern for his own welfare had drowned under the massive debt owed anything you had kept alive for more than five thousand years. He should have thought about Jadzia, though, he realized. It wasn't fair to drag someone else into his moral dilemmas, no matter how closely they were related to the patient.

Still, Jadzia herself seemed remarkably undisturbed by Sisko's warning. "I'd like to see Judith explain to a board of inquiry how she intends to prosecute us for following the wishes of a sentient life-form who is not *individually* a member of Starfleet."

Sisko turned his stormy frown full on her. "She'll argue that you can't know the wishes of a life-form who is barely conscious."

"*I* can." The ancient certainty in her gray eyes dared anyone to challenge that.

Sisko grunted and turned back to the tank without trying to argue with her. Bashir watched the captain rhythmically bounce one fist against the side of his leg for what felt like several hours before finally risking his voice against the quiet of the room. "How did you find out?" he asked plaintively. "I thought I'd been so careful—"

"I knew," Sisko said, with a sigh so deep it was almost paternal. "I knew the moment you first dropped the stasis field that you wouldn't be able to just walk away. And you, old man . . ." When he finally turned to face them, it was with a resigned fondness Bashir hadn't expected to see after his harsh entrance. "I've never known you to do anything but exactly what you want, no matter which body you're in. I doubted that five thousand years in a fish tank would do much to change that."

Dax flashed the captain one of her many flavors of all-knowing smile, and Sisko surprised Bashir again by laughing softly as he shook his head.

"Then you're not going to tell Admiral Hayman?" Bashir asked.

Sisko glanced up at the doctor's question, and a little of the hardness returned to his tone. "I don't have to. You can cover your tracks from here to *Deep Space Nine,* Doctor, but you can't hide the fact that the *Defiant* at Starbase One is now minus one passenger." He folded his arms and leaned back against the tank to gather both officers under his scowl. "Admiral Hayman went to check on the symbiont's status a few hours after the *Sreba* left dock, and found the medical bay cleaned out—lock, stock, and symbiont."

He wasn't sure which was worse—the disapproval in Sisko's voice or the gape of mute amazement Dax turned up at him. He tried to counter them both with a boyish smile. "I suppose stuffing a pillow under the bedsheets wasn't the most effective strategy in this instance."

Neither of them seemed particularly amused.

"Admiral Hayman called me on a priority Starfleet channel just five minutes ago," Sisko informed him, "demanding that we return to Starbase One—with the symbiont—immediately."

Dax leaned expectantly over her knees. "And you said . . . ?"

"I said," the captain answered smoothly, "that I was a liaison officer and not the captain of this vessel. She has to make her request to Dr. T'Kreng."

Bashir felt as though someone had released a choking band around his chest, and relief burst out of him on a sigh. "Thank you."

Sisko flicked him a hard, unreadable glare. "Don't thank me yet, Doctor. Hayman was still talking to Professor T'Kreng when I left the bridge."

"With as eager as T'Kreng is to get within sensor range of the wormhole?" Jadzia relaxed back onto her elbows with an eloquently dismissive snort. "She'll choose a one-hour detour to Trill over the six hours that obeying Judith's order requires, or I don't know my Vulcans."

"Any change in course is completely unacceptable." T'Kreng stepped around Bashir as though her pronouncement rendered him chronodynamically insignificant, and pointedly sank her attention into one of the many science panels ringing the *Sreba*'s bridge. "We will continue for Bajor at maximum speed."

"But . . ." Bashir pulled his arm away from Sisko's hand before the captain could turn his warning touch into a grip.

"Professor T'Kreng," he persisted, following her indifferent back as she moved from station to station, "I don't think you understand. We have an unhosted Trill symbiont—"

"—which has survived without incident for nearly five thousand years. It will survive in stasis a few days longer." She passed her hand across a readout, freezing a string of incomprehensible equations, and turned so abruptly that Bashir almost stepped off the edge of the bridge platform dancing out of her way. She responded to his display of startled emotion by peering down at him with the stoic disdain only Vulcans seemed able to express. "Apply logic to this question, Doctor, not emotion. If we reach the wormhole expeditiously, our actions there will avert the temporal shift which originally brought the symbiont into your possession. Once the temporal shift is removed from our timestream, the symbiont, also, will cease to be part of this reality. Therefore, any efforts to return it to the Trill homeworld are unnecessary."

"Provided," Dax pointed out, "you're successful in preventing the temporal shift."

The Vulcan turned cool eyes on the young science officer. Bashir wondered if T'Kreng would exude such disrespect if she understood that Dax was older than any of them. "My models indicate a 93.789 percent likelihood that I can pinpoint the time and place when the singularity matrix was damaged." She speared Bashir with another glower just on the brink of disgust. "Provided we are not delayed."

He scrubbed a hand through his hair. "Then let me take a shuttle. I can escort the symbiont to Trill by myself, then meet you back at *Deep Space Nine*."

This time Sisko succeeded in stopping him before he could grab at the physicist's arm. "Doctor—"

"I'm not needed here," he insisted. Torn between appealing to T'Kreng and appealing to his captain, he finally turned to plead with the one he felt most likely to understand. "Whatever's wrong with the wormhole isn't a medical problem," he explained to Sisko. "And unlike Professor T'Kreng, I can't ignore the needs of my patient just because there's a high probability it will be dead soon."

"Do you willfully misunderstand my statements?"

T'Kreng asked in what sounded almost like honest curiosity. "Or is this merely a natural error-generating effect of undisciplined human emotion?"

Bashir swallowed the flash of anger that rushed up on him. "Will you give me a shuttle?" he asked again, more slowly. He refused to dignify her racist elitism with an emotional reply.

Tipping her head infinitesimally, T'Kreng's pupils dilated in response to some subtle shift in her nonexistent mood—intrigue at his persistence, Bashir suspected, or perhaps even honest surprise that he didn't rush to appease her the way everyone else around her had been trained to. "The *Sreba* is a scientific research vessel," she said at last, as though still not quite sure why she needed to explain such a thing to Bashir, "not an exploration craft. We have unpowered lifepods in the event of an accident. We have forty-seven unmanned, self-contained probes for purposes of data collection and sample retrieval. We have seven different configurations of launchable sensor arrays. But we have no long-range shuttles."

Bashir wished there were something he could say, something he could do to make one of those useless payloads substitute. Instead, all he could think about was how he didn't seem able to succeed in doing anything to help the symbiont—not at Starbase One, not here, not five thousand years ago. The knot of frustrated anger that had settled into his stomach upon reading the first of his old medical logs twisted silently tighter.

"Is there anything else?" T'Kreng asked at last.

Bashir felt Sisko's hand flex briefly on his shoulder, but couldn't tell if the captain meant it as some kind of signal or just an unconscious expression of his own displeasure with the outcome. "I think that's all for now, Professor."

"Very well." T'Kreng reanimated the display behind her with a succinct motion of her hand, but moved to retrieve a data padd from a researcher nearby rather than attending to the newly reactivated panel. "P'sel," she called without looking up at anyone in particular, "please escort Captain Sisko and his officers off the bridge."

The dark male who rose from the station nearest the doors was young by Vulcan standards, but as cool and tight-lipped as the rest. He didn't really make any effort to escort them, Bashir noticed—just stood by the doors to usher them out with a stiff nod, then keyed the bulkhead shut behind them. Bashir watched the light beside the exterior door control, his irrational human emotion knowing that it would blink from green to red even before the Vulcans inside the ship's bridge engaged the lock. Something about the gesture struck him as delightfully human and petty, but did nothing to abate the awful anger he felt at being so helpless.

"I'll have O'Brien prepare a runabout the moment we reach *Deep Space Nine,*" Sisko said, very gently. "I'd send you with the *Defiant,* but . . ."

Bashir nodded so he wouldn't have to say the obvious. "I understand."

Dax reached out to place her hand on his arm. "Don't worry, Julian. It shouldn't delay us more than forty-eight hours, and with the symbiont in stasis . . ." She shrugged a little, trying on someone else's smile. "It won't even notice."

"No . . ." Bashir pulled his eyes away from the locked door and his thoughts away from the infuriating, inflexible Vulcan within. "No," he said again, "of course not. Thank you." He gave Jadzia's hand a squeeze before placing it back down at her side. He suspected his smile looked at least as wan and ungenuine as hers. "If you'll excuse me, I should get back to my quarters. I've got five thousand years of medical records to read through before we get home."

CHAPTER 7

"DINNER?"

The utterly blank look on Bashir's face made Dax want to laugh and hit him at the same time. There were times when the human medical officer's obsessive focus on his work exceeded even her vast tolerance of alien behavior. She compromised with an exasperated sigh.

"Dinner, Julian. The meal that comes after you quit working for the day and before you go to sleep at night." She paused, eyeing his haggard face critically. "You do remember what sleep is, don't you?"

Bashir scrubbed a hand across his forehead, looking as if she'd reminded him of an unpleasant chore he'd forgotten. "I know, I know—I'm going to get some rest tonight, I promise. But I still have two hours of work to do before I can be sure I've stabilized the symbiont for the journey." He gave her the boyishly appealing look that had won over many a *Deep Space Nine* heart. "Couldn't you just bring me something back and spare me an hour with the patron saint of singularities? I'll get to bed an hour earlier that way."

This time, Dax did hit him, but she was laughing while she did it. "I'll have you know T'Kreng has won not one but *two* Nobel/Z. Magnees Prizes for her work on quantum chronodynamics and singularity matrices. It's going to be an honor to talk to her."

Bashir winced and rubbed at the shoulder she'd punched.

"It's also going to be as dull as listening to O'Brien explain how he reprogrammed the food replicators. I'll pass, thanks."

"If that's what you want." Dax paused in the doorway of the small passenger's cabin, which was filled almost entirely now with tank, pumps, and tubing. Bashir had already bent back over the ancient control panel, his forehead creased into a frown. "Julian," she said, and waited for his impatient upward glance. "Try not to feel so guilty about keeping me alive all this time. I don't know about Earth customs, but on the Trill homeworld, it's the patient who decides about euthanasia, not the doctor."

"I know." He glanced back into the brine tank, a muscle jerking in his thin cheek. "I just wish I could be sure this patient didn't change its mind after the doctor died."

Unfortunately, there was no way Dax could reassure him about that. Her brine-gleaned memories were only clear about the *Defiant*'s final battle—all the rest was a haze of meaningless thoughts and half-remembered hallucinations. She closed the cabin door quietly behind her and left him alone with her catatonic future self.

She found the *Sreba*'s dining room by the simple procedure of following the sound of conversation down the hall from the sleeping quarters. The Vulcan research ship was built along the same spare lines as one of their diplomatic couriers—a bottom deck for engineering and life-support, a top deck for the bridge and the research labs, and a central deck where the dozen or so crew members lived and ate. There didn't seem to be a recreational area on board anywhere, but knowing Vulcans, that didn't surprise Dax.

Inside the small, undecorated mess hall, a handful of scientists sat along a single long table, many of them scribbling equations on notebook screens while they ate. Captain Sisko sat at one end opposite the elegantly icy figure of T'Kreng. His dark face wore no particular expression, but the stiff set of his shoulders told Dax he'd rather be sitting somewhere else. She suppressed a smile and ordered a bowl of *chfera* stew from the replicator, then went to join him.

"—accept the theory that the wormhole inhabitants play any role in stabilizing the singularity matrix," T'Kreng was saying when she arrived. "In fact, I am not sure the current data even support the existence of these life-forms."

"They exist," Sisko said, his voice brusque enough to make heads around the table turn. "I've seen them."

The Vulcan physicist raised a slender eyebrow at him. "According to the reports I have read, Captain, 'seen' may be too strong a word for what you experienced. Is it not true that these life-forms appeared to you only in the guise of human beings from your own past?"

"Yes."

She made an infinitesimal gesture with her free hand. "Then there is no actual evidence of their existence. What you experienced could have been a sensory by-product of your immersion in the singularity matrix."

Dax cut into the conversation before Sisko could reply. "In that case, Professor T'Kreng, why has no other being— not even Captain Sisko—reported such hallucinations? I believe Sterchak's principle states that any complex phenomenon which occurs only once indicates a high probability of sentient life."

A murmur of agreement drifted along the table toward her, making T'Kreng's opalescent eyes narrow. "That is true," she admitted coldly. "Although I would not have expected a Trill to be so familiar with such a minor branch of Vulcan philosophy."

"I *am* a Starfleet science officer," Dax reminded her gently. "And I also happen to have made the acquaintance of Professor Sterchak when he visited the Trill homeworld three hundred years ago." She gave Sisko a glance full of reminiscent glee. "He got especially philosophical after a few glasses of *ghiachan* brandy, as I recall."

The human captain snorted with laughter, echoed by a quieter voice from halfway down the table. Dax looked that way in surprise, and saw one smiling non-Vulcan face amid the slanted eyebrows and serious expressions. It was a young human female, wearing the practical lab coat of a graduate student rather than a professor's ornate robe. The girl dropped her gaze back to her plate as soon as she noticed Dax looking at her, but a small puckish smile still lingered on her face.

T'Kreng made a soft disapproving sound, more hiss than

sigh. "I do not see that Sterchak's drinking habits are relevant to this discussion, Lieutenant. Furthermore, his principle is merely a guide to logical inference, not a fundamental law of nature." She pointed her eating sticks across the table at Dax. "If indeed there are sentient creatures living in the Bajoran wormhole and keeping it open with some unimaginable technology, would they not represent an evolutionary anomaly? They cannot have evolved from nonsentient precursors in such a hostile environment."

"Perhaps they didn't, Honored Professor." It was a distinctly un-Vulcan voice, full of enthusiasm and excitement despite its attempt to sound logical. Dax wasn't surprised to find that it belonged to the young human graduate student. "Perhaps they evolved in a more hospitable environment first, and only colonized the wormhole later."

"Highly unlikely," T'Kreng decreed.

Sisko's dark eyes gleamed with amusement. "As unlikely as humans first evolving on a temperate planet, and then going to live in deep space?" he inquired. "If another race only knew us from our space stations, perhaps they would consider *us* an evolutionary anomaly."

Judging by the Vulcan physicist's elegant wince, Dax thought she might agree with that. "Comparative cultures are not my specialty, Captain Sisko, quantum singularities are. I cannot conjure up the hypothetical development of a totally unknown form of life as blithely as my young human assistant can. However, I can state with confidence that whether or not these wormhole inhabitants exist, they would not be able to withstand or divert the amount of energy the Bajoran wormhole will absorb when it displaces the *Defiant*. If they could, logic dictates they would have done so during the initial propagation of this timeline." She set her sticks at a precise angle across her lacquered eating tray, and lifted her eyebrows at Sisko. "Have I answered your question?"

"Abundantly, Professor."

T'Kreng inclined her head in a minuscule nod. "Then I will leave you to enjoy the rest of your supper with your colleague. We should arrive at *Deep Space Nine* at 0450 hours tomorrow. Please make sure that your chief medical officer is prepared to off-load his cargo with maximum efficiency at that time. I do not wish to remain docked for more than one standard hour."

Sisko's own nod was barely more noticeable than the Vulcan physicist's. "I'll inform him of that."

Dax frowned, watching T'Kreng leave the room in a dignified rustle of silk robes. "I'm not sure Julian can get the symbiont unloaded that fast," she told Sisko in a quiet voice. "He won't want to disengage the stasis field until we're out of subspace."

Sisko gave her a gleam of teeth that was by no stretch of the imagination a smile. "No matter what the Honored Professor thinks, the authority to dock and undock at *Deep Space Nine* still rests with me. If my chief medical officer needs more time to off-load, he'll get it." He rubbed a hand across his strong-boned face and grimaced. "Talking to Vulcans gives me a headache. You mind if I leave you to finish eating alone, old man?"

Dax glanced down at her empty bowl. "What makes you think I'm not done already?" she demanded quizzically.

Sisko snorted. "Dax, I haven't seen you eat just one bowl of *chfera* stew since we signed the treaty with the Klingons." He rose and clapped a companionable hand on her shoulder. "Enjoy the rest of your supper."

She laughed and followed him as far as the single food replicator, standing in line with her empty bowl while two Vulcans waited for their raktajino cups to stop bubbling in the chamber. Someone else came to stand behind her, clearing her throat in a polite but distinctly human sound. Dax turned and smiled at T'Kreng's young graduate student.

"Doctoral thesis?" she asked companionably, nodding at the note padd the young woman had tucked under one arm.

"Why—why, yes." The human's cheeks turned a more rosy shade of pink. "That's why I wanted to introduce myself, although I guess you sort of know me already. I'm Heather Petersen, the Starfleet Academy student who's been helping you analyze the subspace time-distortion data you collected from the Bajoran wormhole last year. Um—you are Lieutenant Dax from *Deep Space Nine*, aren't you?"

"Of course." Dax's smile widened. "And *you* are the brilliant young physics student who finally explained why the wormhole opens with some inherent rotational energy. Did Professor T'Kreng ever allow you to publish that fourth-dimensional time-transit equation of yours?"

Petersen grinned back at her. "After the editors of *Subspace Physical Reviews* accepted it, she didn't have much choice. Thanks for the advice, Lieutenant."

"Any time." Dax pulled her steaming-hot bowl of *chfera* from the replicator, then waited while Petersen ordered Elasian cloud-apple pie à la mode. She headed back to the end of the table, where Sisko and T'Kreng's absence had left a buffer of space between them and the rest of the *Sreba*'s crew. "So, how did you manage to get aboard a deep-space mission like this, Heather? Isn't Starfleet Academy still in session?"

Petersen nodded. "This is my doctoral internship semester, so I'm not actually in any classes." She lowered her voice to a more discreet murmur. "And I think Starfleet wanted at least one person on board with military security clearance, even if it was just a senior cadet like me."

Dax raised her eyebrows, knowing what a mark of trust that was. There must be more to this quiet young scientist than her gentle face and calm voice implied. "You're the only commissioned officer on board? Who's captaining the ship?"

"T'Kreng," Petersen informed her. "She used to be a Starfleet captain, in command of a small science survey ship, before she resigned to get her second doctorate and teach."

"No wonder Admiral Hayman called her in." Dax scraped up the last of her stew, mulling that over. "How much has T'Kreng told the crew about this mission, Heather?"

The young woman gave her an intent look across their empty plates. "Just that there's a high probability of losing the Bajoran wormhole to an accident in the next few weeks. She says she wants to do a high-precision chronodynamic analysis to pinpoint the time and place where it happens." Petersen paused, a slight frown creasing her forehead. "I think there must be some element of time travel involved in the problem somehow, though, because half the scientists she brought along on this trip are time specialists like me, not just wormhole physicists. Do you know if that's true, Lieutenant?"

Jadzia deliberated with her symbiont for a moment, weighing their previous experience with Petersen's intelligence and good judgment against her youth and the gravity of the situation they faced. "Yes," she said at last, and tugged the science student away from the table before she could ask more. "I almost forgot that I promised to bring dinner to my friend Julian tonight. Can you help me carry it to his cabin?"

"Of course." Petersen looked mildly surprised at the sudden change in subject, but made no protest as Dax ordered up a plate of lamb, lentils, and couscous for Bashir's dinner, then handed her a cup of hot raktajino and two orders of cloud-apple pie. "Your friend must like dessert."

"Actually, he doesn't." Dax balanced the warm plate of couscous in one hand and grabbed two forks in the other. "But I do, and it smelled good when you got it."

Petersen chuckled and followed her out into the hall, not speaking again until the chatter of the dining hall had faded behind the echo of their footsteps. "So, Lieutenant. Just how confidential is what you're about to tell me?"

Dax gave her an amused look. "Was I that obvious? Well, let's just say that you're going to be in the company of admirals once you know it."

That got her a grave look. "Then should you be telling me?"

"I need input," Dax replied just as seriously. "Preferably from a scientist a little more knowledgeable about quantum time paradoxes than I am. I was going to ask your thesis advisor, until I saw how unsympathetic she was to new ideas back there."

Petersen snorted with laughter. "T'Kreng can be very sympathetic to new ideas, Lieutenant Dax. They just have to be her own."

Dax paused in front of Bashir's cabin door, juggling plate and forks to press the access panel. "Which is exactly why I'd rather talk to you about what I've been thinking. As far as I know, no one's ever tested this hypothesis before." She heard the doctor's muffled acknowledgment through the speaker, and stepped back as the door slid open. "Of course, that may be because no one ever had the kind of test subjects I do."

Bashir looked up from a screen covered with his ancient medical notes. He'd obviously been deeply immersed in them, since he looked only vaguely puzzled by the sight of Heather Petersen and Dax in his doorway. "Did you want something, Jadzia?"

She made an exasperated noise and skirted a pile of spare tubing to wave the plate of couscous under his nose. "I want you to eat supper, that's what I want. And to introduce you to a friend of mine." Dax glanced back at Petersen, who had come just far enough into the room to examine its odd array of equipment with thoughtful eyes. "Heather, this is Julian Bashir, chief medical officer of *Deep Space Nine*. Julian, this is Heather Petersen. It's all right, she's a research colleague of mine from Starfleet Academy."

The doctor raised his eyebrows, ignoring the plate she'd deliberately set down in front of his screen. "Right now, I wouldn't care if she was a member of the Obsidian Order, if that *raktajino* she's holding is for me."

"Of course it's for you. You know I don't like mine flavored with hazelnut." Dax handed him the steaming cup and one of the dessert plates, then snagged the other for herself. The cloud-apple pie tasted even better than it had smelled. "Heather's doing her doctoral thesis on the time-distortion effects of singularities," she said through a mouthful of pie. "I brought her in for a consultation."

Bashir looked puzzled again. "A medical consultation?"

"No, a quantum-chronodynamics consultation. Eat." She left him poking tiredly at a chunk of lamb, and tugged Petersen across to the brine tank, where the ancient symbiont lay wrapped in the complete silence of stasis once again. "You're familiar with the theory of ansible technology, Heather?"

Petersen looked mildly surprised. "The idea that two twinned quantum particles will resonate in eternal synchronicity with each other, no matter how far you separate them in space? Of course. It's the basis for all our interstellar-communications relays. Why?" She glanced down at the unmoving symbiont below them. "And what does it have to do with this other Trill symbiont?"

"I've been thinking," Dax said slowly, "that ansible technology might work in time as well as in space. Has anyone ever suggested that?"

Petersen shrugged. "I've seen some casual discussions of it on the science nets. But in practice, it would be impossible to test. We can establish true synchronicity between two particles separated in space, but once we separate them in time, there's no way to know if their resonance is truly synchronous."

"But if we were dealing with sentient beings instead of quantum particles—" Dax could sense Bashir's sudden focus on her from the silence behind her back. "—we could test for an ansible linkage just from shared thoughts. Couldn't we?"

Petersen frowned. "But that would require two sentient beings that were absolute twins of each other. Even cloning processes would never work precisely enough to—" She broke off, her startled gaze dropping to the brine tank below them. "Unless this is—Lieutenant, are you saying this Trill symbiont is *you?*"

"Yes," Dax said calmly. "My exact internal self, particle for particle, but separated from me by five thousand years of time."

Like racing shadows, quick realization flickered in the human scientist's eyes. "The accident with the Bajoran wormhole—it threw you back that far? And somehow your symbiont managed to survive until now even though your host body couldn't?"

"Yes." She dropped a hand to the lid of the brine tank, feeling the blend of Jadzia's faint horror and Dax's amused affection that was starting to become familiar. "I'm here, and I'm there. The question is, am I now an ansible?"

Petersen chewed on her lower lip, looking intently thoughtful. "There's no theoretical reason why you couldn't be," she replied after a long moment. "Of course, you wouldn't notice any effects of it with—with your twinned self in stasis and unable to resonate. We'd need both of you awake and thinking in order to test for resonance synchronicity."

Dax glanced back at Bashir, and found him watching her with an odd mixture of awe and disbelief in his pale brown eyes. She guessed what he must be thinking and smiled. "I might not like the idea of living in a brine tank for five millennia, Julian, but that's no reason not to take advantage of the fact that I did it. And this is a scientific opportunity no one else in the galaxy has ever had. Can we bring the symbiont out of stasis?"

The doctor shook himself, as if he were throwing off some waking dream. "No, you may not," he declared firmly. "Jadzia, you may be a brilliant scientist, but you're not being realistic. I'm not sure the symbiont's going to survive the stress of this voyage as it is. Putting it through some kind of scientific experiment now would be the worst possible thing we could do."

Dax frowned. "But we won't be able to run the tests once we get to *Deep Space Nine,* Julian. Captain Sisko wants me to stay on the *Sreba* with him. And if we succeed in keeping the wormhole safe—" She broke off, glancing down at the brine tank with a slight frown. "—this one of me will disappear forever."

Bashir sighed and dropped his fork into his half-eaten food. "How long will these tests of yours take?"

Dax exchanged glances with Heather Petersen. "About an hour, minimum?" she asked, and the young physicist nodded. "Does that mean you'll let us run them now?"

"No, but it means I'll let you run them as soon as I get the symbiont out of stasis and stabilized, before you leave *Deep Space Nine* for the wormhole." He frowned at their glum expressions. "What's wrong with that?"

Dax snorted. "According to the patron saint of singularities, we're only going to get an hour of turnaround time once we dock. Of course," she added thoughtfully, "Benjamin did say that he would make sure you got as long as you needed to off-load the symbiont."

A ghost of Bashir's usual mischievous smile lit his tired face. "Then you just leave everything to me. If I can't manage to transfer this equipment slowly enough to give you two time for your experiment, then I'll just ask O'Brien to help me. That will make it take at least twice as long."

Dax chuckled appreciatively, but Heather Petersen gave them both a puzzled look. "Why will it take longer with someone else helping?" she asked.

"Because the person helping will be our chief engineer," Dax explained. "And he won't be able to look at this equipment, much less move it—"

"—without telling me all the ways I could have put it together better," Bashir finished for her.

Ragged metal tongues curled outward along the edges of the breach, yawning open to the stars like teeth in a roaring mouth. Frost dusted the tips, laid there by the lick of escaping gases some unknown number of hours ago. *Less than ten,* Kira reminded herself as she stroked one gloved hand around the curve of the long rip. They hadn't startled up the militia cell ten hours ago, or stumbled onto the first blown-open vessel. Initially pleased with herself for noticing the derelict on Odo's sensors and stopping to offer assistance, Kira had ceased to feel any satisfaction five minutes into their futile search for survivors. By this, the third drifting, lifeless shell, the only thing inside her was a numb, gnawing anger.

A ripple of movement reflected against the curve of her environmental suit's faceplate. Turning, glad to put her back to the unwelcome expanse of vacuum, she trod carefully across the buckled deck to meet the glossy mass that pooled at the base of one doorframe. It was an old ship, not well built even in its younger days; the force of whatever had blasted the long rip across its belly had blown most of the inner bulkheads askew, sucking out the air they should have protected, and the fragile life within. It had been a huge price to pay just for the convenience of cracks wide enough for Odo to slip through.

The constable swirled up to Kira's height, congealing into himself with his face already set into a waxen frown. Kira envied him his ability to move about in vacuum without a suit, but not the unexpected responsibilities that sometimes came along with it. She still felt guilty for sending him alone to check out the lower decks. *You never have a hardsuit around when you need one.* And no matter how much she griped to O'Brien, she did understand what a danger first-stage radiation could be.

She waited for Odo to press his hand against her faceplate, spreading it into a translucent tympanum, before asking, "Anything?"

"Only what we found before." The vibration of his hand against her faceplate translated only the ghost of his voice to her, a thin, blurry echo that seemed to come from everywhere and nowhere at once. "The reaction mass is gone, and the engine room is completely gutted." All three ships had been old, primitive sublight creepers, getting by with the cheapest fusion mass drivers that private shipmasters could legally buy. "Whoever they are, they're in a hurry—this fusion pile was cut out with the same lack of finesse as all the others. I'm amazed the thieves themselves survived."

Kira nodded, winding her hands into frustrated fists. "No sign of the crew?"

Odo shook his head even as his ghost voice whispered, "Not even bodies. I suspect the pirates either ejected the remains, or weren't particularly careful when they breached the ship and blew the crew out into space."

They weren't taking time to loot the ships of their ore, much less run down individual crew members just to pitch them out the locks. Still, scans of the other two wrecks had found no evidence of organic remnants within a hundred thousand kilometers. Could a ship really decompress with enough force to tumble humanoid bodies so very far away? "How can Bajorans do this to each other?"

Odo cocked his head—curious or reproving, Kira couldn't tell which. "Major, we have no proof the militia was even involved." Ah—pragmatic. She should have guessed.

"Who else could it have been?" She resisted an urge to turn away and pace in frustration, realizing at the last moment that it would break her contact with the changeling and leave him unable to hear her voice. "They were the only ones headed out this way—we were following right behind them!"

"Precisely." Even this dim version of his voice managed to catch her attention with its hard certainty. "Why would they take the time to accost these ships, much less steal their fusion drives?"

"To slow us down. They knew we'd have to stop and make sure there were no survivors."

The snort that rattled against her faceplate sounded more like a flat buzzing. "If I were escaping with an illegal plasma device, I wouldn't take that for granted," Odo said. "Besides, they would have made themselves infinitely easier to track. Any ship carrying three fusion reaction masses will be detectable up to half a light-year away."

Kira lifted her head inside the helmet, startled. "Odo, we're not following them."

He answered with a corresponding jerk of his chin. "But, Major—"

"We've got a runabout!" she blurted, grabbing him by the shoulders as though she could shake him into understanding. "They've got a plasma warhead and enough plutonium to ignite a small sun! Have you ever seen what's left after you detonate a thermonuclear bomb?"

The question seemed to strike him as meaningless. "I've seen holofilms," he admitted with just the faintest of frowns.

Kira nodded, and slowly removed her hands from his arms. "Well, I've seen real life." She turned away from him just enough to glimpse the breach around the sweep of her helmet, and felt him step up close behind her to follow her gaze even though she couldn't hear his movement. "Just three years before the Occupation ended." She walked carefully through the tangle of her memories, concentrating hard on keeping the image of the placid stars foremost in her mind. "Three years before it was all over, the Pak Dorren resistance cell raided an ancient plutonium mine in Veska Province. They wanted to smuggle a shielded nuclear bomb up to Terek Nor, because they thought it would cripple the Cardassians to lose their prefect *and* their base of operations all in one glorious starburst." A bitter smile twisted her lips. "And Pak wanted to be the one whose name we sang." She shook away the memory of her first and only meeting of Pak Dorren, as one of Shakaar's attendant bodyguards when the two Resistance legends came together to argue about Pak's crazy plan. Hateful now even more than then of Pak's smug laughter and conceited grin, Kira made the mistake of closing her eyes. "Instead of winning Bajor her freedom, they mishandled the payload before they even finished constructing the bomb. The blast took out twenty kilometers of countryside when it set off the rest of the mine. That whole valley is still just one big sheet of black glass." *And blistered bedrock, and twisted bodies, and burning stone—!* She jerked her eyes open on a silent gasp. The stars, each one its own sea of nuclear fire, provided little comfort.

If Odo recognized her pain, he didn't seem able to share in it. "The runabouts can withstand a direct hit by a photon torpedo. Even three thermonuclear devices couldn't get past our screens."

"If we meet up with them in space," Kira allowed. "If they go to ground on a colony, or even one of their own moonbases, being the last runabout standing wouldn't exactly make me feel like a winner." She reached up to close her hand around his elongated wrist. "No, we're going back to the station and warning Bajor. I'm not going to let what happened at Veska happen anywhere else." And she peeled him off her faceplate before he could argue with her further.

She let Odo thread himself through her equipment belt before stepping through the breach to the outside. He might be able to hold himself to a gravityless deck within the shelter of a ship's hard walls, but Kira despaired to think about how well he could hang on under a barrage of solar wind and micrometeorites. Clamping her booted feet to the ship's fragile outer skin, she gave herself a moment to find a new sense of "down" beneath this topless sky before looking across the bow of the freighter to where *Rio Grande* waited. Kira had wanted to land right on the nose of the derelict once she found out that the residual radiation prevented a direct transport, but both Odo and the ship's computer had convinced her that the runabout could match the freighter's tumble closely enough to make a short, suited jump reasonably safe. That argument seemed particularly hollow now as three points of blue-white light picked themselves out of the confusion of stars by their brightness and their precise triangular spacing.

Tapping Odo with the side of her hand, Kira waited for

him to reach a pseudopod up to her faceplate before remarking, "I suppose it's too much to hope those are Starfleet ships that just happened to be in the area."

He formed a partial face at what seemed an uncomfortable angle to the rest of his mass, and studied the three nonstars with customary blandness. "Not coming from the direction of the Badlands."

"Hang on." Breaches littered the surface of the freighter like fissures. On the way out from the runabout, Kira had taken the time to navigate carefully around each of the jagged splits for fear of tearing her suit or slicing a bootheel on the edges. Now she kept her strides long and steady, and let momentum carry them over the chasms with a graceful slowness that was still faster than the irregular detours. Even so, it seemed to take forever to reach *Rio Grande*'s waiting hatch and swing into the ship's comforting gravity.

She tore off her gloves the instant the airlock gauge blinked green, throwing them to the floor when the hatch slid open and attacking her helmet stays on the run to the console. "Computer! Identification on ships approaching on—" She glanced aside at the sensor display as she threw herself into the pilot's seat. "—heading three one two one mark seven."

"Working." Lights came up around them like campfires on a summer night, and Odo was only just pouring free of Kira's belt when the system announced, "One Kronos-class dogfighter, registry unknown. One Corsair-class cruiser, registry unknown. One Vinca-class tow barge, registry unknown."

Odo settled into his seat and reached immediately for his panels. "That doesn't sound like a very official gathering."

"Fifteen thousand kilometers," the computer reported, "and closing at warp factor seven."

Kira canceled the autopilot and seized back flight control. "Let's not stick around to see who they're representing."

An ore carrier, no matter how large, had little enough gravitational field, even when fully crewed and loaded down with water and oxygen. Still, leaping into warp too close to anything larger than you were always ran the risk of attenuating your mass across distances stretching into the infinite, and while that was not something Kira had ever seen or even really heard described, it was something she endeavored to avoid whenever given the opportunity. She lifted *Rio Grande* up over the subjective "top" of the freighter—for no reason other than she felt safer, more in control with the greater mass underneath the runabout's belly instead of looming over her head.

When she felt the first jolt, she thought with a flush of self-irritation that she'd misjudged the distances and clipped an engine nacelle on the freighter's hide. Then the second impact slammed them. With all settings at full-go, the *Rio Grande*'s engine readings went redline as she wrenched to a complete stop.

CHAPTER 8

THE LAST THING Benjamin Sisko remembered before toppling into sleep on board the *Sreba* had been asking his room computer unit to wake him when they reached the outer fringes of the Bajoran system. He'd expected the usual polite computer-generated voice, but what dragged him out of uneasy dreams a few hours later was the repeated chime of a two-toned bell. Sisko rubbed his eyes, wondering why an advanced Vulcan science ship would have such an old-fashioned wake-up system. It didn't even turn off when he sat up.

"I'm awake," he growled at the faint ripple of lights that marked the room computer. "Turn that alarm off."

Instead of the instant response he expected, he got a long pause full of continued ringing. "Passengers do not have the authority to issue that command," the computer said at last, in prim Vulcan accents.

"What?" Sisko scrambled out of bed and the room lights rose in response, letting him see the time on the monitor's small display screen. Zero-three-hundred hours—a full hour and a half before T'Kreng's estimated arrival time at *Deep Space Nine.* His sleep-fogged brain finally woke up enough to notice that the doubled tone he heard was the muffled outside echo of the bell still ringing in his cabin.

"What kind of ship alarm is that?" he demanded, diving into his uniform with more haste than care.

"Captain T'Kreng has called an all-hands science alert," the computer informed him. "Passengers are not required to respond."

Sisko snorted. "Well, this one's going to respond whether she wants him to or not." He stamped on his boots and headed for the door. To his relief, it opened for him. Whatever kind of situation produced a "science alert," it evidently didn't involve keeping the passengers locked in for their own safety.

He met Dax out in the corridor, looking sleepy and curious but not particularly alarmed. Her long hair was still wrapped in a sleeping-braid around her head, exposing more of the freckles on her neck than usually showed above her uniform collar. "What's the science alert for?" she asked him, her words stretched around a yawn.

"Exactly what I'm going to find out." He strode down the hall to the *Sreba*'s single turbolift, with his science officer at his heels. A whistle of motion took them to the bridge and into the silent intensity of a Vulcan crew at alert. A quick glance showed Sisko that the most active stations were those monitoring the multitude of long-range sensors that this science vessel carried instead of weapons. Neither the *Sreba*'s shields nor her navigation panels showed signs of hostile activity. He felt his adrenaline-kicked tension ease a little.

"Captain Sisko." T'Kreng glanced up from the most crowded of the sensor stations, her pale eyes glittering with single-minded intensity. "Have your science officer contact *Deep Space Nine* on a priority channel immediately."

It had been his own first instinct, but the Vulcan's arrogant assumption of command irked him. Sisko fought off an irrational urge to disobey her, reminding himself that he was a passenger aboard her ship, and instead sent Dax over to the empty communications console with a silent nod. "You haven't been able to raise the station on a normal subspace channel?" he demanded.

Only the continuing peal of the science alarm answered him. T'Kreng's attention had been sucked back to the sensor screen in front of her, intent on the fire-blue parabolas intersecting and expanding across the screen. It was left to his own science officer to say quietly from behind him,

"There's too much subspace interference coming from the wormhole, Benjamin. I'm having trouble getting even a Starfleet priority channel punched through it."

"From the wormhole?" Sisko let his exasperation lash out in a question so fierce it lifted heads around the bridge. "What the *hell* is going on here?"

T'Kreng gave him a Vulcan frown as delicate and sharp as a paper cut. "A few minutes ago, we began reading an unusual number of subspace oscillations coming from the Bajoran wormhole. It appears to be opening and closing at a rate of—" She glanced down at the sensor screen. "—once every ten seconds."

Sisko felt something twist inside his gut. In all the time he'd commanded *Deep Space Nine,* he'd never seen the wormhole act that rapidly. He glanced at his science officer and saw the same blend of disbelief and foreboding on her quiet face.

"Dax, can that be right?" he asked bluntly.

She was watching the long-range scanner output with nearly the same intensity as T'Kreng. "It could be an artifact of subspace symmetry and our own warp speed," she said after a moment. "Under certain conditions, that might create a quantum reflection, doubling or even quadrupling the frequency of the real signal. Did you check for that?"

Her question startled Sisko, until he realized it wasn't directed at him but at the solitary human on the *Sreba*'s crew, seated at the science station beside her. The young woman nodded without taking her eyes from her own equation-filled screen.

"Yes, sir. We also tested for sensor-ghost errors and for any signs of artificial generation of the signal. All results came out negative. It's a real-time subspace oscillation, Lieutenant, and it's really coming from the wormhole."

"But what does it mean?" Sisko demanded, hoping the young human physicist would answer him even if T'Kreng chose not to. To his surprise, it was the Vulcan who replied, in the crisp pedantic tones of an academy professor. She could ignore practical questions, Sisko thought wryly, but she couldn't pass up an opportunity to lecture him about her specialty.

"One possible hypothesis, Captain, is that we are seeing the reverberation of a massive disturbance in the singularity matrix. The simplest and most elegant interpretation would suggest that it was the same disturbance which threw your ship back in time, although that cannot be proven without a closer scan."

Sisko scrubbed at his face. "Then the wormhole's already been destroyed, without us being in it? But if that's true, why hasn't—" He snapped his teeth shut on the rest of that sentence, but threw a baffled look at Dax. If the ancient symbiont had disappeared along with his timeline, Julian Bashir would surely have let them know by now.

T'Kreng clicked her teeth in a distinctly Vulcan sound, somewhere between impatience and stoic resignation. "You are thinking about this too linearly, Captain Sisko. Singularities like the Bajoran wormhole deform time just as much as they deform space and gravity. Any change in their internal matrix will ripple through the fabric of space-time in *all* directions." She tapped one slender finger against the parabolas twining across her monitor screen. "This reverberation we are seeing—if it is indeed a reverberation—represents the upstream echo of the disturbance in the wormhole."

"Upstream echo?" Sisko repeated, frowning. Wormhole physics always gave him the same queasy feeling that stepping into microgravity did. "You mean we're seeing an aftereffect from something that hasn't happened yet?"

"A crude description, but essentially correct." The Vulcan physicist steepled her fingers together meditatively. "Of course, that is simply one hypothesis. There is another, also theoretically valid although much less elegant. Unfortunately, until we can make contact with your station, we cannot determine which of the two is correct."

"What's the second possibility?" he demanded.

T'Kreng moved her fingers in a tiny circle, which somehow managed to convey the sense of a shrug. "That these oscillations are merely the result of extremely heavy wormhole usage. A multitude of ships, passing through the singularity at ten-second intervals, would generate an identical subspace oscillation."

"Impossible," Sisko said shortly. "It takes at least fifteen seconds for the subspace ripples of a wormhole passage to dissipate. Sending a second ship through any sooner than that is too dangerous to do."

"Under normal conditions," his science officer reminded him from behind.

T'Kreng raised one slim Vulcan eyebrow. "Then perhaps conditions are no longer normal."

Sisko scowled and took two long strides across the small bridge to join Dax at the communications station. "Still no luck getting through to *Deep Space Nine?*"

She shook her head. "I could punch a contact through if I had the *Defiant*'s comm—or if the station's narrow-band receiver were tuned to our transmission—but *Sreba*'s comm just doesn't have enough power to boost our signal-to-noise ratio. I don't think we'll get through until we're within normal hailing range."

"And by then it may be too late."

"If T'Kreng's second hypothesis is the correct one, you mean?" The Trill's blue-gray eyes reflected back his frown. "I don't think even an emergency evacuation to the Gamma Quadrant would risk running the wormhole every ten seconds, Benjamin."

"I'm not worried about an emergency evacuation," he said. "I'm worried about an invasion."

"They're holding us!"

"Magnitude-four tractor beam." Odo confirmed what Kira had already guessed with a quick look at his sensors. "Originating from the Vinca-class tow barge."

Kira growled under her breath. "Of course . . ." She'd been on a Vinca for a year and a half when the Cardassians still used the clumsy ships to tractor salvaged vessels to the maintenance yards. Then someone had figured out that it was cheaper just to vaporize the wreckage and have a ramscoop sweep through the cloud and strain out the raw materials. They could usually salvage enough gold and rare isotopes to fund the building of a new ship and still have cash left over. It had been the scrap yard for the Vincas themselves then—all the ones that hadn't been sold black-market to anyone wanting enough tow power to yank an ore freighter to a standstill.

"It's used to hauling derelicts," Kira said aloud as she diverted shield power into the drive core. "Let's see how it holds up to a real engine."

She pushed the impulse engines until the overrides kicked in and forced a cutback of power, then added maneuvering thrusters to the mix in the hopes that the little bit of extra would snap them out of the *Vinca*'s grasp. Something at the back of the runabout groaned loudly, and Kira felt the panel start to shiver under her hands.

Odo, watching her struggle with her controls, grunted once. "It holds up fairly well, apparently."

Sarcasm from an ill-tempered changeling was the last thing she needed right now. "Can you get the station on subspace?" Kira asked as she knocked everything back down to idle.

He shook his head, running quickly through several attempts while he answered. "They're jamming us." He paused and glanced aside at Kira. "But I am picking up a hail from the *Kronos*."

"At least they're willing to talk to us before they blow us up." She nodded for him to put the call on the main viewscreen, and sat back in her seat so that her tension and frustration might not show so plainly to their captors. "This is Major Kira Nerys of *Deep Space Nine*. You'd better have a real good reason for hijacking a station runabout, because Starfleet tends to take exception to losing its equipment."

The older Bajoran woman who appeared on the viewscreen smiled with a bitter dryness that matched her sparse lines and weathered angles. "Then Starfleet should exercise more discretion about what it does to other people's ships."

Kira found herself drawn to the woman's simple earring, and had to force her eyes away from whatever half-memory it awoke to scowl at the owner. "What are you talking about?"

"We discovered this ore transport and three others like it while patrolling on official business," Odo explained. Leave it to the constable to understand a paranoid's ravings. "We had nothing to do with whatever happened here."

The woman snorted, and her almost-familiar earring jangled. "So you say."

Her easy dismissal of the truth burned in Kira's stomach

"Starfleet's here to help protect Bajor. Why would anyone at the station attack Bajoran vessels?"

"Because you can't protect Bajor without something to protect against. If we're not kept afraid and helpless, we might look up and notice that the Occupation never ended."

"That's not true!" Kira leaned forward over her panel, wishing this woman were more than just a projection so she could grab her and shake her. "If you'd ever worked with Starfleet, and seen how they treat each other, you'd know that it's not true."

The incredible bitterness etched into the woman's face ran deeper than any brief run-ins with the Federation, deeper than anything Kira had personally known, but was still somehow familiar in its flavor. "I know that they may wear prettier uniforms," this older, harder version of herself snarled, "and they may talk with prettier words. But they still lord over us in their Cardassian-built station, too far away to talk to or touch, and they control everything we do." She spat off to one side with a hatred so dry it left only harsh air. "Slavery is slavery, no matter how attractive the masters."

It was the phrase—the phrase, and the gesture. *Slavery is slavery,* a long-ago voice had declared with the same lack of interest other people used to talk about the weather. And Kira remembered being disgusted at the long streams of *chaat* juice Pak Dorren could land with such accuracy even a full meter away.

She'd been younger then, and Pak had been someone she was supposed to respect. And she hadn't. She still didn't. "Does terrorizing your own people with bombs and hijackings make you any better?"

The terrorist's pale eyes glittered, and she smiled a smile still faintly off-color from years of chewing *chaat.* "You know who I am."

Kira nodded somberly. "I thought you were dead."

"I almost was." And the honest grief in Pak's voice startled Kira into feeling a pang of sympathy. "I should have been. I never should have left children to finish something just because I thought it would be easy. I should have known that what came so naturally to me wasn't obvious to everyone." She refocused her eyes with obvious effort, fixing on Kira's face. "I still have nightmares about what I did to Veska Province. It's my greatest regret."

Kira refused to be moved by Pak's contrition. "You don't seem to learn from your mistakes."

The terrorist shrugged with a kind of easy acceptance of herself. "I'm more hands-on now," she explained. As if they were businessfolk, discussing how to maximize their profits. "From start to finish, I supervise every bomb we make. We don't have accidents anymore."

"Now," Odo interjected, "you only kill people on purpose."

Pak smiled again. "Funny you should mention that."

Kira hadn't consciously been waiting for any particular cue from Pak; she just reacted with an instinctive speed that even she didn't fully understand. She launched two torpedoes aft with a single swipe of her hand, then lunged for the helm controls as both missiles impacted against the Vinca's forward shields. *Rio Grande* was just enough below the tow barge's ecliptic that the blast rocked the bigger ship up and back; Kira slammed *Rio Grande* straight downward as powerfully as her engines would fire. If there was one thing she'd learned in a year and a half on a Vinca's crew, it was that tractor beams were damned near unbreakable under direct force, but surprisingly fragile when stressed on the sheer.

The runabout hesitated, a hill rover caught in the mud, then lunged forward so violently that Kira slammed back in her seat hard enough to bruise her neck on the rim of her environmental suit. She flailed for the controls that had been under her hands only a moment ago, caught the edge of the panel, dragged herself forward, and arced the runabout down and behind the ruined freighter without taking the time to verify coordinates. She heard the resounding crash of *Rio Grande*'s tail skipping across the derelict's surface just as one of the ships behind them carved away a section of the ore carrier's hull with a sweep of phaser fire. A roiling cloud of glowing vapor washed across the runabout's path. Kira struggled to level *Rio Grande* as they scraped off the aft side and into clear space, leaping them into full warp. The freighter's massive presence at her back didn't even enter into the equation—this was just one of those times where there were too many odds to play, and she had to pick which one to go for.

They were five seconds into flight before Kira dared to risk a look at her companion to see if they were both still there. She found Odo staring pensively out the front screen, an expression of peevish consideration on his smooth face.

"Still think this is something we can handle on our own?" Kira asked.

"We were following nine fugitives in an overloaded Orion transport when I made that suggestion," Odo pointed out, with more than just a little impatience in his tone. "Given recent developments, I think a return to the station might be in order."

Kira couldn't quite smother her smile. "I'm glad you agree." She laid in a course for the station, then let the runabout steer itself while she watched the cluster of sensor blips behind them recede, and blink, and finally vanish. "We can't let them go on like this," she said. The emptiness where Pak's trio of ships used to be fueled her with an idea she thought she should have had before this. "I don't care what sort of patriot Pak Dorren thinks she is, I'm not going to let her blow apart everything Bajor has worked for." She opened a subspace channel with a definitive flick of her thumb. *"Rio Grande* to DS9. Chief, prep the *Defiant* to leave the station. . . ."

"Captain Sisko?"

Sisko glanced up from drumming impatient fingers on the *Sreba*'s silent communications panel. Even at the top warp speed he'd insisted on, they were still several light-years out of *Deep Space Nine*'s normal hailing range. The wait chafed Sisko's tenuous hold on his temper, each minute dragging with it a different nightmare vision of his station being blasted by waves of invading Furies. Dax had sensed his seething impatience and wisely left him alone, moving over to join her younger human colleague at the adjacent science station. It was the Academy graduate student's voice hailing him now, softly enough not to catch the attention of T'Kreng and the other Vulcan scientists clustered around the main long-range scanner.

"What?" Tension made his voice sharper than he'd intended, and Sisko made an effort to soften it. "I'm sorry, Ensign, I don't remember your name—"

"It's Petersen, sir. I thought you might want to look at this."

"This" was the solitary equation now occupying her screen, full of imaginary numbers and integral signs, but surprisingly short compared with the complex calculations that had been crawling across the screen a few moments before. Sisko glanced at it briefly, then lifted an eyebrow at his science officer.

"Well, what does it mean?"

"No invasion," Dax said succinctly.

He scowled in disbelief. "How can you tell that from here?"

"We applied a moving-detector deconvolution program to get better resolution on the source frequency curve," Petersen said.

Sisko snorted. "Try that again, Ensign. This time in English."

Her apple cheeks turned a rosier shade of pink. "Sorry, sir. Lieutenant Dax and I have been able to find out exactly how fast the wormhole has been opening and closing, by correcting for our own warp speed." She toggled something on her board and the equation rippled off the monitor screen, replaced a moment later by an ice-white curve and a matching scatter of multicolored dots. "There's the actual data and our best-fit curve. It approximates a constant pattern of ten-second intervals, just as T'Kreng said, but the actual pattern is much more complex."

"So?"

Dax leaned forward, tracing the line with one confident finger. "What this shows, Benjamin, is that the wormhole is opening and closing in repeating octets, each event separated by precise inverse-logarithmic intervals of time. Even if an invading fleet tried to maintain a complicated pattern like that for some reason—"

"—the slop of individual ship passage times through the wormhole would destroy it," Sisko finished for her. The cold knot of tension in his gut dissolved a little. "So we really are seeing aftereffects of the wormhole throwing us back in time?"

"We do not yet have sufficient data to reach that conclusion," said T'Kreng's thin-edged voice from behind him. Sisko swung around to meet a crystalline glare, distributed with Vulcan impartiality to all of them. "I would appreciate it, Lieutenant Dax, if you would refrain from making unsupported hypotheses aboard my ship. Ensign Petersen, you know you are not supposed to run full-scale data reductions on the main computer without my direct authorization. And Captain Sisko—" She stepped back with a tiny gesture of two fingers toward the communications panel. "—if you had been carrying out the task for which I believe you volunteered, you would have noticed that someone is trying to hail us."

Sisko cursed and dove for the adjacent communications station. Just once, he thought fiercely, why couldn't this pedantic Vulcan professor give him information in order of its importance rather than its relevance to her own academic concerns?

Two quick focusing scans, and he had the hailing signal locked in, throwing it onto the main screen without bothering to ask permission from T'Kreng. It wasn't until the familiar contours of *Deep Space Nine*'s operations center appeared across the bridge, and he felt the hard knot of ice in his stomach finally melt, that Sisko realized how much he'd feared his station's complete destruction.

Onscreen, Ops seemed unusually noisy, as though many voices were talking just outside the viewing range. Without even looking up from his workstation, a stocky figure in coffee-stained engineering coveralls said, "Approaching Vulcan ship, please be aware that all traffic through the wormhole—"

"Chief O'Brien, it's Sisko."

"Captain!" The engineer swung toward them, a look of quick relief chasing the scowl off his blunt face. "Thank God you're back, sir. I've been trying to get a priority hail through to you by way of Starfleet headquarters, but there's too much quantum interference coming from the wormhole."

"I know." Sisko's internal time clock, calibrated by years

of shipboard service, told him this should be the daylight shift back at the station. "Where's Major Kira?"

O'Brien scrubbed a hand across his face, looking both tired and tense. "She and Odo are out chasing Bajoran paramilitary forces. They've been gone since yesterday night."

Sisko felt his gut clench tight. "Did they take the *Defiant?*"

The engineer shook his head. "No, there wasn't time to get it crewed before they left. The paramilitary cell aboard the station started a firefight when they were discovered, and the major went straight from there to a runabout to follow them. Her latest transmission came from just outside the Bajoran solar system."

The most annoying thing about Bajor's fledgling terrorists, Sisko decided, was their ability to make trouble at exactly the times when you wanted to pay them the least attention. "So you've been in Ops all day? How much traffic has there been through the wormhole?"

"None, sir." The tired lines around O'Brien's eyes creased deeper. "I revoked everyone's departure permits three hours ago, when the wormhole started opening and closing for no reason. Without Lieutenant Dax here, I didn't want to take any chances." He gave Sisko a brief, mirthless smile. "There's a bunch of Ferengi and Orion merchants standing outside Ops right now, screaming about me having exceeded my authority. I expect you can hear them."

Sisko grunted. "Patch me into a stationwide audio loop," he ordered, and waited for O'Brien's confirming nod. "This is Captain Benjamin Sisko, commander of *Deep Space Nine,* declaring a Class Five Sector Emergency. On Starfleet Command authority, all departure permits for the Gamma Quadrant are canceled indefinitely. All visiting crews who have not left the station within three standard hours will be confined to their vessels. Anyone attempting to pass through the wormhole will be stopped or destroyed by station phasers." He nodded at O'Brien to cut the audio echo, then said into the ensuing quiet, "Did that chase them out of Ops, Chief?"

"Like Cardassian voles who just got a whiff of fumigant,"

O'Brien confirmed. "And with any luck, you'll be back here before Quark shows up to complain about his lost profits."

Sisko's mouth twisted wryly. "I expect so. We should be docking in—" He glanced over at Dax, who'd taken over the navigation panel from a disgruntled-looking Vulcan scientist.

"—approximately ten minutes," she finished.

"Good. We've got docking space available on pylon two. O'Brien out." The communications channel closed in a small sizzle of static. When Sisko turned back, it was to find T'Kreng giving him a steely look across her bridge. She had resumed her captain's chair, sweeping her slim fingers back and forth across its small control panel as if to reassure herself she was still in command here.

"I trust you are not including the *Sreba* in your prohibition on travel through the wormhole, Captain," she said flatly.

Sisko met her colorless glare with one he hoped looked just as implacable. "Yes, I am. My chief engineer is right—with the wormhole behaving like this, it's too dangerous to let any ship through. And if I allow you in there, every Orion and Ferengi ship onstation is going to try and go right in after you. Your singularity survey will have to wait, Professor."

Nothing moved on T'Kreng's face, but all its lines and angles took on a severe, glass-sharp look. "If I wait, there will be nothing left of the wormhole to survey. Our only chance of preventing the time avulsion is to locate the exact time and place when it starts."

This time, Sisko didn't have to force a glare. If there was one thing that exasperated him about scientists, it was their single-minded belief that you couldn't solve a crisis without first finding its ultimate cause. "And if you do locate it, then what? We can't risk sending the *Defiant* through the wormhole if the problem's on the other side, and there's no other heavily armed starship within range—even assuming Starfleet would risk sending one into an unstable singularity." He overrode whatever the Vulcan physicist was trying to say by the simple expedient of raising his voice to drown out hers. "And if the problem turns out to be on our side, all we need to do is watch the wormhole and blow up any ship, probe, or object that tries to approach it."

T'Kreng's delicate voice sounded as if it might shatter with the intensity of her restrained Vulcan rage. "That, Captain, is a typical military solution, made in total ignorance of the true scientific complexity of this situation. I find myself forced to remind you that you do not have the authority to revoke my research commission from Starfleet Command."

"But I *do* have the authority to defend the Bajoran wormhole," Sisko retorted. A quick glance behind showed him not only Jadzia Dax's decisive nod of agreement but an unexpected hand gesture from the young physics graduate student sitting beside her. The fingers of Petersen's left hand first curled into a fist and then snapped outward again—a gesture Sisko remembered from his own days at Starfleet Academy. It was the silent hand signal that meant a cadet's assigned ship had been destroyed during a battle simulation.

Sisko scowled and turned back to T'Kreng, who was tapping commands into her control panel as if the argument were over. He dropped his voice to its deepest and most somber note, dragging her reluctant attention back to him. "If the *Sreba* is destroyed during its passage through the wormhole, Professor T'Kreng, isn't it possible that you will trigger the very time avulsion we're trying to prevent?"

The quantum physicist gave him a glacially affronted look. "I believe that to be an extremely remote possibility, Captain."

"But it is—at least theoretically—possible?"

He had her trapped on the unyielding bars of Vulcan logic, and they both knew it. T'Kreng's eyebrows tightened in a look as near frustration as Sisko had ever seen a Vulcan come. "Yes. Theoretically, yes."

"Then until and unless we get a countercommand from Starfleet Headquarters, this ship will be detained as soon as it docks at *Deep Space Nine*," he said crisply. "If you leave station and approach the wormhole, Professor, I'm afraid I will have to apply the same sanctions to you as I have threatened to apply to any other ship at *Deep Space Nine*."

He'd expected a flood of logical Vulcan argument in

response, but T'Kreng surprised him with a minuscule nod. "A strategically defensible move, Captain, even if it is a completely transparent one. You and I are both aware that as long as the Bajoran wormhole continues to be racked by quantum echoes—in fact, quite probably until the very moment of its destruction—we will be unable to contact Starfleet Command on any subspace channels." She lifted one slender shoulder in a shrug so slight it barely stirred the fabric of her platinum robe. "Afterward, of course, it will be too late. The wormhole will be gone."

"Assuming your scientific analysis is the correct one, Professor," Dax pointed out calmly from behind. "We have *Deep Space Nine* and the wormhole in visual range now, Benjamin."

Sisko glanced up at the viewscreen, seeing the familiar crowned silhouette of his station backlit by the disturbing glow of the wormhole as it writhed open and shut. The spiral of singularity-funneled light had lost its pristine symmetry, shredding into tendrils and shreds of bright ionized gas that lingered in phosphorescent shadows even when it closed. Each time it opened, its edges looked more frayed, as if it were eating away at itself from within.

"No one's going through that wormhole again," Sisko said with grim conviction. He swung around to give T'Kreng a hard look. "We've arrived too late for you to do any good here, Professor."

"Do you think so?" T'Kreng asked, a little too politely. "I do not agree."

Compared to the delicate restraint of all the Vulcan's previous gestures, her sudden stab down at her control panel hit Sisko like a blow. He cursed and took a step toward her, guessing what she meant to do, but by then it was too late. In midstride, he heard a familiar hum and felt his muscles freeze inside the paralyzing shimmer of a transporter field. His dissolving senses caught the edge of a surprised cry from Dax, echoed more faintly by one from Heather Petersen, and then nothingness closed in around him.

CHAPTER 9

THEY MATERIALIZED WITH annoying Vulcan precision, directly centered on *Deep Space Nine*'s main transporter pad and so well aligned that Sisko didn't even feel the usual slight drop to the floor. For some reason, the perfection of the maneuver blasted his anger at T'Kreng to an even hotter pitch. He slammed a hand over his comm badge the instant his muscles were released from the beam's tingling paralysis.

"Sisko to Ops," he snarled. "Locate the Vulcan science ship *Sreba*—"

"Medical override!" Bashir snapped out from behind him, and Sisko swung around to see the doctor lunging toward the ancient stasis chamber that had been beamed in with them. Disconnected from the *Sreba*'s power supply, it stood dark and ominously silent on one edge of the transporter pad. "An occupied medical stasis chamber has just been beamed aboard without internal power, repeat *without internal power*. I need immediate onboard transport to medical bay—"

"I'm on it, Julian," said O'Brien's voice from the comm.

"—and technical assistance with the power linkage—"

Bashir disappeared in midword, along with the symbiont's chamber. Dax took one step toward where it had been, then pulled herself up with a visible effort and turned to Sisko. "We have to get to Ops and stop T'Kreng."

He was already heading for the door and the nearest turbolift. "Sisko to Ops," he snapped at his comm badge again. "O'Brien, I want you to stop that Vulcan ship before it enters the wormhole!"

The voice that answered him was Commander Eddington's. "Chief O'Brien had himself beamed down to the infirmary to help Dr. Bashir, sir. And the computer reports no Vulcan ships docked at the station now."

Sisko slammed the turbolift call button with a great deal more force than it required. "It's not docked, Mr. Eddington, it's in transit—"

"Moving at warp five approximately five hundred kilometers out from *Deep Space Nine*," Dax added. "Concentrate your scan toward sectors nineteen, twenty, and twenty-one."

"Yes, sir."

The turbolift doors hummed open at last, slowly enough that Sisko was inside with Dax before they had even finished moving. "Ops, priority one," he snapped at the lift computer. The doors moved with more satisfying speed this time, although they made an ominous screech as they did so. "When was the last time we overhauled the turbolifts?" he demanded irritably of his science officer.

Dax gave him an exasperated glance. "Just last month. Remember, I told you that a lot of them needed to be replaced? *Deep Space Nine* was never designed for the kind of commercial traffic it's getting these days."

He grunted. "That may not be a problem for much longer."

"True."

There was a long, tense pause. Sisko forced himself to concentrate on the numbers that flicked across the lift's location display rather than on the lengthening silence from Ops. He knew all too well where part of his anger was coming from: his illogical but complete conviction that if Kira Nerys had been up in Operations, instead of out chasing a straggle of would-be Bajoran terrorists, the *Sreba* would already be locked tight in the station's tractor beam. She might not be Bajor's best diplomat or even a very comfortable second-in-command, but when it came to anything military, Sisko trusted Kira's instincts and abilities almost as much as he trusted his own.

"Captain, we've located the Vulcan ship," said Eddington's voice from his comm badge.

"Good." The turbolift doors screeched open at Ops and Sisko vaulted through them, feeling the immediate gut-deep reassurance of being in command of his own crew and station again. The main viewscreen showed an infinitesimal *Sreba*, barely visible against the ionization haze of the pulsing wormhole. "Is she out of tractor range?"

"Yes," said Eddington and Dax simultaneously. The Trill had wasted no time reclaiming her usual place at the science station.

Sisko took a deep breath, trying to purge all anger from the decision he was about to make. "Then fire phasers on her immediately, Mr. Eddington."

The Starfleet security commander swung in his chair at the weapons console, staring across at Sisko incredulously. "You want me to fire on a *unarmed* Federation vessel, Captain? Can't we just—"

"Fire your phasers, Mr. Eddington. That's an order."

Eddington's narrow face folded into disapproving lines, but his Starfleet training was far too ingrained to let him make the fierce protest Kira would have in his place. He punched in a firing sequence, with a careful precision that made Sisko's teeth ache with gritted impatience. "Initiating phaser blast now, Captain."

Streaks of fierce white light punctured the space around *Deep Space Nine,* burning a curved path toward the wormhole. Sisko scowled as he watched the increasing deviation of the usually lance-straight phaser beams. He knew, even before Eddington spoke, what he was going to say.

"Phasers off by point-four degrees of arc, Captain. A complete miss." The Starfleet security officer spun around to give him a baffled look. "My weapons system still insists those are the right coordinates, sir. Do you want me to fire again?"

Sisko shook his head irritably. "Dax, what's going on?"

"The wormhole's fluctuations are bending the local curvature of space, Benjamin." Dax looked up, face splashed red and gold by reflections from the computer model now pulsing on her screen in perfect synchronicity with the wormhole. "Either the *Sreba* isn't exactly where our instruments say she is, or our phasers are being deflected away from her by the singularity matrix."

"Can we correct for the curvature?"

The Trill's strong hands were already moving across her control panel. "I'm sending new coordinates over to your weapons console, Commander."

"Too late," Eddington said bluntly. "She's entering the wormhole."

Sisko swung around to stare up at the monitor. The wormhole's once slow and majestic portal, into which ships had skimmed on a sea of calm radiance, now cracked open and shut in a series of irregular bursts, like the grand finale of an old-fashioned fireworks display. The *Sreba* had been a small flake of dark ash silhouetted against that flickering fire, but now it glowed inside an ominous haze of ionized gases, reaching out from the singularity like a tentacle to drag the small Vulcan ship inside. It vanished in a spike of light as bright as any phaser burst.

"Hull breach?" Sisko demanded of Dax, without taking his gaze away from the screen. It seemed to him that the ship's disappearance had been followed by a longer than usual pause in the wormhole's frenetic dance of opening and closing.

"No trace of ship debris or ionic pulses from a warp-core overload," his science officer reported after a moment's intent silence. "I think they made it into the wormhole. There's no way to know if they made it out again."

Sisko slammed one big hand against the nearest non-breakable surface, which happened to be the transparent aluminum panels of his own office doors. His palm stung from the impact just enough to calm his icy rage and let him consider his alternatives.

"Dax, do you remember the *Sreba*'s main communicator frequency?" he demanded after a moment. "Can you bounce a narrow-beam signal to them through the wormhole?"

"It's possible. I'll have to compensate for the space-time curvature effects first, though. Give me a few minutes." She glanced up from the relativistic model on her science monitor, lips tightening in a somber expression that he recognized from his time with Curzon. "I'd appreciate it, Benjamin, if you'd check in with the infirmary in the meantime."

"Of course, old man." Sisko glanced at the mixed crew of Starfleet and Bajoran personnel staffing Ops, then turned and entered the more discreet silence of his own office. He waited for the doors to hiss shut before tapping his comm badge.

"Sisko to Bashir. What's the status of your patient, Doctor?"

The voice that answered after a moment was O'Brien's. "We've got the stasis chamber plugged in and back on-line, Captain." There was another, longer pause. "Julian says the patient survived the transfer better than he expected—no additional physiological trauma and only a little neurological shock. He says it actually seems to have stabilized itself at more normal levels of—um—vital chemicals."

From the engineer's carefully guarded tone, Sisko deduced that O'Brien had been both admitted into the doctor's confidence and given a strict lecture on keeping it. "Tell Dr. Bashir that's the first good news I've gotten since I beamed back aboard." He saw Dax glance up again from her console and gave her a thumbs-up sign through his window. The Trill's face lit with a brief flash of smile before she bent back over the pulsing glow of her monitor. "Has anyone else but you seen our—um—patient?"

"No, Captain. Julian's assistant was off-duty when we got here."

Sisko sat back in his office chair, scrubbing a hand across his beard thoughtfully. If he remembered correctly, the medical assistant was also from Bajor. "Can you rig up some kind of security access panel to isolate that stasis chamber, Chief? I don't want anyone visiting down there unless they've got a Priority One clearance from Starfleet Command."

"I've already designed a portable isolation barrier for the infirmary, Captain." Part of what made O'Brien such a good engineer was his ability to foresee and prepare for the kinds of problems he'd eventually be ordered to solve. "It'll block off this whole wing and give us room to move in a cot and food replicator for Julian. If you don't need me up at Ops, I'll get started on it right now."

"Do that," Sisko agreed. "And tell Dr. Bashir to start thinking up a good cover story for his assistant, to keep any rumors from starting."

"No problem," said the doctor's crisp voice from the comm. "I'll just find a disease I've been exposed to that she hasn't."

"Tartha pox?" O'Brien suggested. "Keiko said they had an outbreak of it in Molly's day-care center on Bajor a few weeks ago. It hit the Bajoran kids pretty hard."

One corner of Sisko's mouth kicked up in brief amusement. "I'd prefer something just a little more deadly than that, Chief. I want to make sure anyone else who might be curious about what we beamed in doesn't decide to drop in and pay poor Julian a visit."

"Garak, for example," Bashir said wryly.

O'Brien snorted. "Or Quark."

"Exactly, gentlemen. Sisko out."

He started to lever himself out of his chair with both hands, his shoulder muscles stiff from too much stress and too little sleep. Before he'd even finished rising, the translucent comm screen on his desk rippled with color, signaling an incoming call. Sisko groaned and fell back into his chair.

"Deep Space Nine, Captain Benjamin Sisko."

"At last." The prim outrage in that voice told him who was calling even before Kai Winn's chilly face had finished coalescing in his screen. "Emissary, I have been trying to reach you for *two hours."*

Sisko scrubbed a hand over his face again, hoping he didn't look as grimy and unwashed as he felt. "I was off-station—on a high-priority Starfleet assignment—until just a few minutes ago."

"Well, perhaps the Prophets know why you had to be gone during such a critical time for Bajor," Kai Winn said, with her usual infuriating blend of dulcet voice and malicious words. "Have you at least begun to address our problem, Emissary?"

For a second time, Sisko found himself silently cursing the absence of his second-in-command. "I believe Major

Kira is currently engaged in tracking the—er—the alleged terrorists—"

"You think that these are *terrorist* attacks?" Winn's pale eyebrows lifted in what almost looked like real amazement. "But why would the Maquis want to attack and destroy ordinary Bajoran freighters?"

"Who said anything about the Maquis?" Sisko demanded absently, his attention shifting past his viewscreen to Dax. She had transferred whatever signal relay she was working on to the main viewscreen of Ops, but so far all she had to show for it was a queasy blur of subspace static. He glanced back at Kai Winn's frowning face, and what she had said finally sank in. "For that matter, who said anything about Bajoran freighters?"

She gave him an irritated look. "I did, Emissary, in my very first message to you. In the last twelve hours, three Bajoran ore-carrying freighters have been attacked and destroyed within our solar system by some unknown force. *Within our solar system.*"

The interior steel that the Kai usually kept hidden under layers of false sweetness gleamed naked and fierce in her final words. Sisko eyed her narrowly. Despite all of Winn's secret maneuverings for power, there was no doubt that her one and only commitment was to her planet's future. Any threat to Bajor that could peel away her hypocritical mask of demure sweetness and expose the tiger beneath had to be real.

"The terrorists I was thinking of were Bajoran—a cell that Major Kira uncovered here on *Deep Space Nine*," he told her. "Could they be the ones responsible for these attacks?"

"No." For once, her reply was as blunt and honest as his question. "I have observers placed in the group on *Deep Space Nine* as well as in the Bajoran militias. Neither has space weapons powerful enough to destroy ore freighters."

Sudden exasperation flared through Sisko. "You mean you knew about the terrorist cell on my station, and didn't bother to inform me about it?"

Kai Winn gave him a sweetly mocking smile. "How could I, Emissary? There was always the chance that some of your own staff might have been involved with it."

And you wouldn't have minded if Deep Space Nine *had been blown up, anyway,* Sisko wanted to snap back, although he knew he couldn't. He gritted his teeth and tried to ignore the frustration that his conversations with the Kai usually devolved into. Unlike the Cardassians, who never much cared if you told them what you thought of them, Winn would stalk off in insulted and uncooperative hauteur if you called her on her manipulative power plays.

"Were there any witnesses rescued from the damaged ore freighters?" he asked instead.

"None." Winn's smile vanished and her elaborately ringed hands tightened in her lap. "Every freighter was found sliced open—completely breached to vacuum, without a trace of crew left aboard alive or dead. We're not even sure what weapons were used to do it." She gave him a glance as cold and hard as latinum. "Our economic recovery depends on our new ore-processing plants, Emissary. Any threat to our freighters is a threat to our entire planet."

"I understand that."

Kai Winn made a graceful gesture, more sweeping than any T'Kreng would have used but somehow exuding the same utter sureness and self-possession. "Then you will have to hunt these raiders down and stop them immediately. As the captain of the only starship permanently stationed in this quadrant, I believe that is your responsibility."

"One of them," he agreed. Out in Ops, he could see a wavering image starting to melt through the static on the monitor. "Unfortunately, right now my main responsibility is to Starfleet and the Priority One operation I'm engaged in. Your raiders will have to wait."

"Emissary." The Kai gave him a hurt and puzzled look, although he could read the shark-swift calculations rippling through her pale eyes. "Surely, you can't mean that."

"I mean it."

"But the only reason we agreed to have a Starfleet presence in this region was to protect us while we recover from the Cardassian occupation. If you can't protect us, we may have to find someone else who can."

Sisko gave her an exasperated glance. "Like the Romulans?"

Winn glanced down at her gently clasped hands, a picture of religious humility. "Perhaps," she agreed softly. "Or the Klingons."

Sisko's lips tightened. "Neither of whom would be very interested in Bajor if it weren't next door to the only stable wormhole in the galaxy," he said bluntly. "Before you start issuing ultimatums to Starfleet, Kai Winn, I suggest you call up some of your university astronomers and find out how stable the Bajoran wormhole is. Or isn't." He paused, savoring the rare gratification of shaking Winn's hypocritical mask completely off. Her face had gone steel-hard with shock, eyes narrowing to suspicious slits. "In the meantime, I'll assign Major Kira the job of protecting your ore freighters, as soon as she's back on board *Deep Space Nine*. Sisko out."

He stabbed the end-transmission button, cutting the Kai off before she could utter the indignant protest he saw gathering on her face. The instant he did, his comm badge beeped, as if Dax had toggled it to wait until the Kai was off-line. "Benjamin, get out here," she said urgently. "We're getting a signal from the *Sreba*."

Sisko rounded his desk in two strides, turning his shoulders sideways to slide through his office doors as they opened. On the main viewscreen, a haze-streaked view of the *Sreba's* bridge had coalesced out of the subspace static, peopled with ghostly Vulcan figures at barely visible monitor stations.

Dax looked up at him from the science panel. "From the way their signal's resonating, I think they're still inside the wormhole," she informed him. "I'm compensating for the subspace fluctuations as much as I can."

Sisko grunted and punched a communications channel open. He could just make out a familiar slight, still figure in the center of the screen. "This is *Deep Space Nine* hailing the *Sreba*," he said. "Can you hear me, T'Kreng?"

"You are interfering with our ability to scan the singularity matrix," said the Vulcan physicist's annoyed voice, oddly clear and sharp from that clouded image. "Stop transmitting at once."

After dealing with the Kai, Sisko was in no mood for

another civilian's condescending orders. "Why are you still in the wormhole? Can't you get out?"

"We were in the process of running our fourth and final scan—" The signal wavered and buzzed with static, then reformed. "—have to redo it from the opposite end now."

"No!" From the corner of his eye, Sisko could see heads turn throughout Ops at the force of that shout. He concentrated all his attention on the ivory smudge of T'Kreng's face. "Whatever you do, don't go out the opposite end of the wormhole!"

Whatever gesture T'Kreng made to her navigator was too subtle to carry across the blurred screen, but her voice sounded less annoyed and more serene. "We are in no danger, Captain. We have identified the onset of the time rift to a high degree of confidence, and have a satisfactory buffer within which to operate. We are proceeding to exit the wormhole now—"

Her voice didn't break off—it was swamped beneath a sudden thunder of explosions, ship alarms, and the bone-chilling roar of air escaping into vacuum. The *Sreba*'s visual signal flared into meaningless prismatic colors, and a moment later its audio plummeted into utter silence.

"We've lost contact," Dax reported, breaking the appalled hush that filled Ops.

"Did they get caught in the wormhole as it closed?"

"Maybe." Her freckled forehead creased with frustration as she scrolled through her sensor readouts. "I can't tell from here what destroyed them. I can't even tell if they made it out into the Gamma Quadrant or not."

Sisko felt the muscles along his jaw tighten. It was fear more than intelligence that told him what to do next. "Put the wormhole back on the main viewscreen."

Dax punched in the command, and a familiar tattered glow of ionized gas replaced the subspace static. Sisko waited, watching for the explosive flash-dance of the wormhole to appear in the midst of that afterglow. A moment crawled past, and then another. Nothing happened.

"Captain," Eddington said sharply, as if he was worried that Sisko couldn't see it for himself. "The wormhole's not there anymore!"

Sisko had thought that nothing could be more unnerving

than the irrational tremors of a singularity opening and closing for no reason. He was wrong. The sudden, inexplicable absence of the wormhole's inner radiance made the skin between his shoulders crawl with dread. He swung around toward Dax. "Has it been destroyed?"

Her hands raced across her science station. "No, not according to my instruments. It's not gone, just closed. Back to normal."

"Back to normal," he repeated softly. A chorus of relieved sighs rustled through Ops at those words, but Dax met his gaze with deep foreboding in her eyes. Sisko gestured her toward his office with a silent jerk of his chin. "Mr. Eddington, you have Ops. Keep a channel open to the *Sreba*, in case she reappears."

"Yes, Captain."

Dax followed him up the steps, still frowning. "Do you think T'Kreng was wrong about the time?" she asked, as soon as the doors slid shut behind them.

"Maybe." He turned to watch the viewscreen through his windows in somber silence. The tortured glow of ionized gas was slowly fading around the wormhole, leaving the screen lit only by the tiny diamond sparkles of distant stars. "She was certainly wrong about something. If the wormhole's back to normal, then whatever was going to happen to it must have either happened already, or somehow been averted."

"I agree," Dax said. "Should I check to see if—if Julian still has a patient?"

Sisko nodded grimly. "Yes. But I already suspect that Starfleet Command won't care what the answer is. They're going to want to know what's on the other side of the wormhole now that it's stopped spasming."

His science officer gave him an intent look. "You think the wormhole's new stability means that the Furies have already finished using it as their jump gate?"

"Yes." He took a deep breath, abruptly thankful that Jake was spending his school vacation as Keiko's field assistant down on Bajor. This situation could only get worse. "What happened to the *Sreba* didn't sound like an accident to me. For all we know, the Furies could be in position to invade us from the Gamma Quadrant right now."

"Possibly," Dax agreed. "Maybe we'd better ask Judith to send us some of those ships she's hoarding at Starbase One."

Sisko clenched a fist around his antique baseball, feeling its normally strong sides yield beneath his fingers. "But the *Defiant* is still the only ship in Starfleet that can scout the Fury fleet and bring the information back without being detected." He looked up and met Dax's somber gaze. "Whether we like it or not, old man, we're going to have to go through the wormhole one last time."

After nearly two days in a runabout with no shower and no bed, the only thing Kira really wanted to do was strip out of her sweaty uniform and go to bed. Duty always complicated things, though. First, duty had kept her diligently awake while Odo puddled in the back of the passenger compartment—embarrassed about being there when the constable was forced to revert to liquid, resentful of having no such good excuse herself for taking a much needed time-out. Then duty had trapped her into a decidedly short and sour conversation with Eddington as she brought *Rio Grande* into dock, all because she thought it proper to ask someone what had gone on at the station in her absence. No, Chief O'Brien wasn't available to talk to her, yes, the station was still all in one piece, and would the major mind very much if Mr. Eddington put off answering any further questions until they could talk face-to-face? As if anything that prissy Starfleet dandy had to say would be worth someone's effort to monitor. Still, it was as good an excuse as any to get him off the comm, and she'd finished docking *Rio Grande* in sleepy, aching silence.

Now, duty had brought her to the airlock just outside the *Defiant's* berth before even letting her point herself toward home. She had some silly notion that O'Brien might be down here, preparing the ship for launch like she'd told him. Instead, two of Eddington's boys in gold stepped up to form a solid wall of grimness the moment she came near the airlock doors.

"Good evening, gentlemen." She meant it to come out politely, but couldn't even remember how that was supposed to sound, so she suspected she spoke more irritably than she'd intended. "Is Chief O'Brien still around?"

The taller of the two slipped neatly into her path when she moved to step around him, not even backing down to avoid their brief collision. "I'm sorry, sir, but this area is restricted to official Starfleet personnel."

She couldn't hold back the sharp laugh that huffed out of her. "I'm the first officer on the station, mister. I think that's official enough."

This time when he blocked her, he at least had the grace to look apologetic. "Not anymore, sir. I'm sorry."

You bet you are. But she quashed that feeling quickly—it wasn't his fault that her last two days had been less than ideal. "Who ordered this?" If it was Eddington, she was going to burn his skinny little Starfleet ass.

"Captain Sisko, sir."

"Captain Sisko?" Not at all the answer she'd expected. "He's not even on the station!"

The guards exchanged what Kira assumed was supposed to be a discreet glance; then the younger of the two volunteered, "He is now, sir. He got back last night."

Well, that at least simplified things more than doing the Starfleet shuffle with Eddington. Slapping at her comm badge, Kira kept a stern glower on the two guards as she called, "Kira to Sisko. I'm just outside the *Defiant's* berth in upper pylon three, and two of Eddington's jarheads are try—"

"Hold that thought, Major." Sisko's voice, as smooth and collected as always, still managed to sound brusquely distracted as he cut her off. "I'll join you in a moment."

This was apparently everyone's day for hustling her off the comm. Crossing her arms—and not caring if that made her look unpleasant or aggressive—she paced back and forth in the stubby stretch of hallway in front of the guards. She wasn't even mad at them anymore; she was tired past the point of being angry. All that was left was a sort of grumpy irritation that she'd been stupid enough to come down here in the first place, and an almost childlike longing for the comfort of her own warm quarters, and for sleep.

She had her back to the airlock—staring down the main hall for Sisko's arrival, even though she knew it was far too soon to expect him—when the airlock door rolled aside with a bone-deep rumble. She jerked a look behind her from habit, and was surprised to see the captain sidestep through the hatchway while it was still barely wide enough to admit him. "Major," he greeted in a tone of polished neutrality. "Welcome home. Commander Eddington got down here just a few minutes ahead of you, and told me you were back."

Kira bobbed up on tiptoe to steal a glimpse of whatever was happening beyond the big round door, but Sisko's height and the artfully placed security guards prevented her from seeing much before the lock boomed closed. "What's going on?"

Sisko nodded toward the other end of the hall—away from the ubiquitous security drones—and Kira was just as happy to oblige him. She only made it half the distance, though, before demanding grumpily, "Why didn't Eddington tell me you were back? I didn't even know you were down here."

"Commander Eddington has a tendency to err on the side of caution, I'm afraid. I didn't specifically ask him to tell you, and he didn't want to appear presumptuous." He slowed to a stop with a dry smile, pulling her around in front of him so that his body blocked her view of the security team. Or blocked her from them, it occurred to her, and the thought gave her a chill. "I'm down here with Dax and O'Brien. We're getting the *Defiant* ready for launch."

At least some things were stumbling along in the direction she expected. "When do you think we'll be leaving?"

"*We* aren't going anywhere," he corrected her with gentle emphasis. "*You* are staying on the station to keep an eye on militia activity while Dax and I go to the Gamma Quadrant."

She was too tired to do more than hiss with frustration. "We already know everything we need to about militia activity! Odo and I just spent thirty-six hours chasing them into the Badlands after they hulled four sublight freighters!" She flashed an angry hand back toward the airlock. "I came back to the station for the *Defiant* so we could finish tracking them."

A certain careful stillness settled over his face. "The *Defiant* isn't available."

She'd seen him like this very rarely—his expression

leached of all emotion, the elegant angles of his face smoothed into planes like coffee-colored marble. And then you looked into his eyes, and you could see the awful power of the emotions he was trapping behind that mask, and you realized that what you dealt with was only a fraction of what this man could call upon if he chose. Kira had seen that frightful coldness slip into place for countless Cardassian Guls who still thought their rank gave them power in this sector, for Kai Winn when she presumed to argue her personal goals in the name of the Prophets, for Bajorans who insisted on making him their spiritual Emissary no matter how he rejected that mantle. Kira had even seen Bashir slapped with that look once when the doctor was foolish enough to interrupt an official subspace transmission. But in all her years of working beside him, Sisko had never turned that face on her.

"You're the commander of this station, aren't you?" she asked, doing the only thing she knew to do with her frustration—lash out. "You could make it available."

The captain's face never stirred. "I'm afraid it's not that easy."

"Why not? Because Starfleet's decided the engine's isotopic ratios are more important than a few Bajoran ore transports?" She'd expected the hint that she'd sensed the importance of yesterday's comm call to at least spark a flicker of surprise in his dark eyes. Instead, he only held her gaze with his own as though trying to will his thoughts directly into her. The sheer intensity of his stare finally forced her to turn away under the pretense of pacing. "I can't believe we're having this conversation. You told me once that you were really dedicated to helping Bajor, no matter what Starfleet's motives for being here might be." She stopped on the other side of the corridor, that little distance giving her the bravery to scowl back at him again. "Isn't that true anymore?" Then, because it was really the crux of her fear and anger, "What did they talk to you about back at Starbase One?"

He opened his mouth to answer her, but Kira could see him swallow whatever he'd originally begun to say even before he gusted a frustrated growl and started over. "Believe me, Major, my concern for this system is greater now than ever. And sometimes Starfleet's motives and the good of Bajor really do run hand-in-hand." He glanced aside, as though conferring with himself, then turned back to her with his mask peeled aside and a confusion of emotions roiling in his eyes. "For right now, all I can tell you is that Admiral Hayman has already ordered the starship *Mukaikubo* to DS9. She's not as heavily armed as the *Defiant*, but she should be able to handle any militia hunting you might need."

Kira wasn't sure what unnerved her most—what Sisko wasn't telling her, or what he'd almost said between the lines. "A rear admiral like Hayman can't possibly care about a little militia trouble in Bajoran shipping lanes. Why is she sending the *Mukaikubo* here?"

"If what we're doing in the Gamma Quadrant is successful," he said with a care that was chilling, "it won't matter why the *Mukaikubo* came."

Kira nodded, understanding enough to know that she hated not knowing more. "And if you're not successful?"

She could see the apology in his eyes, and in the way his jaw muscles knotted with the effort of keeping silent.

"Don't do this to me!" she flared. "Don't leave me in the dark like this!"

"I don't have any choice—I don't really know anything more for certain than you do."

"You know enough to be afraid," she countered.

He met her gaze frankly. "Don't you?"

This time, it was Kira who glanced away.

"The *Mukaikubo* should be here within two days," Sisko went on, almost gently. "Captain Regitz knows you're my second-in-command. She'll give you her full cooperation."

She swung about at the sound of his footsteps, stopping him just before he joined the guards at the airlock door. "What about you?" she challenged. "When are you bringing the *Defiant* back?"

An odd, not-quite smile ghosted across his face. "That's a very good question, Major." He keyed open the lock behind him. "I hope I get the chance to tell you the answer."

CHAPTER 10

"JADZIA, YOU CAN'T do this."

Dax looked up from where she knelt beside the *Defiant's* piloting panel, surprised by the flat intensity of that familiar voice. Bashir was nothing more than a rail-thin silhouette against the flare of light from the flash-welder O'Brien was using beside her, but what she could see of the set of his shoulders and jaw radiated worry. Across the bridge, she noticed Sisko pause in his intent reprogramming of the weapons station with Eddington and give the doctor a long, considering look. As far as she knew, this was the first time since they'd beamed aboard that Bashir had left the infirmary.

"I have to, Julian. We're only taking a skeleton crew through the wormhole with us." Dax glanced down at the optical cables she was holding for O'Brien, to make sure she hadn't joggled them. "Don't worry, my reflexes are fast enough to handle engineering and fly the ship at the same time. That's the advantage of having two cerebral cortices."

"That's not what I meant and you know it." Bashir came closer, squatting beside O'Brien as if to inspect the chief engineer's work. The spit and sizzle of optical cables fusing in the heat of the laser-welder shielded his words from the rest of the *Defiant's* small bridge. "How can you even *think* of taking the *Defiant* to the Gamma Quadrant? Didn't you tell me that the isotopic ratios in the old

Defiant's warp core meant it would be thrown back in time on its very next voyage?"

"Assuming we were still trapped in our original timeline, that would be true," Dax agreed. "But the wormhole's been stable for six hours now. That means there's a high probability the original time rift has been averted."

"Then why hasn't the old Dax symbiont disappeared?" he demanded tightly.

She started to shrug, then realized that would joggle the cable in her hands and forced herself to be still. "Starfleet Command thinks that five thousand years of being embedded in our time flow gave the old *Defiant* and her crew so much temporal inertia that even the elimination of their original time shift couldn't destroy them. It has something to do with conservation of space-time energy."

Bashir looked appalled. "That means the other Dax is going to stay in our timeline forever? As—as a relict?"

"I believe the technical term is 'timeline orphan.'" She watched the last microscopically fine crystal strands of optical cable fuse together in a prism of laser-sparked reflections. "Of course, it's just been a theoretical term until now. The *Defiant* will be the first documented case on record."

"Only if the time rift in the wormhole really has been averted." O'Brien toggled off the laser torch, and replaced the circuit-panel cover with a grunt. "And I thought you said the probability of that was sixty-eight percent, Lieutenant."

Dax gave him an exasperated glance. She should have known better than to give Julian a reassuring version of the odds against them with an engineer as meticulous as O'Brien in hearing range. "That was my minimum estimate," she said, seeing frown lines crease back into the doctor's thin face.

"And what was your maximum estimate?" Bashir demanded.

Dax bit her lip, and scrambled to her feet so she wouldn't have to see his expression. "Seventy-two percent," she admitted, then bent over her piloting board to fend off whatever reply he would have made to that. "I'll start running diagnostics to make sure the engineering circuits are completely tied in, Chief. Why don't you go help Captain Sisko and Commander Eddington automate the phaser firing sequences?"

O'Brien shot Bashir a perceptive glance. "I think the captain's got that pretty much under control. Maybe it would be better if I went back to the infirmary and kept an eye on Julian's patient for him."

"Yes." Bashir rubbed a hand wearily across his face. "I would appreciate that very much."

O'Brien rose and dropped a hand on the doctor's shoulder to give him a quick, admonitory shake. "Take a shower and get something to eat before you come back to work," he advised. "If the lieutenant's right, your medical problem's not going anywhere."

"I wish I knew if that was good news or bad." Bashir leaned back against the base of the piloting console from his seat on the floor and closed his eyes with a tired wince. Dax and O'Brien exchanged concerned glances over his head; then the chief engineer shrugged and walked away.

Respecting the troubled silence at her knee, Dax busied herself punching a diagnostic routine into her hybridized piloting/engineering panel. A sprawl of engineering plans began to strobe across her screen while her piloting grid condensed to an inset window in one corner. She played with the color and contrast controls, trying to find the maximum visibility of both displays.

"Which crew members *are* you taking through the wormhole?" Bashir asked after a moment. Although the words sounded almost absentmindedly, a glance at his tense face told Dax this wasn't idle conversation. "The same ones we saw on the bridge log?"

"No." Dax closed her eyes for a moment, then swept her board with a quick scanning look to see if her helm coordinates were still visible. "Even if the rift hasn't been averted, Benjamin thinks we'll have less chance of getting thrown back in time if we take a different crew. We've whittled it down to three engineers and three bridge officers—me on piloting and engineering, Commander Eddington on weapons, and Ensign Hovan on the cloaking device.

"Who'll handle communications?"

"I will," Sisko said from behind them. Dax swung around

to see the captain checking the miniature comm panel O'Brien had installed beside his command chair. "We won't need to do much hailing, since we'll be running cloaked the entire time. If there really are Furies on the other side of the wormhole, the last thing we want is for them to know we're there. We'll do a quick pass to gauge their strength and numbers, check the status of the *Sreba,* then come back to this quadrant to inform Starfleet Command."

The doubtful look on Bashir's face told Dax he wished he could believe it would be that easy. "What about medical staff?"

"I wanted your opinion about that." Sisko steepled his fingers and gave the doctor an intent look. "How secure is your patient in the infirmary?"

Bashir shrugged. "Chief O'Brien's rigged up an emergency bulkhead to isolate one alcove. But we can't very well ask Odo to provide security guards without telling the whole station there's something more in there than a Vulcan physicist with a case of *mactru* fever."

"I thought as much," said Sisko. "That's why I'm taking your medical assistant on the *Defiant.*"

Bashir's chin jerked up. "Instead of me?"

"How can we take you, Julian?" Dax asked, before the captain could reply. "You have to stay with my—with your patient."

"But if you're wrong about the timeline—"

"Not here," Sisko said abruptly. He rose to his feet, a slight jerk of his chin gathering them up without any further need for words. Eddington gave them a curious look as they left the *Defiant's* bridge, but made no comment.

"Medical bay," Sisko told the turbolift computer, when the doors had closed behind him.

Dax frowned up at him. "There's not much room in there to talk, Benjamin. Wouldn't it be better to use your quarters?"

He shook his head, dark eyes intent. "There's something down here I want the doctor to see." The turbolift doors hissed open on the enlarged hallway that served as the *Defiant's* medical bay. The tiny area, clearly a designer's afterthought on this prototype attack ship, seemed even more cramped than usual to Dax, but it took her a moment to realize why.

Beside her, Bashir said something beneath his breath, so softly she couldn't tell whether it was a curse or a thankful prayer. Dax followed the direction of his gaze, and finally saw the familiar translucent tank that had completely replaced the central diagnostic bed. Its brand-new transparent aluminum panels were set into a shock-absorbing plasfoam column, and in place of the original spaghetti-tangle of emergency fittings, a neat candelabraum of power cables and brine tubes emerged from a dilithium-powered recirculating pump at the base.

"O'Brien," Bashir said, with a wondering shake of his head. "When he insisted on doing a full-scale engineering scan of the symbiont's tank this morning, I thought it was just so he could tell me all the things I'd done wrong. Where did he find that pump?"

"I think he wheedled a couple of them from a liquid-atmosphere merchant ship that's docked here now," Sisko said. "He's replicating another version of this for your patient on *Deep Space Nine,* but I wanted one on board the *Defiant* first." His gaze swung back to Dax, who was still staring at the tank. "Well, old man, what do you think?"

She took a deep breath, trying to sort out the odd swirl of feelings that the sight of the brine tank had evoked. Usually, the emotions felt by her host and symbiont overlapped each other so comfortably that she had stopped noticing whose brain was generating them. That was one of the things that made her Trill pairing so successful. But for once, Jadzia's uneasiness at the thought of deliberately preparing for a five-thousand-year internment found no echo in her symbiont. Instead, the emotion resonating out from Dax was a quiet and ironic amusement. She was reminded again that the passing of time for symbionts, with their millennial life spans, held much less fear than it did for shorter-lived organisms.

"I think," she said calmly, "that I'll have to make sure you don't get in the way of any quantum-torpedo explosions for the next few days, Benjamin. I can't very well put myself to bed in that thing, can I?"

Sisko snorted. "And what makes you think *I'm* going to be able to do it, old man?"

"Well, I've seen how neatly you can filet a trout."

Bashir made an almost strangled noise of protest at their banter, and Dax exchanged contrite looks with Sisko. Whatever happened, she knew the doctor was never going to be completely comfortable with his role in preserving her symbiont. She tried not to think about what a second time rift would do to his sense of mingled responsibility and guilt.

"Don't worry, Julian," she said reassuringly. "Remember, there's a seventy-percent chance we won't need to use this tank at all."

Bashir scowled at her. "That means there's a thirty-percent chance that you will!" He swung around to face Sisko. "My assistant's a medical intern—not a doctor, not a surgeon, and certainly not an expert on Trill physiology. If you want to save Dax's symbiont again, you have to take me with you."

Sisko lifted an eyebrow at him. "Even if that means leaving the symbiont you already saved alone on *Deep Space Nine?*"

"But it doesn't have to." He flung out a hand at the renovated brine tank. "We can bring the old symbiont with us—maybe even manage to wake it up enough to help us avoid getting caught in the time rift this time."

"Hmm. That might work—"

"No!" Dax said fiercely. Both men turned to look at her in surprise. "We're not going to bring the old symbiont with us through the wormhole. I'd rather risk a thirty-percent chance of getting thrown back in time without you, Julian."

"But, Jadzia—"

"Old man, I don't see why—"

She wanted to shake them both. Even at their most sympathetic, humans could never truly fathom the ethics of symbiosis. "Listen to me, you two. As a Trill, there's only one thing that's important to me right now, and that's keeping my symbiont alive. It doesn't matter *which* symbiont that is. If the old Dax can regain its sanity—and with Julian's help, I think it can—then whether I get thrown back in time or get killed going through the wormhole, *one* Dax will still survive to return to Trill and the pools of memory. All of its wisdom and knowledge will still exist." She glanced at Bashir and saw the look of dawning unhappiness in his eyes. "And *I* will still exist, Julian, inside it. You know that."

He nodded, although he didn't look much happier. "But what if Starfleet Command is wrong about this temporal-inertia theory of theirs? If you do get thrown back in time, and if there's no one around to preserve the symbiont for you, *both* versions of it might disappear."

"There are three 'if's in your argument," Dax retorted. "Mine has just one: If we put both symbionts together on the *Defiant*, there's too much chance that neither of them will survive a Fury attack on the far side of the wormhole."

A somber silence descended on the medical bay. After a moment, Sisko cleared his throat to break it. "Dr. Bashir, you'll stay on *Deep Space Nine* and continue to rehabilitate the old Dax symbiont. Your medical assistant will be assigned temporary Starfleet status aboard the *Defiant*."

The doctor nodded reluctant agreement. "I'll put copies of all my Trill physiology references on board, as well as my notes from the old *Defiant*." He ran a hand across the gleaming surface of the empty brine tank, his expression unreadable. "If worst comes to worst, she might even have time to make sense of them."

Sisko didn't want to enter the wormhole.

In the eight hours since the *Sreba* had disappeared, the tortured glow of gas at the portal site had drifted away. Now the region of space where the wormhole opened looked like it always did: backlit by light from Bajor's sun, freckled with distant stars, and far too ordinary to house the galaxy's only known stable singularity.

"Any signs of subspace fluctuation?" he asked Dax.

She punched a command into her combined helm/engineering panel and scrutinized the flicker of output carefully. The pause seemed longer to Sisko than it should have. "I think what I'm seeing is just the normal leakage from the wormhole," Dax said at last, but he knew the Trill well enough to read the shade of doubt buried in her voice.

"What's not right about it?" he demanded.

"The frequency," she said. "It seems distorted—as if the gravity well around the singularity still hasn't returned to its normal configuration." She glanced back over her shoulder at him, inquiringly. "Proceed with wormhole approach?"

Sisko drummed his fingers on his jury-rigged communications console, aware of the watchful silence from Eddington at the weapons panel and Hovan at the cloaking controls. He'd chosen this skeleton crew for their high-level security clearances and their lack of immediate families, which meant they were mostly recent transfers to *Deep Space Nine*. In approved Starfleet style, neither offered an unsolicited suggestion to their superior officer. Deprived of Kira's outspoken opinions, Odo's blunt questions, and O'Brien's resourcefulness, Sisko turned his scowl on his oldest and most trusted friend. Fortunately, she knew him well enough to know it meant he was thinking through his answer.

"We need to know if the wormhole functions," he said flatly. "If it doesn't, Starfleet won't need to worry about a possible invasion through it."

"Agreed," Dax said calmly. "I'll pilot us to the usual trigger site."

Sisko grunted agreement, forcing himself to sit back in his chair while she entered the course coordinates. The *Defiant* sliced through Bajoran space with its usual surging kick of sublight acceleration. Its overpowered impulse engines, designed to give it maximum maneuverability in close-range battles, had an unfortunate tendency to outrun its inertia dampers. Sisko suspected that the gut-wrenching result was one of the reasons this prototype had never been made into a standard Starfleet model. He'd grown so used to it, however, that better-behaved ships like the *Enterprise* no longer felt like they were really moving.

"Approaching wormhole now." Dax toggled something on her board, giving Sisko a glimpse of the same kind of space-time contour maps he'd first seen on board the *Sreba*. He could see the *Defiant* on it, a bright blue dot moving toward the place where those glowing white curves converged. It looked unnervingly like a fly diving headlong into the heart of a spiderweb.

"Engage cloaking device, Mr. Hovan," he said quietly. "We don't want anyone to see us come out the other side."

"Aye-aye, sir." Her voice was commendably steady for a recent Academy graduate on her first crucial mission. The

Romulan cloaking icon glowed to life on his command panel and the *Defiant's* viewscreen flickered its usual initial protest while the cloaking field coalesced around them. Then the short-range sensors compensated for the additional electromagnetic radiation and the flicker was damped out.

"Subspace radiation fields increasing," Dax reported. Sisko saw the glowing white lines on her display begin to move in a familiar swirling pattern, and glanced back up at the main viewscreen in time to see the gold-streaked bloom of the wormhole spiral open directly in front of them. It looked as it always did—immense and impossibly bright with its gravity-defying burst of light. "The wormhole appears to be functioning normally, Captain."

He took a deep, soundless breath. "Then take us through to the Gamma Quadrant."

"Aye-aye, sir." She punched the new course into her panel, and Sisko felt the *Defiant's* usual impulse surge take it straight into the maw of the swirling singularity.

Then everything went away.

"Destruction," said T'Kreng's crystalline voice, "is imminent."

Sisko blinked and swung around, unsure of where he was or how he had gotten there. All he knew at first, from the lost tug of acceleration on his body, was that he was no longer aboard the *Defiant.*

"Destruction has already occurred."

His physical movements had a queasy unreal quality which told him, even before he saw the empty bridge of the *Sreba,* that he wasn't truly on board the Vulcan research vessel. His senses felt correspondingly unfocused, so that T'Kreng's platinum-robed figure shimmered insubstantially at its edges and the banks of machinery behind her looked more like sketches of themselves than actual equipment.

"Destruction is to come."

Despite the years that had passed since he'd last experienced it, this alien feeling—something like sleepwalking, something like fever dreams, and yet far more vivid than either—had been etched forever in his memory. For some reason, the wormhole's time-defying inhabitants had dragged him into their dimensional refuge again.

"Whose destruction?" he asked T'Kreng, or the image of her which the wormhole aliens had borrowed from his memories. "Yours or mine?"

The Vulcan physicist's quartz-pale eyes lifted from the screen she was watching, to meet his with a calm tranquillity she had never possessed in real life. "All beings who live and have lived and will live near the time bridge—"

"—must suffer the same fate." Admiral Judith Hayman stepped out of the *Sreba's* turbolift, her graveled voice less calm and her steely gaze more intense. Sisko wondered if it was his own brain that chose the shapes the wormhole dwellers wore, or if they selected images appropriate for their mental states.

"When the strands of the time bridge are unwoven, all energy escapes."

"So the wormhole is going to explode after all." He curled his fingers into tense fists, feeling and yet not feeling the sensation of pressure. "But *why?*"

"There will be and has been and is too much energy," T'Kreng said simply.

Hayman made an oddly human sounding snort. "We accept the energy outputs your vessels give us, Sisko. They feed us and we use them to sustain the bridge. But the ones who send from the side beyond you send too much for us to absorb."

"We have moved, will move, are moving the time bridge to escape." T'Kreng made an infinitesimal gesture of regret. "As soon as cancellation will be, has been, is no longer possible."

Sisko scowled. "Cancellation of what?"

The bridge of the *Sreba* melted into the bridge of the *Defiant*, with misty images of his crew all speaking at once.

"Ripples—" said Hovan.

"Echoes—" said Eddington.

"Shock waves—" said Dax.

Sisko took a deep, comprehending breath, although he never felt the resulting flow of air. "The subspace fluctuations that were tearing the wormhole apart. You're damping them out from inside."

"We can, have, will," agreed Eddington, his vocal rhythms unchanged despite the shift in form.

"But our resources are finite." Dax gave him another version of Hayman's intense gaze. "We cannot sustain the time bridge at all points in the continuum. Rupture is inevitable."

"Destruction is inevitable." Hovan's voice suddenly held a ringing power that the young ensign would not have for years, if ever. "All times and places are one to us, Sisko. We cannot unmake what for us exists. That is the power of those who live inside the river that we bridge."

Dax nodded. "Those that live inside time. They must take away the energy or suffer the destruction."

"They must go, will go, have gone through the time bridge," Eddington said with surreal calm. "They might come, will come, have not come back."

Fear crawled up Sisko's back. The scene around him shifted again, this time to an alien bridge studded with weapons panels and lit by the glow of external phaser fire. A face like a massive horned gargoyle lifted from a bank of firing controls, breath steaming in the cold of its unknown atmosphere and eyes flame-lit under translucent amber lids. He desperately hoped his own fear had called up that half-remembered image of the enemy from Admiral Hayman's totem figure, and not from the wormhole dwellers' actual experience with them.

"We are holding the time bridge open for your passage to the other side." Despite the Fury's growl, so low-pitched it was almost inaudible, Sisko could still hear the ring of command. "We promise nothing about return. Unless you have prevented the energy from entering, you would do well not to enter yourself."

"I understand," Sisko said curtly. "I'll do my best."

The Fury glared at him a moment longer, then disarmingly shimmered into a smiling image of his long-dead wife. "You no longer live in the past, Benjamin Sisko," she said. "That is good. We wish you to continue."

He opened his mouth to reply, but the sudden tug of acceleration in his gut told him he was back on the *Defiant*. Dax looked over her shoulder at him oddly.

"Captain, did you hear me? I said I'm reading damped-down quantum fluctuations inside the singularity matrix—the same pattern we saw on board the *Sreba*."

"I know." He sprang out of his chair, wanting to feel the impact of real decking beneath his feet. Above him, the *Defiant's* viewscreen roiled with the coruscating energy flows of the wormhole's interior. Sisko tried not to watch it too closely, for fear it would transform without warning into the explosion he was supposed to prevent. "The aliens who live inside the wormhole are cancelling the upstream echoes from the time rift."

"How do you know—" Dax broke off, narrowing her eyes at him with an intensity eerily similar to that of the wormhole dweller who'd borrowed her form. "You mean you saw them again? Did they tell you anything else?"

Sisko sorted through his incoherent memories, ticking off what he was sure of. "That the input of energy which destroys the wormhole will come from the Gamma Quadrant side. That they'll move the wormhole—through time, apparently—to escape it. And that we can't come back through until we've managed to avert whatever that input of energy is."

Dax took a deep, audible breath. "Then Julian was right after all. We *are* still on our original timeline." Her freckled face closed in a little tighter, but otherwise she lost none of her usual Trill self-control. That was the advantage of having several centuries of experience under your belt, Sisko reflected. He wished his own composure were as steady, but he could feel adrenaline fizzing more strongly through his blood with every second they stayed inside the singularity.

"The wormhole dwellers couldn't tell you what the source of this disruptive energy was?" Dax asked.

"No." He paced across the bridge to make a superfluous check on Ensign Hovan's cloaking panel, then prowled restlessly back around the curved perimeter toward Eddington. The security officer was absorbed in running computer simulations of all the automated firing sequences they'd programmed into the phaser controls, apparently in an attempt to fine-tune them down to the last millisecond. Sisko thought about ordering him to stop the needless use of computer time, but refrained. Everyone had their own methods of coping with the stress of wormhole passage, and for all he knew, those milliseconds might prove to be crucial.

He returned to drum his fingers restlessly against Dax's

piloting console. "Is it just me, or is this wormhole passage taking longer than usual?"

The science officer glanced at the clock inset into her display. "Passage times vary depending on initial entrance velocity, and we deliberately came in slow. We're only five percent over the median time interval for the trip." She toggled back her singularity matrix model and pointed at the position of the blue dot among the gently pulsing braid of fire-white lines. "According to this, we should be getting close to the exit."

Sisko bent over her board. "These changes in intensity you're showing here—that's the subspace fluctuation?"

Dax nodded again. "It hit a maximum in the heart of the singularity and has been fading since then. I don't think it will—"

Something changed in the *Defiant's* heading, a subliminal shift of vectors that told Sisko the wormhole was getting ready to spit them back into normal space. He threw a look up at the screen, watching the quantum interference patterns of singularity condense back into star-swept darkness. There were no other ships in view.

"Dax, throttle down the impulse engines to the minimum thrust needed to get us out of the wormhole trigger site," he commanded, feeling his helpless tension settle into the calm, driving rhythm of command. The wormhole washed them with a final bluish benediction of light, then spiraled shut. "I want to leave as little ion trail as possible. Mr. Eddington, give me a long-range sensor scan for enemy vessels."

"Aye-aye, sir."

Sisko swung back toward Hovan. "Are you reading any variations in the cloaking field that could indicate someone's trying to scan us, Ensign?"

Her nervous gaze flashed from the viewscreen down to her controls. "No, Captain. I'm not seeing any fluctuations in field strength at all."

Sisko grunted and glanced across at the weapons panel. "Results of long-range scan?"

"Completely negative, Captain." Eddington scowled down at his station, as if he thought its sensors could somehow have been subverted by the enemy. "No detectable vessels, no leakage from shields, not even any trace of warp-drive ion trails. According to sensors, we're the only ship within parsecs."

Sisko scowled and sank into his command chair, hands clenching in frustration on its padded arms. The one scenario he had not prepared himself for was that they would emerge from the wormhole to find nothing at all on the other side. Something threatening *had* to be out here in the Gamma Quadrant—the destructive energy that would explode the wormhole back in time couldn't have come from nowhere.

"There are no signs of the Vulcan science ship that entered the wormhole before us, Commander?"

Eddington punched in another command, then shook his head. "Not if it still exists as a powered vessel, sir."

"Which it may not," Dax said quietly. "Captain, helm sensors are picking up a microgravity field at nine-thirteen mark three. It's the right size to be the *Sreba.*"

Sisko grunted acknowledgment. "Set course to circle it at ten kilometers."

The *Defiant* kicked its way across deep space, its viewscreen filled with stars whose steady fire was undimmed by planetary atmospheres and nearer suns. Just as they began to slow and angle into their precautionary orbit, Sisko caught a small, drifting flicker of darkness across the starscape of the Gamma Quadrant. Something had momentarily blocked out those stars—something much nearer than they were.

"I think I see our microgravity field," he said softly. "Magnify starfield vector eight-nineteen, Commander Eddington, and put it on the main viewscreen."

"Yes, sir."

The distant stars swung sideways as the *Defiant's* short-range sensors changed their angle of focus. The darkness became more visible, tracing out a spiral of random motion against the starlight. If it was a spaceship, it was a derelict one. Sisko flicked an inquiring glance from Dax to Eddington.

"Analysis, gentlemen?"

"According to our tactical sensors, there's a ninety-eight-percent probability that it's a ship," Eddington said promptly. "And a sixty-percent probability that it's unarmed."

"But the long-range science sensors aren't picking up any trace of a warp core," Dax said.

Sisko scowled. "You mean the *Sreba's* containment field was breached? Or did the warp core actually explode and somehow manage to leave a big chunk of the ship intact?"

"Neither of those can explain this." Dax swung around to give him a baffled look. "I'm not reading any core radiation in that ship at all, Captain, contained or exploded. *None.*"

He scrubbed a hand across his face, feeling as if he'd just emerged from Alice's rabbit hole rather than a singularity. "Well, if they don't have a warp core, they're not going to attack us any time soon. Take us to visual range, Lieutenant."

"Aye-aye, sir." With the *Defiant's* oversized impulse engines, it took longer for the crew to give and acknowledge that kind of command than it did for the ship to carry it out. Sisko watched the dark patch as it seemed to swoop toward them, growing and resolving into a familiar stubby shape. This darkened hulk was definitely the *Sreba*—or what was left of her. Not even a gleam of emergency lights remained alive aboard the Vulcan research vessel.

Eddington whistled softly as the ruined ship enlarged to fill the viewscreen. "It looks like they got *sliced* open, Captain."

"Yes." Sisko eyed the damage with disbelieving eyes. No phaser burns had seared along the *Sreba's* hull, no jagged photon-torpedo eruptions had torn away her flanks. Instead, a myriad of impossibly neat cuts had razored off the roof of her bridge, cut through her warp nacelles, and quarried through her breached decks to leave a gaping hollow where her warp core must have been.

"Dax, have you ever seen weapons damage like this before?"

He could see a distinct shiver run along the Trill's freckled neck. "I don't—no. No, I don't think so." The trace of uncertainty leached out of her voice. "It's certainly not Jem'Hadar work."

"Nor is it Romulan, Klingon, or Cardassian." Sisko leaned back in his chair, glaring at the derelict Vulcan ship as if he could somehow make it yield up its secrets by sheer force of will. "Are there any signs of life on board?"

"Negative, sir," Eddington reported.

"I started a carbon-scan for organic remains," Dax added quietly. "Also negative, Captain."

Sisko frowned. "Can you detect any sign of internal backup power? If any of the computer memory is still on-line, we might be able to download her instrument records."

The science officer punched another set of commands into her hybrid engineering/helm panel. The resulting readout made her stiffen in her seat. "Captain, I'm detecting a strong internal power source inside the ship. It looks like an emergency stasis generator—and it's coming from the area of their sickbay."

Sisko straightened, feeling his pulse quicken. "An injured survivor?"

"Very possibly." Dax swung around to give him an urgent look. "Permission to beam the stasis chamber aboard?"

"Can you do it without releasing the stasis field?"

"Yes."

He vaulted to his feet. "Then let's beam it right onto the bridge and see what we've got. Commander Eddington, Ensign Hovan, keep your phasers trained on the beam-in site in case of hostile action—and Dax, I want a continuous transporter lock on the power generator, so we can spit it right back into space if it turns out to be a Trojan horse."

"Yes, sir." She programmed a series of commands into her boards, her freckled face creasing with concentration. "Ready on your mark, Captain."

Sisko took a deep breath and drew his own phaser, moving to the empty right side of the bridge so they had the beam-in site covered from all angles. Hovan had braced her phaser on her console and Eddington had his locked in both hands, in approved Starfleet style. He hoped neither of them would get so nervous they fired at the seeming motion of the transporter sparkle.

"Begin transport."

CHAPTER
11

THE ENVIRONMENTAL SUIT helmet banged into the back of the locker, bouncing out onto the floor again as though begging Kira to kick it back inside. She indulged it with passionate force, then followed it up with the chest piece, arms, and trousers of the suit. She had to twist her entire body into the throw to make the pieces crash into the cabinet with satisfying violence; even then, she still pulled out part of the suit just to be able to sling it again and again to re-create that sound. It didn't fit very nicely among the other suits without its proper hooks and hangers, but Kira didn't really give much of a damn. As far as she was concerned, this little color-coded, height-proportioned arrangement was just one more example of Starfleet's anal compulsion for rules and order instead of for what any half-minded gennet-herder could tell you was *right*. Faced with that awareness, the concept of returning *Rio Grande's* environmental suit to its assigned position in the public locker seemed an unendurable act of submission.

The *Defiant* had spiraled down the wormhole's maw while she was dragging the suit out of the runabout one and two pieces at a time. Light, as brilliantly refracted as a Prophet's Orb, winked unexpectedly at her through an observation port, and habit had forced her to pause and watch as space unfolded in a helix of color. The ship slid down the singularity's throat like a dim black bead, dwarfed by the wormhole's size and beauty. For just an instant, her traditional twinge of religious respect was beaten back by a fist of anger. She felt like a helpless native whose world, people, and faith had been swept up and put away for safekeeping by well-meaning outsiders. "Play amongst yourselves for a while," Great Father Starfleet seemed to say. "We'll be back later to tuck you in."

But even as the image exploded in her mind while the wormhole peeled in on itself and disappeared, she knew it wasn't fair. She knew it wasn't fair now, as she kicked and rekicked the last boot into the environmental-suit locker. Somewhere in the rational landscape of her thoughts, she knew that Starfleet's presence in the Bajor system had meant more to their growing independence than anyone could ever have dreamed, and Sisko's arrival as the long-prophesied Emissary was one of the most important events in Bajoran history. She should be relieved and honored to be part of such great accomplishments, to help lay the path toward the future with every passing day.

Instead, she felt like a child who'd been given a miniaturized spaceport set for her birthday, only to have her father play with it without her.

This time when a blossom of light gleamed through the nearest window, she almost didn't turn to look. She didn't want to see the wormhole again, and be forced to think about being trapped on one side of it while the man she was mad at was unreachable on the other. But there was always the chance Sisko and the *Defiant* might return this quickly—she hated open-ended time frames—and the thought of not having to wait for the *Mukaikubo* to head after Pak Dorren was certainly appealing. Shouldering closed the door to the suit locker, she trotted over to the window just to satisfy her curiosity so she could go to bed without having to wonder what she missed.

A single Lethian passenger coupe ghosted slowly in and out of the station's shadow, rhythmically catching and leaving the light from the distant sun. Of course. Nothing so useful as the *Defiant* coming home, or the *Mukaikubo* appearing ahead of schedule. She let out a tired snort and began to turn her back on them when one detail about the ship's stately progress prickled the hair on the back of her neck.

Running lights. The Lethian ship was drifting past the station without its running lights.

She tapped thoughtfully at her comm badge as she turned back to the view outside. "Kira to Ops. Chief, are you in contact with the Lethian transport just passing the station?"

O'Brien's voice when he answered carried just the slightest hint of confusion beneath his normally businesslike tone. "We've got no record of a Lethian transport in the sector."

"About fifty kilometers out from runabout pad F, thirty degrees above the ecliptic."

She waited in silence for him to run a scan of the area. The passenger coupe continued its dreamlike glide toward the edge of the window, its elongated nose just disappearing from Kira's sight when O'Brien came back with a short little *hmph!* of surprise. "Composition and size match Lethian registries," he reported, obviously reading from something in front of him. "But it's too light on mass, and I'm not picking up a drive signature."

"That's because it doesn't have one." Kira didn't realize what she was thinking until that whisper breathlessly escaped her; then disbelief and fury tangled together deep inside her. "Chief, tow the Lethian ship into cargo bay four and have Bashir meet me down there." Not that there would be survivors. She was already certain of that.

Still, there was something uniquely infuriating about trotting up to the cargo-bay airlock and finding no one there to meet her but the shapeshifter with whom she'd already spent the last two fruitless days.

"I happened to overhear your conversation with Chief O'Brien," Odo remarked before she even asked him. "I took the liberty of joining you."

"I'm glad you did." The deck under her feet hummed on a note too deep to be heard as pumps somewhere in the station's structure kicked into life. Kira paced impatiently in front of the airlock, glancing toward first one end of the long corridor, then the other. "Where the hell is Bashir?"

"He isn't coming." Odo met her fierce scowl with a serene lift of one shoulder. "He's sending Ensign Maile, so he can stay in the infirmary with Professor Stel." Then, as though imparting some meaningful tidbit of evidence, "One of the Vulcan physicists has a case of *mactru* fever."

Kira threw her hands up in frustration. "Vulcan physicists? *What* Vulcan physicists?"

"The ones who came back from Starbase One with Captain Sisko." Odo's face took on one of his few unmistakable expressions—the one Kira always associated with teachers who could no longer hide their disappointment in an inattentive pupil. "Really, Major, you must learn to bring yourself up to date on station business when you've been away for an hour or more."

She managed a wry little smile for him, and paced back down the corridor to rejoin him at the lock as the bay finished flooding with air and the ready lights blinked green. "Sorry, Odo. I don't have quite your flair for 'overhearing' other people's conversations."

"Pity. It would save us both time and discussion." And he sounded not the slightest bit embarrassed by the major's implication, even when running footsteps announced the arrival of one of Bashir's human medical assistants close enough on his words to have picked up at least the gist of their conversation. Thinking it best to avoid any further gossip in front of the girl, Kira merely nodded her a terse greeting and activated her comm badge.

"Okay, Chief, we're all here. Open up."

A quick exchange of air puffed cold into the corridor as chill, space-touched gases flowed together with the warmer station atmosphere. Ensign Maile unfolded a medical tricorder into the silence, and its shrill song bounced around the huge bay like a springball in a box. Something about the smallness of that sound against the creaks and hisses of the transport warming to the station air made Kira wish for a phaser as she stepped into the open bay.

It wasn't a big ship, as far as passenger transports went. Enough to hold maybe twenty-five adult Lethians, fifty if they didn't mind being chummy. Squat and irregular like the Lethians themselves, it reflected their fanatical privacy as well—no external markings, no windows, no hint as to where it was going or why. The only thing Kira was fairly certain of was that the curling petals of sliced metal gaping open down the length of its side weren't part of the standard Lethian design.

"I'm picking up faint life signs. . . ."

Kira halted, turning toward Maile's voice when it rang out suddenly above the shush of blooming frost. She'd almost forgotten anybody else was with her.

"Inside the Lethian airlock," Maile continued, never raising her eyes from the tricorder's dance of readings. "Or very close to there."

"Lethian life signs?" Odo asked.

Kira thought the ensign hadn't heard him at first, but then Maile shook her head with a little frown. "I can't tell. The hull's carrying a pretty heavy transperiodic charge. It's reflecting more of the tricorder signal than it's letting through."

A radioactive derelict—just what they needed. Kira backed a few more steps away. "Are we safe out here?"

Maile pulled alongside her, nodding. "For at least a half-hour." A somewhat nervous smile played across her round, golden face as she glanced up from the tricorder. "I wouldn't go leaning against any bulkheads, though."

Ah—humor. Something else Kira might appreciate more if she weren't so tired. Or so scared. "Constable. . . ." She swept a gallant gesture toward the ruined hulk, earning a curious tilt of the head from Odo. "If you'd be so kind."

Whether or not he understood her strange, tired sarcasm, he understood what she wanted of him, at least. Lifting one arm shoulder high, he stretched himself across the remaining distance to trigger the passenger ship's outer airlock door. It seemed a pointless exercise to Kira—there were a hundred places to enter the ship through the gashes torn into its frost-speckled hide. But actually boarding the ruined vessel would have required another stint in one of O'Brien's ISHA approved hardsuits, and Kira had neither the patience nor the stamina for another suit walk right now. Besides, she'd seen enough of these ships in the last two days to write up a convincing report without even going inside. What they were doing here now were technicalities—going through the motions, just in case.

Frost and damage had warped the door in its frame. It bumped something deep inside, grinding helplessly, and

Kira could whiff just the faintest trace of something chemically sharp, and burning.

"Wait a minute!"

Maile again, intent on her tricorder and impossibly close to Kira's elbow, the strain of making sense from the small machine's trilling knotting her face and eyes into a tangle of concentration. "I—it—" She pursed her lips in scholarly frustration. "I lost the reading for a moment. Like it moved, or changed, or—"

A great crash of screaming metal exploded through the bay when the door finally let go and slammed open. Kira whirled toward the Lethian ship, instinctively going for the phaser that wasn't there as Maile shrieked and leapt against her. Movement flashed in the suddenly open airlock—dark, smooth, long, low—and Kira found herself jerking aside to free herself of the ensign's clutch in the same instant that Odo recoiled from the skritch-skitter of claws on decking and the ugly, hairless escapee rocketed between their feet to dash across the bay and disappear into the station's halls.

When it was all over and the strange, brittle silence had returned to the ship and the bay, the only thing Kira could think to say was, "Ah, dammit!"

Maile extricated herself with only as much dignity as Kira expected from someone who'd throw herself into someone else's arms in the first place. "Well," she said, a little shakily, as she stooped to retrieve her tricorder, "whatever it was, it wasn't a Lethian."

Kira snorted at this lovely example of well-trained Starfleet attentiveness. "It was a Cardassian vole." Still, she had to admit she was surprised by how much it calmed her to say that out loud. Proving only the power inherent in one ensign's overreaction. "Just what Chief O'Brien needs," she sighed, striving for a lighter note. "Fresh breeding stock."

Odo didn't turn from where he examined the Lethian airlock doorway. "I'll try to break it to him gently."

Kira was just as glad not to be saddled with that chore on top of everything else this ship represented. Drawn by the tricorder's renewed song, she glanced aside at Maile. "Any other life signs?"

The young medic—composed now, but still flushed with

what Kira assumed was embarrassment as she scanned the ship—shook her head. "Not even voles."

Damn.

Beside the opened airlock, Odo straightened. "Four," he said simply, catching Kira's eye.

"Only this one's not Bajoran." She slammed one fist against her leg, longing instead for something to throw, or kick, or break. There were disadvantages to loosing your temper in the middle of a nearly empty hold. "Seal off the bay until O'Brien can get down here to examine the remains," she told Odo. "And put together teams to meet every ship that docks here from now on. I don't want any more militia sneaking on board until we find out what they've done with those engine cores."

The constable called out as she turned to leave, "And you're going . . . ?"

"To talk to Starfleet." She paused in the cargo bay's entrance, clenching her hand into a fist on the jamb as she looked back at the ruined Lethian ship. "Maybe now that a government with more money than Bajor is involved, they can make a little time for us in their busy schedules."

The hum of the transporter faded, replaced by the hiss and crackle of space-cold metal hitting room-temperature air. Dax swung around to see a haze of contact fog blossom inside the *Defiant's* bridge, turning Sisko and Eddington into vague shadows and obscuring Hovan entirely. Whatever she had beamed aboard was hidden behind that pale gray veil, but it was large enough to trigger an urgent buzz from life-support systems. Dax glanced down at the priority screen that had popped up on her engineering panel, noticing that the temperature had dropped fifteen degrees.

"Dax, can you get rid of this mist?" demanded Sisko's tense voice. "I can't see anything inside it."

"I'm adjusting life-support now." She dialed down bridge humidity levels and tapped in permission for heating rates to temporarily exceed standard safety thresholds. A rush of arid air swept through the bridge in response, making her skin prickle unhappily but clearing most of the fog away. What emerged was a frost-spattered gleam of metal, shaped like an upright coffin. It looked like the medical stasis generator she'd expected, although Dax couldn't see if anyone was actually inside it.

Sisko edged farther toward the back of the bridge, craning his head for a better view. He made a frustrated noise. "The window panel's still frosted on this side—Ensign Hovan, can you see through it?"

"A little bit, sir." She looked both surprised and uncertain. "I think there's a Starfleet cadet inside."

"That's Petersen!" Dax engaged the automatic helm controls and vaulted up without asking Sisko for permission. The captain motioned Eddington to cover her station with a silent jerk of his chin, then moved back to allow her to round the deck in front of him. Dax frowned, seeing that he hadn't yet put away his phaser.

"Benjamin, you can't suspect Heather—"

"Can't I?" He followed her to the front of the stasis chamber, where the last of the contact frost was melting into a faint glitter of mist. His dark eyes held a wary look Dax remembered from past battles—something had triggered his cautious military instincts. "Then why is she in that stasis field, old man? Does she look injured to you?"

Dax scrubbed the last of the mist from the transparent aluminum, finding it still achingly cold to the touch, and eyed Heather Petersen's frozen form. Not a trace of blood or battle grime darkened her Starfleet uniform, and her rounded face still held the rosy bloom of complete health. The only thing that looked out of character was the grimace that twisted her quiet mouth and the fierce downward slant of her eyebrows.

"Maybe she had internal injuries," Hovan suggested.

Dax shook her head. "I don't think so, but I'd need a medical tricorder to be sure." She glanced across at Sisko. "Do you want me to get one from sickbay before we drop the stasis field? If the scan is negative, we'll still have to decide whether or not to release her."

He grunted reluctant agreement to that logic. "All right, drop the stasis field—but don't get between me and her."

Dax didn't dignify that unnecessary command with an answer. She leaned forward to press the release controls on the stasis field's internal power unit, then backed away while the seals on the transparent aluminum cover hissed open. A moment later, the glimmer of stasis beneath it transformed into a blur of arrested motion—not a forward lunge but a backward slam, as if Petersen had been pushed violently into the stasis chamber just as it was being closed.

"—can't do this! This is a Starfleet mission, dammit, T'Kreng! You can't—" Petersen's fierce shout died as soon as her gaze focused on Dax. Her eyes widened and she vaulted out from the stasis chamber with a gasp. "You came back?" she demanded eagerly, her gaze moving from Dax to Sisko. Then she took in the black military curves of the *Defiant*'s bridge, and the color faded abruptly from her cheeks. "This isn't the *Sreba!* What's going on?"

"You're on the Starfleet cruiser *Defiant,* Heather, posted to *Deep Space Nine.* We just beamed you in from the *Sreba.*" Dax paused, trying to find a gentle way to phrase the rest of her explanation. "We found your research ship, floating derelict and abandoned here in the Gamma Quadrant. You were the only survivor we could locate."

"But that's—" Petersen broke off, shaking her head in what looked like utter bafflement. "Lieutenant, that's impossible. If the *Sreba* got caught inside the wormhole, the whole ship would have been torn apart by gravity waves. There's no way my stasis chamber should have survived."

"It wasn't the wormhole that destroyed the *Sreba,*" Sisko said quietly. "Your ship was attacked when it emerged from the wormhole into the Gamma Quadrant. You don't remember any of that?"

"How could I?" Petersen demanded, with unusual bitterness. "Professor T'Kreng ordered her medic to put me into stasis five minutes after she beamed your team away. She said it was so I wouldn't be found guilty of disobeying Starfleet orders, but I think it was because I kept shouting at her that what she was doing was illogical. It was making the crew nervous."

"You should be grateful to her." Dax steered the Starfleet cadet around so she could see the *Defiant*'s main viewscreen. Petersen's eyes widened as she took in the breached ruin of the Vulcan research ship floating against the stars. "Whatever attacked the *Sreba* took her warp core, as well as killing or capturing all of her crew. The fact that you were in the stasis generator was probably the only thing that saved your life."

"But *why?*" It was not a grieving or philosophical question. The cadet's gaze when she looked back at Dax was truly puzzled. "At the Academy, they taught us that when you search for an enemy crew, the first place you look for them to hide is in the stasis chambers of sickbay. Surely the Klingons or the Romulans or the Cardassians—whoever it was that attacked us—knew that, too."

"It wasn't the Klingons or Romulans or Cardassians who attacked you." Sisko sheathed his phaser and crossed the deck to the empty weapons panel. A quick stab at the sensor controls brought the Vulcan research ship into closer focus on their viewscreen. The myriad slices through her hull looked even more alien than before, their edges smooth as polished latinum, their spacing uncannily regular. "Our enemy doesn't know any more about us than we know about it."

Dax tilted her head, hearing the new ring of determination in her old friend's voice. "Have you thought of a way to change that?"

A jerk of Sisko's chin indicated the lightless shadow on the viewscreen. "You can learn a lot about an enemy by seeing what they leave behind on a battlefield," he said grimly. "In this case, that's the *Sreba.*"

Over Dax's objections, Heather Petersen had agreed to Sisko's suggestion that she make up the fourth member of their away team. "The captain's right. I'll know better than you will what's normal on the *Sreba* and what's not," she said through a mouthful of toast and cloud-apple jam. Remembering their predawn departure from the *Sreba,* Dax had insisted on feeding the cadet breakfast before they left. "And besides, I want to see if any of our scientific data is still retrievable. That way, at least we won't have made that wormhole passage for nothing."

The scientist in Dax couldn't argue with that. "That's a good idea," she admitted. "If we have enough time, perhaps we can analyze it and pinpoint the initiation of the time rift."

Petersen frowned, as if something had just occurred to

her. "Are you sure it hasn't happened already?" she demanded, pushing her breakfast away half-finished. "I don't remember seeing any singularity fluctuations near the *Sreba*—and the captain said she was attacked right after she came out of the wormhole."

"The wormhole stabilized when T'Kreng went through it." Dax led her out of the *Defiant*'s spartan mess hall and down to the main turbolifts. "Away-team staging area," she told the turbolift computer, then turned back to Petersen. "We initially thought it meant the time rift had been averted, but when we followed you we found out that the precursor echoes were just being damped down by the creatures that live inside the singularity. They told us that an enormous input of energy from the Gamma Quadrant side is going to force them to wrench the singularity back in time in time to escape."

Petersen's quiet eyes lit up. "You saw them, Lieutenant?"

Dax shook her head wistfully. "No, they only spoke to Captain Sisko." The turbolift doors slid open onto a staging deck scattered with environmental suits and zero-g jetpacks. She raised her voice deliberately. "They seem to like talking to him for some reason. You'd think they'd find a Trill more interesting."

Sisko looked up from where he and one of the security guards were sorting their equipment into order. The quick glint of humor in his eyes told Dax that her teasing comment hadn't been lost on him. "You're welcome to stop and chat with them on the way back, old man," he retorted. "In the meantime, I'd like to check out the *Sreba* before whatever attacked her comes back for us. Ensign Pritz and I have pulled together the equipment we'll need for the away team. Find yourselves an environmental suit that fits, gentlemen, and let's get going."

"Aye-aye, sir." Both Petersen and Pritz answered with the well-drilled promptness of recent training. Dax lifted an eyebrow while the two young women swung away to obey Sisko's crisp command.

"With a crew this fresh from Starfleet Academy, Benjamin, you're going to get spoiled," she said, pitching her voice just low enough to be masked by the clatter of gear.

Sisko snorted and threw her an environmental suit. "I'm

sure you'll keep me from getting too used to being obeyed without question. What do you make of—"

"—ten cc's boromine citrate infused in fifteen percent saline, neurotransmitters now stable—"

"Dax?"

She blinked and looked around. "Did one of you just say something about neurotransmitters?" she demanded of Petersen and Pritz, even though the logical part of her mind already knew the answer. Although she rarely noticed which of her two cerebral cortices processed her sensory input, this time she knew it was Dax who thought that familiar voice had spoken through the clatter of suits being donned. Jadzia's brain had no memory of it.

"No, sir," Pritz said in surprise. Petersen shook her head as well, eyeing her worriedly.

Jadzia summoned up a smile for them. "I guess I imagined it, then," she said lightly, while, inside, Dax insisted that it *had* heard Bashir's voice, right here, right now. She turned back to Sisko, now suited up except for his helmet, and saw from his scowl that he wasn't buying her explanation.

"All right, old man, what just happened?" he demanded.

She took a deep breath and began climbing into her own environmental suit. "Sensory separation," she said without looking at him. "Dax heard something Jadzia didn't."

Sisko snorted again. "Then why were you *gone* for a moment while I was talking to you?"

"I'm not sure, Benjamin." She sealed up the suit's single chest seam and bent to scoop up its helmet. The emotion she was trying to hide from Sisko wasn't fear—it was an embarrassingly unscientific excitement at what she hoped this meant. *You can't extrapolate from a single data point,* Dax told herself firmly. *It's premature to think this was anything more than a stray neural cascade, bringing an old memory inappropriately to life.*

With her excitement reined in to hopeful caution, she straightened to meet Sisko's intent gaze. "It might have been some kind of aftereffect from my merger with the other symbiont back at Starbase One." That had the advantage of being close enough to the truth that Dax could say it without faltering. "I don't think it will compromise my performance on the away team."

He gave her a long, unwavering stare. "See that it doesn't."

With a quick snap, Sisko sealed his own helmet down and picked up one of the flashlights and a heavy-duty laser torch. Pritz was already carrying a phaser rifle strapped across her back in addition to her flashlight and hand phaser, while Petersen had hefted the emergency medical kit. That left a flashlight and a tricorder for Dax. She found room for both in her suit's bulky pockets, then slid her hand phaser into its loop on her utility belt.

"Away team prepared for zero-g vacuum transport, Captain?" Eddington's voice asked inside her helmet.

"Affirmative, Commander." Sisko gathered them together with a jerk of his chin. "You're in command of the *Defiant* while we're gone, Mr. Eddington. Whatever happens, do *not* take her back through the wormhole. Not under any conditions."

"Understood, Captain. Four to beam out?"

Sisko gave Dax one last speculative look. She gave him back a nod as confident as she could make it. "Four to beam out," Sisko agreed. "Energize."

Just before the chilly shiver of dissociation swept through her, Dax could have sworn she heard Bashir saying in frustration, "—still not enough isoboromine—"

CHAPTER 12

It didn't even look like the same ship.

Dax splashed her flashlight around, trying to identify the dark emptiness Eddington had beamed them into on the *Sreba*. In the half-day she'd spent aboard the small Vulcan research vessel, she could have sworn she'd seen every public area bigger than a broom closet, but this towering two-story atrium was unfamiliar. She began to ask Heather Petersen where they were, then stopped. The right shoulder pocket of her environmental suit was vibrating—the only evidence in this hard vacuum that her tricorder was emitting an alarm. Dax tugged it out and cursed in Klingon when she saw the radiation readings flashing on it.

"This is where the warp core used to be!" She and Petersen said it in unison across their suit communicators, but Dax's urgent voice overrode over the cadet's simple amazement. "I'm reading high levels of subspace radiation and ionic particle flux in here, Captain. We have to get behind some shielding fast."

Sisko made no reply, but in the braided glow of their flashlight beams, Dax could see his broad-shouldered form trace out an efficient sweep of the chamber. "Looks like a Jeffries tube opening over there," he said, using his flashlight beam as a pointer. "Pritz goes first, phaser drawn. I'll go last."

The security guard acknowledged the command by unslinging her phaser rifle and pulsing her jetpack in one smooth motion. Before the burst of compressed air had faded to glittering ice motes in their flashlight beams, Pritz had disappeared into the dark promise of safety.

"All clear," her terse voice said inside their helmets after a moment. Dax motioned Petersen after her, waiting while the cadet took a slow moment to orient herself to the tunnel's long axis before she pushed into it. Dax angled her belt jets to follow, keeping her flashlight tucked under one arm to illuminate the display panel of her tricorder. The steady glow of Sisko's flashlight from behind provided more than enough light to guide her through the Jeffries tube.

"Radiation levels?" Sisko demanded after a moment.

"Dropping." Dax changed her jet angle to maneuver through a tight coil in the tube, almost bumping into the magnetized soles of Petersen's boots as she did. The tricorder's silent shiver of alarm went still a moment later. "We're shielded now."

Sisko grunted. "Pritz, any sign of an exit up there?"

"Yes, sir. I don't know if it's the kind of exit you want, though."

Dax bumped into Petersen's boots again, this time hard enough to make the insulation of her environmental suit crunch. "Right now, I'll take any kind of exit I can get, Ensign," she said dryly, then became aware that the boots overhead weren't moving. "Heather, are you all right?"

"Um—yes, sir." She sounded a little shaky. "It's just going to take me a minute—"

Dax craned her head to look past the cadet, noticing a patch of darkness ahead that Sisko's flashlight beam couldn't seem to penetrate. She turned her own flashlight up to join his, but it didn't make a dent in the overhead gloom. It wasn't until Petersen wriggled herself around some obstacle and disappeared that Dax finally saw the distant glitter of stars and realized she was looking out at open space.

"We're going out through a hull breach," she warned Sisko.

"With the level of damage this ship's sustained, walking the hull might be the fastest way to get anywhere." He thumped at one of her own boot soles. "I can't get out until you do, old man."

Dax fired her belt jets, undulating gracefully around the ragged lip of metal that partially blocked the Jeffries tube, then floated out into clear space. Petersen and Pritz were already standing upright on the hull, their magnetized boots anchoring them against the *Sreba*'s slight angular momentum. Dax used her jets to brake herself before inertia took her drifting away from the Vulcan ship, and felt the slight tug of renewed spin as the magnetic plates on her boots made contact with the hull.

Sisko emerged from the breached tube more slowly, easing his broad shoulders through the ragged opening to avoid tearing his environmental suit. Dax felt the unsupported hull shudder beneath her when he finally vaulted up to join them.

"Bridge first," he said curtly. "Petersen, can you find it?"

"Yes, sir." The cadet might be awkward and inexperienced at jetting through microgravity, but walking on the outside of a spaceship seemed to hold no fears for her. She turned and headed across the curving horizon of the hull, easily matching Sisko's long strides. They must have added holoexercises in contact walking to the academy since she had graduated, Dax reflected wryly.

She began to follow them, watching her feet to be sure she was making enough contact with each step, then stopped. A long grooved scratch marred the duranium metal cladding beneath her, although the hull hadn't actually been breached here. Pritz paused beside her without being ordered to, phaser rifle still cradled in one arm.

"Something wrong, sir?"

"Something interesting." Dax squatted, keeping her bootheels pressed flat to maintain her position, and ran her tricorder over the gouge. Its small display screen spit back the expected analysis of the *Sreba*'s hull: layered duranium-titanium-steel alloy, approximately ten centimeters thick. Dax frowned and tapped in a request for trace compounds with one gloved finger, then scanned the long scratch again. There was an anomalously long pause before the tricorder display flashed up a single word: difluorine.

Dax let out an involuntary yelp, more of amazement than alarm. Pritz made a reflexive turn on the hull beside her, scanning the field of view with her phaser rifle armed and ready. From out of sight, Sisko's voice said sharply, "What is it, old man?"

"Something I wasn't expecting." She stood and took a careful step back from the scratch she had squatted so casually over, feeling a shiver reverberate up the twin freckle trails of her shoulders. "Try to avoid touching any of the gashes in the hull, or even stepping on them. Whoever attacked the *Sreba* was using chemical weapons."

"*Chemical* weapons?" Sisko's deep voice couldn't rise in astonishment the way hers had, but she heard the sheer disbelief in it. "What kind of chemical can slice through duranium in hard vacuum at two degrees Kelvin?"

"One that's not supposed to exist outside of Starfleet laboratories." Dax climbed over the *Sreba*'s ragged starboard nacelle, and altered course to join the two suited figures standing near the crater that had once been the bridge. Up close, it looked as if a vast section of hull had simply dissolved away here, with no signs of damage even a meter from the edge. She now understood how that had happened. "They used difluorine, Benjamin. The most reactive and the most unstable of the transperiodic elements."

Beneath Sisko's soft whistle, Dax could hear someone—she couldn't tell if it was Petersen or Pritz—draw in a startled breath. "And some of it may still be around?" the captain demanded.

"That depends on what material the difluorine encountered," Dax replied. "A metal alloy like duranium should have simply disintegrated and floated away. I'm picking up only a few parts per trillion here, not enough to breach suit integrity. But with all the carbon-rich fibers and resin alloys down there—" She pointed one bulky glove at the tangle of exploded instrument panels and collapsed plasma displays that was all that remained of the *Sreba*'s former bridge. "—it's a different story. If reaction crusts of difluoric carbide formed on any of those instrument panels, it could be protecting pockets of unspent difluorine." She turned so she could meet Sisko's dark eyes steadily through the clear window of their helmets. "I think it would be best if I ran this solo, Benjamin."

Sisko grimaced, but she could already see the grudging

agreement in his face. "Very well, but I want you to scan every step you take. Petersen, can you guide her from up here?"

"Yes, sir."

"Good. Sisko to *Defiant*."

"Eddington here, sir."

"I want you to use a tractor beam to reduce our angular momentum and keep the bridge area in constant view. Be prepared to transport Lieutenant Dax back to the *Defiant* if her internal suit monitor shows any sign of decompression."

"Aye-aye, sir." The nearly ultraviolet sparkle of a tractor beam shot out from what looked like totally empty space above the *Sreba*. Dax felt the tug and sway of deceleration as the *Sreba*'s chaotic spinning drift was stabilized.

"All right, old man." Sisko gave Dax a shoulder clap she could barely feel through her suit insulation. "Try to download normal ship's sensors first, then the helm, then the scientific data stations."

"Yes, Captain." Dax resisted the impulse to take a deep breath, knowing the sudden flux of carbon dioxide would only confuse her suit's life-support controls. She flexed her feet to break the magnetic seal her boots were making with the hull, then fired her jetpack. The quick burst of compressed air launched her straight down into the heart of the destruction.

"Ship's sensors are to your left, Lieutenant, just past that exposed optical cabling channel," Petersen's quiet voice said in her ear. "No, not that panel, the one next to it."

"I see it." Still hovering, Dax scanned the exploded sensor array with her tricorder. The display showed a strong spike of difluoric carbide, but only trace amounts of the oxidant itself. "It should be safe to touch. I'm going to try downloading—"

"Captain!" Eddington's voice sliced across hers urgently. "I'm picking up warp signatures from two incoming vessels. Tactical computer says there's a high probability that both are Jem'Hadar fighters. Even if they can't see the *Defiant*, sir, they're going to see our tractor beam."

Sisko made a frustrated noise. "Not to mention us

standing out here. Estimated time of arrival, Mr. Eddington?"

"Seven minutes, sir."

"Dax?"

She had already powered up her jets and was maneuvering away from the sensor panel. "Difluorine leaching has wiped the main sensor memory board. Give me a minute to check the helm controls." This time, her tricorder scan showed a jagged spike of pure difluorine. Even though she hadn't actually made contact with the panel, Dax jetted back reflexively. "Helm's contaminated, sir. Do I have time to check the science sensors?"

"Only if you can do it in less than five minutes," Sisko said grimly.

"Try a straight data dump through the optical port," Petersen suggested. "If the memory board is still intact, that will go faster than a scan. We'll just have to sort it all out later."

"Which science station should I use?" Dax demanded.

"The main analytical display in the center of the bridge looks like the least damaged."

She glanced around, spotting one upright plasma display in the midst of the wreckage. Her quick tricorder scan reported much less difluoric carbide here, and almost no difluorine. Dax hoped that wasn't because she'd started the scan while she was still two meters away. She made tentative contact with the decking and felt no immediate outrush of air from her suit. With a sigh of relief she couldn't suppress, Dax reached down to align her tricorder's receptor with the panel's knee-level optical port.

"Jem'Hadar warp signature confirmed, Captain," Eddington's nervous voice said over the communicator channel. "Fighters three minutes away and closing."

Sisko grunted. "Lock on to all away-team comm signals. Prepare to release tractor beam and transport us back onto the bridge of the *Defiant* at my mark. Dax, are you getting data?"

Even though her awkwardly bent posture made it impossible to see the display, the slight vibration of the tricorder in her gloved hand—the vacuum equivalent of steady beeping—gave her the answer she'd hoped for. "Affirmative, Captain. Download in progress."

"Jem'Hadar fighters two minute away and closing."

"Let me know the *instant* that download is finished, old man."

"Don't worry, I will." Dax tightened her grip on the tricorder, waiting for its small vibration to cease. How much data could T'Kreng have collected in one short passage through the wormhole?

"Fighters one minute away and closing."

The tricorder rippled one last vibration into her tense fingers and fell still. "Download complete, Captain." Dax scrambled up from her stooped position, cradling the tricorder in both hands to make sure she didn't drop it.

"Begin transport!" Sisko snapped. "Disengage tractor—"

A shiver of molecular paralysis interrupted him. When Dax could hear again, the background noise of red alert ringing muffled through her helmet told her she was on the *Defiant*'s bridge.

"—beam," Sisko finished, tearing off his helmet and striding to the empty captain's chair. Dax tossed her tricorder to Heather Petersen and went to take her own station at the helm.

"Tractor beam disengaged, sir." Hovan vacated the engineering and helm panel gratefully, and returned to her own cloaking control station. Dax glanced down at the board and saw nothing amiss, then stripped off her own gloves and helmet. At her left, Eddington turned at the weapons panel and said, "Jem'Hadar fighters are just entering visual range now, sir. I don't think they saw us."

"Good work, gentlemen," Sisko said crisply. "Put the Jem'Hadar on the main viewscreen, Eddington. Dax, get us out to a safer distance, but pulse our engines while you do it. I don't want our friends out there to see a continuous thermal signature."

"Beginning pulsed thrust, vector two-nine-zero mark zero-nine-seven." Dax glanced up at the viewscreen, seeing the distinctive silhouettes of two Jem'Hadar attack ships swoop toward them. She glanced back at Sisko. "It looks like they're heading for the *Sreba,* sir."

His intent gaze never wavered from the screen. "Let's

wait until we see them go past us before we start celebrating. Hovan, be prepared to drop cloaking at my mark. Eddington, I want you to target photon torpedoes on both Jem'Hadar ships."

"Torpedoes locked and ready, sir." The security officer's hands hovered over his board, but after a moment he sighed in what sounded like mixed disappointment and relief. "Fighters overshot us by six kilometers, sir. They're falling into orbit around the *Sreba.*"

"Told you," Dax said softly, eyes fixed discreetly on her helm panel. The snort from behind told her that Sisko had heard the comment, just as she'd meant him to. "Maintain position, Captain?"

"Yes. I want to see what they're going to do."

For a long moment, the answer to that seemed to be nothing. The Jem'Hadar fighters circled the ruined Vulcan research ship like two oversize moons, apparently inspecting it. Then, without warning, a double set of phaser beams licked out from each ship, precisely cross-trained on the *Sreba.* It took only a few seconds for that doubled attack to explode the small ship into a cloud of glowing, vaporized metal.

"Why did they *do* that?" Petersen's voice was raw, as if the sight of that final destruction had triggered all the emotion she hadn't had time to assimilate yet. Pritz had reported to her battle station for the red alert, leaving the cadet standing alone and uncertain beside the disengaged engineering console. "All they had to do was scan to see that the *Sreba* was a derelict!"

"I think they did scan—and something they found bothered them." Sisko came to stand beside the helm, watching the Jem'Hadar fighters circle the now empty space where the *Sreba* had been. "I think they're scanning for it again now." He looked down at Dax, his face tightening with swift decision. "Set a course to follow those fighters back to their base. They appear to know something, and I'm starting to think we should know about it, too."

"Aye-aye, sir." She punched in a series of commands to link their flight controls with tracking scans of the Jem'Hadar ships. "Ships are moving off at vector eight-nine-four mark five-one-four."

"Power scans indicate Jem'Hadar ships are engaging warp drive now," Eddington reported. "Warp five."

"Follow at warp five. Stand down red alert and photon torpedoes, but remain cloaked." Sisko glanced back to where Heather Petersen lingered uncertainly at the back of the bridge with Dax's tricorder still in her gloved hands. "Cadet, I'd appreciate it if you went down to our science lab and started examining the data we downloaded. Report anything you find to Lieutenant Dax."

"Aye-aye, sir." She ducked into the turbolift with decisive strides, the trouble in her face eased with the medicine of an important assignment. Dax gave Sisko an approving nod.

"Thank you, Benjamin. She needed to feel like she survived the destruction of that ship for some reason."

"I know the feeling." Sisko laced his fingers together reflectively, watching the stars flash by in their computer-corrected streamlines. "Are the Jem'Hadar fighters keeping to their original vector, Dax?"

She nodded. "We don't have a good survey of this part of the Gamma Quadrant yet. Some preliminary Ferengi records indicate that the Jem'Hadar have laid claim to several of the star systems in it, although they don't seem to use any of them."

"Strategic buffer zones," Eddington suggested.

"No doubt, Commander." Sisko unsealed the chest seam on his environmental suit and shrugged it off, then motioned Dax to do the same while he watched the helm for her. "In which case, we could be heading straight for a major Jem'Hadar stronghold."

Dax paused in the midst of shedding her own suit to give him a glance of restrained amusement. "I got the impression a few minutes ago that that was exactly what you wanted."

Sisko shrugged. "I'd like to keep watch on what the Jem'Hadar are doing, to see if the Dominion has initiated any dealings with the Furies. I'd just rather not try to do it in the midst of constant starship traffic. Our cloaking device can't protect us from a direct collision."

"No, but your pilot can." After a long, tense hour in an insulated environmental suit, the kiss of cool air on Dax's sweaty skin felt like a dip in the Trill baths. She reclaimed her seat, and Sisko sprawled back in his commander's chair. "It does seem odd that the Jem'Hadar would dispatch two fighters from a major stronghold to deal with the *Sreba,* then go straight back again." She turned to meet her old friend's somber frown. "You don't think—"

"—that they know we're back here and are leading us into a trap? It's certainly one possible explanation. Any trace of other warp signatures in the region, Mr. Eddington?"

The security officer shook his head. "No other ship signatures, although I'm picking up a lot of phaser discharge trails and ionic interference. It looks like the aftermath from some kind of battle." Something beeped for his attention on his tactical panel. "Jem'Hadar ships are slowing back to sublight, sir."

"Match vectors," Sisko commanded, sitting up straight again. "Any sign of their destination?"

Dax adjusted velocities, then scanned her boards and saw the telltale peak on one of them. "We're approaching a moderate-size gravity well on heading six-nine-one mark seven-eight-zero. It looks like a small Jem'Hadar base."

"Establish a perimeter orbit around it as soon as we go sublight. Keep us just inside visual range." He steepled his fingers, staring watchfully through them at the *Defiant*'s main viewscreen. A tiny patch of darkness slowly enlarged as the *Defiant* slowed and swung into orbit. Dax upped the magnification factor, and the darkness resolved into a small military starbase. It had the stark, asymmetrical look typical of Jem'Hadar outposts—built for efficiency and ruggedness in battle, with absolutely no sense of aesthetics—but something about it seemed wrong. Dax frowned up at the screen, trying to figure out what it was. Then she glanced down at her helm control and saw the answer in its still-changing distance displays.

"The base is moving!" she said in surprise. "Eddington, can you confirm?"

"Yes, sir." The security officer glanced over his shoulder at the viewscreen, as if he couldn't believe what his own readouts said. "Tactical sensors indicate a sublight speed of point-seven C."

"That's a lot of velocity for a station that size, even one

built by the Jem'Hadar." Sisko sprang to his feet and began pacing, as if some fuse had finally burned down to an internal explosion. "I'm getting a very bad feeling about this. Are their shields up, Commander?"

"No, sir. I'm not reading any weapons systems active at all." Eddington paused, watching his panel again. "The two Jem'Hadar fighters we followed here aren't docking, sir. They've fallen into orbit around the station."

"The same kind of orbit they maintained around the *Sreba?*" Sisko demanded.

"Yes, sir. Sensors indicate they're scanning it the same way."

Sisko paused, bracing both hands against the helm to scowl up at the viewscreen. "Dax, pulse the impulse engines to bring us in a little closer so we can see what's going on down there."

"Aye-aye, sir." She fed in the course change, and felt the *Defiant*'s instant, headstrong response. The Jem'Hadar military base loomed into closer view, occasionally shadowed by the dark silhouettes of the two encircling fighters. Only a few emergency lights blinked along its dark station gantries and bristling weapons towers.

Dax could hear the quick intake of Sisko's breath beside her. "Maximum magnification on the station perimeter," he ordered. She adjusted the sensor controls, and the viewscreen shifted to a close-up rotating view of the Jem'Hadar's thick hull cladding. It looked normal—until a sector pierced with a hundred razor-sharp gashes rolled into sight, trailing escaping shreds of atmosphere and frozen water vapor behind it like white flags.

Eddington whistled softly from behind them. "Looks like this place got hit by the same force that took out the *Sreba.*"

"But not for the same reason," Dax said, scanning the base as best she could through the interference of the cloaking device. "Engineering sensors indicate the internal power source on the Jem'Hadar base is still active. In fact—" It was her turn to frown at her panel displays in disbelief. "—it looks like there are actually *several* power sources inside that station. And at least one of them is emitting the exact subspace frequencies you'd expect from a Federation Mariah-class warp core."

"The type of warp-core the *Sreba* carried?" Sisko demanded. When Dax nodded confirmation, he took a quick stride back to his command console and hit the ship's internal comm. "All hands to battle stations," he said curtly. "Red alert."

Crystalline shimmers a breath of exploding brilliance—steel-gray black spraying metal on metal in the cold dark empty of nowhere, of night—oh, the longness! The heat! The awful heat from every empty spill abandoned to the strangling closeness, to the entrails, to the burst of expulsion as the heat opens up into vacuum, into—

"Julian?"

Bashir jerked upright with a gasp so sharp he thought for a moment that he hadn't been breathing. For a brief, heartbeat instant, fading sparks of memory flicked nonpictures at the back of his eyes—movement swarming black-on-black against a terrible brightness, everything smothered by a fear borne past the point of thought.

Then, just as quickly, whatever he'd almost been dreaming was gone. He was left with his hands dripping where he rested his elbows on the lip of the symbiont's tank, blinking across the contraption at the stocky figure hovering just inside the isolation unit's door. "Chief!" He sounded groggy, even to himself, and he wondered blearily if he was expected to say something more even though his brain didn't offer him anything.

O'Brien shook his head, crossing the small chamber to peer down into the milky brine. "How long have you been sleeping like that?" he asked Bashir, sounding disapproving and concerned all at once, the way only a parent can.

"Like this?" Was he sleeping? Glancing down at the tank, his bare hands, and the symbiont floating placidly in the midst of the medium, Bashir felt the last tattered cobwebs in his brain brushed aside by coherent thought. He'd dropped the stasis field on the symbiont, feeling safe with it for the first time since Hayman showed it to them on Starbase 1. He remembered interrupting its biochemical seizure, then trying to elevate its neurotransmitter levels with a boromine-citrate solution. After that . . .

Bending forward to sink one hand back into the tank, he

grinned sheepishly up at O'Brien as he fished about for the tricorder he'd been holding when he fell asleep with his hands in the water. "Not long." At least he didn't think it had been long. He didn't feel as though he'd slept at all. "Just the last few days catching up to me, I guess. I can't pull all-nighters like I used to." Finally pulling the tricorder up out of the brine, he shook it off as best he could, then searched for somewhere on the front of his uniform dry enough to wipe off the display. "Thanks for waking me."

O'Brien produced an already-stained hand rag from somewhere within his uniform, and offered it across the top of the tank. "Don't thank me yet. Quark's been looking for you."

Bashir paused in accepting the rag to raise his eyebrows. "Quark?"

"Something about a sick customer," O'Brien shrugged. "He wants to see you right away. And he's got *Odo* helping him look for you. That's how we knew you weren't answering your comm badge."

Bashir fingered the insignia on the breast of his uniform, not sure what to say. He couldn't remember the last time he slept so soundly that a comm call couldn't wake him.

"I figured the last thing you needed was the constable snooping around while you were taking care of Professor Stel here," O'Brien continued, gesturing wryly at the very non-Vulcan patient in its equally nonregulation abode. "So I took the liberty of dropping by. Just as well, too, since it seems like I saved you from drowning." He added that last with a puckish grin, but Bashir was too busy closing up the symbiont's tank and gathering his scattered medical gear to do more than flash a tired smile in return.

"What's wrong with this customer of Quark's?" he asked, stuffing tricorder, a hypo kit, and a portable diagnostic scanner into the bag he'd been keeping near the symbiont since leaving Starbase 1.

O'Brien watched him pack with idle interest, shrugging. "Don't know. He's Andorian, and worth a lot of money, that's all Quark would say."

It was something, at least. Andorians had tricky metabolisms—they tended to go into shock with frightening abruptness, no matter how minor their injuries, and

Bashir didn't look forward to explaining to the Andorian embassy why he'd taken so long to answer a sick-call from a bar not twenty meters down the hall from his infirmary. Pausing by the drug cabinet to snatch up an Andorian-specific antigen kit, he'd just slipped the medical bag over one shoulder and turned for the door when his eyes caught on the stasis tank in the middle of the room, and his heart fell into his stomach.

Things were so much easier when there were only two parts of Dax to keep track of. At least they were always both in the same place. While he couldn't very well ignore the rest of his duties and leave other patients untreated, the thought of running out on the symbiont whenever a comm call came in left him feeling nervous and surprisingly guilty. Maybe it was just as well he was falling asleep in the middle of things; he couldn't imagine when he'd next be able to simply lie down and let himself relax.

"I'll stay with it 'til you get back."

Bashir jerked a startled look at O'Brien, still standing with his hand unconsciously feeling out the contours of the jury-rigged coffin. "Can't be that different from watching a three-month-old while she's sleeping, now, can it?" the chief went on with a nonchalance Bashir suspected he didn't really feel. "Besides, when else am I going to have time to rewire some of this mess you call a suspension tank?"

The restless knot of tension in Bashir's chest relaxed by just a little. "Call me if any of its readings change."

"And you keep a couple of hours free the next time Keiko visits the station." O'Brien fixed him with a serious glare that didn't quite match the mischief in his eyes. "There's a Billy the Brontosaur holoplay Molly's been dying to see at the multiplex."

Bashir nodded, smiling gallantly. "I would be honored, Mr. O'Brien. I promise to have your daughter home before dawn."

The faintly horrified expression that washed across O'Brien's face was more than worth the price of the holoplay. "You dating any daughter of mine," the chief grunted as he turned his back on Bashir and started fiddling grumpily with the stasis tank's workings. "That'll be over my dead body!"

Bashir ducked out while the engineer was still grumbling and sorting through the tools he always seemed to carry with him.

The crowded brightness of the Promenade swelled to engulf his senses the moment he stepped out the infirmary door. Noise as palpable as a strong wind buffeted the place, ricocheting off every storefront, every kiosk, every pillar. Bashir had heard of places that claimed to "never sleep," but *Deep Space Nine*'s Promenade was one of the few he'd ever lived in such close proximity with, much less tolerated practically right outside his hospital door. If there wasn't a pocket being picked beside the credit-exchange machines, there was a fight outside the Klingon diner, or an after-hours tongo game whooping it up in the back of Quark's bar. And God forbid that any crisis or accident could ensue without what seemed like half the station's occupants collecting around the scene like platelets around a wound.

That's what first cued Bashir that Quark's dire emergency might not be all that dire—no chaos, no clogging of the station's arteries, no crowding and shoving beyond the normal push and bother of daily Promenade traffic. Aiming for the strident harangue of Quark's voice where it rose above the general hubbub, Bashir wondered if he ought to break into a trot to seem more medically concerned even though the utter lack of gawkers had already told him Quark's patient couldn't be as close to death's door as the barkeep seemed to think. Still, he made a sincere effort to look professionally attentive as he wended his way through the shoppers and the afternoon lunchtime crowd.

Quark bounced up on his toes with a triumphant yelp when he caught sight of Bashir. "There he is!" He stabbed a finger past Odo's shoulder as though pointing out a fleeing felon.

Bashir tried very hard not to sigh as he paused beside them.

"Doctor," Odo greeted him smoothly, sarcasm rampant in his tone. "How nice of you to join us. Is there some reason you weren't answering your comm badge?"

Quark pushed Odo impatiently aside. "What are you

doing down here?" he wailed, grabbing at the front of Bashir's uniform.

The dual questions caught him off guard. "Uh—I was busy," he answered Odo shortly, hoping to stave off further interrogation as he turned an irritated scowl on the Ferengi. "What do you mean 'what am I doing down here'? I thought you had a sick Andorian!"

"No!" Quark bared a serrated grimace of frustration. "I sent *you* a sick Andorian. This morning, just after breakfast." He clasped his hands to the breast of his overembroidered jacket in a show of horror Bashir didn't think was entirely feigned. "Don't tell me you haven't seen him!"

"No one's come to the infirmary all day."

Odo blew a coarse snort. "What a surprise! A wanted smuggler happens to fall deathly ill only moments after finding out the captain is back on the station, then disappears on his way to the infirmary." He angled a skeptical peer down at Quark. "I can't possibly imagine where he got to."

The Ferengi's returning scowl flushed his lobes with what might have been either anger or worry. "Go ahead and laugh! It's not your bar on the line if he lives long enough to sue! Argelian mocha sorbet is very popular with my Rigel-sector customers right now," he explained to Bashir in a voice of almost pleading reasonability. "How was I supposed to know Andorians couldn't tolerate chocolate?"

"Ask them before you serve them?" Odo suggested.

Quark squeaked something indignant in protest to that suggestion, but Bashir lost track of the words under a wire-thin thread of tinnitus that he felt more than really heard. He half-turned to scan the Promenade, his stomach churning with dread. "A transporter . . ."

Odo broke off Quark's ranting with the palm of his hand. "Doctor?"

Blue-white glimmers sprinkled the air near the center of the atrium, and pedestrians scattered in all directions with cries of alarm in an effort to avoid the incoming transporter wave. Bashir gripped the medical bag more tightly under his arm, but stopped himself just short of running out to meet the coalescing figures. It wasn't just common sense that kept him clear of the area of effect—it was the sick anticipation that had been chewing at his stomach ever since Starbase 1, the almost superstitious certainty that something horrible was poised to happen just a tightrope's width away from any moment. So as the transporter's whine rose to a warbling wail and the light and sound braided together into a clutch of humanoid figures wrapped in ragged, soot-stained clothes, Bashir was perhaps the only one not entirely surprised by the scattered, dusty remains that fell to the floor around the group as they solidified—the molecular remnants of whoever had stood near the edges of the beam, too far from the coherent center to make it through.

Whether she responded to the pungent explosion of stench from her less fortunate traveling companions or the shrill chorus of shrieks that suddenly reverberated through the Promenade, Bashir couldn't tell, but the weathered Bajoran woman at the center of the pitiful group had her weapon thrust out at no one, at everyone, before the song of the transporter had completely died. Her wild, pain-shocked eyes found Bashir's on the other side of the atrium, and his heart stopped with a painful lurch as she whipped her phaser around to train it full on him.

"You've got one minute to fetch me your station commander," she called to him in a hoarse, almost tearful voice. "Otherwise, every single one of us is going to die!"

CHAPTER
13

A BLAST OF phaser fire exploded across the viewscreen, disintegrating part of the unshielded Jem'Hadar base. Sisko swung around to confront his replacement security officer, struggling to keep his fierce irritation confined just to the ominous deepening of his voice. He wasn't stupid enough to think that Major Kira would never have fired the *Defiant*'s phasers on her own, but he knew damn well she would never have made the tactical mistake of doing it while they were supposed to remain cloaked.

"I ordered battle stations, Commander, not an all-out attack," he snapped. "Why was our cloak dropped to fire those phasers?"

The Starfleet officer gave him back an almost-affronted look. "Those weren't *our* phasers, Captain. We never lost cloak integrity."

Sisko cursed and swung around to see Dax already adjusting the sensor focus, pulling the viewscreen back for a bigger picture. Stabs of light crisscrossed the darkness as the two encircling Jem'Hadar fighters aimed an unrelenting barrage of phaser fire down at their own base.

"They started firing as soon as their scan was finished," Dax said quietly. "Just like they did at the *Sreba*."

"Then they know it's been taken by the same enemy." Sisko watched the one-sided battle with narrowed eyes, not sure whether he felt more frustrated or relieved at the

Jem'Hadar action. "And we'll never know who it was. Without its shields up, that base won't last five minutes."

"I wouldn't be so sure of that, Benjamin." Dax changed the angle of the viewscreen again, this time focusing on one of the Jem'Hadar fighters. "I think whoever took that base is starting to fight back."

"I'm not reading any signs of weapons discharge from the station," Eddington protested.

"No." The viewscreen was darkening with an odd refractive haze around one of the Jem'Hadar fighters, as if a flurry of small meteorites had taken it into their heads to converge on that exact spot. Sisko felt his gut tighten in grim premonition. "That's because they're not using weapons. Increase sensor magnification, Dax. I want to see exactly what's going on out there."

"Sensors are already extended to their resolution threshold, Captain," she warned. "We'll lose focus if we go in closer."

"Do it anyway."

Dax shrugged and obeyed him. The crisp lines of the Jem'Hadar ship blurred and melted as it grew to fill the viewscreen, but that softening couldn't disguise the crawling organic shapes that now surrounded it. It looked as if a swarm of large metallic wasps had coalesced around the ship, scrabbling across its external shields with jointed claws and blunt segmented bodies that seemed impervious to vacuum.

"Dax, what *are* those things?"

His science officer took a deep breath, dragging her eyes away from the screen just long enough to scan her readouts. "All our sensors can pick up is that they're made of duranium-carbide alloy, powered by small internal dilithium drives." She glanced back up at the viewscreen. "They could be battle robots, Benjamin. They don't seem to notice any pain when they hit the Jem'Hadar's shields."

"No." Sparks of ionic discharge geysered up every time one of the attackers pierced the small ship's defensive forcefields, but those shocks only seemed to slow the metallic creatures down, not stop them. Sisko noticed that despite the seeming randomness of their swarming, they carefully avoided those areas where they could be caught by the rake of the Jem'Hadar's futilely firing phasers. Gradually, the sparks of light kicking up from each contact were getting dimmer and dimmer. Sisko felt an uneasy premonition wash through him. "Is it my imagination, or are the shields on that fighter getting drained?"

"Tactical sensors show his shields at fifteen percent and falling," Eddington confirmed. "His shield generators appear to be getting overloaded by the impacts faster than they can recharge. They'll fall below integrity threshold in approximately two minutes."

"Allowing access to the hull itself." Sisko squinted through the blur of too-close focus to watch as two of the wasplike attackers coordinated a stab at the fighter's sensor array. The failing shields almost let them reach it. "Dax, can you tell if those things are internally piloted?"

"Scanning for internal life signs." Dax paused, then uttered what sounded like a Klingon curse. "That can't be right! The cloaking device must be interfering with our sensor readings."

"What did the scan show?" Sisko demanded. His premonition was crystallizing into bleak reality, born of the combination of sentient purpose and living grace he was witnessing in this blurred confrontation. No spacefaring robot he'd ever seen, not even the ones constructed by the Borg, moved through microgravity with the sleek coordination of a dolphin pod in deep water. These things looked born, not made.

Dax tapped another series of commands into her jury-rigged engineering panel, then glanced back at him with grave eyes. "According to our sensors, there are DNA-based neural networks inside each of those things out there, extending right into their duranium-carbide shells."

"Bioneural computer circuits?"

Dax shook her head fiercely. "I don't think so. I'm not detecting any evidence of internal engineering circuits, not even around the dilithium power cells." She paused, watching the battle on the viewscreen. For a few minutes, the small fighter blurred with the speed of the pilot's evasive maneuvers, but although the dark swarm of attackers rippled and swayed in response, they remained stubbornly attached. "Benjamin, I think those things out there are *alive.*"

"So do I," he said grimly.

The Jem'Hadar's shields flickered with a final pulse of ionic discharge, then failed before the draining mass of metallic bodies that had piled up on them. A shining lacework of vaporous chemicals shot out from each wasplike body, and an instant later ship and swarm disappeared together in the glittering white blast of explosive decompression. When the veils of frozen atmosphere drifted apart at last, the viewscreen showed the shredded hulk of the Jem'Hadar fighter being towed back to its former base by a shadowy host of attackers.

There was a long, reverberating silence on the bridge of the *Defiant*. "Well," Dax said at last, with the sardonic black humor that Sisko remembered Curzon saving for times like these. "At least they're not Furies."

"No," he agreed grimly. "They're not Furies. But they might very well be what the Furies were running from."

"Running from?" Dax snapped a startled look back at him. "You mean the three alien ships we saw on the other side—I mean, in the log record Admiral Hayman showed us?"

"The ones that blew up after firing their phasers randomly in all directions. Sound familiar?" Sisko glanced back at Eddington, wishing now that he hadn't snapped at the Starfleet officer. Unfortunately, the middle of a red alert wasn't the time or place to apologize. "Any signs of the second Jem'Hadar fighter, Commander?"

"It's broken off its attack and is departing the system at warp six." Eddington swung around to face him, scowling. For a brief moment, Sisko thought the other man's anger was directed at him, but the frustrated smack of Eddington's hand on his weapons panel said otherwise. "Tactical sensors can't get any kind of fix on the aliens who attacked the Jem'Hadar fighter, Captain! They don't seem to be putting out any EM emission at all. I have no idea where they are—or where they're going."

"I'll see if we can track them by some kind of targeted sensor reflection." Dax paused to throw a warning glance back at Sisko. "In the meantime, Captain, I'd advise keeping our own EM emissions to a minimum. The creatures seemed to home in on the Jem'Haddar fighter by tracking its phaser fire."

"Meaning if we don't use our impulse engines or fire any weapons, there's a good chance they can't see us?" Sisko nodded curtly. "Acknowledged, Lieutenant. Keep us on our present heading." He swung around to face the wide-eyed ensign at the back of the bridge. "Mr. Hovan, I want you to keep an eye out for any voltage fluctuations in the cloaking device. If those things converge on the *Defiant,* I want to know about it before they start draining our shields."

"Yes, sir." Her voice squeaked a little, then steadied. "I can program an internal alarm to sound if voltage fluctuations exceed normal micrometeorite impact levels, sir, but it'll take me a few minutes."

Sisko gave her a wry smile. "No time to begin like the present, Ensign. Dax, have you managed to get a fix on what our new neighbors are doing out there?"

"Yes, sir." As usual, the Trill's voice held no fear, just the quiet satisfaction of meeting a new scientific challenge. "I'm plotting critical resolution of sensor reflections in the duranium-carbide band on the screen now."

The viewscreen pulled back to show the abandoned Jem'Hadar station, now overlaid by a computer-generated swirl of contoured colors. After a moment's scrutiny, Sisko could see that the brightest peak of white and yellow lay deep inside the station itself, with smaller, moving bumps of green ranged across its surface. Only a few bluish specks glowed in the empty space around the weapons towers and gantries.

"Interpretation, Lieutenant?"

"Approximately four hundred of the aliens appear to be huddled in close proximity to each other inside the Jem'Hadar station," Dax answered. "An additional hundred or so are attached to the station's exterior."

"Perimeter guards," Sisko guessed, and saw Eddington's silent nod of agreement. "What about those reflections you're getting outside the station, Dax?"

"They appear to be fragments of creatures blown up by phaser fire or photon torpedoes. Their DNA signatures are degraded and I'm reading no dilithium power sources."

"Then they *can* be killed." Sisko narrowed his eyes,

regarding the pulsing mass of alien life before him. Despite the fact that it filled only a third of the military base, it didn't seem to be moving. "Have you scanned the station for areas of remaining atmosphere? Or for Jem'Hadar life signs?"

Dax threw him a startled look. "You think some of the Jem'Hadar may still be alive in there?"

"There's got to be a reason the creatures are isolated in one part of the station," Sisko pointed out. "If we can find out why, we might have something we can use against them."

Instead of getting him the sensor scan he wanted, however, that reasonable statement brought Jadzia Dax swinging around to glare at him. "Benjamin, why are you assuming we need to fight these creatures? We can't even talk to them yet! There's no way we can assume they're sentient, much less hostile."

Sisko scowled back at her. "What they did to the *Sreba* and the Jem'Hadar—"

"—might have been an instinctive defense reaction, like wasps swarming to protect their nests!"

"That doesn't make it any less a threat to the Alpha Quadrant!"

They exchanged fierce looks for a moment, until Eddington cleared his throat and intervened. "Lieutenant Dax, correct me if I'm wrong. Didn't we come here to find out what kind of accident was going to throw the wormhole back in time?"

"Yes," she and Sisko said in unison.

"Then before you make any arguments about protecting these creatures—" The security officer tapped a command into his tactical station. "—I suggest you look at where they're moving the Jem'Hadar station to."

The Trill took a deep breath, swinging back to examine the data he'd transferred to her helm display. When she glanced over her shoulder at him again, Sisko saw surprise and a trace of unease flicker through her blue-gray eyes.

"Commander Eddington's right—the vector's too exact to be an accident. They're heading straight for the wormhole."

It was Sisko's turn to take a deep breath, but in his case it was one of grim resolve. "Then we *have* to find out why," he said. "And we have to stop them. How much time do we have before they arrive at the wormhole entrance?"

"With them moving at point-seven light speed? At least fifty hours," Dax said promptly.

"Good." He lifted his gaze to the screen again. "I can't believe every Jem'Hadar on that station is dead—they're not stupid, and they were genetically engineered to defend the Founders against threats exactly like this. Find me some Jem'Hadar life signs down there, Dax. And see if they correlate with areas where life-support is still intact."

She nodded and programmed the search into her sensor controls. "And then?"

"And then," said Sisko, "we're going to find out if these creatures can track transporter beams the way they track phasers."

Even though Bashir had warned her, Kira still couldn't hold back a little sound of disgust as she rounded the corner to the Promenade. It really wasn't any worse than half of what she'd seen in the concentration camps—Cardassian corpse-disposal methods smelled almost as strongly. No, Kira had to admit as she slowed to a controlled, professional walk, it was the hollow, almost mindless expressions on their faces as they trembled, back-to-back, in their little circle that somehow made what had happened here so much more horrible than just what the eye could see.

That, and the knowledge that the two Bajorans who lay screaming were really no different than the molecular dust they writhed in—both were victims of standing on the fringe of a long-range transport when the distance transmitted was too long, and the signal began to decay. It made Kira glad that Odo had been able to clear the Promenade of civilians before any real panic could begin.

One of the still standing militia members said something softly into Pak's ear as Kira neared, and Kira saw the older woman twist around to look at her while she was still too far away to really converse. Still, that didn't stop the terrorist from smiling darkly and waving her phaser toward where Bashir knelt in the once living dust to tend to her injured people.

"Useful as well as decorative," she called, voice as pale of life as her face despite her obvious effort. "Do you share?"

Bashir lifted his head at the question, but didn't turn to look at Kira or interrupt his work. It wasn't hard to read the discomfort in the set of his lean shoulders, though. Kira wondered if he was embarrassed. "Dr. Bashir's services are available to anyone on the station who needs them. Even you." She altered her approach just enough to catch the doctor's eye and order gently, "Get these people down to the infirmary."

He nodded, looking oddly grateful as he tapped awake his comm badge. Kira stepped around him to draw Pak's eyes away so he could finish his work without the threat of either her phaser or her sarcasm.

"First Veska Province," she said, shaking her head at Pak as she came to a stop beside Odo and his own brown-clad security, "now this. You certainly know how to make an impression."

The smile that spasmed across Pak's face was too twisted to really be amused. "Desperate times call for desperate actions." She jerked her chin at Kira, phaser gesturing aimlessly. "Where's your commander?"

"You're talking to her." Kira crossed her arms, trying not to scowl in response to Pak's impatient grimace.

"Good try, but I've seen pictures. The guy who runs this place is a human—not to mention much taller and much browner than you."

"Captain Sisko is off the station just now." *I wish I knew why, and I wish I knew where.* "As his second-in-command, I'm what you get until he returns." She waited until the tingle of Bashir's emergency transport to the infirmary had faded, then gave Pak another few seconds to recover from watching her people vanish into that quick, unforgiving shimmer. "Do we talk?" she asked at last, pulling the terrorist's attention back to her.

Pak looked up sharply, as though surprised that she was still alive to partake in it. "What can I say to make you believe me?"

Kira frowned, studying the older woman's face. "You haven't told me anything yet."

"But when I do," Pak persisted. "When I do, you've got

to believe me, or we're all going to wish this was us." She stomped one foot in the dust that surrounded her.

This wasn't a band of human tourists who'd just survived their first clash with the Cardassians. These were children of the Cardassian Occupation, and veterans of both Veska Province and the Kotar Killing Fields. And Pak Dorren...

You didn't see her, Kira thought at Odo, afraid to break her stare from Pak long enough to whisper to him. *She's not afraid of anything—not of the Cardassians, not of Shakaar, not even of her own damned bombs!* Yet she'd risked a long-distance transport with who knew how many people, and had said nothing, done nothing, to indicate she regretted the results. Just the thought of what could force a woman like Pak to do that made Kira's muscles ache with cold.

"All right, I believe you."

Odo growled softly in frustration, but the strong relief that moved in Pak's dark eyes frightened Kira far more than the constable's disapproval. "What happened?"

Pak took a deep breath and let her phaser drift down to her side. "I think I found out who did in those ore freighters."

"It really wasn't you." Kira said it aloud without meaning to, too surprised by her belief to censor herself.

Pak threw her head back with a short, harsh laugh. "You didn't listen to a damn thing I told you out there, did you? We're in this to *free* Bajor, little bit, not screw up its economy any worse than it already is. We were looking to stop whoever did this just as much as you."

"And you found?" Odo prompted.

The terrorist's face collapsed into a look of bleak honesty. "I don't know." She snapped her gaze to Kira at the sound of the major's frustrated sigh. "I've never seen or heard of anything like this before," she insisted. "We had a dozen ships patrolling freighter routes when they closed in on us...." Her eyes lost focus, clouding on whatever memories stole the animation from her voice and made her gaze drift to one side as she remembered. "Sensors picked up a dispersed mass of duranium-titanium alloy." Her tone was reflective, almost gentle. It occurred to Kira that she would have had a pretty voice if it hadn't been worn raw by drinking and *chaat.* "I thought it must be ship debris from another freighter wreck, and I dropped us out of warp so we could scan for survivors. By the time they hit our shields, I knew we should never have gone sublight, but by then it was too late. . . ."

Kira waited for her to continue. She didn't. "Too late for what?" Kira asked at last. *"Who* attacked you?"

As if the questions yanked her back into real time, Pak shook off her dim distraction and brought her eyes back to Kira's. "Animals. Aliens of some kind. Big, vacuum-adapted *things* that ate up phaser fire and crawled right through our screens." She shrugged at her inability to describe them with an impatient, angry sound. "I watched them peel open three of our fighters like jil-birds on a redfruit; then did my best to call a strategic retreat. They homed in on our engine exhausts, backtracked along our phaser beams, followed the paths of our torpedoes . . ." Her voice began to fade; then she shook her head with a bitter grimace. "I didn't think this transport would work. It just seemed better to die in a scatter of atoms than to let these things blow me out into space."

Strong words, coming from a woman who had once turned an entire valley into glass. Kira cleared her throat, her mind already racing. "We should contact the Bajoran military," she said to Odo, "see if they can get ships up to deal with this before any other freighters disappear."

"You don't get it, little bit, do you?"

She jerked a scowl at Pak, and the terrorist pushed between the three who circled her to cross the empty Promenade. "I'm not talking about calling out the Temple guard. We ran into these things doing point-eight C while on our way to *here!* If they keep going just the way they were when we first found them, they're going to be here in under four hours." She spread her arms wide, as though laying out the implications for any fool to see. "So—do you want to start panicking now, or shall I?"

CHAPTER
14

A BITTER CHILL burned Sisko's skin as soon as the transporter beam released him. He cursed the confidence in Starfleet sensors that let them beam over with open faceplates to what was supposed to be a pressurized section of the Jem'Hadar station. His hand was halfway to his visor before he realized he couldn't feel the relentless suck of vacuum against his exposed cheeks, only cold. He left his visor up and took a cautious breath. Although his nose and throat protested at the bite of frigid air, his lungs assured him it held a reasonable amount of oxygen.

Sisko glanced around and saw his away team ranged around him, still in the defensive back-to-back circle they'd assumed on board the *Defiant*. They'd beamed into a room lit only by the dim phosphorescent glow of emergency lamps. "Nobody move!" he snapped, seeing the tentative turn of one gold-and-black form in the darkness. "Dax, scan for difluorine."

She tapped an order into her tricorder, scanned the sector of the room she was facing, then handed the instrument on to Sisko. He repeated the motion and passed it to the quiet young security guard beside him. While he waited for the tricorder to complete its circle, Sisko surveyed the area they'd beamed into. His dark-adjusted eyes told him the huge room was full of identical waist-high consoles arranged in precise rows. Something about their shape tugged vaguely at his memory.

Dax took the tricorder back from Pritz on her other side, and scanned its readout. Her relieved breath steamed in the frigid air. "No difluorine readings here at all. The aliens must not have used it after they breached the hull and got inside."

"Probably because they didn't want the station to break apart before they got it to the wormhole." Sisko stepped out of the circle and turned to face the three security guards. They waited silently for his orders, phaser rifles cradled and ready in their hands. His own rifle bumped gently against the insulated back of his environmental suit, leaving Dax the only unarmed member of the party. "Goldman and Fernandez, locate and secure the nearest doors. Pritz, you'll guard the lieutenant."

The two young men turned to leave, one of them stumbling over something on the floor before he swung his flashlight down to light his way. Sisko swung his own light in a wide arc and whistled when he saw the random scatter of Jem'Hadar weapons across the floor, fallen like dead branches after a windstorm. Here and there among them, the steel floor plates were splotched and streaked by ugly dark stains.

"It looks like the Jem'Hadar made a last stand here," Dax commented. "Funny that there aren't any bodies. Do you think the survivors took their dead away with them?"

Sisko's flashlight caught on an odd, curving fragment of what looked like metal torpedo casing, except for a clinging inner rind of fleshy strands oozing something too clear and viscous to be called blood. "Not unless they took the alien dead away too," he said grimly. "Dax, what is this place?"

She scanned one of the waist-high consoles with her tricorder. "These appear to be stasis-field generators, but they're much too small for emergency medical use. I think it's a Jem'Hadar creche, Benjamin."

Sisko sucked an incautious breath of frigid air and coughed it out again painfully. He'd just remembered the similar-looking device in which Quark had once found a Jem'Hadar child. "We're in a nursery full of babies?" he demanded, scanning the cold rows of consoles that stretched into the dim distance of the room.

"A warehouse full of neonatal reinforcements," Dax corrected gently. "Waiting to be grown into fighters at need."

Sisko grunted acknowledgment of that. "You said you'd spotted very weak Jem'Hadar life signs from the ship, old man. Could it have been these children you were reading?"

"No." Dax took one tricorder bearing, then moved down the long aisle of stasis generators to take another. Pritz followed a wary step behind her. "Sensors can't pick up biologic activity from a Jem'Hadar in stasis any more than they could pick up Heather Petersen's life signs on board the *Sreba*. And in any case, the original biologic activity I spotted didn't come from here. This was just the closest site where we could beam an away team into the battle wreckage."

Sisko grunted. "It's interesting that the Jem'Hadar children were left untouched by the aliens, the same way Petersen was."

Pritz cleared her throat. "It means they can't know much about the Jem'Hadar, sir. If they did, they would have eliminated these neonatal reinforcements as a potential threat."

"It may be even simpler than that, Ensign." Dax paused to take a third bearing with her tricorder. "Maybe they just can't recognize anything in a stasis field as a living organism." The tricorder whistled to notify her of its completion of some task, but whatever it told her knotted her smooth brow into a frown. "I've got a triangulated fix on the Jem'Hadar life signs, Captain, but—"

"Which way?" Sisko demanded.

"Outside, a hundred meters to our right, but Benjamin—with readings like this, I don't see how this Jem'Hadar can be alive!"

Sisko swung around, spotting the doors by the stationary glow of flashlights on either side. He motioned Dax and Pritz toward the other two security guards. "But he *is* alive?"

"According to his neural patterns, yes. According to his heartbeat and respiratory activity, no."

Sisko paused at the doorway, running his light over the tangle of broken roof beams and fallen ceiling plates that filled the outside corridor. "Can you tell if he'll stay alive for a while yet? It's going to take us some time to get through this mess."

The taller of the two male security guards lifted his phaser rifle inquiringly. "Captain, we could clear out some of this wreckage with controlled phaser blasts."

"Too much danger of attracting attention that way, Ensign Fernandez. Whatever they are, these aliens seem able to track energy discharge. We'll have to open a path by hand." Sisko perched his flashlight on a broken wall panel to light their path, then squatted to slide his gloved hands under the beam blocking the door. Fernandez slung his rifle across his shoulder and did the same. "One, two, three—"

One heave sent the beam crashing down on the far side of the corridor, rolling a wall of cold dust up toward them as it did. Sisko coughed and scrubbed at his stinging eyes. Maybe he should have put his visor down, after all.

"All right, Dax, which way do we go from here?"

Only silence answered him. With a frown, Sisko turned back to face the green glow of the creche. He got a worried look from Pritz, but no response at all from his science officer. The Trill was staring down at her tricorder, but the blankness of her expression told Sisko she wasn't seeing it. He stepped forward to shake at her shoulder, hard.

"Dax? Old man, where the hell are you?"

There was still no reply. Sisko let out a deep breath of exasperation that steamed in the cold, dusty air. This was what he'd been afraid of when they'd first beamed over to the *Sreba*—a relapse into the odd stillness that had come over Dax once before. Her breath and color seemed perfectly normal, but not even a measured slap against her cheek could rouse her.

"Pritz, Fernandez—stay here and guard the lieutenant until she wakes up." Sisko slid the tricorder from Dax's unresisting hands and squinted at the radial coordinates it displayed. "Goldman, you're with me. Let's go."

It took them fifteen arduous minutes to work their way down the debris-choked hallway, following its sinuous curve to a completely unexpected dead end. Goldman glanced across at Sisko, his blue eyes dubious in the mask of dust that now covered his face.

"Where do we go from here, sir?"

"I'm not sure," Sisko admitted, scowling down at the unresponsive tricorder. "I can't triangulate on the Jem'Hadar's biologic activity the way Dax—"

A fierce hiss and screech of metal from the pool of darkness to their left interrupted him. Sisko swung around, stabbing his flashlight into the gloom like a weapon. He caught the quick leveling of Goldman's rifle from the corner of one eye and threw a hand out to stop the young security guard.

"No! Don't shoot—it may be the Jem'Hadar."

Goldman took in a shaky breath as the flashlight beam found a ripple of movement in the dark. "That's no Jem'Hadar, sir," he protested.

"Yes, it is." Sisko had already recognized the serrated bony edge of the genetically engineered fighter's face. He took a cautious step forward to shine the light more directly on his target. Metallic noise squealed through the room again, and this time Sisko could see that it came from the rippling motion of something behind the Jem'Hadar's limply sprawled body.

He lifted the flashlight to reveal a black, segmented form as tall as a man and as flexibly scaled as an insect. It turned more fully to face them, as if the light had attracted its attention, and Sisko heard Goldman curse in a strained voice. From this angle, they could see that the Jem'Hadar was half-engulfed by a wide central orifice on the creature's belly, with two rows of segmented, claw-tipped appendages closed so tight around him that only his legs and shoulders protruded. The Jem'Hadar's head rolled and lifted, eyes staring out at them unseeingly. Blood-crusted lips moved as if they barely remembered how to form speech.

"Kill me . . ." the Jem'Hadar whispered.

Goldman raised his phaser rifle in unthinking response, but Sisko caught the barrel in one gloved hand and shoved the weapon away again.

"Wait," he ordered, despite the revulsion roiling in his own gut. "We might be able to save him."

"How?" the security guard demanded.

Sisko sent the flashlight skimming around the alcove the alien had dragged its prey into, and saw the shadow of fallen roof panels along one side. "Work your way around to the left and find cover. Be prepared to give the alien a glancing shot when I give you the word. If I can pull the Jem'Hadar out while it's distracted—"

"What if it starts throwing out difluorine?"

"You'll be under cover, and I'll be off to one side," Sisko said grimly.

"No use—" The Jem'Hadar braced his elbows against the metallic carapace of his captor and pushed himself upward in one convulsive jerk so they could see the dangle of raw nerves and blood vessels that was left of his spine. "Not enough left to save. Only kept alive—to bring you here. Kill quick—"

Goldman took a deep breath. "Captain Sisko, it's a trap!" A crash of rubble from farther down the corridor triggered the security guard into a whirl of motion. He aimed a phaser blast into the darkness before Sisko could stop him.

"Don't shoot!" Dax's urgent voice rang echoes off the corridor walls. "It's us!"

Sisko cursed and caught Goldman's arm, swinging him around to face the stationary alien in the alcove. "Cover *that!*" he snapped, then turned to light the way for the rest of the away team. Dax ducked under a slanted roof beam and came toward him, followed closely by Pritz. Fernandez took up a defensive position a few meters down the hall.

"Old man, are you all right?" Sisko demanded.

"Yes, of course." Dax came to a halt a stride away from him, her voice resonating with excitement beneath its professional calm. "Captain, I've just been in touch with *Deep Space Nine!* The ansible effect works!"

"The *what?*"

She grinned up at him, gray eyes bright in her dusty face. "It's long physics derivation, but here's the short version: The two Dax symbionts can communicate with each other across space, instantaneously, because they're composed of identical quantum particles. I've become a living ansible, Benjamin."

Sisko scowled across at her. "You're telling me you

were actually in contact with the other Dax back at *Deep Space Nine?*"

The Trill nodded emphatically. "The old Dax still wasn't very clear, but he warned me about aliens who take over—"

Sisko's glance shot involuntarily toward the shadows now hiding the Jem'Hadar and his captor. Dax followed his gaze and froze. It took Sisko a moment to remember that a Trill's night sight was much better than a human's.

"That's it." Even in the dead stillness of the deserted station, her voice sounded unnaturally quiet. Sisko brought his flashlight snapping back to light the intertwined pair in the alcove. More of the Jem'Hadar had been digested, caving his chest in like a rotten melon. "That's the alien old Dax told me we had to—"

She broke off in horror as the Jem'Hadar lifted his head, dark blood spilling down his chin and his unfocused eyes rolling in involuntary response to the motion. "Kill now, use all phasers," he said urgently. "They will track you by your DNA. They will take you back and divide you—"

It was Sisko's turn to freeze, his skin prickling with the rush of implications. "Jadzia, are you saying old Dax already *knew* about these aliens?"

"Yes." Dax took a deep breath to steady her voice. "It told me over and over to find one of them and talk to what it had eaten. I thought it was still confused."

"Then these *were* the aliens we met when the *Defiant* went back in time."

"But how could they be here now?" Dax demanded. "The wormhole still hasn't shifted—"

"No, but this station is about to shift it."

Their eyes met in swift understanding. Before either of them could speak, however, a proximity alarm went off on one of the security guards' belts and a shout echoed off the wreckage.

"Captain, motion detected out in the corridor, two hundred meters and closing!" Fernandez warned, scrabbling close to them. "Multiple sources."

Sisko cursed and slammed a palm down on his combadge. "Eddington, stand by to transport us back to the *Defiant!*"

"Want your DNA," the Jem'Hadar whispered. For some

reason, the alien was now ejecting him in spasmodic, blood-drenched jerks, but his mouth still managed to form a ghost of words. "No human DNA, not yet. *Kill me now!*"

The last command was a shout, spat out even as what was left of the half-digested Jem'Hadar fell twitching out of the alien's central orifice. Freed of its burden, the segmented form promptly lunged at Goldman, who sprayed it with a reflexive blast of phaser fire. The Jem'Hadar's corpse vanished in that barrage, but the phaser energy simply soaked into the dark metallic carapace of its former captor.

"Damn!" Sisko reached back to yank his own rifle down into firing position, aware that Pritz and Fernandez were scouring the corridor behind them with phaser blasts. Goldman had fallen beneath the alien's sinuous scuttling rush and was screaming as it grabbed at him with jointed claws. Sisko aimed a long, sustained shot from his phaser rifle at it, but despite the dance of hot sparks across its metallic back, the alien refused to move.

"Hand weapons aren't working, Captain!" Pritz shouted over the roar of phasers and the background screech of metallic advance. "Aliens fifty meters and closing *fast*."

"*Defiant!*" Sisko yelled into his combadge, still firing at the alien. "Prepare for close-quarters transport with possible enemy involvement. Beam us back *now!*"

The raw ends of the data conduits met imperfectly, but there wasn't time to trim them. Kira wriggled onto her side inside the cramped Jeffries tube and reached behind her to grope the back of the equipment belt she'd borrowed from O'Brien, wishing again that she'd been able to fit everything into the front pockets so she could work by sight instead of feel. Oh, well. Added difficulty only heightened the sense of urgency. It was something she'd grown used to during her years with the Resistance—the brisk, zinging excitement that came from knowing what you did was vital, and you only had a short time to get it done. Not a contented feeling, really, she reflected as she finally found the tape to flash-wrap her splice, but so familiar from her early life that it felt oddly comforting, even with the life of a station and all its inhabitants depending upon her.

She bit off the tape and scooted back from her handiwork,

just in case it didn't hold. "Okay, Chief—take her off-line."

"Aye-aye, sir." He sounded tense and focused, even over her comm badge, and Kira suddenly felt foolish for finding any sort of solace in their hurried work. If an action did no good, was it the end result which judged the work, or the fact that you took action at all? As the light and life inside the Jeffries tube flickered and died, she decided not to do too much philosophizing until they were finished rerouting the systems.

"That's the last data path on your deck, Major," O'Brien reported after another long moment of checking and rechecking whatever warning lights Kira was sure they'd set off in Ops. "If you want to take deck five off the loop, too, you're gonna have to find me another power grid to run it through—we're eighteen percent over capacity as is."

"Then we'll work with what we've got." She scrambled backward until her feet dangled out into air, then pushed herself free of the narrow tube with a grateful sigh. She could only stand to belly-crawl for so long. "You did good, Chief. I didn't think we could cut back this far."

"I'm not so sure we can," O'Brien grumbled morosely. "Ask me again in three hours."

Kira smiled, glancing up to look down the corridor toward the sound of approaching footsteps as she stooped to retrieve the Jeffries tube's cover. "I'll make sure I do that. Kira out."

Odo squatted to take half the door as Kira tapped off her comm badge. "If Pak Dorren is to be believed, we may not be here to worry about power consumption in another three hours."

Kira let him help her wrestle it back into place, casting him a sidelong glance. "You don't think I should have listened to her."

He stepped back as Kira secured the bolts, and she realized that he was truly considering his answer when he still hadn't said anything by the time she turned to start for the turbolift. "She wasn't lying," the constable allowed at last. Neither agreement nor argument—simply a straightforward statement of fact. "Whatever—or whoever—they fought with was frightening enough to drive them onto that transporter. I just don't know that I would evacuate all of the station's outer decks on the strength of one eyewitness report."

She nodded, chewing at her lower lip as a host of conflicting impulses swarmed her for what must have been the hundredth time since she'd met Pak's tortured stare in the Promenade. No matter how many times she swam through her own reasoning, though, she kept coming back to the same simple truth. "You saw those ore freighters." She stopped to pop a circuit box and shut down power to all but one of the deck's turbolift bays. "If Pak's 'vacuum-breathers' really are at fault, then we can't risk sending a runabout just to check up on her story. What have we learned if it just never comes back?" She closed the box with a disgusted shake of her head. "That leaves either waiting for Sisko to get back from whatever field trip Starfleet has him out on, or waiting for the *Mukaikubo* to get here."

"And you can't stand to just do nothing until help arrives."

She wondered sometimes if Odo's stark perceptions were good for tuning her sense of reality, or merely blunt and annoying. "Think of it as a practice drill," she told him, neatly avoiding any real comment on his remark. "If nothing happens, we still get to find out how quickly we can compress station functions without overloading the power grid. If somebody *does* show up, then we've got four decks of buffer for our vacuum-breathers to crawl around in and breach before cutting into vital systems." Distracted by another open Jeffries tube cover, she grimaced in silent criticism of her own sloppiness and squatted to lift it back into place. "All in all, a pretty reasonable trade-off, considering."

At first, she didn't know what made her jerk back from the Jeffries tube opening, only that her breath froze in the back of her throat and a sudden dump of adrenaline into her blood made her feel as though her heart would explode. But it came right on top of the subconscious observation that she'd never been inside this Jeffries tube, and the thought and the movement seemed somehow related until the traveling weight of something hard and heavy slammed the cover plate from behind and threw her backward.

She didn't see it clearly—a flash of dark movement, too

small and amorphous to be humanoid—but she felt its tiny hands scrabbling at the toes of her shoes, and the bright, acidic smell of its sweat burned her nasal passages like fire. Barking a curse she hadn't used since the concentration camps, she heaved against the cover plate to try and rise up to her knees, and the attacker responded by lashing around the edges of the metal until it found a purchase in the meat of her upper arm. The cover plate crashed to the deck between them with a *bang!*

Pain exploded across her senses like a lightning flash; then she twisted sideways so that she'd smash shoulder-first into the wall instead of being yanked deeper into the tube, and the pain leapt back to a more respectful distance. This was the way it should be—pain was a fact of life, not a thing that could destroy you, not a demon to be feared just for itself. Animals gave in to pain—Bajorans used it. Gritting her teeth, she hitched up her legs to make a wedge against the outside of the opening and let her anger eat the pain and feed it to her strength.

A cool, slick rope of pressure snaked across her chest, over her shoulder, around her waist, and yanked her back toward the corridor. She screamed, kicking and jabbing, furious at being ganged up on by some other creature she didn't know and couldn't even see. Whatever had her in its teeth responded with an angry jerk, its tiny metallic fingers feeling out her shape like a swarm of blinded men. The cord around her chest cinched crushingly tight, and cut off her breathing in midscream. Pain, tube, and corridor all splintered into a dull gray cloud, and Kira felt herself yanked back into the tunnel opening so hard that her arm wrenched straight out over her head. A warm pulse of wetness against her cheek smelled sharply familiar; she wondered if she was bleeding, or if some other Bajoran had somehow managed to smear blood all over the decking when she wasn't around.

The edge of the tunnel smacked into her knees, and she clenched herself death-rigid trying to halt her advance. She felt like rag between two warring barsas, pulled inward by the fierce grip above her elbow, outward by the gelatinous hug about her waist. Clawing across her middle for the phaser that should be on her right hip, she closed cold fingers around the pommel and spared only a wisp of thought for what she would do if this were some engineering tool and not her weapon. Then she craned her head back to look into the monster's face, raised her gun, and fired.

An instant's vision of dusty Andorian blue before the phaser's actinic white filled the dark passage and blinded her. The grinding pain of bone on bone washed to nearly nothing as a greater splash of anguish gushed over her arm, her hand, her shoulder. She thought she must have recoiled—she was sure she heard her own scream under the phaser's shrill report—but it wasn't her strength that tumbled her into the corridor, or her voice that whispered urgently, desperately, "Major, get up! Get up and move away from the Jeffries tube!"

I can't . . . ! Even when she felt Odo pushing at her, urging her to her knees, she couldn't seem to find the right nerve pathways to make her tortured muscles answer. It wasn't just the ever-expanding pain that ate away at her thinking—it was the strangely thick distance that had inexplicably spread itself between her and the world. Dulling, muffling, softening all the sharp edges. When a queerly jointed waldo felt its way outside the Jeffries tube to tap and tick at the flooring, no rational awareness pushed its way through that viscous membrane, but the sheer force of her fear slammed her back against the opposite wall. She froze with her feet collected under her, ready to run and too shocky to move as the pain burned into her with a smell like rotten medicine.

"Major . . ." Odo's voice buzzed in her ear from very nearby, sounding eerily wrong and thin. "Please don't fire your phaser while I'm covering you."

At first, she couldn't take her eyes off the creature in front of her. Smooth as brushed metal, almost light-absorbing, but contoured so strangely that she couldn't tell if she was staring at its head or its tail. She could tell that she'd hurt it, though—the eyeless expanse of Andorian blue that had seemed to cover its face now looked like part of its abdomen, and was burned to brilliant sapphire. The only thing Kira recognized for sure was her own blood streaking hieroglyphs on the decking as the not-quite-waldo felt about in patient blindness.

"Major?"

She jerked aside, trying to find him. "Where are you?" But even as she asked, she felt the skin-thin caul across her mouth, and shivered in unreasonable discomfort. "I . . . Odo . . . !" Remembering his request as though from a great distance, she made herself slowly, carefully lower her phaser until it thumped against the floor. Encased in a sheet of softened changeling, it didn't make a sound.

"It doesn't seem able to sense me," Odo remarked with quiet calmness. She realized that he must be vibrating a small tympanum just outside her ear, the way he'd talked with her through the spacesuit helmet in vacuum. "Or perhaps I'm just not to its liking. Either way, this seemed the most efficient option." He fell silent a moment as the thing withdrew into the tunnel, and Kira could hear the fearfully light skitter of its movements as it hurried away. "That's more like it." His mass pushed against her chest—just a gentle pressure, like a quick, chaste hug—and the comm badge on her right shoulder beeped. "Emergency medical transport on this comm badge signal."

"No!" She surged to her feet, stumbling back against the bulkhead as the movement blurred her vision and the pain nearly took her breath away. "Odo, don't do it! That's an order!"

He peeled away from her with almost gentlemanly care, not even slowing as he slipped through the fingers of her grasping hand. "I'm sorry, Major, but I can flow through a Jeffries tube faster without you." He paused at the mouth of the tunnel to form a confident face and look back at her. "Don't worry—I'll file a full report when I get back."

"Odo!" She wanted to grab him, to throw herself on top of him and force him to be transported out along with her so this thing couldn't shred him, or eat him, or find some other way to destroy him. Instead, she managed only one lurching step forward before the itching tingle of the transporter beam folded around her. Her muscles went rigid, the corridor fading away, and the transporter whisked her to nothing even as she drew in the breath to shout her anger.

CHAPTER
15

IT CAME THROUGH the paralysis of the transporter beam like pounding surf with an occasional mutter of distant thunder.

"—*talk to them, the only way we can stop them is from inside*—"

"—much better stability on these neurotransmitter levels today—"

"—*talk to what they've eaten, bring one back and talk to what's inside*—"

For the first time, Jadzia tried to turn the quantum-deep resonance between symbionts into a true conversation. "I've met them," she replied, forming the words clearly in her mind. "The aliens you warned me about are here."

It felt as if a spark had jumped through immeasurable time and space. "—*talked to what they've eaten?*" demanded a fainter, distant echo of her symbiont's familiar voice.

"Yes, a Jem'Hadar. He said they would kill us for our DNA."

"*Not kill, divide. Divide and share the DNA, divide and share the cerebral cortex.*"

"Then they retain the knowledge and memories of the organisms they engulf?" She wasn't sure whether that was Jadzia or Dax asking, but the answer was vehement.

"*Yes! You must try to find one who will help you*—"

"—Chief, will you hand me that thermal diffuser—"

"—while I try to make Julian understand."

Jadzia felt a shiver of sadness run through her, so deep and inexplicable that she knew it must have jumped across time and space along with that transmitted thought. "Understand what?"

"That you should have brought me with you."

"You with us, old man?"

Dax opened her eyes, suddenly aware that the rigid freeze of the transporter had worn completely off. She shook away the pervasive sense of déjà vu that lingered after each ansible trance.

"I'm all right, Benjamin. I just got some more information about the aliens from old Dax." She glanced around, seeing that only four forms in dust-stained environmental suits had returned to the *Defiant*'s ready room. The two remaining security guards were disarming their phaser rifles in grim silence. "What happened to the alien who was attacking us when we beamed out?"

"I don't know." Sisko stripped off his gloves and slapped them against his thigh, raising a violent cloud of dust. "I don't know what happened to Ensign Goldman either. Eddington must have left them both back on the station."

"No, we didn't, Captain." The doors hissed open to admit Heather Petersen, flushed and breathless. She must have run straight from the transporter control room. "I beamed them both into stasis chambers in the medical bay."

"Alive?" Sisko demanded, taking her elbow and steering her back around toward the open doors. Dax dropped her own gloves and helmet on the floor, and followed them down the hall to the nearest turbolift.

"Goldman was alive when we beamed him out, but his vital signs indicated massive internal trauma. I haven't talked to the medic yet, but I don't think we'll be able to take him out of stasis until we reach *Deep Space Nine*."

"Bridge," Sisko snapped at the turbolift computer, then turned his narrow-eyed gaze back on Petersen. "What about the alien that was attacking him?"

"It was picked up, too, but I separated out the transport wave and put it into a different stasis field." Dax lifted an eyebrow at Petersen's matter-of-fact statement, knowing that even Chief O'Brien wouldn't have found that calculation easy to do on the fly. "I'm not sure if it's alive, though. I think only part of it got beamed in."

"That might work to our advantage," Dax said. "If we could selectively activate some of the cerebral matter the alien has incorporated, we might be able to—"

The turbolift doors hissed open on the bridge, its viewscreen still lit by the glowing indicator colors of Dax's targeted sensor scan. Sisko's face hardened in that reflected light. "Let's not run any scientific experiments just yet, Dax. I want to make sure we're safe first." He strode over to drop a hand on Eddington's shoulder, making the Starfleet security officer look up with a startled snort. "Any sign of movement from the Jem'Hadar station, Commander?"

"Not according to Lieutenant Dax's sensor scan, sir." Eddington gestured up at the swirls of whitish green crawling across the surface of the Jem'Hadar station. "The aliens seem to be searching the area near your beam-in site, but they haven't gone out into space from there. I don't think they were able to track the transporter beam back to the ship."

"Good." Sisko threw himself into his command chair, raising a small cloud of dust as he did. "I'd call a senior officer's conference, gentlemen, but I think we already constitute one. Don't just stand there, Dax, sit down."

She threw him an exasperated glance but took her usual seat at the helm. "I'm not going to collapse, Benjamin. I haven't become an epileptic, just an ansible."

"I don't care what you've become, old man. I still can't see through you to the viewscreen." Sisko's gaze lifted to the ominous glow of green and white that mapped out their enemy's occupation of the Jem'Hadar base. "Eddington, what's the latest update on the station's vector of travel?"

Eddington cleared his throat, as if he'd been waiting for exactly that question. "I've refined tactical sensor analysis to plus or minus one-sixteenth of arc, Captain. Bearing of the Jem'Hadar station remains dead-on for the wormhole. Estimated time of arrival is just under seventeen hours."

Sisko grunted acknowledgment of that. The security officer gave him a frustrated look, making Dax duck her head to hide a smile. Anyone who'd served under Benjamin

Sisko for more than a single voyage knew he didn't waste time handing out compliments, but Eddington never stopped trying for them.

"All right, Petersen, it's your turn." Sisko swung his chair to face the cadet. "What have you learned so far from the *Sreba* data?"

Petersen's throat-clearing was much more hesitant. "Um—Lieutenant Dax managed to download nearly all the scientific data T'Kreng recorded on her way through the wormhole. I ran a numerical model of the upstream subspace echoes and was able to pinpoint the precise time and location of the time rift. The singularity matrix will avulse at the Gamma Quadrant entrance in approximately eighteen hours. Plus or minus forty minutes, sir," she added apologetically.

Sisko's mouth twitched. "An acceptable margin of error, Mr. Petersen. That gives the aliens about an hour to detonate the station's augmented power core once they arrive."

"But what reason would these creatures have for doing that?" Eddington demanded. "They barely seem sentient."

"I'm not sure they *are* sentient as we define it," Dax said somberly. "But they appear to have evolved the ability to capture and utilize both DNA and cerebral material from other sentient species. As for why they're doing this—" She paused, feeling the deep swash and pull of the twinned symbionts inside her, like a tidal current running below the bridge that was Jadzia. "—the ancient Dax encountered others of their kind in the time and space the wormhole will be diverted to. The aliens in the station may be planning to travel into the past to join them, or they may be trying to bring their ancient counterparts into our present."

"Either way, we can't let them divert the wormhole to do it," Sisko said flatly. "We'll have to destroy the Jem'Hadar station before it comes close enough to do any damage to the singularity matrix. Ideas, gentlemen?"

"Not an idea," Dax said soberly. "A limitation. Since these aliens home in on energy discharges, we'll have to plan an attack that can destroy the station quickly. Otherwise they'll overwhelm our shields and breach us to vacuum, just as they did the Jem'Hadar fighter."

Sisko scowled. "Won't our ablative armor hold up under difluorine attack?"

"It will resist breaching at first," Dax agreed. "But the protective effect will only last for about a minute."

Sisko swung toward his security officer. "And how long can our shields hold out before they're drained by alien contact?"

Eddington keyed the question into his tactical panel, looking annoyed that he hadn't already thought to do it. "About four minutes, sir."

"Giving us an attack interval of five or six minutes." Sisko drummed his fingers on the arm of his chair. "Estimate of time needed to destroy the Jem'Hadar station, Mr. Eddington?"

This time, the security officer had his answer ready. "It would take a sustained phaser barrage of eight minutes at close range to destroy the station. If we remained at our present distance, the attack time would be doubled."

"Not good enough," Sisko said crisply. "What if we launched all our quantum torpedoes?"

"That would increase our attack range, and reduce attack time to under four minutes. The trouble is, we'd need a complete structural analysis to find and target the station's major stress points first. Otherwise, we can't be sure of total destruction."

"How long will that take?" Dax inquired.

"About an hour."

Sisko scowled up at the slow-moving station on their viewscreen. "This is one battle where we seem to have the luxury of time, Commander. Proceed with your structural analysis and targeting plan. In the meantime—" He vaulted out of his chair and came down to the helm station. "—why don't you see what you can find out about our captured alien, Dax?"

"Exactly what I was about to suggest. Can I take Ensign Petersen along to help me release the stasis field?"

"As long as you take a security guard, too." Sisko reached out a long arm to catch her as she turned away. "And Dax—after you're done examining this thing, see if you can find out how to kill it. I think we're going to need to know."

* * *

"Odo, god*dammit!*"

Bashir whirled without lifting his hands from his patient, as startled by the fury in that shout as he was by hearing it in the first place. This had been a day filled with the unexpected, however—he was getting to where he almost dreaded the sound of the transporter.

"Take him," he ordered his nurse brusquely. She nodded, stepping in front of him to slip the regenerating wand from his hand without interrupting its steady back-and-forth strokes. They were past the point where anything could be done for either patient without a cloning tank and a full rehab unit. Even Pak Dorren couldn't fault him for abandoning her people to an RN's capable hands.

Still, he had to ignore Dorren's shouted "Hey! Where the hell are you going?" as he dashed out of the ICU, and he somehow knew she wouldn't be able to keep from following. She'd been hovering just outside intensive care for the last two hours, volunteering her own medical expertise despite his requests that she stay silent. The image of her haranguing at his elbow during a second emergency was enough to make him want to send her down to Odo on some trumped-up civil charge, or lock her in a supply cabinet, at least, until he was finished.

Then he ducked through the door and into the main infirmary, and all thought of Pak Dorren evaporated on the stench of blood and acid.

His brain cataloged a list of snapshot images as he rushed across the infirmary: the pain-filled hitch in Kira's breathing as she staggered in a clumsy circle toward the exit; the scattered flecks of blood shattering on the deck beneath her; the breathless, devouring sizzle of flesh giving way to some solvent. Ducking to catch her as she crumpled, he grabbed her around the waist, and carefully avoided her mangled arm as he pulled her backward toward an examining table. "Easy does it, Major . . ."

"Let me go!"

She probably would have hit him if she'd had the strength—she certainly tried hard enough despite his efforts to keep her moving. "I don't think so. Not until I've had a look at that arm." A hard, flat surface caught him in the small of his back, and he maneuvered neatly from behind the major to steer her back toward the table he'd bumped into. He spared Pak only the briefest glower as she pushed in beside him to lend her own hands to the effort. "What happened?" he asked Kira, motioning Pak away to fetch a medical kit from the other side of the room.

Kira blinked at him as though only just realizing he was there, then glanced down at the blood and burns smearing her right arm in dull disinterest. "I don't know." She looked like she wanted to lie down, but couldn't quite remember how to do it.

"You don't know?" Pak recrossed the room with a skeptical snort, and thrust the requested medical kit at Bashir without paying much attention to his darkly reproving scowl. "What?" she sneered. "Wasn't your arm with you all day?"

Kira glared at her with an anger so bright, it seemed likely to burn up the last of her reserves. "I'm not sure how to explain it!"

"Well, that's not the same thing, is it?"

Bashir reached out a restraining hand, opening his mouth to banish Pak from the infirmary entirely, as his eyes skipped across the diagnostic scanner's readings by unconscious habit. A single chemical symbol leapt out at him from the morass, and alarm ripped through him like a gunshot. *"Maile!"*

The nurse skidded into the doorway before his voice had even died. He heard her running footsteps, but didn't turn away from lifting Kira's arm clear of the rest of her body. "Bring me the burn kit and basin we were using in the ICU," he commanded, casting frantically about for some nearby something to use in touching Kira's arm instead of his bare hands. "And a full osteodermal regenerator! And a set of polyteflon body drapes. Stat!"

She was already gone by the time he shouted that last, but they'd done this often enough today that he was confident she'd come back with what he needed. Slipping a hypo out of the medical kit, he set the dosage one-handed and injected Kira neatly in the artery thumping at the side of her neck. If she thought she was in pain now, she wouldn't even want to be in her own body in another five minutes—a heavy dose of painkiller was the least he could do until they managed to contain the acid damage. Leaving Kira to keep her own arm suspended out in front of her, he gingerly slipped a forceps inside her cuff and used a laser scalpel to slit the sleeve from wrist to elbow.

"What's the matter?" Kira's eyes, wide and unnaturally dark due to pupillary dilation, followed every careful little movement as he sliced free each bit of fabric and peeled it back to expose the bubbling skin beneath. "What did that thing do to me?"

Bashir glanced into her face with what he hoped was a reassuring smile, then dropped another strip of blood-soaked uniform into the disposal chute beside the bed. The scrap disintegrated with a hiss and a blue-white flash. "Nothing that can't be fixed." *I hope.* "We'll have you back in Ops in no time, Major." *Amazing the strain that transperiodic chemical contamination could put on your bedside manner.*

As Maile returned with the drapes and equipment, Bashir quickly scanned his own hands for traces of the acid while he let the nurse drape the bed and carefully lay Kira across it. "You've got diflouric acid burns on top of some nasty lacerations," he explained as the readings scrolled across the tiny screen, first one hand, then the other. Beside him, Maile continued to flash bits of Kira's uniform in the disposal chute, one blood-soaked strip at a time. "There's also some blood loss, obviously, and a compression fracture of your upper arm. I've given you something for the pain, but it's going to take a little while to neutralize the acid. We'll work on putting everything else back in order once that's taken care of." The last scan came up clear, and his heart gave a painful throb of relief.

"Difluoric acid?" Kira repeated blankly.

"Yes." Bashir set aside the scanner as casually as he had taken it up, and picked up the subspace reverter in its place. "Major, diflourine is such a rare transperiodic element, I don't even know of any stores of it on the station. It would help to know how you were exposed to this."

She looked up at him very seriously. "I was bitten by an Andorian."

Bashir shot her a startled glance, and Pak snorted derisively.

"All right, it wasn't an Andorian," the major growled

before Pak said anything more. "But it looked like an Andorian—I *thought* it was an Andorian. Only . . ." She shook her head, and Bashir recognized the dull distraction in her eyes when the pain medication finally took hold. "Odo went after it . . ." she went on, more drowsily. ". . . he said it couldn't see him . . ."

Her eyes fluttered closed, and Bashir did nothing to prevent it. It would do her good to sleep, especially once they started on the osteoregenerator—the itch of knitting bone could be maddening. Bashir made a final pass with the subspace reverter, then carefully scanned the length of Kira's arm for any sign of diflourine not forced back into the transperiodic realm.

"If your constable's got any silicate in his structure," Pak remarked in a calmly conversational tone, "he'd better damn well hope that 'Andorian' can't see him."

Somehow, Bashir never expected anyone who spent all her time terrorizing populations to even know how to spell words like "silicate." He gave her a sidelong glance, reaching for his tissue regenerator to close off the worst of Kira's wounds. "Exactly what do *you* know about diflourine?"

Pak shrugged, looking just a little surprised. "You can use it with a carbon plug to make a no-fuss timer for bombs." As though everyone should be born knowing what you could use illegally obtained transperiodic elements for. Maybe in her circle of friends that was true.

"Did you have any on board your ship?"

She burst into what sounded like honest laughter. "Are you nuts? Too big a breach risk to just carry around. We keep that stuff in planetary stores until we need to use it." Then she seemed to read something in his face, and cocked her head suspiciously to peer at him. "Why do you want to know?"

"I suspect it's because your crewmen show evidence of diflourine burns similar to Major Kira's," said a dry voice from the door. "Isn't that right, Doctor?"

"Yes." Bashir glanced up, not entirely reassured by the steadiness of Odo's voice. Except for his tightly clenched hands, however, the changeling showed no evidence of having encountered anything out of the ordinary that afternoon. "Did you find the Andorian who attacked Kira?"

"That's what I want you to tell me." Odo lifted his cupped hands in what seemed to be both explanation and apology. Inside the conjoined blob, a thick, segmented worm coiled whitely around itself, stubby legs twitching sluggishly. "I think it might be best to place this in stasis before you study it, Doctor. I've tried everything I could think of on my way down here, but there doesn't seem to be any way to kill it."

CHAPTER 16

THE ALIEN WAS, in fact, still alive.

"I don't see how it *can* be," said Yevlin Meris, the Bajoran medic who had shipped out on the *Defiant* in Bashir's place. "It looks like there's only about half of it here."

Dax eyed the severed section of metallic shell and trailing filaments of flesh that occupied one of the *Defiant*'s emergency stasis chambers. "Less than that," she said. "It was over two meters long back on the station. Are you sure you got life signs when you did the partial stasis release?"

"Watch." Yevlin handed Dax her medical tricorder, then dialed down the stasis control knob. The bluish glimmer of the field faded to an almost invisible sheen, and the tricorder immediately shot up peaks for metabolic processes, cell division and synapse activity. The two jointed appendages that splayed out from the shell began to move, very slowly, as if they were trying to explore the boundaries of their prison. The medic hurriedly swung the knob back to full stasis. "You see?"

"Yes." Dax readjusted the tricorder to map out neural pathways and scanned it over the alien fragment. "I think it's because the creature has a widely distributed cerebral system rather than a single central brain. Even small fragments of it should be able to think and function separately—they just won't be as intelligent as the whole organism." She redid the scan, this time tuning the tricorder's sensors for dilithium and difluorine. "It looks like the alien generates and stores transperiodic elements in the carapace material around its legs." She glanced back at Ensign Pritz, standing just inside the cramped medical bay. "If we keep those areas in full stasis, we shouldn't be in too much danger."

"All right." The security guard hefted her phaser rifle. "But just in case, Lieutenant, I'd like to have a clear shot at the soft tissue. That's the only place phasers seemed to have any effect."

Dax nodded agreement to that. "Yevlin, can you give us a ventral exposure?"

The physician's assistant punched a command into the stasis chamber, and the stilled alien slowly rotated to expose its underbelly. The flesh there was a tangle of thick muscle fibers twined around steel-wire ligaments, with very few sensory organs or other organized structures visible. Crenellated intergrowths of gray cerebral cortex in gel-like pouches were strung throughout the fleshy interior, like loose, moist strings of pearls. Dax looked them over critically, then glanced across the stasis field at Heather Petersen.

"Ensign, can you program the stasis generator to selectively release each of these cortical masses in turn?"

The Starfleet cadet flipped open the control panel and squatted down to eye the transparent array of computer circuits inside. "Probably not each mass, but I think I can release one string at a time. I'll need a phase modulator."

"Here." Yevlin handed her a small, medical version of the standard engineering tool. "What do you want me to do, Lieutenant?"

"Basic genetic analysis on the neural matter." Dax handed her the medical tricorder and picked up her own Universal Translator. "These aliens apparently steal their cerebral cortices from other organisms they engulf and digest. We need to know who those others are before we can talk to them."

"*Talk* to them?" The Bajoran cast a doubtful glance across the stasis chamber at Pritz, who shrugged with one shoulder so as not to disturb the aim of her phaser rifle.

"You think you can actually communicate with bits and pieces of digested brain?"

Dax gave her a wry look. "It does sound insane, doesn't it? But I have it on very good authority that it can be done." She held up the Universal Translator. "I've programmed this to scan for microelectrical synapse activity rather than sound waves as input. We should be able to pick up any conscious or subconscious speech patterns from directly inside the brains."

"How will you talk back to them, Lieutenant?" Pritz asked.

"I won't," Dax admitted. "We'll just have to listen and hope they say something interesting."

This time it was Petersen's turn to look dubious. "But how will the incorporated beings know we're listening to them? Isn't there something we can do to alert them to that?"

Dax exchanged long, thoughtful looks with Yevlin Meris. "Adrenal injection? Microelectrical shocks?"

The physician's assistant shook her head. "An external magnetic pulse would be better. We can send that right through the stasis field, and it will stimulate the neural material to create its own internal electrical stimulation. Given the size of these cortex fragments, I can probably generate enough field strength just by using my tricorder's magnetic resonance sensor at close range."

The young Bajoran medic's quick intuitive leap made Dax smile. Evidently, Julian Bashir was as good a mentor as he was a doctor. "That sounds like our best alternative," she agreed. "Let's start with the cortical string nearest my side of the stasis chamber."

"Releasing stasis on first string." Petersen's phase modulator hummed, and a long stripe of the stasis field vanished. "You might have to align the alien with the field generators to get complete release."

Yevlin adjusted the antigravs, maneuvering the alien until the long, moist strand of gel-encased cortices lay completely within the nullified portion of the field. "Release complete—I'm getting synapse activity along the whole string." She focused her tricorder on the first knotted cortex, then frowned at the result and repeated the action.

"Problem?" Dax inquired.

"The tricorder's database has no record of this DNA pattern, Lieutenant. It's not remotely similar to any known races in the Alpha or Gamma quadrants."

"That makes sense," Pritz said quietly. "Whoever these aliens are, they haven't been in our region of space for a very long time."

"Agreed." Dax glanced ruefully at her translator, then toggled it on and held it over the cortex. "With no language database to draw on, we'll probably only get gibberish out of this, but it won't hurt to try. Magnetic pulse, please."

Yevlin reprogrammed her tricorder and aimed it at the cortical fragment. The Universal Translator promptly squawked and spat out a string of fast-paced whistles and clicks, almost dolphinlike in its vocal range. It was clearly a language, but not one the translator was able to convert to English without extensive exposure. Dax sighed and stepped back.

"Next cortex?"

This time, Yevlin's scan made her tricorder beep decisively. "This one's definitely Jem'Hadar—there's not another race in the universe that has DNA without a single junk genome in it. Ready for a pulse, Lieutenant?"

"Ready." She positioned the Universal Translator over the second, ragged-looking fragment, but this time when Yevlin aimed her magnetic pulse at the alien, the translator stayed stubbornly silent. Dax gave the medic a puzzled look. "You did stimulate it?"

"Positive."

A low grumbling emerged from the translator, and Dax hurriedly dialed its resolution up to maximum. "—Will not obey, will not obey, will not—" said a fiercely determined voice.

"Subsidiary brains resisting takeover." Even filtered through microelectrical impulses and the logic circuits of the Universal Translator, the crystal-sharp arrogance of that second voice was unmistakable. Dax glanced down at Heather Petersen and saw stunned recognition on the cadet's face. "I'm no longer in contact with the other brain strands—"

"That's T'Kreng!" Petersen jumped up and leaned over

the alien, as if she could somehow spot her former advisor among the tangle of muscle fibers and gelatinous sacks of cerebral cortex. "There must be some of her along this neural string—she's communicating with the Jem'Hadar through it somehow!"

"Scan the entire string for Vulcan DNA," Dax ordered Yevlin. The medic punched the request into her tricorder, then swept it along the series of cortices. She paused at the fifth one in the string.

"This one's Vulcan, and female. Should I pulse it?"

"Yes." Dax moved farther down the edge of the stasis chamber to position her Universal Translator over the fifth cortex. It immediately began emitting a stream of precise, Vulcan observations.

"—obvious from nonresponse of ambulatory systems that we're in stasis, and therefore on a Federation vessel. I have lost all contact with Solvik and the Ferengi trader. The strands they dominated either remain in stasis or were detached by edge effects during transport. We knew when we decided—"

"Pulsing now," said Yevlin.

"What?" T'Kreng's crystalline voice sharpened to something approaching irritation. "I assume there is someone out there listening to me. If you cannot communicate more effectively than that, please allow me to talk without inducing unnecessary visual hallucinations."

"That's T'Kreng, all right," Dax muttered.

"I shall start from the beginning. This is Professor T'Kreng of the Vulcan Science Academy. I have been killed and eaten by an alien of unknown affinity, one of a swarm which engulfed my research vessel upon its emergence from the Bajoran wormhole. My cerebral cortex was divided among several of the aliens, but enough remains intact in this individual to allow me almost complete control of its activities."

Dax lifted her eyebrows at Pritz. "I wonder if that's why we found this alien separate from the rest?"

The security guard shook her head in bewilderment. "But if there was a Vulcan in control of it, why did it attack Goldman?"

Petersen looked across at them, her eyes wry. "You have

no idea how ruthless Professor T'Kreng can be. I suspect she attacked that man in order to make us do exactly what we have done—beam her back to the ship and examine her."

"In fact," Dax said quietly, "she may even have kept that Jem'Hadar she was eating alive to draw us to her."

"If you are a member of the Federation, as I suspect," continued the crystal-calm voice from the translator, "I must warn you of the immense danger we all face. These aliens have the ability to keep intact cortical matter from any species they ingest. They string it into the organic equivalent of parallel processors, and use it until each piece ultimately degrades into noncognition. When they congregate into a core mass, they connect their individual neural strings to form immense living supercomputers. These core masses are capable of astonishing theoretical calculations. I speak from direct knowledge. I was part of the one gathered in the Jem'Hadar station, until I managed to take control of this individual and send it away."

Dax shook her head in silent wonder. Only a brain with the Vulcan genius—and driving arrogance—of T'Kreng could have summoned the mental resilience to overcome this most complete of alien captivities. It was hard to remember that the Vulcan physicist was really dead, and that just a fragment of her powerful brain was speaking to them from an organic prison.

"I regret to say that these aliens had no intention of destroying the Bajoran wormhole before they attacked my ship," T'Kreng's silken voice resumed. "They were merely following their species' established way of life. They must have evolved as parasites within a thickly populated sector—they drift randomly through space, attacking any spacefaring life they encounter. They feed off its genetic matter, its sentience, and the power cores of its space vessels. They would have continued doing this forever, but the influx of Vulcan intelligence and astrophysics knowledge into their race has given them both a new goal, and the means to accomplish it.

"I have been able to absorb a little of their history from the oldest fragments of cortex present along these neural strands. As abundant as they seem to be, this species evidently has dwindled to a mere shadow of former hordes which once swept across vast portions of the galaxy and demolished every spacefaring civilization they encountered. They have always desired to return to their former glory. Now, after long hunger and deprivation, they have found a quick way to do it. They will use the Bajoran wormhole to bridge space and time to their last great battle, when they were at the peak of their strength and numbers."

"The battle the *Defiant* got caught in when it was thrown back in time," Dax murmured. She saw the chorus of baffled looks thrown at her by Petersen, Yevlin, and Pritz, and shook her head. "It sounds insane, I know, but things are actually starting to fall together."

"Detonating the wormhole with precisely enough energy to make it connect to the proper place and time is a complex and difficult task," T'Kreng said, in typical Vulcan understatement. "However, the aliens have fifteen Vulcan brains at their disposal—including those portions of my own brain which contain my understanding of singularity matrices. What fifteen Vulcans could barely comprehend individually will almost certainly yield to their combined intelligence, linked together as it is in the alien core mass."

The disembodied voice hardened to a knife-sharp edge. "Whoever is listening, you must believe me when I say that the Federation is in grave peril. If these aliens bring all of their kind forward to our time and our quadrant, the combined forces of the Federation, the Klingons, the Cardassians, and the Romulans will not be able to withstand the invasion. Just as the ancient race known as the Furies could not withstand it millennia ago. These alien parasites are the 'unclean,' the very ones who drove the Furies from the portion of Federation space they are now trying to reclaim. It is perhaps the most ironic part of this affair," T'Kreng added acidly, "that we who grew up on this abandoned battlefield now must fight off both the victors and the vanquished."

"It's only a portion of the creature, obviously."

Bashir nodded absently at Odo when the constable crouched on the other side of the open stasis drawer and peered through the field at what he was doing. The tight weave of subspace fabric rippled as Bashir pushed a needle probe through the meniscus, distorting Odo's already misproportioned face and making the little curl of "worm" at the center appear to be floating in transparent liquid.

"I decided against trying to apprehend the entire intruder when it pushed through a level-two containment field on deck six," the constable went on. His eyes seemed to lift involuntarily to something over Bashir's right shoulder, and the doctor suspected he knew what had captured the changeling's attention. Kira was no doubt still visible through the morgue's open doorway, sleeping deeply if not peacefully while Maile finished tending to her wounds. "And it didn't seem wise to expose anyone else until we knew what we were dealing with."

"Well, I certainly can't argue with that." Especially if Kira was any indication what this thing was capable of in only a few seconds' exposure. Piercing the worm as near to its middle as he'd been able to aim through twenty centimeters of stasis, Bashir made sure the probe was well seated in the field before gently releasing it and turning to activate the scan.

A few meters away, Pak Dorren drummed her fingers on the back of the stool she was straddling, her feet tapping an uneven counterrhythm on the rungs. Bashir would have guessed it was close proximity to the alien fragment that made her twitchy and nervous if he hadn't already spent half the afternoon with her ceaseless fidgeting. Now he just suspected she needed medication. "You think this thingamajigger beamed over with us?" she asked, never interrupting her drumming.

Odo straightened with a judgmental sniff, but Bashir looked up from his equipment to announce definitively, "No," before the constable could do more than cross his arms. He answered Odo's scowl of skepticism by gesturing at the soft white body on the other end of his probe. "This is—sort of—an Andorian antenna." He tried to trace out the gentle arc of its endoskeleton, the disklike flare of its tip, without actually touching the stasis screen. "And Quark reported his Andorian customer missing before Pak Dorren's people even came on board." He shook his head down at the bizarre fragment as the first of the medical readings blinked into existence on the probe's output screen. "If this is part of whatever attacked Major Kira, then your intruder either is that missing Andorian, or *used* to be him."

Odo tilted his head to a decidedly skeptical angle. "He seems to have had a particularly bad reaction to Quark's Rigellian chocolate."

"I'll say." Leaning over the back of her stool, Pak squinted across the room as though intrigued with the worm in the morgue drawer but perfectly willing to keep her distance. "Andorian antennas don't usually have legs, do they?"

"No, not usually." Bashir swiveled the probe screen around in front of him and started scrolling through the complex of readings, searching for something—anything—familiar. He paused the screen and frowned at the broken code of amino acids filling one-half of the display. Sliding the probe clear of the alien body, he backed it out of the stasis field and carefully chose another entry point several millimeters from the first. The probe didn't want to push through the leg joint as neatly as it had through what passed as this sample's thorax, but a little patient twisting finally slipped it into place with a click Bashir almost swore he could hear. Pleased with his handiwork, he rocked back in his seat to watch the sensors cycle through their business and throw the answers up onto the screen.

"Oh, now this is odd. . . ."

"What?" Odo appeared suddenly at his shoulder, and he heard Pak's feet thump to the deck as she climbed off her stool to join them. "What do you see?"

A lot of things, and he wasn't sure how to explain any of them. "Well, this—" He split the screen, quickly sorting through the probe's first set of readings until he found the spiral helix he was searching for. "The chromosomal structure in the body of the sample is almost entirely Andorian. In fact, this particular linkage—" He traced an amino-acid chain with one finger when they both crowded closer to look. "—is characteristic of Haslev-Rahn disease, a congenital disorder endemic to Shesh-caste Andorians. But here . . ." This time he bracketed a length of helix with both hands, and wondered if Pak and Odo could see the differences in it as clearly as he did. "None of these even uses the same amino-acid sets as Andorian chromosomes, yet they're spliced into the very same genes."

"Could the Andorian be infected with something?" Pak asked. She studied the readings with a seriousness Bashir wasn't sure how to interpret. "Viruses can copy and replace parts of chromosomes, can't they?"

The fact that she even knew to ask the question startled him. "There does seem to be a certain viruslike behavior at work here," he admitted, "although not in the way you're thinking." He swung his chair to face them, trying very hard to keep his words slow and his sentences coherent, even though his mind had already raced well past his explanation and on to what it implied. "As a general rule, viruses work to alter their *own* genetic structure, not yours. They take over individual cells in a host body, and coopt those cells' reproductive mechanisms to generate copies of the virus. While it's in there, a virus will sometimes steal bits and pieces of the host's genetic code for insertion into its own. That way it can avoid some of the host's natural attempts to identify and destroy it, and pick up new characteristics which might make it easier to transmit, or harder to kill once it's established an infection." He glanced aside at the morgue drawer and its bizarre occupant. "A remarkably elegant organism, considering it's little more than a string of coded proteins."

"Doctor," Odo broke in. "How is this relevant to what happened to Quark's Andorian?"

He shook off a blur of speculation with some effort. "Well, this isn't a simplified organism with one or two Andorian codons on its chain. This is essentially an Andorian organism with entirely alien functions added to its structure." Drawing their attention to the screen again, he pointed out whatever random codons passed across the display as he moved through the readings. "This codes for digestive enzymes, so this bit of antenna could conceivably 'eat' by absorbing organic material directly into itself. These are for sensing organs—light, heat. This is the crux of a Tholian's electromagnetic organelle. *These*—" He tapped the right-hand side of the monitor, where the convoluted findings from the leg probe scrawled around the sensor scan like a mad man's ravings. "These aren't even something I recognize. My guess is there are at least three separate genetic families represented here, all of them no less than ten millennia old, judging from the extent of genetic decay." He looked back at them over his shoulder. "What we have here isn't an Andorian who's been infected by some alien virus's DNA—we have a viroid life-form that's absorbed an Andorian's genetic code for its own selective usage."

Pak stared at the alien readings as though the force of her attention could make them understandable. "So you're saying my ships were attacked by an Andorian who was chewed up by Tholians?"

"I doubt the Andorian genotype had been added to the mix when you were attacked," Bashir said, "but the duranium-titanium traces you detected might well have been caused by a Tholian carapace, yes."

"Then how did it get on board the station?" Odo asked. "Traffic has been at a standstill since before Captain Sisko returned from Starbase One." He cast Pak a dry look that could have been either disdain or derision for all Bashir could tell. "And sensors haven't exactly been brimming with reports of free-floating Tholians lately."

"The Lethian transport."

Bashir jumped to his feet to intercept Kira as she made her way slowly, stiffly into the morgue to join them. Maile must have disposed of her jacket while cleaning out her wounds, because the major was left with only her trousers and a white cotton shell for a uniform. The dark maroon patches that might have passed for spilled coolant against her rust colored trouser legs, though, stood out in brilliant scarlet on the white undertunic. The contrast only served to make her look more pale and fragile.

"This is what took out Pak's armada?" she asked, jerking her chin toward their innocuous prisoner as Bashir came to take her elbow.

He thought about scolding her for being up and about, for climbing out of bed when the new skin on her arm was still delicate and shiny, and they hadn't had the chance to fully replace her blood volume yet. Then he remembered the flare of organic sludge around Pak's escape party when they beamed in, and the evidence of what they'd run from etched into the broken bodies of her cohorts. If that threat was really aboard the station, walking about a few pints low on bodily fluids would be the least of his patients' problems. "I think it must be," he said quietly.

She seemed to sense how his thoughts must have run, because she didn't shake off his helping hand or resist when he guided her toward the chair he'd abandoned beside the drawer. "Then it's what destroyed those freighters we found." She looked at the alien fragment with open hatred. "And it's what hulled that Lethian transport."

Odo nodded slowly. "The missing crew."

"Of course!" Bashir didn't realize he'd blurted the exclamation until everyone looked to him as though expecting something more. He tried not to sound too professionally excited as he explained, "It must have taken them for their genetic raw material."

Kira clenched her teeth so hard that he could see the muscles bunch in her jaw. "And it came on board with that Cardassian vole."

It wasn't something Bashir had thought of, even having heard Maile's horrified account of scaring up some monstrous rodent from the bowels of the Lethian ship. "I can't tell you specifically if it's from a vole," he admitted, thinking back over the scans he'd examined only a few minutes before, "but it does have Cardassian DNA."

Kira sat back in the chair with a wince Bashir didn't think she'd meant to reveal, and propped one elbow on the edge of the morgue drawer. "All right, then—how can we kill it?"

A simple question, really. For some reason, though, he hadn't expected everyone to turn to him as though he were expected to just produce the answer. Not for the first time since the *Defiant* left this quadrant, he desperately wished Jadzia were here. "I don't know."

Pak spun away with a disgusted curse, but it was Kira rubbing wearily at her eyes with the heels of both hands that stabbed him most keenly with regret for letting them down. "This thing has no circulatory blood supply," he told the major, feeling almost like he ought to apologize. "No real nervous system, and no digestive tract. Yet it's capable of developing all of them even as we speak! We're talking about an organism that conceivably has access to any physical characteristic it might need. If it needs to photosynthesize, it will photosynthesize. If it needs to regenerate limbs or nerves or organs, it will do that. Short of disassembling it on a molecular level, I don't know that we *can* kill it."

Kira tipped her head back to sigh up at him, a look that wasn't quite disappointment but wasn't quite resignation, either, in her tired eyes. The chirp of her comm badge saved Bashir from whatever she'd meant to say.

"Major . . ." O'Brien's voice sounded grim, as though he'd been listening in on their conversation and didn't like the answers any more than the rest of them did. "I think you'd better get up to Ops right away."

Kira pushed the side of her fist against the stasis field, watching the weak corona flare to blot out the frozen alien. "I'm a little busy right now, Chief."

"All the same, ma'am," he persisted, "I really think you'd better come. The *Mukaikubo* just arrived—"

"You can patch Captain Regitz through to me down here."

"That's just it, Major. I can't get Captain Regitz on the comm. In fact, I can't get anybody. As far as I can tell, there's not a single soul left on board."

CHAPTER
17

SOMETIME IN THE last three hours, the wormhole had gone insane.

Lurid ultraviolet lashes curled and whipped across the fabric of Bajoran space, invisibly shattering the starscape like cracks across a darkened mirror. The filters on the Ops viewscreen painted each wave in intricate detail. Kira hugged her arms across her chest, watching the *Mukaikubo* drift sleepily through the swirl and throb of radioactive night, and wondering if she ought to order O'Brien to drop the UV filters, so they couldn't see how bad the outside world was getting.

"I wonder how they got them to drop out of warp." She didn't mean to murmur it out loud, but once it was spoken she couldn't take it back.

Beside her, Odo studied the lifeless starship with a clinical stoicism Kira envied. "Probably the same way they trapped Pak Dorren's people—by reading like ship debris."

It just seemed like it shouldn't be that easy. Nothing should be able to lure a Galaxy-class starship into sublight, then overwhelm it like ants on a peach before it could think of some way to defend itself. Yet here it was, its secondary hull stripped open in a dozen different places, the great flat disk of its primary hull divested of its bridge assembly entirely, as though the whole ship had rotted away from within. Only the busy skitter of alien bodies—the size and shape of ticks from this distance—gave the ship's outer skin any movement, any life. Its running lights were as black as a Vegan's eyes; the darkened husk looked incredibly small, impossibly fragile hung against the wormhole's silent roars.

O'Brien cleared his throat from the upper tier. Kira didn't look up at him, but he must have sensed her shift of attention. "Should I catch her with a tractor beam and bring her to a standstill?" he asked.

She thought about Pak's armada, about the aliens following the paths of their phasers and their engine exhausts. "No." Then, because an officer as good as O'Brien always deserved a straight explanation, "I don't want to draw their attention."

"Well, we've got to do something," he countered. It was what Kira liked about O'Brien—he was never disrespectful, but he always spoke his mind. "She'll drift into the wormhole's gravity well in another thirty minutes or so, and that hoard of engine cores she's carrying will never make the passage without exploding."

"I know that, Chief." They'd been through all this when Kira first noticed the eerie glow in the hull plates along the *Mukaikubo*'s belly, and O'Brien identified its cargo as four separate, unshielded reaction masses. At least now they knew where the stolen engine cores from the ore freighters and the Lethian transport had gone.

"We could try to destroy the ship from here," Odo suggested. "Detonate the payload with torpedoes or phaser fire."

O'Brien made a blunt, unhappy noise that earned an impatient scowl from the constable. "With the wormhole oscillating like it is right now," the chief explained, "an explosion of that magnitude even at this range would collapse it for good."

"And letting the *Mukaikubo* drift into its event horizon won't?"

It would, and all of them knew it, so Kira wasn't surprised when O'Brien answered Odo's question with little more than a growl of frustration.

"We're not going to let the *Mukaikubo* destroy the wormhole." Kira pulled her eyes away from the viewscreen with painful effort, and turned to limp a few steps closer to

O'Brien so she could crane a look up at him from below. "Can we get a transporter signal into the ship?"

He lifted his eyebrows in thought, and looked over her head at the viewscreen. "Her shields are down, and she's well within range, but I wouldn't want to trust that we could maintain a coherent pattern with all the leakage from the wormhole."

"That's all right," Kira told him. "I don't want a coherent pattern."

She held tight to the rail as she hauled herself up the steps to join O'Brien. No matter what Bashir claimed, there didn't seem to be a painkiller in existence that could touch the bone-deep ache in her muscles, much less the pounding tension that had crawled up the back of her neck to burrow in at the base of her skull. She felt like she'd hiked forty kilometers with a field pack and bad boots, never mind the hand-span bruise across the outside of her thigh. The acid burns on her arm were just about the only place on her body that didn't hurt right now.

Odo trotted up the steps close behind her, smart enough not to try and help her move now that she was back on duty and in front of the crew. "What are you thinking?" he asked, his voice dryly suspicious.

Kira eased herself onto the seat O'Brien never used, swallowing a grimace. "Disassemble them on a molecular level, Bashir said. That's the only way to be sure." She stared past O'Brien at the drifting starship on the screen. "I want to transport those things off the *Mukaikubo* and into space on a wide-dispersal setting."

O'Brien nodded, reaching for his panel. "The cargo transporter would work best for that. We could pick them up in loads up to ten cubic meters—still only a handful at a time, given the size of those things out there, but better than the one or two we could get with the personnel transporter." His hands flew across the engineering console without waiting for Kira's reply.

"Pak Dorren said these aliens could backtrack a phaser beam to find an attacking ship." Odo took up a position behind them and peered over O'Brien's shoulder. "What's to stop them from doing the same thing with a transporter beam?"

"Because they didn't," Kira said. "When Pak brought her people here, the aliens didn't follow. That means for some reason they can't, or they don't, and we're going to make use of that."

"It's a higher-energy beam," O'Brien volunteered in the distracted, almost expressionless voice of a man deeply immersed in his work, "but it's got a much shorter duration than the sustained phasers the militia's been using. The aliens probably don't have time to get a fix on the transporter signal." Looking up from his computations, he nodded once to Kira. "Ready when you are, Major."

"Give 'em hell, Chief."

Kira half-expected to hear the whine of the powerful transporter engaging several decks below—she remembered it cycling almost continuously, day and night, when the need to quickly restaff and restock the great station had kept her awake with all its noises and demands. But that had been when DS9 still orbited Bajor, and a cargo transporter was still an acceptable alternative to sending up a freighter. In the years since they'd moved the station three light-hours away from its previous home, she couldn't recall hearing the cargo transporter fired up even once.

So it wasn't the distant hum of the awakening transporter or the rumbling throb of its compensators coming on-line that made her grip the sides of her seat and shoot a nervous glance toward the ceiling—it was the flicker in the Ops main lighting, and the little shudder of brownouts that swept through half the surrounding panels.

"You're going to overstress the capacitors," Odo warned, and O'Brien pressed his lips into a grim line.

"No, we're not."

Even so, the lights took another alarming dip as O'Brien swiftly reversed the beam to bounce back whatever ugly cargo he'd picked up. Kira just barely glimpsed the silvery shimmer of a transporter materialization on the viewscreen somewhere between the *Mukaikubo* and the station, then a thin white line of expanding crystal as the tiny motes of matter wisped away in their silent dance of annihilation and scatter. Ops broke into a ragged cheer of relief.

"There's your first shipment," O'Brien announced over the shouting.

Kira clenched one fist in her lap in grim triumph. "Keep at it," she commanded. It was a little frightening how in control of a situation you could feel once you knew your opponent was killable. "I want that ship empty, no matter how long it takes."

The second pulse and fade of the lights didn't seem nearly so dramatic as the first, and, if anything, the glowing cloud of gassed matter deposited outside the *Mukaikubo*'s walls looked even larger and more luminous than before. A series of urgent chirps from the comm station reminded Kira that the entire station must be feeling the punishment for Ops to be so hard hit by the power drains. Waving for a noncom to handle the calls from the other decks, she looked expectantly toward O'Brien for the third transporter cycle to begin. "Chief . . ."

O'Brien acknowledged her with a quick, frustrated nod, never looking up from his controls. "It's being a little slow about cycling the matter converters. We'll be all right. . . ."

Even as he spoke, Ops sank into near darkness, and a third spray of deconstructed matter dusted the radiation-torn space outside. It seemed to take forever before the power rebounded, though. Kira gave O'Brien fully twice as long to make the fourth transport before prodding, "Isn't there some way we can cut that delay?"

"Not without dumping half those rerouted systems off the grid." He chewed on his lip, swearing almost subvocally as he fought with the controls. "Cargo transporters were designed for pattern capacity, Major, not for speed."

"Then I'd suggest we quit while we're ahead." Odo touched Kira's shoulder and pointed up at the viewscreen. "Our friends seem to have noticed their missing comrades."

Dark floes of what appeared to be oil dribbled from the wounds in *Mukaikubo*'s sides. Kira wondered if this was the acid these aliens seemed to use for breaching starship hulls—and how quickly it could eat through the structure of her station; then the rivulets broke apart into individual motes, and the dozens of mitelike passengers on the surface of the ship scuttled down to meet the outgoing rush.

Kira pushed anxiously to her feet. "Chief . . . ?"

He didn't answer, even when the first wave of aliens leapt out into space toward them on little puffs of steaming gas.

The cargo transporter rang out with a great rumble and disintegrated most of the nearest ones just as half the lights across Ops crackled brilliantly and died.

By the time her eyes adjusted to the almost-dark, Kira couldn't even tell where in the onrushing force O'Brien's blow had been struck. They swarmed as aimlessly as puff-weed spore, driven on by their own expulsions instead of the wind.

"Major . . ."

She ignored Odo, concentrating instead on O'Brien's muttering. "Just one more, you damned thing—one more!" You could tell a lot about your timing just by listening to your engineer swear, she thought absently.

"Major," Odo repeated, more firmly, "this is not going to work."

Of course not. Nothing was working. That didn't mean they had to stop trying. That didn't mean they could run away.

Something deep and urgent moved through the skeleton of the station, and O'Brien crowed "She's coming up! Here we go!" just as the transporter's distinctive whine rose to a wail and Odo shouted her name in honest alarm.

And the first of the oncoming aliens passed the point of no return.

"Raise shields!"

Deflectors flashed into being before the echo of her shout had died. Sparking like steel against steel, two, then three, then dozens of the duranium-shelled creatures bounced against the screens to skitter sideways, and the transporter beam smashed a psychotic explosion of misplaced energy against the inside of the shield as it reached out for a target that was no longer within its reach.

The backlash boomed through the station like an asteroid strike. Kira knew without asking that the jolt and thunder she felt through the decking was the cargo transporter blowing most of its workings out into space, and the shadows that gyrated on the Ops ceiling and floors after the last working light went dead told her there were fires at the stations even before the hoarse roar of extinguishers drowned out the frantic shouts. Somehow, the back of her brain took note of every detail of the mechanical carnage as she leaned over the upper bridge railing and glared her hatred at the distant *Mukaikubo*.

Until the spark and shimmer of alien bodies impacting the deflectors grew too bright to see beyond.

Something was happening down on the Jem'Hadar station. Under ordinary circumstances, Sisko might not even have noticed it, but he'd been concentrating so hard on keeping his gnawing tension under control that he'd forced himself to focus all his attention on the central portion of the Jem'Hadar station. The color contours there were changing, slowly dimming from arctic white in the center to a pale greenish ivory.

"Dax, do your sensors show any changes in alien distribution down on the station?" he demanded.

The science officer tapped a command into her panel and frowned at the answer she got. "There seems to be an overall decrease in alien concentration, but I can't find out where the missing mass has gone. I've scanned the whole system and I'm not picking up concentrations of duranium anywhere but the station."

Sisko felt a chill of distrust crawl down his spine. "Set up a motion-sensing scan around the ship, with the smallest resolution you can manage. I want to make sure we don't get surprised by those things. Eddington, what's the progress on your structural analysis of the station?"

"Eighty-three-percent complete, Captain. Estimated time to targeting is ten minutes."

Sisko grunted. Some instinct was hammering at him, telling him that the luxury of time was no longer on their side in this battle. The logical part of his brain knew he was probably wrong, but his gut refused to be convinced. "If we fired on the basis of our present data, how much chance would we have of destroying the station?"

Eddington gave him a baffled look. "Sixty-three percent. But why would we need to fire now, sir?"

"I don't know. Just be prepared to do it." Sisko vaulted out of his command chair and went to lean over Dax's shoulder. "Have you got that motion detector in place, old man?"

"I'm bringing it on-line now. It's set to trigger a proximity alarm for anything bigger than a micrometeorite."

"Good." He straightened and scowled up at the Jem'Hadar station on the viewscreen. Its color change was more obvious now, with the entire interior painted in shades of green rather than the concentrated whites it had once glowed with. Sisko ran down a mental list of further precautions he could take. "Lay in a course back for the wormhole, Dax, and program the piloting computer to engage at warp five at the first sign of shield penetration. I don't want to risk a diflourine breach."

Unlike Eddington, Dax obeyed him without question. Afterward, though, she swung around in her chair to give him a grave upward look. "You've figured something out about these aliens, haven't you, Benjamin?"

Sisko opened his mouth to deny it, then realized she was right. His subconscious had put together the pieces during the past hour while he had been simply concentrating on staying calm. "You told me these creatures take both DNA and cerebral cortices from the species they attack. Why take the DNA unless they're going to use it?" He paused, glancing down at his science officer to gauge her reaction. She nodded agreement. "Well, what the hell are they using it for?"

"They obviously don't use it to reconstruct the cerebral cortices they take," Dax said thoughtfully. "T'Kreng said they simply keep them intact until they decay into noncognition."

Sisko nodded. "So they either use the DNA to reconstruct other parts of their bodies—or to make themselves completely different bodies for use in different environments."

"Bodies that might still be vacuum-resistant, but wouldn't show up on our duranium scans?" Dax frowned. "But without their duranium carapaces, they couldn't store diflourine safely. How much damage could they do us?"

Eddington looked over his shoulder at them. "They could still overwhelm our shields by sheer mass."

Sisko nodded at him. "And they could also make atmosphere-tolerant bodies, ones that could use the Jem'Hadar defenses on the station—"

Dax frowned. "But they can't shoot at us as long as we're cloaked."

From the back of the bridge, Ensign Hovan cleared her throat apologetically. "Sir, I've been meaning to tell you . . . You asked me to watch out for voltage fluctuations on our cloaking screen? Well, for the last fifteen minutes, I've been reading a consistent loss of fifteen millivolts. It's well within our operating tolerance, and much too small to be due to an alien of the mass we'd seen before—"

Sisko gave her a narrow-eyed look. "But not too small if they can change shape or size? Where is it located, Ensign?"

"Near the aft thermal diffuser panels, sir."

Dax looked disgusted with herself. "Where our waste heat from the warp core is vented to space," she said. "I should have known that any space-dwelling species who preys off spaceships would have developed sensory organs able to detect thermal trails."

Sisko's vague swirl of unease crystallized into decision. "Eddington, target our quantum torpedoes *now*. Dax, I want immediate departure as soon as—"

The blare of a proximity alarm sliced through his orders and made them meaningless. Sisko's fierce curse was lost beneath its banshee echo.

"Motion detector scan has picked up incoming aliens in all sectors." Dax's fingers flew across her panel. "Initial estimates are over two hundred individual entities."

"I'm reading voltage drops across our entire cloaking screen," Hovan added. "They've penetrated the cloak and are approaching shields, Captain."

"Captain, our weapons sensors are picking up activity in the Jem'Hadar phaser banks," Eddington warned. "Someone down there is preparing to fire on us."

Sisko scowled. "Can we track the aliens with sensors for close-range phaser attack?"

Dax shook her head. "I'm getting no response on scans for duranium or other metallic alloys. This version of the aliens must be constructed entirely of light carbon polymers. They're nearly invisible to our sensors." She gave Sisko a quick, sidelong glance. "I'm also reading negative on scans for diflourine."

"That's because these are just the shock troops, designed

to take down our shields so the station's weapons can destroy us." Sisko stared up at the uninformative viewscreen, feeling the muscles along his jaw clench and quiver with frustration. This was an impossible battle, fought against an unseen enemy whose strengths and weaknesses fluctuated too quickly to counter. He began to understand why the Furies had fled before their onslaught. A gentle quiver of contact rolled through the ship as the first of the aliens made contact with their shields.

"How long before we can fire torpedoes, Mr. Eddington?" Sisko demanded.

"Two minutes, sir."

"Status of shields?"

"Holding," Dax said. The *Defiant*'s quiet occasional shivers became a constant growl of vibration as more and more aliens descended on her shields. "But the power drain is increasing so fast that even if the shields hold out for two more minutes, we'll have lost our ability to engage the engines."

"*Damn.*" Sisko took in a deep, decisive breath. "All right, Dax. Get us out of here at maximum impulse, *now.*"

The *Defiant* surged into motion with its usual kick of unbalanced acceleration. Sisko watched in grim silence as the Jem'Hadar station dwindled to a greenish speck in the distance. "Do we still have our passengers, Dax?"

"We've lost some of them, but not all," she replied. "Shield drains are now constant at half of previous levels."

Sisko grunted. "Drop us back to one-quarter impulse." He caught the worried look Dax cast him, and responded with a grim sliver of smile. "Don't worry, old man. I know what I'm going to do will work. Eddington, release one quantum torpedo and detonate it just outside our shield containment radius. Without their duranium shells, those things should be vulnerable to EM radiation."

"Releasing torpedo now, sir." A prism of hyperpowered light exploded just off the port nacelle, rocking the *Defiant* through her shields as it engulfed her in its shock wave. "Torpedo exploded," the security officer added unnecessarily.

"Shield drains have dropped to zero," Dax added a moment later. "The aliens have been destroyed." She glanced over her shoulder at Sisko, one eyebrow lifting quizzically. "How did you know that would work?"

"Because it's how we saved the *Defiant* from these aliens, five thousand years ago," Sisko said bluntly. "The only difference is, this time we had intact shields to protect us."

His science officer winced. "Should I plot a return course to the Jem'Hadar station, Captain?"

Sisko rubbed a hand across his face, feeling the grit of incipient beard under his callused fingers. For the first time in hours, he became aware of the aching tiredness in his bones that came from too much stress and too little sleep. A glance around the bridge told him that his skeleton crew wasn't in much better shape. He shook his head. "Let's head back to the wormhole first," he said. "We've got sixteen hours left before the Jem'Hadar station gets there. And now that we know what we're up against, I think we could use some reinforcements."

CHAPTER 18

WHEN THE BLAST and rumble of faraway damage shuddered through the station infirmary, Julian Bashir glanced toward the ceiling as though that might help tell him what had happened. He'd always thought that an interesting reflex—even if he'd been working in a planetbound facility, it wasn't like looking skyward could tell him anything except the color of the ceiling. Yet it was the first thing humans the galaxy over did when surprised by unexpected sounds and movements. And it probably didn't tell them anything more than it told him now; just as he lifted his gaze from the symbiont's quietly bubbling tank, the lights overhead shivered, flickered, and died. Black rushed in from all sides to erase every contour of the room, and the growling tremor of distant danger passed away into silence.

Which left him in the darkened room with a life-support tank that was no longer bubbling.

He drew his hands carefully out of the clammy brine. Not because he was worried about startling the symbiont, really, but just because it felt wrong to shock the dark with any unnecessary noise now that even the stasis tank had fallen silent. *I should have had O'Brien hook up a stand-alone generator for the symbiont,* he thought, patting about for a rag on which to dry his hands. It wasn't like it couldn't be done—he'd nagged O'Brien into fitting the ICU with an uninterruptable power supply the first month he was on the station—and God knew he had little other use for the three stand-alones currently taking up space in the back room storage locker. But he hadn't wanted to bother the chief when there seemed to be so little likelihood of a power failure, and—deep down inside—he'd also known T'Kreng was right, and there was a very good chance he wouldn't be caring for the symbiont much longer. It had seemed an unnecessary bit of effort for something that might not exist in another twenty-four hours.

Shows what I know. Folding the rag as neatly as he could in the dark, Bashir dropped it onto the chair he'd just vacated and sighed down at the symbiont. "You know," he remarked aloud, "when I said I'd give anything to be locked in dark room with Dax, I rather assumed Jadzia would be there, too."

The symbiont, not surprisingly, didn't answer.

Bashir wasn't sure how much of his vocalizing the symbiont was aware of, but his ancient medical records at least indicated that he'd spent a lot of the last five thousand years talking to it. "Today, taught Dax how to make b'stella," was his favorite of the old entries. Perhaps it was because there was no way he could have kept silent for nearly a hundred years. Or perhaps it was because even a hundred years with the displaced symbiont never erased his gut-deep certainty that it somehow knew and cared when it was being interacted with, even when that interaction was only a heartsick human who could offer it nothing more than one-sided conversation. Whatever the reason, the precedent had clearly been set long ago, so he still talked to it now whenever they were alone.

"I don't know if you've noticed, but we've just lost all power in the infirmary. Which means I'm standing here in the dark, and you're floating in your medium without any of your support equipment running." He found the edge of the tank through the blackness, and curled his hand over it to tickle the surface of the water with his fingers. "I'm going to get a generator from the back room—it ought to be able to run you and a couple of small trouble lights with no problem, so we'll be back in business in no time. I won't be gone long. I promise."

He thought he felt the symbiont's cool, soft mass brush

against his fingertips, but the feeling was gone again before he could be sure.

As impenetrable as the darkness inside the infirmary seemed, Bashir was surprised to discover gradations in its relative depths as he turned slowly toward the examining-room door. The main infirmary glowed an icy gray beyond the adjoining doorway, lit from within by the isolation field at the mouth of the ICU, and from without by whatever illumination leaked through the open front entrance from emergency lanterns on the Promenade. While both those light sources would have been completely inadequate under most conditions, they proved marvelously helpful when compared to the absolute dark in the other parts of the infirmary. Bashir passed from the examining room into the open with a sense of little more than dark against darker, but it was enough to steer him toward the morgue at the rearmost of the infirmary without bumping into anything or tumbling himself head over heels.

He didn't particularly like keeping equipment in the same room where they occasionally kept cadavers. It felt oddly callous to tell a nurse, "Go fetch the dual-organ bypass cart from the morgue," as though all you had was one oversized coat closet that you also stuffed dead bodies into because you hadn't anywhere else to put them. In reality, it was more the other way around. The Cardassians had been quite particular about preserving their comrades' remains while they were occupying Bajor, but either hadn't the finances or the compassion to invest in the large lifesaving equipment that came standard with any Starfleet sickbay. With no interrogations, no lethal disciplinary actions, and at least a good deal fewer liberation operatives romping about the station nowadays, Starfleet's tenure at *Deep Space Nine* had seen a gratifying decline in the number of dead bodies coming through the infirmary. Bashir had been able to remove more than half of the stasis drawers to create some much-needed autopsy and storage space. (Cardassians, apparently, didn't see much use in postmortem exams, either.) Trying to explain that you really *did* have a morgue and you were using it as a coat closet sounded even *more* callous and bizarre, though, so Bashir had a tendency to avoid mentioning precisely where the large equipment was kept. "Nurse

Gerjuoy, could you please go get the bypass cart? I believe you know where it is." It didn't seem to hinder efficiency, but it did keep incidents of anxiety-induced hypertension among the patients at a minimum.

As he slowed at the doorway to the morgue, Bashir pointedly refused to let himself think that the small chamber was now dark as a tomb. He felt as if the walls rushed in to blind him on both sides as he stepped into that darkness, then rebounded to an impossible distance filled with echoes, bigness, and distracting not-quite sounds. He found himself picking his way gingerly across the smooth decking, tiny steps, feet barely leaving the floor, as though the slightest miscalculation would send him plunging into the abyss. That thought alone spiraled a brief moment of vertigo through his head. He was just about to stop to let the dizziness wind down when his hip barked against something jutting out of what should have been empty air, and all sense of place, orientation, and balance evaporated like flash-burned nitrogen. He flailed wildly for a grip on the obstacle, half doubling over it, half tumbling to his knees, and just managed to catch himself before he did more than stumble in an indelicate circle around the end of the barrier. Feeling the hot flush of embarrassment in his face, he was glad for the dark and the privacy as he carefully got his feet back under him and slowly straightened. He bumped something—light and angular—with his knee while still getting his bearings, and it scooted with a dry coughing sound before banging into something bigger and heavier, then fell silent.

Bashir took a deep, steadying breath, and splayed his hands on the cool, flat surface in front of him. *You're in your own infirmary,* he told himself sternly. *You know where everything is—where you are—if you just relax and think about it.* Trouble was, he'd never tried navigating the infirmary's Cardassian-designed rooms in the dark before, and right now the only thing he could think of that should be this tall and smooth and long was the autopsy bench. But he hadn't turned in that direction, or at least hadn't walked that far, and if this was the bench then the door with its view of the brighter main infirmary should be directly in front of him and there should have been no chair where he could kick it—

Steady . . . steady . . . Another deep breath, this one consciously aimed at relaxing the tension across his back, slowing the rapid trip-hammering of his heart. Finding his balance firmly, with both hands on the surface at his waist, he made one more slow inhalation, and closed his eyes.

The character of the darkness didn't really change—no blacker, no less total and pervasive. But instead of being trapped and confused in a room with no lights, now he'd simply closed his eyes. It removed the disorientation somewhat, and left him feeling focused and in control. He carefully imagined the layout of the morgue without trying to place himself anywhere within it. Then he felt out the edges of his mystery obstacle—smooth, wide, only about a table's thickness but without legs or other supports. When his elbow thumped against what felt suspiciously like a wall, he trailed his hand to where his "table" ought to be butted up against the bulkhead—only to have his arm slide past the plane of the wall into more nothingness.

"Oh, this is ridiculous!"

His voice echoed queerly, flat and immediate against the bulkhead right in front of his face, with a hint more resonance from somewhere farther down. This time when he reached in front of him, he found the wall immediately, and instead followed it downward toward the table. His hand found the opening with an abruptness that nearly made him dizzy again, but he was rewarded with a crystalline image of the wall of morgue stasis drawers and realized with an almost physical snap of recognition where he was. Each of the individual drawers could pull out to form an examining table of sorts, creating both a room-crossing hazard and an empty space in the wall that normally housed it. But why in hell had somebody left an open morgue drawer—

Memory washed over him with a knife-sharp gasp: the alien.

Bashir jerked his hands away from the open drawer as though they'd caught fire. He hadn't forgotten about the lethal fragment, precisely. He'd just gotten so tied up in trying to stabilize the symbiont's readings, and it had never occurred to him that the stasis fields in the morgue drawers were dependent on the main station power. Now it had been—how many minutes had it been? Too many, surely. And if you were a motile alien fragment, where would you go?

Whirling, he caught sight of the brighter dark of the main infirmary, with its untended patients and its open outside door.

Any anxiety about dashing through the big room in the dark was burned away by memories of Kira's burned, bubbling flesh and the smell of outgassing carbon and oxygen. He nearly always kept the door to the infirmary open when he was there, so that everyone would know they were welcome even if they weren't human or even Starfleet. Now, as he slammed shoulder-first into the jamb and groped madly for a handhold on the inside face of the door, he cursed himself for his egalitarianism, and wished he were enough of a paranoid to keep every door closed and locked behind him. Then, at least, there'd be less chance that this creature had escaped into the station proper while he was bumbling about.

The doors moved slowly and thickly with nothing to push them but one young man's admittedly meager weight. It occurred to Bashir, as he braced his back against one narrow ledge and pushed with every micron of his strength, that each of the two main doors no doubt massed in at twice his own measure, with Cardassian hydraulics designed to withstand everything short of direct phaser fire. Thank God they didn't have adrenaline, as well, or he might never have gotten them closed all by himself. As it was, when the second door bumped the first and cut the light in the room by nearly half, the sound of their seals mating was as solid and final as a closing coffin. That image pulled a little moan of anxiety from him, and he turned to face the room with his back pressed against the door, his hands flat against its surface and the light from the small, high windows spilling weakly over his shoulders.

Somewhere near the floor and unlocatable, something scuttled through the darkness.

Bashir slapped his combadge without taking his eyes off the shadows. "Bashir to Security!"

The badge hadn't even beeped. His mind registered that only a moment before realizing no one in Security was going to answer him, but he hit it again, harder, because he didn't want to believe he was completely alone. "Bashir to Ops!"

Nothing.

Lightly, like the occasional tapping of sand at a beach house's window, what sounded like the *click-tick*ing of tiny arthropod footsteps punctuated the silence. Bashir tried to follow their progress through the infirmary, but kept losing the delicate clatter to distance, and objects, and the pounding of his own blood in his ears. At the hindmost part of his brain, a tiny, terrified voice screamed at him to *run!*, to put himself outside and leave this thing inside, to let people trained in handling dangerous life-forms take responsibility for what happened in this room. But when he looked across the puzzlework of shadows toward the glowing mouth of the ICU and the absolute black of the symbiont's chamber, the clearest thought in his mind was the 1st Rule of Hippocrates: Do no harm.

"I can't leave the patients." Saying it out loud drove away all fears for himself or his own safety. The patients came first—the patients *always* came first. That had been true when he first set his heart on medical school, when he took up his first scalpel to cut into his first living patient, and when he denied himself a quick, peaceful death for nearly a hundred years to insure that a damaged Trill symbiont could survive. Leaving now when there were patients still needing his protection and help was simply not an option.

The room where he'd been hiding the symbiont didn't seem as dark as it had when they'd first lost the lighting. Bashir could just make out the blurry lines of the jury-rigged stasis tank, and while he couldn't see anything inside the tank itself, he knew the symbiont was aware and waiting for him when it greeted his hurried approach with a soft electric *snap!* and a whiff of ozone.

"I don't want you to panic," Bashir whispered, shoving his chair and work cart aside on his way to the rear of the tank, "but we've got a little bigger problem than just the lights at the moment." He bent to brace his shoulder against the tank's narrow end. "I'm going to move you into the ICU with the rest of Pak Dorren's people. It's got a level-nine quarantine field, which ought to keep out damn near anything, and if it doesn't . . ."

Well, they'd have to fudge those results when they got to them.

Regulation Starfleet boots slipping on the polished decking, he could barely get the purchase to keep from sliding off his feet, much less wrestle the brine tank into motion. He scooted it twice, sloshing medium all over the floor and the back of his uniform, both times accomplishing little more than inscribing an ugly arc in the infirmary's deckplates. He remembered his joke about the tank weighing nearly as much as the Brin Planetarium, and feverishly wished he hadn't been quite so accurate.

"I'll be right back!"

Almost two years ago now, Bashir had requisitioned a pair of light-cargo antigravs after he, Odo, O'Brien, Kira, Maile, Yevlin, Gerjuoy, and Sisko spent the better part of an afternoon serving as lift-and-carry team for a narcoleptic Morn while Bashir muddled his way through inventing an appropriate Vegan choriomeningitis treatment regimen for Morn's species. According to the medical texts, Morn shouldn't have been able to contract the disease at all; Bashir had gotten an excellent paper out of the experience. He'd also gotten the antigravs. Since then, he'd used them a total of once—to move the confocal microscope during one of his late-night "rearrange the infirmary" binges—but he remembered distinctly pushing them to the back of a floor-level cabinet when he was finished, briskly reminding himself not to forget where he'd put them in case he ever needed them again.

Julian Bashir, bless your anal compulsive little soul!

He half-ran, half-stumbled to the bank of cabinets, finding his way more by the feel of the furniture and equipment beneath his hands than by anything he could clearly see. As he thumped to his knees in front of the featureless doors, a sudden certainty of just how dark, and close, and crowded the inside of the cabinet would be clenched his lungs with dread, and he hesitated.

This was not a good time to be crawling about in places where you couldn't see.

He caught the counter above him and pulled himself to his feet. The drawer just above the storage cabinet jerked open with a great metallic jangle, announcing itself as exactly the random-junk collector it was. Lock screws and sleeves that seemed to go with nothing, but looked too useful to just throw away; laser scalpels with one or two damaged focal elements that weren't quite fine enough to use on flesh anymore but would cut most anything else you wanted; O-rings looking for a joint to seal, and scores of broken forceps, probes, and once-hermetic vials. Bashir pawed through the clutter as best he could, seizing on anything of about the right shape and length and circumference, then lifting it up into the paltry light from the Promenade to better determine its dimensions.

He had half the drawer emptied, scattered around the top of the counter, when his hand closed on something cold and hard-shelled that squirmed spastically in his grip. Taking a breath to scream but uttering little more than a strangled cry of disgust, he flung it away from him, toward the morgue, toward the dark. It struck what must have been the top of an examination table, skated across the smooth surface with a wisp of friction, then smacked to the floor with a distinctive rattle and crash that Bashir had learned to identify by the end of his first term as a surgical resident: a jointed *k'fken* probe for xenobiological biopsies, probably a number-four aluminum by the sound of it. Useless and potentially awkward in the wrong hands, but hardly what one would consider dangerous. He sighed shakily, and reached into the drawer more carefully this time to test what was left with the tips of his fingers.

He found the flashlight snugged into the back corner, trying to hide itself against the side of the drawer. O'Brien had forced it on him several months ago when an epidemic of tonsillitis had every parent on the station accosting Bashir in the Replimat, on the turbolifts, at his quarters, demanding that he peer down the throat of their child before he did another thing with his day. "Don't haul 'em down to the infirmary!" O'Brien had snorted. "You know what strep looks like, don't you? Use this, give 'em a peek, and send 'em home. That's all they want."

He'd been right, as usual, and Bashir had carried the small light as though it were Excalibur for almost two months. Now, all he cared about was that it lit when he depressed the end with his thumb, and that it seemed bright enough to drive back space itself after all this darkness.

He climbed back to his knees with the penlight clutched in one fist. Easing open the first of the two cabinet doors, he knelt for what seemed an eternity with only his light reaching into that inner darkness. All manner of useful paraphernalia littered the cabinet's landscape; lots of crannies and hollows for something the size of an Andorian's antenna to hide in. He crouched forward slowly, leading the way with the penlight, carefully examining every contour on every device, supply, or container before shoving it aside.

The farther into the cabinet he worked, the easier it became to steady his breathing and still his shaking hands. It was a closed cabinet, after all—the likelihood of the fragment finding its way inside was astronomically small, and surely the noise and light of his presence would have flushed it out or scared it off by now. If it were here. Which it clearly wasn't.

All the same, his heart throbbed painfully with relief when the penlight's beam danced across the antigravs' storage case all the way at the back of the cabinet. He took the light between his teeth, and went down on his elbows to squirm deep enough to pull on the antigravs with both hands.

Soft, ghostlike scuffling, then the faintest prick of tiny fingers through the fabric of his pants. He jerked back with a startled yelp, banging his head on the top of the cabinet, tangling himself with the doors, the supplies, the equipment as he thrashed to pull out of the enclosure. Halfway up his leg, its thousand limbs digging in like needle stings, a thick worm of movement pressed against the outside of his knee, and started to burn.

Fear more than pain dragged a wild cry from him, and he slammed back against the wall of cabinets rather than clutch at the squirming intruder for lack of anything better to do with his hands. *It's not difluorine!* his rational mind screamed at him. *Whatever it's doing, it's not difluorine!* And in a very real sense, that was all that mattered. Twisting sideways, he struggled to keep his burning leg as still as possible as he pushed himself high enough to slap awkwardly at the top of the counter.

Probes, forceps, and O-rings scattered, going wherever the flashlight had gone when he'd shouted with it still in his mouth. When his hand came down forcefully on a pile of clutter painfully on the edge of his reach, touch sorted what he wanted from the confusion with a speed and certainty that bypassed conscious thought. The scalpel was already humming when he flashed his arm down and slit the pant leg from ankle to knee.

The Andorian-pale fragment smelled like burning walnuts where the laser scalpel cut sizzling across it. For some reason, he half-expected it to squeal or shriek at the touch of pain—instead, it twitched loose in a writhe of silent anguish and scrabbled off into the dark.

It was looking for new DNA. That had to have been what attracted it to him, through the dark clutter of the morgue. And now Bashir knew where it was headed without even having to track its skittering progress. The only other DNA it could sense and want lay across the infirmary in an unguarded brine tank.

"Dax!"

Biting his lip in an effort to pretend his leg wasn't still on fire with pain, he wrenched himself to his knees and took only a moment to lunge after the flashlight in the bottom of the cabinet before surging to his feet. The cold spray of the penlight's beam danced crazily about the darkness as he ran for the symbiont's chamber.

The gentle splash of a body into brine crashed across the small room like a thunderclap. Bashir wailed in despair, the tiny light illuminating the shadowy struggles of a worm that was once a sensory organ now turned voracious attacker. Plunging his hands into the tank, he clapped the wriggling fragment between both palms, interlocking all his fingers, and swept it clear of the brine in a long rooster tail of fluid. He had almost reached the independently powered disposal unit when whatever passed for awareness within the fragment registered that it was in danger. The gush of difluorine across his hands hissed like hot oil over ice.

When he pushed the disposal chute open with his elbow,

he couldn't tell whether or not he was screaming. He only knew that disintegration was his only hope, and that the blinding flash of all its atoms bursting free to seek a new existence was the most beautiful fire he had ever seen.

Nausea crashed over him, nearly buckling his knees. *No!* he thought desperately, catching himself with one elbow as he slewed against the wall. Thrashing, thumping from the symbiont's tank pulled him back across the room when every neuron in his body wanted to slump down into shock. In the dilute glow of the penlight from the bottom of the brine, he could just glimpse Dax writhing and bucking as if to escape, as if—

Oh, God! Difluorine mixed with water produced the most corrosive acid known to science, powerful enough to chew through a starship's hull, not to mention the flesh of a frail, ancient symbiont. *Oh, no please no! Not after five thousand years—I didn't keep you five thousand years just for this!* It didn't matter that his own hands were already seared raw, or that submerging any part of himself in the brine put him as much at risk as the symbiont. He could rush them both to the subspace reverter, banish the acid into subspace, repair whatever tissues melted under the acid's sting. Murmuring over and over, "I'm sorry! . . . Dax, I'm so sorry . . . !" Bashir slid both aching hands underneath the thrashing symbiont—

—and the infirmary around him corroded into starlight and blood, scouring his thoughts off the face of the world.

"Oh, no. Not again."

Sisko glanced up from the entry he was jotting silently into his captain's log, alerted by the half-wry, half-serious tone of Dax's voice. A glance at the viewscreen showed him only the normal computer blur of star trails streaming past them. "What's the matter?"

She glanced over her shoulder from the piloting console. "Engineering sensors are picking up a quantum resonance in subspace, and it's getting stronger as we approach the wormhole."

Sisko exhaled sharply, jamming his note padd back into its slot in his command chair with more force than it needed. "Upstream echoes?" he demanded.

"It looks like it, but I'll need Heather's input to be sure. She's still down with T'Kreng."

Sisko palmed the comm button on his chair. "Ensign Petersen, report to the bridge immediately." He sat back, trying to spot visual evidence of the wormhole pulses the sensors had detected, but all of the stars he could see burned bright and steady, slowing in graceful arcs across the viewscreen as the *Defiant* slowed from warp speed to sublight. "How far are we from the wormhole?"

"We're coming up on it now." Dax cast a puzzled look up at the screen as the *Defiant* braked to a swift, stomach-tugging stop. "That's odd."

Sisko lifted an eyebrow at her. All that showed on their viewscreen was the familiar stretch of empty space that their visual sensors were programmed to lock on to in this region. "It looks normal to me—the wormhole's not even opening and closing."

His science officer shook her head, looking baffled. "But according to our sensors, it *is*. I don't understand—" She glanced up as the turbolift doors slid open to admit an again-breathless Petersen. "Heather, have you been watching our subspace readings lately?"

The cadet's cheeks turned a rosier shade of apple-pink. "No, Lieutenant, I'm sorry. T'Kreng and I were setting up a magnetic communications relay in the medical bay."

Sisko blinked, a little taken aback by this casual mention of the dead Vulcan physicist, but Dax seemed to take it in stride. Of course, to a Trill, the idea of communicating with the preserved sentience of a long-dead person was perfectly normal.

"Well, take a look at these readings." Dax punched them up on her panel, and the two scientists bent to study them together. "Doesn't that look like the wormhole has destabilized again?"

"Worse than before." Petersen tilted her head to study the unremarkable expanse of deep space on the screen before them, speckled with the dim bluish glows of distant stars. "If it's emitting this much energy leakage, it may have shifted below visual frequencies. Have you tried scanning this area with sensors tuned to ultraviolet and microwave frequencies?"

"Not yet." Dax swung around and tapped the command into her jury-rigged engineering controls. The viewscreen broke up into visual static for a moment, then settled into a solid black display. Sisko watched it with a frown. "Dax, I don't see—"

"Subspace pulse arriving now," the Trill said tersely, and the blackness abruptly blossomed into a shriek of swirling white shadows across the screen, like a ghostly negative of the wormhole he was used to. Sprays like snowy avalanches tore across the jet-black emptiness, then fell back into their fiery white center and were gone. "You're right, Heather. The wormhole's downshifted entirely into short-wave ultraviolet display."

Sisko felt the pressure of his frown dig deeper into his tense face. "Does that mean we can't travel through it?"

His science officer exchanged thoughtful looks with the Starfleet Academy cadet. "The ultraviolet by itself isn't a problem," Dax said absently. "Our shields can handle a lot worse in the way of EM radiation. But the instability levels are almost back to what they were before the wormhole-dwellers neutralized them. I don't think anything bigger than a photon torpedo would get through the singularity matrix safely now."

Sisko rasped a hand across his chin, thinking hard. "So even with your ansible connection, old man, we're not going to be able to get any reinforcements from *Deep Space Nine.*"

"No, Benjamin. I'm afraid not."

"That's not our only problem, Captain." Petersen glanced up from the display of subspace data, the expression on her face making it look far older than its actual years. "The wormhole's releasing more energy than our original models can account for. If I didn't know better, I'd say it meant the subspace rift is so close to happening that the wormhole-dwellers can't control the quantum resonance fluctuations anymore."

Sisko scowled. "But since we know the Jem'Hadar station will take sixteen hours to get here—"

"—then it means the time rift will be a lot larger and more destructive than we'd expected," Dax finished. She swung around to face Sisko, her eyes grave. "It's not just the wormhole and *Deep Space Nine* that we'll save by preventing this time rift, Benjamin. It's the entire planet of Bajor."

He shot to his feet, the coiled-spring tension in his gut winching even tighter than before. Jake was on Bajor. Two hundred million other people were on Bajor—and he could only think of one or two who deserved to be swallowed by an exploding singularity. *"How* do we save it?" he demanded, pacing the length of the *Defiant*'s empty bridge in a vain attempt to burn off his angry frustration. "These aliens can track us through our cloak by our waste heat, they can overwhelm our shields, they can pierce our ablative armor, they can apparently even use the Jem'Hadar's defenses against us! What can we do to *them?*"

"Infiltrate them," Petersen said unexpectedly. Sisko shot her an incredulous look, but although her cheeks reddened a little under it, she didn't back down. "It's not my idea, it's T'Kreng's. And seeing this—" She jerked her chin at the fierce white-shifted splash of ultraviolet radiation painted on the viewscreen behind them as the wormhole opened and closed. "I think you better come down and talk to her about it, Captain."

CHAPTER
19

THE ALIEN LOOKED like something from a Tellerite antivivisectionist tract, lying belly-up with its gelatinous strings of crenellated cortical fragments nestled inside loops and strings of gently pulsing flesh. Sisko paused in the door of the medical bay, startled by the absence of any blue glimmer around the creature.

"Dax, I thought you were going to keep that thing in stasis," he snapped. "It almost killed Ensign Goldman."

"A minor miscalculation, Captain." The words were spoken by an electronically generated voice routed through the medical bay's comm speakers, but their silken serenity was unmistakably T'Kreng's. "I intended only to entangle myself with a member of your away team, to ensure you brought me back with you." The two remaining appendages on the alien flexed and went limp again. "Unfortunately, my control of my newly acquired Jem'Hadar sub-brain was not completely established at the time."

Sisko slanted a disbelieving glance across the examining table at Yevlin Meris. "She can hear me?"

The Bajoran physician's assistant nodded. "The medical computer is digitizing all our speech and sending it to her via microelectrical impulses. It was Professor T'Kreng's idea." She pointed at the tiny remote electrodes embedded in one of the larger brain fragments. "She's receiving our words in binary computer code and converting them back to speech almost instantaneously."

"That's remarkable—even for a Vulcan." Dax leaned over the stasis chamber, seemingly oblivious of the diflourine-laced claws waving a few centimeters below her freckled face. Sisko gritted his teeth and resisted the urge to pull her back. "Professor, are you engaging your sub-brains as parallel processing units, the same way the aliens link their separate strings of cortices into a massive processing network?"

"Precisely, Lieutenant Dax." T'Kreng's artificially generated voice still managed to sound unbearably superior. "That is why I had Petersen release stasis on the other strings. I need them to process your voice input correctly."

Sisko cleared his throat. "And you are in complete control of this organism, Professor? It has no volition—no inherent personality—of its own?"

"Only a set of very basic survival instincts and drives, Captain, encoded within its cellular genetic material—which I suspect is not DNA. All higher logic and emotional input is determined by a process of internal competition, cooperation, and dominance among the incorporated cortical fragments. This portion of my cortex had very little trouble taking over the neural strings of the original organism, although I did have assistance from one of my Vulcan associates and a rather irate Ferengi trader."

Sisko scrubbed a hand across his face, trying to assimilate the concept of a clearly sentient species whose individual members had no sentience of their own. "If all the thinking and feeling is provided by the organisms they digest, how can these aliens carry out any consistent actions and goals? How can they even have the desire to bring the rest of their species through the wormhole to join them?"

T'Kreng was silent for a moment, as if that was a question that had not occurred to her. "I suspect that immersion in this alien matrix creates a generic identification with the host for those cortical fragments lacking will and memory. Even parts of my own brain seem to have been affected in this way. On the other hand, cortical fragments which were deeply involved in self-consciousness and personality also appear to retain their anger at being engulfed, even after many hundreds of years of immersion. It is those fragments that I believe will unite to help us."

Dax nodded. "Then all we need to do—"

"*Dax,*" Sisko said sharply, seeing the blankness of an ansible trance start to creep over her face and steal away its expression. The Trill opened her eyes again with a fierce shudder. "You all right, old man?"

Shock leached her face of all color but its freckles. "I am—but the other Dax isn't. Benjamin, some kind of genetically altered creature is in the infirmary, attacking Julian and the symbiont right now! Some of the aliens have already traveled through the wormhole!"

"What?"

"The core sent an advance party of two hundred and fifty individuals through the singularity matrix, long before they attacked my ship," T'Kreng agreed. "Whatever communication method they use between themselves apparently transcends space and time. The alien core here has given their Alpha Quadrant counterparts instructions to rift the wormhole on their side, if they can't accomplish it from ours."

"*Damn.*" Sisko thudded his clenched fists together, hard enough to make his knuckles ache. He saw both Yevlin Meris and Heather Petersen wince, and channeled his roiling temper into the fierce restrained fury of his voice. "Then we can't save the wormhole, even if we destroy the Jem'Hadar station?"

T'Kreng made a sound of crystalline disapproval. "An inability to control all aspects of a problem is no excuse for neglecting the aspects you *can* control, Captain. We must trust that your station crew will be able to deal with the aliens on their side of the wormhole. Our task now is to deal with ours."

Sisko paused, then pushed out a breath of renewed determination. "All right. How many of them are we facing?"

"There were over five hundred individuals inside the Jem'Hadar station when I left it."

"And you think we can infiltrate them? How?"

"By putting an intact cerebral cortex directly into their neural processing core." For once, T'Kreng's reply was as blunt and concise as Sisko's question had been.

Dax looked down dubiously at the string of disembodied brains that was talking to them. "You think a single individual can dominate the thousands of cortical fragments in there?"

"Unlikely," T'Kreng agreed. "But a highly motivated and intelligent cortex could find sufficient allies to dominate a small part of the core—and that part could be used to initiate the station's self-destruct sequence while it is still a safe distance away from the wormhole."

"Could you do it?" Sisko demanded.

This time, he could almost feel T'Kreng's ice-cold irritation echoing through the pause in her speech. "Of course I could, Captain—if I could somehow be reassembled into my original cortical pattern. But you are speaking to less than sixty percent of T'Kreng's consciousness, and I have no idea where the rest of me is. You will have to locate another, more intact cortex to carry out this plan—or you will have to create one."

Dax's eyes narrowed, and she looked across the alien fragment to meet Sisko's equally grim gaze. He put their unwelcome conclusion into harsh words. "You mean, deliberately deliver someone to be attacked and digested by one of the core aliens?"

"And to be killed moments later when the station explodes. Not an appealing strategy, perhaps, but one I know will work." The Vulcan's voice turned crystal-sharp with the force of her conviction. "I can assure you, Captain Sisko, nothing else will. The linked core mind will manage to out maneuver any other attack you make on them."

"We'll see." Sisko straightened to his full height, suddenly wanting to get away from this mangled alien and the impossibly preserved and implacable Vulcan inside it. "We've got sixteen hours and one of the best fighting ships in Starfleet. I'm not ready to send out any kamikaze missions just yet."

"Of course not." T'Kreng's disembodied voice was a cold shiver of silk in the silence of the medical bay. "But in fifteen hours or less, when you will be ready to do it, you can come to me for your final instructions. After that, I suggest that you terminate this entire alien fragment by wide-angle transporter dispersion."

Sisko scowled, caught on the verge of leaving the medical bay by a strange note in the Vulcan physicist's voice. "Is that a strategic suggestion, Honored Professor?"

"No," said what remained of T'Kreng. "It is a plea for mercy."

"We've got to get Dax to the Gamma Quadrant."

Wedged inside the guts of the external sensor panel, her torso weighted down by what felt like the Prophets' own collection of tools and burned components, Kira snorted wearily in response to Bashir's bleak announcement. "Dax is *already* in the Gamma Quadrant, Doctor. If you left the infirmary once in a while, you might know that." She pulled another brace of cracked, cloudy isolinears, and threw them out to join all the others in an ever-growing pile. "Now, do me a favor and—"

"Oh, my God! Julian, what happened?"

The startled alarm in O'Brien's usually calm voice registered on Kira's raw nerves like a breach alarm, but it was Odo's dry observation, "The power loss must have deactivated the stasis field on our little guest," that flooded her stomach with sick dread. She shivered violently under a roil of remembered terror and anguish, overlaying Bashir's slight frame on that horrific memory, and slid herself out from under the panel with a single frantic pull. *Don't let us lose our medical officer!* she prayed. *Don't let me have to explain to Sisko how I didn't even take care of our doctor!*

He stood near the Ops ladder access, his hands held out in front of him as though he wasn't sure what to do with them and his uniform smelling strongly of sour blood and brine. O'Brien reached him first, and had him pushed into a chair with his wrists firmly pinned by the time Kira rolled to her feet and bounded up the steps to join them. She could see the dark sheen of blood on Bashir's palms, and found herself wondering wildly how he could have possibly climbed all the way from the lower decks in such a state.

O'Brien caught the doctor's chin in one hand and glared sternly into his eyes the way only a parent could do. "Don't move!"

Bashir obeyed only marginally after O'Brien released him, leaning forward to keep sight of the chief as O'Brien trotted across Ops to fetch an emergency kit from under a panel.

"What happened to the alien?" Kira asked him, grabbing at his shoulder in an attempt to catch his attention.

"Chief, I'm all right—it's neutralized. . . ." He was shaking so hard, the words stuttered out of him in fits and starts. "We're both neutralized . . . it's fine . . ."

"Julian!" She shook him until he blinked up at her, dark eyes almost without focus in his thin, sallow face. "Julian, what happened to the alien? Where is it now?"

He shook his head faintly. "Gone—I flashed it in the disposal bin."

She remembered the sound and smell of her diflourine-soaked jacket disappearing into that maw, and her guts uncoiled with relief. A small victory, maybe, but better than they'd managed up here so far. Resting one hand on the top of his head in silent approval, she stepped around behind his chair to give O'Brien access to his hands.

To her surprise, the doctor drew back and away from the chief, his face folding into an impatient scowl as he lifted his hands out of O'Brien's reach. "Look, we don't have time to worry about this! We've got to find a way to get Dax into the Gamma Quadrant."

O'Brien dropped the opened medkit across Bashir's lap to snatch at his hands. "Julian . . ." His voice carried a warning that seemed all out of proportion with Bashir's resistance.

"You don't have to worry, Doctor," Kira told him, thinking it would calm his fidgeting. "Dax is already in the Gamma Quadrant."

He twisted a desperate look at her over his shoulder. "Not Jadzia," he said plaintively. "*Dax!*"

"Julian." O'Brien's voice snapped the doctor's head around as though he'd been slapped. "Starfleet's orders—"

"I don't give a damn about Starfleet's orders!" The violence of his outburst startled Kira. "You've got a shipload of viroid life-forms outside draining our power systems, and I've got a Trill symbiont in the infirmary who says it can help us." This time when he looked up at Kira, his face was flushed to an almost normal color for all that his eyes were still cloudy with shock. "But we don't have much time. Whatever's going to happen to the wormhole, it's going to happen soon, and . . ." His gaze drifted to one side, focus fading to somewhere dark and internal. ". . . they're part of it somehow," he murmured, frowning. "I . . . I'm not sure . . . I don't entirely understand . . ."

Odo snorted and folded his arms. "Well, at least we're all in the same position."

Kira silenced him with a sharp glare, then gave Bashir's shoulder a bracing shake. "Why don't you start with explaining what the hell you're talking about?" she suggested tartly. "If you've got Dax, who's with Jadzia?"

Bashir pulled himself straighter with obvious effort, but didn't seem able to look away from O'Brien's inexpert but meticulous inspection of his hands. "When we were called to Starbase One, it was because Starfleet had . . . evidence that Captain Sisko, Jadzia, and I would be . . ." He used the side of his hand to tap one of the regenerators in his lap, and O'Brien plucked it dutifully from the kit to switch it on. "They knew we would be lost in some sort of temporal rift caused by the wormhole," he went on softly as O'Brien played the regenerator back and forth across his palm. "Part of their evidence was Dax—the Dax that *would* be lost, that *was* lost, that . . ." He squeezed his eyes shut and shook his head as though trying to jar his thoughts back into order. "It outsurvived us all, and it's the only one who knows what happened. If we don't get it into the Gamma Quadrant, it's all going to happen again!"

"And this symbiont . . ." Odo leaned back against a panel, his voice fairly dripping with skepticism. "It *talks* to you?"

A thoroughly arrogant clarity flashed into the doctor's eyes. "Of course not. Symbionts communicate electrochemically, both with their hosts and with each other. I . . . this other me . . . I lived with the symbiont for a long time after the others died. I think it must have learned to . . . match my bioelectric patterns, to link with me somehow so that we wouldn't feel so all alone. And now with the tissues in the my hands exposed . . ." His voice trailed away, caught again in the riptide of whatever memories still churned too close to the surface. "I don't hear words, or even thoughts, I just . . . I just *know!* I *feel* things that aren't mine, and see . . ." Another bout of stumbling silence, then he craned desperate eyes up toward Kira and stated with fearful lucidity,

"You've got to let me take a runabout to the Gamma Quadrant. We have to get Dax to the *Defiant* before it's too late."

The thought of letting him pilot anything in his current state was nearly laughable, but O'Brien saved her from having to tell him that by blurting, "Julian, that's impossible! Even if we could get anything bigger than a torpedo through the wormhole right now—which we can't!—those things would home in on your engine exhaust and tear your ship apart before you were a thousand klicks out."

"And if we don't try," Bashir countered quietly, "those things are going to destroy the wormhole and possibly change the course of history."

A foreboding she didn't want to acknowledge shivered through Kira's aching muscles. "How can these things destroy the wormhole?"

"I don't know!" The thin edge of panic crept back into his voice as easily as it had vanished a moment before. "All I know is that if we don't get Dax through the wormhole, it will have spent five thousand years in a brine tank for nothing!" He raked his one healed hand through his hair, knotting it at the back of his neck in frustration. "I can't do that to it . . . I won't."

"Which leaves us with what options?" Odo paced to stand at Kira's side, his crossed arms and downturned mouth radiating a dissatisfaction she suspected related more to having no clear-cut answer than to their impending demise. "We can't send this symbiont outside the station in anything containing a power source, and it certainly isn't going to swim through the wormhole on its own. What else is there?"

When Bashir jerked his head up to whirl a startled frown toward the constable, Kira thought he meant to rail at Odo for his insensitive doom-crying. Then an expression of almost beatific revelation spread across the young doctor's face, and he settled back in his chair to look Odo carefully up and down. "Actually," he said, very slowly, "I do have one idea. . . ."

If there was one bad habit Jadzia Dax knew she had as a science officer, it was her tendency to fidget with the color scales of her sensor displays whenever she was nervous or bored. Right now, she was both. As a result, the color index she had created to display the wormhole's bursts of high-energy radiation on the main viewscreen kept shifting from an angry bruiselike red-violet to an icy borealis shimmer of translucent blue to a deep electric indigo sparked with hot white highlights. No matter how she changed the colors, the wormhole's frantic spasms of opening and closing kept looking more and more ominous.

"I still think we should use the quantum torpedoes," she said, more to distract herself from the silent convulsions on the viewscreen than because she had any hope of being listened to. "They're our most powerful weapons."

"Too much thermal signature, old man." From somewhere under the weapons panel, she heard Sisko grunt as he wrestled off the cover panel from the phaser controls. "A cluster of shelled aliens could intercept them and kick off a premature detonation. Hand me the phase modulator, Eddington, and read me off the wavelength we want."

Dax swung around to watch them work, still frowning. "We could link all the torpedoes into one stationary spacemine, and rig it to go off as soon as it entered the Jem'Hadar station's gravity well. There wouldn't be any thermal signature emitted that way."

"With an untargeted blast like that," Eddington said, "we couldn't be completely sure the reaction core would be destroyed. And we need core destruction—"

"Wavelength," Sisko reminded him curtly.

"Three hundred and ninety-three nanometers. We need core destruction because just breaching hull integrity on that Jem'Hadar station isn't going to stop it from exploding in the wormhole."

"I *know* that," Dax said. There were times when the Starfleet security officer's tendency to restate the obvious became really annoying. "But I'm not sure that tuning the phasers to the resonance frequency of the Jem'Hadar reaction mass is going to ensure core destruction either. There are still four hundred duranium-shelled aliens wrapped around the station's reaction core. They might absorb a lot of our phaser blast."

"Not if we can provide them with a distraction somewhere else." Sisko rolled out from under the weapons panel, his face dusted with feathery flakes of insulating cable. "*That's* where the quantum torpedoes come in."

Dax shifted the viewscreen color scale to a purple so deep it was almost black. The wormhole faded to nearly invisible lacework explosions against the darkness of space. "I suppose I could modify the torpedoes to emit the same power signature as a large ship's warp core," she said thoughtfully. "That might lure a significant fraction of the aliens out to attack them."

"Especially if we send them out on two different headings," Sisko agreed. "How long will it take you to make the modifications?"

A shrill warning buzz yanked Dax's attention back to her engineering sensors before she could answer. She felt the freckles on her neck and back tighten with sudden tension. "That depends on whether we have any torpedoes left to modify, Captain. Long-range sensors show five warships approaching us. Eddington, can you confirm their identify?"

The security officer punched his rewired weapons console back to life and scanned it intently. "They're definitely Jem'Hadar ships, but there's something odd about their warp signature. Oh, my *god!*"

Dax threw him a startled look. Eddington might be annoyingly supercilious at times, but she'd rarely seen him display anything other than the most professional demeanor at his station. Sisko's eyebrows lifted nearly to his hairline. "What is it?" he demanded.

Eddington swung around, his narrow face stiff with shock. "The Jem'Hadar ships—they've all got their tractor beams locked on a joint target, sir. I think it's the station the aliens took over."

"*What?*" Sisko crossed to inspect the weapons sensor output for himself, his dark eyes narrowing with intensity. "Dax, put us on an intercept course *now,* at maximum warp."

"Coming about," she warned, punching the commands into her helm computer. At steep accelerations, the *Defiant*'s undercompensated warp drive tended to throw people across the bridge if they weren't braced. "Intercept in five minutes, visual contact in four."

"Put it on screen as soon as you get it," Sisko ordered.

"All right, people. Why the *hell* would the Jem'Hadar be bringing that station to the wormhole?"

Hovan cleared her throat nervously from her station at the cloaking device. "Maybe the shapeshifting aliens have taken over some Jem'Hadar ships," she suggested.

"It's more likely the Jem'Hadar have just picked the most convenient way to dispose of a problem they want out of their quadrant," Dax said wryly. "If they yanked the station into warp without warning, the aliens couldn't travel out to attack them. Even duranium bodies couldn't sustain warp-level accelerations without tearing apart."

"Too bad we didn't think of doing that, in the opposite direction," Sisko said grimly.

"We'd have had to destroy the station the instant we dropped out of warp," Dax reminded him. "I think the Jem'Hadar will find the aliens coming at them like a swarm of wasps as soon as they recover from warp exposure."

Sisko grunted acknowledgment, then glanced up as the turbolift doors slid open.

"What just happened?" Heather Petersen demanded urgently. "I was running a relativistic analysis to tighten up my estimate for the onset of the time rift—" Her face lifted to the main viewscreen and paled visibly. Dax turned to see five sleek Jem'Hadar warships, blurry with maximum magnification, enter visual sensor range. Their crossed glitter of tractor beams backlit the unmistakable half-ruptured silhouette of the alien-captured station. "Oh, my god. They've brought it here!"

Sisko turned away from the disturbing image on the screen to regard the cadet intently. "What happened to your estimate for the time rift, Ensign?"

Even from across the room, Dax could see that Petersen had to swallow before she could answer. "It suddenly jumped from fifteen hours to forty-five minutes."

An ice-cold shock of fear tore through Dax, although she couldn't be sure if it was coming from her symbiont or from its ancient twin. She closed her eyes and took a deep breath, fighting off the tidal pull of ansible trance.

"The Jem'Hadar squadron has just entered attack range, Captain," Eddington said. "Should I target phasers on the station or on the warships?"

Sisko threw a furious look at the console he'd just retuned. "At that low frequency, the phasers will bounce right off the ships' shields, and we'll have given away our location for nothing. Aim quantum torpedoes at the ships, Commander. We'll try to take out as many of them as we can, then blow up the station."

"Aye, sir." Eddington punched the commands into his station. "Torpedoes ready."

Dax wasn't sure what warned her—a premonition of numbness in her fingers, a dance of odd lights at the edges of her vision. The deepening tidal pull she felt inside confirmed that she was falling into another ansible trance, one too strong to fight off.

"Benjamin!" she called out urgently. "Get someone to cover my station—"

She was barely aware of his shadow falling over her before the *Defiant*'s bridge rippled and went away. Instead of the wet, dark quiet that usually settled over her when she joined with old Dax, she found herself engulfed in a roar of impossibly vivid colors and a glare of shrieking noise. With a jolt of terror, Dax wondered if she was sharing the old symbiont's death throes. There was no way an unjoined symbiont could perceive actual visual stimuli—

"—sensory illusions created by alternation of intense magnetic fields—" The words were very faint, but Jadzia still recognized the voice that spoke them. That unquenchable interest in new experiences, no matter how life-threatening, could only belong to her symbiont. "—insufficient shielding for these conditions, survival uncertain—"

A glowing burst like a tracer torpedo ripped through the slow fade of colors, splashing another bright aurora across her mind. The noise had become a thunderous howl of static, so deep now that she felt more than heard it. Had some catastrophe hit *Deep Space Nine*? She couldn't hear Bashir's or O'Brien's voice in the background—maybe the station was being attacked by the same aliens they were fighting here. If the warp core had been breached, the explosion of subspace energy would send an immense magnetic flux surging through the station.

"—at midpoint, magnetic fields still increasing—"

A fiercer, more chemical jolt shrieked through Dax's

body, and the colors and noise promptly vanished. She tensed, reaching out with all the strength of her joined minds to find the ansible connection again.

"*Lieutenant!*" Fingers dug into the muscles of her shoulders, hard enough to make Dax wince. Suddenly aware that she was back in her real body, she dragged open her eyes and stared up disbelievingly at Yevlin Meris.

"What did you do?"

"Lowered your isoboromine levels." The physician's assistant held onto her tightly as an evasive maneuver sent the *Defiant* skating sideways hard enough to make even Dax's space-hardened stomach lurch. "They were twice normal. Whatever this ansible effect is that Heather keeps trying to explain to me, I don't think it's good for you."

Dax winced and scrambled to her feet. "What's going on?" she demanded, seeing only a spiral of fast-moving stars on the viewscreen. "Where are the Jem'Hadar?"

Sisko never took his eyes off the helm panel he was manning. "We got one of them with our first torpedo blast, but two more split from the convoy and came after us. They're firing at extrapolated positions of our ion trail. Do you have a fix on the lead ship yet, Eddington?"

"If you could give me just a few more seconds on this heading, Captain—"

The *Defiant* slewed into an abrupt downward corkscrew and Dax grabbed at the edge of the empty command chair to steady herself. The viewscreen blazed with the fierce white light of the phaser beam that had just missed them. "Sorry," Sisko said between gritted teeth. "That's as long a targeting interval as they're going to give us before they fire."

Dax frowned and skidded across the bridge to join Eddington at the weapons station. "Have you tried programming the torpedoes to home in on the Jem'Hadar shield signature?"

"Of course. But as soon as they realized that we weren't firing our phasers at them, they dropped their shields."

"Then we should be able to program the torpedoes to recognize the activated metallic spectrum of their hull armor. Running unshielded at these speeds means they're getting blasted with cosmic radiation." Dax took the seat next to Eddington and began to input a series of quick commands into the torpedo-control panel. "If we convert the energy-dispersive scanning system on the torpedoes to an X-ray fluorescence detector tuned to the indium emission peak of duranium alloy—"

The security officer gave her a baffled look. "And that won't make the torpedoes home in on us?"

"Not unless we lose our own shields." Dax finished her reprogramming, and readied two of their last five torpedoes. "I'd suggest firing both launchers together, Commander, so the Jem'Hadar don't have time to put up their shields."

"Whatever you do, do it fast." Sisko swung the *Defiant* into another impossibly tight curve, nearly sliding Dax off her seat. This time, the phaser blast they avoided was close enough to make the ship shudder and the viewscreen flash completely to white. "They're getting better at tracking our ion trail."

"Torpedoes armed and ready," Eddington said. He took a deep breath, then slapped at both launch controls. "Torpedoes launched on homing mission, Captain."

"Good." Sisko yanked the ship into a fierce upward zigzag as two sets of phaser beams crisscrossed the place they would have been in another second. "Estimated time to impact?"

"Five seconds," Dax said, before Eddington could reply. "Four, three—"

The fiery explosion of a ruptured warp core across the viewscreen stopped her. The bridge crew waited in tense silence until a ghostly white gas cloud bloomed in another sector of the screen. "I think that one raised his shields at the last minute," Dax said thoughtfully. "But the torpedo still came close enough to clip him."

"Close only counts in horseshoes and hull breaches." Sisko pushed himself away from the helm station. "Thanks, old man. Now, can you plot us a course back to the wormhole? We still need to intercept that damned station before the other Jem'Hadar dump it into the wormhole."

"They can't have kept up the same acceleration with only two warships tractoring it." At the back of the bridge, Petersen let go of the back of Hovan's chair and took two steps forward. Dax skirted around Yevlin Meris, who was cautiously rising from her braced position against the disconnected engineering panel. "If we can convince them to alter course away from the wormhole and release it at warp speed—"

Sisko gave the cadet a wry look. "I don't know what they teach you about the Jem'Hadar at the Academy, Ensign, but in all my interactions with them, I don't think I've ever convinced them of anything but their own superiority."

Dax typed in the course changes and sent the *Defiant* surging back toward the wormhole, now several thousand kilometers away. "I'd suggest hitting them with our last quantum torpedoes before they even know we're there."

Sisko gave her a curt nod. "Provided they're not so close to the wormhole that the torpedo impact will accomplish the very thing we're trying to prevent."

"Heather should be able to tell us that." Dax sent the cadet an inquiring look and got a confident nod in return.

"Good." Sisko sat back in his command chair, looking far too calm for a captain who'd just piloted his ship through the fiercest dogfight of its life. Only the occasional jerk of his fingers into an impatient fist betrayed that this was anything other than a routine cruise of the Gamma Quadrant. "Any sign of the Jem'Hadar station on long-range sensors?"

Dax swung back to her engineering panel. "I don't—no, it just entered visual range." She frowned, eying the readout on her panel. "That's odd."

"What?" Sisko demanded.

"According to this, the Jem'Hadar ships and the station have all come to a halt, just outside the wormhole's gravitational field."

Sisko's forehead creased. "They're not moving any closer?"

"No. They're just—stationary."

The captain scrubbed a hand across his face. "You think the aliens are already attacking them?"

"Perhaps." She glanced over her shoulder at him. "We'll rendezvous with them in two minutes. Orders, Captain?"

"We'll come in cloaked and establish a minimum-thrust orbit around the station, just like we did before," Sisko decided. "If the aliens have swarmed out to attack the Jem'Hadar ships, we won't have to worry about using our quantum torpedoes to divert them. We'll fire phasers immediately at maximum sustained power directly into the station's warp core."

"*No!*" Heather Petersen's voice sounded more like a startled squeak than an articulate protest, but the panic in it was sharp enough to jerk all their heads around. "Captain Sisko, that would set off a subspace explosion big enough to trigger the time rift, even at that distance!"

Sisko blew out a distinctly frustrated breath. "Well, what do you suggest we do, Ensign?"

Petersen dug her teeth into her lip, looking as stymied as Dax felt. "I don't know, sir," she said at last. "All I know is that we can't do *that*."

"Jem'Hadar ships are now in attack range," Eddington reported. "Revised orders, Captain?"

Sisko paused, watching the two fighters and the towed alien station congeal out of darkness on the viewscreen. Dax toggled her color display to overprint the screen, and the purple-black explosion of the wormhole appeared just behind the stationary ships. "Remain cloaked and establish minimum-thrust orbit," he said again. Dax punched the course into her helm, and the *Defiant* rolled into a soft, energy-conserving ellipsoid around the Jem'Hadar station. "I want to see what's going on here before I decide what to do. Dax, scan for alien distribution."

"Scanning." She diverted one of the sensors from its focus on the wormhole, dimming the dark purple display to near invisibility. A flare of white-and-green alien concentrations bloomed inside the station when she reprogrammed it to scan for duranium, but not even the isolated blue specks of individual shelled aliens appeared in the surrounding space. "It doesn't look like they're doing anything to the Jem'Hadar ships, Benjamin. The aliens may need a while to recover from the unprotected warp exposure they just got."

Sisko smacked a fist into his palm with a frustrated slap. "Then why the hell did the Jem'Hadar stop short of the wormhole?"

From behind them, Ensign Hovan cleared her throat. "I might be wrong, sir—but I think that left-hand Jem'Hadar ship has switched its tractor beam to something else beside the station."

Dax frowned up at the viewscreen, seeing the slight

switch in angle and extension that meant Hovan was right. "I'm increasing magnification to see if I can detect what they're pulling in." The Jem'Hadar ships and station enlarged to fill the entire screen, and Dax focused in on the altered tractor beam, tracking it past the alien station to where it now terminated: at the tiny silhouette of a single floating figure in a radiation-shielded hardsuit. In the glittering phosphorescence of the tractor beam, the suit's markings were easy to read.

Sisko cursed, in a raw, startled voice Dax couldn't remember ever hearing from him before. She wasn't sure how he managed—the image on the viewscreen had left her completely speechless.

"What's the matter?" Heather Petersen glanced around the bridge, the puzzled look on her face deepening as she took in their stunned expressions. "All I see is someone in a hardsuit, getting hauled in from EV work. Maybe the Jem'Hadar had to stop for emergency hull repairs."

"I don't think so, Ensign." Although the shock had faded from Sisko's voice, he still sounded as amazed as Dax felt. "They wouldn't be using a hardsuit marked with *Deep Space Nine* insignia—and with no life-support attachments on its back."

"No life support?" Petersen repeated blankly. The distant suited figure was deliberately turning, as if it wanted to be sure the Jem'Hadar could see its tankless exterior. "How can someone be alive inside a hardsuit without life-support?"

"As far as I know, there's only one possible way." Sisko slammed a palm against the control on his makeshift communicator panel that opened all Starfleet frequencies. "Sisko to Odo. What the hell are you doing here, Constable?"

CHAPTER
20

"WE'VE GOT A hull breach!"

Dammit! Kira whirled away from the observation port near *Deep Space Nine*'s smallest airlock, turning her back on the spasming wormhole, the lingering image of Odo's tiny figure spiraling down that flaming abyss, and the bleak sadness on Bashir's face as he stared after Odo and the symbiont in uncharacteristic silence. She was almost glad for the interruption, relieved to drive off the melancholy with some form of productive action. "Where, Chief?"

"Habitat ring," his voice answered promptly, "section three."

A hollow, ringing bang echoed through the station's bones before Kira could even place the coordinates in relation to her and Bashir's position, then the brief, chilling roar of air blasting out into vacuum with such explosive force that it barely left a sound behind.

"And another in section twenty!" The sheer urgency of O'Brien's shout would have told Kira how nearby that was even if she hadn't felt the bulkhead's fracture. "Damn, but I was afraid of this!" he reported grimly. "I'm getting multiple duranium readings from all over the outside hull. Major, we're compromised."

But they'd had to drop the screens in order to send Odo through, and not sending him had ceased to be an option the moment Kira had knelt in front of the cloudy brine tank to speak to its ancient occupant. Any discussion about the wisdom of their actions was pointless now.

"Chief—" Bashir pulled himself away from the window with what Kira thought a very definitive resolve, drawing her with him down the hall as though he hadn't been the one holding them back. "Isolate those hull breaches as much as you can. If I'm right about what draws them, the viroids will be trying to reach the Promenade safe zones, and I don't think they'll let a little thing like bulkheads stand in their way."

The very thought of ripping the atmosphere from halls still lined with people made Kira's head ache. Grabbing Bashir's arm, she urged stiff muscles into a limping run.

"What about the shields?" she asked O'Brien, dragging the doctor down a side corridor to take them deeper into the station.

"Are they back up?"

"For now. I've still got fifty or sixty buggers skating around the screens on the side of the station we left shielded, and another hundred or so on the ship." He sounded as tightly stretched as a Vedek's drum. "I don't know how long we'll last."

"Pick off as many as you can inside our defenses," Kira ordered. "And use the personnel transporter in Ops, not the cargo unit!" Even if the delicately repaired power systems could survive the big transporter's draw—which Kira thought less likely by the minute—she didn't want to risk beaming entire sections of the station out into space until they ran out of other options.

O'Brien made a grumbling little sound of unhappiness. "That'll be slow going."

"It's only for starters." The deckplates shivered with another surge of brittle creaking, and Kira felt the heavy *thud-thud-thud* of emergency bulkheads slamming into place in corridors too empty of air to transmit sound along with the sensation. She tried to ignore the thin chill threading the metal of the turbolift controls when she punched at the call button with the heel of her hand. "I'll see if we can't initiate something faster from down here. Just buy me a little time."

"Not exactly something we're swimming in at the moment," the chief said morosely. Kira found herself smiling at the accuracy of his complaint as she pushed Bashir into the arriving lift. "I'll do what I can, Major. O'Brien out."

Bashir moved back against the wall of the lift, giving Kira room she didn't feel she needed as he crossed his hands behind him to grasp the inner rail. A few minutes with the tissue regenerator and a hypo full of stimulants had worked wonders—although dark smudges of exhaustion made his eyes seem even bigger and more attentive than usual, his complexion had rebounded to a dusky cinnamon that left him looking weary but reasonably functional. "What are you thinking?" he asked, his voice as calmly polite as if he'd been inquiring what she'd ordered for lunch.

Kira sighed and leaned back against the wall opposite him. "That we can't just wait for Sisko to solve his problems and come back here to save us," she said, meeting his earnest face with what she hoped was equal sincerity. "We've got to get rid of these things on our own."

The floor heaved powerfully, spastically beneath her, and Kira crashed to her knees with a horrible certainty that everything was finished, the station had died. Then her eyes locked with Bashir's where he'd fallen to all fours on the other side of the lift, and the unnatural stillness registered on her nerves like an electric shock: they were no longer moving.

A thump like the landing of a hundred booted feet thundered on the top of the lift. Craning a look skyward, Bashir suggested dryly, "Whatever your plan is, it had better be a doozy."

She was across the car before the last word left his lips, jerking one arm out from under him to knock him to the floor and clap her hand across his mouth. His eyes narrowed into an impatient scowl, and Kira felt his mouth twist with annoyance as he peeled her fingers away. "They're vacuum-adapted, Major," he told her while the busy clattering on the roof of the lift grew louder. "I doubt they've much in the way of ears."

Kira leaned half her weight into gagging him this time, and bent to put her lips almost against his ear. "Maybe not," she whispered fiercely, the words little more than angry breath, "but they just ate an entire Starfleet crew with perfectly good hearing, and I don't want to find out how quickly they can use that DNA!"

His eyes above the clench of her hand widened in silent horror, but he made no effort to comment. *Wonders never cease.*

The clamor overhead collected into a single knot of intense thunder, and Kira pushed away from Bashir to scrabble for the turbolift doors. They were the same ornate, clumsy slabs of metal the Cardassians had installed a dozen years ago, with only enough strength to keep the passengers from falling out and a lip almost as wide as Kira's hand to curl your fingers around. Her back complained with a waspish twinge as she struggled to haul one door aside, but Bashir scrambled to his feet to join her before she'd done more than grit her teeth against the discomfort, and their combined force wrenched the door open with deceptive ease.

Exposing a blank stretch of dull gray wall. *Between decks.*

Kira slammed a fist against her thigh, cursing silently, and Bashir mouthed a wide-eyed *What now?* as the entire lift trembled at a blow from above.

Good question. She put her back to the exposed shaft wall and swept the inside of the car with eyes that had once been well-practiced at seeing the weaknesses in machines. Without even knowing what she reacted to at first, her attention zeroed in on an access panel only as wide and as tall as the length of her arm. Access panels led to compartments. Compartments led to outside walls.

Outside walls could be broken.

She had the panel yanked off and resting awkwardly across her knees before Bashir had left the door to squat beside her. He took the door, settling it flat on the floor some meters away with amazing delicacy, then squeaked in inarticulate protest when Kira used both hands to tear a huge tangle of workings from the hole.

"Major—!" He managed to sound remarkably shocked, considering the circumstances.

She pushed the wad of circuits and cables at him, motioning for him to get rid of them as he had the access door. "It doesn't work anyway," she hissed, ripping out another load. "Do you want to get out of here, or don't you?"

He frowned, but disposed of the torn-out workings with the same swift efficiency he'd applied to the door. Kira was tempted to point out that they could requisition new components for the turbolifts—only the aliens had a similar option available for their bodies. She suspected he'd come to the same conclusion, though, when he leaned past her to tear out the next clot of workings on his own.

The outer skin of the turbolift trembled faintly from the pounding overhead when Kira found it with her hands. Feeling frantically along the edges, she bumped the ridged heads of permanent bolts instead of the inner hatch seal she'd expected to find. No access panel, then. Just standard Cardassian plating. Acid chewed at her stomach, and she squirmed back out of the hole with her mind racing in a ratlike whirl.

Sometimes, it was best not to think too hard before plunging down a path you'd been forced into following. Pulling her knees up to her chin, she grasped the rail above her head and blasted a two-footed kick at the outside panel without bothering to warn Bashir. Bootheels against metal rang through the lift like a warp-core explosion, jarring her teeth together with a painful *clack!*, and popping the sheet off its rivets with a scream of stripping threads. Reaching back to grab Bashir by the collar, she yanked him toward the opening as the plate tumbled away down the shaft below.

The scrabbling on the roof of the lift fell silent.

Bashir cocked a leery peek over his shoulder. "So much for subtlety."

"Go! Go!" She pushed him through the opening with both her hands and feet, trying not to beat him in her own panic to clear out of the lift and be gone. Time paced itself to the pounding of her heart instead of seconds, and the few moments she was sure it must have taken Bashir to crawl through the access seemed an anguished eternity. Halfway through, he squirmed onto his back, scraping for purchase on the floor of the lift with one foot, then slid cleanly out of sight. She hoped desperately that he'd pulled himself through somehow, and hadn't had unwanted help from above.

Beside her, something struck the deck with a fragile little

tick, and a ragged circle of metal next to Kira's hand began to bubble.

A great, curving scythe pierced the roof of the lift. There must have been some sound, some scraping of monster on metal, but Kira heard nothing as they split the car open as though it were soft butter. Fluid the color of plasma drizzled from a huge claw tip, cutting a sizzling line across the floor, and Kira grabbed the edges of the hole to shoot herself through without waiting to see what intended to follow the acid inside.

Her legs hit open air beyond the outside edge of the access, and hands gripped her ankles in almost that same instant, guiding her toward a narrow bar that she could hook with her feet even as an arm looped strongly about her middle and pulled. For some reason, she hadn't expected Bashir to be so athletic; he clung to the emergency ladder by the virtue of one hand and one leg locked around an upright, pulling her across to join him by bracing his other leg against the side of the car for leverage. Kira grabbed at the rungs with a breathless nod of startled gratitude. "Keep moving!" Then she hooked her feet around the outside of the ladder, took the uprights lightly in her hands, and let artificial gravity take her on a quick slide straight down.

She didn't pay attention to decks, or distances, or anything besides the damnably unchanging contours of the wall beside her. Only when it swelled open into a lift-sized tunnel of black did she tighten her grip on the ladder and jerk herself to a stop. Discomforting warmth itched across the surface of her palms, and she suspected she'd left more than just a few layers of skin behind on the slick metal. A small price to pay. Swinging sideways into the tunnel, she jigged on adrenaline overload, blowing on her hands, and waited for Bashir to climb in behind her.

And waited.

There was no doubt in Sisko's mind that the person in the hardsuit had heard him—even at this distance, he could see the involuntary turn of the head that followed his inquiry, although he knew there would be nothing to see with the *Defiant* cloaked. A moment later, a familiar dry voice emerged from howling static to say, "—moment, Captain, I am attempting to convince the Jem'Hadar—"

Sisko scowled. "Dax, can we boost Odo's signal?"

The Trill shook her head without taking her eyes from her sensor controls. "Hardsuit transmitters aren't designed for ship-to-ship distances, Benjamin. All you can do is reduce the static from the wormhole by attenuating all frequencies except the central band."

Sisko grunted, toggling switches on his makeshift communications board. The banshee howl faded to a more bearable hiss. "Odo, repeat transmission."

With the static reduced, the exasperation in Odo's voice was plain to hear. "I said, at the moment, I am attempting to convince the Jem'Hadar that they shouldn't dump their garbage into other people's wormholes. Do you have an objection?"

"Not in the slightest." Sisko scrubbed a hand across his face, blessing his security chief's adamant sense of right and wrong. Without even knowing what was going on, the one being whom the Jem'Hadar would obey without question had managed to avert catastrophe, at least for now. "Can you order them to—"

Dax swung around before Odo could reply. "It's too late for the Jem'Hadar to do anything, Benjamin. Look at the station."

Sisko cursed. Fountains of white-green fire were exploding from the ruptured Jem'Hadar station as the aliens inside boiled out with the wasplike fury Dax had predicted. "Odo, tell the Jem'Hadar to release their tractor beam so we can transport you to safety!" He didn't wait for a reply, leaping down to join Dax at the helm. "Prepare to beam Odo over as soon as he's free. Any sign that the aliens are heading for us?"

She shook her head. "The cloaking device and our low-energy orbit aren't attracting their attention—and I've routed our waste heat to the internal heat exchangers this time. They should be able to soak it up for at least an hour."

"According to Petersen, that's all the time we'll have anyway." Sisko glanced up at the viewscreen. The onslaught of alien attackers had begun to crash down on the two Jem'Hadar warships, making their shields glow and spark with contact. Both ships began to fire their phasers in return, in random sprays of short-range energy. The translucent glitter of the tractor beam was still pulling Odo's suited figure closer to the maelstrom. Sisko scowled and stabbed at his communicator controls.

"Odo, have you told the Jem'Hadar to release the tractor beam?"

"They don't appear to be paying much attention to me right now, Captain," his security officer said dryly. "I recommend you come up with an alternative strategy."

Dax glanced up at Sisko. "If we drop our cloak for a moment, we can send out a tractor beam programmed to neutralize theirs," she suggested.

He nodded. "We'll have to decloak to transport Odo aboard anyway." A quick glance over his shoulder caught Heather Petersen's expectant gaze. "Ensign, get down to the transporter room and prepare to lock on to Odo as soon as we drop our cloak. Hovan, I want minimum decloaking exposure. Synchronize your controls and make sure you get us cloaked again as soon as Odo's on board."

"Aye-aye, sir," they said in unison; then Petersen shot toward the turbolift, leaving Hovan to reprogram her cloaking controls. Sisko swung back to the viewscreen. The shields of the right-hand Jem'Hadar ship were dimming beneath the piled mass of alien bodies, and its random phaser bursts were slowing, a sure indication of power drain. "Status of battle, Mr. Eddington?"

"Starboard warship has shields at twenty percent and phaser controls at fifty percent," the weapons officer reported. "Destruction expected in two minutes or less. Port warship is less heavily engaged and may survive another four minutes before destruction."

Sisko made a swift decision, and opened all hailing frequencies on his communicator. "This is the *U.S.S. Defiant*, hailing the Jem'Hadar," he said curtly. "You are in imminent danger of destruction. If you drop your shields on my mark, we will beam you to safety."

A Jem'Hadar face appeared on screen, its serrated chin plates dripping with condensation in a ship's atmosphere overheated by failing shields. Sisko couldn't be sure which of the two pilots he was seeing. "Why should I believe you?" the warrior demanded. "You attacked us first!"

"Only to prevent the destruction—" Sisko broke off as the viewscreen flashed with the vapor-white explosion of a hull breach washing over them at close range. He shot a fierce scowl at Dax. "Is that tractor beam still on?"

"I'm afraid so." Her slim fingers flew across her panel faster than any human's could have, powered by the ferocious intellect of two cerebral cortices working in unison. "Our neutralizing tractor beam is ready to engage. We can drop cloak on your command."

Sisko stabbed at his communicator controls again. "Jem'Hadar warship, this is your final chance," he said to the last warship, glowing fiercely now under its swarm of alien attackers. "Drop shields when you see us decloak and we'll transport you aboard along with the Founder."

There was no reply. Sisko cast an assessing look at the shortening distance between Odo and the flare of battle, and felt the muscles of his jaw tighten with decision.

"Hovan, drop cloak *now,*" he commanded. "Dax, engage tractor beam. Petersen, prepare to transport."

As sometimes happened in high-precision starship battles, the actual maneuver took less time to perform than his orders.

"Cloaking device disengaged—" said Hovan.

"Tractor beam locked and nullified," said Dax, in overlapping echo. The fierce glitter of their own tractor beam, dark gray to the Jem'Hadar's pale silver, slapped out like a snake striking through the darkness. "Petersen, begin—"

"Transporter beam locked and activated," said Petersen's voice, before Dax had even finished speaking. "Transport complete, Captain."

"Cloaking device reengaged," Hovan reported promptly. "We're cloaked again, Captain."

Sisko took a deep breath, cut off abruptly when the screen frosted with another ghost-white hull breach. He waited until the outward burst of gas and vapor had cleared around them, leaving the *Defiant* alone with the alien-occupied station. The bright sprays of white and green that marked high concentrations of aliens were swirling like angry wasps around the shattered remnants of the Jem'Hadar fighters. "Any sign of aliens heading in our direction?"

Dax shook her head. "I'm not picking up anything, on either the duranium-keyed scan or the close-range motion sensor. They may not be sensitive to short energy discharges like that tractor-beam pulse."

Sisko grunted and turned toward Eddington. "How fast is the station heading toward the wormhole now, Commander?"

Eddington answered in the slightly-too-fast voice of a man still running on battle adrenaline. "One of the Jem'Hadar's tractor beams was still attached when it was breached. The residual momentum from that is actually pushing the station farther away from the wormhole right now. I don't know how long it will take the aliens to realize that and make course corrections, but it's in no immediate danger of falling into the wormhole."

"Good." Sisko stretched with a sudden bone-cracking release of tension. "That gives me time to find out why Constable Odo decided to take a slalom ride through an unstable wormhole. Dax, you have the comm. Notify me the instant that station reverses direction."

His science officer swung around to give him a severely meaningful look. "With your permission, Captain, I think I should come with you down to the transporter room."

Sisko lifted an eyebrow, recognizing the fierce Joran tone that meant he disagreed with the Trill at his peril. "You want to talk to Odo, too, old man?"

"No," she said bluntly. "I want to talk to myself."

Kira knew Bashir was dead.

She knew it with a certainty that made her stomach burn as she leaned out into the shaft and looked back up the ladder. If the aliens hadn't caught him and torn him into pieces smaller than the fragment Odo had found, Kira would do it for them, just to pay him back for fraying her nerves to such a splintered jangle.

"Doctor!" No sense trying to be quiet anymore—it wasn't like the aliens didn't know they were there. She watched Bashir's brisk hand-over-hand progress down the ladder with her fingernails dug into her palms, knowing it was dangerously fast for someone not accustomed to working on ladders every day, fearing that it wasn't fast enough. "*Hurry,* goddammit! We're supposed to be fleeing!"

He glared down at her without slowing. "I'd rather not break both my legs in the process, if it's all the same to you."

Kira growled, wishing he were close enough to hit. "I'll break both your legs . . ." she grumbled. But she didn't pull back into the tunnel, afraid he'd vanish for real if she let him out of her sight.

The stench of corroded metal blossomed through the open shaft. What seemed only an arm's length from her face, acid twisted in a sparkling ribbon, and Kira jerked a horrified look toward the stopped car above them just as it shuddered, tilted, and dropped a dozen rapid meters.

"Julian!"

Fear stiffened him so sharply, Kira was afraid he'd freeze while still within the aliens' reach. Instead, he didn't even waste a glance at the crash and scrabble overhead. Straddling the ladder, he tucked his chin to his chest and surrendered to the controlled fall. Kira stepped out onto the rungs, into his path, and braced herself to stop him before he could slide past. He hit her with less force than she expected, but still enough to jar her feet off the rungs and send her heart leaping into her throat as she flailed to recover her hold. She lost track of which of them clambered into the side passage first—all she knew was that the light in the turbolift shaft seemed to constrict abruptly, roaring like a summer storm, and she felt the weight of the Prophets rushing down toward her head just as she tackled Bashir and dragged him away from the tunnel's opening.

The turbolift crashed past in an angry blur. Flat, segmented forms clung like ticks to its roof and sides, looking too much like machines themselves to be easily separated from the metal. Kira recoiled instinctively, blind to any thought but her inborn compulsion to protect anything more helpless than herself. Locking her arms around the doctor despite his indignant yelp, she whirled him away from the entrance and beyond the snaking grasp of one of the viroid creatures.

It slapped the deck with a thick, three-fingered paw,

curling its digits to grip at the decking as its black-mantled body hurtled past. *It'll slip!* Kira thought, a desperate wish as much as a realization. *Its weight'll pull it down the shaft!* But the bang of its carapace striking the wall outside only dislodged its grip by a millimeter, and three glossy talons the color of polished hematite halted even that tiny movement by shooting down into the decking as though it were cork. She couldn't see muscles flex through the translucent sheen of its carapace, but she heard the crack and grind of its power along every joint and seam. A second, more insectoid appendage joined the first, tapping daintily at the walls, and the creature hauled itself above the lip of the passageway to peel open the long vertical slash of its mouth—

—only to vanish in an ear-shattering blast. Three deep, sharp grooves torn into the floor of the shaft were all that marked where it had gone. High overhead, a shrill whoop of triumph clapped off the turboshaft walls.

"For some jobs, nothing beats explosive percussion!"

Kira wondered if she was supposed to feel lucky, or if they'd just traded one problem for another.

When they crawled to the mouth of the tunnel, Pak grinned down at them from a distinctly nonregulation rift in the wall high above where the turbolift had been. Switching the heavy, wide-bore shotgun over to her left hand, she snapped Kira a manic salute, and loosed another exultant howl.

"Well?" she hollered, waving them up with such exuberance Kira was sure she'd overbalance and fall. "Close your mouths and get up here—we've got bugs to kill!"

"All right, whose idea was this?" Sisko growled.

Fortunately, Odo was as impervious to human fury as he was to Ferengi whining. "According to Dr. Bashir, my passenger was the one who insisted on coming." His stern dignity wasn't even hindered by the enormously pregnant bulge in his abdomen, at which Dax was looking with a mixture of disbelief and dismay. Inside, according to Odo, was a volume of hyperoxygenated and isoboromine-spiked brine sufficient to maintain the ancient symbiont on their passage through the wormhole. That hadn't seemed to reassure Dax much—after a momentary ansible trance, she'd sent Heather Petersen running for the spare brine tank Bashir had sent with them. "He said you would need it to save the wormhole."

Sisko exchanged a long, assessing look with Dax. "That has to be true," the Trill said at last. "Julian would never have agreed to send the symbiont into danger otherwise—"

"Which means the ancient symbiont knows something about this mess that we don't." Sisko stepped back as the transporter room doors hissed apart to admit Petersen and Dr. Bashir's assistant, rolling a cartful of tank and tubing before them.

"Considering all of this is déjà vu for it, I'd say that's understandable." Odo's bulging midsection abruptly flowed up and out to engulf the cart in streaming liquid changeling, making the Bajoran medic gasp and step back. The tank abruptly filled with a glittering wash of brine and squirming symbiont. Dax had both hands immersed and wrapped around the symbiont before Odo had even finished recongealing into his humanoid form. Sisko watched the worried lines on the Trill's face smooth into the now-familiar blankness of trance.

"All right, Constable," he said softly, so as not to break Jadzia's concentration. "How bad are things aboard *Deep Space Nine?*"

His security officer made a gruff noise that was not quite a snort and not quite a laugh. "Bad enough that sending me in a hardsuit through the wormhole seemed like our best alternative. Need I say more?"

Sisko scowled. There were times when he wished Odo had a little more Starfleet training and a little less of his own peculiar sense of humor. "Is the station being attacked by the aliens on the other side of the wormhole?"

Odo cocked his head, his equivalent of a lifted eyebrow. "If by aliens, you're referring to viroidal vacuum-adapted organisms who appear to steal DNA and ship reaction masses with equal facility," he said with careful precision, "the answer is yes."

"Are they on board *Deep Space Nine?*" Sisko speared the changeling with a fierce glare. *"How many?"*

"When I left, only one," his security officer replied.

"Outside, there were enough to take out three Bajoran ore freighters, one Lethian transport, and the starship *Mukaikubo*, not to mention an entire wing of the Bajoran militia. My guess is about two hundred. We managed to disassemble some of them with the cargo transporter, and Major Kira has closed down all the station's outer decks as a hull-breach buffer. I think she hopes to lure them in there and kill them."

"Luring them's not the difficult part," Sisko said grimly. "It's killing them afterward that's hard."

"So we've noticed," Odo agreed.

A soft splash from the brine tank yanked Sisko's attention back to his science officer. Dax was still staring down at her immersed hands, oblivious of the wetness soaking up her uniform sleeves, but a horrified expression had replaced her previous blankness. The wetness glistening on her cheeks could have just been splashed brine, but something about the rigid way she was breathing told Sisko differently. He went to stand behind her, his hands dropping to her shoulders and squeezing hard.

"What's the matter, old man?" he demanded.

The Trill dragged in a spasmodic breath. "The old symbiont—it heard us talking about T'Kreng's plan to infiltrate the aliens, Benjamin. It's coherent now and it thinks it should be the one to go—" She took in another heaving breath. "And *Dax* agrees with it!"

Ah—so this was Jadzia talking. Sisko bit back the acid comment he would have made to Curzon and replaced it with a carefully neutral question. "You don't?"

"No!" She swung around to scowl up at him. "A Trill's first responsibility is to keep her symbiont alive, you know that! I can't sentence any version of Dax to certain death—"

"Even if it means saving another version from five thousand years of solitary confinement?" He shook her gently. "Jadzia, stop thinking of the old Dax symbiont as a thing you have to protect! It's an extension of you—and don't tell me you wouldn't sacrifice yourself *and* your symbiont if that was the only way to save the entire quadrant from this alien invasion."

"Of course I would," she said without hesitation. Then

her blue-gray eyes darkened. "But it's too late now, Benjamin. Even if we infiltrate the alien core in the Jem'Hadar station, we can't blow it up. It's too close to the wormhole."

"We can tow it—" he began.

Dax shook her head. "Not from a dead stop. I did the calculations just before we came down here. The *Defiant* is powerful, but it can't match the acceleration of five Jem'Hadar warships. That's the minimum thrust we'd need to get the station into warp fast enough to keep from being attacked."

Sisko vented his frustration in a snarl. "Don't tell me there's nothing we can do now, Dax, because I *don't* want to hear it. After everything we've gone through—and everything Odo's done to help us—I refuse to stand here and just watch the wormhole be destroyed!"

From across the transporter room, Heather Petersen cleared her throat hesitantly. "Um—Captain? Remember you asked me if I could think of some other way to destroy the Jem'Hadar station, beside firing our phasers at their reaction core?"

"Have you?" he demanded intently.

"I think so, sir." The cadet glanced at Dax. "Isn't it true that most self-destruct sequences are designed to release the containment fields around the reaction mass before they explode it, so it scatters harmlessly into space? Just in case other vessels are nearby?"

"Yes, of course."

"Do you think the self-destruct sequence programmed into the Jem'Hadar station would work the same way?"

Sisko frowned. "Probably," he said before Dax could answer. "But that doesn't do us any good, Ensign. We can't initiate the Jem'Hadar's self-destruct sequence without the proper code."

"I know," she said. "But I thought maybe you could convince him to give it to us."

Sisko's frown became a scowl. "Convince *who?*"

"The Jem'Hadar pilot I beamed out of the second warship when it dropped its shields." Petersen turned toward Dr. Bashir's assistant, oblivious of Sisko's astounded expression. "He wasn't hurt too badly to talk, was he, Meris?"

The Bajoran medic shook her head. "No. In fact, he

called me so many names while I was treating him that I finally had to put him in stasis just to shut him up. He certainly didn't seem very happy to be rescued."

"Probably because he didn't drop his shields on purpose," Sisko guessed. "They must have failed at exactly the moment you were trying to beam him out, Ensign."

Petersen winced. "Then I suppose he wouldn't agree to give the self-destruct sequence to us." She glanced back at Sisko apologetically. "Do you think we can drug or hypnotize him into doing it, sir?"

"I don't believe that will be necessary, Ensign," Odo said with dark amusement. "Just take him out of stasis and leave him to me."

CHAPTER
21

THEY BROUGHT THE old Dax back to the medical bay with them. There was really no good reason to, since the self-contained brine tank O'Brien had made would have functioned perfectly well wherever they left it, but Dax couldn't bring herself to leave the ancient symbiont alone with the transporter that would soon be sending it into a suicidal battle.

"—not a millennium too soon—" Even standing in the turbolift, Jadzia could hear the echo of her other self in her mind, although it wasn't possible to reply without sliding into the concentration of ansible trance. The pleasure she heard in the ancient symbiont's voice confirmed what her physical contact with it had already told her—it was not only coherent again, it was totally committed to carrying out T'Kreng's battle plan. "—I've been waiting for this ever since Julian died—"

Dax shivered at that matter-of-fact statement, then caught the concerned glance Sisko threw at her. "You okay, old man?"

"Jadzia's a little shaky, but both Daxes seem to be fine," she admitted ruefully. "Between the three of us, I think we'll manage."

Odo snorted, flattening himself back against the turbolift wall so Yevlin Meris could wheel the occupied brine tank out into the passageway. "I hope so, Lieutenant. Otherwise, we'll all be collecting our pensions by the time we make it back to *Deep Space Nine*. Assuming these viroids don't destroy civilization as we know it in the meantime," he added acidly.

Sisko paused in front of the medical bay to give his security officer an exasperated look. "Constable, have you ever heard of the power of positive thinking?"

"I was taught about it on Bajor," Odo admitted, following him inside. "As I recall, they considered it one of the defining myths of the human psyche."

"Well, it was a myth that Curzon shared," Dax retorted. She paused beside the brine tank, which Yevlin had tucked into a back corner of the medical bay, and pressed a hand against its reassuring warmth. An ivory glimmer emerged from the gray-green brine and pressed itself urgently against the glass on the other side.

"—talk to the entrapped Vulcan—" said the ancient symbiont's voice in her mind. "—things I must know—"

Dax nodded and glanced over at the stasis tables. The alien fragment still lay belly-up under the nearest pale-blue shimmer, unmoving. The other stasis field guarded the surviving Jem'Hadar pilot. He'd lost one leg and half his facial crest to whatever explosion had destroyed his shields, and most of his chest glowed pale-pink with regenerated flesh, but his expression was still one of frozen fury, not pain. Dax wondered if the genetically engineered warriors *could* feel pain.

"Captain, the other Dax wants to ask T'Kreng some questions," she said quietly. "Can Petersen and I release her from stasis while you talk to the Jem'Hadar?"

Sisko lifted an eyebrow at her. "How will you ask her questions if you're entranced at the time, old man?"

Dax gave Yevlin Meris an inquiring look. "You said my isoboromine levels rose when I went into trance. It may be that losing consciousness is due to that side effect, not to the ansible connection itself. If you could monitor my isoboromine and keep it stable—"

"It might work," Yevlin agreed, and went to get a hypospray from a supply cabinet.

"If it does," Dax said even more quietly, for Sisko's ears

alone, "I'll be able to tell you as soon as Dax succeeds in taking over the alien core—or as soon as it fails."

Sisko nodded grim agreement. "In which case, we'll try the tuned phasers as a last resort." He gave Odo an ironic look. "Ready to play Founder, Constable?"

Odo nodded. "I'll restrain him as soon as you drop the stasis field. That should keep his—er—irritation with us in check."

"And if not, I've got a phaser." The blue glimmer rolled into invisibility as Sisko released the control, and Odo's hands closed around the Jem'Hadar's wrists with a steely snap. The warrior spit out a long curse that sounded like a hyena's bark.

"Are you ready to try talking to T'Kreng, Lieutenant?" Petersen asked. Yevlin Meris stood at her shoulder, hypospray ready in one hand.

Dax spread her fingers across the front of the brine tank, catching a faint hint of the symbiont's electric sizzle through the transparent aluminum. For some reason, she didn't want to move away from that tingling connection. "Can your microphone pick me up from here, Heather?"

"No problem." The cadet squatted beside the stasis table, fitting her phase modulator over the controls. "Dropping stasis now."

The second blue glimmer of stasis faded. "Well?" demanded T'Kreng's silk-cold voice. "Have you failed yet in your attempt to destroy the aliens with your ship's weapons?"

Dax saw Sisko cast an irritated look over his shoulder at the second stasis table. "Yes," she said, before he could start to argue with what was left of the Vulcan physicist. "And we plan to infiltrate the core as you suggested—"

"Tell me the self-destruct sequence of the station you were towing here," said Odo.

"I have heard of you. You are not a true Founder. And I will not cooperate with Federation scum!" the Jem'Hadar pilot snarled. "These vermin probably came from their side of the wormhole—" He nodded at Sisko and the others.

"—but we have some questions to ask you first," Dax finished, hoping the Vulcan's partial brain could sort out the several conversations going on around her. She took a deep breath and nodded at Yevlin Meris, then reached down into herself for the tidal swash and pull of the ansible connection, ocean-deep now that the second symbiont was only a few centimeters away. She barely felt the cool hiss when Yevlin injected the isoboromine suppressor, but the white haze that had begun to thicken around her senses boiled away again, leaving her feeling vaguely disconnected but quite aware of what was going on around her.

"I need to know how to establish connections with like-minded subsidiary cortical masses," she said, and although it was Jadzia's lips making the words, it was the mind of ancient Dax that thought them, "in order to establish a network which can dominate all preexisting networks inside the core."

"That is indeed the crux of the infiltration problem," T'Kreng's crystalline voice agreed, sounding a little surprised by her perceptiveness. "The neural connections are not a problem. The aliens' messenger RNA will establish those on a cellular level as soon as you come in contact with them."

"And they can be used as communications networks immediately?" Dax asked.

"Yes," said T'Kreng. "My strategy was simply to broadcast my identity through the neural network in as many languages as I could, and listen to the replies I got. In my immediate alien environment, I found one of my shipmates that way, as well as one like-minded Ferengi. While I was still connected to the larger core, I also got echoes from others of my crew, as well as several other engulfed minds, old and new, who appeared to understand Standard English. Including several Jem'Hadar."

"Who speaks of Jem'Hadar?" The warship pilot's eyes rolled sideways and widened at the sound of T'Kreng's voice emanating from the fragment of bloody flesh next to him. "I knew it! The vermin are members of the Federation!"

"No, the vermin have *eaten* members of the Federation." Odo thumped the Jem'Hadar soundly against the table when he tried to lunge at the alien fragment. "The same way they've eaten Jem'Hadar. And they'll eat a lot more of you, if you don't tell us the self-destruct sequence for your station!"

"I'll tell you *nothing,*" the warrior shouted fiercely. "You're lying!"

"No," said a new and deeply graveled voice. "He's not."

The Jem'Hadar jerked against Odo's hold, his dark eyes rolling sideways again. A wash of almost supernatural awe swept the fury from his face at last. "Commander Kaddo'Borawn?" he demanded. "Where—where are you?"

"Dead," the Jem'Hadar voice said bluntly. "And eaten by the alien vermin, just as this Federation Founder told you. But I survive as a mind inside it, as do many of our brothers. They must be freed to real death, Manan'Agar. The station must be destroyed."

The Jem'Hadar warrior made a frustrated movement of his hands, as if he would have slammed his fists into something if Odo hadn't been holding them in his steely grip. "Exactly what we planned to do, Commander!" he said hotly. "We would have cast the station with its vermin horde into the wormhole to be crushed, if these awards had not stopped us."

This time, the hyena-bark cursing sound came from Dax's jury-rigged Universal Translator. "The alien vermin would have abandoned the station before the wormhole destroyed it, as they always planned to do once they arrived there. And our brothers would have lived forever inside that vile imprisonment—as I would have, if not for the Federation female who controls this vermin fragment. We must destroy them outside the wormhole, Manan'Agar, and we must destroy them utterly." The gravelly Jem'Hadar voice paused. "I would tell them how to do it, myself, if this part of my brain remembered. It does not. You must tell them how to blow the station up. And then you must make sure they do it. Will you honor this command from a dead man?"

The Jem'Hadar warrior swallowed convulsively, then jerked his head sideways in what Dax hoped was a Jem'Hadar nod. Sisko made an ominous growling noise, and Odo shot him a reassuring look. "I believe Manan'Agar has just agreed to cooperate with us," the security chief said. "Hasn't he?"

"Yes." The warship pilot's voice sounded almost sulky. "But you must promise to kill me afterward."

Sisko let out an exasperated breath. "I'll add you to my list," he said. "Provided there *is* an afterward. Now, what's the self-destruct sequence for that station?"

The Jem'Hadar took a deep breath. "Self-destruct."

Dax saw Odo and Sisko exchange skeptical looks. "That's it?" the security officer demanded. "All you have to do is say 'self-destruct' and the entire station blows up?"

"Of course." Manan'Agar drew himself up on his elbows, looking baffled. "What else would you need?"

Sisko cleared his throat. "How about a voiceprint security identification? Or a seconded command from another officer?"

The injured pilot made an impatient coughing sound that seemed to signify irritation. "Starfleet bureaucrats may need such things, but the Jem'Hadar do not. Any one of us must be able to destroy our stations alone, because after a lost battle, one may be all that is left. And if that one is injured or dying, why make it more difficult than it needs to be?"

Odo shook his head, looking baffled himself. "But if an enemy came on board, how would you prevent *them* from giving a self-destruct order?"

"Simple." Manan'Agar's dark lips pulled back to bare his scaled teeth in a grimace that might have been meant to convey anything from amusement to disgust. "None of our enemies knows our language. We are careful never to speak it around them."

The information reached Jadzia through a serene detachment that seemed to settle on her like snow the longer she stayed linked with the ancient symbiont. It might be coherent now, she thought in sudden realization, but millennia of solitary confinement had still left their mark on its psyche. She took a deep breath, and threw off the numbing tranquillity with an effort. "So that's why the Jem'Hadar always speak the language of their adversaries?" she demanded.

Odo grunted. "They do it because they are genetically programmed to learn languages within moments of first hearing them, Lieutenant. It gives them a distinct tactical advantage over races that depend on Universal Translators." He frowned down at the Jem'Hadar. "All right, then. How *do* you say 'self-destruct' in your language?"

Manan'Agar's dark eyes flashed with scorn. "I will not tell *you* that. I will tell only the one who goes to destroy the station."

Sisko cast an exasperated glance at the brine tank beside Dax. "That may be a little difficult. Right now, the—er—organism we're sending to destroy the station can only see and hear through its mental link with my science officer."

The Jem'Hadar's puzzled gaze traveled from the tank to Dax, still standing with her palm pressed to its window. "Then your science officer will be going with it to the station?"

"No," Sisko said flatly. "We'll be transporting it straight into the aliens' central core—straight into their brain."

Manan'Agar spat out another untranslatable curse. "Impossible. When we tried to transport a photon torpedo into that mass of vermin, the output of subspace energy from their stolen power cores disrupted the beam and made it totally incoherent. And that was not even a living organism!"

"Damn!" Sisko swung around to scowl at Dax and Heather Petersen. "Are we going to have the same problem?"

Dax threw a questioning look at the younger scientist, knowing she had more expertise in transport physics. Petersen chewed at her lower lip for a moment, looking increasingly worried. "I'm afraid so," she admitted at last. "We could try to compensate by increasing the confinement field on the transporter beam, or we could just try to get a coherent beam in as close to the core as we can—"

The cadet broke off abruptly, but Odo finished her thought with his own relentless logic. "—and send the symbiont in with someone who can carry it the rest of the way."

"Unacceptable, Constable," Sisko said flatly. "We'll have to find another way to get the symbiont into the core."

Dax frowned at him, feeling a tidal wave of urgency crash through the ansible link. Before she could find the words to express it, however, T'Kreng's crystalline voice had already broken the somber silence. "That may be an ethically responsible goal, Captain Sisko, but it is one that will be impossible to achieve. The singularity matrix will undergo irreversible chronologic displacement approximately thrity-five minutes from now."

"Well, that gives us enough time to—"

"No!" The Vulcan's voice rose to an unexpected shout, buoyed by a sudden infusion of Jem'Hadar ferocity. "The Trill symbiont you're sending will need *at least* that much time to form a neural network strong enough to dominate the rest of the core. Every minute—every second!—you delay now could cost it the time it needs to save the wormhole."

Dax exchanged troubled glances with Sisko and Odo, seeing the same bleak acceptance creep into both their faces. She took a deep breath, flexing her hand against the chill of the brine-tank window. "Then it's settled," she said at last. "One of us has to take the symbiont into the alien core."

"Yes." The steel-hard set of Sisko's jaw told Dax he had finally accepted the necessity of what they had to do. "How do we decide who goes?"

"That's the easy part, Captain." Odo's pale eyes glittered with sardonic humor, although Dax had no idea what he could find amusing about this situation. "All you need to do is ask for a volunteer."

"What the hell are you doing down here?"

They'd had to wait for what felt like an hour while Pak and her cronies hunted up a length of purloined bulkhead to lay a makeshift bridge. It wasn't hanging on the ladder that had eaten away at Kira's patience as much as the awareness that very little prevented the aliens from scuttling across them again. She didn't want to count on being so lucky the next time.

"What do you think I'm doing down here?" Pak tossed a crooked grin back at Kira as she caught Bashir by one elbow and pulled him off the ersatz platform to relative safety. "I've still got another twenty-three of those things to kill before I start to break even for what they did to us."

Bashir flicked a disdainful wave at the gun balanced across Pak's shoulder, and Kira noticed that his hands were shaking, ever so slightly. He was running on nothing but the stimulants and adrenaline by now, she realized. It wouldn't be long before they lost him to exhaustion completely. "If that's what you've been using," Bashir told Pak in a voice already hoarse from too much excitement, "you haven't killed any of them. At best, you've inconvenienced them a little."

Pak shrugged and nodded her people off down the corridor ahead of them. "I'll settle for inconvenienced until somebody thinks of a better idea."

"I'm working on that. But first—" Kira flashed her hand up behind Pak's neck, snatching the still-warm barrel of her antique weapon and sweeping it out of her grasp. The old-fashioned weapons had been popular among the resistance when Kira was young—easier to stockpile than phasers, since the Cardassians' weapon scans only looked for more modern energy weapons. The militia had probably managed to hide this one on the station in much the same way. Pak grumbled with an adolescent pout, but didn't resist when Kira slipped back the gun's chamber and pulled out all six of its remaining slugs as they walked. "The last thing we need is you putting a 100-caliber hole through the bulkhead."

"I didn't hear you complaining a few minutes ago." She stretched out her hand to reclaim the gun, then grimaced again when Kira switched it to her other arm to keep it out of reach.

"What about the rest of your crew?" Kira demanded. "Are there more of these?"

"Maybe," Pak shrugged. "Probably. My people had weapon components stowed all over this station. It took me a while to find all the pieces for this one, but I've got enough spare parts to say there's probably at least two more of 'em scattered around. Why?" She grinned wickedly and bumped Kira with her elbow. "You want some more?"

For just an instant, Kira was sorry she'd emptied the gun. "I want to know that I can trust you! I want to know that while I'm trying to haul our butts out of the fire, you're not running around behind my back screwing everything up!"

"Since when does saving you and pretty boy from the lunch rush count as a screwup?"

"You know damn—!"

"All right, both of you, *stop it!*" Bashir pushed between

them with a force that startled Kira, shoving her back against one wall of the corridor and Pak against the other. "I don't know if either of you has noticed," he whispered fiercely, "but we're not exactly in the best position to indulge this little androgen display right now." An angry sweep of his arm encompassed their whole section of station. "There are aliens crawling all over these decks! Instead of butting heads to decide which of you is really queen of the hill, you should be getting us to the Promenade ahead of the viroids!"

Kira wasn't sure which was worse—being in debt for her life to the dictionary definition of "militant radical," or being lectured on duty by a Starfleet doctor whose idea of a rough childhood was having to pay for your own tennis lessons. Fighting back a scowl of embarrassment, she clapped an arm around Bashir's shoulders and pulled him alongside as she pushed through the little knot of militia.

"That's the second time you've mentioned the aliens heading for the safe zones," she said. "What do you know that I don't?"

Bashir tipped his head in uncharacteristic reluctance. "It's only a theory. . . ."

Pak jabbed at him from behind. "Spit it out!"

Kira tossed the militia leader a warning scowl, but if anything, Pak's rough insistence seemed to wake up some of the doctor's usual enthusiasm.

"Well, we already know that they coopt DNA." He ducked out from under Kira's arm, turning sideways so he could face the small group and still keep them walking at the brisk pace Kira had set. "It's obviously vital to the structure of their own genetics, vital to what their bodies do and how, probably vital to whatever passes among them as reproductive success. It only makes sense, then, that they must have some way to analyze the genetic makeup of their potential victims. If they didn't have some built-in drive to seek out genetic material not already assimilated into their structure, the behavior itself wouldn't persist. They'd make do with a finite set of traits, and pass those on to future generations the way every other life-form does."

Catching sight of a cross-corridor that led deeper into the station, Kira turned them without warning and had to lean out to snag Bashir and guarantee he made the turn with them. "So what you're saying," she prompted as he jogged to catch up, "is that if they've never 'assimilated' a Bajoran before, that makes them *want* to eat Bajorans?"

"In a manner of speaking, yes."

Pak snorted loudly, spitting dryly toward the wall. "These things have eaten plenty of Bajorans."

Bashir shook his head, lean face youthfully earnest. "We don't know that." He held up his hands to silence her before she could do more than open her mouth to disagree. "We know they raided four ore carriers," he elaborated hastily, "and that you lost twenty-four of your people. That's perhaps fifty Bajorans, all total. There are *hundreds* of those things out there—they can't *all* have assimilated Bajoran DNA. Even if they have, they most likely *haven't* encountered Ferengi, or Vulcans, or Tellerites, or Klingons." He turned plaintive eyes on Kira, as though to make sure she was listening. "We've got all of those and more gathered down in the safe zones."

She'd been more than listening. She'd been thinking two steps ahead. "No wonder you thought they'd make their way to the Promenade."

Bashir nodded bleakly. "They shouldn't be able to resist it."

"So what are we waiting for?" Pak skipped eagerly forward, drumming her palms on Kira's back as though they were wartime comrades and soul-tight friends. "If we know where they're going, let's meet them there and do some damage!"

"Because people might get hurt!" Frustrated anger flushed Bashir's face with color, flashing brightly in his exhausted eyes. "The point is to *stop* the aliens from reaching the station inhabitants, not to use the safe zones as bait!"

A shocking kick of realization brought Kira to a standstill. "Not the safe zones, maybe . . ." Heart racing with something she didn't dare yet call hope, she grabbed at Bashir's arm. "You examined one of them. Do you think you could make a good guess as to what sorts of DNA they *haven't* already absorbed?"

He frowned down at her, clearly torn between answering

her question and railing at her for wasting time with unimportant details. "Remnant DNA traces from various species place the viroids along the eastern spiral arm for at least the last five millennia," he said at last. "If nothing else, species from the galactic core and western edge should be completely new to them." The faintest flicker of understanding seemed to skip through his eyes, and he answered Kira's grip on his arm with one of his own. "Why? Major, what are you planning to do?"

It made too much sense. The idea exploded to fill her mind with intricate detail, and she couldn't avoid following it to its inevitable conclusion. "Draw them away from the station. Put together a meal ticket their instincts can't say no to, and launch it into space."

Bashir tried to pull away from her, horrified. "You can't do that! That's tantamount to condemning whatever spacefaring race they next come in contact with to death!"

"Send 'em to the Cardassians!"

"No!" She spun an angry glare on Pak, shaking the empty shotgun at her in a silent warning not to challenge her on this of all points. "I'm not going to dump my problems at anybody else's door." She tried to gentle her voice as she turned back to Bashir, knowing how much she hated what she was about to say, knowing he would never really see that. "We lure them out away from the station, all to a single place, and blast them down to molecules, just like you suggested. A couple torpedoes to the *Mukaikubo's* warp core ought to do it."

Silence swept around them like a cold wind, and Kira almost couldn't look at Bashir as understanding settled tragically across his face.

"You heard what O'Brien said." He sounded younger than she'd ever heard him before, his voice nearly a whisper, as though he didn't want Pak and the others to hear. "If you destroy the *Mukaikubo* while the wormhole's still in flux, the subspace surge will collapse the singularity. You'll be trapping everyone in the *Defiant* on the other side."

But that was the nature of command—to know, to feel, to hate the hard decisions you were forced to make, and then to make them anyway so that innocents like Bashir would never have to.

"You can't have it both ways." The calmness of her words lied shamelessly about the sick despair tearing her up inside. "We either save the Alpha Quadrant, or we save the *Defiant*. Which will it be?"

His eyes burned into her with stark misery, but he didn't voice an answer. She hadn't expected him to.

"You know what you guys really need?" Pak laced her hands behind her head and tipped herself back against the bulkhead with a maddeningly contented grin. "You need some piece of low-tech wizardry powerful enough to waste alien butt without throwing any subspace crap to interfere with your wormhole." She sighed like a woman remembering a favorite lover. "You need a good ol'-fashioned fusion bomb."

Kira resisted an urge to kick the terrorist's legs out from under her. "And you know where we can get one on short notice?" she snarled, too mad at herself and the terrible constraints of necessity to suffer sarcasm gladly.

Pak Dorren only smiled even wider, and winked at her in broad delight. "Why, little bit, as a matter of fact, I do."

CHAPTER 22

THE BRIGHT GLEAM of the transporter effect flashed over two shapes on the *Defiant's* bridge, making their silhouettes glow like wind-gusted candles just before they vanished. The high-pitched drone of the matter-to-energy converter faded a moment later, leaving a somber silence behind it. Dax closed her eyes, feeling the ansible link vanish for the few seconds the ancient symbiont was in transport, then rematerialize much farther away.

She heard Petersen's relieved voice from the auxiliary transporter control panel to her right. "We got coherent beam arrival, sir, six hundred meters away from the reaction core. They're in."

"Good work." Sisko's command chair hissed as he swung it around. "What's the station's current vector, Mr. Eddington?"

"It's completing the turning maneuver they started five minutes ago, sir." Dax opened her eyes to see the ruptured Jem'Hadar station stabilize itself with synchronized bursts from its impulse engines. Behind it, the wormhole's ultraviolet corona was strobing from indigo-black to wine-dark red on her color scale as its energy output intensified. "It's now headed directly for the wormhole entrance, at point-zero-three of light speed."

"Estimated time of arrival?" Sisko demanded.

"Twenty minutes, assuming they don't accelerate."

"That doesn't give us much time to infiltrate the core." Sisko slapped at the communicator controls beside his command chair. *"Defiant* to away team. Report." A long silence filled with the tense crackling static of the wormhole was all that answered him. After a moment spent listening to it, the captain finally exploded. "Dammit, I *knew* this was a bad idea! Dax, give me the Jem'Hadar translation of that self-destruct code. I'm going over there."

"Oh, no, you're not." Dax swung around to face him, recognizing the outburst of fierce frustration that could overwhelm Sisko's common sense when he wasn't the one carrying out a crucial maneuver. "Give them time to get their bearings."

"And keep in mind that the Jem'Hadar are programmed for maximum self-reliance," Odo added dryly. "The first report you get from Manan'Agar may be when the station blows itself up."

"That's *exactly* what I'm worried about, Constable." Sisko vaulted out of his chair and began prowling the bridge, as if he could no longer stand to sit and wait. "I'm afraid he'll try so hard to destroy the station himself he'll forget that the main point of his mission is to deliver the symbiont to the alien core."

Dax shook her head. Faint but steady through the ansible connection, she could feel the vibration of water sloshing around her other self. "No, Benjamin—the symbiont can feel that it's moving. Wherever Manan'Agar is trying to go, he's taking the brine tank with him."

"Not surprising, since he's using its antigravs to support himself," Odo reminded her. "If I had to guess what he's doing, I'd say he's trying to find a part of the station that still has power, so he can deliver the self-destruct command himself."

Sisko paused in front of Dax's jury-rigged engineering panel. "Can we see where the aliens are still running power through the station?"

Dax recalibrated one sensor to scan the Jem'Hadar station for live power circuits, then scrutinized the results. "Aside from the engineering sector they're occupying, the aliens are only supplying power to the station's impulse engines and navigational thrusters." She pointed at the strands of light that ran like faint spiderwebs through the station's darkened outline. "And those areas are all breached to space."

Sisko grunted, a little of the tension fading from his face. "So if Manan'Agar's heading for a live power circuit—"

"—he's going in the direction we want him to." Odo slanted Dax an inquiring look from his seat beside Eddington at the weapons console. "Can you pinpoint exactly where your counterpart is on the station, Lieutenant?"

"No." Dax closed her eyes again, trying to glean whatever sensations she could from a naked Trill symbiont enclosed in brine. What she got back was a fierce sense of impatience and determination, accompanied by the prickle of a hallucinatory aurora. "They must be getting closer to the stolen reaction masses, though. The symbiont is feeling some kind of unshielded magnetic flux—"

She gasped and broke off as a violent lurch of motion slapped the ancient symbiont against one cold aluminum wall of its tank. The ansible connection between them skated into screaming white haze. Through it, she was vaguely aware of Sisko swinging around, then coming to join her at the helm. *"Yevlin!"*

Dax couldn't hear what the physician's assistant said or did in reply, but a moment later a shock of cold rippled through her, and her senses returned. The first thing she saw was Yevlin Meris's intense Bajoran frown, a few inches away. "I can't keep depressing your isoboromine levels forever, Lieutenant," she said grimly. "If the ansible connection gets cut off, your internal suppressors may rebound and send you into systemic shock."

Dax took in another gasping breath and tightened her grip on whatever was supporting her. "I don't think—this will take forever—"

"What's going on, old man?" Sisko demanded. *"Talk to me!"*

Both symbionts responded to that familiar whip-crack of command. "We think Manan'Agar's been attacked—" Dax said. "Something heavy hit the brine tank a moment ago. And now—"

She broke off again, feeling another lurch of motion in the brine, along with the fierce vibration of ripping metal. Then came the worst nightmare a Trill symbiont could have: an uncontrolled splashing fall through released water, followed by the horrid thud of unprotected neural matter against a bitterly cold surface. Dax gasped in shared shock and pain.

"—tank's ruptured—I've been thrown out!" She reached out to grab at the nearest hard surface, her fingers scrabbling blindly over her helm panel until they reached and clutched around the strength of Sisko's wrist. Something lifted the symbiont in a harsh metallic grip, something turned and twisted it, nearly breaking its fragile cortical envelope. "An alien has picked me up—" Dax screamed and convulsed against the surge of transmitted agony, barely feeling Sisko catch at her shoulders to keep her from falling. "Oh, god, I'm being *eaten*. . . ."

"And it's a winner! They're takin' the bait!"

Kira sighed with such explosive relief that she fogged the inside of her helmet. For a moment, the immediacy of their danger seemed almost lost behind that cloudy sheen, but her memory held fast to the image of a lone runabout lifting away from the station on a preprogrammed course, its onboard transporter sprinkling a chum line of exotic DNA behind it. Then the hardsuit's internal environment controls compensated for the rise in humidity, and her vision cleared just as O'Brien announced, "You're on, Major."

She nodded, even though several meters of station separated her from the chief up in Ops. "I read you." There was something bizarrely comforting about watching alien carapaces slough off the station like scales, drifting and swirling like windblown leaves in the runabout's wake. Even from here, she could see that one of those wriggling bodies wore a shape different from the rest, with a streak of Andorian blue staining its hematite-colored carapace. Some fierce inner part of her wished suddenly that she hadn't left her phaser rifle behind to lighten her trip. *It wouldn't have worked anyway,* a more rational part of her brain reminded her. With an effort that felt almost physical, Kira dragged her gaze away from the alien that had attacked her.

"We're on our way," she told O'Brien, unnecessarily, then stepped out of the airlock. The transition from the station's artificial gravity to the free-floating world outside the hull washed Kira's muscles with a wave of weary relief. She'd almost forgotten how much she still ached until that ever-present pull was gone; the release from it now almost made her want to go back inside. In the great scheme of things, pain was fairly easy to ignore—comfort had a way of sneaking up on you and making you complacent.

"I hope you're planning on making this quick," Pak Dorren complained, shuffling her own suit over the threshold between Starfleet's regulation Earth-normal and space's zero-g. "I hate this EV stuff. I don't want to be out here any longer than we have to."

Kira waited for the terrorist to creep up beside her, but didn't offer a hand to help. "It was your idea to hide the bomb outside."

"My idea," Pak snorted, "but not my job." She turned her head to show Kira a wan smile, then flailed her arms as though that tiny motion had stolen away her balance. "That's the point of being the boss, little bit," she gasped, throwing herself at Kira's arm and wrapping it in a bear hug with no consideration for whether Kira was interested in helping. "You don't have to crawl around on the outsides of ships unless you really, really want to."

Or someone has a weapon to your head. Peeling herself free from the other woman, Kira shifted her grip to the storage hook on the back of Pak's torso, thinking that might reassure Pak without slowing them too badly. "In the Shakaar resistance cell, we were taught that the point of being in charge was that you did your own dirty work."

Pak gave a rough grunt, but let Kira push her gently forward. "Yeah, well, Shakaar was an idiot."

Kira would have been disappointed if a woman like Pak felt otherwise.

Dark, silent, the station's exterior looked deceptively placid compared with the turmoil inside. They'd stepped onto the hull opposite most of the gaping breaches, and the abrupt lack of aliens crawling about the screens left the starscape to all sides as clear and still as a summer night. Even the wormhole seemed to have quieted to its usual darkling simmer. Only the clumsy bulk of their hardsuits and the radiation gauge on the edge of Kira's display betrayed how much the wormhole was vomiting outside the visual spectrum. That, and the lacy-fine whispers of ultraviolet fluorescence that frosted bits and pieces of the station like morning dew. Kira wondered if they'd have been able to pick up the radiation signature of Pak's hydrogen bomb through all this noise even if Pak hadn't thought to hide it within the blind spot of the station's own sensor array. Considering the range and volume of the wormhole's output when compared with even the most poorly shielded bomb, it seemed rather unlikely.

"Step it up, Pak." Kira resisted an urge to poke her in the small of her back, aware that there was always the chance it would send Pak tumbling out into space, and they actually needed her now if they were going to make sure the bomb was functional. "You're the one who said you wanted to hurry."

Pak wheezed a hoarse little sound that might have been a laugh. "Little bit, for me this *is* hurrying." She came to a sudden clumsy standstill before breaking her foot's contact with the hull to lift it over a conduit box. "I told you I didn't like EV."

It wasn't until that moment that Kira realized Pak hadn't actually pulled her feet loose from the hull plates since they stepped outside the airlock doors. She been shuffling, sliding the magnetized soles of her hardsuit's shoes across the station's surface like some ridiculous ice skater. Irritation and amazement overcame Kira in equal measure. "You're not afraid of hydrogen bombs, but you're afraid of spending fifteen minutes EV."

On the other side of the conduit, Pak planted her second foot carefully beside her first, and took up her snail-like shuffling again. "Hey, honey—that's why they call it a phobia."

But at this rate, the runabout would be at Organia before they could get to the bomb.

"O'Brien to Kira. Major, we've got a problem."

She lifted her head, startled by the river of static roaring underneath the chief's transmission. Constant but distant, as if someone had left the faucet on. "What's the matter, Chief?"

"The buggers," he reported urgently. "They're all over

the runabout like voles on a cat. Julian's got the onboard replicators producing his DNA concoction at top capacity, but once they destroy the stand-alone generator and the replicators shut down, they'll do away with the whole load in under a minute."

She was suddenly viciously resentful of having to remove the bait runabout's engine core. Glancing keenly in the direction she knew the little ship had taken, she was only slightly surprised to find she couldn't pick it out from the other flecks of brightness that were the surrounding stars. "Start pulling the aliens off with the transporter," she told O'Brien, stepping intimately close to Pak and wrapping her arms around the older woman's middle. "We've got to decrease the load on the runabout or it won't last long enough to receive the bomb."

"That'll mean dropping the shields, Major, and with you right out there in the open—"

"We'll just have to hope Bashir's concoction smells more appetizing than we do. Kira out." She cut off their comm channel without waiting for his acknowledgment, then tightened her grip around Pak with a warning bump from her helmet. "We're going to jump."

She could feel Pak's body stiffen even through both heavy suits. "No, we're not!"

"Yes, we are. Hold on!" It wasn't like she'd meant for Pak to have a choice.

As far as double-time suit jumps were concerned, the surface of DS9 was one of the more convenient locations to navigate. An irregular moon, where gravity's bothersome pull could interfere with your trajectory, was far harder to sail across, and the spinning outer hull of a centrifugal cylinder ranked among the worst suit walks of Kira's life. *Deep Space Nine*—a steady, immobile behemoth wider in girth than some of Bajor's colonies—released her into her leap with no jealous efforts to pull her down, no spiteful rotational movement to spoil her aim. She caught herself neatly against an upthrust communications antenna, pausing a few seconds longer than perhaps absolutely necessary to make sure Pak's added mass had equalized alongside hers before stepping into the last short hop as though she were stepping through an open door.

To her credit, Pak made not a sound during their rapid flight. She didn't struggle, or curse, or do anything that might have jeopardized their safe arrival at the station's upper tier. *She may be phobic,* Kira thought as her feet clanged and locked on the sensor array's outer housing, *but she's not stupid.* Using one foot to stomp on Pak's boots and ensure they were firmly mated with the hull, Kira carefully released her passenger and squirmed around in front.

"Okay, Pak, what do we—"

Catching one glimpse of the terrorist's face, Kira cut herself off with a sigh. Pak stood rigid as a statue, her face the color of frozen cream, her eyes and mouth clamped so resolutely shut that Kira almost wondered if she was breathing. *My fault,* the major chastised herself. She should have known that anything Pak Dorren was afraid of frightened her through-and-through.

"Dorren . . ." Rapping her knuckles on the other woman's faceplate, Kira did her best to keep the worst of the irritation out of her voice. "We're at the sensor array. You've got to open your eyes and look—you said the bomb was here, but I don't know what we're looking for."

Pak slitted her eyes as though afraid of the light, but nothing else about her stance or expression dared to change. Kira stepped aside, giving her a clear view of the crowded array, and waited as patiently as she could for Pak to scan the workings for what they needed. Thinking of the overwhelmed runabout and its load of priceless genetics, she felt a tickle of sweat trace its way down the middle of her back. "Pak, you've got to tell me. Where is it? Where's the bomb?"

Her eyes as wide and sightless as dabo wheels, Pak lifted her shoulders in only the most tiny of helpless shrugs. "I don't know," she whispered. "I just know it's not where it should be. It's not here."

Rehk'resen.

The alien word glowed like a spangle of light in the darkness, warmed Dax like a shivering flush of color melting its way through coils of translucent gel. In this floating state of barely liminal consciousness, it was all Dax knew, without even knowing what it meant. But remembering it was crucial. *Rehk'resen. Rehk'resen.*

Something tugged at Dax's awareness, in the vague nerveless way things happened in fever dreams. *Maybe I'm sleeping,* Dax thought. *Maybe I'm sick.* With an effort, Dax tried to crawl free of the floating numbness, and only succeeded in making the surrounding nothingness feel more like a tight, strangling shroud than the warm blanket it had been a moment before. *Maybe I've been drugged.*

The mental tugging came again, this time sharper and more electric, as if tiny circuits were plugging themselves directly in. Dax tried to focus on that feeling, tried to pin down what was happening. There was a familiar funneling rush, eerily similar to the rush that happened when a symbiont first connected to a brand-new host and began pouring itself in to share their brain. Except this time, what Dax's blind, encapsulated consciousness poured itself into wasn't a Trill brain trained and disciplined to receive it. It was utter chaos.

Mental links stretched out in all directions, linking to five thousand moving appendages, five hundred digestive systems, a thousand light-sensing organs all transmitting shared images like the faceted eyes of a bee, except that each of them saw something different. A warp exhaust, a portion of breached hull, a curve of duranium carapace ... too many disparate images to make sense of. And hearing was no better. From every direction came the roar of hundreds of overlapping mental voices, some speaking, some screaming, some making only mindless animal grunts. Dax reeled under the cascade of random sensory input, choked on the wild schizophrenic explosion of voices. This was insane! What kind of host was this?

Rehk'resen, said an urgent internal voice, closer to Dax than all the rest. The alien word stirred a ghost of memory, like ashes floated by a vagrant breath of air. This was no host. This was an alien life-form, and Dax was here to do something to it, with it—but could not remember what!

"... can't lower her isoboromine any more than that ..."

"... have to know whether the infiltration is working ..."

Now, there was something different about *those* voices. Unlike the surrounding crash and babble of sound, those came from a more distant place, through the soothing swash and ripple of familiar Trill host-mind. Dax pulled back from the chaos of sight and sound that was the newly formed neural connections, and concentrated instead on the internal channel that seemed to link with someplace else.

". . . old man, can you hear me? Do you know where the symbiont is now?"

"Benjamin?"

With enormous effort, Dax opened what seemed to be someone else's eyes, and had a dizzying moment of seeing the clean lines of the *Defiant*'s bridge overlaid on jigsaw-puzzle insanity. The sight of the breached Jem'Hadar station on the viewscreen above her brought memory crashing back, cold and heavy as an avalanche. Her twinned symbiont had just been linked into the alien neural core on that station. Now it had to learn how to bend that group mind to her will and use the Jem'Hadar self-destruct code before it was too late.

"Rehk'resen," she murmured, only vaguely aware of her own real voice above the fitful clamor around the symbiont. "That's the Jem'Hadar code for self-destruction."

"You with us again, old man?" A strong hand slid behind her head and turned it so she could blink muzzily up at Sisko's face. "What's happening on the station?"

"Symbiont is linked in . . ." She swallowed past an odd dryness in her throat, hoping it was just a side effect of all the medication Yevlin had been injecting her with and not a precursor of systemic host-symbiont shock. "How much time . . . ?"

Sisko's voice turned bleak. "Twelve minutes, maximum. The station's accelerated to point-oh-five of light."

"Can't tell time in there," Dax warned him. "You'd better keep us posted. . . ."

"Us?" Sisko demanded.

She nodded and closed her eyes. "The symbiont can't do this all by itself. I'm going back to help. . . ."

It was easier sliding back into the chaos of the alien group mind, now that she knew her own name and self and purpose. Dax felt herself merge into the familiar Trill symbiont-mind that was her ancient counterpart, feeling again its fierce millennia-old determination to stop the wormhole from rifting. She grounded herself in that shared emotion, then stretched her mind—their minds—out along the newly grown nerve pathways that bound her to the other mental entities trapped in this strangest of alien prisons.

"I am Dax of Starfleet! Who will join with me?" She launched the demand in Standard English like a quantum torpedo, using the mental force of three joined brains to power it through the babble of voices. It made a surprisingly loud explosion in the chaos, followed by a short, startled silence. Just as the random chatter began to rise again, she repeated the words in her own native language. The musical rise and fall of the Trill speak/song echoed down the neural network, and this time the silence lasted a little longer. Dax identified herself over and over again, first in Vulcan, then in Ferengi, then in Klingon—

"Dax of Starfleet!" It was a Ferengi voice, not far away, sounding half insane with frustration. Dax felt an electric crackle of power rush through her as another mind added its control of the network to hers. "I'll join with you, I'll do anything you want. Just get me out of here!"

"Dax of Starfleet!" A half-familiar Vulcan voice, echoed by others a little farther away. This time, the power surge was enormous but far more controlled, connecting to her through what felt like miles of precisely calibrated computer circuits. "If you're here to rescue the wormhole, the crew of the *Sreba* will join with you. We have already formed a network around the navigations controls. Tell us what we can do!"

"Dax of Starfleet!" It was a distant thunder of Klingon voices, their accent the archaic growl of a previous millennium but their lust for battle undiminished by their time inside the group mind. Dax felt the power of their joining roll through her like the shock wave of an earthquake. "Dax of Starfleet, wherever that kingdom is, you speak our language. We hold the territory near where the fires of hell burn brightest. Share with us your battle plans."

"Dax." The faint, tired whisper barely reached her, from somewhere very deep inside the alien core. A jolt of recognition and disbelief shivered through Dax as the familiar mind-pattern overlapped hers. "This is . . . Jadzia. I've been waiting for you, for so long . . . tell me what we have to do to save the ship."

CHAPTER 23

"NOT HERE?" KIRA GRABBED AT Pak's gloved hands, martialing every ounce of her control not to shake the terrified woman senseless. "What do you mean the bomb's not here? You said it was hidden on the sensor array!"

"It's supposed to be!" Pak screwed her face into a pale semblance of her normal vinegar, and Kira was afraid for a moment that she was going to spit inside her helmet. "Those lazy little sons of raskers—I should've known they'd cut corners somewhere." Tipping her head back, she shouted in the general direction of the alien-covered runabout, "I'd kick your sorry asses clear to the Prophets' Temple if you hadn't already been eaten!"

An understandable sentiment, considering their circumstances, but not immediately useful. "Kira to O'Brien." She released Pak and turned away to survey the station's wheel laid out below her. "Run a sensor sweep on the outside of the station. Can you find any evidence of stray radiation *anywhere?*"

The few seconds it took to run the scan seemed to stretch on forever. When O'Brien's voice came back to her through the wall of static, Kira could barely hear the words past the growl of his frustration. "The wormhole's got everything in the vicinity so excited, the only things I can pick out of the background are the engine cores on the *Mukaikubo* and that leaky weapons sail we were working on the other day."

The other day ... Time flies when you're having fun, stretches days into eons when your life is on the line. Kira shook her head at the tall weapons sail, and tried to remember what it felt like to have your biggest problem be explaining the word "no" to an obsequious Ferengi toad.

The radiation gauge on her helmet display blinked as something in the wormhole rearranged itself beyond the threshold of sight, and she paused, caught by the spiraling numbers. Caught by a fragment of memory that hadn't quite been there before. "Chief . . . do self-diagnostics still show everything as normal in weapons sail two?"

"For what it's worth," he answered slowly, "yes, sir, they do. And it did all right as far as bug zapping before. But, Major—" She could tell he was striving hard to retain a tone of respectful objectivity. "—figuring out what's wrong with that weapons sail isn't exactly our first priority anymore."

Kira twitched a little smile and smacked one fisted glove into the other. "Maybe it is." She turned awkwardly in her suit, only to find Pak squatting with her hands folded over her head and her eyes screwed tightly shut on the world. "You're right, Pak." She knew the terrorist could hear her, whether or not she would look. "Your cronies were lazy. It's a shorter jaunt from the closest airlock to the sail housing, and they wouldn't have to try and sneak the bomb through as much of the station." She threw a defiant gesture toward the arcing sail, her heart starting to race with a fierce and angry thrill. "It's the bomb, Chief," she announced triumphantly. "The radiation leak in the weapons sail is Pak Dorren's bomb."

"Jadzia—" A surge of horrified pity swept through the Dax aboard the *Defiant,* and she reached out with all the power of her three linked minds to pull that long-lost fourth into the joining. Another, deeper jolt of completion echoed down the ansible link, as ancient host and ancient symbiont reunited after milennia apart. Dax used the resulting sense of doubled power to project her mental voice down every neural pathway she could find, speaking first in Standard English, then in Klingon.

"My plan is to make this station self-destruct. I know the

code, but we need a mouth to speak it and a powered computer junction to hear and implement it. Where can we get them?"

"We could fashion a vocal apparatus from the DNA these creatures hoard," one of the Vulcans suggested.

"Too slow," said the ancient Jadzia fragment, with a certainty that came from centuries of gleaned knowledge about these aliens. "My other selves tell me we have only a few minutes before we enter the wormhole and our group mind scatters again. We must find an existing mouth to use."

Flickers of searching thought sparked through the alien core like heat-lightning. "I've got one!" crowed the Ferengi voice after a moment. "The shell right next to mine is digesting a dead Jem'Hadar—"

"Manan'Agar." Dax suppressed an unexpected swell of remorse, reminding herself that the warship pilot had known he was going to certain death when he volunteered to take the ancient symbiont to the aliens. "Can you see if his mouth and throat have been destroyed?"

From out of the kaleidoscope of a thousand visual images that crowded in on her, Dax got a stronger flash of Manan'Agar's bony-plated face, disappearing into an alien that had apparently already swallowed the rest of him. She winced, but the ancient Jadzia merely made a thoughtful noise as she sampled the image with her. "Looks like they've already extracted most of his cerebral matter," she commented. "We'll have to incorporate that neural strand into our network." Then she added, in perfect archaic Klingon, "Lords and officers of Qu'onos, you are best suited to wage this battle. Can you conquer the territory that's being added to the enemy's kingdom?"

"The assault has already begun," a Klingon voice growled in reply. Dax got another flashing image of Manan'Agar's face, jerking to a stop just before it was swallowed. "We have wrested the main roads from the enemy's control, and stopped their advance," reported a distant member of the Klingon network. "Where shall we link the newly acquired land? It does not seem to speak our language."

"Let me have it." Dax felt a smooth scuttle of motion as the Ferengi-controlled shell maneuvered around the outside of the alien core until it could burrow beneath its neighbor. She felt the electric jolts of connection as the newest neural strands were woven into the Ferengi's network, but no sense of Manan'Agar's furious personality came with them. "Hmm—looks like this joker shot himself in the back of the head when the shells caught him. Smart guy."

"Is there enough neuromuscular tissue left to issue commands to his voluntary muscles?" Dax demanded.

"Just barely." Another flash of compound vision showed her Manan'Agar's head at close range, his lips moving in a convulsive jerk. "Now, where's the closest powered section of the station?"

Another bright explosion of mental searching flickered through the group mind, and this time it was a Vulcan voice which spoke first. "I have found the main power switches." This time, the flash of vision Dax got was in a lighted corridor, where a duranium-shelled alien had plastered itself up against what looked like a cracked-open engineering panel. "If we can take control of this entity, we can simply reroute power to the Ferengi's location. But it is one of the enemy—its captured minds have no will of their own to join us."

"Then let all of us combined bend this one quickly to *our* will," a Klingon voice growled.

"Heads up, old man," said Sisko's unexpected voice, sounding light-years distant now. "You've only got five more minutes. . . ."

"Time is running out," Dax warned her allies, then reached out through the neural network to her ancient counterpart and felt her determination redouble. "Send all your excess power to me—*now!*"

Mental energy cracked like lightning across the chaos of the group mind, joining and growing like a river in flood as it channeled into Dax. For a moment, she struggled to contain it, but the strength of four Trill minds in complete ansible contact rose to the challenge and hammered the energy into a single flaming bolt, then flung it onward to its mark. She saw the targeted alien jerk as the attack reached it. One by one, the cerebral nodes inside the duranium shell tried to ward off their joint assault. One by one, each of them failed.

As the last one shattered beneath her assault, Dax grabbed control of the neural strands that ended in slender, claw-tipped digits and the ones that fed in vision from a pair of thick-stalked eyes. She swiveled those eyes to regard the power grid beneath her, seeing a dim glow in only one of its hundred circuits. The aliens were releasing only a trickle of power from their hoarded reaction masses, just enough to run the navigational thrusters.

". . . three minutes, old man . . ."

"Tell me the instant you have power," she ordered the Ferengi, then began tapping each circuit in turn, diverting the power trickle to other parts of the station. She was slow at first, but as her new neural connections solidified, she gained the ability to move her alien fingers faster and faster until she could make the dim glow of connected power race across each row of the circuit board. She heard the Ferengi's anguished mental yelp two lights past the correct one, but it only took a few seconds to backtrack power to his sector.

". . . two minutes left, Dax . . ."

She left the ancient Jadzia holding the enemy network in check, and reached the rest of her mental presence back through the network of her allies to join the Ferengi-dominated shell. *"Rehk'resen,"* she told him urgently. "That's what we've got to get the Jem'Hadar to say. *Now!*"

"I'm working on it." A flurry of energy sparked out from the Ferengi's local network, and in a fragment of her compound vision, Dax saw Manan'Agar's slack jaw clench and quiver. A faint hint of sound trickled back into their neural network, gleaned from the Jem'Hadar's own ears.

"Reeh—" It came out sounding more like a groan than a word. "Reehek—"

". . . one more minute. Old man, whatever you've got to do, do it now!"

With one last desperate effort, Dax shoved her consciousness past the Ferengi's startled mind and down into the inert dead nerves of what was left of Manan'Agar, forcing air through his stiffening throat muscles and vocal cords. "Rehk!" he shouted abruptly. "Resen. *Rehk'resen!*"

And with the blinding speed that the Jem'Hadar built into all their military equipment, every containment field on the station's reaction mass exploded outward. The last thing Dax remembered was a violent swell of joy from the trapped minds in contact with hers, just before the pure white fire of superheated plasma seared them into nothingness.

"Okay—" Kira took a deep, steadying breath, and fixed her gaze on the towering weapons sail in front of her until the pit of her stomach ceased its twisting. *It was just a simple leap—no tethers, no controls, but still a simple leap.* The stalwartly rational chant in her head had started to sound decidedly hysterical about halfway across the long, empty expanse between the sensor arrays and here. Faster than walking, perhaps, but not conducive to an intact stomach lining. Kira hoped she'd bought enough time to make the future health of her insides a legitimate worry. "I'm at the weapons sail."

"That fast?" Pak Dorren's voice scratched across the wormhole static as relentlessly as ever, no matter that she still crouched with her eyes presumably shut in the shadow of the sensor array. "I don't even want to know how you got there."

Kira played clumsy gloves across the sail's exterior door controls. "Don't worry—I wasn't going to tell you." As the hatch slid aside in vacuum silence, she stepped forward into her past from just a few days before.

The sail stretched up into what seemed an impossible distance, pinching in to a dark point somewhere far above the crowded floor. Kira moved carefully among the confusion of torpedo handling equipment and targeting brains, leery of touching anything now that she knew O'Brien's radiation threat was more than just some minor capacitor leak. "I'm in the final delivery chamber," she reported to Pak as she worked her way toward the center. "This is where the phaser capacitors charge and where the photon torpedoes are armed before launching."

Pak grunted. "The idiots probably thought that would hide the radiation signatures from the plutonium and tritium."

"Good thing they were wrong." All unbidden, a vivid, glowing image of Veska Province blasted into Kira's mind, and she forced herself to crush the panic in her clenched fist as she instructed, "Tell me what I'm looking for."

Suit joints cracked and clattered across the open channel, and Kira heard Pak make an odd little grunt. She hoped the terrorist wasn't trying to move herself. They couldn't afford to have their only bomb expert go catatonic just now. "It's gonna be a two-part contraption." Her voice sounded a margin more steady, and the sounds of her suit movements had ceased. "The first part is the plutonium detonator, which should already be inside a delivery shell. Look for something about as big around as a disposal bin, maybe half a meter long. If there's someplace where your torpedoes stockpile—like waiting for arming, or something—that's probably where the morons put it."

She'd moved herself to where she couldn't see, Kira realized. Of course. If you couldn't see a danger, it wasn't really there—if you stared at the welds surrounding a brace of deck rivets, you couldn't notice that a gentle flexing of your feet would send you sailing off into infinity. With only a plutonium detonator and nightmare images of Veska Province to keep her company, Kira wished her own fears could be so easily avoided.

She remembered studying the diagrams—years ago, when she'd been sent to the station as a teenager on some idiot mission to incapacitate the weapons systems. Torpedoes were stored deep inside the station, away from the habitation areas, shielded to protect them from detonating every time a rival force managed a direct hit to the station's hide. For that very reason, the Cardassians never stockpiled torpedoes in the weapons sails. Better to lose the sail and all its associated phaser batteries than to suffer the damage of forty photon torpedoes all going up in concert. Instead, the torpedoes stayed in stasis until needed, then were conveyored to the sails and armed for launching. It was an elegant design that the Bajoran Resistance had bitterly resented—what they could have accomplished with a single suicidal operative "if only the Cardassians weren't so anal with their weapons" had been everyone's favorite pointless debate.

Now that Starfleet ran the station, protecting against constant bombardment and sabotage were no longer primary concerns. Still, the torpedo system was already there and well designed; the only difference in Starfleet's procedures was what became of the weapons after they were loaded into the sail and armed for launch. Any duds among the Cardassian supplies were summarily launched into space—after all, just because a torpedo couldn't arm didn't mean it couldn't still explode, and keeping it inside the sail still posed a significant danger. Starfleet took a dimmer view of such wanton technological pollution; Starfleet had built a special storage rack along the arching spine of the sail, and this is where her duds went to rest until engineers with nothing better to do could come outside and repair them.

There were two sleek black casings waiting in the rack now—far fewer than the Cardassians threw out in a single day, Kira noted, and this was no doubt the dregs from the last time Sisko had ordered torpedoes armed more than a month ago. No wonder Starfleet could be so gracious about cleaning up its own messes. It was probably a lot easier when you didn't make much mess to begin with.

She couldn't see the higher of the two torpedoes from where she stood at the foot of the rack, but a dim, roseate glow against the empty sling above it caught her attention as it silently came and went and came again. Planting one foot on the wall of the sail, she gave herself a moment to reorient to the new position, then walked up what now felt like a gently sloping floor to stand beside the blinking casing. Just above the beautifully embossed Starfleet emblem and neatly printed PROPERTY OF DEEP SPACE STATION #9, the message ribbon embedded in the torpedo's nose shouted redly, ERR 3453 'RADIATION CONTAMINATION HAZARD.' REBOOT AND RELOAD.

Kira thought at first that it must mean that something inside its own structure had malfunctioned and flooded it with a fatal load of subspace radiation. Then she noticed the first-stage indicator in her rad meter as it sailed steadily redline, and she realized just whose radiation this forgotten torpedo was reporting. It slid easily into another holding bracket when she pushed it, exposing the slim silver casing of someone else's bomb tucked underneath.

Kira read the elaborate scrawl winding its way around the narrow casing's nose. "'The Hand of the Prophets.' Very subtle."

On the other side of the station, Pak chuckled dryly. "Do yourself a favor, little bit. Don't even try to pick that up and move it. Just unscrew the nose and slide out the workings until you see the cup where the tritium goes."

Kira touched her suit fingers to the casing as lightly as possible, wishing she could somehow unscrew it without having to actually make contact. The instant the nose cone swung open, she jerked her hand away to let the workings slide out by themselves. "It's open." She wished her voice didn't sound so stretched tight and breathless. "Now what?"

"Now you slip the tritium inside. It's plasma, inside a magnetic bottle, about as long as your forearm. I'd suggest checking among your phaser batteries for that one."

But it wasn't hidden somewhere within the batteries, or underneath the second torpedo, and there was nothing to open or move among the targeting equipment that was big enough to hide anything larger than the palm of her hand. Swearing, feeling tears of frustration burning at the backs of her eyes, Kira aimed a useless kick at the bottom of the phaser optic tower.

"Little bit?"

The force of her kick shivered through the body of her hardsuit, breaking her contact with the deck and setting her spinning lazily several meters above the floor. It didn't matter—nothing mattered. They were one step away from assembling a functional bomb, and unless she could locate the tritium, they might just as well have played tongo until their whole world rolled to an end. Putting out one arm to catch herself against the optic tower, she took angry satisfaction in the jolt of discomfort that sent shooting up her arm. *Serves me right. I can't even put together a hydrogen bomb! What have I got to be careful about now?*

A brilliant glitter high overhead danced its reflection across her faceplate, then swept out of her sight as she rotated.

Her breath catching in her throat, Kira grabbed the tower in both hands and pulled herself toward the ceiling so hard her helmet cracked against the upper optical mount before she could slow her ascent.

"What are you doing in there?" That panic was the most honest thing Kira had heard come out of Pak since she'd met her. "Little bit, what happened? What'd you drop?"

"Nothing. I just hit my helmet on the ceiling." The magnetic bottle was more delicate than she'd expected, thin and sparkling, like a cylinder of summer sun. "I've got the tritium."

"Good! Now put it in the detonator. Make sure it clicks into place. You'll know it's seated right when the lights in the control display come on."

She was already on the floor and halfway across to the weapons rack. Walking carefully, calmly up the curving wall, Kira eased the magnetic bottle into its cradle as though it were a sleeping baby. It fit more perfectly than anything she'd ever seen, and even the sudden brightness of the lights jumping to life around it did little to take away from its luminance.

"That's it!" O'Brien's cry was so obscured by static, Kira was barely certain that she heard him. "I've lost all power readings from the runabout, Major. You've got one minute!"

One minute's all I need! "Get a lock on the transponder, Chief!" She dug the little clip out of its carry pocket on the leg of her hardsuit and placed it with exaggerated care on the bomb's sleek outer shell. Then, as her hoarse breathing slowly obscured the inside of her faceplate, she used the smallest finger on her glove to punch the seconds into the blinking timer. She could just make out a blurry number ten when she slipped the tray of workings back inside and gave the nose cone a two-handed spin.

"Energize!"

The transporter's telltale sparkle danced across the silver metal housing just as Kira shoved off from the weapons rack and headed for the floor. She wasn't sure what she expected. Some impossible shock wave, maybe, or some searing blast of heat such as once wiped Veska Province from the face of Bajor and laid a platter of glowing silicate in its place. Instead, she stepped out of the weapons sail in time to see only the reflection of brilliance as it dashed itself against the station's parts. Like the striking of a match in the middle of darkness. Or fireworks underneath a cloudy sky. A shriek of cheering voices swelled to fill her hardsuit helmet, and Pak Dorren sighed with a murmur of quiet contentment. "Now, that's what I call beautiful."

Kira climbed to the top of the nearest docking light, turning away from the contaminated weapons sail and toward the secretive wormhole. Her suit comm rang with a clarity that seemed almost unnatural, and the station all around her lay undisturbed and dark. "Chief . . ."

"We're doing some last mopping up with the transporters, Major." He sounded giddy and restless, and ready to drop on his feet. "Not that there are many left to worry about. That was one hell of a bomb."

Instead of the smug response Kira expected from Pak, all she heard was silence. "Pak?" she demanded.

Still no answer. Worried that the terrorist had finally gone catatonic with fear, she slid over the far edge of the docking light's gantry to bring her into view. All she saw below her was an empty curve of gunmetal hull. Exasperation and suspicion burned through the last of Kira's mindless relief. *"Pak!"*

A gravelly chuckle, devoid of the slightest traces of fear, greeted her across the comm. Behind it, Kira could hear the rush of air whirling into an activated airlock. "Hey, you did good, little bit. And don't worry—no one's going to blame you for being so busy saving the wormhole that you let one sneaky old Resistance fighter slip through your fingers."

She'd been faking it! Kira should have known that any woman who could stare a nuclear bomb in the face without flinching couldn't possibly be afraid of something as simple as open space. She couldn't believe she'd fallen for a ploy that any first-year Resistance fighter should have seen through.

Kira growled and swung herself out to follow Pak into the station. Before she could do more than reach for her next handhold, however, an outward blast of released air from a shuttlebay nearly knocked her off her precarious perch. She cursed and clung to it with scrabbling fingers. "Chief! What just happened?"

O'Brien sounded even more irritated than she felt. "The

Platte just took off from docking bay three with your friend Pak inside, that's what happened. We didn't have enough controls on-line to stop her."

"Not the *new* runabout?" Kira felt like banging her head against the station's hull in frustration. "I'm going to *kill* her."

"Good luck, little bit," said Pak's mocking voice, this time with a chitter of Starfleet machinery behind her. "But you have to catch me first, you know. Boy, I can't wait to see how much tritium this baby ship will trade for on the black market. . . ."

Kira lifted her head abruptly, her attention caught, not by Pak's taunt, but by the lack of static behind it. "Chief," she said again, this time in wonder, "am I hallucinating, or is that a stable wormhole I'm not hearing?"

O'Brien didn't answer for a long moment, and the stark clarity of the silence on the comm made Kira scrabble around on the docking light to view the velvet dark space behind her with a weary laugh.

"Well, what d'you know," O'Brien said in an awkward attempt at levity. "I guess fusion bombs fix wormholes."

She tipped her head sideways to prop her helmet against one hand, and watched the first azure streamers swirl stationward as the wormhole blossomed into life. "I don't think so, Chief."

It exploded across the sky with a blinding radiance that made her heart swell almost to bursting with its beauty. This is what the Prophets' Temple was supposed to be, a thing of life and mystery—the future of Bajor, not its destruction. As the fleck of black that was an arriving ship flowed out of that giving mouth and into reality, Kira dared to send the smallest prayer toward the gods who had watched over her people for so long. *Thank you.*

"*Defiant* to *Deep Space Nine*. Request permission to dock and off-load this weary crew."

She sat up straighter, her hands on her knees, and smiled as the Temple twined its doors tight shut behind the stars. "*Defiant*, this is DS9. Permission most happily granted, Captain. Welcome home."

CHAPTER 24

THERE WAS SOMETHING wrong with the silence.

Awareness drifted back into Dax, slow and cool as the water that trickled through layers of salt travertine to feed the brine pools of Trill. Even after she felt mostly awake, she kept her eyes closed for a long, puzzled moment, trying to decide what she wasn't hearing in the silence. She knew she must be in the *Defiant*'s medical bay—she could hear the discreet chirps and clicks of sickbay diagnostics overhead counting off her pulse, her breathing rate, and all her other metabolic functions. Beyond that quiet machine noise, there was only a slow whisper of life-support fans circulating refiltered air, and the gentle, occasional rustle of someone else in the room. It all seemed normal, but something *was* missing, Dax knew. There was a sound she should be hearing, a sound she had grown so used to she couldn't even remember what it was now that it had gone.

Then liquid splashed very softly in the distance, and memories of the tidal swash and pull of her ansible link with the ancient Dax symbiont flooded into her mind. Dax gasped and sat up, reaching out with all the force of both her joined minds. She met nothing but silence. The ancient symbiont was gone.

"Jadzia." Something clattered against a table nearby, and a moment later a gentle hand brushed across her forehead. "Are you really awake?"

Dax's eyes flew open. The thin, dark face bending over her in concern was the last one she'd expected to see. "What are *you* doing here?" she demanded.

One corner of Julian Bashir's mouth kicked upward in a wry smile. "Well, at least that was more original than 'Where am I?'" He glanced up at the diagnostic panels above her head and made a satisfied noise. "Isoboromine levels back to normal, and all your other neurotransmitters steady as a rock. Looks like you're fit to go back on duty, Lieutenant."

"But, Julian, if you're here—" Dax broke off, seeing the wider contours of *Deep Space Nine*'s infirmary behind him instead of the *Defiant*'s cramped sickbay. She took a deep, disbelieving breath. "I'm on board the station? We saved the wormhole?"

"You saved the wormhole," Bashir confirmed. His brown face hardened into more finely drawn lines, as if he'd remembered something that made him unhappy. He turned away from her gaze, picking up the steaming mug of raktajino he'd left across the room. "You and the old Dax symbiont."

It wasn't the sadness in Bashir's voice that worried Dax—it was the underlying wash of bitterness that told her he blamed himself for the symbiont's long-overdue death. She took a deep breath, choosing her next words with care.

"We had some help," she told him quietly. "The Vulcan scientists from the *Sreba,* a lost Ferengi, a phalanx of Klingon warriors . . . and another Jadzia host."

"What?" Bashir slewed around to face her so abruptly that hot liquid slopped out of his cup and ran down across his hand. He cursed and set the cup down again. "Jadzia was *there?* Inside one of the viroids?"

She nodded. "Enough of her to help us. She told us the best way to use the alien core to destroy the Jem'Hadar station."

"Oh, my god." The doctor sat down on the bed across from her, horrified realization darkening his eyes. "When the *Defiant* was attacked on the other end of the timerift, it must have been by the viroids, not the Furies!"

"Yes," Dax agreed. "Benjamin used one of our own photon torpedoes to blow most of them off the ship—"

"—but with shields down, Kira and O'Brien got killed doing it," Bashir finished for her. "While the captain only survived long enough to find us a hiding place in that cometary fragment."

"And Jadzia got so much radiation damage that she separated from Dax and sacrificed herself to lead the rest of the viroid aliens away. That's when she was attacked and digested by the viroids."

"We must have known by then what they were," Bashir said softly. "We must have captured one and seen the living brains it contained."

Dax nodded, clasping her hands around her upraised knees thoughtfully. "That's why the ancient Dax was so insistent that we talk to what the aliens had eaten. It wanted us to find the ancient Jadzia."

"Yes." Bashir suddenly seemed to notice the wet stickiness on his hands and cursed again in a more normal voice. He jumped up and went to fetch a cleaning swipe from one of his dispensers. "That must have been what kept it alive all those centuries. It knew it had to save her."

"See, it wasn't just your selfishness after all."

He gave her a startled and oddly guilty look. "How did you know—"

"That you were afraid you'd only kept Dax alive to keep you company on the *Defiant*?" Dax shook her head, sighing. "Julian, you've always been a medical ethics debate looking for a place to happen. It makes you a wonderful doctor—"

"—but an inconvenient friend," he finished, smiling wryly. "Yes, I know. Garak tells me that all the time." His comm badge beeped for attention, and he tapped it reluctantly. "Bashir."

"Doctor, is Lieutenant Dax awake yet?" The breathless voice on the other end was definitely Heather Petersen's, but Dax couldn't imagine what had put so much excitement into it. "I really need to talk to her."

Bashir grimaced. "She's only just woken, Ensign. I really don't think she's up to critiquing the rough draft of your new subspace-physics article—"

"It's not that—it's the wormhole! It's doing something wonderful. Something that she *has* to see."

Bashir's voice had settled back into doctorly steadiness. "I'd really like to keep her under observation for another hour or so—hey!" He lifted his hand from his comm badge and scowled at Dax. "What are you doing?"

"Discharging myself." She sat up straighter in the bed, patting about beneath her for the drawer that should hold her uniform and comm badge. "You said I was fit to go back to duty. Now get out of here, so I can get dressed and see the wormhole."

"For a Trill who's just recovered from systemic shock, I really can't recommend—"

"Julian, scram!"

Dax found Heather Petersen standing together with Kira and Sisko at the large observation port on the Promenade. Outside, the usual darkness of space had been blasted into luminescent brilliance. A waterfall of light poured from the wormhole: fierce volcanic crimson melting into iris bronze, soft apple green shading to translucent glacial blue. Kira watched it with almost supernatural awe, but Sisko only looked tense and tired. He glanced up at Dax as she joined them, his worried look easing into a smile of welcome.

"Well, old man, it's good to see you on your feet again." He clasped Dax's shoulder warmly and drew her closer to the thick transparent aluminum of the observation port. "What do you make of the fireworks out there?"

Dax watched the steady outpouring of light for another moment, then glanced over at Petersen. The cadet was engrossed in whatever readouts she had linked to her portable data padd, but there was no fear or tension in her face. Dax relaxed, her own suspicions confirmed by the excited smile the younger scientist turned on her.

"Energy equalization?" she asked, before Petersen could say anything.

The cadet's smile widened. "Yes, exactly! How did you guess without seeing the subspace matrix scans, Lieutenant?"

"I've been living with this particular subspace matrix for a long time, Heather." Dax watched a vivid purple corona sink into ultraviolet invisibility for a moment, then flash back to dark dragon's-blood red to start the cycle all over again. "And there's clearly no destructive patterning to this—it's just pure energy release through the visible spectrum. That's the part of the EM spectrum," she added for

Sisko and Kira's benefit, "that poses the least threat to living organisms."

Kira made a sound of vague comprehension. "So the Prophets are doing this on purpose? It's some kind of release—"

"—of the excess chronodynamic energy they've absorbed over the last fifty hours," Dax finished, nodding. "It would be a lot more thermodynamically efficient for them to release it in a few high-intensity bursts, but they appear to know that would be hazardous to our health. So they're sending most of it five thousand years into the past. What we're seeing is the visible-spectrum backwash."

"Which proves beyond any scientific doubt that there really are sentient organisms in the singularity!" Petersen was flushed and breathless again. "I can't wait to write *this* up for the *Journal of Subspace Reviews!*"

"Five thousand years in the past?" Sisko's face went blank. "Tell me, Dax, what will happen—what did happen—when those bursts hit the Fury fleet?"

Dax thought for a minute. "That much energy shooting out of the wormhole would cause major subspace tunneling. The Furies could have been thrown anywhere in the galaxy. Anywhere at all."

"An energy blast we caused," Sisko said, his voice heavy. "So they were right. We did it. We banished them. Threw them out of 'heaven.'"

"Or saved their lives," Dax, said, a little too lightly. "It's all in how you look at it." The two of them turned back to the circular rainbow of shifting colors outside the viewport, which now seemed much more than a pretty light show.

"How long will this backwash last, old man?" Sisko asked, his eyes still fixed on the expanding rainbow colors.

Dax consulted Petersen's data padd, tapping in a quick energy-decay curve and plotting the wormhole's current emissions against it. "Oh, I'd say it'll last for at least another day or so. After that, the wormhole should be safe to travel through again."

Kira's quick glow of smile chased the lines of strain from her face. "That's wonderful! That will give us time to fly the Kai and all the Vedeks up from Bajor to observe the Prophets in action."

Sisko gave her a considering glance. "And mend some of the bridges we burned by misplacing Pak Dorren? That's not a bad thought, Major. Why don't I issue those invitations personally—"

"Oh, no!" Kira brought both hands up to shoulder height, as if to ward off a threat instead of an offer of help. "No, Captain, you're going to be *much* too busy explaining to all the Ferengi and Orion traders on board why they're going to have to wait here another day before they can travel into the Gamma Quadrant. I wouldn't dream of taking up more of your time."

"Actually, I was hoping that you—"

"And it looks like your first customer is already here." Kira stepped back hurriedly, making room for Quark to scuttle in to join them. "I'll start on those invitations right away, sir."

Dax laughed, seeing the exasperated glance Sisko threw after her. "I'll give you a hand with the traders, Benjamin, if you really need one."

"Be careful, old man. I may take you up on that." He gave in at last to the repeated tugging on his uniform sleeve, and looked down at the impatient Ferengi beside him. "What is it, Quark?"

The Ferengi cleared his throat, giving Dax an oddly respectful glance. "Did I just hear the lieutenant say that the wormhole's going to be closed for another day or two?"

Sisko rolled his eyes, but answered patiently enough. "Yes, you did. Do you want to register a protest now or later?"

Quark drew himself up to his full, unimpressive height. "In emergency circumstances like these, registering a protest is the last thing I would do," he declared with ringingly false sincerity. "I know how much strain a ban on wormhole traffic puts on this station."

"Do you?" Dax asked, curiously.

Quark threw her a glittering Ferengi smile. "You wouldn't believe how profits—I mean, alcohol consumption—rises at times like these. Now, Captain, it occurs to me that what you need is a distraction."

Sisko inclined his head toward the prismatic waterfall of

color pouring out into deep space. "You don't think the fireworks display out there is distracting enough?"

"Not to hardworking spacers looking for a profitable way to fill their time." Quark insinuated himself between Sisko and Dax, sliding a hand through both their arms. "No, what I had in mind was a little gambling tournament—"

After

Out here where sunlight was a faraway glimmer in the blackness of space, ice lasted a long time. The cold outer dark sheltered it in safety, preserving the last debris of the nebula that had birthed this planet-rich system. Inside that litter of dirty ice, the random dance of gravity sent one dark mass grazing too close to a neighbor, ejecting it into the unyielding pull of solar gravity. Unburdened by internal fragments of steel and empty space, no longer carrying memories of distant strife and blood and battle, the comet began its first journey toward the distant sun. It swung past the captured ninth planet, past the four gas giants, past the ring of rocky fragments and the cold red desert planet. Then, for the first time, it began to glow, brushed into brilliance by the gathering heat of the sun's nuclear furnace. By the time it approached the cloud-feathered planet that harbored life, it had become brighter than any star. Its flare pierced that planet's blue sky, amazing the primitive tribes who hunted and gathered and scratched at the earth with sticks to grow their food. They watched and wondered at it for a few days, until the comet's borrowed light began to fade. Then they forgot it, while the tumbling ice began its long journey back to the outer dark.

It would return to the sun again, regular as the turning seasons if more slow. As the centuries and millennia passed, it would trace its elliptical path fifty more times, growing smaller each time it neared the nuclear fire it orbited. It saw dim fires glow to life on the nightside of the bluish globe that harbored life. It saw the fires brighten and spread, leaping across vast oceans. It saw them merge to form huge networks of light, outlining every coast and lake and river. And it saw them leap into the ocean of space. Out to the planet's single moon at first, then later to its cold, red neighbor, then to the moons of the gas giants. Finally, out beyond all of them, to the stars. . . .

**The
Invasion
Concludes
in**

BOOK FOUR

The Final Fury

by

Dafydd Ab Hugh

There is no fear. There is no pain. There is no emotion . . . let it fade and disappear. Pure logic; logic fills your brain. Thought is symbol, and logic gives you complete power over all symbols.

The meditation helped, but Lieutenant Tuvok still found himself caught in the grip of illogical emotion, the DNA memory of a hundred thousand years ago perturbing his endocrine system, triggering the release of Vulcan vidrenalase, which affects Vulcans as adrenaline affects humans. Tuvok trembled; he could not control the fine motor skills. It was the best he could do to maintain a veneer of logic and rationality across a sea of barbaric feelings and impulses.

He stumbled along behind the Fury, behind the captain and Neelix, through the warm, moist tunnel. Even in his nightmare state, he could not help but notice that it was like a return up the birth canal; but rather than fascinate him, as it should have, the image filled Tuvok with the unaccustomed *emotions* of loathing and disgust.

Like the impulse to kill the interlocutor, Navdaq, and every other demon on the planet, all twenty-seven billion of them. It was worse than the *pon farr*—at least the mating madness was carefully channeled by ritual. Tuvok had no ritual to deal with the primitive emotions that these creatures stirred in him. Only his meditation.

Tuvok was not bothered by the darkness of the corridor, nor by what the captain considered disturbing architecture: angles that did not quite meet at ninety degrees but looked as thought they ought to, tricks of perspective that made walls or ceilings seem closer or farther than they were, or strange tilts that threw off a human's sense of balance, which was tied so completely into visual cuing.

But he was disturbed by the sudden intrusion of a long-forgotten cavern in the Vulcan mind, the genetic memory of defeat and slavery so complete and remote it left no trace in the historical record, which was thought to have stretched back farther in time than the conquest.

Evidently not, thought Tuvok, clutching at the logical train of thought; *apparently, there are significant gaps in the historical record. I must write a report for the* Vulcan Journal of Archeology and Prehistory. Then he shuddered.

In our innermost beings, we are not very different from Romulans after all, he thought. With bitterness—another emotion; they came thick and fast now.

In fact, Tuvok realized they would never stop . . . not until he forced himself to confront the Fury. Gritting his teeth against the terrors, Tuvok increased his stride until he stood but an arm's length behind Navdaq; then with a quick move, before he could disgrace his race further by losing his nerve, Tuvok reached out and caught Navdaq by the shoulder, spinning the creature around to face him.

Tuvok looked directly into Navdaq's face—and felt an abyss open inside him deep enough to his hearts.

I know you! he thought, unable to keep excitement and emotion even out of his thoughts. *You are Ok'San, the Overlord!*

Ok'San was the most despised of all Vulcan demons, for she was the mother of all the rest. The mythology was so ancient that it was consciously known only to a few scholars; even Tuvok knew only dimly of the stories, and only because of his interest in Vulcan history.

But all Vulcans knew and—to tell the truth—feared Ok'San, for she represented *loss of control* and *loss of reason;* there was little else that a sane Vulcan feared apart from the loss of everything it meant to be a Vulcan: logic, control, order, and reason.

In demonic mythology, Ok'San crept through the windows at night, the hot, dry Vulcan night, and crouched on the chests of her "chosen" dreamers: poets, composers, authors, philosophers, scientists, political analysts . . . the very people whose creativity was slowly knitting together the barbaric strands of early Vulcan society into a vision of a logical tomorrow, who groped for shreds of civilization in the horror of Vulcan's yesterday.

She crouched on a dreamer's chest, leaned over his writhing body, and pressed her lips against his. She spat into his mouth, and the spittle rolled down his throat and filled his hearts with the *Fury of Vulcan*.

The Fury of Vulcan manifested as a berserker rage that flooded the victim and drove him to paroxysms of horrific violence that defied the descriptive power of logic.

Tuvok had tried to contemplate what must pass through a Vulcan's mind to drive him to kill his own family with a blunt stick, striking their heads hard enough to crush bone and muscle and still have force enough to destroy the brain. In one of the few instances of the Fury of Vulcan to be well recorded by the testimony of many witnesses, a Vulcan hunter-warrior named Torkas Torkas of the Vehm, perhaps eighty thousand years ago, grabbed up a leaf-bladed Vulcan Toth spear and set out after the entire population of his village. He managed to kill ninety-seven and wound an additional fourteen, six critically, before he was killed.

Tuvok had always believed Ok'San was the personification of the violent, nearly sadistic rage that filled the hearts of Vulcans before Surak. The Fury of Vulcan always seemed like a disease of the nervous system; yet it was curious that there were no recorded instances of the Fury within historical times . . . not a one.

Diseases do not die out; and it was unlikely in the extreme that primitive Vulcans who had neither logic nor medical science could have destroyed the virus that caused the Fury.

It was an enigma, until now.

Look for
STAR TREK® VOYAGER™
Invasion! Book Four
The Final Fury
Wherever Paperback Books Are Sold
Available from
Pocket Books

**It is the Day of Reckoning
It is the Day of Judgement
It is...**

STAR TREK®
THE DAY OF HONOR

**A Four-Part Klingon™ Saga
That Spans the Generations**

**Coming Summer 1997
from Pocket Books**

THE UNIVERSE IS EXPANDING

STAR TREK
— COMMUNICATOR —

...ENGAGE

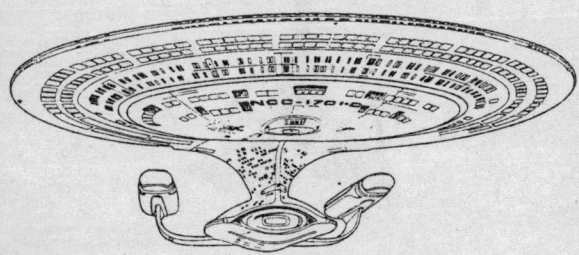

A PUBLICATION OF THE OFFICIAL STAR TREK FAN CLUB ™

SUBSCRIPTION ONLY $14.95!

Subscribe now and you'll receive:

★ A year's subscription to our full-color official bi-monthly magazine, the *STAR TREK COMMUNICATOR*, packed with information not found anywhere else on the movies and television series, and profiles of celebrities and futurists.

★ A galaxy of *STAR TREK* merchandise and hard to find collectibles, *a premier investment for collectors of all ages.*

★ Our new subscriber kit. It includes a set of 9 highly collectible Skybox Trading Cards and exclusive poster, and discounts on *STAR TREK* events around the U.S. for members only.

TO SUBSCRIBE, USE YOUR VISA OR MASTERCARD AND CALL 1-800-TRUE-FAN (800-878-3326) MONDAY THRU FRIDAY, 8:30am TO 5:00pm mst OR MAIL CHECK OR MONEY ORDER FOR $14.95 TO:

STAR TREK: THE OFFICIAL FAN CLUB
PO BOX 111000, AURORA COLORADO 80042

SUBSCRIPTION FOR ONE YEAR– $14.95 (U.S.)

NAME _____

ADDRESS _____

CITY/STATE _____

ZIP _____

TM, ®&© 1994 Paramount Pictures. All Rights Reserved. STAR TREK and related marks are trademarks of Paramount Pictures. Authorized user.

STVFC

INVASION!
The Fury ships were closing.

In the captain's chair of the *U.S.S. Voyager,* Commander Chakotay could think of only one way out. *But do I have the guts to take it?* he asked himself. Chakotay shrugged, feeling his heart begin to race just at the thought; but he had no choice . . . he had to get the Furies off his tail, and that meant they had to think the *Voyager* was dead.

"B'Elanna," he said after a moment, "how long would it take you to reconfigure the shields to metaphasic?"

"About two minutes; but why would I want to . . . Chakotay! You *can't* be thinking of—"

He nodded, lips pressed together either in a grim smile or an amused grimace. "Set a new course," he said, "directly into the sun."

Look for STAR TREK Fiction from Pocket Books

Star Trek: The Original Series

The Ashes of Eden
Federation
Sarek
Best Destiny
Shadows on the Sun
Probe
Prime Directive
The Lost Years
Star Trek VI: The Undiscovered Country
Star Trek V: The Final Frontier
Star Trek IV: The Voyage Home
Spock's World
Enterprise
Strangers from the Sky
Final Frontier

#1 *Star Trek: The Motion Picture*
#2 *The Entropy Effect*
#3 *The Klingon Gambit*
#4 *The Covenant of the Crown*
#5 *The Prometheus Design*
#6 *The Abode of Life*
#7 *Star Trek II: The Wrath of Khan*
#8 *Black Fire*
#9 *Triangle*
#10 *Web of the Romulans*
#11 *Yesterday's Son*
#12 *Mutiny on the Enterprise*
#13 *The Wounded Sky*
#14 *The Trellisane Confrontation*
#15 *Corona*
#16 *The Final Reflection*
#17 *Star Trek III: The Search for Spock*
#18 *My Enemy, My Ally*
#19 *The Tears of the Singers*
#20 *The Vulcan Academy Murders*
#21 *Uhura's Song*
#22 *Shadow Lord*
#23 *Ishmael*
#24 *Killing Time*
#25 *Dwellers in the Crucible*
#26 *Pawns and Symbols*
#27 *Mindshadow*
#28 *Crisis on Centaurus*
#29 *Dreadnought!*
#30 *Demons*
#31 *Battlestations!*

#32 *Chain of Attack*
#33 *Deep Domain*
#34 *Dreams of the Raven*
#35 *The Romulan Way*
#36 *How Much for Just the Planet?*
#37 *Bloodthirst*
#38 *The IDIC Epidemic*
#39 *Time for Yesterday*
#40 *Timetrap*
#41 *The Three-Minute Universe*
#42 *Memory Prime*
#43 *The Final Nexus*
#44 *Vulcan's Glory*
#45 *Double, Double*
#46 *The Cry of the Onlies*
#47 *The Kobayashi Maru*
#48 *Rules of Engagement*
#49 *The Pandora Principle*
#50 *Doctor's Orders*
#51 *Enemy Unseen*
#52 *Home Is the Hunter*
#53 *Ghost Walker*
#54 *A Flag Full of Stars*
#55 *Renegade*
#56 *Legacy*
#57 *The Rift*
#58 *Face of Fire*
#59 *The Disinherited*
#60 *Ice Trap*
#61 *Sanctuary*
#62 *Death Count*
#63 *Shell Game*
#64 *The Starship Trap*
#65 *Windows on a Lost World*
#66 *From the Depths*
#67 *The Great Starship Race*
#68 *Firestorm*
#69 *The Patrian Transgression*
#70 *Traitor Winds*
#71 *Crossroad*
#72 *The Better Man*
#73 *Recovery*
#74 *The Fearful Summons*
#75 *First Frontier*
#76 *The Captain's Daughter*
#77 *Twilight's End*
#78 *The Rings of Tautee*
#79 *Invasion 1: First Strike*

Star Trek: The Next Generation

Kahless
Star Trek Generations
All Good Things
Q-Squared
Dark Mirror
Descent
The Devil's Heart
Imzadi
Relics
Reunion
Unification
Metamorphosis
Vendetta
Encounter at Farpoint

#1 Ghost Ship
#2 The Peacekeepers
#3 The Children of Hamlin
#4 Survivors
#5 Strike Zone
#6 Power Hungry
#7 Masks
#8 The Captains' Honor
#9 A Call to Darkness
#10 A Rock and a Hard Place
#11 Gulliver's Fugitives
#12 Doomsday World
#13 The Eyes of the Beholders

#14 Exiles
#15 Fortune's Light
#16 Contamination
#17 Boogeymen
#18 Q-in-Law
#19 Perchance to Dream
#20 Spartacus
#21 Chains of Command
#22 Imbalance
#23 War Drums
#24 Nightshade
#25 Grounded
#26 The Romulan Prize
#27 Guises of the Mind
#28 Here There Be Dragons
#29 Sins of Commission
#30 Debtors' Planet
#31 Foreign Foes
#32 Requiem
#33 Balance of Power
#34 Blaze of Glory
#35 Romulan Stratagem
#36 Into the Nebula
#37 The Last Stand
#38 Dragon's Honor
#39 Rogue Saucer
#40 Possession
#41 Invasion 2: The Soldiers of Fear

Star Trek: Deep Space Nine

Warped
The Search
#1 Emissary
#2 The Siege
#3 Bloodletter
#4 The Big Game
#5 Fallen Heroes
#6 Betrayal
#7 Warchild

#8 Antimatter
#9 Proud Helios
#10 Valhalla
#11 Devil in the Sky
#12 The Laertian Gamble
#13 Station Rage
#14 The Long Night
#15 Objective Bajor
#16 Invasion 3: Time's Enemy

Star Trek: Voyager

#1 Caretaker
#2 The Escape
#3 Ragnarok
#4 Violations
#5 Incident at Arbuk
#6 The Murdered Sun
#7 Ghost of a Chance
#8 Cybersong
#9 Invasion 4: The Final Fury

For orders other than by individual consumers, Pocket Books grants a discount on the purchase of **10 or more** copies of single titles for special markets or premium use. For further details, please write to the Vice-President of Special Markets, Pocket Books, 1633 Broadway, New York, NY 10019-6785, 8th Floor.

For information on how individual consumers can place orders, please write to Mail Order Department, Simon & Schuster Inc., 200 Old Tappan Road, Old Tappan, NJ 07675.

THE FINAL FURY

DAFYDD AB HUGH

INVASION! concept by John J. Ordover and Diane Carey

POCKET BOOKS
New York   London   Toronto   Sydney   Tokyo   Singapore

The sale of this book without its cover is unauthorized. If you purchased this book without a cover, you should be aware that it was reported to the publisher as "unsold and destroyed." Neither the author nor the publisher has received payment for the sale of this "stripped book."

This book is a work of fiction. Names, characters, places and incidents are products of the author's imagination or are used fictitiously. Any resemblance to actual events or locales or persons, living or dead, is entirely coincidental.

An *Original* Publication of POCKET BOOKS

POCKET BOOKS, a division of Simon & Schuster Inc.
1230 Avenue of the Americas, New York, NY 10020

Copyright © 1996 by Paramount Pictures. All Rights Reserved.

STAR TREK is a Registered Trademark of
Paramount Pictures.

A VIACOM COMPANY

This book is published by Pocket Books, a division of
Simon & Schuster Inc., under exclusive license from
Paramount Pictures.

All rights reserved, including the right to reproduce
this book or portions thereof in any form whatsoever.
For information address Pocket Books, 1230 Avenue
of the Americas, New York, NY 10020

ISBN: 0-671-54181-1

First Pocket Books printing August 1996

10 9 8 7 6

POCKET and colophon are registered trademarks of
Simon & Schuster Inc.

Printed in the U.S.A.

THE FINAL FURY

PRELUDE

THE WAR RAGED FOR A HUNDRED THOUSAND YEARS.

The Furies once were hosts of heaven; but heaven was all but closed to them now. The Unclean swept across the vast expanse of space, across the 217 million star systems known mapped, and held in heaven by the Furies. The new enemy was unlike all those who had preceeded it: alone among the sentient races of the galaxy, the insectoid Unclean were unaffected by the Terrors unleashed upon the disobedient by the lords of heaven.

Taken by surprise, the host—six hundred and sixty-six separate races bound together into a single people—were driven first from the planets at the rim of the galaxy, whence the Unclean invaded, drinking energy and draining away the life-force of entire armadas of a million ships or more. Perhaps the Unclean were the cursed union of vermin and castaway subjects, fleeing their rightful lord on the Throne of the Autocrat. Perhaps instead they came from *outside,* and were not of this galaxy at all; the latter was the more popular speculation among the war leaders among the Furies—it mattered not, for the Unclean burst upon the righteous hosts like an ocean upon the volcano, washing them away.

A fragment of a story dating from that dark time hinted at a greater darkness: that the subject races cast their lot *with the Unclean,* rebelling against their righteous masters. They stood their ground even when the Furies sent the Terrors. Though the subject races died like bugs beneath the Fury heel, and though the Terror lash was used against them over and over, still they maintained, fighting until the end of the first millennium—when the Furies were forced to retreat from the rim of the galaxy.

The farthest provinces were lost.

For century after century, the Furies retreated. There were battles—many times, the hosts stood against monstrous swarms that flew through the starry void without ships, without life-support. The first great stand engaged 93,109,907 Fury vessels carrying enough warriors to people a hundred planets against Unclean too numerous to count; but the records left by Subcrat Ramszak the Ok'San, who stood four meters tall and sported a hand where one ear should have been, gave the count as more than ten Unclean for every Fury.

The *last* great stand involved a mere fifty thousand ships, give or take, with warriors spread thin among them. Tiin, the Cannibal Whose Bed Would Not Be Shared, commanded the final defense, this time from the Autocrat's chair; Tiin traced his ancestory back through an entirely male line for a thousand generations to Ramszak himself, but he fared no better than his illustrious but defeated ancestor.

A small fleet of a few thousand ships lured the main contingent of the wasplike Unclean by attacking them from out of the black. The attack broke a four-century truce; but the hosts of heaven were not bound by promises made to insect minds.

The Unclean responded to the taunt. The entire remaining *field-unity* of Unclean pursued the marauding fleet; and when the last Fury ships retreated, they numbered twenty-one out of more than four thousand.

The enemy approached them from different vectors; but

when the swarms assembled for attack, and the Furies prepared to die, a blast of light engulfed them. The Furies fell through nonspace, their minds reeling from the passage.

The enemy made to follow the hosts . . . but as they approached, the light changed, their space-born, space-living bodies melted, fused, reduced in seconds to atoms, and then less than atoms, and everything at last, after many steps, over the space of microseconds, transmuting to dead.

The light was so great that scientists among the subject races would be able to detect it even after three or four millennia. The swarms were decimated but not annihilated; the remaining wasps fell upon few remaining Furies as they passed through the swirling, gaseous debris that had once been living members of the Unclean.

Tiin was unprepared for his responsibility; he was, in the end, a poor representative of the line that had begun with Subcrat Ramszak. He lost control of his few ships, and the captains panicked, firing wildly . . . almost as if they were suddenly bathed with their own Terrors—though all Furies were, quite simply, immune to fear themselves.

Against the backdrop of a sky turned negative, black suns silhouetted against a sky yet white from the collapsing stars, a single, small host made the journey along the entirety of the wormhole, a trip that took four years—or no time at all. When they reached the other side, the light faded. Wherever they were, there would be no return to their bright black heaven.

It was not until they found and settled a planet that they realized the enormity of the Unclean victory . . . for the Furies were trapped in a hellish realm of space, so far from heaven that they sickened and began to die from sheer loneliness. The Fury surgeons studied the disease for hundreds of years. The symptoms were always the same: black depression, followed by ennui, then anomie, the loss of all ethical and moral boundaries. They grew their population, even while the best and most promising were struck down in their prime of intellect and will by the Factor, as it was called.

D'Mass, the greatest Autocrat-in-Exile, who was the last to unite all the Furies, himself diagnosed the Factor: they had lost their way, their purpose, their reason for existing. The hosts of heaven were born to *rule* heaven, not watch it from so far away that the light they observed was generated by the stars of heaven at precisely the moment when Ramszak had staked everything on an all-or-nothing bid to destroy the Unclean . . . and had lost.

Under D'Mass, all of the Furies worked together to develop and construct an artificial wormhole to bring them back home. But when D'Mass died, his two sons fell to quarreling between themselves.

In the end, D'Vass sought to leave with nine-tenths of the Furies to found a new world and forget about heaven; while his brother Bin Mass chose to stay and direct all efforts to the artificial wormhole. But Bin Mass could not afford to lose the talent in D'Vass's host; they battled from dawn until dusk, then slept together as brothers, only to wake and do battle again. Millions of Furies died in the war, slain by their brothers out of heaven. At last, D'Vass fled—but with a greatly diminished host, a mere forty thousand.

Bin Mass had conquered the hearts of his people; and by rededicating the Fury hosts to reclaiming heaven, no matter how long it might take, he conquered the Factor as well. No longer were the Furies lost and wandering; now they were focused and driven.

They would eradicate the Unclean from the blessed place, no matter what the cost. The time would be ripe someday; the moment would come. And when it did, the galaxy would tremble once more to the cold, brittle voice of the Autocrat.

CHAPTER 1

Captain Kathryn Janeway of the U.S.S. Voyager sat behind the desk in her quarters, swaying gently, trying to avoid actually becoming ill onto the stack of duty rosters littering the desktop. The ship rolled back and forth, causing the fluids in her inner ear to perform acrobatics.

Well, I knew it was going to happen, she thought; this far from the Federation, from the nearest starbase, without any chance for maintenance or repair other than what the crew did themselves, Janeway knew the ship systems would begin to fail, one by one.

Unfortunately, the most recent one to fail was the inertial damper/gravitic stabilizer system. Motion that ordinarily would be damped down to a slight vibration instead became a lurching, rolling gait that was causing terrible havoc with crew health . . . and morale.

Is this the torture that sailors on the old oceangoing ships had to endure? she wondered, swallowing several times. *If it is, I wonder how anyone survived to cross a small lake, let alone an entire ocean!*

She stood, feeling the air clammy against her sweaty skin.

STAR TREK: INVASION!

Like most everyone else in Starfleet, Captain Janeway had ridden on sailboats, sloops, four-masters—in the holodeck. Controlled by a friendly computer that understood the unpleasantness of seasickness and minimized the roll, pitch, and especially yaw.

But the present nauseating dance was constant, uncontrolled, interminable . . . and worse, it included the fear, haunting the back of her mind, that if the ship hit a subspace fiber bundle, they would lurch violently—as they already had once, throwing everything, including Captain Janeway herself, to the deck in a heap.

Or into a bulkhead, headfirst; the holographic doctor was already treating one crew member who had fractured one of his vertebrae and suffered a serious concussion; the next time, someone could be killed.

Janeway cleared her throat, swallowing again. "Janeway to Torres," she croaked; her voice was so strained, it took the computer a moment to recognize her.

"T-Torres here," said the equally strangled voice of the *Voyager*'s chief engineer, Lieutenant B'Elanna Torres; Janeway felt an uncaptainlike pleasure when she noted that Torres's vaunted Klingon half did not prevent her from being as spacesick as the rest of the crew.

"Do you have a new time estimate?"

There was no need to specify any further; the only problem on anybody's mind on the ship was the failure of the gravitic stabilizers.

"Estimate . . . excuse me, Captain." The sound cut off momentarily. When it returned, B'Elanna Torres's voice sounded a bit weaker. "Estimate unchanged. Twelve to twenty-four hours, depending on . . ."

"On?"

"On whether we can fix it at all, using these damned bureaucratic, stupid, useless—"

A new voice chimed in, annoyed; Lieutenant Carey rose to defend Federation procedure against unorthodoxy.

"Depending on whether someone who shall remain nameless will just stick to the process, instead of trying a hundred so-called shortcuts!"

Damn, thought the captain; *they've been doing so well!* It must be the nausea, she decided; everyone was edgy, including Janeway herself.

The captain reached into the depths of her soul, bypassing as well as she could the depths of her stomach; she spoke with the Command Tone she had learned at the Academy. *"That is enough,* people. We're in a difficult enough situation without you two bickering. Torres, would it help if I were to reconfigure the stabilizers to run off the replicator-holodeck power grid?"

"Nothing will help," said the half-Klingon engineer, letting her pessimistic human side take over. "We'll never get the ship steady. I'm sick, and I just wish I were back in a nice, safe Maquis ship without all this weird, bioneural circuitry!"

Janeway forced the conversation back to solutions. "I'm going to redirect the power; keep working, stop arguing, and give me a better time estimate in fifteen minutes. Janeway out."

The captain stood; it was hard to maintain balance with the deck rolling beneath her feet, but the nausea was less intense. If the *Voyager* struck another subspace fiber bundle, she would just have to hope she didn't break anything on the way down.

Her stateroom was spacious by Starfleet standards . . . almost as large as any bachelor apartment in a minor city on any insignificant planet in the Federation. But she loved it; it was hers. The entire ship was her stateroom.

A voice full of peeved indignation invaded her space. "Neelix to Captain Janeway!" Neelix, the ship's Talaxian cook, had never quite caught on to the fact that he did not need to bellow when initiating communications; the computer would figure it out at normal speaking volume.

"Janeway here. What's wrong, Neelix?" She was glad not to be in Neelix's kitchen; she could imagine the carnage wreaked upon pots, pans, and vats of food by the failed stabilizers.

"What's wrong is this insufferable turbulence! I'm trying to prepare a bravura meal for the crew, and I can't even keep my ingredients from flying off the counters onto the floor!"

"Neelix, don't you think if we could stop the rolling, we would have already?" *Ouch! Didn't mean to be that harsh.* "We're working on it, Neelix." She leaned against her desk as the ship lurched again; a stack of reports fell to the deck with a loud clatter.

"Well, why don't you simply *stop the ship* until you fix the problem? Surely we can afford one or two days' delay. But we can ill afford a crew too sick to even enjoy the simple, culinary pleasures."

Janeway rolled her eyes, grateful that the comm link was auditory only. She waited a couple of beats until she could speak calmly. "Neelix, if we stop the ship in our present situation, without gravitic stabilizers, the angular velocity of the warp-core reaction itself will cause the ship to start spinning like a top."

"Really? What an odd design decision."

"We're going the speed we're going precisely because it minimizes the roll."

"This is the minimum?"

"This *is* the minimum, Neelix. Now please return to your duties and let me return to mine. Janeway . . . wait, what did you say you were cooking?"

"I didn't say. I'm cooking pate of Denethan bloodbladder, Ocampan cream punch, and a Federation dish whose recipe I found in the computer . . . Three-Cheese Quiche!"

"Oh," said the captain, feeling her stomach begin to roll in the opposite direction from the ship. "Very—very good. Carry on. Janeway out."

Swallowing repeatedly, she shuffled forward through the door and onto the bridge. "Captain on the bridge," chimed the computer protocol program, but as usual nobody paid any attention; Captain Janeway was long on performance but short on ritual.

Everyone on the bridge looked grim-faced but determined; *determined not to disgrace himself by actually succumbing to spacesickness,* she thought. The curved bridge console actually seemed to warp slightly, another trick of the instability. Lieutenant Tom Paris used his elbows to steady himself against the helm; his hands played across the console, making minor adjustments. Janeway didn't know whether they did any good; perhaps it just made Paris feel better to be "doing something."

Ensign Harry Kim hunched over his console, staring at his viewer; he had nothing much to do at the moment, but he continued scanning the sector anyway . . . probably for the same reason Paris made continual course adjustments.

Janeway was surprised to note that even Lieutenant Tuvok, who normally stood at his tactical station, was seated.

She stood at the door to her ready room, preventing it from closing, and surveyed the bridge crew more carefully, assessing their health. Paris looked jovial and full of bonhomie; but he sweated profusely, and his face was white. Tuvok appeared at first glance to be unaffected by the ship's motion, but Janeway knew him well enough to understand that he felt as sick as everyone else; he simply placed the feeling in the same category as an emotion—something to be ignored and suppressed.

Commander Chakotay, sitting in his command chair, looked inquiringly at the captain, his face asking whether he should relinquish command. His face also looked slightly green.

Janeway smiled, gritting her teeth. "I see the ancient nausea remedy of your people worked no better for you than it did for me."

Chakotay tried unsuccessfully to smile. "It only works when the water comes from the Long Woman Mountains, not the replicator."

Of all the crew on the bridge, Kim was the only one completely unaffected by the rocking and rolling of the ship . . . a fact that Captain Janeway found both annoying and perplexing.

She sat heavily in her chair, whence she checked the forward viewer; the computer stabilized the image, but it couldn't stabilize Janeway's head. Thus, she saw the stars as jagged lines, rather than dots; the effect was disconcerting, to say the least.

"Ensign Kim," she called.

Harry Kim eagerly swiveled his chair around. "Yes, Captain?"

"I wrote a—excuse me—I wrote a program that transfers power from the replicator-holodeck power grid to the gravitic stabilizers. Implement it."

"Aye, Captain."

"Activate Emergency Medical Holographic Program."

The doctor's face suddenly appeared on the viewer; Janeway found him much easier to look at than the star jags.

"Please state the nature of the emergency," said the doctor as programmed; but he immediately appended "that is, if it's something different from the emergency I'm already very busy attending to."

"Doctor, *please* tell me you can do something."

If it was possible for a hologram to look pained, the doctor managed it. "Captain, the situation is unchanged. As I've told you, all my remedies lose efficacy over time. I presume that the ship will at some point, actually stop rolling. If you insist upon allowing the ship to continue rolling indefinitely, there is nothing I can do.

"The situation is unchanged here as well," said Janeway, softly.

"Correction," said Lieutenant Tuvok from his station; "the situation has changed rather dramatically."

The captain held up her hand to the doctor and turned to her science officer.

"Captain," continued Tuvok; "I am picking up a distress call."

"From whom?" asked Janeway, simultaneously grateful for the distraction and irked at the poor timing. "Is it any race we're familiar with?"

"Yes," said Tuvok, "we are quite familiar with the signal. The distress call is coming from a Starfleet shuttlecraft."

In the shocked silence, Captain Janeway asked, "Another wormhole? Is the signal current?" Once before, they had been fooled by a communication that came through a freak wormhole; but that transmission from a Romulan ship turned out to have come from decades in the past.

"The signal is of the type currently in use by Starfleet," said Tuvok; "it comes from a Galaxy-class starship shuttlecraft, the *Lewis,* which Starfleet records indicate is attached to the *U.S.S. Enterprise.*"

"Does its stardate match ours?"

"Yes, Captain. I do not believe the signal is coming to us through a wormhole. The indications are that the shuttlecraft is, indeed, in this quadrant, approximately two-point-one-five light-years distant."

Tuvok stood; Janeway noted that even the Vulcan had to grip his console to steady himself. "Captain, it is reasonable to assume that we are not the only representatives of the Federation in this quadrant. Despite the distance, which ordinarily is far beyond our capacity to scan in any detail, I picked up a single life-form aboard . . . a human male. He is not moving but is alive."

"How is this possible, Tuvok? That you could scan him, I mean."

"I can only conclude that something is boosting both transmissions, our scan and the shuttlecraft's distress call."

Janeway sat back, nonplussed. A *Federation* ship and pilot? She had dreamed of such a break for so many months; and now, maybe . . . maybe . . .

She dismissed the daydream. As captain, she had a job to do; she had a ship to protect. She could not allow her reason to be overwhelmed by what she *wanted* to be true.

"Shall I lay in the course, Captain?" asked Paris.

Captain Janeway hesitated. Under ordinary circumstances, she would have assented even before Paris finished the question. But the circumstances were not ordinary.

She looked at Lieutenant Paris, who still wore his frozen smile, holding down his nausea by a great act of will. He sat poised over the helm console, ready to engage the course he had already computed.

Everyone stared at Janeway. *Oh well,* she thought, *I guess this is why they let me wear the four pips.*

"Stand by, Lieutenant Paris." She raised her voice. "Janeway to Torres. Lieutenant, have you been monitoring the distress call?"

"I just picked it up," came the engineer's voice, stronger now. "Captain, it might be a trap! We're being lured closer. . . . There couldn't possibly be a Federation ship out here."

"I might point out," said Tuvok, with impeccable, Vulcan logic, "that there *is* a Federation ship out here: the *U.S.S. Voyager.*"

"Tuvok's right," said Janeway; "if we can be sucked here by an unknown force, so can someone else."

"I can feel in my gut that there's something wrong with this entire setup," insisted B'Elanna.

Again, Tuvok spoke up. "Captain, Starfleet protocols require that we—"

"I am well aware of Starfleet protocols," sighed Janeway.

The question was, did the safety of her ship take precedence over a shuttlecraft distress call? And so far away from the Federation, was there even a Starfleet, let alone protocols?

As soon as she asked herself the question, she knew the answer. Wherever there was a Starfleet ship, there was Starfleet. "Lieutenant Paris, lay in a course and engage. If the door opens in one direction, perhaps it will open in the other direction as well."

"Everyone hold tight," warned Paris; "without the stabilizers, this is going to be a rough turn."

The captain braced, but she wasn't prepared for what she felt: the *Voyager* felt as though it suddenly accelerated *backward* at several g's. It was a trick of perspective; all the rolling was ultimately an illusion. *Under classic subspace theory,* she recalled, *the ship doesn't really exist at all at warp speed;* as near as Janeway could judge from watching the crew sway, no two members of the crew reacted to precisely the same motion.

They all reacted to a horrific forward force when they turned, however. Janeway felt as though she were dangled upside down by her feet with a kilogram weight attached to each eyeball; but when Paris completed the turn, the ship returned to the familiar enemy of stomach-churning rolls.

"En route to intercept the shuttlecraft," gasped Paris, swallowing hard.

"En route to intercept the shuttlecraft," gasped Paris, swallowing hard.

We had better have a plan of action long before we arrive, she decided. "In my ready room," said the captain, rising as smartly as possible under the circumstances.

The senior staff assembled around the discussion table—or the "peace rock," as Chakotay jokingly thought of it. Chakotay looked around the room, trying to gauge reactions: B'Elanna looked suspicious, Paris excited, Kim nervous, and Janeway worried.

The captain turned to her helmsman. "Mr. Paris, how long to reach the shuttlecraft?"

"I'd give it a good two days to be sure."

Chakotay spoke up. "We might be able to shave that down to twenty-four hours by accelerating to warp seven, but at that speed, we might lose some crew members to sudden gravitic neutralization."

"I'm not willing to risk killing my own crew," said Janeway. "The castaway will have to wait the extra day."

She looks haggard, thought Chakotay; *she's lost track of her spirit guide. Of course, so have we all,* he mentally appended; when mind and body were out of balance, mistakes became more likely.

"Mr. Tuvok," asked the commander, "how did you first pick up the signal?"

Tuvok still controlled the spacesickness that had laid low everyone else except Harry Kim. "Commander, the signal appeared mysteriously, already activated. I cannot be certain, but I believe I caught a faint echo from the wormhole itself. I was only able to scan at such a long distance by using the distress beacon as a carrier wave."

Janeway typed at her console, possibly playing with some equations. "People," she said, "I've modeled every variation for power-boosting I could think of, and I simply cannot come up with a scenario by which a shuttlecraft could project a distress beacon two light-years. A starship, maybe . . . but the power is simply not present on that shuttlecraft."

"The signal must be boosted somehow," said Tuvok.

B'Elanna Torres, sitting next to Chakotay, called up the schematics of the shuttlecraft; the commander watched over her shoulder. "You're right," said B'Elanna to the captain. "I *knew* there was something wrong with this entire scenario! It *is* a trap, and this proves it. We should get as far away from here as possible, Captain."

Ensign Kim sat on Chakotay's other side; the young man appeared to want to say something but was worried about interrupting his elders. Chakotay knew how he felt. "Mr. Kim, you have a comment?"

"Sir," said Kim, "when I was a kid, my best friend and I had a pair of communicators his mother gave us. We used to talk late at night, when we were supposed to be asleep, comparing interpretations of Paganini and Bizet."

B'Elanna stared at Kim for a moment, seemingly embarrassed. She opened her mouth to speak, but Chakotay put his hand on her arm.

Kim continued. "Then Alex moved to Singapore, far outside the range of the hand communicators we had. But we were still able to communicate: at prearranged times, we each got near the local comm-sat repeater, and it picked up the weak communicator signal and bounced it off the satellite. We sort of piggybacked the signal."

Tuvok had been quietly typing on a terminal from the moment Kim mentioned a repeater. "Captain," he said, "the signal does show evidence of having been boosted by a repeater, similar to Ensign Kim's scenario; the records indicate a faint subspace echo in the original signal, which our computer filtered out before we heard the message."

"Lieutenant Torres," said Janeway, "are you satisfied with this explanation? Does it seem reasonable?"

B'Elanna hesitated a long time, her rational, human side arguing with the warrior mentality of her Klingon side. She gave a questioning glance at Chakotay, who reassured her with a smile; *you are taken seriously,* he tried to convey. "Well . . . it *is* possible, I guess," she said. "I—I withdraw my recommendation that we ignore the signal, Captain."

"Good; I don't like to buck my senior crew. I much prefer we all sign on to a particular course of action."

Chakotay blinked. "Say, does anybody else notice anything different?"

B'Elanna was the first to speak. "Yes; the ship isn't rolling anymore!"

"To be precise," corrected Tuvok, "it is still rolling at approximately twelve-point-three percent of the former range of motion."

"I can live with that," mumbled Paris, his face slowly returning to a more normal shade. His smile did not look quite so strained to the commander.

"So," said Torres, "it seems I was wrong about your power-shunting trick as well, Captain. I seem to have been wrong about everything. Not the best quality in a ship's engineer."

Uh-oh . . . Lately, Chakotay had noticed B'Elanna's self-confidence dropping. He knew her better than anyone; *this is more serious than a momentary phase,* he realized. He would definitely have to talk to Janeway about it.

The captain tried to reassure her engineering officer. "B'Elanna, it was just an idea I remembered from an systems problem set back at the Academy."

"Maybe I should have stuck it out at the Academy."

"You're a good engineer, B'Elanna. Just because you didn't take the full course at Starfleet doesn't mean—"

"Captain, may I return to my station? I want to fully incorporate your innovation to eliminate the final twelve percent of roll."

Worse, thought Chakotay. B'Elanna's Klingon half would never allow her to admit her insecurity; she would not be able to turn to anyone, not Harry Kim—not even Chakotay himself.

"Certainly, B'Elanna," said Janeway. "Let me know when you think *you'll* regain full control of the stabilizers."

Chakotay winced as he heard the captain emphasize *you'll* in the order; B'Elanna picked up the emphasis in a heartbeat, and she took it as patronizing. He had known B'Elanna for a long time, and that was definitely the wrong approach. Chakotay could see her stiffen visibly.

"I think we've discussed about all that we usefully can

before arriving at the signal," said Janeway. "Now, let's get back to work."

B'Elanna Torres left the ready room and returned to the engineering deck and quickly brought up a visual representation of the wave equation the captain had uploaded. Torres told herself the slight tremble in her hands was a lingering effect of spacesickness.

Spacesickness also accounted for why she had not seen before what was so clear now: that Janeway's casual idea was the nucleus of a damping field that could entirely replace the gravitic stabilizers. *Of course; the stabilizers are basically redundant using the new system. All the time I spent repairing them was just wasted time, now that the captain has solved the problem by waving a magic technowand.*

You failed, whispered the tiny voice in B'Elanna's ear; *failed failed failed failed—and here comes Carey to gloat.*

Lieutenant Carey sat down beside his division officer, obviously very upset. "Sir, I'm really sorry I undercut you like that in front of the captain. I was very queasy, but that's no excuse."

"Thank you, Carey. But you were right about Starfleet procedures, and I was wrong."

"Well, I didn't figure it out either! It's the captain; she's just so—well, if she weren't a captain, she'd be the best chief engineer in Starfleet. Let's forget about the argument and just get on with the job. Deal?"

"You're right," said Torres without emotion. Without *audible* emotion; even she did not know which statement she was agreeing to, what Carey said out loud or what B'Elanna was convinced he really meant.

Within thirty minutes, building on the brainstorm of her friend and commanding officer, Torres fully controlled the ship's roll. She went through the remainder of her duties hollowly, wondering when the axe would fall, when Janeway would realize that Torres was really just an impostor in a Starfleet monkey suit.

CHAPTER 2

JANEWAY CHEERFULLY GAVE THE ORDER TO INCREASE TO MAXImum sustainable speed; the jury-rigged stabilizers held, and the *Voyager* shaved the travel time from two days to just under one day; but the distress signal ceased transmission only three hours into the journey.

When the signal died, so too died the sidebanded scan by which Tuvok could still report a living but immobile human being. The captain sailed into inky blackness, unable even to tell whether any sort of reception committee awaited them.

She lay on the couch in her quarters, staring up at the ceiling. Her door chirped; it was Tuvok and Chakotay, arrived at last. The Vulcan had detected an anomalous reading regarding the star nearest the distress signal, and Janeway's executive officer had thought it important enough to bring to her attention. Tuvok's first words, however, were "I suggest we not discuss this matter with the crew."

"Why not?" asked Commander Chakotay.

For a former Maquis, you have an odd antipathy toward secrets, thought Janeway.

"I fear the data may spark more fears of trickery."

"What's the reading?" asked Janeway.

"Captain, the spectral signature of the star indicates that it should be emitting a great deal more radiant energy than I detect. The light is redshifted far more than it should be, considering the distance, indicating some force drawing energy from the system."

"What could suck energy out of a star like that?"

"I would suggest a very high gravitational field, except the star's gravity appears to be normal for its position on the main sequence. The planets orbit at their proper distances and speeds."

Janeway thought for a long time. It was not that she did not trust B'Elanna Torres; it was just that . . .

"Why throw gasoline onto the fire?" muttered Chakotay.

"Gasoline?"

"Yes, Captain," said Tuvok; "the highly inflammable liquid used—"

"Yes, yes, I remember," said Janeway; "but what do you mean, throw it on the fire, Chakotay?"

"Why encourage further controversy?" explained the commander.

"All right. If both of you think we should keep it quiet, I'll have to agree. But slow our approach as we near the system; keep us out of sensor range—assuming there's anyone to scan us. And assuming they have sensors roughly equivalent to ours."

For the next eighteen hours, Janeway and B'Elanna between them tweaked the gravitic stabilizer into holding; at last, Janeway gave the order to match velocities with the star.

"Put it on visual," she said, standing in front of her command chair with her hands behind her back. She had found she generated more command presence when she stood, the obvious center of attention.

"Shall I scan for life-forms?" asked Harry Kim, currently manning Tuvok's station while the Vulcan joined Torres in engineering.

The captain almost said yes from force of habit, but she

caught herself. "No! Let's leave the searchlight turned off, shall we, Mr. Kim?"

He looked perplexed for a moment; then he nodded. "Passive only, Captain: here's what we can see from this distance."

The tiny image of a bright dot of light appeared on the forward viewer. "Full magnification," said Janeway, but Kim was already magnifying the image.

The dot exploded into a disk that nearly filled the viewer. The image wavered, giving the captain a headache; they were so far out still that not even *Voyager*'s image-enhancing computers could fully compensate for the slight vibration of the ship.

Janeway saw a peculiar grid design against the star's image. She squinted, just about to say something when Tom Paris asked first.

"What are those lines? Is that an interference pattern in the buffer?"

"I'll check," said Kim. He worked diligently, then shook his head. "No, Lieutenant; those lines are in the original image."

"But what are they?" wondered the captain.

The image was crisscrossed by thousands of great circles, forming a faintly fuzzy mesh around the star.

"We'll have to get closer, Captain," said Kim. "I can't get any better resolution."

"Computer," said Janeway, "open a comm link to engineering and maintain it. Mr. Tuvok, can you get a better focus on the image down there?"

"Negative, Captain; you're seeing our enhanced image already."

"Are those lines natural or an artifact?"

"Unknown, Captain. But if they are artificial, then we are dealing with a civilization that is far advanced over our own . . . at least in the field of astronometric architecture."

Janeway caught herself fiddling with her hair; she lowered her hands and carefully placed them behind her back again. "Ahead two-thirds impulse. If you detect any sensor sweeps, Mr. Kim, tell me."

They approached carefully but detected no scanning. The turbolift doors slid open and Neelix entered, followed by Kes.

"Neelix, are you familiar with this star system?"

Neelix stared at the screen. "What are those funny lines across the star? Is your video equipment malfunctioning?"

"Well, that answers that question," said Chakotay quietly.

"No, the lines are actually there, Neelix. We were hoping you could tell us what they were—and where we were."

Neelix shook his head. "I've never been here before in my life."

"Without being able to make a sensor sweep," said Kim, "I can't tell if this star system is inhabited or not. There's no coherent electromagnetic radiation, but that might just mean they use fiberoptics, tightbeam transmissions that don't leak, or channeled subspace broadcast. There are no ships that I can detect . . . and I still don't pick up the shuttlecraft's distress call."

Well, did it repair itself and fly away? Or did someone find the beacon and turn it off? The latter possibility disturbed the captain far more than the former.

"Tuvok," said Janeway, "I want you and Torres to make a complete, passive scan of the area for an ion trail that a shuttlecraft would leave behind. If it came through recently enough, maybe we can track it to wherever it landed. Take us in a little closer, Paris."

The *Voyager* closed inside the orbit of the only planet; Paris abruptly declared, "I don't believe it. It's impossible!"

It was a reasonable reaction. What had looked like an optical illusion from the cometary halo was in fact a wire-mesh sphere or cage that surrounded the sun at a radius of seventy million kilometers, or approximately four lightminutes.

The cage comprised millions of cables, each thicker than a Starfleet shuttlecraft, crossing in an elaborate pattern of X's and stars. The "holes" were hundreds of kilometers wide . . . and even they were strung with smaller filament that passed beyond the limits of resolution without an active scan. Janeway was willing to bet a hundred bars of latinum that *those* gaps were strug with even finer filament, as well.

She scowled, still perplexed. "What *is* it? A protective field? Some kind of shielding?"

A soft female voice spoke up from near the turbolift. It was Kes. "Um . . . Captain? Is it possible it's an energy-collection grid?"

Everyone turned to stare at the Ocampan. "Energy collection?" demanded Paris. "From the *sun?*"

"Yes, Tom. It just occurred to me because it looks like a huge-sized version of the energy-collection grid that the Caretaker used to transmit energy to us, before he—died."

"I suppose it is theoretically possible," said Janeway, "but why would anybody want to?" *Why not just power the planet with clean fusion or dilithium crystals? Why not—*

As if reading Janeway's mind, Tuvok answered through the comm link. "We have found water to be comparatively scarce in the Delta Quadrant; perhaps the planet's supply was too precious to use for hydrogen fusion, and perhaps they never discovered dilithium."

"But are they still here?" asked the captain. "If so, why haven't they detected us and made contact?"

Nobody had a good answer to her question, so she asked an easier one. "B'Elanna, have you found any ion trails yet?"

"Yes, Captain," answered the engineer. "I tracked one recent trail, and Tuvok's laid it into the navigational computer."

"Engage, Mr. Paris. Full impulse. Let's find the ship and survivor quickly and get a safe distance." *Maybe we can continue our investigation after we talk to the pilot,* she decided.

The trail followed a hyperbolic arc, indicating that the shuttlecraft had very little power and was not fighting the natural orbit much. Every so often, the trail bent sharply where the pilot suddenly burned the engines at 105-percent rated power to lurch into a graceless turn.

"This guy was either drunk or half-asleep when he plotted this course," griped Paris.

"Or unconscious," added Kim.

The ion trail led away from the single, large planet toward a moon locked into perpetual, stationary orbit: at the L-4 position, sixty degrees ahead of the planet in the same orbit, the three bodies—moon, planet, sun—formed a stable triangle, never varying with respect to each other. From any one body, the other two were always at the same position in the sky.

The moon was small and not very massive; gravity at the surface was about one-eighth that of Earth. Janeway stared suspiciously at it on the viewer; the entire surface appeared to be sheathed in metal of some sort, as if the aliens had armored the moon, for some bizarre reason.

"I don't like this," said Janeway. "Somebody built a chicken coop around the sun and armor plating around the moon; so *where are they?* Why haven't we already been met by a whole fleet of ships?" *I would almost prefer being shot at to being ignored,* she thought. *Well, almost.*

"I don't like this one bit, Captain," said Neelix. "There's something creepy about this system. And I don't like the fact that I've never even heard of this huge cage."

"Should you have?"

Neelix looked pained. "Captain, it's the sort of thing that people talk about from one end of the quadrant to the other ... the entire sun as an energy generator! Certainly a seasoned traveler such as myself should know of it. It's fantastic, astonishing—but completely unknown."

"Either nobody's found it before," concluded Chakotay, "or else nobody who ever found it returned to tell the tale."

"Now, that's a gruesome thought," said Neelix. Janeway noticed that the Talaxian moved closer to Kes, probably unconsciously.

Paris followed the ion trail more closely than he seemed to be following the conversation. "Captain, I think I figured out what he's steering toward: a moon or tiny planet orbiting about the same distance as the planet, at the L-four stable-body point."

Captain Janeway hesitated, then made a decision. "Ensign Kim, go ahead and scan the moon—active scanning, I mean. I think we're safer figuring out who all is here than remaining rigidly silent. Shields up."

Kim smiled. "Aye, *aye,* Captain!" He quickly passed the scanners across the planetoid that the ion trail pointed at; when that provoked no apparent response, he scanned them more thoroughly.

"Captain! It's artificial."

"The moon? The entire moon?"

Kim nodded. "Well, it's small; but it's constructed out of an alloy of titanium, nickel, copper, and some ceramic I can't analyze through the scanners."

"Do you see a shuttlecraft or wreckage?" Captain Janeway was starting to worry that they might have bitten off more than they could chew.

"Not from this angle. It might be on the other side of the planetoid; we'd have to get closer."

"Captain," said Tuvok's voice, "I conducted my own scan after Mr. Kim's. You may be interested in the results."

"Enlighten me."

"I have scanned the debris of between fifteen and seventeen other planets besides the large, intact one we see; one of the destroyed planets was a gas giant, the others were small, rocky, and very far from the sun."

"Were they destroyed by some natural phenomenon? Or were they mined to death?"

"All precious minerals have been removed from the debris, leaving only carboniferous husks. Since there is no known natural force that could do that, I suggest the most likely scenario is that the single, large planet is or was inhabited, and they mined their other planets to produce the satellite and the energy-collection grid."

Janeway picked at the most important hole in their analysis. "That's the big question, Tuvok: is . . . or *was?*"

"They have not hailed us, sir; and we are rather obviously in their space."

"Mr. Paris; take us to the moon. I want to find that shuttlecraft, rescue the pilot, and get out of here."

Paris turned half around in his chair. "We're not going to investigate? A grid built entirely around a sun, and we're just going to walk away?"

Good question, Janeway asked herself; *are we just going to walk away? This is still a mission of exploration!*

STAR TREK: INVASION!

She stepped close behind Paris, aware that others—Chakotay, Kim, even Neelix—were waiting to hear her response—a certain, very specific tone of response.

"After we get the pilot," declared Janeway, "we will debrief him if possible . . . then we definitely will send an away team to investigate. This is certainly a strange, new world to explore."

Paris turned back, satisfied. "Aye, Captain."

They approached the moon at half-impulse; but as soon as the *Voyager* closed to 363,000 kilometers from the artificial planetoid, the entire solar system exploded into a frenzy of activity.

"Captain," said Ensign Kim, "the moon just changed its alebedo significantly; I think protective shutters opened along the entire surface. Captain, we're being scanned!"

"From the moon?"

"No, Captain; the *planet* is scanning us."

"And hailing us," said Cadet Chell; the chubby, blue Bolian was manning communications while Tuvok was in engineering. Chell was progressing nicely under the Vulcan's merciless tutelage.

"Are we in a position to scan the rest of the moon?" demanded Janeway.

"Just barely," said Kim, checking his instrument graphic.

"Then all stop, Mr. Paris. I guess we just rang their doorbell . . . let's see who answers. Yellow alert. Ensign Kim, continue the scan."

"I already have, Captain. There is no shuttlecraft or wreckage that I can find. It might be under the surface."

"Captain," said Chell, "the planet is still hailing us . . . should we answer?"

Chakotay put his hand on Janeway's arm and spoke quietly, for her ears alone. "They might already have destroyed one Federation ship. Perhaps it would be better . . . ?" He nodded his head toward Neelix.

Janeway gave the cook a come-hither gesture.

"What, *me?* You want *me* to answer?" Neelix was astonished.

"Unless you don't want to get involved."

THE FINAL FURY

"No, no! I was just flabbergasted. Of *course* I should be the one to answer; you need somebody who's able to negotiate with these unknown aliens. After all, I've made first contact at least a hundred times!"

Eager for the chance, the crested Talaxian hurried to the command chair. Kes started to say something, then clamped her mouth shut.

Janeway smiled; she had noticed that Neelix didn't say how many were *successful* contacts. "Computer, tight visual on Mr. Neelix; do not show the rest of the bridge. Mr. Chell, open a channel at the same frequency they hailed us."

Janeway waited until the Bolian said "channel open"; then she silently pointed at Neelix, like a holoplay director saying *You're on*.

Neelix straightened his tunic in the Snappy Standard Starfleet Stretch, just as it was taught in the Academy course on Uniform Wear and Maintenance. Janeway was impressed; Neelix must have been watching her closely.

"This is, ah, Captain Neelix of the . . . the Maufansian ship *Songbird*. Um . . . good morning?"

"Why have you entered our territory?" politely demanded a voice that identified neither itself nor the planetary system. No visual appeared on the viewer; audio only.

"The, ah, *Songbird* is a merchant vessel bound for ah . . . Talaxia. We . . ."

"Distress call," whispered Janeway, almost too faintly for Neelix to hear; the computer would automatically scrub any noise softer than a certain threshold, screening out background noise from transmission.

"We heard a distress call and came to investigate." Neelix smoothly incorporated the suggestion into his spiel; Janeway was impressed with how effortlessly and believably the cook spun his tale.

"There is no distress call," said the voice.

"Well, there *was* a distress call," insisted Neelix.

"It was an inconsequential matter, already handled. You may leave."

Janeway bristled; she hated being patted on the head and told to go home.

Neelix considered for a long moment before answering—possibly getting his temper under control. Again, Janeway couldn't help but admire her negotiator's sang froid.

"Um . . . if you don't mind my asking, what was the problem and how did you handle it? Just as a lesson for my own insignificant self, of course."

"The call was made in error. You may leave. Unless"—the voice got noticibly perkier—"you're curious to learn about the true faith."

Chakotay and Janeway looked at each other. Janeway shrugged and nodded to Neelix, who caught the gesture out of the corner of his eye.

"We, ah, we're just a trading vessel; but we always appreciate an opportunity to learn about new cultures we've not met before." Suddenly Neelix smiled. "My trade ambassador, Cap—ah, Vice-President Janeway—and I would be delighted to learn all about your culture and the true faith."

The voice over the audio comm link sounded downright triumphant. "Please pilot your ship to the following coordinates," it said. The aliens transmitted the necessary data. "Do you understand the coordinate system?"

"We'll manage," said Neelix, a bit stiffly. *"Captain* Neelix out."

"We're off," confirmed Chell.

Janeway glared at Neelix as she returned to her command chair. "Vice-president? Trade ambassador?"

"It was the best I could come up with at the moment! Could you do better?"

She shook her head. Neelix had neatly trapped her: now she *had to* allow him onto the away team; anything less might be seen by the aliens as an insult!

The little Talaxian gets his chance to buckle yet another swash.

Tuvok spoke up through the comm link from the engineering deck. "Captain, I suggest I go with the two of you. It may be beneficial to minimize the number of humans on the mission. The injured pilot is a human."

"The away team will consist of Mr. Tuvok, Neelix, and

myself. Let's rendezvous in the hangar bay in twenty minutes."

"And may I suggest," continued the Vulcan, "that we *not* use a shuttlecraft?"

"Mr. Tuvok, if the aliens don't know about transporter technology, why should we alert them?"

"Captain, they may not know about transporters; but they definitely know what a Federation shuttlecraft looks like. They may not appreciate a visit from the owners of the ship they may just have destroyed."

"Point taken, Mr. Tuvok. We'll meet you in transporter room two. Mr. Kim, beam us down about a half-kilometer away from the coordinates they gave us; we'll walk into the area." *And give us a chance to acclimate,* she thought.

"We'll maintain a transporter lock," suggested Chakotay.

"Well, you're going to have a lot of company," said Ensign Kim. "I've just completed a full scan of the planet. There are twenty-seven *billion* dominant life-forms on the planet—of hundreds of different species."

"Twenty-seven *billion?*"

"Yes, sir. Billion, with a *b.*"

"Ready to transport as soon as you get down to the transporter room, Madam Vice-President," said Paris.

Ignoring the gibe, Janeway rose to her feet. "Departing in twenty minutes. Ensign Kim . . . I'd still like to get a look at that artificial moon. Maybe we can find out what happened to the wreckage and the pilot."

"Yes, Captain."

"You and Paris take a shuttlecraft across as soon as we leave and scan the entire surface. Report whatever you find back to Commander Chakotay and Lieutenant Torres."

"Aye, Captain."

"Captain Neelix, you're with me."

Kes sucked in a breath and caught Neelix by the arm as he headed for the turbolift. He gallantly detached her hand and chivalrously raised it to his lips. "Have no fear," he said; "nothing will happen to the captain and Tuvok, not with me there to protect them!"

Janeway rolled her eyes as the turbolift doors slammed shut on his reassurances . . . probably not quite what Kes wanted to hear.

Janeway raised her eyebrows. "Twenty-seven billion. Either these people live like ants, or they've got one hell of a tourist season."

CHAPTER 3

TOURIST SEASON INDEED, THOUGHT CAPTAIN JANEWAY, standing in the transporter room with Neelix; Tuvok entered, carrying a tricorder and three phasers.

"The inhabitants have thoroughly utilized their remaining planet," observed the Vulcan in a voice approaching awe—as closely as it was possible for a Vulcan voice to approach anything. "Their life-form readings are evenly dispersed from the surface to a depth of twenty kilometers. There are no uninhabited patches... no deserts, no oceans."

"Hear that, Neelix?" said Janeway. "No deserts." She was thinking of the Kazon-infested surface of Kes's planet, where they first had met Neelix, Scourge of the Delta Quadrant.

"No dessert," said the cook. He stood frozen, staring at the transporter pads and looking puzzled, as if not quite sure why he had so neatly maneuvered into coming.

"Neelix," said the captain, "why do you let your mouth run away with your common sense? This is a dangerous mission; why did you force us to bring you along?"

All doubt vanished in an instant from his face.

"Captain—I predict that before we're ready to return, you and Tuvok both will thank me for coming along!"

Janeway sighed. Talking sense to a swashbuckling Talaxian was tougher than frightening a Vulcan.

With a gigantic smile, Neelix pushed past Janeway and Tuvok, leading them onto the pad.

As the transporter chief began the dematerialization, Janeway could only ask herself, *How did I manage to end up on my way to meet twenty-seven billion potentially hostile aliens?*

Correction, she thought; *we're the aliens. And we know what most races think about alien invaders.*

The *Voyager* faded around them while Janeway held her breath.

"Chakotay to Paris," said the commander. "Launch now." From the bridge, Commander Chakotay watched the shuttlecraft swiftly depart. Tom Paris and Harry Kim were on their way toward the artificial moon to try to solve the mystery.

"Blow lots of impulse power," ordered Commander Chakotay to the sometimes edgy Ensign Mariah Henley, who had the helm. "Spray a contrail all over the system. There is a good chance the aliens will miss the shuttlecraft in the fireworks."

Henley smiled. It was an old Maquis trick; Chakotay had done it many times, but this was the first time Henley had gotten to be the "Roman candle."

Janeway, Tuvok, and Neelix materialized in a dark but crowded plaza on the planet . . . or more precisely, *in* it. Planetary air suddenly surrounded them, causing Janeway's ears to stuff up momentarily. She pinched her nose and blew, and her ears popped. *High pressure,* she thought.

She noticed an overwhelming, extraordinary odor of *rot*, ten times worse than a Florida swamp in August. For a moment, Janeway's eyes widened; then she gritted her teeth and forced herself to breathe through her nose, trying desperately to get used to the stench.

A second later and they felt the heat wave. The temperature was a balmy forty-six degrees at 105-percent humidity . . . possibly higher, since the "air" was not quite the same oxygen-nitrogen mixture she was used to; fortunately, the oxygen content was somewhat higher than Earth-normal.

Twenty-seven billion bodies all crammed together, she thought miserably. *Join Starfleet; see the universe!* Tuvok, standing next to the captain, was unaffected, of course; he probably appreciated the warmth, much closer to the temperature on Vulcan.

They had materialized inside a building so huge that at first Janeway thought they were outside on the nightside. Staring up, however, she could just barely see a dark metal ceiling—iron, perhaps—arching overhead. Smaller buildings sat within the larger building, much like ordinary buildings on a city street. But the winding paths between the buildings, unlike streets, avoided any possibility of a right angle.

Everywhere she looked, she saw metal . . . rusty metal, dark and dank, looking almost as if every surface were coated with dried blood. Janeway shuddered in spite of herself; the alien planet was like every human nightmare stitched together in a surreal quilt. The effect was not comic, despite the cartoonish overkill.

They were surrounded by an extraordinary horde of beings hustling along a complex traffic pattern. They were various shapes and sizes, and many were not even bipedal; but all wore loose clothing that hid their limbs and mummy-like facial wraps that covered their features. Looking up, the captain saw a roof that looked like hot iron, very uninviting.

"I suggest we find a lane and begin moving with the traffic flow," said Tuvok; "we are attracting some attention."

Janeway slid immediately into a queue that was going approximately the right direction. She noticed that the people kept their heads down; if two happened to meet by chance, they both made a big ritual of looking down and away to the left. She whispered her observation to Tuvok and Neelix.

"Possibly a series of rituals to symbolize some element of privacy," said the Vulcan, clearly fascinated by the culture. "I do not know yet whether it is religious or merely traditional."

Janeway wished she had something to wrap around her face; it would be very convenient, spoiling any chance that the alien interlocutor would spot her for a human. Nobody noticed their strange clothing and unwrapped faces; or at least, no one was rude enough to point it out.

The plaza's darkness was no aberration. Following as straight a line as they could toward the rendezvous coordinates, the away team cut from one queue to another, flowing down long, dank corridors of blackness like the dead lining up for hell. Everything was gloomy. The only windows were slits high in the walls, letting in some dim light that gave just enough illumination for them to avoid actually tripping over the monklike figures in front of them.

An occasional glowtube supplemented the window slits. *If these guys were transported to Jorba during the Dead of Night celebration,* thought Janeway, *they'd feel right at home.*

The air was hot and very wet; Janeway's throat began to ache as the caustic moisture scored her throat. "The whole planet is an oven," muttered Neelix behind her. "I could bake pies in here!"

"That is an exaggeration, Mr. Neelix; the temperature is only forty-six point one degrees, quite a comfortable temperature on my planet."

"I'm not *from* your planet, Tuvok! And I think it's absurdly hot."

Janeway tried to follow a basic direction, working from her tricorder; but the disorienting, twisting streets made it difficult to keep on course. She saw more of the alien planet than she really wanted to; the captain felt sudden claustrophobia, as if the iron buildings were falling over on her, the mobs pushing around her too tightly for her to breathe.

Janeway glanced at the tricorder. The coordinates were only fifty meters distant; looking in the proper direction, she saw a figure lurking in the darkness of a monstrous doorway, too far away for her to make out any more details about the figure other than "tall and heavy." The doorway was the "mouth" of a huge, skull-like design. Janeway felt a premonitory shiver, strange in such heat.

"I think we're about to meet our missionary," she announced. "Neelix, you should be first to speak."

"Thank you, Captain; I accept the honor."

"For reasons of protocol only," she explained, smiling. "After all, you're the *captain;* they'll expect to meet you first."

Janeway stood behind Neelix, out of direct line of sight. She preferred to wait until "Captain" Neelix summoned her and Tuvok before stepping out, so as not to startle the aliens into attacking in an excess of xenophobic self-defense. There was the distinct possibility, she told herself, that they already had attacked the previous representative of the Federation.

"Greetings on all five points of the pentagram," said a strange voice; the Universal Translator gave their host's voice an odd, rumbling twang, like a moose from Texas.

"Greetings, magnificent being. I am Captain Neelix, master of the *Songbird* trading vessel. I come to discuss trade possibilities and, uh, learn about the true faith."

"Abandon false hope, all ye who enter here, and find strength in the Returning."

"Oh—thanks awfully."

Janeway softly cleared her throat, quickly regretting her action; not only did it hurt, somehow it made the odor stronger.

"May I introduce my trade negotiators?" asked Neelix smoothly. "This is Kathryn Janeway, a—a Veermaan from the planet Verminius; and this is Tuvok, a Vulcan from the planet, ah, Vulcan."

"Greetings on all five points of the pentagram," boomed the host. On cue, Janeway stepped close—and halted in horrified amazement.

She stared straight into the face of Satan.

Easy, girl—he's just . . . he's just a . . . Janeway recoiled in horror, actually falling back a couple of steps before she got hold of her emotions and forced her feet to stop moving.

What is it—what is it? She forced herself to stare the

creature in the face. The face wasn't a devil's mask. It didn't have the normal, physical characteristics she associated with the devil; and if it had, so what? Did not Vulcans and Romulans have just such features, except for the missing horns?

But the alien's face, while angular and roughly triangular, held something altogether sinister, something wild and bestial. It was sculpted from every imaginable sign of evil, every conceivable sin, every foulness or violation ever practiced by Man upon Man stitched together.

The mouth was too small, just the *wrong* size; the eyes were narrow; the cheekbones high, but cruelly high. The thin lips held such promise of torture and murder that Janeway's heart suddenly shifted into warp speed.

Its lips parted to suck in a breath, and the inside of its mouth was covered with writhing worms. Ripples flickered across its skin, vermin infesting its flesh! They crawled across the hideous face, and the captain felt her knees weaken.

She had never experienced such a reaction. Every specific or particular about the alien's face could be rationalized and accepted—*in theory*.

But the universe contains not theories but concrete actualities: and the actuality of the alien face was a nightmare of half-buried, demented, squirming little childhood fears, night terrors, seizures and suffering, flickering malevolence, befouled, spoiled beauty.

It—the thing could not possibly be dignified with a sex— it bore the Mark of the Beast.

When Kathryn Janeway was a little girl, her mother had read her that Kipling story. Rationally, even at so young an age, Kathryn had thought it absurd that the horses would detect some horrific evil lurking beneath what should have been a normal man's skin; nevertheless, it had terrified her.

Now she understood why. But she did not understand her sudden feeling of uneasy familiarity; *she had seen these monsters before,* somewhere ... pictures, at least. But where, *where?*

A minute had passed while Neelix casually chatted of nothing with the alien, and Janeway finally got her respirations and heart rate barely under control. She turned to look at Tuvok instead and saw a sight she had never imagined to see in a hundred years: Tuvok the Vulcan was absolutely frozen with fear.

All the fears of a moment before, the fears Janeway thought she had overcome, jolted through her body like a monstrous static discharge. Tuvok was *frightened?* Tuvok was terrified!

The captain had never even imagined a Vulcan could feel such powerful emotions. She knew they "felt" the same emotions as everyone else but simply suppressed and ignored them ... a talent they had to learn as children, for they were of course not born that way. But the thought had never crossed her mind that some emotions were simply too powerful to suppress, even for a Vulcan.

But how could a mere alien cause such a savage disruption in Vulcan neurophysiology? *Unless Tuvok remembers them too,* thought the captain, *and remembers not just the image, but whatever horror they brought with them.* Janeway shook suddenly with vague loathing; why had she thought that, the "horror" they brought?

Janeway was pulled back against her will to stare at the alien, which she dimly heard introduce itself as Navdaq, and she understood how.

She heard little but the slush of blood in her own ears and felt faint from an explosively high blood pressure. But her reaction was nothing compared to Tuvok's, for the Vulcan left finger-sized indentations in the rusted, iron doorframe.

Navdaq, to be polite, turned its gaze to include her every now and again. Janeway died a little with every glance, the look of the basilisk turning her to stone.

Neelix turned to the captain, his mouth moving animatedly. He stopped. He moved his mouth again, but Janeway could hear nothing but her own pulse. He scowled, confused by her incomprehension.

Words filtered through, though she still saw Neelix only in peripheral vision, staring pop-eyed at the demon. "Assistant ... long journey ... exhausted." He was making excuses for her, thank God, saving her from having to talk to Navdaq and allow it to steal her soul in addition to flattening it where it sat.

Demon? Oh my Lord, where did I get THAT from? She felt herself shrink second by second, cringing in embarrassment that she could not stop herself from staring in horror at the—the demon. Trapped in a nightmare where her will was not her own, Janeway knew her torment was nothing compared to Tuvok's hell of humiliation. A Vulcan who couldn't control his own emotional response!

Then at last, the *thing* turned its face away and stalked into the black horror of a corridor, followed by Neelix. Janeway felt her mortification finally relent to nothing more than a deep, red flush spreading across her body, mercifully hidden by perpetual, artificial night and a uniform. She could follow, albeit numbly, like a robot; she followed. She could walk; she hurried after the pair.

Tuvok forced his legs into a staggering step. He could think of nothing but the black terrors from a Vulcan night so long before bright logic touched his life that he could not even rationalize his fear. His hands shook with emotion so great, only a Vulcan could experience it: this Navdaq creature, this—this *Fury!*—had thrown Tuvok back to the age of the First Ones, a Vulcan from the time before the immortal Surak brought order, logic, order, reason, and order to his disorderly race.

Tuvok's hands shook with palsy, and he fought a wild urge to cover his eyes and run into the blackness, left or right, anywhere to escape *it*.

There is no fear! he desperately told himself. *There is no fear, no monster, no demon, no god, no devil, no angel, no past, no future; now is always now; a race is just a race; a Vulcan is logic and order; emotion is the enemy! Eliminate the enemy!*

Tuvok nearly sprinted after his captain, and a tiny moan forced its way past the paper doors of his useless, laughable self-control. A Vulcan! He should be banished to Romulus with the rest of the bloodtasters.

Choking down a sudden spurt of vomit, almost as terrified of permanently disgracing himself—pride, another emotion—as he was of *it*, Tuvok squinted his eyes and listened only, unfocusing his gaze and allowing himself to see only enough of the passageway to avoid actually bumping into walls.

Neelix spoke to the *thing*. The Talaxian cook and guide seemed utterly unaffected, oblivious of *its* hideous presence. "I am very pleased to meet your Autocrat, great Navdaq. What? No, a preliminary survey. Yes, to find out what you need that I might be able to supply. Well, no, heh, I haven't heard of the true faith; but I'm sure I will find it fascinating and enlightening."

"We missed your ship," said the interlocutor. "How did you slip through our orbital sensors?"

"We, ah, parked it a ways away," extemporized Neelix, squirming nervously. "Um, we didn't want to interfere with your port traffic."

The interlocutor did not respond, but Tuvok got the distinct impression he was not persuaded.

Janeway stumbled as she walked on wobbly knees behind her supposed "captain," and she realized she was trying to follow with her eyes firmly shut; anything to avoid having to see even the back of Navdaq. *This is insane,* she argued; *it—he is just an alien life-form, nothing more! I've seen dozens, races whose facial appearances should turn my stomach. . . .*

The Viidians, sick with the phage, their faces literally falling apart in clumps; the wormlike Knipa of Barnard II, whose flesh cracks and splits before your eyes, oozing rivulets of black oil that they suck up through vacuum appendages.

Let's be objective about this, Janeway told herself sternly; *Navdaq has nothing in its face or flesh to even begin to compare to these horrors, and I face them without a twinge!* Yet she still sweated, perspiration dripping down her forehead and into her eyes.

Slowly, the fear began to ebb. Perhaps her adrenal glands were running out of juice, she reasoned; her panic faded, and even though her heart still pounded when she looked directly at Navdaq, she could look without gagging.

* * *

STAR TREK: INVASION!

The Vulcan Tuvok felt his captain start to relax slightly; her quotient of fear and revulsion appeared to ebb.

But Tuvok found no such comfort. An invisible fist continued to punch him in the stomach every time he caught sight of *it,* and nothing he did or told himself to do made the slightest difference. Tuvok knew deep in his core, so deep it never could be rooted out, that this was a monster that had come to pass horrible judgment upon the Vulcan race. Tuvok knew the Fury would tear into his fleshy meat and strip him to the bone, soon, very soon. His mind couldn't say no to his endocrine system.

Then without warning, Navdaq stopped and whirled to face them. Tuvok barely kept his feet; Janeway sagged against a bulkhead, face whitening again.

Captain Janeway could neither close her eyes nor turn away as the alien seemed to grow; it leaned forward, suddenly inspired by the breath of Mars, Bringer of War and Destruction. Its face exploded into a prismatic display of emotions bottled for more years than the alien had lived. "You are about to embark upon a spiritual journey," prophesied Navdaq; "thousands of years of devotion, preparation, and countless sacrifices, culminating in the final crusade against the most diabolical beings in the galaxy. And the righteous shall win; and you shall join us, an armored fist from behind the back. You shall come; you shall *come!*"

Janeway turned her face to the bulkhead, feeling a tear upon her cheek. She had been chosen by the Fallen One, and her soul was damned to hell!

CHAPTER 4

Time, and rationalization, finally drove away Captain Janeway's entirely unreasonable fear. She still felt a weird, irrational revulsion for Navdaq whenever she looked at it; and she began to wonder whether somehow, there had been ancient contact between its people and early protohumans, contact that was decidedly horrific for the humans. Psychologically—perhaps genetically—all the features of Navdaq's race were implanted into the human neurophysiology as the synecdoche of hatred and loathing.

As crazy as the theory sounded, it resonated so *right* that she couldn't shake it.

Just as a baby that has never fallen will still scream hysterically when placed upon a tall glass table, Janeway reacted to the screams of her ancestors—even though she, personally, had nothing against Navdaq.

The strangest corollary was that Tuvok reacted even more strongly than she did; evidently some Vulcans had some sort of genetic memory of Navdaq's people, a memory that dated to a time before the great philosopher Surak taught them the path of pure logic.

Still, however, Janeway could not shake the feeling that *she had seen these aliens* somewhere before . . . not just in her "DNA memory," but in the real world—in the past, long ago, back in—

No, that's ridiculous. She had been about to think she had seen them when she was a cadet at the Academy. But that was. . . . Janeway pursed her lips, pondering; bits and pieces, they started to return. She decided not to force the memory; it would come—she was sure it would eventually come back to her.

Tuvok seemed to have gotten his emotions nearly under control; only Janeway or some other close friend, perhaps Chakotay, could have seen the Titanic struggle that still roiled just below his skin.

Neelix was unaffected; to him, Navdaq must be a member of just one more alien race, interesting and unique, as were they all. Janeway felt a surge of utterly irrational hatred of the Talaxian. *That's insane!* she railed at herself. *Thank goodness at least one of us three is still rational.* But the bile would not dissipate, a remnant of her barely controlled fear.

Navdaq led them through long, dank, creepy halls, "caverns measureless to man," as Coleridge might describe it. Or in the words of Radolph Na, a twenty-second-century poet that Janeway was just beginning to read,

Cold cupped hands
Squeeze
Squirt like Paq seeds into deep night. . . .

Everything she saw, wherever it led them, was a living nightmare; Janeway reacted so strongly to it all that she started to berate herself for being so easily manipulated. If Navdaq were to move to the Alpha Quadrant, it could make a fortune designing a haunted-house holodeck program!

It talked incessantly, and after a time, Janeway was actually able to listen without flinching or cringing at the voice.

* * *

Neelix followed Navdaq smartly, trying to pick out the one or two useful spices of information from the rambling, bland pudding of religious catechism.

"Captain" Neelix noticed that Janeway and Tuvok appeared to have contracted some extraordinary phobia; they were struck dumb! The Talaxian felt anxious about them, wishing Kes had come along; she had the most remarkable talent for getting right inside a person and soothing the real cause of his distress, whether he knew what it was or not.

"What was that distress call about?" asked Neelix, rising to the necessity. If the captain and the Vulcan were so oddly incapacitated, it was Neelix's clear duty to find out where the missing human was.

Navdaq twitched in some satisfaction. "One of the *Unclean* invaded our temporary home, doubtless a scout for the filth who are its masters, they who envy and fear the Holy even in exile . . . and rightly so! For when the righteous finally move, the hosts shall rout the *Unclean* and destroy the last representative of the vermin that infest our true home!"

"Ah, well thank goodness for that! But tell me . . . what was that distress call about? An ion trail led through your system and to that artificial moon of yours . . . I, um, happened to notice when I was waiting for a representative of the Autocrat to contact me."

"Think nothing of it. The *Unclean* launched a treacherous attack and destroyed a very important tool; but they are mindless beasts, for the crusade shall proceed unimpeded. We have captured the *Unclean* alive and hold it for interrogation."

Neelix forcibly suppressed a triumphant whoop; the Starfleet pilot was alive! Alive, and *held*. Neelix smiled in relief. His boast back on the transporter pad had surely come true . . . in triplicate!

Tuvok was a hollow shell of a Vulcan . . . but he had finally managed to lock outside, for the moment, all the distasteful, dangerous emotions he had felt. He forced himself to Observe and Report; his captain would eventually need any intelligence he could gather.

Navdaq has never once mentioned beaming, noted Tuvok; *he wondered where our ship was docked.* It was a simplistic observation: no race they had yet encountered in the Delta Quadrant, except for the Caretaker, had transporter technology. But it was cold, rational, logical. It was Tuvok's first logical act since seeing Navdaq.

Everywhere Tuvok looked, he saw mechanical locks on doors . . . either external padlock-type devices, or integral card-key slots built into doors. *They have no shields,* he thought—without emotion.

The heat revived the Vulcan; it reminded him of home. He could not see very well in the darkness that Navdaq and those of his race evidently preferred; possibly the aliens saw by means of infrared? But Tuvok's ears were much sharper than a human's, and he had followed the conversation ever since he began to regain control of his long-suppressed emotions.

With control came a shred of memory: true, rational memory from his own experience. It was during his first assignment under Captain Sulu; something happened . . . a war, a fight with another ship. Tuvok read about it in the message traffic but paid it little mind until he saw the single image included in the subspace broadcast; the image evoked such revulsion in the young Vulcan that he quickly minimized the icon and stored it in the archives, never opening the file again.

Could these creatures be the same aliens who fought against Captain James Kirk and the *U.S.S. Enterprise?* Tuvok firmly pushed the thought from his mind; it held no practical value, just a distraction from the very real and immediate problems faced by his current assignment, *Voyager* and its crew.

Though they encountered no one along the route they followed, a very circuitous route, perhaps deliberately avoiding contact, Tuvok could hear movement and breathing behind virtually every door they passed. The planet was immeasurably crowded, many times the population of

Vulcan or even Earth in significantly less space: the planet had a diameter only sixty percent that of Earth, which meant it had a surface area only thirty-six percent of Earth's.

The aliens accomplished the improbable by stacking their population some twenty kilometers deep, and Tuvok heard large crowds of people noisily walking across metallic catwalks beneath the floor and above his head.

The time has come, thought the Vulcan, *to drive the last traces of emotion from my mind. I must confront my fear and destroy it.* Calming himself by meditating upon the IDIC, the symbolic heart of Surak's philosophy, *Infinite Diversity in Infinite Combinations,* Tuvok lengthened his stride and approached Navdaq's back.

"Sir," said the Vulcan—his voice sounded like metal grating on stone—"you have alluded to an ancient history when the Unclean drove you away from your home."

Navdaq stopped and slowly began to turn. Tuvok caught himself starting to rush the question to spit it out before seeing the Face again; he deliberately slowed and waited until he could look directly at it. "Will you elaborate?"

The Vulcan actually felt physically ill, as if he had eaten a spoiled *Tolik* fruit. He had to force his breathing and forcibly stop his hands from lurching forward of their own will to gouge thumbs into Navdaq's eyes and tear the alien's throat out.

I am not a strand of imprinted DNA, Tuvok told himself; *I am a Vulcan. I am in control.*

Navdaq considered him; it did not recognize Tuvok, either by memory or genetically. *Of course not; we were the victims. They must have enslaved and terrorized us; it is no mystery that Vulcans and humans imprinted the aliens' faces with terror and utter despair, and the aliens did not imprint us at all.*

"You shall hear the truth," said Navdaq, "and you shall understand."

It shifted its gaze upward and pressed its hands together like claws with long, sharp nails that slid out of its fingers. Tuvok was on the verge of yanking the captain away, lest the alien forget himself in hypnogogic reverie; but Captain Janeway herself backed hastily away from the suddenly lethal claws.

"A hundred thousand years or more ago, we ruled heaven. It was given unto us, and we took what was offered. Some speculate we may have come from another corner of the galaxy and only settled heaven when the Dark Ones invited us in. I offer no opinion; be it known we had been allowed inside, and we jealously guarded our blessing.

"We treated the subject races with compassion; we forbade the wanton killing of slaves and allowed them to grow and prosper within the limits ordained by their condition."

Tuvok glanced at the captain; she was not visibly reacting to the tale. *She can be as unemotional as I have ever seen a human,* he noted with some satisfaction.

Janeway presented an unemotional front, but it was only because her body seemed finally to have run out of adrenaline. The capacity for fear burned itself out. She felt sick revulsion, but that was easier to contain.

Navdaq was casually talking about its race having enslaved other beings for tens of thousands of years before somebody or something drove them away. She felt an irrational impulse to strangle Navdaq, as if she were somehow the substitute for the enslaved races and it symbolized the conquerers.

"Then came the *Unclean* to disrupt the natural, ordained order," said Navdaq, a dark tone of disharmony creeping into its voice. "They did covet heaven and came from a far place to cast out the Holy unlawfully. We are told the tragic battle lasted thousands of years; in the end, we were driven through the great gate, the longest wormhole that has existed in this galaxy, and brought to this place."

Navdaq's face lowered. "Then came our shame, for the elder son of D'Mass, D'Vass, rebelled against the holy quest: his brother Bin Mass fought without surcease eleven days and eleven nights; then he lay down next to his brother, and they slept hand in hand—only to arise and fight for eleven more days and nights. D'Vass was exiled with some of his rebels, and the rest of us are descended from the loyal hosts of Bin Mass."

"If you were in heaven," asked Janeway, surprising herself with her own unemotional voice, "how could the Unclean cast you out? Weren't you—protected?"

"The *Unclean* made alliance with the subject races, who envied the Holy their place in the order. And the subject races laid down their tools and their yokes, and laid *themselves* down, and refused to fight.

"We sent the Terrors, and still they refused. We sent the Terrors louder and louder, brighter than ever we had before, letting them see the true horror that disorder brings; but still they refused, and they fell into madness and tore each other apart in their fright. They fought and killed . . . but not for us; they killed for fear, and for the madness."

We SENT the terrors . . . Beneath her own disgust, Janeway felt a small lump of worry begin to grow.

Shortly before the Caretaker yanked *Voyager* millions of light-years across the galaxy to strand her in the Delta Quadrant, Captain Janeway, sporting a brand-new fourth pip on her collar, heard about a discovery in the Alpha Quadrant: a helmet that could project telepathic images over long distances.

Suppose Navdaq's people had similar toys . . . but instead of projecting communication, what if they had relentlessly projected mind-numbing fear and terror to sap the will of their *subject races,* their slaves?

It was a chilling thought. *The fear I felt upon first seeing Navdaq could only have been a dim, distant echo of the terror they could "send" if they used their projection device.*

If the aliens chose to *send their terrors,* they could probably enslave Janeway herself and her entire crew.

There was only one ray of hope. If Navdaq was telling the truth—assuming he knew the truth—then at least once before, the *subject races* had managed to pull off a strike at a critical moment . . . and maintain it despite the fear projector.

It worked; the aliens were defeated. But the effects of the projector on maximum drove many of them violently insane with fear.

Was it a fair trade-off? she wondered.

"For centuries," continued Navdaq, "we have planned our counterattack."

"You still intend to return to heaven?" asked Tuvok. Janeway jumped; they were the first words her Vulcan friend had spoken for many long minutes, ever since he first forced out the question about the early history of heaven. Tuvok's voice was clipped and strained; probably nobody but Janeway or another Vulcan would have noticed. *Maybe he's going to be all right after all.* . . .

"We were punished for our laxity, our complacency in power. We were meant to learn vigilance and focus; we were meant to learn that the *Unclean* cannot be allowed to remain in the Holy, not as conquerers, not even as slaves. And we have learned well our lessons. Yes, we shall return to heaven . . . and you come at a great moment, for the hour is at hand. We shall return to heaven, whence we were cast out, and cleanse it of all *Unclean!*

"Heaven was meant for the Holy—and heaven shall be cleansed of all *but* the Holy . . . this we say, and this we say! Now come, my guests; you have come on the eve of the momentous war of righteousness, and I cannot think that is mere accident. Let us go unto the Autocrat, and he shall listen to your tale and scry why you truly are here."

Navdaq turned about and strode into the creeping darkness, and Janeway and Tuvok had no option but to run to catch up.

Lieutenant Tom Paris and Ensign Harry Kim cautiously approached the artificial moon in the shuttlecraft, alert for any more robotic alarm systems—or defense systems. Kim licked his lips nervously; his engineer's mind conjured up all sorts of nasty possibilities for technoalarms, land mines, and booby traps.

Ever since the *Voyager* approached close enough to ring bells, the moon had sent a continuous data stream to the small planet; Kim monitored the data, looking for anomalies and discontinuities.

"It's repeating the same packets over and over," he announced; "it hasn't changed since we've gotten closer."

"Has the modulation changed? The frequency, anything that could convey more information?"

"No, Tom. It's absolutely identical to what it was just after we first triggered it."

Paris considered for a moment, then shrugged. "Harry, I think we've just got a beeping rack-alarm here. The only thing we have to worry about is the owner eventually coming back to shut it off."

"A beeping what?"

"Oh, that's right . . . where you come from, there is no crime. But at the Federation Penal Settlement in New Zealand, where I was hanging out with my buddies before Janeway hired me, we quickly learned that the most common method of intimidation was to burglarize someone's room while he was on work detail or at chow."

"Burglarize? People actually *broke into* your own, private room? You mean"—he glanced pointedly at Paris—"the way you broke into *mine?*"

Paris laughed, a short, ugly sound. "You did lead a sheltered life, didn't you? Yeah, Harry, they actually broke into my space. They went through my things. They left them just slightly moved . . . enough so I'd wonder if anyone had been there, not quite enough to know for sure."

Harry shook his head, savagely poking a button to change the scan range. He had read about burglary in history classes; but he could not imagine what it must feel like to have a stranger, a *criminal,* rummage through his most personal possessions. *Maybe they would even steal my clarinet,* he thought; the image made the hair on the back of his neck stand straight up.

"So one guy, Hasty Kent, made rack-alarms," Paris continued, "and the rest of us bought them. We paid him in synthehol, or homemade alcohol, if someone smuggled some in. We didn't have any latinum, usually. Huh, now that I think about it, maybe Kent was the one burglarizing the spaces, just so he could sell more alarms."

"What's that got to do with the data stream, Tom?"

"Hasty Kent didn't want to bother making the alarms very sophisticated; so he just made them start ringing when the space was violated and keep ringing until someone came and shut them off.

"So naturally, the burglars quickly figured out that if they set off lots and lots of alarms all the time, people would get tired of coming back to check . . . and they could burglarize a space while the alarm was going, and no one would ever know."

Harry thought for a minute. "Let's poke our nose in, shall we, Tom?"

"I thought you'd never ask."

Paris took manual control of the shuttle and dove toward the moon, while Kim scanned for weapons power-ups or any changes in the data stream. They looped around the back side, and Harry whistled.

"Here we go! Take a look at this, Tom." He put the scan on the forward viewer.

They saw the remains of an extraordinarily huge dish antenna, easily a hundred kilometers high and seventy kilometers in radius. It had been destroyed by a fist from heaven, an object punching out of the stars at a velocity somewhere between 0.1 and 0.7 light speed—something very like a starship shuttlecraft.

"The ion trail leads right into the impact crater," said Paris. "Harry, I think we've found where the distress signal emanated from. The only question is . . ."

"Where the heck *is* it?" Harry Kim completed.

There was no wreckage from a Starfleet shuttlecraft, not a scrap. And there was no life-form reading.

"Somebody's already done some tidying up," deduced Ensign Kim. "They've been here, seen the damage, swept up the wreckage, and removed the pilot to a hospital."

"Or more likely a prison cell."

Kim looked at his shipmate. "You think they would put someone in prison for this? It was an accident."

"Oh yes," said Paris; "I think people would put other people in prison for just about anything. If they were angry enough."

My friend, thought Kim, *you're a hell of a nice guy and a great pilot . . . but you have a dark, cynical side that scares the hell out of me sometimes.*

As they continued their orbit around the moon, Paris had to adjust the impulse engines to keep them on course; the moon's gravity was so low that true orbital velocity would be an interminable crawl. "Hey, Kim, here's another antenna. This one's an innie, not an outie."

They passed over a huge, perfectly circular indentation with a dish at the bottom five times the size of the one that had been destroyed. On impulse, Kim turned his sensors around and scanned in the direction the antenna pointed.

"This is interesting," he said. "The moon's rotational orientation is set so that this antenna always faces the sun."

"The grid—Harry, Kes was right . . . that *must be* an energy-collection grid around the sun, and this is where the energy beams to. *Holy—!*"

Tom Paris yanked the controls up and to the left; at exactly the same instant, the red-alert klaxon automatically sounded.

The shuttle veered violently to the side; Harry Kim grabbed his console to avoid being flung out of his chair. He stared wildly at all of his instruments, trying to figure out what Paris saw that made him swerve so suddenly.

"That would have been a hell of a spectacular death, Kim," said the pilot in question with a grin. "I suddenly realized that if the grid was beaming that much energy to the moon, we'd better not get between it and the collection dish with our shields down!"

Shaking, Kim adjusted his scanner. "There's energy all around this thing. I didn't think to look for microwaves; it seems so . . . primitive. Sorry, Tom; I should have been paying more attention. I almost got us killed."

Paris nodded, which Kim took as acceptance of his apology. "Now," said the lieutenant, "what's on the inside of this puppy?"

Kim shook his head. "I can't scan through the hull, Tom."

"Shields?"

"No. There are no shields anywhere I've detected in this

system. But the hull of the moon is made of some super-dense material that our scans can't penetrate."

"Don't tell me that we can't beam through it either."

Kim considered a moment. "All right, Tom; I won't tell you."

"But we can't?"

"I wasn't the one who told you that. But you're right."

"Figures. So how do we get in? We can't go down the energy-collection shaft; too much microwave radiation."

"Well . . ." Kim ran over shield-configuration equations in his head while he fiddled aimlessly with the controls. He suddenly realized he was "keying" the console as if it were a clarinet, playing "The Slionimski Variations."

Paris waited, then said, *"Yes?"*

"Maybe we can go down that shaft," said Kim, "and right through the collection antenna. I *think* I can adjust our own shields to give us a couple of minutes of protection."

"Think?"

"Hey, this is Starfleet, Tom: risk is our business!"

Paris gave him a look; pretending not to notice, Kim continued. "It won't be good for us; we'll probably get some pretty serious sunburns."

"The doctor can fix us up later. Let's do it!"

"And if you mess up the piloting, there won't be anything left to cure."

Paris raised his brows. *"Moi?* Look, you got a needle? I can take this baby right through the eye while hanging an elbow out the window." He winked.

"All right then, modifying shields now—just a minute—all right, Tom, we're ready."

Lieutenant Paris nosed the shuttlecraft over into a dive toward the gaping hole. Kim gritted his teeth, seeing his life flash before his eyes; it didn't hold his interest. "Tom," he said, just before they passed the lip of the hole, "you know if we make a smoking crater, I will never speak to you again."

Paris snorted. "Don't tempt me!"

CHAPTER 5

THE SHAFT WAS STRAIGHT, DRIVING DIRECTLY TOWARD THE center of the moon for more than a hundred kilometers. Paris kept the shuttle steady in the center, trying not to think about the walls closing in around him, about the radiation—about how they were going to get back out again without taking a lethal cumulative dose.

The first eight kilometers were nothing but shielding, the unreasonably dense material that Paris dubbed "baloneyum" when Kim informed him that chemically, it could not exist. "If you say it can't exist," said Paris, "maybe I should test your theory by ramming the wall." Kim didn't respond, not surprisingly. Tom Paris reacted to tension by incessant joking; Kim tended to clam up.

The shaft started to narrow, and even Paris ceased harassing his crewmate, concentrating on the piloting job.

"Paris," said Kim, interrupting a long silence, "you've got to pick up the pace; we're starting to get some serious leakage through the shields. If we're not out of direct view of the microwave beam in the next four minutes . . ."

"Yeah, yeah; got it. Hang on, here we go."

Paris tapped the throttle, pushing to twenty-five kilometers per minute; it would have been a snail's pace in free space, where sublight velocities were measured in kilometers per *second*.

But the space was decidedly unfree; they drove through a narrow shaft, dodging spars and pieces of equipment, guy lines, and the walls of the tunnel itself, being buffetted by the microbursts of energy "wake turbulence" that their own ship stirred up and threw ahead of them at half light speed. Ensign Kim gripped the sides of his seat, and even Paris felt his stomach clench as they careered wildly from one side of the shaft to the other.

Easy, easy! he warned himself; fried or shredded wasn't much of a career choice.

"My mother makes the greatest kimchee," Kim said; the nonsequitur helped break the tension . . . slightly.

"Does she? So when are you going to invite me over for a Korean feast?"

"Soon as we get back. Um, glass noodles—chap che, bibimba, maybe some barbecue . . . she makes wonderful, traditional side dishes."

"Gosh. All my mom ever made was meat loaf."

"Really? I love meat loaf."

A spar suddenly loomed in front of them. Reacting at warp speed, Paris swerved to avoid it; suddenly the shuttle slid out of control!

The ship rolled, inertial stabilizers straining to keep up; for an instant, Paris actually felt zero-g, and his stomach lurched.

"Yak!" he shouted, yanking the shuttlecraft back in the other direction.

Tom Paris fought the irrational but almost irresistible impulse to squeeze his eyes shut. "Watch it!" bellowed Kim. Ahead of them bulked a dense web of gold-colored wires strung across the outer perimeter of the shaft.

Grimly, Paris bent the shuttlecraft back into the center in a move that the manual insisted could not be done with the ship in question. He rotated the shuttle impossibly fast, and the ship just barely slipped through the small resonance gap in the center of the array, neatly clipping off a dozen strands of wire on both left and right.

THE FINAL FURY

"So," Kim said weakly, "when are you going to invite me over for a meat-loaf feast?"

"I'll cook it for you myself back on the ship, if we can tie up Neelix and use his kitchen."

"Cook it? You?"

"Man learns many things in the Maquis, especially when replicators are hit-or-miss. Hang on, Kim, here comes the antenna."

"Getting hot in here, isn't it?"

Paris wiped the sweat out of his eyes. He glanced at the temperature gauge: 52.2 degrees. They were roasting alive! "Actually, I feel kind of a chill. Did we bring my jacket along?"

Paris tapped the throttle high, then higher yet. He had adjusted the throttle scale way, way downward; at the normal range, a small tap like the one he had just given would have accelerated them to a quarter light speed. The shuttle would have drilled a neat, shuttlecraft-sized hole all the way through the moon, coming out the other end a shuttlecraft-sized ball of ionized plasma.

As they closed, Paris saw to his dismay that the antenna was not just a simple dish he could edge around. Instead, they would first encounter an inner ring, the energy-focusing mechanism, that was only *thirty meters* in diameter—followed in mere seconds by an outer dish.

Millions of threads of strong filament connected the inner ring to the shaft wall, keeping it in place like the muscles of the human eye keep the corona facing the right way. The shuttle could not simply bypass the inner ring; they would have to thread it, diving straight into microwave hell.

Paris did not need Harry Kim to tell him that in between the inner ring and the dish itself, the electromagnetic radiation would rip through the shuttlecraft's shields like a hot knife through butter, cooking the two of them in moments. Their only hope was to maintain thirty kilometers per minute all the way through.

That meant that the only way to thread the inner ring and then clear the outside rim of the dish was to perform a patented maneuver that Paris had invented flying Gawkhoppers as a kid: the Swoop of Death.

He clenched his teeth, but smiled coolly for Kim's benefit. The kid was all right, but he really was not prepared to die, not yet; best not tell him the maneuver they were about to perform had only a thirty-three-percent chance of success.

Hell, I'M not prepared to die just yet! Alas, Paris could not lie to himself; he had attempted the Swoop of Death only six times in his life—and successfully completed it twice.

Of course, never before had the name been quite so literal. As a kid, he dove around purely holographic barriers; and if he missed and blew through one—well hell, then his buddy won that day's bet.

The inner ring loomed. Through it, Paris could actually *see* the energy, as the intensity of the microwaves produced so much heat, such intensity of infrared echos, that they actually registered on the human eye.

The Swoop of Death required exceeding the design limitations of the inertial dampers by a huge margin. Twice.

"Hold on, Harry," said Paris softly. "You like zero-g inversions?"

"No, I *hate*—"

The shuttle shot through the inner ring, into the electromagnetic maelstrom. *Now or never!* flickered across Paris's cerebrum.

He grabbed the attitude slideswitch and pulled it all the way back, pitching the nose up toward a ninety-degree angle from their direction of motion.

For a fraction of a second, the inertial dampers held out manfully, throwing off the force-load as free heat; then, with a loud click, they gave up the ghost.

A fist weighing 9,600 newtons crushed down on Paris . . . twelve times the normal force of gravity; he gasped under the strain—*Can't black out—can't lose consciousness!*

Tom Paris's world turned dull gray as he closed in on unconsciousness; under heavy-g, with blood pouring out of the brain and down toward the buttocks and abdomen, the retinal cones are the first to go, and the subject loses color vision.

Then Paris's world turned into a weird tunnel as he lost peripheral vision as well.

He strained and grunted, drastically raising his blood pressure to force the heavy, sluggish blood higher; if the brain blood pressure sank too low, he would pass out and be unable to execute Phase II of the Swoop of Death . . . and they would pound into the shaft wall at nearly half a kilometer per second.

There might be some debris left for the *Voyager* to find.

Three, two, one, NOW! Just as they attained level flight, the g-forces dropped off, and the beleaguered dampers finally kicked on-line again, Paris viciously spun the shuttlecraft rightward, rolling it 180 degrees, exactly upside down from its previous orientation.

It was a necessary part of the Swoop of Death; no human could survive twelve g's straight *up* without losing consciousness; Paris had to switch "down" and "up" to avoid making a smoking hole in the shaft hull.

Then he again yanked back, pitching the nose "up" toward ninety degrees. If he pulled it off, they would be headed in the same direction they had started—but jogged a kilometer sideways. And with a reverse up-down orientation.

They would clear the antenna . . . *if* Paris pulled it off.

As soon as he began Phase II, Paris realized instinctively that he had blown the timing. He had pulled too late. They were not going to clear the shaft wall.

Color, which had just begun to flicker back, disappeared again; Lieutenant Paris's vision tunneled down, and he once again strained against the horrific acceleration that crushed him into his seat.

Wow. We're going to die. Sorry, Kim; been a slice.

Oh, what the hell . . . If they were going to go out, decided Paris, they might as well go out spectacularly.

He jammed the attitude control all the way back, pulling the shuttlecraft so hard that not only were the inertial dampers exceeded, so were the structural design limitations of the shuttlecraft hull itself.

The g-meter climbed; Paris's tunnel vision narrowed and narrowed until he skated on the merest, monomolecular thread of consciousness.

From somewhere he heard a distant thud. He blinked. Without knowing quite why, or whether he had actually cleared the rim of the dish or simply hallucinated seeing it fly past, he willed his lead-filled arm to creep forward, pushing the attitude control and killing the acceleration.

Slowly, the g-meter dropped; the crushing gravity lessened. Then the inertial dampers finally caught up with the maneuvering, kicking on-line again with an annoyed whine.

The computer spoke, but it sounded like a dream, far away; it warned him that he was making maneuvers that exceeded his shuttle's tolerances.

"Thanks," he gasped through a throat parched and burned; he realized he had jumped from one hell to another: the interior temperature was *sixty degrees.*

Another instant in between the two antennas and their lungs would have been cooked beyond the ability of the EMH program to fix.

Maybe Neelix had a recipe for parboiled pilot and Korean barbecue.

Kim! Paris quickly killed the shuttlecraft's forward velocity—they were past the antenna, and the shields could block the small bit of microwave leakage indefinitely; no more rush. He turned to his friend and crewmate.

Kim was unconscious. Paris put his ear to the ensign's mouth; to his great relief, he heard the faint stirring of breath. Placing his hand on Kim's chest, Paris felt it rise and fall at the limits of perception.

Then Ensign Kim suddenly wheezed and groaned, rolling his head gently from side to side.

Paris fell back into his command chair, feeling his own blood pressure drop slowly, slowly back to normal. He was so exhausted, fighting both the acceleration and the unbearable heat, that he could not move.

He forced his eyes open after a few seconds; the temperature had dropped to normal. He glanced at the g-meter.

They had pegged it at fourteen g's . . . a new record for Tom Paris, and without a combat suit!

He lay back in the chair, waiting patiently for Harry Kim to wake up.

* * *

THE FINAL FURY

Ensign Kim blinked back to some semblance of consciousness in a white room filled with white noise. He was surrounded by some sort of instrument panel.

He decided he really should know what the instruments were for; for that matter, he really should know who he was.

He remembered nothing—not even his name. *Easy... steady—I'm thinking, so I'm alive. Something happened to me ... if I can just figure out ...*

A name floated back—Kim; Harry Kim, that was who he was! *Ensign* Harry Kim, of the *U.S.S. Voyager.* But he was not on the *Voyager,* was he?

No. He was on a shuttlecraft, the shuttle with—Tom Paris!

Kim started to turn to Tom, to ask him the stupid question "Did we make it," when the pain struck.

Kim's eyes flew wide open as a white-hot needle slid through his skull, an astounding shear of agony that lasted—a second, perhaps two. Then it was gone, leaving only a dull ache, and he blinked back to full consciousness.

He stopped himself before asking the obvious. "Uh ... scanning ... Tom, the hull here is much thinner."

"Thin enough to beam through?"

"Yes. Yes, I think it is; and there's a livable enviro inside the hull. No life-forms."

"What are we waiting for, Harry?"

Kim set the computer to monitor and warn them of any approaching ship or anybody beaming across, as unlikely as the latter was; then he and Paris equipped themselves with phasers, tricorders, and exploration packs and beamed inside the artificial moon.

They materialized in a long corridor that stretched forward and back as far as they could see before dropping out of sight owing to the moon's curvature.

The corridor's "walls" were actually massed pipes and cables, bundles of fiberoptics and power conduits. There was no catwalk; they had to stand directly on the bottom fiber bundle.

There was also no artificial gravity, and they were nearer the moon's core than not. Kim jumped at the sudden feeling of near-weightlessness ... a serious mistake, as he bounded into the air, squawking and flapping his arms. He banged his head on a conduit, rebounding back toward the bottom; Paris caught Kim's trouser leg and reeled him in.

Rubbing his head, Kim worked his tricoder and announced, "From fifteen g's to less than a twentieth g. My bones are going to ache worse than my sunburn when we get back."

Paris gave an experimental hop forward, traveling a long distance but having to ward off the overhead with his hand. The pair required several minutes of practice before they caught the pattern of long, shallow jumps; thereafter, they moved far more quickly than they ever could have on a planet.

Kim kept up a long-range scan, finally finding a cross-corridor; they turned and followed it for a few kilometers before running across a deep, wide chasm . . . a circular pit in the deck.

"You want to go for it, Tom?" Kim indicated the hole.

Paris leaned over to stare, holding his light as far down as he could and stepping up the brightness to maximum. "I can't see a bottom, and the sides are smooth as glass. No ladder. You know, if a thirty-meter fall can kill you in normal gravity, then a six-hundred-meter fall can kill you here. Maybe we should think about this."

Kim monkeyed with his tricorder. "Huh. You know, I've always wanted to do this, ever since I saw those animated holoplays as a kid."

"Do what?"

Kim pulled a thermal blanket from his pack. "Tom, in this low gravity, I think we really can do it!"

"Do *what*, dammit?"

Kim grinned. "Use a blanket as a parachute."

"Cute. So how do we get back up?"

Kim rummaged in his kit. The packs were generally stowed in shuttlecraft storage bins for use by away teams exploring new planets; they contained everything an explorer could possibly need, including plenty of provisions, water blastules, binoculars, tricorder, blankets and tents, inflatable rafts—and mountaineering equipment; lots of it.

The ensign removed a coil of incredibly thin rope; an attached tag read **1000 M**.

They tied off the rope to a very solid-looking, shielded bundle of fiberoptics, then tied the other end to one another, leaving ten meters of separation between the two of them. Then they stepped to the rim of the pit.

"Harry, I take back everything I ever said about you in the mess hall. Are you *sure* this is going to work? I'm a little nervous about just jumping off a cliff."

"Don't you trust me?"

"No."

"Well, how about my calculations?"

Tom Paris considered. "All right, them I trust. Geronimo!"

"Who?"

"Ask Chakotay," said Paris mysteriously. They each took hold of two corners of the gigantic blanket and stepped over the edge.

The two Starfleet officers wafted gently down the airshaft like oak leaves lazily dropping from the tree in October. Kim discovered that he could steer after a fashion by tugging on the corner in the direction he wanted to go; he kept them in the center of the shaft, away from the sides.

They dropped for a long, long time. Kim estimated their rate of descent holding steady at somewhere between 1.5 and 2.0 meters per second . . . which meant it would take anywhere from eight to eleven minutes to reach full extension.

It took just about nine by the chronometer in the pack; he was pleased at his close estimate.

The shaft suddenly opened up into a vast, gaping room, easily two kilometers in diameter; at the same moment, the rope above Kim suddenly became taut, jerking them to an ignominious halt a kilometer down from the top, yet still half a kilometer at least above the deck. They dangled like fish on a fishing line, high above the most complex, gigantic machine Kim had ever seen.

With no idea what he was looking at, Kim aimed his tricorder and began to scan the room.

CHAPTER 6

"ALL RIGHT. WE'VE SEEN IT. NOW, WHAT IS IT?"

Kim did not answer right away; he continued imaging as much of the machine as he could. *Whatever it is,* he thought, *it's the biggest whatever I've ever seen!*

"It's something to do with a huge amount of energy," he replied at last. "Those power conduits are more than a hundred times as large as the conduits on the *Voyager*, and there are hundreds of them. The grid is obviously throwing some significant fraction of the sun's radiant energy at this moon, maybe five or ten percent . . . but what the hell are they doing with it, Tom?"

"Wish I knew. But we'd better find out; it could be a weapon, and if we're going to try to extract that pilot—"

"Shh!" Kim waved his hand at Paris, indicating *Shut up, the walls might have ears.*

"Aw, hell, nobody's listening; if they were, we'd be in custody already."

"We can't take that chance!"

"I think I'd know if we were about to be captured."

"Why? You missed it when you were a Maquis."

Paris closed his mouth and frowned at Harry Kim. On

Tom Paris's first mission as a Maquis, he had been captured by Starfleet, ending up in a penal facility in New Zealand . . . whence Captain Janeway had recruited him.

"Well," said Paris stiffly, "unless we're going to unhook and drop down to the deck, possibly never to get back out again, we'd better climb back up."

"We, ah, could break out another rope and tie it off. But I guess there's no point; if we can't figure this thing out from up here, I don't think we'll understand it by getting up close and personal." He did not add that at the moment, he hadn't a clue.

"I think we have enough to take back to the ship. We'd better start putting some pieces together, or when the captain gets back, she'll be mighty pissed."

Climbing up one kilometer was almost as easy as dropping had been. A typical, adult, human male weighs anywhere from 730 to 950 Newtons; but on the alien moon, Kim and Paris each weighed no more than thirty-five Newtons.

Kim gave the rope a vigorous tug, easily giving himself a velocity of three meters per second. This lasted six seconds, during which he covered nine meters.

They rested after every eleven tugs . . . about every hundred meters. Kim coiled up the rope during the rest stops.

Counting resting time, they made it to the lip of the pit again in just under forty-five minutes. Ensign Kim was surprised at how tired his arms were, considering he had never lifted more than the weight of a Starfleet field pack in the entire journey. Of course, he had lifted that pack more than a hundred times. Paris took it in stride; if his arms ached, he did not let on.

They backtracked their trail, Kim following the heat trail with his tricorder—directly into a solid bulkhead. He pulled up short, staring at the obstacle. "Tom, correct me if I'm wrong, but . . ."

"You're not wrong, Harry. That wasn't there an hour ago."

"Didn't we come right through here?"

"You've got the bloodhound. But I sure think we did."

Harry Kim rotated in place and scanned 360 degrees

around. "There's a parallel bulkhead about a meter to the left that goes past this block. If we can somehow get to it, maybe we can get close enough for beam-out."

They returned toward the pit, but it had disappeared. Instead, the corridor they walked along veered abruptly right, then right again, debouching into the parallel corridor they sought.

"The *walls* are moving!"

"No, really? Maybe we're hallucinating."

"Cute, Paris; I just think it's . . ."

"Weird?"

"Unnecessarily complex."

Kim stared at the solid-looking walls. Far in the distance, they heard a scrape as other bulkheads presumably went wandering. "It's almost like . . ."

"Like?"

"Nah, it's silly."

"Come on, Harry, what were you going to say?"

"Like the entire moon is a gigantic logic board, with synapses opening and closing."

Kim adjusted the tricorder and rescanned. "The electrical impulses are following patterns remarkably like, you know, neurons. Some sort of planetwide neural net—or series of nets, actually; I think the walls are connecting and severing the connections between networks.

"The next evolutionary phase," he continued, "is a neural net assembled from millions of smaller neural nets. Like a fractal: each small part is a fuzzy model of the whole thing."

"Harry? Let's get the hell out of here."

They dodged through the maze; once, Lieutenant Paris almost got caught when a bulkhead suddenly came marching toward him. Kim yanked him out of the way at the last moment, and the wall brushed past, implacable, while Kim's heart raced at his friend's close call.

At last, they got close enough to contact the onboard shuttlecraft computer and request beam-out. Kim sighed with relief as he felt in his gut the familiar tingling of the transporter beam.

Back on the shuttle, they paused to figure a strategy. Paris was worried. "Look, Kim, I don't want to go through the Swoop of Death again. We made it once; let's not push our luck. I need more time to do a smooth, sideways transition."

"Tom, it's microwave soup in between those lenses! There's no way we can hang around for more than three or four seconds without our shields being ripped to shreds."

"So?"

"So we wouldn't have anything left for the rest of the shaft out of here."

"So?"

"So—" Kim scowled; he tapped gently on the computer console. "Well, maybe we wouldn't be too badly burned if we turned around and backed out of the shaft. There's more physical plating on the aft end of the shuttlecraft."

"Just give me twenty seconds between the lenses, and I'll back us out of here so fast you'll leave your eyeballs on the forward viewer."

Kim tore open a panel and set to work, desperately wishing he had gone for the doctorate in engineering instead of opting for command school. *I could have been a brilliant starship designer,* he swore to himself.

Twenty minutes later, he cleared his throat. "I can give you eighteen seconds."

"You're on. Strap up and let's get the hell out of here."

Paris slapped Kim's seat, and the ensign hustled to his spot.

Paris turned the ship around before creeping around the dish antenna, not wanting to waste time turning around under radiation bombardment. He skillfully backed up and over the dish, through the central focus like a thread through a needle's eye, then backward along the long, deep shaft toward the surface.

Kim felt sicker and sicker as they progressed, his temperature climbing way past body-normal. His skin turned so irritated and tender, he could hardly keep his mind on his task: watching the ultraviolet count to make sure they did not blind themselves. That, even the grumpy, holographic doctor might not be able to fix.

"Better hurry, Paris," he said almost inaudibly when they were three-quarters of the way out. Paris did not waste attention responding.

Kim found himself blinking rapidly, watching sweat pour down the face of Tom Paris. Paris's skin was so fair, his face turned command-red and began to peel. Kim turned away; he did not want to see it.

Just as the ensign was starting to see small, dancing bugs all over the ship, electromagnetic stimulation of the retina—a bad sign—they burst out of the shaft into the cool blackness of space. Kim was giddy, swaying in his seat; he grimly clung to consciousness as if it were a clarinet that someone was trying to yank from his hand. The universe swam; he dimly wondered how Paris could point the shuttle at the *Voyager* when Kim couldn't even point at the moon they had just left.

But Tom Paris pointed the shuttlecraft, activated the distress beacon on a tight beam to the ship, and engaged . . . all before slumping over in his seat.

"Emer—emergency—medical—beam-out," gasped Kim to the comm link. "Tractor—shuttlecraft. . . ." The young ensign lost the battle as last, loyally following his friend into the Land of Nod.

Paris woke on the doctor's operating table. For a moment, he panicked; he had dreamed that all his skin charred off, and he was dancing in agony, his muscles and organs simply exposed to the knifey open air.

But the illusory doctor was playing a simple skin stimulator back and forth across his face and hands.

"Oh. You're awake. I suppose it was inevitable."

"Hello to you too, Dr. Schweitzer."

The doctor raised his eyebrows. "I ceased using that name a long time ago, Mr. Paris. I hope you were just being sarcastic, and you haven't suffered a loss of memory."

"Pure, unadulterated sarcasm."

"It figures. I'm programmed to ignore such maldirected attacks."

"Oh, don't be so humorless, Doctor; I can see right through you."

"Is my imaging system malfunctioning again? Oh . . . another joke. Har de har har. I don't suppose it would do any good to tell you to stay off your feet for a couple of days?"

"Not a chance, Doc."

"I didn't think so. You and Mr. Kim deserve each other." The hologram snorted. "Kes, give these two the usual advice, which they will ignore, and a temperature monitor."

Kim sat up on the next table, blinking groggily. "Gentlemen," said the doctor, "you will call me if your temperature sensors register a fever?"

"You bet," said Paris. Ensign Kim nodded; *probably doesn't even know what the hologram just said,* thought Paris.

"Good. Sickbay to Chakotay: Commander Paris and Kim are ready for the debriefing."

"Understood, Doctor," came Chakotay's calm tones. "If they will join me in the ready room? And doctor—I'd like Kes to be present, as well."

"Why not? After all, certainly I can't have any need for her . . . I'm just a hologram, after all. Holograms don't have needs."

Paris rolled his eyes. Just what he wanted to hear: a grand holo-opera with the woman he—but the woman he could never—

Kes sighed, putting her hand on the doctor's arm. "It's all right; I'll come right back. I do want to finish the test . . . it was really challenging this time."

"It was? I mean, you really were challenged?"

"Oh, it was brutal! I'll be right back, Doctor."

"Yes . . . yes, of course you will."

There is no fear. There is no pain. There is no emotion . . . let it fade and disappear. Pure logic; logic fills your brain. Thought is symbol, and logic gives you complete power over all symbols.

The meditation helped, but Lieutenant Tuvok still found himself caught in the grip of illogical emotion, the DNA memory of a hundred thousand years ago perturbing his endocrine system, triggering the release of Vulcan vidrenalase, which affects Vulcans as adrenaline affects humans. Tuvok trembled; he could not control the fine motor skills. It was the best he could do to maintain a veneer of logic and rationality across a sea of barbaric feelings and impulses.

He stumbled along behind the Fury, behind the captain and Neelix, through the warm, moist tunnel. Even in his nightmare state, he could not help but notice that it was like a return up the birth canal; but rather than fascinating him, as it should have, the image filled Tuvok with the unaccustomed *emotions* of loathing and disgust.

Like the impulse to kill the interlocutor, Navdaq, and every other demon on the planet, all twenty-seven billion of them. It was worse than the *pon farr*—at least the mating madness was carefully channeled by ritual. Tuvok had no ritual to deal with the primitive emotions that these creatures stirred in him. Only his meditation.

Tuvok was not bothered by the darkness of the corridor, nor by what the captain considered disturbing architecture: angles that did not quite meet at ninety degrees but looked as thought they ought to, tricks of perspective that made walls or ceilings seem closer or farther than they were, or strange tilts that threw off a human's sense of balance, which was tied so completely into visual cuing.

But he was far more disturbed by the sudden intrusion of a long-forgotten cavern in the Vulcan mind, the genetic memory of defeat and slavery so complete and remote it left no trace in the historical record, which was thought to have stretched back farther in time than the conquest.

Evidently not, thought Tuvok, clutching at the logical train of thought; *apparently, there are significant gaps in the historical record. I must write a report for the* Vulcan Journal of Archeology and Prehistory. Then he shuddered.

In our innermost beings, we are not very different from Romulans after all, he thought. With bitterness—another emotion; they came thick and fast now.

In fact, Tuvok realized they would never stop . . . not until he forced himself to confront the Fury. Gritting his teeth against the terrors, Tuvok increased his stride until he stood but an arm's length behind Navdaq; then with a quick move, before he could disgrace his race further by losing his nerve, Tuvok reached out and caught Navdaq by the shoulder, spinning the creature around to face him.

Tuvok looked directly into Navdaq's face—and felt an abyss open inside him deep enough to swallow both hearts.

I know you! he thought, unable to keep excitement and emotion out of even his thoughts. *You are Ok'San, the Overlord!*

Ok'San was the most despised of all Vulcan demons, for she was the mother of all the rest. The mythology was so ancient that it was consciously known only to a few scholars; even Tuvok knew only dimly of the stories, and only because of his interest in Vulcan history.

But all Vulcans knew Ok'San, but preferred not to think about her, for she represented *loss of control* and *loss of reason*. There was little else that a sane Vulcan dared not consider apart from the loss of everything it meant to be a Vulcan: logic, control, order, and reason.

In demonic mythology, Ok'San crept through the windows at night, the hot, dry Vulcan night, and crouched on the chests of her "chosen" dreamers: poets, composers, authors, philosophers, scientists, political analysts . . . the very people whose creativity was slowly knitting together the barbaric strands of early Vulcan society into a vision of a logical tomorrow, who groped for shreds of civilization in the horror of Vulcan's yesterday.

She crouched on a dreamer's chest, leaned over his writhing body, and pressed her lips against his. She spat into his mouth, and the spittle rolled down his throat and filled his hearts with the *Fury of Vulcan*.

The Fury of Vulcan manifested as a berserker rage that flooded the victim and drove him to paroxysms of horrific violence that defied the descriptive power of logic.

Tuvok had tried to contemplate what must pass through a Vulcan's mind to drive him to kill his own family with a blunt stick, striking their heads hard enough to crush bone and muscle and still have force enough to destroy the brain. In one of the few instances of the Fury of Vulcan to be well recorded by the testimony of many witnesses, a Vulcan hunter-warrior named Torkas of the Vehm, perhaps eighty thousand years ago, grabbed up a leaf-bladed Vulcan Toth spear and set out after the entire population of his village. He managed to kill ninety-seven and wound an additional fourteen, six critically, before he was killed.

Tuvok had always believed Ok'San was the personification of the violent, nearly sadistic rage that filled the hearts of Vulcans before Surak. The Fury of Vulcan always seemed like a disease of the nervous system; yet it was curious that there were no recorded instances of the Fury within historical times . . . not a one.

Diseases do not die out; and it was unlikely in the extreme that primitive Vulcans, who had neither logic nor medical science, could have destroyed the virus that caused the Fury.

It was an enigma, until now.

CHAPTER 7

THIS IS THE FURY, THOUGHT TUVOK, STARING INTO THE FACE OF Ok'San . . . albeit a male aspect of Ok'San. *I am the Fury— and everyone within my grasp is in grave danger.*

The rage was so barely under his control that Tuvok did not even hear Navdaq ask a question, presumably a variation on "What do you want?"

Trembling still, Tuvok forced himself to speak: "Sir— your features—they are—fascinating—yet others do not all—all share. Are—are—are you all one?"

Navdaq smiled, ratcheting up the emotional response another notch inside the Vulcan: the interlocutor's smile began to trigger even more genetic memories of the horrors of the occupation.

"The Holy are many, but they are one. They have come from many planets, but so many years back it disappears into the haze of memory, even for them; they joined in heaven as the only rightful heirs of the divine."

"But you still—maintain the separateness . . . ."

"The divinity of the Holy manifests as many points of a many-pointed star; but the pentagram describes the five great classes of being. I myself am of the family Sanoktisandaruval, of the second great class. My divine ancestors ruled as kings under the Autocrat. The Holy, though one, are yet separate species and cannot mix together, cannot dilute the separateness of the points."

Ruled as kings . . .

There was not a shadow of a doubt in Tuvok's ravaged mind; the Sanoktisandaruval were the Ok'San, and they had ruled over Vulcan.

Perhaps they were benevolent kings under their own, internal standard. But tiny crumbs of ancient memory broke loose from the abyss and floated to the surface, where Tuvok could stare at them.

A smoldering furnace—perhaps a fusion power plant remembered by ancients who had no reference beyond a wood cookfire . . . a lake of fire, or radioactivity, or even liquid helium; slaves writhing in agony, suffering the torments of the damned—or perhaps struck repeatedly by the terror-projection machines . . . mountain-sized demons filling the field of view—holographic projections to convey orders quickly to a large group of slaves?

I am a slave of the household of Javastaras. I rise from a fitful three hours of dreamless sleep in which waking dreams torment me. I am compelled forward to crawl on my stomach alongside six other slaves before the hell-princess Meliflones, whom Javastaras wishes to conjoin. She is pleased, laughing and clapping her hands in childish joy.

But we are forgotten as Javastaras and Meliflones court, and I crouch on my knees, afraid to move lest I call attention to myself.

It was Tuvok's first conscious genetic memory.

More frozen images: trapped and bound in a tiny room while demons ripped and tore at the flesh. Doctors, surely, giving inoculations or engaging in medical procedures, perhaps without anesthetic. Many-tentacled monsters screaming and thrashing their limbs . . . pumps, hydraulics, electrical cables? A threshing machine?

But the genetic memories that were not simply misconstructions were the pain, the terror, the physical abuse and overwork to the point of death, and most especially the invasion of the most private corners of a Vulcan mind, for there dwelt the Terror and the Fury—and there the Furies touched most deeply.

I am a young girl now, performing in the drama. And they make me stand frozen while a young boy approaches jerkily, anguish on his face but blood on his hands....

For Tuvok suddenly remembered the slave torcs, metallic collars worn around the throat that melded into the mind, controlling the slave's every action, every word, every *thought*. They became no longer Vulcans but animals, beasts of the field, bowing and capering and doing their masters' will instead of their own. Tuvok "remembered" the shows, the degrading fantasies in which Vulcan slaves played the role of mythological beings, talking animals, children, even rocks and other scenery. Dramas of torment and humiliation in which one captive was forced to murder another, the limbs of each controlled by his slave torc.

I am an old man. I am tired. I hurt, but I cannot stop. I work incessantly; I am possessed. The demons wish me dead. I feel a pain in my lower heart, and perhaps they will get their wish after all. I haven't the strength to fight anymore, so I am useless. They discard the useless.

To genetically "remember" such specific incidents in such detail must mean, Tuvok reasoned, that they had occurred again and again, over a period of tens of thousands of years. And the worst memory of all was the utter helplessness... they could never even free themselves; they had to wait for the Unclean, whoever they were, to arrive and drive out the Furies for their own reasons.

It was a bitter truth to vomit up; but now that he had dragged it from the black abyss of the Vulcan unconscious into the light, where reason and logic could analyze it, the emotional charge of the memories began to fade.

It happened in the blink of an eye, though it felt like a hundred years to Tuvok. But Navdaq turned away, the conversation over, and resumed its trek to the Autocrat, leading Janeway, Neelix, and Tuvok himself while the Vulcan began finally to come to peace inside himself, suppressing the powerful emotions behind the mask of logic and restoring his natural equilibrium.

The gods had arrived, to drive away the Furies and demons.

The "gods" were hideous! Enormous, bloated, black wasps, horrors of fiber woven with metal—Tuvok caught only glimpses of writing mouths sucking the life-energy out of entire ships, *in deep space*. The gods did not need boats to sail the celestial waters; they crawled the vasty deep naked and horrible, bodies puffing out with internal pressures, mandibles and hundred of multifaceted eyes causing Vulcan slaves to fall face to the ground and sometimes even die of terror.

The Ok'San turned their terrors on the wasp-gods; the weapon had no effect on insectoid, soul-feeding horrors. In fear and fury, the Ok'San turned on their own slaves, throwing them into combat against the gods; the slaves died by the tens of thousands, split and eaten live before their paralyzed fellow slaves.

The Ok'San fell back, beaten for the first time, frightened and astonished at these beings over whom they had no power! And the Furies fled, enraged but impotent, helpless—but vowing to return and reclaim *what was owed*. But as Tuvok watched them leave, logic help him, he cowered . . . he was *afraid* that the Furies were leaving; he wanted them back!

Shame burned in his face at the racial memory, another powerful, unaccustomed emotion. Tuvok bowed his head in retroactive shame and humiliation.

Thenceforth, history fell back into the rhythm that Tuvok had studied. The wasp-gods, the Unclean, were uninterested in the Vulcan ex-slaves. There was no economically viable reason to maintain slavery in any spacefaring culture; the only reason was arrogance, the sheer joy of oppression itself. The Unclean had no motivation or interest; they saw the Furies as a threat . . . they removed the threat.

And the Vulcans, suddenly granted freedom, their fondest wish, fell to warring among themselves, for they could no longer contemplate life without the overseer's whip. They mistook custom for natural law and sought to perpetuate the vile institution of slavery.

Savage wars erupted, acts of bloodthirsty vengeance and

preemptive barbarity became commonplace. And from the chaos of "the war of all against all," as the human philosopher Hobbes had described, rose the cleansing logic and system of Surak, resurrecting Vulcan high culture on the operating table of reason.

Slowly, Tuvok began to remember who he was and, more important, *where* he was. He blinked back to the present in a dank, dungeonlike hole—the antechamber of the Autocrat. Navdaq was gone; they awaited its return.

Another stupid, useless meeting, thought B'Elanna Torres; *another chance to find out that I'm unnecessary on this ship; a supernumerary, a third engine pod, a white elephant.*

Ensign Kim cleared his throat. He and Paris had been trying, with limited success, to describe the vast machinery they had seen inside the moon.

Commander Chakotay, Lieutenant B'Elanna Torres, and Kes turned toward the young ensign. "You have something to add?" asked the commander, command duty officer in Captain Janeway's absence. B'Elanna tried not to let her annoyance show. If she could change just one thing about Harry, she would make him bolder about offering his own opinion. Half the time, it seemed he allowed Paris to speak his lines for him, as if he weren't even present.

"Actually, a suggestion, sir. Can we adjourn and go down to the holodeck? I could feed the dataclip from the holocam into the computer and simulate the machinery."

"Yeah," said Torres, a little too quickly; she was overanxious to please—and knew it. "I second! Let me get a look at it. I promise I can figure it out."

Torres was uncomfortably aware that she had contributed very little to the discussion so far; actually, Paris's description had not been particularly helpful, but she did not want to say that. It sounded too much like an excuse.

Chakotay shifted the debriefing. Ten minutes later, they stood on an invisible platform, hovering half a mile above the gigantic machine . . . exactly the position from which Kim had used the tricorder.

B'Elanna stared down between her boots; she tried to get

an overall impression of the *flow* of the system as a whole before getting a close-up. The entire apparatus was too large to comprehend any other way.

"Power obviously comes in through those conduits in the southwest quadrant. Computer: superimpose bearings over the image. There—the conduits at one-zero-seven and one-zero-eight. That's the power supply."

She paced back and forth, absently rubbing her Klingon brow ridge . . . an unconscious habit of discomfort. She noticed and stopped herself.

She held her hand out, palm down, tracing the probable movement of power from the input into the guts of the machine. "Subspace channeling gear . . . some kind of compression device—really huge, 10^{20}, 10^{25} watts. Imaging gear—never mind, just for aiming, I think. Commander? They're right on the knife edge of transporter technology, but they go off in some funny direction. I can't tell exactly what it is. But I don't think we're going to like it."

"Why not?"

"I think when you put the whole thing together—and I have no idea if it's operable yet—you somehow have the power to reach out and crush something. Maybe even through subspace."

"Something?"

"I don't know . . . a ship, a planet, empty space, a sun. Something—and crush it really hard, I mean; hard enough maybe to turn a sun into a neutron star, or even a black hole, if it starts out big enough."

"Are you sure?"

B'Elanna Torres flushed . . . an alien reaction for a Klingon; it came purely from her human half. But both sides understood doubt and embarrassment. *He thinks I'm crazy,* she thought. *He doesn't trust me anymore.*

Or am I just paranoid now? She licked her lips nervously, uncertain what to say or do next. She felt a terrible pressure to *do something,* anything! Say anything. Something, for Kahless's sake!

"Chakotay," said Kes, "I think B'Elanna's right. I recognize some of this technology . . . it's similar to the way the

Caretaker taught us to build our energy-distribution centers."

Chakotay nodded. "If an engineer and a technician agree, then that is good enough for me. Ensign Kim?"

Kim shrugged; he didn't know enough engineering to offer an opinion. Nobody asked Paris.

"Let's review what we know," said the first officer. "The aliens have built an energy-collection grid around their sun; it captures perhaps ten percent of the sun's radiant energy, but beams it via microwaves to this artificial moon. The moon contains a giant apparatus—or more likely many such devices—that takes this enormous energy and converts it into a beam that can project a crushing force, possibly through subspace, powerful enough to turn a star into a neutron star. Is that a fair statement?"

"Put that way," said Torres, "it scares the hell out of me." She tried to imagine what anyone would want with such a collection of dangerous toys.

Chakotay nodded. "Scares the hell out of me too. We also know the aliens have captured a crashed shuttlecraft and possibly a still living pilot . . . and currently, they have Captain Janeway and Lieutenant Tuvok as guests."

Chakotay stood silent, thinking. B'Elanna could almost read his thoughts by watching his expression . . . he glanced at the empty space they unconsciously reserved where Janeway would have stood; glanced down at the huge machine a half-kilometer below their feet; fingered his comm badge.

At last he spoke. "I believe we should request the captain's immediate return and tell her what we saw; I don't like this picture."

"Aye, aye, sir," said Ensign Kim. "Request permission to return to the bridge."

"Does anybody have anything else to say?" asked the commander. No one spoke. B'Elanna especially didn't speak; all she had to say was *I agree* . . . and Chakotay didn't need a yes-person. "Then the meeting is adjourned. Kim, return to the bridge and contact Captain Janeway. Paris, stand by for an emergency beam-out, just in case. Torres, you monitor the moon; tell me if there is any sudden power surge . . . I want to know if they power up their weapon. Dismissed."

The rest of the senior crew scurried off about their tasks, but Torres remained behind with Chakotay, staring down at the huge machine . . . the huge weapon.

"Chakotay? Why would anyone want to crush a planet through subspace?"

"Let's hope that's all they can do," said the commander. "I'm afraid . . ." He did not elaborate his fear, and this time she couldn't read his thoughts; eventually, B'Elanna decided to give him some space to work it out.

"Captain," said Tuvok hoarsely. Janeway and Neelix each grabbed one of his arms and sat him down on an iron bench. The bench was decorated with skulls and spiderwebs. *My God,* thought Captain Janeway, *he's just passed through the dark night of the soul!*

"Tuvok, don't try to speak just yet," said the captain; "you've had a very bad reaction to—"

"Captain," he whispered, "I am well aware of my reaction. I am perfectly all right now; I have controlled the outbreak."

"Maybe we should contact Commander Chakotay . . . the doctor should look you over."

"I assure you, I have regained full control of myself. It is an effort, but there will be no future outbreaks of emotion. Captain, I must warn you about something, who these Furies actually are."

"Furies?" Janeway sat back, surprised by how *right* the name sounded. At once, her vague memory clicked into place. She had learned about the Furies—could they be the same Furies?—in her second-year Academy class in military history. A previous captain of the *Enterprise* had encountered hideous beings some six or seven decades earlier in Federation space; they almost destroyed his ship—they almost overran the quadrant!

At the time, she found the tale of marginal interest; she was worried about a term paper on rotating Okudagrams, and the adventure was just one of an improbable number of similar stories attributed to that ship and that captain.

THE FINAL FURY

Captain Kirk had not been stretching the truth; the similarities were too great. But if James Kirk discovered any special clues or insights into the nature of the Furies, that information did not remain in her faded memory of an Academy lecture. If the Furies were more than just monstrous-looking aliens, Janeway and Tuvok would have to "remember" for themselves, staring back along their own DNA histories.

She stared around the antechamber in which Navdaq had deposited them. The room was not quite round; the walls were not quite perpendicular; the room was an iron stewpot, indifferently formed by a careless ironmonger. A bench tilted against one side, and Janeway and Tuvok sat upon it, recovering their self-control; but Neelix paced anxiously in front of the bench, keyed like an animal that smelled danger. His yellow cheek-streaks looked like burnt umber in the faint, red glow from the walls.

Janeway considered the Furies, wondering what Tuvok might remember; Vulcans had been civilized far longer than humans; there might be records.

"Well . . . I know they used to live somewhere else and hold other races as slaves. They used a fear projector, some kind of device to project terror into their slaves to prevent a revolt. But I don't know *how* I know all that. It's as if . . . "

"Oh right," said the Talaxian, more peeved than usual; "like you were there!"

"Yes," said the Vulcan. "As if I were there."

Tuvok closed his eyes. Calmly, unemotionally, he recounted the hell he had journeyed through for the past thirty minutes . . . and the memories it had raked up. Janeway listened with rapt attention, astonished and a little chilled by how close it struck to her own vision.

"We did encounter these Furies once before in recorded history," concluded the Vulcan.

Janeway nodded. "Yes, I remember: the original *Enterprise* fought them to a standstill some decades past. I read about it in Military History 120 or 140."

Tuvok raised an eyebrow. "Indeed. I read about it in the message traffic at the time."

The captain stared. "Tuvok, that long ago?"

"Indeed, I confess I did not pay sufficient attention at the time to benefit us now."

Janeway strained to remember everything she had heard or read about the Furies in years past; the intelligence amounted to a very little pile after all. "But why bother to come to Federation space?" She turned her hands up. "What's wrong with all this? Why isn't this enough for them?"

"Captain," concluded Tuvok, rational as any Vulcan, "I believe that heaven, as Navdaq calls it, was in the Alpha Quadrant. And the subject races included Vulcans . . . and doubtless your own."

"You mean—but we were never . . ." She pressed her lips together; it would indeed explain much about her own reaction, the unexpected and irrational fear and disgust she felt on first seeing Navdaq.

A hundred thousand years ago, humans might have had no reason to feel such horror at these Furies—early men might think them gods or demons, but they saw gods and demons everywhere!

Yet *something* had made the entire human race, and even the savage, violent Vulcan race, simply give up and allow themselves to be enslaved for tens of thousands of years, if Tuvok's racial memory was accurate; all so long before history began that there was no record . . . except in the DNA.

And then she recalled, with a chill, Navdaq's words: *We shall return to heaven, whence we were cast out, and cleanse it of all Unclean. . . . Heaven shall be cleansed of all but the Furies.*

She stood, blocking Neelix's path; he almost ran into her before noticing and stopping.

Janeway felt a sense of unreality. She had no illusions. Biologically, humans of today were not that different from humans of a hundred thousand years ago.

If it worked then, it would work now.

The hour is at hand . . . .

"Captain, did Navdaq describe the Unclean? I confess

there were many minutes when I heard nothing of what was said."

"I wasn't listening very well myself," admitted Janeway ruefully. She and Tuvok sat quietly for a moment until Neelix broke the silence by clearing his throat.

"Well, I was listening the whole time . . . and it did paint a reasonably complete picture of what it called the Unclean. It described them as a cross between a virus and a machine."

Janeway shook her head. "That's no race I'm aware of in the Alpha Quadrant, at least not in the Federation or the Klingon, Cardassian, or Romulan Empires."

"Yet we encounter new races every day," said Tuvok. "We may yet meet with their remnants in a few years. They may not be able to help us against the Furies, however; they have clearly degenerated far enough over the millennia to lose control over 'heaven' after once defeating Navdaq's people."

"Tuvok, I get the queasy feeling that we're the thin, red line." She glanced at the iron-red walls that gave no heat; unconsciously, she stepped away.

"I am unfamiliar with that reference, Captain."

"British Army, five hundred years ago. We, my friend, are the first defense of the entire Alpha Quadrant against this terrible invasion . . . assuming they're serious."

"I don't think Navdaq is lying," said Neelix. "He seems quite sincere and passionate."

"Then we are in trouble, Tuvok. It's one ship against twenty-seven billion invaders. Been practicing with that phaser?" She smiled, taking the edge off the cut.

"Your point is taken, Captain."

Neelix interrupted. "Why always look at the dark side? You should count your blessings that you found out in time. We can overwhelm them and stop the invasion!"

Janeway glowered at Neelix. Just what she needed: more swashes to be buckled! "Next question: why all the nightmare architecture, the darkness, the moist, rotting air?"

Tuvok, fully himself again in Navdaq's absence, extracted his tricorder and scanned the local area. "I detect a great many microorganisms in the atmosphere, far more than on Earth or Vulcan."

"You mean germs?" worried Neelix. "Are we inoculated against them? I don't want to come down with some bizarre, alien disease."

"It is not likely, Mr. Neelix, that alien microbes would even recognize any of the three of us as food. In fact, I believe these microorganisms are closer to plankton than to viruses or bacteria: simple, single-celled plantlike organisms with no capability of reprogramming a cell's DNA."

"Plankton?" Janeway thought for a moment. "Tuvok, is it possible that Navdaq and the other Furies are filter-feeders?"

"I believe that is a very likely scenario. The horns and tendrils on the heads of most of the races we have seen so far, and the wormlike cilia in Navdaq's mouth, may well be organs that suck in moist air and filter out the microorganisms for nourishment."

"And the darkness and musty smell simply encourage the fungi and plankton to grow," she mused. "I wonder . . . the remote ancestors of both humans and Vulcans used to dwell in holes in the ground, tens of millions of years ago. Yet now we associate being underground with death and damnation. When did we first begin doing so?

"Could the Furies have given us that fear, too?"

They fell silent, and fifteen minutes passed. There was still no sign of either Navdaq or the Autocrat. Janeway almost touched her commbadge to ask Chakotay what was happening on the *Voyager;* but she suddenly felt reluctant to announce that the brooch on her chest was a communications device—just in case they were being observed.

After a while, Janeway opened another line of inquiry; in fact, she had decided to initiate as many logical speculations as possible to keep her Vulcan lieutenant firmly grounded in his natural element.

"Tuvok, why is Navdaq being so open with us, with the very people the Furies once enslaved?"

"If I had to speculate, I would conclude that he does not see us as the enemy. After all, we are here, not there; we are in the Delta Quadrant, and the Unclean are in the Alpha Quadrant."

"I'm getting a bit worried, Tuvok. Navdaq has been gone a long time, leaving us alone in this giant saucepan. I think we're being deliberately delayed . . . and maybe our cover is blown after all."

"Blown? Do you mean they've figured out who you are?" Neelix began to glance suspiciously into every dark, dank corner, as if expecting a horde of Navdaqs to pop out with pitchforks.

Almost as if in response, a crack as bright-red as fire opened in the iron wall immediately opposite them; slowly, an oilwood door began to creak open.

Beyond it, they saw only the red glow of more "hot" iron.

"I believe the doctor will see us now," muttered Janeway.

CHAPTER 8

I NEVER UNDERSTAND WHAT SHE'S TALKING ABOUT, THOUGHT AN annoyed Neelix as they rose and slipped through the door. The red walls were not particularly hotter than the rest of the planet; they were noticibly brighter. Neelix wondered whether such comparatively bright light bothered the Furies; was the corridor intended to put local suppliants off their game, make them nervous before meeting their Autocrat? It had the opposite effect on the Talaxian, tired of the black gloom.

The glowing-iron corridor wound around a series of bends that were perfect right angles; the floor remained on the same level; the ceiling lowered, then in a trick of suddenness exploded up and out of sight. The glow grew steadily brighter until even Neelix had to squint against it, a glow like metal heated to the searing temperature. The walls, ceiling, and floor were all of a color, so that the *Voyager*'s guide had a hard time telling exactly where one ended and the other began—the corners were lost in the glare. He could not see how far the corridor extended, and *that* disturbed him.

I'd better be ready to defend the crew, he thought, casually brushing the phaser on his belt. Then belatedly: *I'd better not die down here, or Kes will kill me.* Somehow, the Fury planet brought up the most morbid thoughts.

Not being able to really see when the corridor turned, the away team several times piled up against the wall, thankful that it was not as hot as it looked.

Then they turned and saw a black spot in the distance, the only disharmony of color since leaving the antechamber. It was a door, a simple dungeon door of some local oily wood. A mechanical lever—mechanical!—jutted from the bottom. Neelix boldly squatted down to yank on it.

The door flew open with a bang, wrenching itself from the startled scout, who yelled and lunged backward, flaring his arms to shield his companions from whatever was coming through the door—nothing, as it turned out.

Inside was a room so bright it hurt all three pairs of eyes, bright and hellish white: a combination to strike terror in the guts of a local, used to musty darkness as they were. Neelix did not need the captain's tricorder to know the air was dry and sterile, devoid of comforting plankton-food and yet another blow to the self-confidence of a Fury.

A huge figure sat in black silhouette at the far end of the room. The Autocrat's face and flesh were obscured by the difference in light; but his bulk was unmistakable. Seated, he towered even over Tuvok, while his shoulders were as wide as he was tall. His neck and arms articulated in the wrong places, and Neelix's stomach turned slowly.

There was something dreadful about the Autocrat. He slowly rose and fell, groaning up to full extension and slithering down against the desk.

As Neelix's eyes adjusted, he began to scope the room. Again, it was badly fitted, walls meeting at strange angles, alien geometry that made Neelix dizzy. The light was so intense, it hurt even Neelix's eyes. A gigantic, U-shaped desk and riveted-iron chair occupied one entire side of the room; there were no other chairs, and the three supplicants had to stand before the Autocrat like accused criminals. Beyond the Autocrat, or behind the away team, Neelix could see little because of the intense lighting.

The voice was the dry rattle of bones down a chimney, a

serpent's sound, the voice of a deadly Thrack Gourd-Shaker lizard. "So. You. Have come. For trade deal."

Neelix answered earnestly, pretending to be unaffected by the sights and sounds. "Quite so, O great . . . potentate. I am Captain Neelix of the merchant vessel *Sunbird.* I—"

Janeway, standing to Neelix's side, shifted slightly as if by accident and trod upon his foot.

"Ow! Of the merchant vessel *Songbird,* and these are my assistants. Lowly, unimportant assistants. The clumsy one on the left is Vice-President Janeway, while on the right is—"

"But what. Have you. For our interest?"

"Ah, why, we can probably find in, er, storage any item from the vast reaches of the Delta Quadrant you desire . . . the fabled Britelflowers of Dazan Two, whose merest odor fills the heart with intense longing for the object of one's affections—that is, if you have need of such an item here. A necklace made of the teeth of the Drugga Bear, the most beautiful, symmetrical carboniferous crystal teeth you've ever . . . no? Well, surely no person of discriminating taste could pass up an opportunity to buy Distak 'nk'Arat lava-water, the most intense intoxicant in the quadrant, and no lingering aftereffect! A special price, half the going rate . . . special introductory offer for new customers only."

The Autocrat began to make a peculiar noise that sounded like the death-gurgle of an animal dying of pain and thirst. *He's laughing at me,* thought Neelix in a flush of anger.

"We have no."

"Well, if you don't have—"

"Need for such. Items of frivolity. What have. You for. Our holy quest?"

"You—mean weapons? Navigational charts?"

The Autocrat rattled at a much higher frequency. "Arifacts! Have no. Need for tools. Can make ourselves. What can you. Offer of. Spiritual nature?"

Neelix opened his mouth for a moment, then shut it. He repeated the action, then a third time. *Honesty!* he told himself. *Why not give it a whirl? When all else fails . . .* "I'm sorry," he admitted, "I have no idea what you're talking about."

Abruptly, *Navdaq's* voice spoke from behind the Autocrat. Neelix had missed the huge Fury in the glare. "He means, you tendrilless coward, that all that the Furies really need is the *courage* to face the Unclean; the *purity* to gain heaven; the *loyalty* to obey without pause; the *cruelty* to war without mercy against whoever wishes to keep us from our destiny! But we find such values in short supply aboard the *Songbird*. Or was it the *Sunbird?* We've lost track."

Uh-oh. "Sir, you impugn my motives and my character!"

The Autocrat "laughed" again, sending a chill down Neelix's spine. "Yes! Yes yes. You understand! It is good."

The captain's commbadge beeped; Neelix jumped, startled by the sound. "Captain," said Chakotay's voice, "we've detected a fleet of ships lifting from the planet at constant bearing, decreasing distance. Prepare for emergency beamout."

"Chakotay, get the ship out of—!" shouted Janeway. From nowhere, from behind, a hand with suckers and squirming, wormlike digits wrapped around her mouth, cutting off the rest of her command and her breath. Quick as Nick, Navdaq stood before her; he ripped the badge from her uniform, tearing a strip of cloth and exposing her undertunic. He flung the badge across the room, while more Furies did the same to the commbadges worn by Neelix and Tuvok.

Neelix held his breath, desperately hoping the *Voyager* had gotten a lock before the reference point headed south. But he felt no welcome uneasiness of dematerialization.

"Your emergency weapon beam will do you no good, no good. *Unclean,* and ally of the *Unclean* who destroyed our projection antenna! You are nothing before the rage of the Furies. You will live to see your filth cleansed from heaven. And you, traitor to your own, friend of *Unclean*—" Navdaq turned his fury upon Neelix, who was doing his best to maintain dignity and doing a remarkable job. "You made your impious way along the right-angle path, and so shall you share now their fate. Favored, take them below."

Neelix struggled uselessly for a few moments while the

"favored" gripped his wrists in a grasp of steel to push him directly toward a painfully bright wall. The wall contained a loophole, invisible in the glare, and the guard propelled him through.

He stole a glance at Janeway and Tuvok; they were docile, allowing themselves to be gently shepherded—brawling was hardly an option, outnumbered as they were—by two of twelve massive creatures, hexapedal, a rim of what must be vision organs around their heads protected by alien visors.

Damn! Damn my instincts—and why didn't I LISTEN to them? He had no answer; it was a humiliating position for an interstellar explorer of Neelix's repute.

Neelix relaxed and went where they pushed him. They made progress into an immediate corridor as dank and dungeonesque as would warm the feeding-tendrils of any self-respecting Fury. When Neelix's eyes adjusted to the midnight dark, he saw that the favored had removed their visors, revealing six eye-orbs: two in front, two in back, one each on the side. Their limbs were articulated so that there was neither front nor back; they could move or act in either direction with equal facility.

Once in thieves' blackness, the favored dropped to four of their limbs and began to gallop, forcing their bipedal prisoners to sprint to stay ahead and avoid being knocked down and trampled. The favored steered them through hall after hall, down a spiral staircase on which Neelix tripped and fell hard on one wrist, then across a courtyard full of gaze-averting natives.

The Talaxian caught a quick glimpse of metal-grate floors and oilwood walls, of high, iron ceilings and buildings that rattled like fiery furnaces. But he could not track the route, for they were dragged too quickly.

Any thought of escape was thwarted by the breakneck speed of the hunt and the single, unyielding hand that closed around both of Neelix's wrists. No one so much as glanced up; the prisoners were stampeded through the ruly crowd, then under a skull-bedecked archway to a pit.

The favored yanked them all to a stop. Janeway and Tuvok were out of breath, but Neelix was destroyed! His heart pounded like the Autocrat's laugh, and he could not catch his breath. *I'm too old for this nonsense!* he bemoaned, not for the first, tenth, or last time. The one problem with swashbuckling as a profession was the tremendous demand placed upon the physical body.

Neelix's eyes were screwed shut, his mouth wide open sucking in the acrid, burning stench with its minute trace of oxygen, a mere contamination (so it tasted to Neelix) of an otherwise caustic gas.

The favored conversed, Neelix guessed, in extremely high-frequency, highly compressed data packets. The much-ballyhooed Starfleet Universal Translator did nothing, could not even detect that the occasional squeak they made to each other was an unreasonably speeded-up monologue; when two or more squeaked in unison, they were probably interleaving a conversation faster than the ear—or Neelix's ear, in any case—could follow. After the conference, the mob set off again, somewhat slower.

Down, down, down they continued, through dungeon and cavern tilted alarmingly, throwing off Neelix's balance, wrapped by walls of indifferent, disordered joining that seemed not quite right to the eye. Now they began to pass barred cells, and Neelix's sides ached, his lungs a searing agony. There was no oxygen at all! He was going to pass out from the exertion.

But he staggered on, driving himself forward more by pride than fear: Neelix would not be the one who collapsed; he would not shame the captain and Lieutenant Tuvok.

The favored wrenched the away team to a halt, nearly pulling Neelix's arm out of its socket. He kept his feet, though his knees buckled. He leaned over at the waist and focused his mind on one breath, then another.

He turned his head to the side, still seeing stars. Janeway's face was pale in dim lamplight, her eyes unfocused; she was having no little trouble of her own. But Tuvok remained unperturbed; his eyes were half-lidded, face impassive, Vulcan chest rising and falling in slow rhythm. *He comes from a hot, dry planet,* Neelix reassured himself, *none too different from this, save for the humidity.* He still felt a hard lump of resentment.

One of the favored skittered forward and extracted a

ridiculous key, a *physical key* from some sort of pocket somewhere—Neelix could not see where. It inserted the flat card into a slot and the cell door slid noiselessly open.

The favored did not move. When Tuvok began to move toward the cell, his favored let him go. Janeway began to join him, but she hesitated a moment at the cell door; a limb struck her back with brutal force, smashing her to the ground at Tuvok's feet. The Vulcan helped her up.

Neelix stepped briskly into the cell with the other two. The guard pulled tight the door; with a rush of wind, the favored departed along the corridor in the same direction they had been traveling.

Neelix let out a breath, sucked in another greedy lungful. "I was afraid"—he gasped—"they would slap me—in my own cell—out of respect for—my local status."

The beginning of a stately, old, human poem by Samuel Taylor Coleridge kept running through Captain Janeway's head; she couldn't stop it:

*In Xanadu did Kubla Khan
A stately pleasure-dome decree:
Where Alph, the sacred river, ran
Through caverns measureless to man
   Down to a sunless sea.*

Janeway began to prowl the cage while Neelix caught his breath. She was annoyed more than anything else by the spectacularly bad timing of Chakotay's communication, forcing her to reveal to the Autocrat what the pendants were. If the damned Furies had just held their horses a few minutes longer and attacked the *Voyager* after the away team was slapped in chokey, the favored might never have guessed that the pins were devices.

Without communicators, they had no prayer of being beamed out, even if the ship was still in orbit . . . which she doubted. Chakotay would obey his order to protect the *Voyager,* which meant getting the hell out of orbit, considering the odds they faced.

THE FINAL FURY

She felt the bars; metallic, very hard, the alloy not one she was familiar with at first glace, though she would need a tricorder to tell for certain. Tuvok joined her, and the Vulcan cautiously pushed his hand between the bars as far as he could, up to his forearm.

"Captain," he said, "I do not believe there is any force shield on this cage."

"You mean all that's standing between us and freedom are a few lousy steel bars?" Janeway shook her head, staring in amazement up and down the corridor at the long rows of similar cages in the cell block. The cells faced each other with no privacy; even the lump that must be the toilet was placed in the middle of the room, in full view of the rest of the cages—not to mention the other prisoners that would be held in the cell itself, which was obviously designed for four inmates. It was barbaric . . . unless the Furies did not have even the concept of actual privacy, which made a certain amount of sense; presumably, if a Fury prisoner used the facilities, the rest would avert their eyes, as they did when passing in the "streets" (which were actually underground corridors).

"The bars are not exactly steel; but your point is, in essence, correct."

Janeway sighed. "This is such a strange quadrant. They have warp drive, directed energy weapons, subspace communication—but no shields, replicators, or holodecks; and they seem to have room here for a few hundred prisoners in this block alone, and who knows how many other blocks there are? I always thought our different pieces of technology would go hand in hand . . . and all would go together with freedom."

"Evidently, our society is more a fortuitous accident than we like to believe," said the Vulcan.

"But what the Furies *don't* have is so easily deduced from what they *do* have!" She paused, considering; on the other hand, the Federation had no idea how to make an artificial wormhole. They couldn't bring people back by cloning them from the dead body. They couldn't just use the transporter to disassemble an injured or sick person and reassemble him without the medical problem. Neither could they make a deflector shield they could beam through, create a tractor beam powerful enough to bend a phaser beam, fly ships as fast as subspace communications—and for that matter, they hadn't even managed to move beyond the need for a huge fleet of starships to protect them from marauders and looters.

How long before they developed powers like the Organians? Evidently, forever.

"The view back is always sharper than the view ahead," quoted Neelix. He sounded annoyed; he didn't seem to appreciate being reminded that in some ways, his quadrant was backward compared to the Alpha Quadrant.

"Maybe so," said Janeway, not wishing to offend. "But the important point is how we get out of this cell. As a famous poet once remarked, 'Stone walls do not a prison make, Nor iron bars a cage.'"

Tuvok, still methodically testing each bar, absently muttered, "I believe you will find that the author is Richard Lovelace, and the poem is *Lucasta*, 'To Althea: From Prison,' 1649."

"I'll take your word for it."

"Well," said Neelix, "*these* walls and *these* bars look an awful lot like a cage to me."

"Damn; I wish we still had communicators. It would be easy for the *Voyager* simply to beam us out. We *have* to figure a way to stop the invasion!"

Neelix looked surprised. "You don't have a communicator?"

"Neelix . . . you saw Navdaq take them, along with our phasers and tricorders, anything we could use as a weapon or communications device."

Neelix looked incredulously at the captain. "Are you trying to tell me that, as useful as those things are, you don't carry *spare* communicators?"

"No, why should we?"

"In case someone takes it away from you!"

Janeway felt her face begin to flush; she didn't like to think of herself as unprepared—but Neelix had a point. "Great idea, Mr. Neelix—'the view back is always sharper than the view ahead.' Did *you* happen to bring a spare communicator?"

Neelix looked pained and offended . . . his natural expression, when he was not looking officious and self-important. "I most certainly did!"

Pained, offended, officious, self-important, touchy, jealous over Kes, and a highly *idiosyncratic* cook—he was all those things, thought Janeway; but he was also right more often than he was wrong—and he'd gotten them out of a number of scrapes—and he was a tiger in combat—and it looked like Neelix had once again been the prescient one. *What would we do without him?* she thought, highly irritated that she had to think it once again.

The short, chubby Talaxian sat on the edge of one of the bunks in the cell and pulled off one boot; a commbadge slid out onto the floor, tinkling loudly.

Janeway's flush deepened. She envied Tuvok, who could suppress any feelings of being unprepared. "In fact, I brought two," added Neelix, removing his other boot.

"I, ah, don't suppose you brought a spare—"

Neelix pulled free the second boot, and a second commbadge fell out. A phaser followed, and Janeway bit off the end of her question.

Wordlessly, Neelix picked up the phaser and both commbadges and handed them to Janeway, who handed one of the badges to Tuvok. The cook-guide-adventurer-equipment-storage-locker frowned. "I can't imagine why it's not standard Starfleet procedure to issue each crewman a half-dozen of the little things . . . or better yet, with your extraordinary medical technique, why don't you simply have communicators surgically implanted?"

Janeway had no good answer; Tuvok merely raised one eyebrow, the standard Vulcan expression meaning anything from *Did I just hear you correctly?* to *I think we all just learned a lesson here,* depending on context. Janeway gave Neelix a smile that was actually closer to a wolf baring her teeth. "Good thinking, Mr. Neelix. I'll enter a commendation for you when we return to the ship."

A good captain had to know when to yield gracefully and cut her losses.

She tapped the commbadge. "Janeway to Chakotay . . . Janeway to *Voyager,* emergency away-team beam-out, these coordinates. . . ."

Nothing happened; there was no response.

She exhaled through clenched teeth. "Either there's a communications shield, or else Chakotay took the ship far enough away that they can't hear us."

"The Furies have not shown any propensity for constructing shields. I suggest that the ship has problems of its own and is either maintaining a communications blackout or is out of range."

"All right," she said, "stand back from the bars. Let's get out of here under our own steam." Captain Janeway aimed the phaser at the non-iron bars that a very effective cage made.

Neelix backpedaled, turning his face and covering his eyes, in case the Federation weapon decided to bounce. Just before the captain fired, however, Neelix heard voices approaching.

"Wait!" he whispered urgently.

Janeway paused, staring curiously. "What? Why are we waiting?"

Oh, why can't humans hear anything! fumed the Talaxian. Tuvok the Vulcan suddenly cocked his larger, pointed ear. "I believe I hear Furies approaching."

"You do? Oh, wait; now I hear them too." Evidently, Captain Janeway didn't hear the sudden note of tension in Tuvok's voice; Neelix heard it clearly. The Vulcan did not react outwardly, but he was still strangely affected by these aliens.

The team waited until the Furies ambled past, staring curiously at the human, the Vulcan, and the Talaxian. *Tourists!* snorted Neelix to himself. Irritatingly, the last one lingered, peering at them from under its hood and cloak. A strange odor permeated the cell; the Fury had been dunked in some sort of perfume or cologne.

But Tuvok relaxed, surprising Neelix. Of course, this batch of Furies included many races, but not the race to which Navdaq belonged. *That must be the one that enslaved his homeworld,* Neelix realized.

By the time the last, dawdling sightseer finally decided it had seen enough and moved on, Neelix's sensitive ears picked up *another* pair of Furies coming the opposite direction along the cell block.

Captain Janeway waited, frustrated, while again the Fury spectators stared at the most fascinating creatures they had ever seen in their lives—actual Unclean from heaven! Neelix began to notice various odors: *Maybe they tell one another apart by scent, not by visual image? Or is that how they distinguish rank or position?* It made sense in a low-light situation; the powerful smell was quite identifiable, even for citizens who offered a form of privacy by averting their eyes from any passing strangers.

Two more sets of sightseers simply insisted upon finding occasion to stroll down to the dungeon and check on the prisoners . . . something which must have been a terrific violation of etiquette—unless the rule was that the Unclean have no rights and so cannot be offended or insulted. "Captain" Neelix had never been considered a patient man, even among his fellow Talaxians, nor a sociable man who enjoyed large mobs of people. He'd spent most of his life in space. He especially didn't like being the object of a mob of gawkers. More than once, he wished he had kept the phaser, instead of generously and loyally giving it to his captain, so he could . . . *Well, it wouldn't be a smart move,* he consoled himself.

Captain Janeway herself looked ready to chew her way through the bars with bare teeth by the time the fourth batch of tourists finally rolled on down the corridor, leaving them alone. "All right, let's do it quickly, men—before a whole guided tour shuttlebus comes driving down the cell block . . . stand back!"

The captain pointed the phaser at the nearest set of bars and followed Neelix's lead, covering her eyes against the possibility of the unshielded metal shattering under the energy impact. She pressed the button, firing a thin beam at the most powerful setting.

The bar glowed dullish red at the point of contact but was not otherwise affected. She ceased firing, and the glow faded immediately.

Tuvok put his hand near the bar, then touched it. "I do not believe the phaser fire affected it, Captain," he announced unnecessarily. "Perhaps if we had a high-powered cutting phaser."

Neelix stared in surprise. "Don't you carry a spare high-powered cutting phaser? It seems like a remarkably useful tool." It was cold, he knew; but he couldn't resist; he managed a sober expression, as if he were serious.

"Mr. Neelix," said the captain, "unless you have one tucked under your shirt, would you please shut up?"

CHAPTER 9

NEELIX ALMOST REACHED OUT AND TOUCHED THE BARS IN HIS astonishment; the Federation phaser had done nothing, they weren't even glowing! But he refrained, just in case.

"Tuvok—explain!" said the captain, seemingly as startled as the Talaxian.

Never put all your faith in technology, Neelix thought; *it's what I've always said—trust people, not playthings.*

Lieutenant Tuvok leaned close to the metal tubes, fingering them so gently that for a wild moment, Neelix wondered whether he was mind-melding with them—*excuse me, Mr. Bar, but why weren't you phasered out of existence?*

"Captain, I cannot say for certain without a detailed analysis, but this metal has some of the same properties as the metal that Mr. Kim scanned on the artificial moon. I suspect the Furies use this as an all-purpose shielding material—which does imply that they have the capability of scanning, else there would be no reason to shield against it—and in any event, no ability to do so."

"Can we cut it?"

Neelix stared at the bars, as thick around as his forearm and dark as *thrat* blood. *Cut it? With what, a pocketknife?*

He said nothing, only sat on one of the beds; it was uncomfortably hard and had no blanket.

"I do not believe so," answered Tuvok; "not with the materials we have at hand. I do not now believe a cutting phaser would work, even if we had one."

"Captain," said Neelix, "I'm sorry for that jest about the—"

"Bend it? Freeze it? Break it?"

"We have no means of freezing the metal," continued the Vulcan, "but if we did, it might become brittle enough to shatter. As far as bending, the tensile strength required for construction of the artificial moon is approximately . . ."

Tuvok half-closed his eyes, apparently making warp-speed estimates using rules of thumb and constant engineering coefficients. "Three point one times that of steel. The metal may be stronger than that, but probably not much stronger, as that would render shaping difficult."

Neelix stared at the lock, a boxlike device colored so black it was almost blue. If there was a weak spot, that was it.

"But can we bend it? Even a little?"

"Captain, Lieutenant, maybe we should look at the—"

"Not with the tools we have available, I'm afraid."

The captain hestitated for a moment, listening for more guards; still quiet. "Captain," began Neelix again; but she held up a hand. Then she turned the phaser on the wall for a few moments.

Fuming, he let her make another futile gesture. The wall was even less affected than the bars; it did not even glow. "Damn," she muttered.

Janeway tried to push her arm between the bars; she had better luck than Tuvok, getting just past her elbow to her biceps; but there she stuck. In fact, she retrieved her arm back through the bars only by bracing with her foot and pushing.

"I can't get much of my arm through; but that's all right—I haven't a clue what I'm reaching for, anyway."

Neelix leaned back onto the bed, searching for the proper way to talk the two Starfleeters out of brute force and into an approach that depended upon some finesse. He sat up

THE FINAL FURY

and stared through the bars at the cell directly opposite, studying the locking mechanism as best he could, remotely. *How do you open a lock? Well, how about with a key?*

"Captain," said Neelix, "why not just wait for the next troop of Furies to wander by, stun them with the phaser, and take their key-cards?"

Janeway paused for a moment, looking slightly embarrassed. "What if they're wearing some of that metal as phaserproof armor?"

Immediately, Neelix saw the problems with his first-draft idea. Flushing, he started to withdraw it; but before he could, Tuvok administered the coup de grâce: "There is also the problem, Mr. Neelix, that the guards may not have the appropriate key-card. They may fall out of reach. They may return fire and wound or kill one of us. For a number of reasons, we must reject the naive approach of violence."

"I'm sorry," said Neelix, his feelings wounded. "I was just trying to help." *Great help! You've just undone weeks of effort getting these people to start taking you seriously!*

"Captain," said Tuvok, "I believe that the weak point of the cell is the locking mechanism itself. We cannot affect the bars or the walls, but the lock might perhaps be activated by means of a tool other than that which was intended for the purpose."

"You mean we might be able to pick it," said Neelix quickly. Too quickly; in fact, he had just been about to make the suggestion himself, but the Vulcan beat him to it.

"I believe that is the vernacular, Mr. Neelix."

"With what?" asked Janeway.

"I have not yet thought of a suitable alternative."

Janeway crouched to stare at the annoying box at eye level. "Tiny, little electrical thing, isn't it? Almost cute. I'd like to fire a photon torpedo . . . into its keyhole."

"How about the phaser?" gingerly suggested Neelix. "Can you shoot it into the lock and short it out?"

"Wait—" said Neelix, this time answering his own second-draft idea. "You'd probably just fuse the locking mechanism so it would be impossible to open."

Janeway and Tuvok continued to nag each other, but

Neelix tuned them both out. He stared around the room . . . something, *something* tickled the back of his brain, something they could use. Something—not phasoelectric; more primitive. Something . . .

I demand a brilliant idea . . . I want a light panel to go off in my head! He lay back on the slab the Furies called a bed, staring up at the ceiling.

The bright ceiling.

The bright, illuminated light panel in the—

"I see the light!" shouted Neelix, jumping up. The captain and Tuvok stared at him curiously. "Can't you see it? Look, the light!" Neelix pointed triumphantly at the light panel.

"The light?" asked Janeway, looking up. The light was bright by Fury standards, illuminating the cell to approximately two hundred lux, or half the light of a reasonably well lit room on the *Voyager*.

"That's your energy source!" announced the Talaxian. "Use that to blow the lock."

Janeway nodded slowly, obviously impressed for once by Neelix's suggestion. *Hah, take that!* he beamed.

"How many watts, do you think?" she asked Tuvok.

"I cannot begin to estimate. I do not believe much would be needed to overload the locking mechanism."

"Only one problem." Neelix stood on the bed to stare up at the tube. "How do we get the electrical current from *here* to over *there?*"

The distance to cover was approximately four and a half meters from the light to the cell door; but it might as well have been four kilometers . . . not even Captain Kathryn the Great could carry electricity in a bucket.

She fingered her hair; Neelix noticed that she did it unconsciously in times of stress. A ghastly thought was beginning to gel in his mind.

"Can we pop the light-panel cover and see whether we can even get at the electrical connection?"

Neelix went and stood directly underneath the ceiling-mounted light panel, supporting it; Tuvok began working the end closest to the bars, while Janeway stood on the bed to try to wriggle her nails under the opposite end.

After much rocking back and forth—interrupted once by another group of curious, staring Furies—the away team managed to work the cover down low enough that they could peer inside.

They saw an intricate swirl of light tubes, almost like a small intestine, irregular in shape and connected at one end by a four-pronged plug and socket.

"Looks like an old excited-gas system," the captain mused; "I haven't seen such a museum piece since—well, since the last time I visited the Hieronymous Museum of Irreproducible Technology on Urbania. If we shatter the tube, we might be able to connect directly to the leads."

"With what?" asked Neelix, his aching arms souring his mood. "Our fingers?"

Captain Janeway frowned. "Now, that's the best suggestion you've made all day, Mr. Neelix."

"What do you mean? I only wanted to know what . . ." His voice trailed off, and the spikes on his ears spread wide. He felt his face flush bright orange. "Oh, no! Oh, no you don't! You are *not* going to get me to stick my fingers in a light socket just to see what happens!"

"I wouldn't dream of it, Neelix."

"Well, thank goodness for small favors."

"Tuvok is going to stick his fingers in the light-tube socket, and you're going to hold Tuvok's other hand while he does it."

"What!"

"And I'll hold your hand."

"Captain, listen to me closely—you're overworked. I'm not one of your Federation doctors—I'm a real person—but I prescribe a long rest, a cup of my very best Dyzelian coffee, and —"

"Very intriguing, Captain," said the Vulcan, unperturbed by Janeway's wild, harebrained scheme, "but how do you propose to complete the circuit with the lock?"

Janeway played with her hair again, but to a purpose, this time. "With this," she said, extracting one of the pins that held her hair in its severe bun.

Tuvok raised his eyebrow. "I believe the hairpin is

indeed the traditional tool for extralegal operation of a locking mechanism."

Neelix sighed; he hadn't meant to be so loud, but both the captain and Tuvok turned toward him. "You're determined to do this, aren't you?" asked Neelix peevishly. *She's going to get herself killed!* he thought, but said nothing. He certainly was no stranger to being determined to do something dangerous and foolhardy.

"Neelix," said the captain, "there is no other way to get out of this cell . . . and it's more than just our lives at stake; we have to think about—"

"Yes, yes, I know, Captain." Neelix drew himself up to his full height, staring her directly in the collarbone. "I once had a planet too. Remember?"

"I'm sorry, Neelix. I didn't mean to condescend."

He shrugged. "It's a human thing; I understand. But Captain, if you're *really determined* to electrocute us all trying to blow the lock . . . then I absolutely insist that *I* be the one to stick his fingers in the light socket."

Instantly, a small voice inside Neelix's head screamed *Are you insane? You'll die!* Oddly, it sounded like Kes's voice. Janeway didn't know what to say; Lieutenant Tuvok merely raised one eyebrow—a Vulcan thing.

Now, why in free space did I volunteer to do that? Neelix wondered. But the answer was clear: Talaxians understood duty, and Neelix especially understood risking his life in a good cause. The Furies had nothing to do with the destruction of his homeworld . . . *But they might as well have,* he realized; they were tyrants and slavers—how different were they really from those who all but destroyed his home?

But how could he convince Janeway? "Captain," he began. For a moment, he floundered; then his natural glibness asserted itself. "We Talaxians have a—special resistance to electricity. It doesn't injure us the way it does you humans, or Vulcans."

"You have not mentioned this before," pointed out the stubborn Tuvok.

Neelix snorted. "You've never asked me to stick my fingers in a light socket before!"

Even Tuvok had to concede the situation had not come

up previously. But Janeway still looked dubious. "Are you sure? A special resistance?"

"Special resistance to electricity," repeated Neelix, sticking to his yarn. Rule Number One when lying, he had been taught: Don't change stories in midstream!

"I hope Mr. Neelix is not being literal," said the Vulcan. "We need a current flow, not resistance." Several moments passed before Neelix wondered if this was a droll sort of Vulcan pseudo-joke; but by then, the Talaxian was too nervous to ask.

The captain took off her slightly torn uniform jacket, pushing her bare arm as far through the bars as she possibly could; when it stuck just past the elbow, she compressed her biceps with her other hand and pushed even farther.

"Um, Tuvok," asked Neelix, "isn't the current going to short at the bars?"

"No," said the lieutenant firmly. "The metal does not conduct electricity at all . . . it is too dense. It is not properly even a metal. If it did, the phaser would have disrupted the electrochemical bonds and vaporized the bars."

Janeway gritted her teeth; probably the pressure was cutting off the blood flow in her brachial artery. *It's going to tingle a damn sight worse,* sighed Neelix.

She still could not quite reach the lock with her hairpin. "Tuvok," she called, wincing against the pain, "I need your help. You've got to get my arm farther through the bars."

"It is a dangerous maneuver," said the Vulcan; "you may get your arm so wedged in that we cannot extract it. If the circulation is cut off long enough, serious damage may occur."

"If we wait here for the Furies to execute us, serious death may occur."

"You have a point." Tuvok put a hand on either side of Janeway's muscle and began to squeeze. He got her arm just far enough through the bars that she could hold the hairpin between her middle and ring fingers and insert it into the card slot.

"Quick! Neelix, do it now—my hand's going numb—I'm going to drop the pin!"

Swallowing hard, Neelix grabbed Tuvok, who seized Janeway's groping hand. The Talaxian swallowed hard, his heart pounding at triple speed. *Am I really going to do this?* His own hand trembled; he moved quickly before she could see. *This is for you, Kes,* he swore to himself; he didn't believe his own lie, but it worked anyway.

Neelix reached up and shattered the tube and closed his eyes tight, then licked his fingers and pressed them firmly against the pair of leads.

Ice hands clutched both sides of his body and dug their spirit fingers into his flesh. Exquisite ecstasy flashed through him, burning away the mortal corruption, the cobwebs that accumulated around a person's life. He convulsed as a jolt of high-voltage electricity ripped through his body. He could not let go! His hand crushed that of Tuvok, who crushed the captain's hand in turn.

Neelix heard a loud crackle and smelled roasting meat; but with the current disrupting every nerve and neuron in his body, he could not even think about any damage it was doing, let alone worry about it.

Then as suddenly as the surge began, it ended. Blinking his eyes back into focus, Neelix noticed two things simultaneously: he lay on the floor all the way across the cage from the light panel . . . and *the cell door was slightly ajar.*

The lock was fried.

Alas, so too was Captain Janeway's arm, nearly so. "Tuvok—I don't want to open the door until we can start running, in case there are guards. But I've got a problem. . . ."

Tuvok and Neelix quickly moved to her side; past the bars, her arm was bone white. "Captain, can you move the arm?" asked the Talaxian.

She tried; her hand twitched slightly, but all she felt was pins and needles. "Maybe the nerve is pinched," she gasped.

Tuvok tried to compress her arm to extract it as he had wedged it in; but the only result was a stifled scream from the captain. The arm was stuck solid.

"Neelix," requested the Vulcan, "would you happen to have any sort of lubricant? Oil, or soap, perhaps?"

Neelix shook his head sadly. "Captain, I'm terribly, terribly sorry . . . I do usually carry machine oil, but today I was using it in the kitchen."

"Not, I hope, in your latest culinary offering, Mr. Neelix." It did seem that Tuvok was on a roll, perhaps trying to distract Janeway; but Neelix glared him down.

Janeway smiled wanly at the attempt; but she was in too much pain to be distracted.

"Certainly not!" said the sometime-cook. "I was oiling a sticky—"

"Captain, I believe your brachioradial and pronator muscles are in spasm, and they have contracted so tightly they are now wider than the gap between the bars. If we had a muscle relaxant, we could probably extract your arm without difficulty."

"Do you—want to try—borrowing one—from the guards?"

"Your joke may in fact be worth exploring. If we make sufficient commotion that the guards hear and come to investigate, they may be able to administer medical aid."

"Or else they may just cut her arm off in retaliation," snapped Neelix, exasperated with these Starfleeters who never could seem to think their way out of problems. "Tuvok, they don't even think of us as people . . . we're animals to them—*dangerous* animals! We can't rely on them to help the captain."

"I fear you may be correct, Mr. Neelix."

"We've got to get her arm out—*we've* got to get it out, because we can't count on anyone else. And I, for one, will not leave unless she leaves with us."

"No one is suggesting abandoning Captain Janeway. But we need some means of relaxing her muscles, or we shall all remain here until the guards come and notice the open door. Then the question becomes moot."

"Well, can't she just relax it? Meditate, or something?"

Janeway tried to calm herself; she breathed deeply. But the pain interfered with her ability to concentrate. After a few seconds, she gave up, her arm throbbing rhythmically with every blocked beat of her pulse.

"Can't—concentrate. . . ."

At once, the odd idea struck Neelix. Why not stun her? After all, they had a phaser, didn't they? Stunning relaxed the entire body.

While Tuvok futilely tugged on the bars, the arm, the bars and arm in combination, Neelix strolled over and picked up the nearly forgotten phaser lying on one of the beds. He started to explain his idea, but Tuvok was busy tugging and Janeway was busy agonizing. *You know, maybe it's best they don't know until after I do it. . . .*

Neelix studied the phaser. The power setting looked relatively straightforward, though in the past it had usually been handed to him preset by whoever led the away team. He thumbed it all the way over to one side. "Stand back," he said to Tuvok, barely giving the Vulcan time to get clear before he pointed it at Captain Janeway, and pressed the contact. The beam lashed out, glowing orangeish in the red light of the Fury world, and Janeway grunted loudly; the noise faded into an extended sigh. Rubbery legs collapsed slowly, bringing her to her knees.

The swelling ebbed. She relaxed and fell into a trance, nearly unconscious. Every part of her became liquid, supple, soft. Smooth.

Slippery.

Neelix and Tuvok gently worked her injured arm backward; it stuck, he pushed . . . suddenly, she fell back onto her rump, dizzy and confused, blinking back to conscious awareness. As if waking from a particularly vigorous, muscular dream, she rubbed her arm, her face a mask of confusion, as though wondering where she was.

Then full awareness returned.

"Neelix—you *shot* me!"

"Yes, Captain," said the Talaxian, nervously smoothing his hair back. "You don't mind much, do you?"

"Good thinking."

Neelix smirked, aware that he had not just recovered lost territory, he had forged ahead in his plan to prove to the Starfleeters that he was as good a swashbuckler as he often claimed. "Tuvok," said Janeway, "let's get the hell out of here. I think I hear more 'tourists' coming!"

Tuvok and Neelix helped Janeway to her feet and dragged

her behind them. She was having trouble making her legs move swiftly enough. "Wait," she whispered, just as they stepped into the corridor.

Stooping, she forced her recovering arm to reach forward; numb fingers picked up the hairpin. She had to do it by sight; it was obvious that she still could not feel a thing.

"Let 'em wonder," she explained, as they ran away from the approaching footsteps into the comforting gloom.

CHAPTER 10

COMMANDER CHAKOTAY WANTED TO PACE BACK AND FORTH across the bridge. He wanted to run to every duty station and take personal charge. He wanted to scream and shake his fist and pitch somebody down the turbolift shaft. He sat calmly in the command chair, doing nothing but casually crossing his legs, not allowing the young crew to see any emotion but calm certainty.

The captain and Tuvok were down on the planet; Paris and Kim were back in the infirmary, arguing with the emergency holographic medical program about his prescription of "rest and recuperation." On the bridge were Chakotay, a single officer to handle all science, and engineering, and ops—B'Elanna Torres—and three crewmen: Dalby, Chell, and Jarron. Torres had been remarkably silent, saying nothing except in answer to a direct question.

The *Voyager* played "hunters and buffalo" with now *six* alien ships, a veritable battle fleet; the *Voyager* kept dodging from one bearing to another, sliding around the planet, trying to keep the ships in line, so only the lead ship could shoot . . . easily deflected by the shields. But if Chakotay gave the wrong order or the helm officer responded too slugishly, the aliens could open fire with four or five ships; then the *Voyager* could be crippled or killed.

The situation taxed Chakotay's renowned inner calm to the limit.

"Turn right, bearing zero-two-zero degrees, mark forty . . . back up, bearing one-eight-zero, one-quarter impulse . . . good. Hold this position; let's see if they're going to fire again."

The alien ships paused; they too were tired of the game. They had begun to realize that the *Voyager* was more maneuverable and faster than their own ships. So far, they had utterly failed to box her in.

But there were some close calls: once, Chakotay had ordered the helm to turn starboard, then port too quickly, luffing the ship; while it wallowed in its own impulse wake, three alien ships had locked on and fired their directed-energy weapons from the port side slightly below.

Dalby's quick thinking saved them. Without orders, he engaged a course of 000 mark 90—straight up. The shots missed by a few hundred meters.

"Good initiative, Crewman Dalby," said Chakotay laconically; inwardly, he was kicking himself in the rear for screwing the turn . . . he had been thinking of his smaller Maquis ship.

"Gentlemen," said the commander, "it is good to remain at large with hull integrity intact; but we can't dodge their disruptor shots forever. We must find an end to this duel, but an end that allows us to close within transporter range of the planet to extract the away team."

"Perhaps we should fight them, sir," suggested Dalby from the helm. Fortunately, Chell had the weapons . . . Dalby's impetuousness had been good, as when he dodged the phaser blasts; but this was something else.

"No, we can't fight them, Crewman," said the commander; "they still have the captain. And may I remind you they also hold Lieutenant Tuvok and Neelix?"

Dalby grunted in resignation. Recently, Dalby, Chell, Jarron, and Henley—all former Maquis—had developed a solid working relationship with the Vulcan, who trained them in a mini-Academy course.

"Couldn't we just go out of the solar system?" suggested Chell.

"And abandon Captain Janeway?"

"No no! I mean we could shift into warp and whip around the system, coming back from the opposite side of the sun and hide there."

Chakotay answered immediately. "Chell, think about it a moment. The aliens have impulse power; they have warp. They would simply follow us the whole way."

At once, Chakotay realized to his astonishment that the impossible had occurred: *the Starfleet ship had an entirely Maquis bridge crew!* The commander smiled; *my wildest dream come true—we've finally "stolen" a Federation starship right out from under them . . . and we can't do anything with her!*

He heard a faint cough, paid it no mind. It repeated, followed by a voice so meek and uncertain that at first, Chakotay could not even tell where it came from. Then Jarron, the Bajoran, repeated himself. "Sir . . . if we were— I mean if they thought we were destroyed, they wouldn't— you know, follow . . . never mind. I'm sorry."

"Keep talking, Jarron."

"Well, if—I mean, if they thought we were destroyed, you know."

"Do you have anything in mind?"

"Well—if we dropped debris, or something?"

Chakotay shook his head. "Not enough; they would board us to investigate."

"I'm sorry."

"Don't apologize, you're on the right track. Anyone else have any follow-up?"

Dead silence. Dalby stared at the screen, watching the immobile alien ships in case they decided to attack again. Chell stared in anguished astonishment at the commander, his normal expression. And Jarron, who had shot his only arrow, returned to his navigation console and tried to cringe inside himself.

THE FINAL FURY

Suddenly feeling the expectance of speech from behind him, Chakotay turned. B'Elanna Torres opened her mouth, starting to make a suggestion, then closed it again. When she had repeated the maneuver twice more, Chakotay asked, "Do you have any sort of idea, B'Elanna?"

"I, ah, don't mean to butt in, but it occurs to me . . ." She faded out.

"Go on," said the commander, still aware that Torres' confidence had taken a severe nose-dive.

"If they—" Torres's Klingon side suddenly seemed to assume control, disgusted at the human side's indecisiveness. "Commander," she snarled Klingon-style, "if they thought we had burned up in the sun, they wouldn't bother looking for us."

"Let me see if I've got this straight. You propose to take us into the *sun?*"

"We have shields," explained B'Elanna; "they don't. Our shields might protect us from the intense heat and pressure; their ships would be crushed. They'll think we destroyed ourselves because our mission was a failure."

"You seem to understand them well, B'Elanna."

"They're a lot like my people. Half of my people."

"You said the shields *might* protect us. I don't like the sound of that *might.*"

B'Elanna was silent for several seconds. When she spoke, she sounded somewhat more human than Klingon. "This isn't good. I just did a simulation, and it shows us being crushed and incinerated in forty-two point six seconds."

"The shields give out?"

"Yes, Commander."

"Well . . . can we increase power to the shields?"

"I calculated for max shield power."

"But did you calculate including every bit of power on the ship, including engines, backup battery, replicators, the holodeck, and life-support? Everything but the Doctor . . . I suspect we'll need him."

"No, I didn't! Wait just a moment." She added a belated, distracted "sir" while recalibrating. "Amazing . . . Commander, the new calculation shows us surviving for almost a hundred and fifty seconds."

"Two and a half minutes," mused Chakotay, "can be a very long time indeed. Start making the necessary modifications, Torres." She turned away. "And Torres—good initiative."

"Commander!" cried Chell, stricken. "The aliens have powered up their weapons again—they're going to shoot!"

"Are the shields still at full strength, Mr. Chell?"

"Yes, sir."

"And they're still bottled up in a line? Then let's wait to see what they're going to do. I have a good notion... there's a tactic I've been expecting them to try for an hour now, but so far they have disappointed me."

A new voice spoke from the turbolift; Lieutenant Paris had just entered the bridge. "Would you possibly mean... the *starburst* maneuver?"

"You're familiar with it?"

"I have a nodding acquaintance." Paris winked, but Chakotay did not understand the reference.

"Do you want to take the helm?"

Dalby looked sour, his face flushing. He still was not used to being a junior member of the crew, after having lived the exciting life of a Maquis helmsman.

Paris noticed Dalby's reaction—and was impressed that the normally irrepressible motormouth said nothing. "Nah, I think I'll just watch, come up to speed. Change in watch in fifteen minutes; I'll wait."

"Thank you, Mr. Paris. Mr. Dalby, let me know the moment you have confirmed a starburst maneuver."

"Commander, what's a starburst maneuver?"

"You'll know it when you see it," said Paris cryptically.

"—They're moving, sir." Dalby watched for a second. "Oh! I see what you mean—starburst maneuver, sir!"

The alien ships each took off in a separate direction, exploding like a fireworks rocket in a cone surrounding the *Voyager.* In a moment, every ship had a clear shot; all six immediately opened fire on the sitting-duck Starfleet ship.

"Mr. Dalby, flank speed, bearing zero-zero-zero mark zero."

THE FINAL FURY

The *Voyager* shot straight forward, toward the core of the starburst . . . the one spot where there were no ships. "Now if we're incredibly lucky—or they're incredibly stupid . . ." Chakotay allowed himself a small smile of expectation.

"I don't believe it!" muttered Lieutenant Torres. She stared at her scanner. "Sir, you're not going to believe this."

"Try me."

"But their guns are following us. They're going to hit—correction, they *have* hit one of their own ships. Two of their own ships—three!"

Chakotay turned to look at Paris, who was unsuccessfully trying to stifle a laugh behind his hand.

Chell finally recovered his wits to make a report. "Sir . . . as we passed between them, all but one of the ships continued to fire, even when their own fleet was in the line of fire."

"Running the gauntlet," muttered Paris, still breaking up.

"One alien ship destroyed," reported B'Elanna Torres, "two others damaged, one seriously."

"Not bad for still not having fired a shot," said Chakotay soberly. He had tremendous empathy for Tom Paris; were it not for Chakotay's own tremendous self-control, he would be holding his sides and laughing like a hyena.

"Commander," said Torres—she did not appear to be on the verge of laughter . . . *more's the pity,* thought Chakotay—"I've completed the modifications to the shield power grid. I can send full power to the shields on your order."

After a moment, when Chakotay remained lost in thought, B'Elanna asked, "Sir? I said I've completed—"

"I heard you, Lieutenant." *Do I have the guts to do it?* he asked himself. Chakotay shrugged, feeling his heart begin to race just at the thought; but he had no choice . . . he had to get the Furies off his tail, and that meant he had to think the *Voyager* was dead meat, *glop* on a stick.

"B'Elanna," he said after a moment, "how long would it take you to reconfigure the shields to metaphasic?"

"About two minutes; but why would I want to . . . Chakotay! You *can't* be thinking of—"

111

He nodded, lips pressed together either in a grim smile or an amused grimace. "Directly into the sun," he confirmed. "Do you think they'll follow?"

Nobody responded; Chakotay took the first step along the trail.

"Jarron, open a channel to the alien flagship, assuming it isn't one of the damaged ones."

"It's damaged but not seriously," mumbled Jarron; Chakotay had to strain to hear him. "Channel open."

Chakotay leapt to his feet, turning himself beet-red and screaming so violently that spittle flew from his mouth. *"We will* never *be captured alive! We won't spend even an* hour *in your torture chambers! We'd rather die like* men *than live like* animals! Songbird *out!"*

Jarron was so startled, he almost forgot to kill the transmission. As soon as the red light went dark, Commander Chakotay sat back down in the command chair, perfectly calmly, and wiped his mouth with his hand.

"Mr. Dalby, lay in a course directly for the sun, full impulse, and engage immediately."

It took the entire crew several seconds to recover from their astonishment and perform their tasks. Chakotay frowned; he could not help thinking that a Starfleet crew would probably have responded three times as efficiently.

He did not like his inevitable conclusion that there really was a qualitative difference between a crew trained by Starfleet and a Maquis crew. He made a mental note to speak to Captain Janeway about expanding Tuvok's mini-Academy to include the senior officers . . . including himself.

They certainly had plenty of time, even for the full, four-year Academy course.

The sun suddenly surged forward, growing in size until it filled the viewer. The smaller, individual strands of the grid began to come into focus, silhouettes against the filtered yet still painfully bright image of the star.

"Ah—Commander?" Torres seemed a bit nervous. "Shall I transfer power to the shields?"

"Time to contact with the sun's corona, Mr. Dalby?"

"How far out? The corona extends from—"

"It's a G2 star. Let's say the photosphere, about a million kilometers from the center. Should be about six thousand degrees at that point."

"Seven minutes, fifty seconds, sir."

"Chakotay—six thousand is hot enough to boil the hull of the *Voyager.*"

"Can the shields as they currently are protect us?"

"For a few seconds!"

"Chill the ship as cold as you can make it, Mr. Torres, before you transfer environmental power to the shields. It's going to get mighty hot in here while we're in there; let's get a head start on the heat exchange."

Lieutenant Torres, at least, responded instantly. Within less than a minute, Chakotay began to feel distinctly cold as the cryogenic unit whined into action.

"Pursuing," announced Jarron, so loudly that at first Chakotay did not recognize the boy.

"Are they firing, Mr. Chell?"

"No. Wait—yes! No, I don't thin . . . yes, definitely yes."

"Mr. Chell!"

"My mistake. Yes, Commander, they're definitely firing."

"You can't commit suicide," declared Paris, dryly speaking as the alien fleet captain. "We have to execute you!"

"Reinforce the aft shields, Mr. Torres."

"Aft?" she demanded, incredulous. "But the sun is directly ahead of us!"

"And the hostiles are directly behind us."

"Would you rather be fried or shot?" inquired Lieutenant Paris.

"Reinforce aft shields, Lieutenant Torres. Don't even think about firing, Mr. Chell. Find something constructive to do, Mr. Paris."

The cryos began to strain against the heat of the sun, now only partially shielded. The *Voyager* closed to within 0.25 astronomical units from the sun.

Some of the crew paradoxically began to shiver violently; the internal temperature was down to -15° centigrade. A voice cut through the cacophony on the bridge.

"This is the emergency medical holographic program . . . what the devil is going on up there? I have crew members all over the ship collapsing from the cold. . . . Oh, I see. I have just scanned the computer log. We will all be dead in a matter of moments."

"Not now, Doctor—please."

"My, but you people lead exciting lives. Emergency medical holographic program out."

"Jarron!" called Chakotay, a little too loudly. "Alert me when we're approaching the collector."

"We're . . . we're approaching it now, Commander. Aren't we?"

"Don't ask me, *tell* me!" *Come on, he doesn't respond well to being shouted at.* "Jarron, tell me when we're within twenty seconds."

"Aye, sir. We're within twenty seconds now, sir."

"Mr. Dalby," said Chakotay, getting his voice under control, "how wide are the strands at the widest point?" Seeing the sun loom so large, Chakotay unconsciously reached up and wiped his brow, despite the chilly bridge temperature.

"Commander, we've got plenty of room—eight or ten meters on each side if we hit it just right."

Eight meters! Chakotay ordered Paris to take control of the helm . . . either Paris would come through, or they would all die.

The grid rushed toward them. This close, Chakotay could see that it was not, in fact, a uniform color, but a prismatic spray of the entire visible spectrum, as if the strands functioned like tiny light prisms, scattering the sunlight in every direction. *Probably captures each frequency separately,* he thought . . . while not forgetting to admire the sheer, overwhelming beauty of it. His father had always taught him never to lose the hawk in its feathers.

Swallowing hard, seeing the inappropriately called "strands" loom larger and larger—they were in fact monstrous cables nearly ten meters in diameter—Chakotay silently commended his soul to the Sky Spirit, but asked if perhaps he might be allowed just a little more life.

The gap loomed—they were off course! Dalby made a strangled noise in the back of his throat and tapped frantically. The *Voyager* jerked gracelessly, barreled into the web . . . and burst through! Chakotay heard the faintest ping as they passed.

"Well," said a white-faced Paris a few moments later, "I guess I overestimated slightly." He grinned sheepishly, but Chakotay had more important details to be concerned about.

"Coming up on the photosphere," said Paris, sounding preternaturally calm. "Thirty-five seconds." Under the stress of the moment, he had passed beyond emotional reaction to pure action—*an admirable quality for a future Starfleet officer,* noted Chakotay for his internal record.

"Torres!" barked the commander. "You have thirty seconds to tell me that you've finished adapting to metaphasic shielding."

"I'll have it ready in twenty!" she snapped from down in engineering.

"Then, Mr. Torres, prepare to re-norm shield concentration and feed the extra power on my mark. Twenty seconds. Ten seconds . . . five, four, three, two, one, mark."

"Metaphasic shielding is on-line, and functioning nor—"

"Sir," interrupted Paris, "entering photosphere in . . . five, four, three, two, one, mark."

"Helm, full reverse! Don't pop out the other side of the sun! B'Elanna, pump full warp-engine power into the shields, and let's call upon our ancestors to help us wait them out."

The impulse engines strained backward, their whine rising so loud that everyone, Chakotay included, had to cup his hands over his ears. Again, they overloaded the inertial stabilizers, subjecting the entire ship to the instantaneous equivalent of more than fifteen times the force of gravity straight forward—for a tenth of a second.

Chakotay felt like he had been kicked by a mule. He rocketed forward into Chell, who sprawled across the console. Within a couple of microseconds, however, the rebuilt stablizers compensated, reducing the forward acceleration to a mere four g's.

After four seconds, even that cut off as the ship almost literally screeched to a halt.

Dazed, Chakotay noticed that Paris *had* found something

constructive to do: he had sat down with his back against the forward bulkhead next to the turbolift.

Chakotay floundered, dizzy and stunned; but Paris was up the second the gravity returned to normal—fortunately, for the entire rest of the bridge crew lay unconscious.

CHAPTER
11

PARIS WORKED THE CONTROLS. THEY WERE VERY SLUGGISH . . unsurprising, considering that the *Voyager* sat in the middle of a G2 star.

It was all Paris could do to maintain position; convection currents inside the sun buffeted the ship fiercely, threatening to tear it to shreds long before the heat and radiation fried them, were it not for the supercharged shields.

He could hardly complain. In his single (required) astrophysics class at the Academy, Paris had learned that without such currents, it would take *tens of billions of years* for the very first photon to random-walk its way from the steller core, where it was produced by hydrogen fusion, to the surface.

In other words, without convection currents to bring the photons up like gas bubbles in water, the surface of every star in the entire universe would still be black as ink and cold as the depths of interstellar space.

"I don't care," he snarled aloud; "they're damned inconvenient right now!"

Fighting the bucking bronco of a ship, Tom Paris backed

away from the opposite side surface to a point about a third of the way toward the stellar core; closer, he dared not go—the core temperature was several million degrees, and he was not sure even B'Elanna's modified shields would guard against that much energy.

He almost made the mistake of a lifetime. He almost snapped on the sensors.

He stopped with his hand just touching the panel, shaking with suddenly awakened fear. Turning them on would have been like flipping on searchlights. The aliens would immediately know.

Instead, he activated passive sensors only. He would have to hope to pick up random, subspace fluctuations from the aliens' warp cores. "Computer, begin record, all readings."

Certainly it was absurd even to check for ion trails; he was sitting in the biggest ball of ionized plasma for billions of kilometers!

Spotting the alien ships was like sitting inside an antimatter reaction chamber, trying to detect someone using a communicator outside.

The hull temperature steadily climbed, despite the shields. It reached three hundred thousand degrees, and still no one else had awakened.

As Torres materialized on the surgical table, the doctor swiftly moved to her; without the chief engineer, the ship might never make it out of the sun intact.

He injected a cortical stimulant, then gently slapped her face. She groaned but did not respond.

Oh, well, thought the doctor; *she is a part Klingon, after all.*

Winding up, he slapped her across the jawline.

Torres bellowed like an angry bull and vaulted to her feet in a defensive posture. She swayed, then fell to one knee, clutching her head in agony.

"The pain will pass quickly," said the doctor; a useless piece of advice, since it would have already passed before he finished the sentence. The pain was caused by the sudden return of bloodflow to the cranial arteries after they had been drained by high acceleration.

THE FINAL FURY

"We're in the middle of the sun," explained the doctor quickly.

"What? Already? But we had a couple of minutes to—"

"Microamnesia. Goodbye."

Without another word, he beamed B'Elanna Torres directly to engineering.

As soon as B'Elanna Torres faded in, her brain thoroughly muddled from two sudden and complete changes of perspective, her commbadge started beeping insistently. "Paris to Torres! Are you there? Repeat, are you all right?"

"Am I *where?*" she replied crossly. "I'm in engineering . . . I think. Where am I *supposed* to be?"

"That'll do. Quick!" demanded the thoroughly annoying Thomas Paris. "Without using the fire-control sensors, tell me if there are any ships left outside the photosphere . . . we've got to get the hell out of this hell, or we're going to melt like butter!"

She turned to the sensor-array control apparatus, so dizzy she had to grab a bulkhead to keep from falling to the deck. She powered up VLAs two and seven, looking nine to three and three to nine, respectively—the full hemisphere forward and the full hemisphere aft.

She studied the blips, starting to sweat heavily in the extremely hot, dry air. "Yeah. Two ships. Both aft of us. Wait . . . a third ship just passing bearing two seven zero. It's rounding the sun, checking to see if we came out the other side."

"Damn. I was hoping they would just go home."

"How long have we been in here?"

"Two minutes, fifteen seconds."

"Damn—Paris, ships or no ships, we've got to get out of here *now.*"

"No way, Torres. We've got to give your trick time to work. The shields are holding out better than expected. They're still at seventy-two percent."

"They *are?*" She checked the power-decay curve and overlaid the projection. "You idiot! That's three percent *below* the projection!"

"How long do we have?"

"According to my model, the shields will fail suddenly and rather spectacularly in about ten seconds."

"How long will the hull hold out after that?"

"About ten seconds."

"Don't touch the controls."

Torres held on, counting silently to herself. She had reached five when suddenly she said, "Paris! They're leaving orbit, heading back to the planet!"

"Can they still see the back side of the sun?"

"Yes . . . but wait for it—wait for it—Shields just failed. Lasted two extra seconds. Well, lover, been nice knowing you. Goodbye."

"Can they still see—damn, I can't touch the controls they're so hot! No time, no—"

Paris punched the button, she thought; the *Voyager* lurched forward, ripping through the flesh of the sun and just clearing the corona as the hull temperature hit two hundred thousand degrees.

B'Elanna stared at the internal temperature gauge in mounting horror as it hit two hundred degrees—but it lasted only a couple of seconds.

Over the next hour, the ship slowly returned to normal operations. Chakotay and the rest of the bridge crew recovered, the hull cooled, the shields returned to normal, and the cryogenic units cooled the interior of the ship to a manageable thirty degrees . . . uncomfortably hot, but not catastrophic. B'Elanna returned to the bridge, taking the longer, scenic route by turbolift this time.

The aliens were nowhere to be sensed. They had swallowed the con without demur.

Paris parked the ship a couple of million kilometers off the surface of the sun, on the opposite side from the planet. He matched velocities with the alien planet, using the impulse engines to maintain his altitude above the sun—for of course, the *Voyager* was moving too slowly to hold an actual orbit at that point.

Captain Janeway clenched and released her fist, pins and needles dancing up and down her arm, as she, Tuvok, and Neelix skittered down the cellblock hallway, seeing neither prisoners—not the shuttlecraft pilot—nor more guards. The escape was not long being discovered, however; the lights began to flicker, growing nearly bright enough for a human for a fraction of a second then dropping to their normal gloom. Since the bright light probably hurt the Furies' eyes, Janeway deduced it was the equivalent of a red alert.

At first, the captain insisted upon stopping and looking sharply into each cell on left and right; after a minute, she merely glanced to either side. "Neelix," she said at last, hearing the wild hunt of pursuit not overly far behind them.

"Captain?"

"You look in the left cells, I'll check the right. Tuvok, keep an eye behind us . . . we've got to find the pilot and get the hell out of here!"

They ran full speed, hoping they would not turn a corner and smash into a favored. The cells in their section were all empty; evidently, the Furies had no intention of allowing different batches of Unclean to mingle.

Each cell was a replicator-quality copy of their own: six by five meters, two bunks along walls and even floors that did not quite meet at right angles. As Janeway ran, she frequently stumbled when the floor went funny.

Dammit, there's a limit to Lovecraftian geometry! she insisted to herself. Evidently, the Furies disagreed.

The away team bolted down a long corridor, counting eighty-four cells, including their own. At its end was a locked door.

Janeway stopped at the lock; she heard a shout of triumph behind her. "Tuvok—got any bright ideas for picking *this* lock? It's mechanical, for goodness' sake!"

"Yes, Captain. May I?"

Janeway stepped aside. Tuvok stepped back, raised his foot, and kicked the door just above the handle. The jamb splintered with a noise like Baba Yaga gnashing her iron teeth and the door sagged inward. Tuvok shouldered it open and the away team ducked through as the guards fired a badly aimed shot.

A large, five-sided room; a door directly opposite. "I've got this one!" shouted Neelix.

He barreled toward the door with a shoulder lead; just as he reached it, it dilated, four pieces pulling back from the center. Neelix sailed through without a sound, until they heard a muffled thump.

Janeway and Tuvok glanced at each other, and the captain grinned. Tuvok merely raised one eyebrow, meaning . . . Before Janeway could fill in the meaning, they head a scuffle from the room Neelix had just entered so dramatically.

Rushing to the door, which opened as politely as before, Janeway saw her cook writhing on the floor with a horrific, slithering serpent with stubby legs and muscular arms. She jumped through the doorway, reaching for her phaser.

Before she could get off a shot, however, Neelix twitched in a way she could not follow, and the snake-man stiffened and slid to the floor. Neelix stood over him triumphantly.

"Captain," said Tuvok, "may I point out we have only scant seconds before the guards enter this room, and they are armed far better than—"

Without comment, Janeway raised the phaser and fired a full-power blast at a small box jutting from the wall next to the door. "Now we've got all night," she predicted.

Moments later, they heard a terrific pair of thumps as the point and second-point of the guard squad ran full-tilt into the unexpectedly inoperative door. They began to pound, shouting dire threats about immortal souls, bright lights, and parting the Unclean on a square.

"May I suggest the window?"

"Not much choice, Tuvok. Can you see out? Is there anybody waiting for us?"

Tuvok stood on tiptoe, peering out the dark, volcanic obsidian. "I cannot see very clearly, but I do not see any witnesses," he said.

Tuvok used his elbow, tapping tentatively on the black glass, then winding up for a full-strength strike. The glass cracked; two more blows and it finally shattered.

Janeway used the phaser butt to break off the sharp points sticking into the window space. "Hoist me up," she said.

In the courtyard, the captain looked up, hoping to see sky; outside, they might possibly be able to contact the *Voyager*.

Alas, she saw overhead only the same grayish metal that neither phasers nor sensors were able to penetrate. "Don't these guys ever want to look at their own sun?"

"To crowd twenty-seven billion sapient life-forms onto this planet," said Tuvok, "one must assume a certain uninterest in outdoor scenery."

"Hm. To each his own, but I sure wouldn't want to live here."

They prowled the perimeter of the courtyard; the wall was iron, rusted in many parts, and it enclosed a large series of rounded, stone artifacts. "Are these . . . burial sites?" guessed Janeway.

"Without a tricorder—"

"You can't tell where the bodies are buried. I know, I know, Mr. Tuvok. I'm amazed at how much cuing we took from our captors . . . virtually everything associated with them now scares humans to death."

"There are many ancient Vulcan symbols of bad fortune and terror as well, Captain."

"Great!" interrupted Neelix. "Now, if you two amateur anthropologists are finished comparing historical notes, can we get back to the escape plan?"

The courtyard bent around an L shape, then stretched on for more than two kilometers. Past the bend, the yard was full to overflowing with ghastly Furies, wandering purposefully with faces down and eyes averted.

"I think we'd better get lost in the crowd," suggested the captain.

They approached. "Captain," said Neelix quietly, "maybe we had better liberate three hooded robes? We don't exactly look like Furies."

She shook her head. "We don't dare get into a fight now; we're no way prepared to attack a body of them. We'll just have to trust our luck and the pseudo-privacy of the Furies. Maybe they won't look up and see us, or won't know who we are if they do."

Breathing deeply to calm herself, she slowly advanced along the courtyard until they joined the crowd, melting into a train of aliens—two snake-men, a shambling, red-eyed *thing,* and one Fury who looked like Navdaq's species. The crowd pressed in on either side, crushing the away team by sheer weight of numbers.

"Take my shirt," Janeway called softly over her shoulder. Neelix caught on at once, grabbing her undertunic. She caught Tuvok's jacket ahead of her.

The crowd surged around them, ebbing and flowing; its movements were best described using the language of fluid flow. Were it not for the tight grip they held to each other, they would have been separated for certain.

"Captain!" shouted Neelix in Janeway's ear, startling her. "Look over there."

She followed his finger. Ahead and to the right was a group of six Furies of yet a different species: skins so wrinkled they looked like rhinoceri, pink in color, covered in dense, bristly hair, and with unshod feet that looked remarkably like hooves from a distance. They showed a series of tails running up their spines.

But the most remarkable thing about them was how they were dressed: they wore Starfleet uniforms.

Wait, thought Janeway, *not exactly....* But she saw a mixture of yellow and red shirts and black pants and ankle-boots. True, some of the jackets were both yellow and red; still, they looked extremely similar to the away team's clothing. The captain, science officer, and cook clawed their way through the wall of flesh to the group, falling in step behind them, heads bowed, looking neither left nor right.

All this while, they had walked alongside a building so massive, they had not even recognized it for what it was. The ceiling even bent up, rising toward infinity. How far down from the surface were they? As soon as they cleared the building, Janeway glanced to the side from the corner of her eye and saw what could only be computer terminals ... dozens of them lining the building's other face like public subspace communicators.

In a second, Janeway yanked on Tuvok's shirt and tugged him in the direction of the terminals; Neelix followed, of course.

"If these connect to a central guard database," she said,

"I might be able to get into the system and find out exactly where the shuttle pilot is being held."

She stood in front of a terminal about halfway back, hoping not to attract attention.

Janeway chewed her lip, tapping the flat screen here and there, getting a feel for the system.

"Can you get in, Captain?" asked Tuvok.

"If I can't," she muttered, "then I guess I'll never make chief engineer." She winked at her Vulcan friend and began to work in earnest.

CHAPTER 12

Tuvok and Neelix stood on either side of the frantically tapping Captain Janeway, keeping watch.

The Fury computer system used a sophisticated, one-way keycode security encryption. Poking around the edges, Janeway determined that it wanted a seven-hundred-character password.

"Well, no possible way to guess that," she muttered.

"Captain?"

"Nothing, Tuvok. It looks like we're sunk." She scowled; this was silly—to be stopped by a mere schoolboy encryption scheme! Janeway pulled the commbadge out of her pouch to make another futile attempt to contact the ship.

"Wait—belay that. I think I know how to . . ."

She faded out, staring at the commbadge.

"Yes." Smiling cryptically, she placed the badge on the terminal. The badges had a simple, artificially intelligent dataclip in them that detected an open-communications command, such as *Janeway to Commander Chakotay*. The The clip was simplistic, a moron compared to the ship's computer.

But it was still a computer, and it was the best they had.

THE FINAL FURY

"Commbadge," said the captain, "identify your model and year."

She jumped as a voice, the *computer's* voice, popped out of the badge. "I am a Starfleet general-issue Tang Bioelectrics Model 74-A communications badge manufactured at Rivendell Prime in 2362."

Neelix stared. "I never knew you could do that."

"I never thought of trying before." She licked her lips. "Commbadge, locate a receiver circuit in the terminal unit you're sitting on. Signal when you have done so."

After a silent second, the commbadge beeped.

"Transmit the following commands through the Universal Translator to the receiver circuit. Activate prisoner manifest." She watched the screen; after a moment, it went blank, then displayed a screenful of unfamiliar but clearly not encrypted characters.

"Fascinating," said Tuvok. "She has bypassed the entire encryption system by jumping over it, as it were, and communicating directly with the brain of the terminal."

"Um . . . I'll take your word for it."

"I never told you I was half-Ferengi, did I?" said Janeway with a wink. "Command: Display schematic of prison cells; highlight cell containing the Unclean captured on the moon."

An architectural drawing of a series of huge, roughly rectangular buildings (none was quite right-regular) appeared; one of the buildings then displayed a schematic of the cells. The building expanded until it filled the viewer, and a cell at the inner end glowed blue.

"Command: Show location of this terminal in relation to the highlighted cell."

A dot appeared on the side of the very building they wanted. All three stared at the wall they faced, then back toward the front they had seen. "Show all entrances to the building." She studied, memorizing the map. The nearest entrance was on the back side of the huge cell block.

Janeway paused; the next command was the big one. "Command: Unlock the door to the cell in which the Unclean is kept."

The terminal hesitated, then flashed a legend in the Fury's language, or one of them. Then the entire terminal went blank.

"Unauthorized access or command," guessed Tuvok. "Captain, I strongly suggest we remove ourselves from this location before the nearest guards arrive."

Resisting the urge to bolt, they slowly continued down the side yard toward the back.

The back of the building looked exactly like the front: featureless, the angles all wrong, dark and chilling, even in the heat of the Fury planet. But in the center was a ghastly, leaning, leering doorway that beckoned like an open mouth.

Janeway approached, ready to find a door that was open, locked with an electronic or mechanical lock, or ready to dilate as soon as she got close enough. She held her phaser ready.

In fact, the door was none of the above. It was closed and locked with a peculiar contraption that she only dimly recognized as a centuries-old *padlock*. The padlock actually dangled from an eyelet in the handle.

"Amazing," she said, shaking her head. The mix of modern and stone-age on the Fury planet was beginning to get under her skin.

The padlock was made out of the same indestructible material they were unable to cut through earlier. Janeway paused, temporarily defeated. Then she smiled, set her phaser on high, and proceeded to cut a Janeway-sized hole in the door itself—the door was made of mere steel-bound wood, an oily, warped wood. For once, the Fury peculiarities worked in the away team's favor.

She left the last centimeter of the top attached; when the edges had cooled—Neelix remembered himself this time—the three of them peeled back the flap with some difficulty. The flap did not drop or make any great noise; they ducked underneath into the building.

The layout was similar to their own cellblock: a door leading to the cells dilated as they approached; long corridors marched into the distance, all of them lined with metal-barred cages, each with its corresponding key-card lock. The away team kept close to the sides, in shadows deeper even than the normal gloom of the Fury world; it was a good thing, for when they rounded the corner that led to the block containing the pilot's cell, according to the database, Tuvok saw a strike team of guards checking out the cell.

He silently waved the captain and Neelix back. Around the corner, Tuvok whispered. "They must have responded to the attempted unlock command, Captain. The guards must realize some unauthorized person accessed the database. They will not leave the prisoner now."

Janeway nodded. "I agree. We've run out of options."

"You mean we're just going to let him rot in there?"

"Certainly not, Neelix. We've run out of *peaceful* options. I'm getting damned sick and tired of being poked, stared at, and imprisoned—me and the rest of you, including the pilot. I think this has passed far beyond the Prime Directive territory and deep into the realm of self-defense."

"I concur, Captain. These aliens are conspiring to launch an invasion of the Federation, and as such they are outside the domain of any treaty or law . . . including General Order Number One."

"It's time we showed them what Starfleet officers can do. Mr. Tuvok—you take the right flank. Neelix, you're on the left to prevent anyone from escaping for reinforcements. I'll take the middle two. Neelix, make believe Tuvok is your enemy; you look more like you could be a weird species of Fury. Ready?"

They rounded the corner, easily; Janeway lay on her stomach in the shadow, while Neelix and Tuvok walked deliberately toward the cell. The guards had closed the door, leaving a lump in a vaguely recognizable, burned and shredded Starfleet uniform; now the Furies surrounded the cell, seven strong. As soon as they caught sight of the pair approaching, they leveled their weapons.

Tuvok put his hands in the air, while Neelix pushed him none too gently in the small of the back. "Get along there, you!"

The confused guards backed up, still leveling their weapons but unsure what was happening and who they should believe. Capain Janeway kept as still as a corpse . . . she presumed the Furies could see in the dark; she counted on their vision being based around movement, as was human and Vulcan vision. If she stayed still enough, she might not attract any notice.

"Holy ones," said Neelix, "I have captured one of the prisoners. Ah . . . should I hand him over to you?"

The guards stared back and forth between Neelix and Tuvok. Almost certainly, the former was violating numerous social cues and unspoken protocols—the away team had had no time to study the society to be able to successfully blend.

While the guards puzzled out that paradox, they allowed the pair to close within arm's length. "Sirs," said Tuvok, his hands still in the air, "I wish to make a complete confession." He lowered his hands onto the necks of the two of guards on the right and used the Vulcan neck-pinch . . . it worked as well on Furies as it did on most other races.

As soon as they started to sag, before the others had a chance to react, Janeway opened fire from her position on the floor, steadying her aim for the long-distance shot by planting her elbow and using her hand as a tripod. She stunned two before they could fire a shot.

Two of the remaining three bolted toward her in the confusion. Tuvok turned and gave one of them a solid push as he stumbled past; the guard sprawled full length on the ground face-first, grunting in pain. She tried another phaser blast at the one who still approached, but this time he was ready; the guard ducked under the shot and connected with Janeway at her midsection, pounding the air out of her. The pair went down in a tangle of bodies.

But Janeway was a captain in Starfleet, and she had received hundreds of hours of armed and unarmed combat training. The guard was too big for her to handle by herself—but she was *not* by herself. After a few seconds, she managed to get the heel of her palm against the Fury's chin and press his head back a little bit.

It was enough. Tuvok stepped over the guard on the ground, who still struggled to get up, and pinched Janeway's assailant into the Land of Nod. The captain rolled to the side, getting a clear shot around Tuvok, and stunned the

THE FINAL FURY

sixth guard just as he got to his knees. He fell heavily to the ground once more.

Kathryn Janeway blinked, then suddenly remembered the last guard: when numbers five and six had bolted *toward* her, the seventh turned tail and made a laser-line for the opposite door. Suddenly realizing the danger, Janeway leapt to her feet and tried to get off a shot; but Tuvok was in the way, and the guard was far, far out of her reach.

A yellow blur flashed across her field of vision: Neelix charged after the last guard, leaping onto his back just before the Fury reached a lever-style switch. The cook tackled the guard centimeters away from the alarm switch.

"Did we get them? Is that all of them?" Janeway quickly checked each of the seven, making sure he was unconscious. Then she returned to the cell, accompanied by Tuvok. "All right, got any good ideas about opening the lock from the *outside?*"

"Not at the moment," said the Vulcan. "The light panels in this hallway are mounted high enough that I doubt we could reach them."

The captain was in the process of removing her hairpin as a preliminary step when Neelix gently coughed. "Um, Captain—maybe I'm being dense, but can't you just use this?"

He handed her the key-card that had been carried by the guard he coldcocked.

Flushing slightly, Janeway inserted the card in the slot; nothing happened. She removed it, and the cell unlocked and hinged open with a noise like a rusty wheel rolling along cobblestones. They entered and discovered what once had been a man, a human Starfleet officer. He wore command red, but they could hardly tell, for most of the fabric was burned beyond recognition, probably in the fiery crash of the shuttlecraft. His commbadge was missing; whether it fell off or he removed it was unknown. He once had been a tall man; now he was stooped. He once had boasted bright, red hair; now, only a few, discolored wisps remained, and the rest was gray and frayed. Ugly brown spots and blotches covered his skin; they might once have been freckles, now grown monstrous under tortures that must have involved ultraviolet radiation. His eyes were vacant and stared far out over the horizon. The man's skin was pallid where it wasn't spotty, with bloodred cracks marbling the surface.

Tuvok carefully felt his carotid artery pulse and declared him alive. He bled from a dozen serious lacerations, and his shoulder was dislocated. He had a crushed wrist and fractured ribs—this much determined by a cursory examination of his swollen joints and chest. But whether he would live or die, whether indeed his brain was functioning somewhere under the trauma, pain, and incoherence, only the doctor could tell. The man was not talking; he stared at the away team with no shock of recognition or relief and did not respond to their urgently whispered questions. His pupils were dilated and reacted sluggishly and unevenly to light.

Janeway hesitated only a moment. "Gentlemen, we have to get this patient to the ship; he is our top priority. Besides, I'm fresh out of ideas for stopping the invasion . . . but maybe if we can figure out where he came from, how he got all the way out here, maybe we'll have a clue how to get back ourselves and warn the Federation."

"Or perhaps," added Tuvok, "we can covertly accompany the Furies when they invade and take that opportunity to issue our warning. I believe our best chance to return to the Alpha Quadrant is at hand."

"Either way, we have to return to the ship—which means we have to find the surface of the planet somehow . . . or at least coordinates we can beam from."

"How about the place we beamed to in the first place?" asked Neelix.

"Can you find it again?"

"I—can't say for certain, but I think I can. I can try."

"That's more than Tuvok or I could do; we were in no condition to note the route."

Tuvok grabbed the lieutenant around his waist and hauled him to his feet. Miraculously, he stuck there, swaying a bit; but his eyes still stared into nothingness. Janeway gave the man an experimental push, and he staggered forward a couple of steps, then stopped. By a combination of pushing and turning, they got him moving; the captain supported him with her shoulder to speed things up.

Janeway led them back through the dilating door to the plaza; then Neelix took over. They tried to get into the Fury mode of walking, keeping their heads down, eyes averted, really getting into subsuming their individual identities in the crusade of the group to recover a particular piece of real estate at the expense of their entire multicultural existence, if necessary.

After all, what could possibly outweigh the chance to storm heaven? That is what Janeway told herself, and evidently it worked, for they were neither stopped nor questioned while Neelix led them down one blind alley and along another false trail. Each time, he added "—but *now* I know where we're going!" and the Starfleet officers patiently followed, each supporting one of their new companion's arms. He felt clammy to the touch.

At last, Neelix insisted, "Wait, this time I *really* know where we are . . ." and that time, he was right. He led them around another pair of corners, across a courtyard that Tuvok agreed looked familiar, down some more passages where Neelix agreed the geometry was loathsome, to a square that even Janeway admitted was the original beam-in spot. They returned to the approximate location they had entered, and the captain touched Neelix's secret commbadge. "Janeway to *Voyager*—Chakotay, are you out there?"

The voice crackled with static, but it was unmistakably her executive officer. "Captain! We have been trying—"

"Four to beam out right now, Mr. Chakotay—lock in on the communications signal."

"Yes, Captain, it'll be a little tricky, but we'll get you out."

Janeway turned back to Tuvok and Neelix. "All right, we've got the ship; now all we have to do, gentlemen, is survive until she gets here."

"That may not be as easy as it sounds," declared Tuvok. He pointed at the guards, including the feared favored, boiling out of the building they just left and out of two others just like it. "We might possibly escape detection by remaining within this crowd," suggested the Vulcan.

The captain of the guards made a peculiar pinging noise that might have been the equivalent of a human's whistling for attention. The guards gathered around—except for the favored, who inched close enough to hear but remained proudly aloof from the ordinary guards. The guard captain spoke animatedly, his oddly articulated limbs gesturing in impossible directions. Then he whipped out a bulky, boxlike item. *Now what?* thought the captain; she didn't appreciate new rules introduced into the game in such a late round.

"It could be a Fury tricorder," guessed Neelix.

"New plan: We take our so-far unrescued prisoner and get as far away from here as possible. I'll leave the commbadge carrier signal operating, so as soon as Chakotay gets close enough, he can lock on."

Janeway took one arm of the prisoner around her neck, and Tuvok took the other; they hurried as fast as they could, with Neelix dashing forward a few meters, then dashing back, looking remarkably doglike. "Get behind a building," Janeway suggested; "maybe their own tricorders are no better at poking through it than ours."

"We will have gained little," said Tuvok; "they can still follow our life signs."

"Yes, but they'll have to *follow* us then . . . they can't head straight toward us. We can lead them in circles."

"The idea is not without merit."

Janeway shifted to their rear, poking her nose around the corner to watch the guards' progress. Temporarily safe, at least until they had to move on to the next building, thirty meters away, Janeway looked up at the ceiling high overhead and tried to mentally *will* the *Voyager* to materialize right that instant and beam them out.

Neelix joined her, watching the guards.

Tuvok began trying to revive the shuttlecraft pilot; they would make much better time if he could be induced to move under his own power. But none of the standard means of bringing an unconscious human about worked; although the man was semiaware—he groaned and occasionally rolled his head from side to side and attempted to wrap his arms protectively around his head—the Vulcan could not get him fully awake, not even enough to move his legs or balance on his own without swaying like a sapling in a wind.

"Uh-oh," said Neelix, "they've figured it out . . . they're casting for us—wait, they're going the wrong way!"

Janeway held her breath as the guards, the favored in front, crowded around the door they had just exited, weapons out; then the biggest favored rolled forward like an armored fighting vehicle, gathered speed, and burst through the cut-out hole, firing his disruptor-like weapon as he went. His bulk ripped off the flap that Janeway had left; the others followed him through, and there were a few moments of confusion while they determined that they had followed the scent in the wrong direction—a fifty-fifty chance in that sort of tracking operation.

Janeway spoke up: "Now's our chance—Tuvok, let's move quickly before they figure it out!"

Neelix and Tuvok again picked up the pilot and followed Janeway around the building. "Captain," said Tuvok, panting, his voice nevertheless cutting through the noise, "can you cross and recross our own trail several times? It might serve to confuse our pursuers further."

Keeping a wary eye on the door—the Furies had left a guard, of course—they dodged into the courtyard again, slipping from one line of pedestrians to another. Janeway could feel the Furies' confusion and resentment at being jostled, probably a severe breach of politeness; but she jumped from one conga line to another, slowly enough that Neelix and Lieutenant Tuvok could follow, and worked her way back to a spot she remembered traversing. She walked their own trail for a few meters, then cut to the left; she zigged in the other direction, into the mob again, followed it around a circuitous route, then zagged back across the previous path at right angles.

Then she got nervous. The guard outside the building leaned through the hole and talked to someone just on the other side; then he looked around as if searching for them. "Neelix—move it, quick! Behind the next building over there!"

Just as Janeway feared, the guard reached through the

hole and took the tricorder from its previous owner; then he idly scanned the area.

He froze suddenly, then pointed directly at the fleeing away team. Janeway and crew bolted for cover, but it was too late; they were spotted. The guard produced his own version of the pinging noise, and his cohorts leapt back out through the hole.

The guard captain was the third one back through, and he made the smart tactical decision not to wait until he had regrouped. He pointed directly toward them and shouted something loudly enough that the away team's Universal Translators picked it up: "Give chase to the Unclean, for if they escape, we shall all be excommunicated!"

That is a potent threat indeed, thought Janeway, *when all of society is ordered around the Great Holy Crusade.* To a Fury, being excommunicated probably meant losing all reason for living. Suicide might follow quickly, if they were a race capable of such self-immolation.

She thought this as she ran as fast as she could, carrying her burden, expecting with every step the harsh blow of an energy weapon in the back. Or worse, the terror projector. *What hell would that be?* she wondered frantically.

Tuvok gave only the tiniest portion of his consciousness to willing his legs to move; running away from the Furies was something he literally could do in his sleep, so deeply was his fear of them ingrained in the wilder parts of his psyche. He passed his left hand around the pilot's back and up to touch his left temple, then pressed his right hand to the pilot's other temple. The Vulcan tried to find and extract the tiny ball of consciousness he hoped existed somewhere inside the wall of pain, the fleshy prison. Tuvok was trying a Vulcan mind-meld on the run, something that had never before occurred to him.

Here and beyond, Tuvok caught fleeting images of horrific memories—an alien ship, an attack; battle scenes, the dying, explosions and confusion—panic, the shock of being hit—the pilot lay in sickbay, he was in pain, he was trying to protect a friend . . . another Starfleet officer . . .

Tuvok almost drew back out of the man's mind; he was

well aware of the essential, ultimate invasion of privacy the mind-meld required . . . and clearly, the man had suffered severe trauma . . . but it was not so clear whether the Vulcan should continue or back out of the man's thoughts.

He hesitated only a moment; then Tuvok recalled the central tenet of the Vulcan philosophy, a saying attributed to Surak himself: The needs of the many outweigh the needs of the few . . . or the one.

But would the pilot himself agree? Would Captain Janeway? Humans were not Vulcans, and they had a peculiar love-hate relationship with such obvious, logical, utilitarian philosophy.

In the end, Tuvok decided that the decision was his own, and he had no problem with it. The away team needed rescuing; the Federation needed saving; and both required the pilot to become at least somewhat conscious. The man's own need not to have his most private thoughts violated must take second place in importance.

Tuvok again entered the pilot's mind, forcing himself deeper and deeper, trying to find the lowest portion of the brain. Along the way, he saw many more images, horrors etched in the man's brain—the man . . . a name floated past, and Tuvok grabbed it.

The man was Lieutenant Redbay.

Then, just behind the name, Tuvok found what he was looking for: he found the reptile center, the site that controlled such simple activities as walking, balancing, running. *Open,* thought Tuvok, trying to restart the segment; *let me in . . . I am a friend. Your life is in danger; you must revive and begin running.*

Then Tuvok was surrounded and attacked by the mind's I, the "Redbay" of Redbay's mind. *Invader! Assassin! Murderer! Get out get out get OUT of my head, get out, get—*

Do not be afraid of me; I have come to help. You are in danger; you must begin moving immediately.

—devils hurling terror before them like lightbeam tearing through the ship invading invading! in mortal danger must take the shuttlecraft through the wormhole before . . .

Tuvok was fascinated; a wormhole? What wormhole?

Could they return through it and warn the Federation of the impending attack . . . an attack about which they knew no operational details?

But perhaps Redbay knew. Tuvok pressed harder. *Sir, you must return to consciousness, whether you are to fight me or the ones who did this to you. Follow my voice; follow me. . . .*

Tuvok backed slowly away; the "Redbay" grabbed hold, trying to wrestle Tuvok's consciousness to the metaphorical floor—but the Vulcan was the stronger; and slowly, inexorably, Redbay was pulled out of his self-built prison . . . a prison that might have saved him from total madness.

The only logical conclusion was that Redbay had been exposed to the Furies' terror-projection device.

The pilot groaned again; but it was a groan with more purpose than his previous ones. Janeway felt him straighten under her arm; when he stood, he was taller than she, of course, which made her suddenly a burden, not a support. She hastily let go, simply helping him to balance on his hind legs.

Neelix had been watching the three of them, transfixed; then he turned back and started squawking: "Run! Run away—*they're here!*"

The away team bolted, and astonishingly enough, so did the shuttlecraft pilot. He staggered after them under his own impulse power. The quartet ran across the courtyard, under the iron "sky," pursued by those guards who had made it back out—which did not include any of the favored, fortunately, else the *Voyager* team would have been trampled in seconds. *The favored are evidently swift of foot but not of mind,* thought the captain.

But the other guards were fast enough, motivated, and unencumbered by a still-woozy comrade. They gained and steadily closed the gap, reaching for Neelix, who brought up the rear.

At last, Neelix dug in his heels and whirled to face the angels of death, straight-arming the first one. The rest came for him with a roar.

They whirled their facial tentacles in rage; they screamed and leapt at him like wild animals; but they leapt at an empty patch of air as Janeway, Tuvok, Neelix faded into noncorporeality in front of the Furies' snakelike snouts.

Janeway discorporated and disappeared, leaving a confused, enraged, and terrified mob of cops in her dust... cops who would soon face their own, even more terrifying commanders with a story of failure quite unlikely to be believed.

Captain Janeway almost—*almost*—felt sorry for them as she rematerialized on the *Voyager* transporter pad.

CHAPTER 13

"Am I dead?"

Kes waited anxiously in the transporter room, standing first on one foot then the other, while the away team took about nine years, an entire Ocampan lifetime, to materiallize. The stranger, an emaciated human who looked like a ghost, sparkled into view with that horrible question on his lips: "Am I dead?"

After Kes embraced Neelix, she propelled the stranger—Redbay, according to Tuvok—straight to sickbay, while everyone else headed bridgeward.

In sickbay, Kes watched, concerned, while the Doctor checked Redbay quickly and determined that there was nothing physically wrong with him aside from a few broken bones, deep lacerations, bruises, and general ill treatment.

Kes desperately wished she knew if Neelix were safe; but she remained with the doctor. Redbay suffered from a deep psychological wound that would be difficult to cure while still on a starship . . . perhaps impossible, as soon as the young lieutenant recovered sufficiently to realize their dire predicament. He had lost quite a lot of weight and had clearly been tortured physically and psychologically. The man looked like a walking corpse. His color was bad, bone-white, and he did not lose the long-distance stare.

"Am I dead?"

"No," said Kes; "you're aboard a Starfleet starship." *Lost in space, forever, never to return. You may as well be dead,* she did not add.

The doctor took up the conversation.

"You have some severe injuries which I will now heal, if you'll stop squirming long enough to let me do so. You may feel some discomfort and stiffness for a few days, especially in the wrist. Try not to use it as much as usual. In fact, try not to use it at all."

"This is the *U.S.S. Voyager*," said Kes, "but you're still in the Delta Quadrant. My name is Kes, and this is the doctor. The captain's name is Janeway; she's the one who rescued you with the Vulcan. Neelix, the other one who rescued you—not the Vulcan, the *third* one—is my . . . a Talaxian native.

"Kes is my assistant," the doctor explained.

Kes watched Redbay carefully; in fact, she had struck up the conversation, hoping to jar his mind away from his morbid hallucinations.

"Is this hell? Am I in hell now?"

Kes sighed and began telling Redbay all about the *Voyager* and how it came to be in the Delta Quadrant. *I'll entertain him all night, if I have to,* she decided bleakly, concerned about the patient's frame of mind.

Janeway slid into the command chair as if she had merely stepped out to eat a quick meal; the ordeal behind her, she wanted her ship back in hand. "Mr. Chakotay, what's happening? Pursuit?"

"Glad to have you aboard, Captain. We worried we had lost you for a time. Mr. Paris?"

"Nothing yet . . . I plotted a course that stayed well away from the aliens' moon; that's how they caught us last time."

"Where are we now?"

Kim answered. "We shot around the sun, beamed you up

on the fly, and now we're right back where we started: on the opposite side of the sun from the planet; except now we're far enough out for a real orbit."

Janeway nodded. "Continue correcting course to keep from being seen."

"Did you miss me?" The voice sounded from the turbolift.

"Welcome back, Neelix," said Kim. "Of course We missed you . . . especially around dinnertime. Lieutenant Paris drew the black marble and had to cook."

"Mr. Neelix," said the captain, "you performed with exemplary courage, as did Mr. Tuvok, under difficult conditions. I will make an entry to that effect in the log. But right now, we have a serious problem. Senior officers to my ready room; I have to tell you what we discovered. Activate—I mean, Janeway to the doctor."

"Yes, Captain."

"Doctor, how is Lieutenant Redbay?"

The doctor frowned on the viewer, putting his finger on his chin in an eerily human gesture. "Physically? I've done my usual brilliant job. But he still has some lingering psychological problems. Kes is talking to him now—I think he'll be able to leave sickbay in a short while."

"Kes!" shouted Neelix. "Can you hear me? Are you there?"

The Ocampan moved into the frame. "Neelix, I was so frightened when we couldn't find the away team. I thought you might have been captured."

"We were! We had to break out—the captain used her hairpin to pick the—"

"But are you all right? Can you come down here?"

"I'm sorry, Kes," said Janeway, "but I need Neelix up here for right now. He's fine. I'll send him down as soon as I can. Janeway out."

Chakotay was staring at her. "What did you pick with your *hairpin?* This I have to hear."

"In good time, Commander. Senior officers in the ready room. Mr. Kim, contact Torres and and get her up here."

* * *

Chakotay sat back and listened to his captain. He was surprised how relieved he was to have her aboard again. *A few months ago, I would cheerfully have left her behind*, he realized.

"That is as much as we could glean of the Furies' plans. They may represent the biggest threat the Federation has ever faced . . . perhaps even greater than the Borg.

"When they invaded the Alpha Quadrant one hundred years ago, a *single ship* fought the Constitution-class starship *Enterprise* and a Klingon fleet to the death. If today, they chose to send a dozen ships, or a few hundred or *thousand,* how could we possibly respond?

"My words might be inadequate to convey the dire situation we face; but if you had been there with us, if you had *seen them* and felt the mindless, paralyzing terror they induce, even without their terror-projection weapon, I wouldn't need to explain anything."

Tuvok spoke into the well of alarmed silence. "The captain has been deliberately vague about my own reaction to the Furies. She wishes to spare my feelings, for my emotional reaction disgraced my logical heritage. But I have no feelings to be hurt; and if it will help make the rest of you understand the gravity of the threat, I will accept whatever opprobrium my reaction deserves."

Pausing a moment, Tuvok told Chakotay, Kim, Paris, and Torres exactly what he had felt, sparing no raging emotion, no disgraceful, illogical reaction.

When he finished, the commander was stunned. Without even having seen the Furies, he began to understand.

"There are twenty-seven billion—well, *demons* on that planet," said Janeway. "If we allow them to invade our quadrant with even a significant fraction of that figure, we will face an enemy greater in sheer numbers than any we have ever faced since before the Federation was the Federation, and before the human race was really human. And then there are the projected terrors; thank heaven we didn't have to face those. But if they do invade, we will."

"We failed to effectively resist conquest the last time," added Tuvok; "although we are closer to them technologically, the Furies could overwhelm us with sheer numbers."

Chakotay frowned. Fatalism did not sit well in his craw. "It's not just our technology that has changed. We're older now, as a people; we're more sophisticated. We are civilized, and we have met many new and some would even say horrific life-forms. Wilson's Worms on Dalmat Seven; the Viidians, even the Vulcans look a little like human demons."

Janeway shook her head. "When a human encounters a Fury, he is no longer older, more sophisticated, civilized, or even human anymore. He is once more what he was in the past: a terrified slave driven to obedience by irresistible fear."

The ready-room door slid open, and a picture of walking death loomed in the doorway. Chakotay almost winced at the vision: flesh sunk to the bone so it appeared a living skull, skin pallid as death, clammy and dry, sliding across the joints and muscles like a poorly upholstered chair trod upon to reach a high place . . . the man in the doorway did not so much fill his Starfleet lieutenant's uniform as offer it a wire frame on which to hang. Redbay—who else would it be?—listed to the side, like an ocean ship taking on water just before sinking beneath the waves.

He lurched into the room, arms outstretched, and Chakotay impulsively jerked to his feet though the lieutenant had only grabbed for the table to steady himself on legs too weak to support even his emaciated weight. He had crashed only a few weeks earlier, judging from the distress beacon; but it might as well have been years in a prison camp undergoing the punishments of the damned.

Kes accompanied the young ancient into the ready room. She caught him by the arm, levering him gently into a chair; then she sat beside him and put his hand in hers but did not attempt any more emotional greeting. *They are very private souls,* thought the commander.

"I have seen hell," croaked Redbay, and no one in the room dared contradict the audacious statement. Even Tuvok simply folded his hands and let the words hover overhead.

"You're still alive," said Kes, reassuring the young man.

THE FINAL FURY

"No one should see hell," insisted Redbay, "and survive."

"But you have survived," said the captain; "and you must help the rest of us survive. You know what the Furies intend? I see you do. Then you'll help us now."

Redbay closed his eyes—then quickly opened them again, evidently seeing more to fear in the blackness than in the light. He turned expectantly to Janeway, who began the inquiry.

"Yes. Well, we know the what. What do we know about the how? B'Elanna?"

B'Elanna Torres cleared her throat. Lieutenant Carey and I have continued to analyze the tricorder recordings that Ensign Kim made of the machinery inside the moon, and there is no question what it is: the moon is set up to receive a single burst of energy so catastrophic that it will destroy the moon microseconds after it begins to be absorbed."

She tapped on the console, causing a three-dimensional, holoprojected schematic of the machinery to materialize above the conference table and rotate slowly. Chakotay stared curiously, but it meant little to him; it was a big, bulky machine.

"The system Kim and Paris saw was built to channel a massive amount of energy. . . . The moon will be bombarded by a burst of energy; it has to be a burst—the circuits wouldn't last longer than fifteen milliseconds. But that hardly matters, because within a hundred milliseconds, the moon's surface will first liquefy, then a quarter of a second later boil away into ionized gas."

Paris shook his head, confused. "If the whole system breaks down in a quarter of a second—"

"Nowhere near that long," corrected Lieutenant Torres; "only one-point-five *hundredths* of a second, really, before the circuits fry."

"All right, one-point-five *hundredths* of a second—what could it possibly do in that length of time?"

"It projects energy, Paris. Enough to cause a subspace rift and probably enough to puncture through many folds of the fabric, whatever you want to call it, of the universe. It creates something very much like an artificial wormhole."

B'Elanna Torres paused. Chakotay silently pondered the hard-to-miss implication: The Furies planned to send an awful lot of them *somewhere,* and mighty fast, too.

CHAPTER 14

"I DON'T REALLY UNDERSTAND IT," CONTINUED B'ELANNA; SHE felt annoyed at not understanding. But worse, she had to wonder if she would understand, if she had stuck it out at the Academy.

"You really need a subspace physicist here. But while the heavy-particle radiation, the actual guts of the exploding star, crawls toward the moon at only about a twentieth of light speed, say thirteen thousand kilometers per second, the first burst of massless, energetic neutrinos crosses the gap at light speed itself. They strike the neutrino collectors, here." Torres caused a series of thirty-eight gigantic coils of some thin wire, like metallic spiderwebs, to glow blue on the red, floating schematic.

"In the first three hundred nanoseconds, the neutrinos are converted to Bela-Smith-Ng subspace pumped-wave energy, the same stuff we use to send a subspace message—except every particle raised fifteen or sixteen 'orbits,' or levels of energy. Theoretically impossible, of course . . . according to *Federation* science." She smiled, pure Maquis satisfaction.

"In the next fourteen hundred nanoseconds, this Bela-energy is run a few million times around a circular coil, here." She illuminated a different section of the diagram; but she could see Kim and Paris staring blankly, trying to absorb the gist, at least.

"What does that do?" asked the ensign, more to himself than Torres. B'Elanna almost put her hand on Kim's arm; he had always said he would have gone to EDO School to become an engineer if he hadn't gotten the *Voyager* billet. *He's upset that he doesn't see it immediately,* she realized; for a moment, B'Elanna felt very close to Kim, sharing the bond of imagined inadequacy.

B'Elanna Torres answered quickly. "Edvard Bela, who lived on a colony now at the core of Maquis resistance to the Cardassian-inspired treaty, thought that if Bela-energy were forced into a circular path—and I've never seen anyone even attempt it before, but that's what the Furies are doing—it would created a subspace tunnel of such intensity that it would explode along its only available expansion points . . . forward and back."

Janeway gasped. "They really *are* building a wormhole!" she exclaimed.

"You're way ahead of me; but yes, that's the conclusion Carey and I came to."

The captain continued so quickly, even B'Elanna had a hard time following. "They've built a device to focus some monstrous burst of energy into the creation of an artificial wormhole, which they're going to project. Calculations probably would show its other end pointing to the Alpha Quadrant . . . then they'll send their ships through. Have to be fast, though; they've already burned up, what, two milliseconds? And they only have fifteen, say ten for safety's sake? Eight milliseconds . . . they're not going to send their ships through the wormhole. They're going to create the wormhole *around the ships!* So the first warning sign would be when they mass their fleet in one spot. B'Elanna, what's the beam spread? What kind of radius would we have to look for? And where in the universe do they expect to get a burst like that? To vaporize that whole moon, you must have calculated them using an astronomical amount of energy. There's no way they can . . ."

She paused, scowling. Lieutenant Torres opened her mouth; but before she could speak, Tuvok drew the obvious conclusion: "There is only one source for an energy burst that large," he said. "The Furies are planning to trigger their own sun to go supernova."

In the stunned silence around the conference table, B'Elanna Torres could have dropped a molecule and made everyone jump at the crash.

Redbay smiled, but the gesture turned into a grimace of loathing. B'Elanna tried not to look at him; he frightened her.

"Yes," admitted the chief engineer. "They're going to blow up their sun. We—passed through the sun a while ago." Torres glanced at Commander Chakotay, who had said not a word. As Torres expected, Janeway stared at her executive officer in astonishment.

"You took *my* ship into the *sun?*"

Chakotay inclined his head for a moment, and the captain sat back, frowning but saying nothing more.

Torres continued, feeling embarrassed, as if she had betrayed a confidence. "And Paris thought to conduct a full scan of the immediate environment . . . passive only, so we wouldn't alert the Fury pursuers that we were still alive. I've been going over the data since, and I discovered that the core is already in an advanced state of collapse: there are hardly any bosons to speak of and nowhere near enough heat to sustain the fusion reaction . . . but the neutrino count is through the roof. And yes, I know the sun isn't anywhere near big enough to collapse on its own—or anywhere near as hot as a supernova, which can generate core temperatures of six hundred million degrees."

"A Bela-Neutron device," declared Tuvok.

"Of course. Another conceptual breakthrough by Professor Bela . . . the devices, millions of them, absorb heavy particles like hydrogen and helium nuclei and reemit neutrinos plus electrons and positrons. Neutrinos don't interact with anything except neutrino collectors, so most of the sun's energy is pumped away uselessly . . ."

"Leaving not enough energy to hold the sun's diameter apart against the crushing pull of gravity," completed

Janeway, "and the star collapses like a popped soap bubble."

"An overly poetic metaphor," said Tuvok, "but essentially accurate."

"And when it collapses," concluded B'Elanna, *"boom."*

Paris's mouth had opened wider and wider during the explanation. He might have barely passed the minimum physics credits at the Academy, but he could add two and three. "Damn, talk about burning your bridges behind you!"

Tuvok raised his eyebrows. "Mr. Paris brings up an interesting question: Once the Furies create the wormhole to transport their fleet, collapsing their own star into a supernova, what is their plan for the rest of their population? By my rough estimate, this star is large enough that a supernova would extend its radius far past the inhabited planet. Every life-form on the surface of the planet would be incinerated. There would be no survivors."

B'Elanna nodded grimly. "We wondered about that, too. The sun goes supernova, and seven and a half minutes later, the neutrinos and photons strike the moon. In a total of four milliseconds, the wormhole is projected to a target point. Eleven milliseconds after that, the circuits fry, and the wormhole begins wobbling, collapsing in maybe seven or eight seconds.

"But the moon is the same distance from the sun as the planet, in the L-four position. The moon *can't* eclipse the sun. No matter what, their planet will be vaporized, or at least biologically cleansed, by the same blast."

"Of course, the Furies live deep underground," mused Tuvok. "They might survive."

"But they'd have essentially no sun! Captain, I never answered your other question about the radius of the wormhole. That's because we can't. Nobody has any experience with this sort of pumped-wave subspace energy—it doesn't exist as far as Federation science is concerned! So it could be anything from a few meters to a few thousand kilometers . . . neither Carey nor I can narrow it any further than that."

Janeway sat at the head of the table, cupping her chin in her hand. "We didn't see any evidence of a huge fleet of ships while we were on the planet. Of course, we were pretty confined, to say the least."

Ensign Kim spoke up. "Sir, we saw nothing from orbit. I can have the computer review the records, looking for areas of the planet we never got to see; we weren't in orbit long before we were attacked."

"Do that, Mr. Kim."

Chakotay's turn. "Captain, I don't think you'll find any battle fleet, or escape fleet, for that matter."

B'Elanna listened intently; she knew that tone . . . Chakotay had just had, or was on the verge of having, an insight, a satori.

"Why do you say that?"

"I don't know. But I have a feeling that we're shooting into an empty tree. Call it a hint from my spirit guide; but there is an aspect of this we're all missing . . . including myself."

"What do you mean?" asked the captain.

"I don't know yet, Captain." Chakotay considered a moment, then shook his head. "We're missing something. But I don't think we'll find any battle fleets, and I don't think they have any intention of letting any of their people die in the supernova."

"Commander Chakotay," asked Tuvok, "I did not detect any noticible compassion or concern in either Navdaq or the Autocrat for the Fury population."

"I don't mean they're too nice to let them die, Mr. Tuvok; I don't believe they're willing to sacrifice even a single soldier who might aid their cause. It would be wasteful and inefficient . . . and I think that's how they would look at it."

Redbay giggled slightly. Disconcerted, B'Elanna turned to him; but the lieutenant had nothing to say.

"Well, the commander was right about one thing," said Kim, looking up from the screen. "The computer has just reviewed the entire planetary scan and found nothing that could possibly be a fleet of ships."

Paris added his own two strips of latinum. "There wasn't

anything on the moon that looked like a launch bay or docking port. I don't think they even think about fleets of ships."

Kim continued. "There's no ship activity around the planet, no traffic between the planet and the moon, and nothing else in the solar system."

"Lieutenant Torres," said Chakotay, "are there any nearby stars with habitable planets we passed on the way here?"

"Yes sir. Two stars, one with two habitable planets, the other with four."

"Any life-form readings?"

"None that we detected, Commander."

Chakotay looked at Janeway. The captain smiled. "So we've determined the Furies aren't very sociable and aren't interested in colonization, trade, or contact with other beings. This doesn't explain why they don't have a battle fleet on the eve of an invasion."

"Captain," said Torres, "those ships that tried to corner us . . . they were sluggish and completely inexperienced at space combat. But why didn't they shoot their terror-projection beam at us? That's the question that worries me."

Lieutenant Redbay's giggles had become more and more frequent and distracting; now he broke into loud, stentorian laughter. B'Elanna slid away from him, as did everybody at the table except Chakotay and Tuvok.

It was the crazy-man laugh of a person who no longer cared what anybody thinks of him or his sanity. Redbay lurched to his feet, yanking his arm away from Kes's restraining grip.

"A *fleet?* You wanted a *fleet?* Oh, they gave us a fleet, all right—a nice, big, fat, rosy fleet, fit for any invasion!

"And you want the terror lights? Oh, yes, indeed, they did have those, indeed indeed . . . just tell me more about the *Furies* and the fleets they don't have and the terror beams they can't project! *I'm all ears!*"

Redbay danced around a bit, pacing left and right, only a step or two. Kes rose to pull him down again, but Neelix snatched her back out of reach. *Good man*, thought B'Elanna; *no telling what Redbay might do next.*

Redbay remained nonviolent, however; he started walking energetically around the table, hugging himself, glazed eyes overlooking a starscape both alien and terrifying that only he could see. "They came out of the black; we didn't see them, but at first we thought only that they were another race, and we were explorers! But no, they came—they didn't come to explore but to conquer . . . us! Conquer us. Conquer us."

"Go on," said Janeway; Tuvok glanced at her with a questioning raise of his brow, but she shook her head.

Redbay told his tale. He told of the meeting with the Furies, the negotiation, Captain Jean Luc Picard's futile attempt to find a settlement.

Janeway's mouth twitched; it had all happened shortly after the *Voyager* was grabbed by the Caretaker and propelled through an artificial wormhole into the Delta Quadrant. Had she known of the encounter by the newest *Enterprise,* she would have put two and two together and realized the Furies were ready to go Viking again at the drop of a proverbial terror-beam.

B'Elanna squirmed, unsettled indeed to learn how intransigent and monomaniacal their enemy really was, how bloody-minded, and how he would fight to the last soldier, the final ship—to the end without a thought for treaty or compromise!

Redbay sank at last into his seat, but he was not finished. Holding his face in his hands, his voice quiet and shaking, Redbay whispered of the terror projector and how it tore at the mind, leaving it bleeding and raw and wide open to virtually any command or demand that would *make the horror stop*.

"You don't fight. You don't fight. You fall down and do what they say and anything they say is your heart's desire, anything to stop the fear that sucks you out of yourself, and you'd cut your own throat or sell your captain as a slave if they would just turn it *off!* Turn it off, turn it off, *turn it OFF!*"

Kes touched Redbay's arm; the lieutenant began to cry softly. He did not care who watched. B'Elanna sat very still, uncomfortably wondering what tearing of the mind would be necessary to make B'Elanna Torres fall to broken pieces of madness like this man. She did not like the answer.

No one else vented his fear; no one but Redbay had the guts—and he had nothing left to lose.

We're Starfleet, all of us, she thought, noticing all of their responses to a sobbing lieutenant, some uncomfortable, some sympathetic. She smiled behind steepled hands, knowing she was no different: like the rest of the crew, if the Furies projected their terrors at Lieutenant Torres, she would fall obediently to the ground and give them anything, even her Klingon honor, to make them stop. It was purely biological.

"Lieutenant Redbay," said the captain, her voice firm and in control, but gentle, "we have to know how they will come. If you destroyed their fleet—if destroying the antenna destroyed their power source—then where is the new fleet? Where will the attack come from? We can't find any other fleet of ships."

Redbay did not move. He spoke to the table. "Don't you know yet? Don't you know, know how they're coming yet? They're coming, and fear rides alongside."

"But *how* are they coming Lieutenant? Do they have another fleet around another star system? Is the fleet already in the Alpha Quadrant still operable? Mr. Redbay, *we have to know.*"

Redbay remained silent, face still in his hands. But Janeway decided the time had come for the man to begin returning to himself, to his duty.

"Look at me," she said. When he did not move, she repeated herself: *"Look* at me, Mr. Redbay, when I'm talking to you."

Her command tone shook him enough that he sat back slowly and stared wonderingly at her, like a spoiled child slapped for the first time in his life. B'Elanna was impressed.

"Talk to me," Janeway continued. "In words. Tell me how the Furies are going to invade the Alpha Quadrant. Tell me now; I have to know."

"They're—they're invading."

"How are they invading, Lieutenant Redbay?"

"Invading..."

"How are they invading?"

"They—create a wormhole—artificial wormhole, and..."

"We already know they create an artificial wormhole, Lieutenant. Report: *Where is the Fury fleet?*"

Redbay had held himself rigidly erect, staring at the captain. Now he deflated, slumping forward, more relaxed in defeat than he had been since his rescue.

"There is no fleet," he softly said. "The wormhole is... is for them."

"For them how? How will they invade?"

"For them. For the planet."

B'Elanna froze momentarily; then she heard her own pulse beating in her temples. *For the planet?*

"The wormhole—is for the planet."

"Captain," said Torres, "that's it! That's the missing piece Commander Chakotay was talking about—they're going to send their *entire planet* through the artificial wormhole!"

"With all twenty-seven billion aboard?" demanded Tom Paris.

"Yes!"

"But..." Neelix looked confused; he was having a hard time with the concept. "But even if they did, how would they move? They don't have enough ships!"

Redbay stroked the table, the smooth texture of replicated oak. "The... planet."

Chakotay leaned forward. "Redbay, the entire planet is a ship?"

Redbay reluctantly nodded; he gripped his hands together, fighting the residual compulsion to serve his masters in any way they desired—and not to reveal their secrets to the Unclean.

Janeway stood, towering over the table by command presence alone. "I knew we had a problem. But I was not aware of the full extent of the danger.

"With this new intelligence, I now realize we have no idea at all how to stop the invasion of an entire armed planet of twenty-seven billion soldiers. We haven't a clue how to stop their jumping to Federation space and launching the most terrible war we have ever faced.

"The war will be a holy crusade, and it can end one of only two ways: either the Federation, the Klingon and Cardassian Empires, and all the nonaligned races will end up enslaved to these demons . . . or else we will have to kill them, every last one of them, down to the last Fury. Twenty-seven billion self-defense homicides on our consciences.

"Both these alternatives are unacceptable. You will come up with another option, fast. There is nothing more to say here; dismissed."

Grimly, the entire staff except Tuvok rose to return to their duty stations; B'Elanna wondered how they could possibly obey their captain's last command. Lieutenant Tuvok stayed behind in the ready room.

Lieutenant Redbay stayed as well. Janeway understood. *They have a bond,* she thought.

She followed the rest of the crew out of the ready room, leaving the Vulcan and the dead man alone.

CHAPTER
15

"THEY MUST HAVE PLANNED THIS INVASION FOR CENTURIES," muttered B'Elanna Torres. She sat backward in a chair in engineering, resting her chin on the back and staring at part of the schematics of the moon. *Centuries!* The thought frightened her human half—and awed her Klingon side.

"You think so?" asked Captain Janeway from behind Torres. The chief engineer jumped; she had thought she was alone on the deck.

"Captain! I didn't hear you come in."

"You said they've been planning this for centuries. How do you know?"

B'Elanna said nothing for a moment; then the Klingon forced out the information deduced by the human. "Because of the mathematics of it," she said; "twenty-seven billion Furies, figure a thousand—no, *ten* thousand in a ship, they would need a fleet of two-point-seven million ships."

"That's a hell of a fleet."

"That's a ridiculous fleet! Compared to that, the entire Federation has only a handful of starships, and none of them can carry anywhere near ten thousand people. The

Federation, Klingon and Cardassian Empires, and everybody else in the quadrant have combined fewer than fifty thousand ships of any type, maybe a total carrying capacity of twelve-point-five million people if we pack them like Klingon fish."

"So you figure the Furies were planning on sending their entire planet all along."

Was Janeway making fun? *No, she's not the type.* "Right. I mean, yes, Captain. This isn't a desperation maneuver; it's what they always intended to do. The other invasions were just attempts to establish a beachhead."

"And it would have taken more than a century to build all this technology?"

"Captain, they had to develop it from scratch. If they'd had the ability to send their planet through a hundred years ago, they would have. They were planning this decades years ago, when they met the first *Enterprise,* and they must have planned it for decades before that." B'Elanna stared at the warp core, watching it pulse red, fade, pulse. The regularity comforted her in the face of timeless, implacable enmity—"vast, cool, and unsympathetic" stuck in her mind from somewhere.

"I wish we could plan that far ahead," said Janeway. "So what do we do about it? What's my third option, Torres?"

B'Elanna ground her teeth. She had thought for a couple of hours; at least, still stumped, she had finally hooked up with Lieutenant Carey, Maquis cleverness combined with Starfleet thoroughness.

Together, they had come up with one possibility—but it was impossible. Carey was back in his quarters racking out; Torres could not sleep herself, so she was left to bear the torch herself.

"Well, Carey and I have only a vague thought. Frankly, I can't see how we would implement it." Pulse, fade. Bright red, and the control console behind her was cold, hard.

"It is?"

"Destroy the moon. Blow it up somehow. No power—no wormhole."

Janeway absently toyed with her hair, distracted. The

captain's eyes flicked across the instrument readouts behind B'Elanna; *she never stops, not even for a second,* thought the engineer. B'Elanna felt the rough fabric of the chair against her chin; she felt an old dream stir, the dream of command and four pips on her collar. If only—

"All right, that sounds promising," said the captain; "how do we do it? Can we penetrate the hull with our phasers?"

"Nope."

"Photon torpedoes? How about if we rammed it, even if that meant taking out the *Voyager* itself?"

Ouch. "No, and no. We could try taking the shuttlecraft in again, but all the important guts of the system are deep inside, where we can't go."

Janeway closed her eyes; when she opened them, she stared right through B'Elanna's Klingon skull and bored into her brain. "There's another point here you haven't mentioned."

"Um . . . well, yeah." Torres started to squirm but caught herself. "If we blow up the moon . . . well, the sun still goes nova. And the planetary surface will be fried."

"I told you that wasn't necessarily acceptable."

Necessarily? "Captain, you said it wasn't acceptable at all to kill the Furies. Now you're saying *maybe?*"

Janeway pursed her lips. She frowned. "Actually, Lieutenant, I'm not saying. Not yet."

B'Elanna was careful not to exult; Janeway, like most humans, suffered from too much sympathy for her enemies. Best not to play with the inertial dampers when the ship was finally headed the right direction. The captain continued her rapid-fire questions: "How about driving a shuttlecraft up inside and transporting an armed photon torpedo onto the moon?"

B'Elanna raised her brows. "You know the shuttlecraft wouldn't be able to make it out."

"Of course not."

"No good. Transport the torpedo *where?* What are the vital links? It does no good at all to take out this circuit or that circuit; this thing has so much redundancy built into it, because it's absorbing the energy from a *supernova,* that you could take out half the circuits and it would still probably work!" *Was that really admiration in my voice?*

"So what do we do?"

Torres closed her eyes and shook her head, scraping her chin against the chair. "I don't know. And neither does Carey." She kept her eyes shut for a long moment; when she opened them, Janeway was gone without even a goodbye. For a moment, B'Elanna stared, startled. Then she shrugged and got back to work.

In her ready room, Captain Janeway repeated engineering's half-plan to Chakotay. The commander frowned. "Have you considered the moral implication?"

She waited patiently; he didn't like to be interrupted. She stood facing Chakotay.

"If we blow up the moon, Captain, then there will be no wormhole. But that will not stop the sun from going supernova."

Janeway looked her commander in the eye. "Yes, Chakotay, I thought about that."

"Kathryn, that means that . . . twenty-seven *billion* people will die as a direct result of our actions."

"It's a sobering thought, Commander."

Chakotay turned away, not meeting her eyes. "I don't believe I could kill even that many Cardassians, let alone these people with whom I have no history."

Janeway wondered, for a moment, whether she could even contemplate such a savage act. So far, she had kept the moral part of her brain sealed off in order to work on the engineering side; but she couldn't do that forever. "You do have a history with them, Chakotay; you just don't remember."

"That's the whole point, Captain; I *don't* remember. Maybe if we all were to meet them."

"No time; according to Torres, the sun will go supernova very soon, a day or two. Besides, I can't run the risk of the Furies' using their terror device on my crew and maybe forcing them to mutiny." She crossed and sat—the symbolic finality of command.

THE FINAL FURY

Chakotay turned to her. "You *are* the captain, Kathryn. You have to make a decision, and quickly."

She nodded, now staring at unmoving stars, the brightest pinprick shortly to go nova. "This changes everything . . . I never imagined myself *killing* people beyond my ability to count. I don't know if I can do it either, even if I decide I have to.

"All right, you have the conn again, Commander; I'm going down to work with B'Elanna on just what we could do to destroy the moon . . . just in case. Give us three hours, then convene the senior officers. I will decide then. Definitely then."

Janeway walked morosely toward engineering, hands clasped behind her back. *Sometimes,* she thought, *command is the cruelest mistress of all.*

Kathryn Janeway showed up late to a bridge-crew meeting for the very first time in her life. She entered bruskly with B'Elanna Torres twenty-two minutes after the scheduled start. The cast was a virtual rerun of the meeting nearly a day earlier, except for the absence of Lieutenant Redbay. Kes looked distracted, as if she'd rather be down in sickbay with her patient. *Or anywhere but here,* thought the captain.

"We still don't know whether we can destroy the moon," she said abruptly while sitting. B'Elanna sat beside Kim, as usual. "First, we must decide whether we *should* destroy the moon. You all know what that means."

B'Elanna Torres sounded frustrated. "Whether we *should?* How can we not? The fate of the Federation and the Empire are both at stake!"

Janeway looked across the table at Kes, who opened and closed her mouth. The Ocampan said nothing, and Neelix moved his arm to cross hers familiarly.

Chakotay spoke into the sound vacuum. "It's not as easy a decision as you make it out to be, Torres; no human—indeed, no single life-form—has ever killed on the scale we're so casually discussing. Never on any planet in the quadrant."

"We've never faced conquest and enslavement on such a huge scale, either!"

"But *do we have the right* to kill twenty-seven billion . . . even to save ourselves from being enslaved?"

Janeway frowned. The ready room seemed unnaturally dark, as if she were back on the Fury planet. *Dammit, I have to make this decision rationally—not on the basis of my own genetic horror!*

"People, people!" interjected Neelix. At the urgency in his voice, the half-heard, whispered conversations ceased. "I believe Kes has a point to offer."

"Have you considered," she said in a small voice, "that many billions of the dead will be innocent children who have nothing whatsoever to do with the feud?"

Captain Janeway began to fret; she had her own opinion on the subject—a critic might say her own agenda—but she was not a Cardassian captain and could not simply impose her will on such a terrible issue. Definitely not if she were a "majority of one."

But Chakotay and especially Kes were beginning to have an impact on everyone's mood. Janeway turned to Tuvok, but the Vulcan maintained an enigmatic silence, arms folded.

Neelix lovingly put his arm around his beloved's shoulders. "I agree with Kes. How can you even contemplate killing twenty-seven billion people? I can't even imagine such murder on my conscience, no matter what the provocation!"

Tom Paris offered his thoughts, sounding far more sympathetic and reasonable than the captain would have expected of him. "I understand what Kes and Commander Chakotay are saying. It's a horrific thing to think about, killing more people than have ever lived on Earth. But . . ."

He paused; real pain flickered across his face, memories of Maquis friends he had seen killed in his first and only raid. A friend he might have helped kill—somewhere else. *Bad decisions, an overactive conscience,* thought the captain.

Paris continued. "But as huge as the number of Fury dead would be, it's still smaller than the number they would enslave and eventually murder—if not their physical bodies, at least their spirits. The sympathy shouldn't be all so one-sided, that's all I'm saying."

Good words; Janeway nodded and turned to Ensign Kim, one member of the discussion who hadn't yet discussed anything. "We're contemplating a deed, Mr. Kim, that will either save the soul of every person of every race in the Alpha Quadrant, or will be the most staggering act of genocide ever committed in the galaxy, at least that we know of. You must have an opinion, Ensign."

Kim took a deep breath. "My people have a, uh, long history dealing with this sort of thing, on both sides. I've always wondered whether I would risk my life to escape from slavery. I think I would. I'd be scared, but I could overcome that fear, because I'm an intelligent being."

He paused. Janeway nodded again, encouraging him to continue.

"But what if my fear was artificially magnified so enormously that I biologically *could not* overcome it? That's so much more horrible than—I know this sounds weird— mere slavery or mere murder that I think . . . I think *anything* we do to stop it is right."

"Lieutenant Torres," said the captain. "I want to hear from you, too."

"Kim spoke for me," she snarled.

She's in full Klingon mode, thought Janeway. Now the tone was making her uncomfortable in the other direction—all thought of the innocent victims they might be about to kill vanished in the passion of resisting the oppressor. "I want you to speak for yourself."

"Fine. Captain, I am so terrified of these Furies, I can hardly think straight, like an engineer . . . I saw that moon, saw the power they're so casually tossing around. Sir, they may not have transporters and shields, but they're centuries ahead of us in power manipulation."

Janeway sat back, surprised; B'Elanna's anger came from her human engineer side, not her Klingon warrior side!

She continued. "Not to mention creating and exploiting artificial wormholes, which we don't have even the faintest idea how to do! Captain, what the hell makes us think we even *can* beat these guys and destroy their moon? I think it's more likely to be another Narendra Three. We'll die valiantly; big deal. They'll still jump through and enslave us all."

"Activate EMH program," said Janeway.

"Please state the nature of the emergency," said the doctor, appearing on the screen in the middle of the table. He looked around in surprise. "Again? Are these conferences to become a regular feature?"

Paris could not contain himself. "You're kidding! The fate of the human race depends on the opinion of a *hologram?*

Janeway was angry, and she let Paris have it with all phaser banks. "You've had your say, Mr. Paris. Now be quiet, unless you wish to be stripped of your rank and confined in the brig for the next six months."

"Captain, I apologize. Why bother asking? The hologram is programmed to be a doctor; we already know which way it will vote."

"This is not a vote, Mr. Paris; I will make the final decision."

She returned attention to the screen. "There is an emergency, Doctor, and I need your advice." Crisply, she outlined the two possibilities. "I must have the input of every senior staff member, and that includes my chief medical officer—even a holographic one."

The doctor's face softened; he actually looked touched. Not for the first time, Janeway wondered whether a hologram generated by biologically based circuitry might not very well qualify for consciousness, an actual life-form.

"I'm grateful you asked me. Surprised, but grateful. My position is clear: Destroy the moon."

"What?" demanded Kes. The rest of the crew except Tuvok registered astonishment; even the normally implacable Chakotay's mouth parted in surprise.

"I take it you disagree with me, Kes," said the doctor. "I know why . . . your people live only nine years, and forgive me for being somewhat brusque—it's my programming—but you were virtual pets of the Caretaker. You don't have a realistic idea of what it means to be a free person . . . and responsible for yourself."

Chakotay spoke sardonically. "And you do understand being a free person?"

"Yes. I think I do. I know what I want, and I understand that gap between my want and the physical reality. I don't know if I'm a person . . . I *feel* like one, but maybe that's just more programming.

"But I know what just such a small change as—as giving me the power to turn myself on and off has done for me. I know how I would feel if you took that away from me tomorrow."

Janeway followed the exchange avidly. Certainly, no one would ever say all sides hadn't been considered.

"But you're a doctor!" cried Kes. "How can you say . . . whatever happened to the Hippocratic oath you taught me? Above all else, first do no harm. You're talking about murder!"

"No, Kes. I'm talking about *triage.*"

"Triage?" She fell silent, stumped.

Janeway smiled; she understood at last . . . and understood how to articulate and justify her decision. Triage was a concept as well known to commanders as to doctors.

"Sometimes," the doctor explained, "sometimes we have to let one person die so that others can live. Like in ancient human wars, where there weren't enough doctors or operating tables to save all the soldiers . . . so the ones whose medical care would take hours were allowed to die so that instead, the doctors could save three or four other people with different injuries."

"You're not letting them die. You're killing them!"

"No!" insisted Kim, evidently finding the elusive point he had sought many minutes before. "We didn't start the sun going supernova; that was the Furies themselves. They wanted the energy—they set the collapse in motion. All we're doing is stopping them from *using* that collapse to invade the Alpha Quadrant!"

"It's the same thing. You're not just stopping the invasion. You're stopping them from escaping their sun going supernova . . . and they'll all die, each one of them."

"First, do no harm," said the doctor quietly. "Can we

even measure how much harm is done by slavery and the living hell of the terror projector?"

Janeway turned to Tuvok; still, the lieutenant and her closest confidant said nothing. She shook her head, angry and confused. "I said this wasn't a vote. Too bad: for the action, we have Paris, Kim, Torres, and the doctor; against, we have Neelix, Kes, and Chakotay . . . we would have a majority and a decision." She glanced at Tuvok. "With one abstention.

"But the decision is ultimately my responsibility, and I will be the one to make it. Alone. I wanted your input; but I'm not simply going to count noses. I'm going back to my quarters and make my decision."

"We don't have much time," said B'Elanna quietly.

"I know how much time we have," said the captain, a bit too harshly. "Thank you for reminding me; I'll make my decision quickly."

Janeway turned and exited. She passed through the bridge to her quarters, sat behind her desk, behind the unreviewed stack of reports, duty rosters, petty complaints, projections, and performance evaluations, and rubbed her throbbing temples. *They'll call me Bloody Kate the Executioner,* she thought. She was under no delusion that they could ever fully explain the tale of what happened here, not once they finally made it back to the Federation. And she had no doubt they would find a way back before seventy years had passed.

Or perhaps this is it, she suddenly realized. She opened her eyes, astonished no one had even mentioned it.

They were looking at a system to project an entire planet all the way to the Alpha Quadrant in one jump!

Maybe the *Voyager* could just . . . piggyback?

And then what? This small ship's crew were not going to be able to stop twenty-seven billion! They would be killed, and the invasion would proceed apace.

Unless . . . was there a way to stop the Furies from passing through the wormhole, yet slip through themselves?

It was a thought. It wanted exploring . . . soon. But not immediately: her immediate concern, as Torres had pointed out, was to decide within just a few minutes whether they were going to destroy the moon, dooming the Furies, including the children, to fiery cremation, or maybe try to send a subspace message of warning through the same wormhole, letting the Federation know—that it was about to be overwhelmed and destroyed, and all its citizens, and the Klingons, Romulans, and Cardassians, would henceforth be slaves to demons from hell.

Her door chimed. She felt suddenly nervous without any good reason to be. If there were an emergency, Chakotay would have called her on the comm link. But who else would disturb her at this moment, and why?

The door chimed again. "Enter," snapped Captain Kathryn Janeway, in command of herself again after a momentary self-mutiny.

CHAPTER 16

Tuvok entered, hands behind his back. He waited politely; Janeway waited impatiently; both waited for somebody to say something. *Vulcans have the greater patience,* he thought serenely.

The captain cracked first. Of course. "All right, spill it."

"You are using the idiom meaning to reveal one's information."

"When a Vulcan gets pedantic about human expressions, it means he has something to say, and he's uncertain how to say it."

Tuvok stalled, trying mentally to articulate what he had to say in a way that a human could understand it. "An astute observation about my race. What I have to say may seem peculiar, coming from a Vulcan. But there are some things worse than dying, and the Furies promise just such things."

"Living in slavery?"

"No, Captain; that is not worse than dying. A normal slave may dream about being free someday, and may even plot an escape. Ensign Kim has a cogent point here. He drew a distinction between merely being held against one's will by threat of death, and having one's mind biologically altered to make one less than a person, an animal."

"Go on."

Did she not yet understand the special threat the Furies represented to a Vulcan? "For the Furies to return to Vulcan and make my people again what they once were, before Surak, would be far worse than merely destroying us en masse. We would be alive; but we would no longer be Vulcan. And worse—we would have the memory of what once was and never could be again."

"All right. Point taken. It doesn't make the decision any easier."

"I did not expect it would. I did not come here to explain Ensign Kim."

"You came to . . . ?"

"To remind you of your duty. Captain, you took an oath when you joined Starfleet, as did we all. You swore to uphold, among other things, the ideals of the United Federation of Planets; to defend it against all enemies, external and internal; to guard the freedom of its citizens."

"The people who wrote that oath never contemplated killing twenty-seven billion life-forms, including billions of innocent children, to carry out that oath."

Tuvok nodded; he turned to contemplate a new sculpture from Aton-77 the captain had replicated; it must have cost her many days of replicator credits.

"Nevertheless, the oath was written, and you freely offered, in the words of another great document, your life, your fortune, and your sacred honor. You cannot turn your back on that oath now. Not even in the face of killing billions of innocent children."

Janeway abruptly slammed her hands down on the desk, angry and frustrated . . . more human emotions getting in the way of rationality. Tuvok did not turn around; he did not want to see her like that.

"Mr. Tuvok! Do you imagine I don't remember that oath?"

"No. I know that you do. I do not believe you are taking it seriously enough."

"An oath! What's more important, the words, or the *ideals* the words were intended to protect?"

Tuvok said nothing, but he turned around. He had never seen Captain Janeway so racked by self-doubt, so tortured by indecision. He wished he had a magic answer that would make her see what she had to do; but that was irrational.

"The reason we don't go around wiping out races we think are evil, Mr. Tuvok, is not because we're such goody-goodies that we can't imagine fighting and killing. We've fought almost everyone in the damned Alpha Quadrant, at one time or another. It's because *we're not gods*. We don't know what would happen if we started on some great jihad to destroy evil . . . we could end up destroying ourselves!"

"That is a risk we sometimes must be prepared to assume."

Janeway sat slowly, leaning back in her chair and staring up at the overhead. "And if we have to destroy the village in order to save it, was it really worth saving in the first place?"

"If it was worth creating, it is worth preserving. Even at the cost of billions of innocent lives—if that is the only way."

"Tuvok, do you hear what you're *saying?*"

"I am in full possession of my faculties. You do not wish to do this because you do not want the guilt. But your clear duty requires you to take this guilt upon your head. That is the price you must pay—we all must pay—for the freedom we have enjoyed."

"Tuvok, you remember, via your DNA, horrors so traumatic you cannot even contemplate them. I reacted with terror as well . . . but I didn't remember anything in particular about that time. Maybe only the Ok'San were as bad as you recall; maybe only Vulcan suffered like that."

"Perhaps. The suggestion is illogical and unsupported, but possible." He leaned close to the sculpture. *Water*, it was called: a straight column of thin graphite with a hairline blue crack.

"And in any case," continued the captain, "it was thousands of years ago! Who's to say the Furies haven't changed some? Navdaq didn't seem to represent ultimate evil, even if he did throw us in jail. He might just be a petty tyrant. The galaxy is full of them."

Oddly, the sculpture, *Water,* soothed his eyes. "He might. But the evidence we do have indicates that the Furies conquered the Alpha Quadrant once before, were driven off by aliens who no longer exist, and are now planning to return."

"But we don't *know* that they're really going to attack us . . . I agree, it's likely, but not certain."

"If we cannot state for certain they will rule as demons, so to speak, we also cannot say they will not . . . and the odds favor repetition." Tuvok turned his full Vulcan attention to Captain Janeway. "Duty dictates that we cannot take that chance."

Janeway said nothing; Tuvok forbore pressing his case—he saw that she was deep in thought, and she might well be arguing the case better than he could.

She leaned back in her chair, massaging her temples. "Perhaps the doctor could alleviate that pain," suggested Tuvok, more to remind her that he was still there than to tell her anything she did not already know.

"I don't want him to. It's my pain, and I'm going to keep it."

What a peculiar thing to say . . . but so stubbornly human. "If the Furies conquer our quadrant, you will not have even that freedom."

She opened her eyes. "I've decided we're going to destroy the moon. But it's not because of any of your arguments."

"Indeed?"

"It's the argument you didn't make that decided me . . . this vessel, the *Voyager,* is the first and last defense on this side of the wormhole. We're alone—and we're either a projection of Starfleet into the Delta Quadrant, or else we're nothing but just one more ship caught far, far from home.

"And sometimes, my friend . . ." Janeway paused; she stared to the side, as if her mind had wandered from the point. Tuvok refrained from interrupting; *she is listening to a voice humans have, a voice beyond reason, that nevertheless speaks truly to them.* It was that voice the Vulcan hoped someday to understand, to explain, to map.

"Sometimes, my friend, survival takes precedence over everything," she concluded. "I hate it like hell—but sometimes, you just have to shoot the SOB and rationalize it all later." She looked directly at Tuvok with a penetrating stare.

"Tuvok, I asked myself, if not us, who? If not now, when? It sounds terribly trite, I know. But that's how trite things get that way . . . by being true." She touched her commbadge. "Janeway to Commander Chakotay."

"Chakotay," responded the commander's voice from everywhere and nowhere.

"Tell the senior crew we're doing it."

"I am not surprised. Have you figured out how?"

She rose and stared at *Water,* frowning. She turned the blue crack toward the wall, ruining the composition, for the sculpture had a jagged red line along the backside. "No; I'll get back to you. Have Torres and Carey meet me in engineering in five minutes. Janeway out."

"Thank you, Captain," said Tuvok.

"I didn't do it for you, Tuvok."

"Thank you for that, too."

The Vulcan waited until Janeway realized he was done. Then she dismissed him, contemplatively. He ghosted out in silence, thankful he never had to stoop to the argument by which she finally persuaded herself.

Captain Janeway rose and headed for the engineering deck. They had a scant few minutes to design a bomb powerful enough to destroy an entire artificial moon, and she had no idea at all how to proceed.

But Carey and Torres were not in engineering. Janeway waited for a moment, then asked the computer to locate the errant pair. "Lieutenant Torres and Lieutenant Carey are in holodeck two," said the impersonal voice.

Janeway's curiosity—what could they be doing on the holodeck?—was satisfied the moment she entered. Carey had set up a scale model of the moon, using all the data they had gathered. Far away, barely visible on the scale, was a representation of the Fury planet.

The sun was represented by a sharp, bright star far in the

distance. The two engineers eerily floated in the empty reaches, like gods.

"Captain!" cried Torres, sounding ecstatic and worried at the same time. "Commander Chakotay just told us of your decision."

"The decision is made. Now tell me how we're going to do it."

Carey frowned; this was one of his fortes. "We're here, behind the sun," he announced. A tiny dot flickered red and green, so far away it was hard to see. "Here's the first scenario we considered."

The dot broke orbit, swooped around the sun, and dove toward the moon. As it approached, the moon began to flash red, like an angry red-alert indicator.

"We checked the records and figured out the distance at which the moon alerts the Furies," said Carey in a quick aside.

The *Voyager* continued to close as an intercept fleet launched from the planet. *Voyager* barely had time to launch a single spread of photon torpedoes and fire phasers at the moon on the first pass before it was engaged by six Fury ships. The captain frowned.

The *Voyager* ignored the gnatlike ships, firing another spread . . . but then *Voyager* turned bright white, hurting Janeway's dark-adapted eyes. *What the hell—?*

"Terror projector," said Carey. "The end."

"That reminds me—I never did hear Chakotay's theory why they didn't shoot the *Voyager* with the unholy terrors when you fought them. He seemed about to tell us when Redbay interrupted."

"In my opinion, Captain, they had no idea at first where we were from . . . and the ships they sent up simply didn't have terror projectors installed."

Torres spoke up. "We had to make an educated guess when they would fire their projectors. Now that they know where we're from, we figure they'll equip their ships with the devices."

"The range, spread, and speed of transmission are unknown," added Carey.

"When the ship flares," concluded B'Elanna, "it means we've been hit by the projector and we're—slaves of hell."

"But what about the moon?" asked the captain. She stared at the holographic projection; it looked remarkably intact.

"Well," said Carey, "that's what we found. According to the computer, even hitting the external hull with thirteen photon torpedoes and several direct phaser blasts would not penetrate the armor plating, which ranges between three-point-two and four kilometers thick."

"Between three and four *kilometers?*" Janeway was daunted; for a moment, she stepped back, despairing of being able to do a thing against the Furies.

"It was built to withstand the energy of a supernova for several seconds, for heaven's sake."

Janeway sighed. "All right, let's see some other scenarios."

Voyager loped closer to the moon, and the alarm bell went off. Ships uplifted from the planet surface, while *Voyager* expelled an experimental photon torpedo, flying as a "remotely piloted vehicle."

The ship was quickly sprayed with the terror-projection weapon, driving the crew to a madness of fear . . . but the photon torpedo escaped, racing into the long shaft that Kim and Paris had found!

Closer and closer it drove to the antenna . . . a Fury ship gave chase, flying down the same shaft; it fired round after round, using a special, wide-spread, disruptor-like weapon that would not significantly damage the antenna if it missed the torpedo.

The torpedo was never meant to sustain repeated damage. It was not a ship. It exploded harmlessly, the contained antimatter expanding outward to explosively interact with the shaft walls, "scraping" off a few centimeters of ablative material that would have burned away in milliseconds anyway when the sun went supernova.

The mission failed—and the Furies completed their jump.

Voyager loped toward the moon. Again, as the swarm of Fury ships leapt upward, Janeway launched a photon-torpedo RPV; but this time, the torpedo had been fitted with a single-use shield system.

It dropped down the shaft, heading toward rendezvous with the radiation-collection antenna... the Fury ship followed, frantically firing at the torpedo—but this time, the shots were absorbed by the shield.

The probe closed on the antenna as *Voyager* flared white and vanished in an explosion of mind-shredding horror. Closer, the Fury ship accelerated to ramming speed and—

Voyager loped toward the moon.

The RPV was faster this time and equipped with auto-tracking phasers pointing backward.

The Fury ship accelerated to ramming speed... but as it closed, the torpedo itself opened fire!

The power phaser beam held the Fury ship at bay as the photon torpedo crossed the last gap. It struck the antenna at 17,500 kilometers per second, simultaneously detonating its matter-antimatter compression bomb.

The explosion was terrible to behold. The Fury ship only added to it when it ploughed into the expanding sphere of electromagnetic radiation and blew apart itself.

The detonation was so intense, it blew a *Voyager*-sized hole in the thirty-square-kilometer surface area of the antenna... destroying slightly more than 0.003 percent of its collection surface.

The mission failed.

"This isn't getting us anywhere," said Janeway, testily. "Wait—how about sending a shuttle up the shaft and transporting a photon torpedo inside the hull?"

Carey pondered for a moment, then programmed the computer.

Voyager loped toward the moon, setting off the alarm when it got close enough. Just before the Fury ships arrived, the launch-bay doors opened and a shuttle squirted out, accelerating to maximum impulse while still in the hangar.

It bolted toward the shaft, two Fury ships in hot pursuit, and sallied down the rabbit hole, aft shields guarding it from the Furies' disruptors. As the shuttlecraft neared the antenna, successfully deflecting the energy weapons, the Furies began to bathe it with the terror-projector beam.

The shuttlecraft glowed white-hot, and—

The *unmanned* shuttlecraft bolted toward the shaft, two Fury ships in hot pursuit, and sallied down the rabbit hole. As it neared the antenna, the Furies, in a last, desperate gamble, accelerated their ships to ramming speed.

But just before contact, a phaser beam lanced out of the rear of the shuttlecraft, sending one ship careering into the other. The blinding explosion would have obliterated the shuttlecraft as well, were it not for the shields already up, protecting the aft quarter.

Limping, the shuttlecraft approached and veered around the antenna, finding the "soft spot" that Paris and Kim had identified earlier, where the hull was thin enough to permit beaming.

The ship reversed thrust, braking to a quick halt. The torpedo, already strapped down on the transporter pad, was beamed aboard the moon directly to the huge room that Ensign Kim had recorded.

Within seconds, the torpedo detonated, and—

The holodeck simulation froze. Ghostly letters hung in the air, flashing over and over: EFFECT UNKNOWN, EFFECT UNKNOWN.

Captain Janeway stared at the letters floating like the voice of Fate, mocking them. For two minutes, she pondered.

"Carey, Torres," she said at last, "that's just not good enough. 'Effect unknown' is simply too vague to pin the life or death of freedom in the Alpha Quadrant on."

"We have one more scenario," said Torres.

"She has one more scenario," corrected Lieutenant Carey, glaring at the deck.

B'Elanna gave him a hard look. "Computer, activate simulation z-nine." She turned to Janeway. "I haven't run this one yet. Don't know what will happen."

Voyager loped toward the moon . . . but as the swarm of Fury ships tore away from their home planet on an interdiction course, the Federation starship aligned itself with the shaft—and accelerated to warp 9.9, the theoretical maximum that *Voyager* was capable of attaining. At that speed, the engines would automatically shut down in ten minutes.

It did not matter; a single minute was eternity cubed, for the ship would impact with the moon in four hundred nanoseconds.

Instantly, the simulation froze, ticking forward at a rate of ten nanoseconds per second. Janeway saw her ship jump forward jerkily as it accelerated. The initial impact with the shaft was uneventful: the ship was too wide for the shaft, but at first, it was the shaft that gave way; *Voyager* carved a pair of furrows down the rabbit hole where the saucer section impacted, like hot skates across an ice rink.

Then, over the space of a couple of frames, the edges of the ship vaporized. The energy released imploded laterally toward the center of the ship, causing the hull to buckle, then shred.

Janeway felt no emotion, though she watched a simulation of the death of everybody aboard her ship; as visceral as the thought was, it was still too surreal for her to feel it.

The ship might have shredded, but the shards were still moving in a warp field some three thousand times the speed of light. They continued forward, of course; where else could they go? Certainly nothing known in the universe could *deflect* shrapnel moving at such a speed, impossible under normal physics.

But that very point worked against them—for if nothing could deflect such hypervelocity shrapnel, *neither could anything absorb such energy* . . . and if what you want to do is create the biggest bomb ever seen, the target must *absorb* the energy. Otherwise, it just . . .

Voyager punched a *Voyager*-sized hole through the antenna, continued along the moon's axis—creating its own *Voyager*-sized and -shaped shaft—and out the other side. In one second, Janeway knew, the remains of the ship and crew would be a billion kilometers away, no further threat to the Furies or anyone else.

When *Voyager* passed through the antenna, it destroyed slightly more than 0.003 percent of the collection surface . . . about as much as had the single photon torpedo.

"I told you," said Lieutenant Carey pettishly. "I'm not afraid to die; I just knew it would be a useless, futile gesture."

The captain silently pounded her thigh in frustration. "What if we go slower? Will the antenna absorb more of the impact energy?"

B'Elanna glared at the holodeck simulation. "To force the antenna to absorb sufficient energy to blow it up," she growled at last, "we would have to approach no faster than zero-point-six times light speed . . . which is impossible: it's three times faster than full impulse, but much less than warp one."

"And warp one . . . ?"

"Is too fast. At maximum impulse, we *might* destroy a significant fraction of the antenna's surface—maybe thirty percent."

"That could be enough," mused Janeway; "it's certainly the best option I've seen so far."

"You're forgetting one little factor," said Carey from his corner. "At impulse power, we won't be able to get all the way along the shaft before the Furies come in after us . . . and as soon as we're in line of sight . . ."

"They fire the terror projector at us," finished Janeway.

"And then command us to stop, turn around, and exit the shaft. Checkmate."

"Dammit!" shouted the captain, startling everyone, most especially including herself. "You two—I want options! I want them now, or . . . or I'll transfer you both to maintenance detail. As a team!"

Furious most especially at the lack of a target for her fury, Kathryn Janeway stormed out of the holodeck toward nowhere in particular.

CHAPTER 17

As she stalked angrily, blindly down a passageway, Janeway's arm was suddenly yanked, whirling her around. She snapped into a defensive posture, hands raised, ready to put the assailant on the deck with a heel-hand or a snap-kick to the kneecap.

Commander Chakotay retreated gracefully out of range.

"Are you back from the land of spirits?" he asked.

"What the hell are you talking about? What do you mean by jerking my arm like that?"

"I had to get your attention somehow."

"Why didn't you just try saying, 'Excuse me, Captain?'"

"Excuse me, Captain . . ."

Janeway felt her face flush. "Oh. Sorry; I was . . . thinking."

"That much was obvious."

"Chakotay, we're absolutely stuck here! We—Torres and Carey and I—just cannot come up with a way to destroy that moon; either we can't generate enough energy, or if we can, we can't get the machinery to absorb enough of it to fry itself."

Chakotay shrugged. "Too bad we can't unleash you on it hand-to-hand. That's an interesting style of fighting; I don't recall that from the Academy."

"Stop trying to distract me. I *like* brooding." Janeway leaned against a bulkhead, at ease in the presence of the man who once was her prey and was now her executive officer.

The commander smiled. "I like new styles of self-defense. Got a name?"

"Just something based on ancient Japanese judo; my father taught me years ago. You turn the enemy's own power against himself. Well, that's the idea, in any case; usually, I just get him off balance and rabbit-punch him." Despite Janeway's determination not to be distracted from her brooding distraction, she began to thaw.

"We should spar sometime. I would like to see what it feels like to have my own power turned against me. Say," he continued, struck by a thought, "too bad you can't use that judo stuff on the moon—turn its own power against it. Can you?"

Janeway raised her eyebrows. "You know, that's not a bad suggestion, especially coming from the engineering impaired."

"Captain!"

"Oh, you know what I mean. I can't see exactly how we can do it, but dammit, it's something to try, at least."

She turned to the bulkhead and pushed against it, almost like isometrics: she closed her eyes, letting the thoughts form their own images. She wanted the image of a great force, a tremendous force—the Fury supernova—being turned against itself to trip and fall. She felt the weight of the *Voyager* pressing all around her, but that wasn't enough of a force.

"Well," Chakotay said, "this engineering-impaired commander came up with another idea. I've been talking to Lieutenant Redbay about the terror-projector weapon."

"Does he remember anything?"

"Enough to convince me that if we could jigger the shields somehow to make them kind of wedge-shaped, like this . . ." Chakotay pressed his fingertips together and held his stiff arms and hands forward like the prow of an old-fashioned water ship. "We might be able to deflect the beam just long enough to dodge to the left or right and avoid it."

Janeway smiled. "More martial arts?"

"It's something to try, at least. Unfortunately, I haven't the faintest idea how to make the shields buckle like that." She visualized the shields, not as physical objects in Einsteinian space, which they technically weren't, but as vectors in phase space—the way they were *meant* to be visualized.

"They're designed to do just the opposite; a direct hit by a phaser or disruptor right on the seam would probably blow the shields away, and even a glancing blow would leak through and damage the ship if you monkeyed with the shield geometry."

Chakotay rubbed his chin. "Captain, the Fury disruptors were powerful, but we could probably survive a couple of direct hits. Certainly a lot better than we could survive a single hit by the terror weapon."

"I know," said Janeway, dropping her gaze. "I don't think it will matter, Chakotay, whether *Voyager* takes a few hits or a dozen. Commander, nobody gets out of here alive."

"We just need to survive long enough to destroy the moon," said Chakotay, completing Janeway's thought.

She opened her eyes and looked up at him. "Take Carey; I can't spare Torres. Besides, Carey has studied our biotech shield systems more than Torres has . . . possibly because Klingons think shields are for cowards." She smiled; Chakotay kept his face impassive.

"And take Tuvok, too. He knows the basic science better; Carey might tell you it's impossible, and it will be critical to have Tuvok backing us up."

"Thank you, Captain; and good luck."

The two parted in three different directions: Chakotay to engineering by way of Tuvok's quarters; Janeway to the bridge; and the captain's dark storm clouds back over the horizon. Having a clear goal for a change performed a miracle on her disposition.

* * *

Commander Chakotay discovered that his first obstacle was to convince *Tuvok* that the shield-wedge idea was possible; far from backing up Chakotay, the lieutenant insisted that the shields could not possibly be bent into such a strange geometry.

He stood in the Vulcan's quarters, quietly admiring the simplicity of decoration: no flashy, splashy prints on the walls or nonfunctional knickknacks cluttering up the work surfaces. Vulcans were Spartan in taste compared to most humans.

Chakotay listened patiently into the third minute of a basic science lecture before finally interrupting. "I don't want to speak before my turn," he said, "but we don't have much time, Lieutenant. I understand you believe the shield-wedge is impossible. But I don't want you to say that to Lieutenant Carey."

Tuvok frowned; he, too, stood, out of polite respect for Chakotay's rank. "Vulcans are not prone to lying."

"Then creatively avoid the truth."

"We do not dissemble."

Huh, you did a great dissembling job to me *when I was a Maquis and you were a Federation spy!* "Then don't, Mr. Tuvok; bore him to death with such a detailed analysis that he tunes out before you get to the part where you say it can't be done."

They stood staring at each other, dueling with utmost politeness; the commander wished Tuvok would sit, so they could converse without such stiff formality.

"You want me to be overly detailed and pedantic?"

"Yes."

"That, Commander, I can do with no trouble."

Chakotay bit off the smart remark that formed in his throat. He and the Vulcan left Tuvok's quarters and wandered down to the engineering deck, where they found Carey sitting slumped before the huge, curved console, B'Elanna Torres having already been summoned to the bridge. The lieutenant was tapping so diligently at a keypad, he didn't even notice their arrival until Chakotay cleared his throat, causing Carey to jump guiltily.

"No," said Chakotay patiently several minutes later, still

trying to explain to Carey, "a *wedge:* two flat planes meeting at about a forty-five-degree angle."

Carey shook his head, befuddled. "But . . . that's impossible, sir! Didn't you ask Tuvok? I'm sure he told you it can't be done." Carey gestured emphatically at the Vulcan, who did not react in any way. After a moment, Carey nervously dropped his hand.

"Tuvok?" asked Chakotay, turning to the lieutenant; Chakotay invoked his spirit guide to lead the stubborn Vulcan to back his commander. *Show time!*

Tuvok looked down at Carey as if noticing him for the first time. "Actually, Mr. Carey, the problem is not so glib or obvious as you might at first suppose."

"Isn't it? You can't make the shields bend in the middle!"

"Have you researched Admiral Anton Wilson's seminal work, 'Shield Geometry as a Function of Differentiable Manifold Dynamics'?" The Vulcan raised one eyebrow. *Beautiful!* thought Chakotay.

"Not exactly," hedged Carey; "I read the abstract. It said you can't have a shield with a discontinuous derivative . . . like a bend. Didn't it?"

"Reading the abstract is not exactly the same as reading the article itself. You depend upon the person who wrote the abstract understanding nuances and finding them important enough to discuss. I strongly advise you to read the article itself; I think you will find it illuminating—and very apropos our present difficulty." Commander Chakotay barely suppressed a smile; Tuvok was a natural at saying everything by saying nothing.

Carey nodded, his lips moving silently. "Oh, thanks, Lieutenant. I'll start reading it immediately. You really think there's something in there telling how to put a *bend* in the shields?"

"If it is not found there," declared Tuvok with finality, "it is not found anywhere."

Leaving Carey to his task, Chakotay grabbed Tuvok's arm and beetled rapidly away before the Vulcan could slip up and answer directly—and truthfully.

They paused in the passageway beyond earshot. "There, that wasn't so hard, was it?"

Tuvok frowned. "I cannot help but think I have conveyed an untruth somewhere in the exchange, though I confess I cannot find a single statement of mine that is technically false."

"Yes . . . but suppose Carey actually figures it out? Then that makes your whole part in the conversation retroactively truthful."

Tuvok raised the other eyebrow, the intragalactic Vulcan facial gesture. "I do not anticipate that the laws of physics will change to suit my present needs."

"You're too cynical," said Chakotay. "I always try to believe six impossible things before breakfast, as the Red Queen said to Alice."

"Is that reference part of the ancient lore of your people?"

"In a manner of speaking." *Yes, if "my people" includes Lewis Carroll,* thought Chakotay, amused but impassive.

"Perhaps I should return and help Lieutenant Carey," suggested the Vulcan, glancing back toward the engineering-deck door.

"Perhaps you'd better not," said Chakotay, thinking of Tuvok and his guilty conscience, which as a Vulcan he would never admit to having, but which might drive him nonetheless to confess his deception.

"As you wish, sir."

"You're more urgently needed helping B'Elanna and the captain figure out how to make the radiation collector blow itself up. I think they're on the holodeck." Tuvok left in search of his commanding officer, and Chakotay breathed a sigh of relief . . . but kept his fingers crossed. Ancient lore of his people.

Captain Janeway and Lieutenant Torres were engaged in a staring contest with a holodeck mockup of the cabling Kim and Paris had seen inside the moon; Tuvok joined them, opening a door in thin air and walking across the invisible platform on which they all stood. The mockup mocked them from half a kilometer below their feet—the distance at which Kim had recorded the scene in the first place.

Janeway was trying to get B'Elanna to hazard an estimate of what they could destroy to wreck the mechanism. "Be the ghost in the machine," urged the captain, hoping Torres could see something that so far eluded Janeway herself.

"It's just . . . this is ridiculous! Captain, we don't know what these cables do. We're just guessing!"

"Torres, guesses are all we have now." Janeway looked up to see the Vulcan impassively observing the inactivity. "Oh. Hello, Tuvok. Torres, all we need is a reasonably clear picture in our heads of the *sort* of connections to look for; we'll have to figure out the exact match on the moon itself."

"No. No way. I can't—it's impossible!"

"Commander Chakotay," announced Tuvok, "was taught to believe six impossible things before breakfast."

Janeway turned, nonplussed by the unexpected reference. "Yes," she said, "as the Red Queen said."

"But I'm not Alice, and this isn't the looking-glass!" snapped B'Elanna.

Tuvok looked perplexed. "I must make a mental note to research the original source legends; it is a powerful mythos that holds sway alike over Native American tribes, human Anglo-Saxons, and Klingons."

Janeway turned back to B'Elanna Torres, exasperated— at herself more than the engineer. "Just try! Try anything, Lieutenant."

"No, there's nothing I can . . ." B'Elanna's voice trailed off as she stared downward. "This is really weird."

"What? What's weird?"

"Captain—suddenly, it all makes sense! I can *feel* how the power flow goes . . . I can feel it! Look, that—that cable bundle is the feedback control . . . it's got to be! That tells the rest of the circuitry when a particular socket is stuffed and the energy needs to redirect itself. And . . . !"

B'Elanna fell silent, moving her hands in a complex, magical ritual that mapped the energy flow in her head.

"Kahless the Unforgettable!" muttered B'Elanna Torres. Janeway was surprised—*she almost never uses Klingon expressions.*

"What? What did you find?"

"Captain . . ." B'Elanna stared up at Janeway, mouth

open, eyes wide. "Captain, we can do it . . . we can reroute the energy flow and *blow up the whole moon!*"

"Are you sure?" Janeway held her breath; she had been disappointed once too often on this mission to leap for joy.

"Logically? No." Torres licked her lips like a starving wolf eyeing a roast. "But I can *feel* it this time. This time, I think we've got a winner."

"What is it? Tell me the plan; we'd better both know, in case something happens."

But Torres shook her head, frustrated. "That's just it, Captain. I can't tell you; it's somewhere inside here—" She indicated her skull. "—but I can't pull it out and put it into words. Yet. I'll . . . just have to do it myself."

Janeway nodded. "You lead the away team," she said. "You'll find I can take excellent direction." She started to rise to prepare for the trip; but Tuvok gently put his hand on her shoulder and quietly cleared his throat.

"Captain, I do not think your participation is a good idea."

"Why? What do you mean?"

"You are more urgently needed on the ship. Commander Chakotay is an excellent executive officer. But he simply does not know starships, and in particular *this* starship, as well as you."

"So? He also isn't a trained engineer, and I am."

"I would not suggest Commander Chakotay accompany Lieutenant Torres. She needs a first-rate pilot, a person who can fly a ship as big as the shuttlecraft through that narrow shaft with the expectation that it will arrive in one piece."

Janeway glanced at B'Elanna; the engineer turned her face back down to the holoprojection. Pulsing lights from the monstrous engine five hundred meters "below" them colored her face blue, red, then yellow; but it remained shadowed in mystery. Janeway could not tell what B'Elanna was thinking.

"I see what you're driving at, Mr. Tuvok; but I can't spare Tom Paris, not even for this mission. I need him flying *this* ship."

"I did not have Mr. Paris in mind, said Tuvok. "In fact, was thinking of our recent guest."

"Redbay?" Both engineers turned, stunned.

"I have examined that part of his record which was transmitted to *Voyager* via routine message traffic before the Caretaker transported us to this quadrant. I am convinced that Mr. Redbay can almost certainly pilot the vessel better than any other member of this crew, including Mr. Paris."

"Don't tell Paris."

"Yes, emotional beings do not like to be reminded that there are others better than they at their chosen professions."

B'Elanna opened and shut her mouth like a fish. She muttered something unintelligible—Janeway caught only the words "basket case" and wisely chose not to hear the rest.

"Find Lieutenant Redbay," she ordered, cutting off any protest from B'Elanna. "Torres, gather what you need and return to the shuttlebay by 0430."

When they had left, Janeway stared down between her feet at the holodeck simulation of what little they knew of the moon's circuitry. Something was there . . . she could feel it, taste it—but she could not quite put it into words. Kathryn Janeway would not be satisfied until she could write an instruction set, at least in her head, for creating a feedback loop.

Neelix hovered outside the infirmary, rocking from one foot to the other, wondering how he was going to say to Kes what he needed to say without mortally offending her . . . or worse, making her *reevaluate their relationship.*

He straightened his waistcoat, smoothed his hair back, took a deep breath—repeated twice—and strode purposefully toward the door.

As the door slid open and Neelix charged through, full of the words that refused to fall into place, he crashed directly into the holographic doctor, knocking both to the ground.

"For a hologram," snapped the cook, "you sure are solid!"

The doctor made himself insubstantial and disentangled, then stood up, more crotchety than usual. "I maintain solidity when I interact with patients and equipment, of course! What did you expect, a ghost? Now what's wrong with you, aside from myopia?"

"Your what?"

"Where does it hurt!"

"Oh. Nowhere . . . I just wanted to talk to Kes." Neelix stood up; his face paled toward green, and he collapsed back down to the deck, gripping his knee and biting back a scream.

"Well," said the doctor, eyeing Neelix's agony, "I'm certainly glad you're not in any pain."

"I am now, you ninny!"

Rolling his eyes and grumping, the doctor squatted and moved his medical scanner up and down Neelix's kneecap, which the cook had cracked on the deck when he went down and the doctor landed on him. Neelix felt the tingly feeling of the bone knitting. The pain ebbed over several minutes, leaving only some residual stiffness.

Just as they finished their unexpected appointment, Kes entered and dashed across the room. "Neelix! What did you do? Are you all right? Is he all right?"

"Aside from some difficulty seeing large objects directly in his path, your friend is fine. Kes, did you finish abstracting those articles from the *Journal of the Federation Medical Association?* How did they compare with the archived abstracts?"

"Yes. They were the same. Neelix, come over here; lie down—you shouldn't be on your injured leg like that! How do you feel?"

She made such a fuss that Neelix flushed again; how could he find the words now, after all this, to tell his beloved that her deepest, most sympathetic urges were innappropriate?

How could Neelix look into his love's eyes and tell her that it was Janeway, and not Kes, who was right . . . that they simply must destroy the moon, even though it meant the deaths of twenty-seven billion souls?

And would Kes ever speak to him again when he did?

CHAPTER
18

COMMANDER CHAKOTAY AND LIEUTENANT CAREY STOOD IN A cramped, experimental laboratory just off the bionet salt-transfer monitoring equipment on the lower engineering deck. The room was Lieutenant Carey's private space, no one else allowed except by special dispensation.

"My . . ." marveled the lieutenant. "I can't believe it! It can't be done . . . but I can do it!"

Chakotay smiled, invisible behind Lieutenant Carey's back. "Can you?"

"No. But yes. But this is ridiculous . . . what *idiot* abstracted that article? Look—look at the wave function for the shield soliton."

Carey vigorously rubbed his thinning hair as he popped an incomprehensible equation onto the viewer. Chakotay stared. He could make out some of the terms: variables for the shields and tractor beams he studied when he took Space-time Engineering at the Academy; but there were six other terms in the equation he had never seen before in his life.

They probably drop out under normal shield geometry, he thought, *so they don't even teach them to us.* The only problem with Academy classes is they were ruthlessly practical: if Starfleet did not think a command-track officer cadet needed to know a large section of the engineering details of a particular system, they not only did not teach it, they did not even bother telling the cadets they were not teaching it! This left functional, efficient officers who nevertheless had gaping lacunae in their understanding of possibly critical systems . . . evidently including the standard "shield solution" of the impulse-soliton wave function.

"Here is the term," whispered Carey, pointing in excitement to one of the missing sections of the equation; his tone of voice indicated veneration, perhaps outright worship. "In the standard model, we always assume gamma of s and t must be a continuous function. But look! Professor Wilson flatly states that that assumption is not proven, either theoretically or by experiment!"

"And if you make gamma discontinuous . . . ?" Chakotay pointed at the appropriate term and tapped the viewer significantly. He actually had no idea what he was asking, but it worked to prod Carey into further thought. The engineer began writing invisible equations with his index finger, as if writing on a class stylus-screen.

"I'll be . . . scuppered. Either the shields will actually bend . . ."

"Or?"

"Or the ship rips apart like an egg in a wind tunnel."

"Really." Suddenly, Chakotay wondered whether unleashing an engineer and Coyote-tricking him into thinking an impossible problem was possible was the best idea after all. But desperate times called for desperate deeds.

"I don't *think* the ship will be destroyed; it seems more likely that the shields will bend . . . that's the least-energy solution if we allow gamma to have a line-discontinuity right at the front of the ship."

"Thank the spirits for least-energy solutions." Chakotay still understood only every third or fourth word Carey said; but he was not about to let the engineer know that.

Carey looked back at the commander with near awe. "If this is the Maquis way, it's a wonder you guys haven't taken over the Federation already. Be sure to tell Tuvok that I was wrong and he was right all along . . . it definitely *is* possible, once we suppress our 'continuity prejudice.'"

"Oh, I definitely shall tell Tuvok," said Chakotay with a mystery smile. "How long will it take to have a working shield-wedge?"

"You want me to go ahead with it?"

The commander thought for only a moment; they had no options, and he knew Janeway would agree. He rubbed his forehead, where a killer headache was forming. There was no time to go see the doctor.

He nodded. "Yes, Mr. Carey. Go ahead and do it. Can you give me a time estimate?"

"Sure, just a minute." Carey punched a few keys on his console; Chakotay had noticed that many engineers preferred to use a keyboard rather than the voice interface, for some reason. "Okay, got it."

"How long will it take?"

"What?"

"The shield conversion," snapped Chakotay.

"Huh? I just did it."

Chakotay felt a chill; he did not let it show. "You mean, the ship could have blown up just now, and we never would have known it?"

Carey looked puzzled. "But it didn't."

A ghostly finger touched the commander's heart; the pain in his head suddenly vanished in the adrenal rush. He nodded brusquely. "Good work, Lieutenant."

"Thank you, sir; it's on-line now. I'll rig a special controller for the captain's console."

"Make it for mine; she'll be rather busy when the fertilizer starts to fly." Chakotay exited the engineering lab and got all the way back to his own quarters before the shakes started.

Lieutenant B'Elanna Torres strapped a utility belt around her hips, checking the sixteen pouches to make sure she had every tool she might conceivably need to attack the moon's circuitry; and at that, she knew she would not be at her job for ten minutes before she would be wanting something she had left behind on the ship.

She mustered what little grace Klingon genetics and Maquis society had left her to utter a stiff "Good morning, Mr. Redbay" when her pilot slunk aboard, carrying nothing but a hand phaser. *Why a phaser?* she wondered with distaste. Redbay's only answer was a shrug. Torres decided that Redbay did not trust *her,* so he carried a weapon good only for antipersonnel warfare.

Torres had brought coils of fiberoptic cable, nylon climbing line, pliers, an assortment of spanners and mag-drivers, three specially programmed tricorders, each to record different types of electronic impulses . . . and no weapons.

She sat at the copilot's console of the shuttlecraft without another word, ostentatiously strapping herself into the seat. She meant it to sting, but Redbay only strapped himself in as well.

Captain Janeway stood at the hatchway of the shuttlecraft but said nothing as the door slid shut. Redbay fired up the engines, commenting only that one of the engines was running hot, and B'Elanna should keep an eye on it. Janeway stepped back out of harm's way; Redbay powered up and quickly ran through the engine-start and launch checklists. Then he picked up the ship and rotated through the bay door. As soon as they cleared *Voyager*'s shields, Redbay announced "Shields up" and flicked the switch.

Torres sat quietly, admiring his piloting skill in spite of her resolve to hate everything about him. Redbay drove directly toward the sun, veering at a comfortable distance and skimming the corona, keeping the hull temperature below ten thousand degrees but remaining in the plasma field as much as he could. They had no communications, but neither could the Furies easily see them. B'Elanna was impressed.

Then at the perfect moment, almost without thought, Redbay yanked the ship up and out of the sun's corona, aimed it toward the planet-moon system, and kicked in the warp engines. Diving straight out of the sun as they were, the odds were excellent that nobody would spot them until they approached the moon itself.

B'Elanna looked in the rear viewer; *Voyager* followed the

shuttle's trail exactly, giving the Furies but a single cross-section to spot.

At warp four, the shuttlecraft crossed the gap between sun and moon in five seconds; then Redbay cut off the warp engines, letting them drift behind the moon before shifting to impulse. B'Elanna turned on every passive sensor there was. Approximately two hundred thousand kilometers from the moon, two klaxons and a buzzer erupted with noise as the moon signaled it was being attacked and screamed for help.

No fewer than *twelve* Fury ships lifted off to intercept, and that was when *Voyager* sprang into action. The big ship pretended that it, not the shuttlecraft, had set off the alarms.

Getting interesting now, thought B'Elanna, keyed to the excitement.

Redbay began a long, slow turn to the right and pulled tighter and tighter, as the inertial dampers struggled against the high-g turn. B'Elanna Torres felt her entire body and a river of blood compressing downward as the g-meter climbed. She began to strain, forcing the blood back up her abdomen to her brain—whatever happened, she could *not* allow herself to fade to black.

Two Fury ships stayed with the shuttlecraft; the rest followed *Voyager* the opposite direction. The bogies started trying to lock weapons on the shuttle, and B'Elanna was kept busy operating the subspace countermeasures, trying to slip disruptor locks.

Janeway sat silent in her command chair. There was nothing to say. Tom Paris could pilot better without someone shouting in his ear, and Tuvok and Kim were perfectly capable of handling shields and weapons respectively by themselves. The captain followed the entire battle, keeping tabs not only on the Fury ships, the weapons and shields, and the piloting, but on crew performance, Maquis and Federation; on Commander Chakotay, who ran back and forth between the normal crew and crewmen Dalby, Jarron, Chell, and Henley, who stayed in the dead spots that were called "bullpen." Each crewman watched his normal duty station, ready to leap into the gap if someone was incapacitated.

The ship pulled hard in every direction. Paris preternaturally sensed where the Furies would head next, and he pulled exactly the right heading to keep them shooting at each other instead of *Voyager*.

Janeway's emergency inertial dampers held, but barely, responding sluggishly; the crew were yanked hard to left and right, driven forward, and pressed back into their seats at a very high g-force for fractions of a second until the juryrigged dampers caught up. *Too bad B'Elanna's not here to see this,* thought the captain; *maybe she wouldn't feel so bad.*

Janeway began to get dizzy, and the old feeling of nausea returned with a vengeance. Paris fought it off, dodging left and right to slip the Fury weaponry. The aliens had not yet fired their terror projector . . . or had they? "Ensign Kim—can you identify every weapon fired so far?"

Kim, who looked distinctly pallid and sweaty, clutching his console, shook his head. "Negative—Captain; they've got—disruptors and old-fashioned fusion bombs, but—still some kind of beam—I'm not sure what it is, but it's causing interspace flux-ulp."

"Has it struck us?"

"One shot—brushed the neural switches—on deck thirteen—don't know if the shields—stopped it."

"Reports of damage?"

"No. No reports at all."

"They're dead silent down there?"

Kim nodded.

"Dammit . . . I think somebody down there just got a taste of Fury terrors." She squeezed her eyes shut, fighting back a tidal wave of guilt. "Activate EMH program."

"Please state the nature—"

"Deck thirteen, neural switchboard; send orderlies and security . . . tell them to be prepared to deal with probably the most horrific panic attack you've ever seen, Doctor."

"I understand, Captain," said the doctor—sadly? *Can a hologram feel sadness?* she wondered. "Team is on its way," said the doctor.

"Chakotay, how is your shield-wedge holding out?"

THE FINAL FURY

The commander looked down at a readout on the special screen at his side, then back up at Janeway; he crossed his fingers and held them up.

"Did the shuttlecraft escape undetected?" Janeway asked.

"Negative, Captain," said Tuvok, looking none the worse for the shaking. "Two Furies followed them toward the moon. They are evading but not returning fire."

"Don't want to attract any more attention," muttered Paris, barely audible.

"Crewman . . . Dalby? Dalby. Get us some antinauseoid from the replicator."

"Aye, sir!" Dalby shouted, sliding along the wall toward the machine and trying to avoid being sent flying across the room.

"Are you sure, sir?" asked Chell. "It didn't do much last time." He looked a much greener shade of blue; Janeway presumed that indicated the same with Bolians as did pallor with humans.

"If it helps at all, it is worth it, Mr. Chell," answered Tuvok without taking his nose from the sensor-array console.

The captain took a deep breath. The time had come. "Commence firing, Ensign Kim; let's give the—ow—the Furies something else to concentrate on for a while."

The battle was joined; *Voyager* fired her first shots in anger in yet another Delta Quadrant star system. *Cross another one off,* thought Janeway gloomily; *at this rate, the Federation will be about as welcome in this quadrant as the Borg were in ours.*

CHAPTER
19

ONCE MORE INTO THE BREACH, THOUGHT CAPTAIN JANEWAY—she made a point not to say it; Cliché Day was tomorrow.

She dropped the *Voyager* straight "down" relative to its orientation; the maneuver often took by surprise the younger spacefaring races—or in this case, races that had had virtually no contact or conflict in space for centuries or even millennia.

The Furies had no quarrel with anyone from the Delta Quadrant, those of no consequence who shared their realm of exile. They wanted only heaven. All war and conflict of the past century had taken place there, according to Lieutenant Redbay—and no one had come back alive.

Their best fighters had been lost in the Alpha Quadrant. The remaining forces of the Furies left behind had little experience fighting in three dimensions with a gravitational field to contend with—obviously, for Paris evaded attack after attack, and the Furies often as not moved only in a planar direction . . . and often fired when their own ships were in the way. Janeway gave orders only when absolutely necessary; mostly she just let her crew crew the ship.

But the Furies learned quickly; and after a few minutes,

they grouped into a coordinated unit and began to take direction from their command ship. "Now, Mr. Paris," ordered Janeway, "turn tail . . . let's see if they'll play follow-the-leader."

Voyager fired a last salvo from the forward phaser batteries; the beams lanced out, striking the unshielded ships . . . but the superdense material, a meter thick, absorbed and dissipated the blast, abating slightly.

As Paris reluctantly turned the ship around and took off at full impulse, Tuvok reported: "Captain, the Fury ships can take a lot more damage before their hulls will be dangerously abraded."

"I've got interspace fluctuations all over the board," Ensign Kim shouted. They're powering up the terror projector again!" He was frightened enough that his tone cut through his spacesickness.

"Rotating the wedge backward," announced Chakotay calmly; the announcement was hardly necessary, since the move was obvious . . . but his calm, measured voice reassured Kim and the cadets.

Janeway's eyes flicked from one to the other.

"Kim," said Lieutenant Paris, "I've given you copilot status; keep your sensors sharp, prepare for evasive maneuvers."

"But—"

"I'll pick up on it, don't worry; I won't fight your course changes."

"The Furies are powering up warp engines," announced Tuvok.

Here we go . . . ! "Jump to warp six," said Captain Janeway. "Don't let's lose them in front of us. . . . Paris, stay just ahead of them; match their velocity and add a shade."

"Aye, aye, Captain."

"Warp six—correction, warp eight," said Paris. "Nine-one, nine-three . . . damn, these guys are quick!"

"Are they—"

"Catching up still! Blast it, I can't get to nine-nine; something's wrong, we're dragging somewhere!"

The captain slapped her commbadge. "Janeway to engines. . . . Carey, what's going on? We need full power!"

The voice crackled over the comm link, full of static. "Captain, it's not the engines—it's the shield-wedge . . . it's acting just like an airbrake in an atmospheric aeroplane."

"Can you fix it?"

"I can revert to normal geometry . . . you've got your choice: a shield-wedge or warp nine point nine. Not both!" Carey sounded desperate. The captain watched the rear viewer, mouthing silent imprecations.

"We're holding at warp nine point six-six-six," shouted Paris, not turning around. "The Furies are making maybe nine point six-six-six-three; they're catching us, but *very* slowly, Captain."

"Ensign Kim," said Janeway, cutting through the chatter, "drop some torpedoes out the rear, one at a time. No juice, proximity fuses."

"Floating mines," muttered Chakotay next to her.

"Maybe it'll slow them down a bit," she explained.

Kim nodded wearily, still sick despite the antinausea drug he had taken. "Fire one . . . two . . . three."

"Yes!" exclaimed Tom Paris. "They're pulling back."

"They've figured out we can't outrun them," said the captain. "Now they're content to run us out of town." She smiled; this was exactly what she had hoped for. "We still have the whole pack, except for the two who went after Torres and Redbay?"

"Yes, Captain," said Kim. Then—"Wait . . . correction! I only count nine Fury ships!"

"Did we destroy one?" asked Commander Chakotay.

"Negative," said Tuvok; "there is no debris anywhere back along our path." He looked up from his console, impassive face unable to completely conceal the faint overtones of concern. "Captain, I'm afraid one of the pursuers has broken off and returned to the system. If he scans for ion wake, it will lead him straight to the moon."

"And he can communicate with his buddies. Paris, we're going to have to turn and fight. It's the only way to keep their minds off the moon."

"Aye, Captain!" exulted the lieutenant. *The secret Sea*

Wolf within Tom Paris burst its chains, thought Janeway grimly. She knew the feeling: she, too, wanted the fight so intensely she could taste it.

The Furies were simply too dangerous to be left alone.

"Ready, Mr. Paris—Mr. Kim, ready to slip the terror projections—cut the warp, accelerate impulse to combat velocity, *now.*"

Voyager virtually halted as Chakotay shifted the shield-wedge back to the front. The Furies flashed past at warp speed, then backtracked and dropped out of warp near the *Voyager.*

"All right, people," said Janeway, "let's show them what a Federation starship can really do."

The ship suddenly lurched left, leaving them all disoriented and dizzy. Only grim-faced Kim was prepared, hunched over his console, desperately scanning for more terror projections. It was he who swerved. "Incoming," he explained, voice shaky.

Lieutenant Redbay flew the shuttlecraft tight to the moon, skimming the edges of structure. Uneasily, Lieutenant B'Elanna Torres cleared her throat: "Lieutenant, the shaft mapped by Kim and Paris is bearing—"

"I know where it is," he said softly. But he continued in the wrong direction.

It took B'Elanna another minute before she realized he had no intention of heading anywhere near the shaft while the Furies remained in hot pursuit. A second later, she was mentally kicking herself for not realizing sooner that they could not allow themselves to be trapped flying up a long, straight shaft with two enemies behind them.

I guess that's why I'm in engineering, not security, she thought.

The Furies pulled within phaser range, and Torres was occupied for some minutes trying to pop off a shot or two while Redbay did his tilted best to spin the universe out from under her feet. She *thought* she scored a pair of direct hits on the lead ship; but despite its lack of shields, it did not blow up or crash. *I must have missed,* she decided. *Great. Now I can't even shoot straight.*

She hunched over the phaser array and focused every erg of conscious will on aiming her shots by a combination of spatial visualization and Klingon "Zen." At last, she definitively *saw* one shot take the tail Fury directly amidships . . . but astonishingly, it kept on moving!

For a primitive people, without transporters or shields, they sure built tough hulls. Until that moment, B'Elanna had not really credited Tuvok's report of a material so strong and dense that phasers could not penetrate it.

But it did not matter; for if the Furies could invent such an unreasonably strong material—they still could not alter the basic laws of physics! If the substance were superdense, then that meant it was supermassive for its volume.

And that meant less-maneuverable ships, for mass becomes *inertia* when you get it moving.

"Redbay," she said tersely, "keep pulling tight turns, the tighter the better; I'm sure they outmass us."

Redbay obliged, pegging the g-meter max indicator three times, the last at a bone-crushing *twelve* times the acceleration of gravity. If Torres were not half Klingon, she realized, she would be a smear of guava jelly after some of Redbay's maneuvers.

She could not quite figure out how he himself had survived. But he seemed unaffected; bones that looked brittle and skin so blue-white it was virtually transparent came through every turn intact and unbroken.

Redbay yanked and banked the shuttlecraft, threading the tall towers that were probably comm links from one part of the moon to another, diving *under* a series of gantries in a move that almost caused B'Elanna to lose her lunch, then heading directly toward a huge block of that superdense material and rolling out left at the last moment. B'Elanna found herself clutching the sides of the seat and wishing for a combat harness, despite the inertial dampers.

The Furies struggled to follow . . . but B'Elanna was right at last: their ships were simply too massive, unwieldy, unmaneuverable; the first moment of pure joy occurred when one of the ships, trying to follow them under the gantries, simply could not pull out of its dive in time. It struck the surface, ploughing a six-kilometer-long furrow in the protective rock and vaporizing itself in the process.

But the second ship clung grimly to its task. Its pilot had to be half dead, thought Lieutenant Torres; he was pulling fifteen g's to the shuttlecraft's twelve! The Fury planet was of normal-range gravitation, slightly less than Earth, in fact; so the alien pilot must have suffered the tortures of the damned with every dive and turn.

But he stuck. Like a magnet, he stuck.

Then he began to fire a weapon that was neither disruptor nor torpedo. B'Elanna watched, mesmerized, as the pilot struggled to play the beam across their ship. She fired back automatically, without awareness—for her only conscious thought was to ponder what it would feel like to be flooded with abject, utter, belly-crawling terror.

Ahead, Redbay must have spotted a new needle eye to thread. B'Elanna saw a building and tower approaching. At first, they appeared to connect; then she saw a tiny sliver of a gap. This was the gap at which Lieutenant Redbay pointed the nose of the shuttle.

B'Elanna leaned back in her seat, baring her teeth and gripping the console, as if that would have any effect if Redbay misjudged the gap . . . and indeed, it certainly looked as though he had. The crack was never wide enough to fit the shuttlecraft!

"Lieutenant—watch out!" she hollered.

But Redbay neither stopped nor veered aside. He continued barreling toward the sliver at 105-percent impulse.

Torres forced her eyes to remain open: whatever happened, she swore she would stand before the great judge proudly, like a Klingon warrior, and never cringe.

The moment came.

The moment went. The shuttlecraft squirted through the eye after rolling sideways, a clean half-meter of space on either side.

And—B'Elanna realized with an exultant surge that the Fury ship *was not going to make it!* It was too wide; it could not clear the tower.

And it was too late for the pilot to veer around it. But not too late to open fire for one parting shot.

The terror projection sheered between the two buildings and struck them in the aft part of the shuttlecraft. The shields were never intended to stop such exquisite forms of energy.

For an instant, Redbay and B'Elanna Torres were caught in the full force of the terror-projection beam. Then the luckless Fury turned one whole side of the large building into a smoking hole.

But an instant can be an eternity.

CHAPTER 20

THE FIRST INKLING B'ELANNA TORRES HAD THAT ANYTHING WAS amiss was the overpowering and rather horrifying certainty that she was about to start crying.

The last time the Klingon had wept was when she was three years old. Her mother's explosive reaction convinced her that it was not the Klingon way.

The knowledge of what was coming, then the feel of salt water on her cheeks, gripped her heart like two giant, icy hands squeezing the life from her body. A Klingon crying! Like a baby!

But a moment later, whimpering, she realized the *true* danger . . . it was the console! It was about to short, sending hundreds of thousands of amperes through her body, frying her instantly.

With a gasp of horror, she jerked away from the death-trap, then clawed frantically with violently shaking hands at her harness, unstrapping it with terrible difficulty. She fell backward out of the chair, rolling onto her belly.

There she stuck, afraid to move forward or back, her mind virtually shut down by the paralyzing realization that the hull integrity of the shuttle had been breached, and the precious, life-giving oxygen was all squirting into dead space.

Crawling forward, whimpering like a slave, B'Elanna the Klingon felt the sharp, torn-up deckplates cutting her palms and knees, felt the diseased germs infesting her body, working their way up her veins to her heart and brain. The worms grew inside her, expelling larvae throughout her body that would grow and grow, finally eating their way out.

Terrified suddenly by the certainty that Redbay was as stricken by the weapon as was she—all her fault, for she didn't dodge that last bolt!—she tried to turn and look. But the fear was too great; she was frightened into rigid immobility, unable to see what was happening.

She could not help hearing Redbay's cries of despair, however. She did not need to turn and look; she knew they were both doomed. And the mission would fail. And all for the want of a tenpenny engineer!

The wave of horrorterror subsided. *Is that it? Is that all? It's over. That's all the stupid useless terror weapon does.*

Over? The surge of B'Elanna's adrenaline awoke a deeper fear that had only been slumbering beneath the surface, allowing the petty phobias of first contact to run dry.

The real fun had barely begun.

B'Elanna folded into a fetal position, locked her arms around her head, and screamed and screamed until she lost her wind and her voice failed. She barely saw, without comprehending, Redbay slap a button in panic before he, too, collapsed. Then a dark curtain of mindless despair shrouded her brain. And she knew nothing more.

Slowly, Lieutenant Torres came back into herself, realizing she *was* a lieutenant, even if brevetted. She had disgraced her new Starfleet, her old Maquis, herself, and her race. She still did; she lay in the dark half pressed inside a cabinet as if trying to escape the starfear by climbing back inside the womb. She still gibbered; she still sobbed, tear ducts now dry. But she had long passed the moment when mere humiliation meant anything anymore. She was alive; they had stopped the punishment. She would do what they ordered . . . *whatever they ordered.*

Unfortunately—fortunately—there was no one around to order her to do anything. She dropped her face into her arms and cried relentlessly, piteously, begging for someone to come along and give her an order she could follow to atone for her apostasy.

After five minutes of such self-abasement, B'Elanna realized how remarkably stupid her whole reaction was. Her face flushed. With still an occasional whimper, she crawled backward out of the hole. She clawed up a bulkhead to her feet, then crept along the wall to her chair.

Redbay already waited for her. He seemed hollower, colder, but no worse otherwise . . . not like big, bold B'Elanna the Klingon Warrior.

"I will re-resign my com-commission as soon as we return," she said, feeling the blood drain from her face.

"Don't be so dramatic," said the skeletal visitor.

"I disgraced myself. I am not fit to wear my uniform."

"It was an energy weapon. So now you know what I knew."

At once, Klingon pride and Maquis stubbornness stiffened B'Elanna's posture, and human rationality asserted control.

She swallowed, controlled herself. She suppressed her raging Klingon side—raging at herself, her own inadequacies—and accepted what she could not change.

"Very well. Where . . . ? Oh." Torres stared at the inside of a tunnel—presumably *the* tunnel. "How the hell did we—?"

"Autopilot," said Redbay, shrugging. "I programmed it with . . . Paris, is it? With Paris's route before we left."

"Lucky thing."

Redbay turned and stared at Lieutenant Torres. "Planning. I knew this was a possibility. I knew the devastation that terror projector caused. I maintained just long enough to engage the preset course before succumbing."

After a moment's pause, B'Elanna Torres said, almost too softly to hear, "You seem to have recovered pretty quickly."

"You were out for an additional eight minutes. I'm more used to it. I haven't as many phobic pressure-points; you've really never been frightened before—I have."

The engineer said nothing. Evidently, she was not allowed the luxury of sulking, either. So much for the simple pleasures of Starfleet life. *May as well go back to the Maquis,* she thought, not meaning it as an insult; *they were more tolerant of childish behavior.*

"We're here," responded Redbay to her unasked question, *What now?*

"I missed Paris's Swoop of Death. I was kind of looking forward to it."

"Maybe we'll survive and do it on the way out."

B'Elanna laughed, an ugly sound . . . recovery proceeded apace. Survive? What a joke. She knew as well as Redbay that their mission was pretty likely to be a one-way ticket: with the power capacity of the moon, built to receive and channel the electromagnetic energy of an exploding star, the odds were they would electro-fry themselves trying to short-circuit the works. And if they didn't, how long before the Furies sent out a massive counter force, as soon as they realized someone was monkeying with their precious machine?

"Got your . . ." She hesitated, staring dubiously at Redbay's phaser. "Got your equipment? Ready to beam over?"

"I brought a phaser."

"Good. Maybe you can shoot us a moon rat for lunch. Let's do it."

They beamed across to the same point from which Paris and Kim had begun their expedition, what seemed like three or four centuries ago. B'Elanna activated the "walkabout" program in her tricorder. She held it up in front of her right eye, looking past the tricorder and down the corridor with the other eye. The screen projected a realtime, three-dimensional model of the corridor ahead, with ghostly, glowing arrows floating spectrally ahead, pointing the path. "Follow," she said curtly, walking forward and doing her best to follow the path—though often it pointed them directly *through* gray bulkhead walls . . . logic gates that were open to Kim and Paris but had closed in the intervening time.

An hour's walk convinced her that their task was not

going to be easy . . . perhaps not even possible. No matter how hard she tried to stick to the path, she simply couldn't! When gates shuffled open or closed, they reconfigured the entire geometry of the warren, so much that they were led farther and farther astray. Finally, even the tricorder couldn't lead them back.

"All right," she muttered, "we'll have to carve our own path."

"What are we looking for?"

"The, ah, primary power switches."

"And we'll know we've found them when . . . ?"

B'Elanna Torres shrugged. "When we stop and sabotage them."

"Thank you."

"Always happy to oblige." *What a stupid question!* Torres had no more idea what they would look like than did Redbay, and he should have known that.

B'Elanna shifted away from the sarcastic. "My guess would be that they're roughly in the center of the moon. Eight hundred kilometers thataway." She pointed straight down.

"Got any suggestions? How we can travel eight hundred kilometers in the few hours we have?"

Torres slowly shook her head. "Only speculation. There *must* be some way for repair crews to get down there, isn't there? It must have broken sometime in the last few thousand years."

"Well, maybe they just transport to the proper coordinates."

She shook her head, emphatically this time. "You don't know, do you? This quadrant never discovered transporter technology, or at least no race we've encountered out here has it. Nope . . . if these Furies want to get to the center of this asteroid, they have to do it the old-fashioned way . . . a mag-lev railway or something equally primitive."

"Look for a shaft," suggested Redbay, though B'Elanna was already doing so, scanning the tricorder in a slow circle.

"This way," she said; "call it north, because it's toward one rotational pole."

Redbay nodded without expression. They set out northward, tacking left and right as the movable walls required. Lieutenant Torres swore she caught movement out of the corner of her eye many a time on the ghost moon. It always scuttled out of sight just before she turned and stared.

Redbay, as always, seemed utterly unaffected by the hallucinations.

CHAPTER 21

A BEAR TURNS, CONFRONTS THE PACK OF HOWLING WOLVES THAT have pursued it—drawn after by the bear's cunning. Momentarily, Captain Janeway pressed back her head, eyes squeezed tightly shut, wondering if the forced metaphor was wishful thinking. Wondering why it so often came down to this, to a brutal fight in the cold deep. Wondering whether the bear would be pulled down this time—they don't live forever, bears.

Dangerous job. Somebody's got to do it. Be the bear.

The Furies drew back, paused before the final assault. They learned; they were people, not wolves, and they knew enough to beware the loping bearclaw swipes. Now they coordinated, and Tom Paris lost the banter that was normally so much a part of . . .

The *Voyager* rocked behind the pounding blow of a disruptor-type weapon. Janeway jerked back to present-time, leaned forward, and began conducting the battle. Her crew was good; she was good. The Furies were better than they had been. It was a hell of a fight.

Four small ships wheeled and attacked flank left, high and

low. *Voyager* had no option but to cut in the opposite direction, and this time the jaws of the trap got clever and made no effort to aim: the Fury ships to flank right simply fired spreads into the blocks along the obvious flight path.

There was no place to evade, and the Federation ship flew directly into several fusion missiles.

They rolled like an ancient cutter on the high seas, staggered and rocked by blow after blow against the shields. The shields were meant to take the force of phasers and photon torpedoes; they would not be breached by ion-powered nuclear missiles. But if the disruptors should happen to open a hole, and if a missile snuck past, detonating against the hull itself—then *Voyager* would vanish inside a spreading, white glow, "brighter than a thousand suns," hotter than the stellar core they had just passed through.

Each hammer blow shook the ship and rattled their brains, until Janeway heard a sound like ivory dice shaken inside a hollow skull ... her own. She shouted orders that she could not hear herself—she could hear everyone else, but her internal voice was drowned out by the rattle.

Abruptly, Ensign Kim jumped up, threw himself across Paris, and in a frenzy, jabbed his thumb into the helm console. The ship lurched straight down so quickly that Janeway and doubtless the entire bridge crew (except for Tuvok) left their stomachs up on the ninety-ninth floor.

Janeway stared at the ensign, who hung his head sheepishly.

"Terror beam," he said. He sank back in his seat, watching his sensor array ... but keeping one hand close to Paris's station.

Lieutenant Paris went back to his task of bobbing and weaving, dodging disruptors, terror beams, and big, dumb rockets. For a moment, Janeway worried that Paris might feel some resentment. With a shake of her head, she dismissed the thought.

No time, no time! She fell into the rhythm: duck and bob, bob and weave.

The shield-wedge served well to ward off the most fearsome of the Furies' weapons, the terror projector; but it weakened the structure and could not repel ordinary weapons as well. Life was a trade-off. "Shields at seventy-four percent," announced Lieutenant Tuvok, unflappable . . . but his words sent Captain Janeway into an internal frenzy she could barely conceal. She deliberately leaned back in the command chair, conscious of many eyes and many more hidden fears turning her way.

Whenever the shields began to fail, the captain's heart leaped up her throat. It was a synergetic engineering effect: the more their effectiveness sank, the more they were damaged by incoming missiles and disruptors.

Then the ship itself began to take blows, as the shields started developing "holes"—weak spots where the laminar flow was disrupted, leaving a singularity that was weaker than the surrounding shield-stuff. A shot to one of those holes shivered the timbers and rattled *Voyager*'s bones, lurching Janeway half out of her seat.

The Furies took to crossing in pairs or triplets across octants of heading. After a few minutes, Chakotay warned, "They're *herding* us back toward the planet!"

Captain Janeway saw it in the same moment: "Mr. Paris! Duck the assault and return to the previous heading . . . don't let them drive us back." While Paris complied, Janeway added more softly, "We can't let them return while B'Elanna is still back there—we must give her the time." But the ship was being pounded into flotsam and wouldn't last the time that she needed. Not unless—

Janeway spied a gap where the confusion of battle had driven the Furies too far apart. She seized the moment: "Paris, bearing zero-seven-zero, mark thirty, full impulse . . *punch it,* mister!"

The helmsman obeyed, yanking the *Voyager* clear of the wolves. For a moment, they headed directly back toward the system. Then Paris cut obliquely and accelerated to their maximum impulse, whipping around the star. The Furies followed, but lost the order of their battle.

At last, free for the moment—a brief moment!—from the urgent necessity to dodge and cross their own trail, Janeway leapt out of her chair and attacked Kim's weapons board. It was marginally quicker to do it herself than tell him what to do, and mere seconds were all they had. She savagely programmed the board to fire shots in rapid succession, much faster than a human could aim.

When the Furies rounded the sun, the computer laid multiple spreads of photon torpedoes and spewed a lattice of maximal-strength phaser blasts . . . and *two Fury ships* were broken, shattering like anvils under a hero's sword.

"Got 'em!" shouted Kim with little dignity.

Immediately, the board flickered and died.

It started up a fraction of a second later; but a chilly fist lodged in Janeway's stomach. "What the hell was that?"

"Captain," said Tuvok, looking up from his science console, "stellar activity increased significantly, evidently some time ago; we are nine light-minutes from the sun, and electromagnetic radiation interference has just reached this part of the sector."

"Can we still see?" asked Janeway.

"With increasing difficulty, Captain."

"Mr. Kim?"

Kim opened and closed his mouth like a fish. "Losing . . . losing sensor contact, Captain. No, wait; it's back again!"

Janeway nodded. "Expect to see waves of interference with increasing frequency as the stellar core collapses by steps."

"With every collapse," continued Tuvok, "core temperatures increase until they ignite fusion of atoms at higher atomic numbers—helium, lithium, beryllium, and on up the periodic table of elements." It was unclear to whom he lectured; presumably, everyone present had taken first-year nuclear physics.

Janeway leaned forward, speaking urgently. "Mr. Kim . . . can we still operate the transporter?"

Kim shook his head. "I don't know, Captain; unfortunately, the only way to find out is to try it."

As soon as the weapons board came back on-line, Kim reactivated the captain's program and unleashed another barrage of hell upon the Furies. Evidently, the electromagnetic pulse had scrambled their sensors as well, for they foundered, drifting along Newtonian orbits while they powered up their systems again. "Like shooting drunks in a barrel," muttered the ensign, picking off first one Fury, then another by concentrated firepower.

Quickly, before the Furies could fully recover, Paris backed the ship away at full impulse speed, dropping photon torpedoes in his wake with speed-killing acceleration to park them in orbit . . . depth charges. The Furies were forced to swerve around them, throwing them into nonmatching orbits through the stellar gravity well.

Then the second electromagnetic-pulse (EMP) wave struck, and *Voyager* was deaf, dumb, and blind, every sensor kicked off-line. "Visual!" commanded Janeway; Kim quickly switched to pure video, and they could see—Janeway thanked her lucky stars they weren't traveling at warp speed at that moment; the visual distortions of pure, unfiltered video feed at warp were stomach-turning and horrifying . . . few could watch for more than a second or two.

Captain Janeway stared at the screen with eyes that were sharper, thanks to modern medical tech, than those of the ancient Greeks who had invented astronomy; she looked for parallaxing stars that would indicate the enemy ships. If they were smart . . .

If WE were smart, she thought. "Paris—shut down impulse engines; all stop! Mr. Kim, keep working on those sensors . . . passive sensing. We can't see them . . ."

"They can't see us," finished Paris, in sudden comprehension, getting it at last.

"Blind man's bluff. Wait, there's one—heading about two-eight-five, bearing—"

"I see him. Them."

"Magnify."

"Captain," said Tuvok, "without the sensors, the magnified picture will be unsteady."

Janeway was adamant; one picture was worth a thousand frets. "I want to see him . . . how badly did the pulse damage him?"

Kim touched a button, and the forward viewer replaced the starfield with a shaky, long-distance visual of a Fury ship. The ship was tumbling, and in a second, Janeway saw why: the aft end, which should have displayed three fusion engines, showed only one operating on one side. When the ship rotated again, they saw a bright white light and hot plasma escaping from one side; this unexpected "rocket" gave the Fury ship a tumbling motion.

"Containment field must have shut down," said Kim; "poor people."

"I doubt there are any people left alive to feel sorry for," said Tuvok matter-of-factly. "I would guess the radiation count aboard that ship to be—"

"Please don't," said the captain, closing her eyes. *Get used to it,* she ordered herself; *try to imagine what it will feel like to kill twenty-seven billion of them.*

She blinked; a tear rolled smoothly down her cheek, but she ignored it. It wasn't really there.

"Captain, there are two Furies left," said Lieutenant Paris; "both are negative bearing, at about two-eight-zero and zero-two-zero."

Can't be much more exact than that, she realized. "Damaged?"

"Not obviously. I think their engines are back on-line, but we haven't been tagged with fire-control sensors yet."

"Maybe they were burned out for good."

Paris turned back to his private viewer. "Maybe you're right; they're firing up and accelerating in a search pattern."

"Are we in the projected cone of search?"

Tuvok quickly punched up the same image. "Negative, Captain," said the Vulcan. "If they maintain their present systematic search, they will not locate us for another five hours."

"They're not going to wait," muttered Janeway. No one heard her, so she was spared the curse of successful prediction when, five minutes later, the Fury ships rendezvoused clumsily—by dead reckoning, the captain guessed—and headed back toward the planet.

"Mr. Kim," asked Janeway for the third time since shutdown, "how long do you estimate for the sensors to be back on-line?"

Kim shook his head. Again. "I . . . couldn't say, Captain. I'm working on it, but—the pulse fried everything!"

Janeway settled back; she began to realize how much she truly depended upon Lieutenant Torres. B'Elanna would have had the sensors back up in—no, that was unfair; Kim wasn't an engineer; he was doing the best he could. *If you really want results,* she told herself, *you'd better take over the repairs yourself. No? Too busy? Then stop whining about Kim's engineering ability!*

"Paris—follow them. Not too closely; if they start heading toward the moon, we have to stop them."

"Aye, aye."

The Furies maintained top impulse speed, evidently deciding that navigating at warp speed through a hurricane of plasma, electromagnetic radiation, and gravity pulses was not conducive to long life. After forty minutes, the two Furies and their surreptitious shadow pulled into the inner solar system. For a moment they slowed, hesitated—then altered course directly toward the artificial moon.

"Dammit!" swore Janeway in a rare loss of cool. "Paris, get ready to—"

"Captain!" shouted Ensign Kim, stricken. He pointed at the screen, and Janeway followed his finger.

A tiny sliver of white streaked away from the moon at high impulse speed. Even at this range, the sliver was perfectly familiar. It was a shuttlecraft . . . their own shuttlecraft.

The Furies accelerated to attack speed and shot after the sliver; *Voyager* took up the chase, far behind.

Janeway half stood in her chair, staring at the drama unfolding before her eyes, out of reach; she was helpless! Yet somehow, she must help.

"Almost there . . ." muttered Paris, hunched over his console. "Almost there—just a few more—"

The first Fury ship opened fire on the shuttlecraft. The second ship fired just as Paris fired a spread of torpedoes.

Voyager's shot ran directly up from behind the two ships, where the armor was weakest. Simultaneously, the powerful Fury disruptor beam sheered through the shuttlecraft, a knife through butter.

The photon torpedo caromed the Fury ship into its comrade, flying in formation next door. The resulting fireball destroyed both ships in a microsecond.

But the shuttlecraft exploded in a burn of white noise, hurling pieces of knucklebone shrapnel in all directions.

Janeway stared, numb and sick at the same time. She didn't know whether to rage or collapse in mute sorrow. "Ensign Kim," she said, "as soon as you restore communications, try to—try to contact the away team. See if there are . . . survivors."

Incredibly, all she could think was *I wonder whether they rigged the moon before they died?*

CHAPTER 22

B'ELANNA TORRES KICKED AT THE JAMMED DOOR, KICKED again, then threw herself bodily at the obstacle. How embarrassing! They had trekked six kilometers through a shifting maze of passages, all alike, betimes diving sideways to avoid Brobdingnagian columns sliding murderously across the slotted floor of electrical connectors and fiber sheaths—only to be frozen scant meters before the shaft by a *locked door!*

B'Elanna exhausted herself, Klingon fury seizing control while the human half sat back in amazement at her futile, repetitive folly . . . unable to stop herself, able only to stare from a height while she beat her hands bloody and finally collapsed, gasping, in a crumpled heap on the floor.

"May I try?" asked Lieutenant Redbay, calm and collected—comatose would be the fairer description.

"You? What can *you* do, scarecrow, if I can't even budge the damned thing?" She realized she was whining—human side giving vent to the frustration of the Klingon.

Redbay grunted.

He drew his phaser and blew the door out of existence.

B'Elanna stared reproachfully at the hole where the door

had been, the edges of the slide still glowing, radiating warmth. Without a word or backward glance, she rose and pushed through, followed by Redbay. There was something terribly unaesthetic about . . . She sighed, staring at the image on the tricorder.

By rights, they should already be *in the shaft;* but she saw nothing but more corridor. "It should be here," she muttered, turning in a slow circle, scanning.

"Are you sure? Dial up the scale."

"Maxed. Maybe we just have to walk forward another— awk!"

The last noise disappeared down the hole that opened suddenly at B'Elanna's feet; the floor gave way like a hollow pie crust, and she dropped twenty meters into blackness, landing on a raised track. Had they been in Earth-normal gravity, she surely would have broken a hind leg, and Redbay would have had to put her down.

"Are you killed?" he called from above, sounding not too terribly interested either way.

"No. I don't think so. Unless we both are."

A thump sounded in the darkness as Redbay leaped down beside her. Torres fumbled around, hunting for her dropped tricorder. Suddenly, the ground was illuminated by a bright light from Redbay's phasoelectric torch. *Must've been stashed in his boot,* she thought.

B'Elanna swept her tricorder in a short arc. "Power generator this way. This track is set up for magnetic levitation, and it's still powered. I think we might actually find a working subway, Redbay." They sped down the corridor, aware of passing time, and almost ran headlong into a low, flattened car with pointy edges; the exterior was blue and yellow with bright-red highlights. "I guess we know why the Furies prefer dim lighting: because if the lights were turned up, they'd all die of terminal color-clash," said Redbay.

"Ho ho." The tricorder still picked up no life-forms, but B'Elanna continued to half-see them on the peripheral edges.

Curiously, the door was manual; they had to yank it open by brute muscle—Redbay didn't want to blow it off, since they might need the airseal. Inside, the car was stuffed with seats, three different varieties, only one of which looked comfortable for humans. The "control panel" was nothing more than a blank panel with a narrow strip of hieroglyphs running along the top edge.

The interior was mostly white and mute gray, the seats molded plastic, and no seatbelt harnesses.

"How does this work?" asked Torres, touching the panel.

The car lurched forward, accelerating hard enough to hurl Redbay to the deck. B'Elanna would have joined him except she wrapped her arms around the "pilot's" seat, which had no piloting controls that she could see. The car accelerated at a rate of at least three gravities toward . . . what? The shaft *looked like* it headed into the planetary interior . . . but where? Anywhere near a power-conduit junction? Redbay struggled to his feet against the acceleration and scrambled into a crash chair designed for humanoids; but B'Elanna Torres dangled where she was, though her arms quickly began to ache from the strain.

After two minutes or so, the acceleration suddenly ceased. Torres squawked and flapped her arms in the sudden shift of "down." She fell into place in the command chair, guessing they were now traveling somewhere around three and a half kilometers per second.

The first indication she had that the car was actually sinking lower in the moon was when she begin noticing a distinct lessening of gravity. She checked with the tricorder and discovered gravity had indeed dropped from 0.2 g to nearly 0.1 g; as they neared the core, the gravity continued to diminish . . . a process that would reach the limit of zero-g at the very center, assuming it was hollow.

Many minutes passed, more than half an hour, and they were still barreling along. They said nothing to each other; they had nothing to say. Temporary crewmates did not always become fast friends.

"This might be awfully rough when we decelerate," said the skeletal pilot. B'Elanna did not respond, but she understood the problem: the human body can stand far more acceleration forward than it can backward. But moments later, the seats in the cabin, including the pilot's chair, slowly began to rotate. As soon as the seats were roughly opposite to the line of travel, the car shuddered and braked hard, just as hard as it had accelerated.

In the same length of time, two minutes, the car brought itself to a complete halt and automatically opened the cabin doors.

They were now so deep that gravitation was detectable only as a faint tug toward the floorplates—0.005 g, according to the handy tricorder, one two-hundredth of Earth's gravity. A slight movement pushed B'Elanna out of her seat and set her drifting toward the roof. Redbay was more circumspect, moving along the car and out the open door; after some fumbling around, Lieutenant Torres followed.

At the far-end platform, they tethered themselves as best they could with hands and feet, staring in silence. The platform dropped away in a kilometer-tall cliff face; the open space was so vast that the other side vanished into the blue haze of the moist air. Directly below them, the valley resembled nothing less than a monstrous dataclip packet, a power router with power conduits that must have been big enough to swallow the *Voyager,* and hundreds of thousands of kilometers of fiberoptic cable as thick as small tree trunks; a number of logic switches that B'Elanna dizzily estimated to be in the low millions; spark gaps wider than Hero's Gulch on the Klingon Homeworld; and arcing over the entire valley, forming a glittering gold dome, a godlike version of Kubla Khan's Xanadu, was an inverted, convex power-grid antenna. It was made of the same filament wire as the Faraday cage surrounding the sun. And oddly enough, though the sun grid was built to a scale unimaginably bigger than the one that spread now before them, B'Elanna Torres was more shaken by the current, smaller version. She felt her stomach contract to a tight fist, felt her breath catch in her throat: the problem with the grid surrounding the sun was that it was *too* big; it defied the mind's ability to comprehend . . . so her mind gave up and accepted it as an intellectual proposition only.

But the current grid was possible to take in all at once—perhaps the maximal size an object could be and still actually register as a single thing—unlike, say, a continent; no one walked around marveling at the size of a continent.

"Kahless's beard," she breathed, taking in the entire vista in one eyeful.

Redbay grunted. "Damn thing's big enough to scare the brass off a bald monkey," he said. "Don't tell me . . . that's the central power router, diffuser, whatever it's called. Isn't it?"

Setting herself to slowly rotate like a top, B'Elanna scanned in all directions. "There's nothing else of this magnitude anywhere in the moon," she confirmed. "This is it, Redbay."

He sighed. "I suppose there's no way to blow up the diffuser grid."

"Not unless you have about two hundred photon torpedoes in your pocket."

"Just a fallen star. No, I have no explosives; I don't even know where you would get any."

"I brought tools, not bombs. Oh well; have to leave the antenna alone. But maybe we can reroute some of those fiberoptic cables . . . well, the smaller ones, anyway." She mused for a moment, slowly drifting back to the deck after her scanning rotation. "I would bet the Furies built a thousand redundancies into the system; they couldn't know exactly how the power would flow during the supernova, and they wouldn't want to waste an erg. We can't just destroy systems; we have to set up an actual feedback loop that will channel the energy itself into an adjacent sector, frying all the circuits."

"Cut and paste."

"You got it. But how do we get down there?"

Redbay twisted sideways, placed his feet against the edge of the cliff, and launched himself out over the valley. B'Elanna gasped, then realized instantly that the gravity was so low he couldn't possibly get hurt.

Lieutenant Torres gritted her teeth; she had never before felt any twinges of acrophobia, but she was feeling it now, a huge boulder of phobic panic crushing her so she couldn't breathe. Residual from the terror beam? She thought she might be jumping at shadows for a long, long time to come. Refusing to allow a mere human to show her up, she planted herself and launched just as Redbay had, trying to mimic his trajectory as best she could.

Nevertheless, they landed a kilometer apart. Leg muscles simply weren't precise enough engines to calculate a good parabolic intercept.

Tapping her communicator, B'Elanna said, "Torres to Redbay; look toward the center of the valley . . . see that tall spike? I'd guess that was the focus collector for the antenna."

"All the power flows through there?" asked Redbay's disembodied voice.

"All the power flows through there. That's our target, Lieutenant; if we can loop those circuits around into a feedback loop, we've got a good chance to divert all the power long enough for the supernova to destroy the moon itself, and—"

"And the Furies get to sit and watch the tidal wave roll in." For the first time, B'Elanna heard real emotion in his normally grim, sardonic voice; she heard pure, malicious joy at the prospect of twenty-seven billion dead Furies.

A day ago, B'Elanna would have been appalled and sickened. But her whole life had changed since then. A day ago, B'Elanna Torres had never felt the whisper of the terror-projector needle into her brain.

Yesterday, she had not yet experienced the degrading horror, the humiliation of paralysis, the mind-numbing, marrow-freezing terror it induced.

Today, she would pull the switch herself, instantly, to fry all twenty-seven billion without a second thought.

"Head for the needle?" asked Redbay.

Torres nodded, then realized he could not see her. "Rendezvous at the needle; we don't have much time if we want to return to *Voyager*."

Redbay laughed, then signed off. *Now, what did I say that was so hysterical?* she thought angrily.

CHAPTER 23

PLANTING HER FEET, B'ELANNA TORRES LEAPED AS HIGH AS SHE could—more than sixty meters. She scrutinized the pole as it rolled past, looking for a panel, a door, an access port—a knob, anything. The antenna was smooth as glass all the way up; it was smooth as a mountain lake all the way back down.

She followed a slow spiral around the base; it was easier to move on her belly, as if she were climbing a cliff. The gravity was so close to zero that her stomach couldn't tell the difference; she was falling—a horrible feeling. She had dreaded every zero-g exercise at the Academy, and she still didn't like it.

At last she found something promising. At first, she didn't recognize the panel for what it was: it was colossal, an octagon with a diameter of eighty-four meters. She crawled the perimeter, at last finding a pair of three locks that evidently wanted a key . . . but not an electronic key; the tricorder told her there were no circuits—it was purely mechanical. The locks wanted an actual hunk of metal with teeth and notches to insert and turn!

She was staring reproachfully at the locks when Redbay finally joined her.

"Ancient locks," she said, pointing. "We need to find a—what did they call them?—a key ring."

"No we don't," said the dead-voiced lieutenant.

It took her a moment, but B'Elanna suddenly realized what he meant. She jerked away . . . a bad move under the circumstances, as Torres catapulted across the deck, landing twenty meters distant.

Redbay leveled an all-purpose lockpick and slipped it into the lock. Silently, the access hatch swung open.

Inside, they found at last the mother lode: bank upon bank of fiberoptic cables that carefully routed the electromagnetic pulse from surface, mirrors, and the giant collector into the various logic gates and circuits.

They had found the nexus where everything came together, the one piece of the system for which there were no failsafes, no redundancies, no dead-man switches to kill the power and try again. The Furies knew it would be a *one-shot deal* when the sun went supernova: there would be no second chances. Either the system would work, and they would be hurled through a brief, artificial wormhole to the Alpha Quadrant . . . or it would fail; and they would be dead, turned into ionized plasma by the stellar explosion.

But there are half a million of them! We can't make a difference!

B'Elanna had just removed one cable to read it when suddenly a horrible screech startled her. She dropped the pile of fiberoptics, and stared about wildly for the sound, nine-tenths convinced they had activated some ancient alarm system, and that soldiers were at that moment materializing out of nowhere, surrounding them. . . .

Redbay looked down at his commbadge. "Oh. That's for me."

"What the—!"

"I instructed the computer aboard the shuttlecraft to take whatever steps were necessary to lead the Furies away from us if they followed us here; that sound means they found the shuttlecraft . . . which has now left the moon."

"Left . . . *the moon?* You mean here? We're stranded here?"

"I'm afraid so, unless the shuttlecraft can outrun the Fury interceptors, which it can't."

B'Elanna stared at Redbay, who shrugged. "Torres, if they found the shuttlecraft parked just outside, how long do you think it would be until they came right here? If we can figure out that this is the Achilles' heel of the power collector, don't you think they can?"

"So that's it. We're . . . win or lose, we're not leaving."

Redbay said nothing, returning to stripping off the heavy sheathing designed to protect the cables from the electromagnetic pulse preceding the matter stream that would tear the moon apart.

B'Elanna hesitated only for a moment; then she resumed testing every major cable to find the critical ones. All the while, she tried to summon up the Klingon warrior within, the one who would rejoice to die killing her enemies. But all she felt was numbness. B'Elanna Torres had spent so many years brutally suppressing her Klingon side that now she was unable to readily call upon it when needed.

If I get through this alive by some damned miracle, she thought, *I hereby resolve never to suppress my Klingon side again.*

Her commbadge beeped, startling her. She slapped at it, but the beep died in the middle of the second sound. "Torres. Is someone there?"

Silence; then the commbadge clicked alarmingly, a startled beetle. Then silence again. B'Elanna frowned; it was a creepy feeling, to be buried deep within an artificial, alien moon, waiting for a supernova to destroy her—and to be called by a mysterious ghost who refused to announce himself.

After another minute, her badge beeped again. "Torres!" she snapped, hitting the metal repeatedly.

This time, she heard a staticky sine wave—a faint, ghostly voice almost seemed to overlay the white noise, as if she were listening to a conversation in another sector, thousands of light-years away, underwater.

"I don't know if you can hear me," she said, "but if this is *Voyager,* please come closer!"

B'Elanna removed her commbadge and attached it to the tricorder, boosting the gain and expanding the antenna. After another minute, the call returned . . . but this time, she actually made out most of the words.

"Janeway to Torres—[unintelligible] destroyed—do you read? Do you [unintelligible] assistance?"

"Captain! This is Torres; comm link breaking up, can't make out everything. We're fine. We need more time, more time, more time. Keep the Furies off us!"

"Torres—[garbled] shuttlecraft destroyed."

"We're fine. Redbay and Torres alive, working. What is happening? Is the ship all right?"

Suddenly the voice became clearer; the computer was beginning to compensate for the high level of electromagnetic interference put out by the collapsing star. "The ship is operational. Do you require assistance?"

"No, we're all right. We just need more time. Are we under attack?"

"We were, but we're [unintelligible]. How much time? In three minutes [unintelligible] be able to beam you back if the sun explodes."

In three minutes what? They would, or *wouldn't* be able to beam them out?

"Say again, please," said Torres, holding her breath.

"Radiation levels increasing. [Unintelligible] inoperative in three minutes. You must decide whether to [garbled]."

Well, that answers that stupid question.

"Stand by, please, Captain." B'Elanna had been cutting through one of the massive fiberoptic cables with her phaser welding-torch while she spoke; now the cable severed into two pieces. Grunting, she hefted the "hot" end up to an input cable, into which she had already bored a hole.

They were in near zero-g; but the cables were so stiff and massive, it still took all of her considerable strength to bend them into a loop. They kept wanting to spring open.

Redbay held the cable in place while Torres applied the polymer bonder and almost decided. "Captain, I . . ."

Torres stared helplessly at Redbay, who wouldn't look at

her. She didn't need to tell him what Janeway was really asking; he knew as well as she. They had no shuttlecraft, and it certainly would be too dangerous to send one from *Voyager* to pick them up after the sun went supernova.

Now that the ship had found them again, their only chance of escape was the transporter: but they would have to leave immediately, or they would lose the last window of opportunity.

B'Elanna Torres clenched her teeth, a lump rising in her throat. *Before I heard the captain,* she told herself, *I already accepted the inevitability of my own death.* Really, there was no choice to make. She had a duty that both human and Klingon could understand.

And Redbay—he lived for his revenge. He would be no problem.

"Captain—we won't be transporting out now. We have . . . there's too much to do. We'll let you know when we're finished."

"You won't [garbled] able—breaking up—[unintelligible] getting worse. This may be the last comm—[unintelligible]—chance—are you coming?"

B'Elanna finished gluing the cable and began cutting the next output. She stared down at her work. "No. Thank you, Captain. I really enjoyed serving under you . . . and I even kind of enjoyed being in one of these uniforms again. I wish—well, I wish things hadn't turned out quite as . . ."

Sometime during her speech, she became aware that the comm link had broken, and her voice trailed off into silence. There was a lot of work to do.

An hour flew past unnoticed until B'Elanna looked down at her tricorder. "Hey, it's getting pretty thick . . . uh-oh!"

"What's the problem?" asked Redbay with all the apparent enthusiasm of the man behind the complaints counter.

"Do you feel sick at all?"

"No."

"Well. You're going to."

"Radiation?"

"Not just EM; heavy particle radiation, hydrogen and helium nuclei; big, slow particles. Gamma, X-rays. It's getting dangerously high."

"You knew the job was dangerous when you took it," said Redbay comfortingly.

Torres's voice was small; she tried to make it bigger, but it trembled instead. "I just hope we survive long enough to make a difference down here." It wasn't exactly what she had been going to say, but it *was* what she should have said.

Redbay stared at their handiwork for the last ninety minutes, loops of fiberoptic cables as big around as a human leg, dangling from other cables like Christmas tinsel. He had always celebrated Christmas . . . before reporting aboard the *U.S.S. Enterprise,* the ship of his buddy Will Riker. Dead? Alive? When Redbay had driven through the wormhole, he might as well have left behind a dead world . . . for he could never hope to see any of them again.

And he was dying; every breath told him, sharp pain knifing down his lungs. He was feeling feverish, dizzy; he hadn't told B'Elanna, who seemed all right for the moment. Probably the Klingon genes. But he was sicker than he ever had been in his life.

And it would never get better; it would get worse and worse until he collapsed, entire columns of cells being crushed and collapsed by the blundering nuclear particles. A dead man; a walking, working dead man. But it didn't matter, because he was already dead. He died the day he discovered what waited for him beyond the grave. In the Furies' terror projector, Lieutenant Redbay discovered what lay beyond the curtain: *nothing*.

When he died, he knew he would cease to exist, utterly and terribly. No afterlife, nothing to live on. His despair was as great as his terror . . . and it was a rarefied terror indeed. He had screamed and crawled just as Torres had done; but it was a different thing. She was too young and hadn't seen what the Furies could do—her fears were more visceral; and when the terror projector stopped, so did the fright, after a decent interval.

But Redbay's horror was total . . . for it *never stopped*. He had looked into the eyes of tomorrow's death and seen only empty pools of endless gray. Redbay staggered under the weight of such existential agony, the certainty of pure chaos.

He stared toward his own death with a terror that mounted minute by minute, until it threatened to overwhelm even that fragile peace earned by acceptance of his own nothingness. Like he never was, never would be again; Redbay looked into the mirror and saw only the empty walls of the room, no reflection.

His hands shook as he held up another heavy cable to be polymer-glued into place. He and Torres were systematically connecting outputs to inputs, bypassing the power distributor that was supposed to channel and filter the raw energy. They were constructing the fiberoptic equivalent of a blast furnace, turning the moon's own energy collection back onto itself—where the staggering power unleashed would tear apart the tough construction of the moon and destroy the circuits that produced the giant, artificial wormhole.

That is, if they could short enough cables. *At this rate,* thought Redbay, *we should get it done—in about a year and a half. Dammit!*

He looked at B'Elanna, and suddenly he saw her as a woman, a beautiful woman; the human trapped within Redbay's shell of iron reached out for a last touch of humanity. "B'Elanna . . . would you—do you want to—be close one last time before you die?"

"No," she answered curtly.

So much for the brotherhood of humanity, he thought bitterly. Then he smiled, though she could not see; odds were he couldn't have done anything anyway, not sick as he was!

"Just a thought," he added, voice cold iron again. The brittle vulnerability was gone. He couldn't tell whether she had even hesitated before turning him down, but it didn't matter. The cables mattered; making sure twenty-seven billion Furies died by their own hand mattered. "How much longer?"

"At least forever," said B'Elanna Torres, using the same tone of voice with which she had refused him.

"Maybe we'll live that long."

Torres grunted, bending up another stiff cable.

CHAPTER 24

Captain Kathryn Janeway sat on the bridge, staring in utter fascination at the viewer, where the image of the Furies' sun seemed to roil visibly. They had powered the ship up again, and again she could look directly at the sun and watch the astonishing process of collapse.

The Bela-Neutron devices—cosmic nanotechnology—were already absorbing so many hot bosons, the heavy particles like protons and neutrons, and leptons, the electronlike particles, as well as photons, units of light, that the sun was startlingly dark and cold. A human could almost stare at it directly... but not quite. The surface temperature remained a steady six thousand degrees, but the core, which had jumped dramatically when the sun suffered the first collapse from hydrogen-fusing to helium-fusing, was dropping again as the Bela-Neutrons gulped energetic particles and pumped out useless neutrinos.

Momentarily, the core temperature would drop cold enough no longer to be able to support helium fusion... and the sun had already contracted too tight to be held apart by mere hydrogen fusion. It would collapse again, causing the core temperature to rise staggeringly high . . . hot enough to begin fusing the next atomic element, lithium. Repeat as needed.

Eventually, the sun would blow itself apart in a colossal supernova. The Bela-Neutron devices would absorb a significant fraction of that energy, flinging it away uselessly; but the remainder would be more than enough to power the creation of a wormhole large enough to swallow the entire Fury planet and belch it forth into the Alpha Quadrant. The entire planet . . . twenty-seven billion warriors determined to rid heaven of all the Unclean.

Twenty-seven billion . . . and certainly some way to move the entire planet as if it were a starship, probably at warp speed. The Furies made the Borg look like pishers.

And 1.5 hundredths of a second after projecting the Fury planet through the momentary wormhole, the moon would vaporize. B'Elanna Torres would vaporize, and Redbay, too.

Or would they? A strange thought occurred to Janeway: Given the characteristics of the Bela-Neutron device, the energy that actually reached the moon might not be enough to rip the molecules apart. She shook her head; it was an impossible equation to calculate or even estimate, since no one had ever *made* a real, working Bela-Neutron device, so far as Janeway knew. But what if—what if the energy were enough to crack the moon like an egg, blowing it apart, but not enough to turn it into an ionized plasma of constituent atoms?

What if B'Elanna and Redbay were on the dark side of the tide-locked moon when it blew? Would they be flung into space to die horribly? She shuddered; far better if they were killed in the initial explosion.

Such thoughts made her morose, tempering the edge of her excitement. As a captain, Kathryn Janeway had several times ordered men, and one woman, to their deaths. But never with such certainty before. She started to feel the pain and quickly closed off the empathic section of her brain. She could not afford emotions now; she must become like Tuvok, for a few moments, at least . . . lest she try some wild, harebrained stunt to try to rescue them and lose the entire ship as well.

They're gone. They're already dead, she kept telling herself over and over. *They're already gone!*

She closed her eyes and saw B'Elanna spinning through the black, starry sky where once a planet had orbited, clawing piteously at her mouth, desperately trying to find air where there was only interstellar dust. She opened her eyes again and stared at the sun.

The ship's intercom beeped; the tense silence, as all waited for the inevitable, was broken by the doctor's voice. He sounded tense and agitated—an odd state for a hologram to be in. "Captain! Captain Janeway, I just had either a small epiphany or a ridiculous dream."

"A *dream?* Doctor, are you functioning properly?"

"I think so. Hold on a minute—yes, all systems are functioning within normal parameters."

"How did you come on-line?"

"Well . . . the truth is, nobody remembered to turn me off after I finished treating casualties from your little escapade with the Furies."

"I thought we gave you the ability to turn yourself off."

The doctor looked pensive, another neat trick. "So you did. But I . . . more and more, I find myself preferring to stay conscious. Conscious? Is that the word I want? I *feel* conscious."

Janeway felt herself getting impatient. "Doctor, is this going somewhere? What was your epiphany?"

"First, I have to ask you an engineering question: How violent will the explosion be by the time it gets to the moon?"

Janeway's eyebrows shot up toward her hairline. It was disconcerting in the extreme to have one's mind read by the emergency medical holographic program. "I've just been thinking about that very problem. I could run some simulations . . . but my gut tells me the explosion will destroy the moon—or at least the side facing the sun—but will not be powerful enough to vaporize it."

"What about the other side, the dark side? How much damage?"

"I don't know. Maybe it will remain mostly intact. Maybe my gut is wrong, and the entire moon will turn into a white, glowing plasma. Where are you going with this?" Despite her short tone, Janeway thought the doctor might well have something somewhere that would mutate a *Kobayashi Maru* exercise into something winnable, the way that James T. Kirk had reprogrammed that particular futile exercise.

"Well . . . I know it's a bit unorthodox, but it occurs to me that the human body may be a lot tougher than we generally think. I assume you know what happens when a human is suddenly subjected to a vacuum?"

"Um—explosive decompression?" It was only a difference of one atmosphere, like ascending through the water from a depth of ten meters to the surface. "Um, I think blood vessels in the lungs would rupture."

"Excellent; are you sure you don't want to join Kess as a medical student? I've run a few simulations while we spoke, and there are a lot of things that will go wrong to kill the human . . . but none of them *instantaneously*. The skin will freeze—but in empty space, it's not easy to radiate heat away, as you well know from your engineering studies. That won't happen as quickly as if the patient were dipped in liquid nitrogen, which is not as cold but transfers heat faster."

"Yes . . . yes—Doctor, are you saying that a person . . . ?"

"Blood vessels will rupture in the lungs, nose, and eyes; the patient will suffocate, but that would take longer than anything else."

"Doctor . . . what are you saying?"

The doctor paused; he was probably simply running all his simulations one more time to be sure, but it gave Janeway the impression of a man hesitating before suggesting something that might sound crazy.

"Captain, I believe the particular radiation that wreaks havoc with our transporters is the heavy neutrino flux from the Bela-Neutron devices, is it not?"

Janeway nodded, and the doctor continued.

"And after the shock wave of the supernova passes by us, the Bela-Neutron devices will be destroyed—and we'll regain functionality on our transporters."

Captain Janeway said nothing; her nod was barely perceptible.

"Then, Captain . . . if the away team is standing at the far side of the moon when the shock wave hits, and it is less severe than a normal supernova because of the Bela-Neutron devices, then they may survive the destruction. And if they do, Captain, I believe—I will stake my medical reputation that *they can survive the vacuum of space* for a few seconds, as long as ninety seconds, before they lose sufficient heat to be unresuscitatable.

"We can beam them directly to sickbay, Captain. One or both might survive."

Janeway stared, feeling a peculiar numbness touch her hands and feet. It was insane—let yourself be blown out into space, gambling that the *Voyager* can find you, lock on, and beam you aboard before you die? She had never heard of such a thing in all her years in Starfleet.

On the other hand, no one had ever seen an artificial supernova used to power an artificial wormhole, either. *The universe,* said the ancient Earth biologist J. B. S. Haldane, *is not only queerer than we suppose, but queerer than we can suppose.*

"Doctor, prepare sickbay to receive a pair of very, *very* cold crew members."

"Aye, Captain. EMH program out."

"Commander Chakotay, you have the conn."

"Yes, Captain. Where are you going to be?"

"Engineering. We *must* find a way to communicate with Torres and Redbay and tell them to get to the dark side as soon as they're able. Chakotay, monitor the sun using subspace sensors . . . when it goes nova, we'll have—what? seven minutes before the electromagnetic pulse hits, and another three hours for the shock wave of thrown-off star stuff to arrive. Keep the shields up; we'll ride out the explosion as best we can, then return and start fishing."

Janeway hopped up, more energized than she had felt in hours, and almost ran to the turbolift.

B'Elanna Torres let go the fiberoptic cable she had just epoxied and went limp. She was amazed how beat she was, even working in near zero-g . . . she was drenched with sweat, her hair plastered to her skull by the surface cohesion of salt water. She drifted on the random air currents, her feet pinioned to prevent her from drifting entirely away. She panted, eyes shut and mouth open.

Lieutenant Redbay held on to the cable, watching her; he seemed unaffected by the long, hot, sweaty work.

"Can't you even be a *little* exhausted?" she demanded angrily.

Redbay smiled, and B'Elanna shuddered. *His rage gives him all the energy he needs,* she realized.

They had done good sabotage. Scores of enormous cables now looped output directly into input, or directly into circuitry, input to input, output to output—anything that seemed likely to fry the ability of the moon to channel the energy of an exploding star into a productive, wormhole-producing beam of coherence.

She opened her eyes, unhooked her feet, and did a slow, 360-degree pirouette; and B'Elanna's heart sank, even in zero-g. It was not enough.

It was nothing! Nothing compared to the hundreds of thousands of cables still left, snaking "down" from the antenna to the power-grid circuitry beneath their feet. B'Elanna shook her head, gritting her teeth to hold back a scream of frustration, anger, and futility.

What? What do we damn well have to do? *We're not even making a dent here!*

"Do you really think this is going to stop the projector?" asked Redbay suddenly.

Torres gasped, staring at the mysterious lieutenant. Was he a psychic? Did he have one of those much-discussed human wild-talents? "Why did you ask that?"

"I followed your gaze. There are a hell of a lot of cables, aren't there? Are we making any difference?"

B'Elanna shook her head, defeated.

"Then maybe," suggested Redbay, "we should think of doing something else."

"Oh, thank you! Nice suggestion, Lieutenant . . . what do you suggest? Set the phaser on overload and blow up the moon? Spin the whole damn thing around to point into empty space? Stick a cork in the barrel of the wormhole cannon?"

Redbay smiled crookedly, like a homicidal Klingon just before going on a rampage with a *bat'leth*. "Now, *there's* an idea."

"Put a cork in it? Dammit, we don't even know where the barrel is!"

"No, the one before that."

"The phaser on overload? There's not enough power to—"

"No, no! The *middle* suggestion . . . turn the moon to point the wrong way."

"Turn the . . . ? Redbay, we can't turn the whole—"

"Look, the moon is tide-locked, right? And we all assumed that was because it needed to be pointed at the sun to collect the energy from the grid, right? But it's not just tide-locked; Torres, it's in the L-four stable-orbital position with respect to the sun and the Fury planet, isn't it?"

"I—did we ever check that? Probably . . . it's in the same orbit as the planet, about sixty degrees ahead of it. Yes, that would be the Lagrange-four stable-orbital point."

"And that means the sun, the planet, and the moon do not move with respect to each other, right?"

"That's the definition of L-four."

"Torres, don't you see it? They're not in L-four to point toward the sun . . . that's easy! It's the brightest thing in the solar system; you can't miss it.

"Torres, they're in the L-four spot *so they'll always point toward the planet.* They have to be pointed at exactly the right spot, or the wormhole won't form . . . or it will form away from the planet, and they won't pop through it or it'll take them the wrong direction—something!"

B'Elanna stood with her mouth open for a moment, mentally performing dozens of simulation calculations. "Blood of my enemies—you're right! It has to be! Redbay, do you know what this means? The slightest jar, the slightest change to the aiming mechanism, and the wormhole might miss the planet entirely!"

CHAPTER 25

"It's been a couple of hours since *Voyager* lost contact with us," said Redbay. "How long before the explosion?"

B'Elanna shrugged; she had no special knowledge. "No possible way of telling; as short as thirty minutes or as long as six hours."

"Then we'd better get moving fast, Lieutenant; we've got to find the aiming circuits soon, like yesterday, and start hooking up cables to short them out."

For nearly forty-five minutes, B'Elanna Torres scanned with her tricorder, reprogrammed the search pattern, and scanned again. Redbay alternately clenched and relaxed his hands. B'Elanna basically knew what she was looking for: a delicate mechanism surrounded by inertial and subspace navigation sensors with a direct connection to a point near the fulcrum of the eight-hundred-kilometer-long tube that was doubtless the "barrel" of the wormhole projector. The problem was that the description still produced a depressingly large number of possible "hits," which had to be sorted and evaluated by B'Elanna herself.

But she learned. When she found a potential valley site, she narrowed the focus and carefully worked up a three-dimensional picture of the location. Each was a bust, one way or another: insufficient energy to move the barrel, no line-of-sight to the planet . . . B'Elanna refined her search engine until, finally, she found a site she could not eliminate, not after ten minutes of fiddling.

"All right—I think . . . I think I might have it here. It's the best shot, anyway."

"We'd better take it," said Redbay, staring at his chronometer. "We can't afford any more time. It's this one or nothing, and we fail."

"Five kilometers, bearing, uh, thataway."

Torres in the lead, they hopped like antigravity jackrabbits. The five kilometers flew beneath them in a few minutes, and Torres finally brought them down within a few hundred meters of the objective.

The beam-navigation chamber was not on the valley floor, but two hundred meters straight down, though *down* was a weak term this far toward the center of mass of the moon. There was no obvious access panel, and Redbay used his phaser to burn a path to the circuitry. Then, at B'Elanna's direction, he phased off thirty huge fiberoptic cables. The hand phaser was rapidly becoming the most useful tool they had brought with them, much to B'Elanna's annoyance; it was the only tool she hadn't foreseen.

They polymer-bonded one end of each cable to power-out junction boxes and pushed the other ends into the hole Redbay had carved. Then, together, the two lieutenants slid over the hole, grabbed the edge, and propelled themselves two hundred meters downward.

They worked feverishly, attaching cables to every delicate-looking circuit they could find, praying they could stick enough before the unseen sun went supernova—if it hadn't already. . . . It would be more than seven minutes, B'Elanna calculated, between supernova and the power surge striking the moon. The shock wave would be almost an afterthought, arriving a few hours later, depending on the violence of the explosion. When it did arrive, it would shred the moon like confetti.

It might already be all over. *We might be walking, talking dead people,* thought B'Elanna grimly.

Captain Kathryn Janeway—temporarily self-demoted to chief engineer—nervously wiped her hands and rearranged her hair bun, staring at the viewer on which was projected her newly devised comm-link procedure. Could she? Would she?

An hour's worth of brutal brainwork had convinced Janeway that there *was* a way to power up the communications link and punch through the radiation interference; but to do so, they would have to take the wedge-shield off-line and risk collapsing it utterly. The same modification that Carey had found to put a bend in the shield allowed Janeway to *extrude* the shield several hundred thousand kilometers in the direction of the bend.

That meant it could actually shield the comm link from the background radiation, but at a price: the shield would stretch so thin it would not function as a shield anymore. In fact, it might well stretch thin enough that the two sides touched; that would short out the circuitry, and the shield would flicker out of existence—permanently. Or at least until they repaired it—hours, maybe.

Dared she risk it?

"Lieutenant Carey, I need some input. How likely is the shield to break?"

Carey licked his lips. *He hates being put on the spot for an estimate when there's simply not enough data,* the captain thought. "That would depend on how far we extrude the shield, Captain. The farther, the—"

"I'm looking for a number, Carey; a percent chance."

Carey stared blankly. "Um, I'd give it a thirty-seven-percent chance, Captain," he said. His face flushed; he was starry-voiding, and she knew it. *I wonder where he pulled that number?*

Janeway knew it was fictitious; but she didn't care. "Thirty-seven," she said, pretending to take the number seriously. "That's not so bad. Done—prepare to extrude the shield, Mr. Carey."

Shaking, Carey nodded. "Aye, Captain." He placed his finger over the viewer, waiting for Janeway's command.

She swallowed. "Engage, Mr. Carey."

Carey touched the screen over the ProgStart label; Janeway watched the graphic in horrified fascination as the shield pulled together into a spike curve, the sides coming perilously close as the point extended for kilometer after kilometer. She watched the process, a mother cat watching her kittens; then she jabbed a forefinger and stopped the shields at just a hundred thousand kilometers' extension.

"I'm afraid to go any farther," she admitted. "Now, let's get down tight and dirty on that moon and get that comm link up!"

Lieutenant B'Elanna Torres worked in a frenzy, feeling the fool-killer creeping up behind her, his hands almost touching the back of her neck. Any minute now the sun would blow; any minute, any—

She felt driven, out of control, truly understanding Redbay for the first time since he was hauled aboard the *Voyager*. She had felt the secret terror; she knew. Never again could she calmly consider whether stopping the Furies was worth twenty-seven billion deaths. She knew.

When her commbadge beeped, Torres didn't respond. The sound seemed almost unreal. Then it beeped again, startling her out of her reverie, and she answered hurriedly.

"Torres, this is Captain Janeway. We have a brief window; I must tell you of a strange, new tactictal development." So the captain began; B'Elanna found the theory wildly implausible and faintly cowardly, but she was lured by the thought of being the first Starfleet officer to take a swim in deep space without a suit and live to tell about it.

If she did live. "B'Elanna, I won't lie to you. I don't think this procedure has much of a chance for success."

"It's better than zero, which is what we have now."

"Yes."

"You'll be able to scan for our bodies?"

"I think so. Probably. Is there any way for you to get to the other side of the moon? Maybe you'd better start now."

"Actually, we have our ways. How long from when you detect the final collapse until the sun actually explodes?"

"We're not sure, Lieutenant; maybe as long as thirty minutes."

"That's all? That's pushing it . . . we might not make it to the other side. Captain, can you warn us as soon as you detect the final collapse?"

"Yes. You'll leave immediately for the other side?"

"Aye, Captain. Wait . . ." B'Elanna trailed off as she got busy gluing another fiberoptic cable into the beam-aiming system.

"We'll call you as soon as the sun collapses. Janeway out."

As soon as the captain signed off, Redbay spoke. "I thought they couldn't contact us again."

B'Elanna shrugged. They had not wasted time discussing the obvious. Evidently Janeway, with her magnificent grasp of engineering, had even figured a way around *that* problem. She returned to her new, gainful employment as a saboteur. After a moment's thoughtful gaze into the ceiling, Redbay appeared to dismiss the unexpected miracle chance for survival and get down to the serious business of stopping the invasion.

Captain Janeway ceased communications, but she kept open the comm link. Almost immediately, Ensign Kim's voice came over the ship's intercom. "Captain . . . solar flux increasing significantly. We're having some trouble with navigation; the heavy-particle stream is interfering with our sensors."

"Ensign, stay in this orbit! Don't drift away . . . this is a very fragile comm link. Is Lieutenant Paris still—"

"Aye, Captain," interrupted Kim—a rare occurrence. "Paris is preoccupied keeping the ship on—"

"Well, don't let's break his concentration. Should I come up?" Janeway held her breath, then got the answer she was looking for.

"No, Captain; I think we're all right if we just shut off the thrusters and orbit naturally. We'll be less likely to . . . *Holy—!* Captain, we're drifting!"

"Oh, no." Janeway stared as the field began to stretch,

growing narrower and narrower. "Janeway to Paris! Lieutenant, why are we moving?"

"Captain," said Paris, "we've got a stuck impulse throttle! Trying to compensate . . . The radioactive bombardment—"

"Kill the engines, now!"

"I've been trying," said Paris's professionally calm voice. "Controls are frozen . . . it's because we don't have enough shielding from the ambient solar-radiation flux."

Janeway let out an exasperated sigh. "Great! Paris, without this shield extrusion, there wouldn't be any reason to *be* here in the first place!"

"Captain," said Lieutenant Carey, "I don't want to intrude, but the extrusion is stretching dangerously thin."

Janeway stared. Carey was right. "Carey, prepare to terminate shield extrusion. Paris, get that damned engine under control! Carey, on my signal: three, two—"

Kathryn Janeway never got to zero. As she said the word *one,* at the tip of the extrusion, the two sides of the shield-wedge touched. The shield was not infinitesimally thin; it had a thickness . . . and when the total diameter shrank below twice that diameter, the opposite sides had no choice but to contact each other, like stretching a rubber balloon.

With not a bang but a whisper, all shield-intensity readings across the engineering console dropped immediately to zero. The pointers rotated all the way counterclockwise to the idle amplitude. The forward shields were dead.

They had lost their corridor; within a few hundredths of a second, they lost their comm link. Janeway stared in shock, realizing it would take hours to restore the shields; and in the meantime, if *Voyager* were facing toward the sun when it exploded, then the ship would end up slagged like the artificial moon itself.

"Paris," she said, grabbing control again, "turn the ship directly outboard the sun and *hold that position;* keep the sun aft!" That was the most important point; the aft shields would probably be sufficient to protect the ship, *if* they kept their stern pointed directly toward the sun.

Carey looked stricken. "Captain . . . should I—?"

"Start rebuilding the forward shield? Yes . . . and get that wedge into it so we can try to restore the comm link . . . move it!"

They wouldn't be able to warn Torres and Redbay. All Janeway could think was that she had promised to warn the away team, and now they weren't going to get that chance. B'Elanna and Lieutenant Redbay would have no idea the explosion was coming until the force of it struck their location, turning the moon into a floating cenotaph.

CHAPTER 26

B'Elanna Torres tried to uncramp her fingers, but her hand remained stubbornly clenched around a lump of fiberoptic cable. "Damn," she muttered. She strained back; the epoxy held, welding the cable end to the aiming circuit, but her abused muscles held as well, and she flapped uselessly from the cable like a flag attached by only one stanchion. "Don't just float there," she snapped, "pull me off!"

"You look so picturesque," offered the deadpan Redbay, "wafting gently in the breeze."

"You need sleep. You're hallucinating. It's a human thing; Klingons don't need—"

"*My* hand isn't locked in the On position," pointed out the expatriate lieutenant.

"Shut up! Just unhook my fingers. When the hell is that Federation going to call us? She should at least check in and let us know the comm link is still up."

Redbay stared unblinking. "If it *is* still up."

Suddenly filled with the sense of something urgent forgotten, B'Elanna slapped her commbadge. "Torres to Janeway.

Torres . . . Captain, do you read? Does anyone read? Great! Just peachy! It's down—it's been down for . . . for I don't know how long—the sun is probably gone supernova, and we're going to be fried in about seven minutes!"

"Torres, I think we've done about as much as we can here." Redbay gestured; all but three limp cables had been attached to various junctions and black boxes on what they hoped was the wormhole cannon aiming system.

"We're not done yet."

"If you want to live, I suggest we leave."

"We're not done yet."

Looking into B'Elanna's determined face, Redbay shrugged. *It's all the same to him,* thought the Klingon; *he died fifty thousand light-years back in the Alpha Quadrant.* Redbay pried her hand loose from the cable, and she flexed it while Redbay took over the glue job.

They took fifteen more minutes; as the hours had progressed, they became steadily faster at attaching cables to inputs, outputs, and logic switches.

"Well, Princess, can we leave orbit now?"

B'Elanna tapped at her tricorder with aching fingers. "I think there's a subway shaft heading toward the surface, opposite the sun, about six kilometers away; bearing one-one-one."

Taking long, slow, graceful leaps, they made the distance quickly. The shaft began some two hundred and fifty meters above their heads; evidently, the maintenance workers who serviced the valley would have used some sort of transport vehicle to get around . . . a not unreasonable guess, anyway.

But a quarter-kilometer was a long, long way to jump—even in such a low gravity. Redbay looked dubious. "That's like a jump of over a meter on Earth," he muttered, shaking his head.

"So?"

"I don't think we can make it."

"We? What do you mean *we?*"

Redbay looked at her. "Oh? How high can *you* jump?"

"I may be half human, but I'm also half Klingon. We value athletic ability. I can make it."

"If it's all the same," said Redbay with a cryptic smile, "I think I'll help you a bit. And I really have enjoyed working with you."

"Oh . . . uh, thanks." *What was he talking about?* B'Elanna shook her head; humans—Starfleet officers— were unpredictable even in the best of circumstances, let alone under pressure.

Redbay made a cradle with his hands; B'Elanna stepped into it and he launched her. She timed her leap to give her maximal push-off from his hands. B'Elanna Torres sailed into the air, closer and closer to the ladderlike rungs of the end of the subway shaft.

Her upward motion slowed and peaked . . . thirty meters below the target; slowly, like a petal in the wind, she fell back to the valley floor. They tried once more with even less effect; this time, B'Elanna got a bad push-off and rose only about fifty meters.

Redbay stared upward. "Shame you don't have three hundred meters of rope."

"Eh? I have plenty of Nylex rope."

Redbay stared at her. "More than two hundred and fifty meters?"

"Four hundred."

Shaking his head incredulously, he asked for it. "You wouldn't happen to have a grappling hook, would you?"

"A what?"

"Hm." He tightened the beam on his phaser to a fine, thin cutting blade and proceeded to cut away a hunk of some strange alloy—not the phaser-impervious metal—and shape it into the rough form of a three-pronged hook. Then he tied it off to the rope and began to cast. It took him eleven tries to finally hook the grapple through one of the ladder rungs. He tugged a few experimental times, then pronounced it fit to climb. "Torres," he asked, puzzled, "why didn't you tell me you had the rope? And *don't* say because I didn't ask."

Torres swallowed the reply she had been about to make. "I was just going to tie it off on the shaft so you could climb up."

"You were going to . . . ?" He shook his head, amazed. "I thought—only one of us was going to make it out."

"Don't be a jerk. I am human, not just Klingon."

"You are Starfleet," he said softly, "not just Maquis."

She glared, then took the rope and began to climb.

The shaft led straight up seventy meters, then debouched onto a sloping mag-lev track. No subway car waited for them. "Look for a button," B'Elanna suggested. The feeling of impending doom tightened her gut. Any moment now, the sun could—or maybe it *already had*. There would be a lag time of seven and a half minutes until the energy pulse hit them, perhaps another hundred and eighty before the heavy particle bombardment, the expanding explosion, tore the moon apart. At the core, even if they survived the initial explosion, it would take the *Voyager* too long to sort them out from all the other debris. They would die, either incinerated by the residual radiation left behind by the supernova . . . or, if the Bela-Neutron devices absorbed enough of the energy, frozen in the interstellar vacuum.

B'Elanna checked her trusty tricorder, a device she was more and more beginning to think of as her lifeline back to the light, out of the long darkness of their suicidal mission. She stared, seeing a strange reading. It took her a few moments to figure out what was rushing toward them. "Hey, Redbay—what did you press?"

"Nothing. I haven't found any—"

"The subway's on its way; we should see it in . . . hell, there it is!"

The blur in the distance raced closer, alarmingly fast; then it braked to a rough, angry halt scant meters from where the two stood, immobile with surprise. The doors popped open; quickly, before it could change its mind, Redbay and Torres launched toward the open hatch. B'Elanna missed slightly, grazing her head on the hatch rim. She struggled to a chair and pushed herself into it, using her feet against the seat ahead of her; only then did she clench her teeth and rub her injured scalp, which bled profusely. The blood drifted out and finally down, bright globules of red darkening visibly as they wafted toward the deck.

The train started with a lurch—Redbay had touched the forward panel—and B'Elanna was kicked back into her seat with an acceleration eight hundred times what they had lived in for the past seven hours.

She fell back into her seat in agony, unable to breathe, still dizzy from the blow. Her inner ears refused to orient themselves; her balance insisted she was lying on her back on a terribly dense planet, being slowly crushed to death.

At last, after two minutes, the acceleration ceased abruptly, and B'Elanna Torres could breathe again. She gasped for air while gravity slowly returned to the "bottom" of the car, increasing perceptibly with every second's travel of five kilometers, some of it upward.

"Now—comes—the long wait," she wheezed. "We going—to make it?"

Redbay did not answer. Looking across the car toward the front, B'Elanna saw that the man was sound asleep.

She debated waking him, then realized that he would have plenty of time to wake up and panic when the explosion came, the explosion that would almost certainly kill the pair of them anyway. Both would have the same chance to get a last breath before being blown into free space to die horribly.

They were virtually at the surface itself, by the tricorder's estimation, when suddenly the lights flickered. A huge, loud thud jarred B'Elanna's sensitive ears; the whole car skewed violently to one side, and she heard a loud scraping noise. It took her a second to realize that the car had lost all power . . . the electrical power was gone.

With a chill, Lieutenant Torres realized that the electromagnetic pulse had just struck the moon. *It's all over,* she thought in near panic; *either we won or we lost . . . either the Furies jumped to the Alpha Quadrant, and when we return, we'll return to a dead, alien battlefield, or they didn't make the jump, and—*

And what? There were too many possibilities. "Redbay," she called, as the train ground slowly to a stop, friction eating away at even their terrific speed. "Redbay, wake up!"

"I'm awake," he said, bleary-voiced. "Who turned out the—"

"Start the timer, Lieutenant. The car didn't make it all

the way to the top before the pulse fried the power circuits. We've got about a hundred and eighty minutes before the explosion . . . three hours to make—looks like two point five kilometers. A little less than a kilometer per hour, straight up." It was harsh, but just barely possible in the low gravity of the moon.

"B'Elanna? It was a pleasure working with you. I'm glad we—"

"Redbay, didn't we go through all this? We're dying in battle, of a sorts, with the greatest enemy our quadrant has ever faced. Isn't that enough?"

Silence. Then Redbay responded, cynical and sardonic as ever. "Sure. My little heart is all aglow with the honor of it."

B'Elanna closed her eyes. The tricorder was programmed to give her a signal every hour, then at the final thirty minutes, ten minutes, and a big alarm the last minute before the explosion, to give her time to hyperventilate, supersaturate her tissues with oxygen, a last-ditch technique she had discussed with Redbay.

It would alert her. She could close her eyes, offer a last prayer for an honorable death to Kahless the Eternal. They started the long climb up the ladder that ran along the inside of the shaft. Three hours for two and a half kilometers—not impossible on level ground. An absurdity climbing a ladder.

She smiled; she would finally get a chance to see whether she was human or Klingon in the end.

CHAPTER 27

COME ON, URGED CAPTAIN JANEWAY SILENTLY TO HERSELF; *come up—just for a moment, just long enough to warn—*

Not for the first time, Janeway wondered why they don't teach the most important command course at the Academy: how to be in two places at the same time. She was in engineering, monkeying with the shields; she desperately needed to be on the bridge.

"Captain," said Lieutenant Tuvok from the bridge, "I must inform you that we are being bombarded by subspace chroniton particles. I believe the final, chain-reaction collapse has just begun. In approximately one and a half minutes, the star will experience full collapse and will explode into a supernova. We have about nine minutes before the radiation front arrives."

"Mr. Kim . . . ?"

"We're not at a safe distance, Captain."

"Mr. Paris, take us into the moon's shadow. If we're lucky, that's where Torres and Redbay will be anyway. I'm on my way to the bridge. Carey, keep on those shields! Damn—I wish we had sensors." Janeway cut off the rest of her complaint; the radiation levels were simply too high.

"Aye, Captain." Paris pressed an illuminated square on his viewer, and the ship changed course.

Janeway continued her frenzied work, trying with Lieutenant Carey to restore the forward shields and give them their new wedge shape, so she could extrude the shields and restore communications—or work the transporters—despite radiation interference. But the bioneural circuitry of the *Voyager* had reacted badly to the short when the shield walls touched; in fact, if the doctor were to examine them, he would probably pronounced the cells "in anaphylactic shock," as if they were truly biological and suffering a severe allergic reaction to each other.

Now she stepped off the turbolift; ship safety had just taken precedence even over the shield operation. Chakotay rose and shifted to the his seat as Janeway sat down.

"Kept it warm for you," said the commander with a wink.

"Janeway to all ship's personnel," said the captain. She waited a beat, then spoke to the entire ship. "Attention, crew; this is Captain Janeway. As I explained, the star is just now collapsing and will momentarily become a supernova. There may be disruption of critical systems; I'm putting the ship on red alert.

"The *Voyager* will easily survive the explosion. I want all transporter manned with a double staff, immediately.

"Thank you all; it is as always a pleasure being your commanding officer. That is all."

Janeway waited a moment for the computer to realize her transmission was over. "Activate EMH program."

"Please state the nature of the emergency," said the doctor from the viewer; then he nodded. "Ah. I see you are about to engage in some dangerously theatrical maneuvers in the middle of a supernova. Do you, by any chance, expect any casualties?"

"This isn't the time for sarcasm, Doctor. Prepare sickbay for crew injuries and for the imminent arrival of Torres and Redbay."

"Aye, Captain. The ERT crash-crew is already standing by."

"Good. Now all we have to do is wait for—"

"Captain," interrupted Tuvok, "two large Fury ships off the starboard bow." His laconic voice belied the shocking intelligence.

"What? Where?" Instinctively, Janeway glanced first at her own sensor-slave display on the arm of the command chair.

"The sensors do not register them because of the radiation. They are, however, visible on the forward viewer."

Janeway looked up. The two Fury ships were nothing like the small patrol craft they had fought earlier. These were long, cigar-shaped, sporting hundreds of metallic tendrils with pods on the ends—weapons? Sensors? Fighter spacecraft? It was impossible to tell until they did something, by which time it might be too late.

"Paris—how'd they get so close?"

Lieutenant Paris squinted. "Um . . . they're not very close, Captain; by the magnification and the parallax effect, I'd say they were, oh, a couple of hundred thousand kilometers."

The bridge fell silent, everyone doing the same calculation. "Tuvok," said Janeway with quiet authority, "check my math on this: assuming Mr. Paris is correct, *how* big are those ships?"

"Mr. Paris's estimation is essentially correct," concluded the Vulcan, "and the Fury ships are approximately two hundred and eighty kilometers long, seventy kilometers in diameter, and the pylons supporting the pods extend some three hundred kilometers from the center. By the albedo and color, I suspect their hulls are made of the same dense metal we observed on the Fury planet."

"Mr. Paris, come about one-eight-zero degrees," ordered the captain without hesitation.

"Turn *around?*"

"Yes, Lieutenant. Turn and run like hell."

A bright flower bloomed at the forward end of a pod, then another at another pod; while Paris turned the ship, maintaining a video feed at the ships in the upper half of the forward viewer, Janeway watched seven more flowers bloom bloodred from seven more pods.

"Evasive maneuvers, Mr. Paris; those are weapons of

unknown strength—but probably a damn sight more deadly than the scout ships' disruptor cannons!"

The *Voyager* began an intricate, preprogrammed series of evasions—Janeway recognized the pattern as EMP 11-Delta—but the flowers kept turning to track. They moved somewhat slower than photon torpedoes, but faster than the nuclear missiles the smaller ships had occasionally fired.

"Kim," snapped Janeway, "can you get a phaser lock on the missiles?"

"Uh . . . uh . . . no, ma'am! I mean Captain! The sensors won't—"

"Mr. Kim, photon torpedoes; program them to home by visual image on the missiles. Fire as soon as you've set the program."

"Aye . . ." Kim pounded frantically at the console, muttering below the audible range.

Janeway sat in her command chair, staring at the screen, forcing herself to remain outwardly calm, confident, in command: the consummate starship captain. Inside, she was screaming in utter panic; these Fury ships dwarfed the biggest thing the Borg had ever thrown at the Federation . . . and *the Voyager had no forward shields!*

One of the missiles had already tracked too close for a safe shot by the photon torpedo; fortunately, the torpedo's own programming caused it to bypass the near missile and focus on one farther away. The torpedoes and the flower-missiles met in empty space; the explosions lit the starry sky with a flare so bright that the viewer could filter it only by whiting out the entire field of view, both ahead and behind. In the brief flash before the light flared, Janeway could actually see a shock wave spreading at about half light speed; six hammer blows struck the ship's rear shields, sending the *Voyager* skittering in a random direction, tumbling so hard the inertial dampers could not keep up, and the crew were flung against their combat harnesses.

The tumble saved them; the shock waves blew the ship out of the first missile's path, and it could not turn fast enough to track. It brushed past and continued into nowheresville, out of sight and out of mind—so Janeway thought.

THE FINAL FURY

"Damage report!" she shouted, trying to be heard over the residual explosions and the red-alert klaxon; "and shut that bloody noise off!"

Tuvok killed the klaxon while he rattled off a list of decks damaged by the multiple explosions.

"Captain," said Kim, his face paling as he stared at the rearview viewer. "One, two, three, four more rose-missiles launched from the second Fury ship!"

"Wonderful," snarled the captain. Then she smiled. "Mr. Paris—hard about one-eight-zero again; let's try driving right down their throats . . . see how smart their missiles really are."

Paris grinned; but it was a bloodless smile. He manhandled the ship hard about and began dancing and dodging toward the closest Fury.

"Captain," said Tuvok, cutting through the soldier's fog that had seized the bridge crew, "the missile we evaded has turned around and is closing on us again."

"Still? What's the intercept ETA?"

Tuvok closed his eyes for a moment; in a pinch, the Vulcan could calculate quicker than consulting the computer. "At the present velocity and course, it should strike us just about the time we intercept the nearest Fury ship."

Janeway leaned back; she was so awash in adrenaline—battlefield pump—that she was actually intoxicated on it. She smiled, mirroring Paris. "Gentlemen," she said slowly, "have you ever played the ancient Earth game of chicken?"

"No," said Kim.

"Of course," said Paris simultaneously. Chakotay merely sucked a breath through his teeth.

"I am not aware of such a game," added Tuvok pettishly. "How is it germane to our present difficulties, Captain?"

"Mr. Paris: dead-on toward the closest Fury ship, constant heading. Ramming speed," she added thoughtfully.

"Aye, *aye,* Captain!" Paris changed course to point directly toward the gigantic target and increased the *Voyager*'s velocity to full impulse. "Show *them* who's chicken," he mumbled.

The two ships closed at a terrific rate, and behind *Voyager,* the missile gained on them both. As they cracked the hundred-thousand-kilometer range again, a number of smaller weapons on the pylons opened fire on the Starfleet ship. Energy beams, the terror projector, and tracers flared across the gap, trying to focus on the incoming kamikaze.

"Captain," reminded Chakotay, leaning forward, chin in hand, like Rodin's *Thinker,* "we have no forward shields. One shot and we're dead."

"If *we're* flying blind, *they're* flying blind. Ensign, return fire, photons and phasers. Aim manually using the computer . . . let's see whose fire-control system is the better!"

Like two wounded duelists riding toward each other firing their flintlocks, thought Janeway, slipping into a fantasy from the era of her favorite holodeck program, *one of us ends up with a pistol-ball in his gut.*

Tuvok called the distance: "Fifty thousand . . . forty . . . thirty . . ."

Paris's hands began to tremble as they hovered over the helm console, ready to pull away. But Janeway did not give the order.

The ship loomed so large it overflowed the viewer; Paris stepped back the magnification, but within seconds, they stared at a solid wall of metal at normal view.

Lieutenant Paris aimed *Voyager* for the largest viewport—the window alone could swallow the entire Federation ship.

At ten thousand kilometers, Tuvok began ticking off each thousand: "Nine, eight, seven, six—"

Captain Janeway crossed her legs. She folded her hands neatly in her lap. She said nothing. She quickly lost all perspective: the Fury ships were as large as good-sized asteroids! Dark in color with few reference points or markings; seconds before impact, an impact that would destroy the smaller ship, Janeway hallucinated that they were divebombing an enormous city of the dead—or Pan-Demonium, City of All Demons in hell.

Next to her, Chakotay leaned back in his chair, gripping the sides. The computer continued firing, aiming at the weapon sites up and down the pylons. Still, the Fury fire-control computers had not been able to lock on to the onrushing starship.

Chakotay sucked in yet another huge breath, face white as porcelain. He grinned through clenched teeth, unblinking. Janeway understood perfectly; she wanted to duck and put her head under her arms—but she was "driving," in a real sense.

"Two thousand—one thousand—seven six five four—"

At one hundred fifty kilometers, Paris evidently couldn't stand the suspense. He grabbed the console in a panic, not waiting for orders, and threw the guidance control all the way right and forward.

The shriek of ripping metal—*not the hull!* begged the captain—cut through the bridge silence like needles through a drumskin. Janeway was pulled so violently against her seat that for an instant, less than a second, she blacked out. When she blinked back to consciousness, she saw nothing but the artificial moon ahead of her; in the rear view, she saw the Fury ship illuminated against a flash as bright as a stellar core.

A fraction of a second later, the shock wave from the hunting missile struck the *Voyager*.

The bright blue glow of hell surrounded the ship in all directions, matting out the stars, the missiles, the faint, twisted threads that once were Fury ships. For a brief instant, before the video feed in all directions went blank, Kathryn Janeway saw the outer skin of the moon boiling away like water on a hotplate.

The supernova's radiation front had finally arrived.

CHAPTER 28

STILL GROGGY, JANEWAY STARTED TO RECOIL BEFORE REMEMbering she was looking at a video—a video that had just vanished, as the external holocams were fried by an electromagnetic pulse of many giga-ergs.

She staggered to her feet to rouse the others, but Tuvok was already doing so. The Vulcan lieutenant appeared unruffled, but it took the two of them to get Kim and Paris back to consciousness; the weapons officer had struck his head on his console when he was slammed down by one of the explosions.

While Tuvok revived his auxiliary cadet crew members, Janeway took command of the situation. "Kim, get that viewer repaired."

"Captain, the exterior monitors are gone." Kim held his hand to his head; Janeway could see blood dripping from the slash, but she couldn't spare the ensign, not even long enough to send him to sickbay.

"Replicate new ones and send someone EVA—in a rad suit—to replace them . . . we've got to have our eyes! We don't have much time. Janeway to EMH program."

THE FINAL FURY

"EMH here."

"Doctor, how many injuries?"

"I was already treating twenty-two casualties. I've got a lot more now, mostly minor."

"Casualty report?"

"There are no deaths among the crew, Captain. Seventy-two reported injuries so far, mostly from falling and striking body parts against panels, railings, and consoles."

"We've got a head injury up here; can you send a medtech up for Ensign Kim?"

"On her way, Captain."

"Thank you. Janeway out. Paris! How long before we can see again?"

"Uh . . . looks like engineering is estimating two hours to get the monitors back on-line."

"Two hours! We only have three total!"

"Well, that's what they're saying," responded Paris reproachfully.

"All right, get 'em hopping. Offer them time and a half."

"Offer them *what?*"

"Never mind. Old Earth reference. Sensors?"

Tuvok answered. "You will not be able to use the sensors for at least seven hours, unless you depart the immediate vicinity of the supernova. There is too much radiation of all types at every frequency."

"Great. We have to get those monitors up. Get all nonessential crew members to viewports—*filtered* viewports. When that shock wave hits, the moon will literally disintegrate. I'll want every eye on this ship watching for B'Elanna and Redbay. Report any sighting immediately to Lieutenant Tuvok for relay to the transporter teams."

The turbolift doors slid open and Kes hustled into the room, carrying a medikit. The elfin Ocampan stood over Ensign Kim and expertly repaired his split scalp. "It's nothing major," she said, loudly enough that Janeway could hear.

The captain fidgeted, waiting for Kes to make some cold point about what they had done; but Kes surprised her, saying nothing. The Ocampan finished with Kim, then tended to the rest of the cuts and bruises on the bridge. "The doctor is handling the serious cases in sickbay," she said, wiping the sweat from her eyes with the back of her hand. Her hair was matted; she looked harrowed. *She's not going to sleep very well,* thought Captain Janeway. *I wonder if any of us will.*

The last thought echoed around the caverns of Janeway's skull as she nervously felt behind her for the captain's chair, trying not to show the hollow emptiness she felt.

She sat down again. "Well, that's it, gentlemen. Whatever was going to happen, happened. Either the Fury planet disappeared . . . or it's not going to." She paused, almost afraid to ask the next question. "Well . . . ? Can anybody pick it up on visual?"

Chakotay leaned into the ship's intercom. "Attention, all crew; this is Commander Chakotay. All nonessential personnel are to report *immediately* to any *filtered* viewport on decks seven through nineteen. Do not, repeat, *DO NOT* use the viewport on the hangar deck, since it has no radiation filter.

"For right now, each crew member should look for the Fury planet. Our external sensors and monitors are inoperative . . . we're down to eyeballs, people. So look sharp; senior officer or petty officer in every viewport stateroom report to the bridge what you saw. Chakotay out." He turned to Janeway. "Well, now we sit. And wait."

"Damn, I hate this," she said quietly. "I wish there were something more we could do. I can't stand just sitting. Chakotay, you have the conn; I'm going to inspect the ship."

"Captain," said Tuvok, "I do not wish to overly alarm you, but I suggest you continue working on restoring the shield extrusion instead."

Janeway frowned. "I was going to make a damage inspection of the ship and see to the wounded in sickbay."

"Our aft shield is too flat; when the stellar material strikes us, it will act as a sail on an early sailing vessel, propelling us forward. Captain, unless you restore the wedge-shield and point the bow toward the supernova, we will be blown far off course by the particle barrage . . . perhaps into the moon itself at twelve thousand kilometers per second, sufficient energy to destroy the ship with or without a shield."

"I hadn't thought of that. Yes, the wedge would deflect the particle stream to either side and stabilize us."

"And unless you re-create the shield-extrusion formula, we will find ourselves unable to lock on to Lieutenants Torres or Redbay to beam them aboard, even should we find them."

I forgot about that too! she raged to herself. *I'm fading fast—what's the matter with me?* But outwardly, she nodded and said, "Yes, I know." The captain of a starship had a duty to appear calm and confident in front of the crew.

Commander Chakotay spoke up, interrupting his stream of commands to various departments on the *Voyager*. "If it's all right with you, Captain, I'll conduct the inspection and visit the wounded. I had a lot of practice patching up ruptures in my old Maquis ship."

Janeway smiled. "Ganging up on the captain, eh? Banishing me to engineering? Well, good luck. Kim, keep a sharp eye out for more Fury ships. And Paris—recalculate the moon's orbit assuming . . . assuming the Fury planet suddenly vanished. Just in case."

"I've finished," said Kes. Janeway jumped; she had completely forgotten about the Ocampan.

"Finished?"

Kes's hair hung in front of her eyes, muting her look—for which the captain was profoundly grateful. She did not want to meet Kes's stare, not yet. "Yes, Captain. I've finished tending the wounded. May I leave? The doctor may need me in sickbay."

"Disappear." As Kes turned to leave, Janeway added, "Oh, and Kes? If you get a chance when the time comes . . . take a look out a viewport. Might see something. Every eye counts." Janeway smiled.

Kes, standing at the turbolift doors, nodded slowly; but she said nothing, just turned and left. During her entire visit, she hadn't said a word about the Furies, the dead, the potentially inconceivable destruction.

In a way, thought the captain, *I almost wish she had.*

Janeway rose; just as she was about to enter the turbolift,

Chakotay stopped her with a word. He listened grimly, nodding occasionally, though the communication was audio only—directed so that only Commander Chakotay could hear it. He looked up as he severed the connection. "Captain," he said, his voice at once sad and sympathetic, "I've heard back now from four view stations, including two department heads."

Feeling a cold hand grab her intestines, Janeway asked the sixty-four-kilobar question: "Is the planet still there, Ex?"

Chakotay said nothing for a moment. The invisible hand squeezed hard; it was all Janeway could do not to double over from the pain . . . was it stress?

"No, Captain," said the executive officer at last. "The planet is no longer in orbit around the sun. It has . . ."—he turned his hands palm-up—" . . . vanished," he concluded.

Utter silence reigned on the bridge. Not a man or woman there did not know what that meant. All their plans, all their—

"Captain," interrupted Lieutenant Tuvok, "I have an anomalous reading."

"Yes, Mr. Tuvok?" Janeway suddenly was so weary, she could fall asleep on her feet.

"The reading is difficult to isolate because of the extreme level of electromagnetic radiation enveloping this system. But tetrion particles are singularly transparent to high-energy photons, and are produced in copious amounts in the vicinity of a wormhole.

"Using the stream output, I was able to make a reasonable estimate of the main direction the wormhole occupied.

"Captain, wherever they went, they were *not* heading toward the Alpha Quadrant."

Janeway hesitated. "They weren't? Which way were they headed? Where does the wormhole terminate?"

Tuvok checked his screen. "I cannot tell without better sensors where the wormhole terminates; but the part of it I can readily see is heading in the general direction of the Lesser Magellanic Cloud."

Janeway could not figure out what Tuvok was saying exactly; but she knew enough to relegate it to the back burner, so she could concentrate on the most important task: restoring the shield system, wedge and extrusion and all, before the wave front arrived and flung the *Voyager* millions of kilometers away.

Lieutenant B'Elanna Torres hauled herself up another hatchway, flopped over the lip, and lay on the floor, exhausted. She had never before in her life attempted to climb a kilometer straight up; even in the relatively low gravity, every muscle in her body felt as if it had been seared by red-hot iron bands. Her only satisfaction, a grim one, was that Redbay's strength of despair had long ago given out; he could only climb a few rungs up each ladder and wait for B'Elanna to help him the rest of the way up.

At first, he had suggested she leave him behind. But this was not the warrior way: a Klingon did not leave fellow warriors behind . . . and the human side of B'Elanna rebelled at the thought of letting a fellow human die, even if he was Starfleet. Killing enemies in battle—that was acceptable, even heroic! But not letting former enemies be blown to pieces in a lifeless moon.

This time, however, Redbay could not even make it to the ladder at all. He lay on the deckplates, a level below Torres, panting.

Lieutenant Torres unslung the tricorder she had stubbornly carried up meter after meter. She checked the time: two hours and twenty-eight minutes; they had exactly thirty-nine minutes until the tricorder timer read 03:07, B'Elanna's best estimate of the time from the explosion—seven and a half minutes before the mag-lev failed. It took light and other electromagnetic waves seven and a half minutes to travel from sun to moon; the expanding shell of stellar matter that would destroy the moon would take twenty-five times longer to reach the moon.

Unless, of course, it's moving faster than I expected. She had not shared that worry with Redbay; it was a silly fret . . . after all, the star stuff could just as well be moving slower. Without analyzing the supernova itself, there was no way to tell.

"Call it thirty-five minutes," she announced between gasps, "to make—half a klick. We're doing well, Redbay—come on, just a half a kilometer . . . move!"

Redbay glared up at her with the first honest emotion he had shown toward anyone but the Furies: desperation beyond words. He looked down, utterly spent.

B'Elanna climbed back down. "You *think* you're exhausted, but you're not. You can always take just one more rung, one more, one more, until you make it or you die from the effort." She dropped lightly to the deck, faking strength and breath she really didn't have. It worked; Redbay struggled pathetically to his feet. B'Elanna steered him toward the ladder, then climbed right behind him to push him forward.

They slogged the last, bitter half-kilometer, while B'Elanna deliberately did not stare at her timer. She even turned off the alarms when they began sounding faster and faster . . . it made little difference whether they hyperventilated if they were still a quarter-kilometer below the surface.

But they made slow progress. At last, they reached the surface. B'Elanna whipped her tricorder around and stared at it.

T plus fourteen. T *PLUS* fourteen . . . so much for time estimates!

"Well, Redbay, we're fourteen minutes late. Fortunately, the particle front is no prompter than we. Better start hyperventilating; it probably will strike at any—"

As darkness closed around B'Elanna Torres, she heard and felt the distant impact of a Klingon warhammer against her entire body. Then she floated in timeless discontinuity.

CHAPTER 29

For the thirtieth time since Captain Janeway and Lieutenant Carey began trying to reconstruct the forward shield, introduce the fold to make a wedge, and re-create the extrusion formula, the captain hallucinated exactly the right figures that indicated success.

For a moment, her heart rate rose to full impulse; then she checked herself. Twenty-nine previous hallucinations tempered her momentrary feeling of triumph.

But this time, the figures did not melt back into the real numbers, different enough to turn success into total failure. In fact, this time, the more she stared, the more the figures looked like a real, bona-fide solution.

"Lieutenant," she said, "check my eyes on this. What does the bioelectrical Griffin potential read?"

Carey turned his own glazed eyes onto the screen; he squinted, shook his head, then sat bolt upright. "Captain, the shield's up," he breathed, so quietly it was almost as if he were afraid to shout for fear of knocking over the fragile thing with too boisterous a shout.

"Time check."

Carey looked at his screen timer readout. "About, what, four minutes?"

"Janeway to bridge: Chakotay, the forward shield is up."

"Yes, Captain, we just noticed."

"Turn us around while—"

"We already have, Captain. Give us a wedge . . . hurry!"

Janeway smiled. "Aye, aye, Commander. *Captain* Janeway out."

The minutes ticked by as Janeway followed exactly the recipe she had used successfully to introduce the fold the last time. After a time lapse, she glanced at the ship's chronometer. Eight minutes had passed; they were already into overtime. "Let's hope it's a really slow explosion," she muttered.

"Two more sequences," hissed Carey, hands trembling as he typed the instructions.

Janeway forced herself not to watch the viewer; the wave front would come when it came, and watching would only waste more time. Carey, however, was not so circumspect. "Captain!" he said. "I can see it—*I see it coming!*"

"Thank you, Lieutenant. Now stop staring at the viewer and type!" Carefully, checking each character, Janeway typed her last command, a direct, bioneural assembler-code sequence . . . the final piece of the Carey formula: the command sequence was actually a set of construction instructions that forced the neural-net shield-control computer to conform to a discontinuous function . . . the shield bent, and bent, and suddenly *folded* neatly along the line of force-equilibrium.

"Got it," announced Janeway, smiling in triumph muted by the grim possibilities awaiting them after the wave passed them and struck the moon.

"Fifteen seconds to spare," said the captain; "hardly even a ra—"

The expanding shell of superenergetic debris, nearly ninety percent of the former sun's mass, struck the *Voyager* head-on. The ship jerked with the shock and was driven backward at 0.15 impulse speed, about 11,500 kilometers per second, the speed of the impact shell. Slapping her commbadge, the captain bellowed, "Janeway to bridge: compensate!"

If there was an answer, she didn't hear; the ship rumbled like thunder, shaking violently. Janeway had once felt a 7.9 earthquake on Sprague XI, the hedonistic paradise sometimes used for shore leave; the shaking was nothing compared to what her own ship now suffered.

In the viewer down in engineering, the stars were jagged streaks where they weren't obscured by the roiling mass of superheated plasma bursting past the *Voyager;* without the shields, the ship would not have lasted a microsecond. But Tom Paris kept it on course; the computers compensated for the buffeting, and the great part of the particles deflected off of the forward shield-wedge and broke to either side, stabilizing the ship left to right; the impulse engines took care of the relative movement up and down, and Chakotay and Paris refused to allow the ship to be driven backward.

The shaking was worse than when they were en route to the Fury star system and the gravitic stabilizers broke—was it really a thousand years ago?—and again, Janeway caught herself fighting back nausea. Lieutenant Carey lost the battle.

Then suddenly, it stopped; the bulk of the shell continued past, headed toward the moon, which it would batter apart in just a few seconds.

Captain Janeway lurched to her feet, fumbling for her badge. "Janeway," she croaked. *"To the moon,* Paris!" Then she dropped back down; nausea or no, she had to restore the shield extrusion immediately, as in yesterday.

B'Elanna floated back to consciousness, feeling nauseated, sore, and dizzy, with a head big enough for its own set of moons. Three questions lined up for attention; the first was *What the hell was I drinking?*

Then she woke fully. "Why the—the hell is there still *gravity?"* she demanded aloud. Belatedly, she allowed the third question: "And why is it pinning me to the ceiling?"

She staggered up and discovered she had no sense of balance. She fell heavily, weighing more than she would on the *Voyager*. Redbay was across the upper chamber, which was dark, lit only by light streaming in the jagged holes in the bulkheads. He lay against the floor, upside down by B'Elanna's reference, as if he were glued there.

Jagged holes? In a flash, B'Elanna Torres realized what had happened: The entire chamber had been ripped loose by the shock wave, and it spun through space, pressing the two away-team members against the perimeter by centrifugal force.

Spinning through space! By itself—and the hurricane rush past her ears indicated the air was rapidly gushing out the gashes in the metal seams, the superdense Fury metal torn apart like cardboard.

B'Elanna wasted precious moments gawking; outside the rips, the vast, black abyss of space was neither, filled with glowing gas that lit the inside of the chunk with a hellish glare.

"Redbay!" She belly-crawled along the perimeter, fighting the increased acceleration when she got into the corners, which were nearly one and a half times as far from the axis of rotation as where she had been thrown . . . which meant they dragged her down at one and a half times the gravity.

She reached the stricken lieutenant and shook him into semiconsciousness. "Red . . . bay," she gasped, becoming lightheaded in the thinning air. "Get up, get—breathe deep!—get . . . get out—find us—beam . . ." B'Elanna fell over, panting with the exertion. Already, the sound of the air was growing distant and tinny, her own voice sounding like it came from the bottom of a well. The thin air didn't carry the sound.

She summoned up some strength and slapped Redbay, rousing him fully. He stared at her, looking sick, miserable, and at last showing some real, honest fear. He had come back to himself—only to come back to a nightmare.

"Breathe!" she screamed, costing her enough oxygen that her head pounded and she almost fainted. Weakly, she pointed at the nearest rip.

Hyperventilate, she warned herself. She began to pant like an overheated dog, and Redbay noticed and imitated her. She could not watch the stars and bright mist swirl past the rips; it made her sick, and the very last thing she needed at that moment was to waste precious time and invaluable air vomiting.

The room seemed unnaturally white; her peculiar, oxygen-starved brain spat up the most useless piece of information it could find: that the low pressure and lack of oxygen was affecting the rods and cones in her retinas, washing the color from her vision.

EYES! She remembered. "Close . . . eyes," she croaked, pointing to her eyes. Redbay nodded, terrified beyond words.

Together they rose to hands and knees and crawled toward the rip, toward death and emptiness. Toward the only silly hope they had left. They panted, trying to suck down as much air as possible to prolong the agony before their brains finally suffered fatal damage due to oxygen deprivation.

Redbay balked; Torres grabbed him by the seat of the pants and hurled him out the rip. *Bones of my ancestors,* she thought sickly; *that's the first time in my life I've ever thrown someone out the airlock into deep space.* She flopped over the hole in what felt like the floor, though it looked like a bulkhead, and was hurled, tumbling, into interstellar nothingness.

B'Elanna shut her eyes tight and rolled into a tight, tight, fetal ball, wrapping her arms around her to preserve as much heat as she could. It was unnecessary; the instant she was out and unshielded, she felt searing fire across her back, her legs, and her arms. *It's a million degrees!* screamed her shocked and tortured mind. *It's the debris, it's superheated gas from—*

The shock bit deeper into B'Elanna's body and brain, and consciousness slipped deeper and deeper beneath her thick, Klingon hide.

She was—she was going—she was going to—

Kes pressed so hard against the window port, her nose began to bleed. She didn't notice Neelix, crowded right next to her and everyone else. But they were too busy staring and squinting, trying to pick out a pair of tiny figures who might lurk anywhere within the bright, expanding gas cloud, which the *Voyager* followed at an altogether indiscreet distance.

"There!" Neelix shouted, pointing at a speck.

"No," she said, "that's a piece of conduit."

"Are you *sure?*"

"Yes . . . wait! What's that over there?"

Neelix shoved against the port as if the extra millimeter might make a difference. "Yes, it could—I think I can see— yes! No!" He pulled back involuntarily, angrily swatting the transparent aluminum as if it were to blame. "No, no, no! It's just another . . ."

Ocampans had good eyes, better than human eyes. She liked to think Neelix's Talaxian eyes were better. In the far, far distance, to the left, Kes just barely made out a speck. It was at the limit of her vision. The ship was paralleling it, and it was growing no larger.

"Neelix," she breathed, suddenly faint, "I think I might have something solid."

"Where? Where?"

Keeping her eye on the dot, Kes moved behind Neelix and pointed past his face—"To the left," she whispered in his ample ear; "further . . . now up a bit—there."

Neelix stared for a moment. Then he touched his commbadge. "Neelix and Kes," he said. "We've got one."

"Coordinates," snapped the unemotional, uninflected voice of Tuvok.

"Um . . ." Neelix felt his heart race; he wasn't used to the Starfleet system. "It's a little to the left and—"

"What port are you standing at?" interrupted the annoying Vulcan.

"Um . . ."

From behind Neelix, Kes shouted, "Number UV-eighteen!"

"There is no need to increase your vocal volume," said Tuvok. "The comm link includes you as well."

On the bridge, Tuvok said, "Captain, I suggest we turn to heading one-nine-seven."

"Proceed, Mr. Paris," said Janeway. "Increase to thirty meters per second." Paris engaged the new course. "It's

THE FINAL FURY

crunch time," continued the captain. "Mr. Kim, extrude the shield . . . but on your ensign's pips, *don't let the shield walls touch.*"

Licking her lips, Janeway touched her commbadge. "Captain to engineering. Mr. Carey—are you ready with that modified monitor?"

"No," said the acting chief engineer.

"Good. Turn it on anyway; let's see what we can see."

The forward viewer, a blank wall at the moment, flickered and displayed a few dozen diagonal lines of color. "I told you it wasn't ready," said Carey.

"Extruding the shield now," announced Kim to an unappreciative audience. Sweat rolled down his face; it was one of the most terrific responsibilities he had yet faced on his first, and probably last, ship assignment.

"Dammit, Carey, we can't see a thing!"

"Something must be loose, a connection."

"Do something—kick it!"

"Captain, it's probably in the monitor itself! That's outside . . . I'll have to go EVA and—"

"Kick the stupid interface! It's right in front of you!"

Tuvok looked puzzled. "Captain, I fail to see what good—"

The image lurched, then settled into an oddly flat picture of bright splotches of color—hot, ionized plasma gas—with here and there a star visible through the glow. The image was bizarre, disorienting; with so many of the ship's systems off-line, including the replicator, it was the best they could do. It was weak, dizzying; but they finally had eyes . . . or rather, one eye.

After a moment, she stood from her chair. "I see them! One of them; Tuvok, can you get a visual lock and send it to transporter room two?"

"Not yet, Captain," said the science officer.

"Janeway to transporter two; prepare to area-beam a humanoid directly to sickbay from coordinates that will be transmitted by Lieutenant Tuvok. Janeway to EMH program; prepare to receive a patient, Doctor."

"I have a visual lock now, Captain; transmitting to transporter room two."

"Energize when ready, transporter two."

Tense seconds passed. Janeway stared and stared; but before she could make out anything more than two arms and two legs, Tuvok announced, "It's Lieutenant Redbay." Before Tuvok finished the sentence, the speck dematerialized.

"Doctor to Janeway," said the disembodied voice of the emergency holographic medical program. "I have Lieutenant Redbay. I am initiating CPR now."

Janeway nodded, absurdly since it was a voice link. "Where is she—*where is she?*"

The universe moves by strange and bizarre turns. With all the eyes on the bridge scanning the glowing plasma cloud for B'Elanna Torres, it was Chell, of all people, who spotted her. Chell, who was only on the bridge as an observer—with no responsibility except to watch and observe.

Tom Paris yanked the helm to port without waiting for an order from Captain Janeway; she barely had time to say "Proceed, Mr. Tuvok" before the sharp-eyed Vulcan oriented the jury-rigged monitor to center Lieutenant Torres and transferred the coordinates to the transporter room.

"Energizing," said Transporter Chief Filz.

CHAPTER 30

VOYAGER MATCHED VELOCITIES WITH THE TINY, REMAINING CORE that used to be the Fury star just an hour earlier. Commander Chakotay, Lieutenant Tuvok, and Ensign Harry Kim slowly took measurements as the frenetic crew got the ship's systems back on-line after both the electromagnetic pulse and the plasma shock wave. The bridge crew measured traces of chroniton particles, neutrino flux, subspace folding effects, residual superstring twists, alpha-particle radiation levels and directions, and residual heat in the form of radio echoes.

But Captain Kathryn Janeway had a more pressing problem down in sickbay.

The doctor circled around and around Lieutenant Redbay, whose skin was burnt bright red over a disturbing pallor. Redbay's eyes were open, but the pupils did not respond. Neither did the eyelids blink; Kes, the doctor's assistant, reached across every few moments and rehydrated Redbay's eyes from an eyedropper of saline solution.

"There is as yet no brain activity from Mr. Redbay," said the doctor; "well, for either of them. But I'm more worried about Redbay. I have applied cardiac stimulators, but as

STAR TREK: INVASION!

yet, his body is not even producing autonomic nervous responses."

"B'Elanna is doing better?"

"Lieutenant Torres is unchanged. She is not on life-support, but we took her off six minutes after she was beamed here. She required only a few forced breaths to begin breathing on her own . . . but she, too, is still in a coma."

Janeway closed her eyes. When she opened them again, the scene had not changed. She was so tired, but it wasn't all just a dream. "Will they recover?"

The doctor shook his head. "That is up to Torres and Redbay. There is little I can do except monitor and—"

"Doctor!" interrupted Kes. "B'Elanna just went into cardiac arrest!"

The doctor raced to Lieutenant Torres and ran a fast scan with his medical tricorder. "Cortical seizure," he diagnosed. "I'm going to try to stabilize her with a cortical stimulator."

"What's happening?" demanded the captain. "Doctor, you said she was doing all right! Why is she—"

"Be quiet!" snapped the doctor.

Janeway clamped her mouth shut, then backed swiftly away. After a moment, she commanded herself to turn and leave the sickbay. It was the hardest order she had ever given or received.

She waited in the passageway, pacing back and forth. Kes and the doctor didn't need her inside distracting them; they most decidedly did *not* need her presence at that moment.

The doctor frowned. *I'm not supposed to feel anything,* he thought; *I can't feel—I'm just a hologram!* But it certainly felt as though he felt concern, worry—even fear. Evidently, the programmer, Zimmerman, did a more thorough job than anyone had imagined, least of all the doctor himself. He had experienced quite a few feelings lately.

"I stabilized her," he announced, "for the moment, at any rate. How is Mr. Redbay, Kes?"

Silence. The doctor turned to find Kes standing over Redbay's bed. The Ocampan looked stricken. "Doctor, you'd better look at this." She held up her own tricorder. "Lieutenant Redbay's neural receptivity is failing. The cortical stimulator can't maintain the electrocolloidal circulation . . . he's dying, Doctor."

The doctor stared. There was no need to check Kes's readings; he had trained her well. "I might be able to rebuild the pathways," he said.

"The operating table is prepped. Which patient should I transfer?"

The doctor looked back and forth. "This is the worst part about being a doctor, Kes," he said, voice firm. "Remember what I said about triage, during our conference? Well, here it is in all its ugliness."

Triage: deciding who would live—and who would be left to die. This case was different . . . but really the same. There was no truly *medical* reason to choose one patient over the other. The doctor scanned his entire library of writings on proper triage and found no comfort, no help. Redbay's case was the more difficult; but with the proper care, he stood a good chance of living . . . neural receptivity collapse—"cortical stiffening"—was better understood than Torres's cortical seizure.

But in reality, neither was a textclip case; because, simply put, no one had ever before been fished out of deep space without a spacesuit in the middle of an exploding supernova.

The doctor ran every computer program in his limitless—he had thought!—medical profiles; but no mere program could convincingly tell him whether to save Lieutenant Redbay or Lieutenant Torres. Of course, each program picked one of the two . . . but there were as many hits for the first as the second.

It always comes down to this, he thought, exasperated and concerned; *it always comes down to the gut feeling of the doctor. But holograms don't HAVE guts.*

There was, he concluded, no *convincing* medical method to resolve the triage dilemma; each patient had his own reasons to live, to die, to sacrifice for the other.

"Doctor?"

What do I do? What do I do? He swiveled his virtual,

holographic head back and forth, virtual mind wrestling with a very real dilemma. No amount of prior programming could help him. *You make a decision, that's what you do!*

"I'll call the captain," said Kes, reaching for her commbadge.

"No!" the doctor almost shouted, grabbing her wrist. "I'm the doctor . . . this is my responsibility." *But WHAT DO I DO?*

He turned away, covering his holographic face with unreal hands. "How can I be torn like this? I'm not even a real man!"

After a moment, Kes spoke, so quietly the doctor had to increase his receiver gain. "You're real to me, Doctor."

"Maybe that's what being real means: making decisions that can't be made by a . . . by an emergency medical holographic program."

"You have to choose. B'Elanna's cortical stimulator can't stabilize her—" Kes fell silent, allowing the doctor to speak, to choose.

"She's a member of this crew. And—and I guess she's my friend. I know her—I can't make this decision!"

"Should I call the captain?"

"No! Help me—wait for me. Trust me, I know the time! I can't help knowing; I'm a computer program."

"You're real. You're a man and a doctor. And my teacher."

"But I have no objectivity!"

"Not every decision should be objective."

At once, the doctor relaxed. His virtual shoulders slumped. He turned around with a deadpan expression. "Transfer—B'Elanna—to the surgical table, Kes. I'll—I have to—"

Without another word, the doctor crossed the distance between the tables, reached out, and removed the cortical stimulator from Lieutenant Redbay. "Med—Medical log: Lieutenant Redbay pronounced deceased." Almost angrily—a comic sight, he thought—the doctor swiftly removed the respirator and pacemaker as well, laying them on one of the other beds in intensive care.

Kes had already transferred B'Elanna to the surgical table

using the antigravs and begun fitting the neurosurgical helmet over the lieutenant. By the time the doctor approached the table, Kes had already activated the holoprobe and microscanner and focused both on the outer portion of B'Elanna's cerebral cortex.

"Prepare to terminate the cortical stimulator," said the doctor, forcing himself not to look at the convulsing Redbay . . . a man already dead, dead ever since he fought the Furies the first time; a man who didn't know he was already dead, who fought it for nearly a minute.

"Terminate the stimulator, Kes; and get ready to immobilize her with repeated shots of desoasopine. She's half Klingon, and I think she's going to fight us every step of the way."

"Captain to the bridge," said Chakotay's voice from nothingness, startling Janeway. "On my way," she said, grateful for the excuse to cut and run. She had dreaded being called in and told that B'Elanna had suffered irreparable brain damage; irrationally, Captain Janeway half convinced herself that even standing in the hallway would "jinx" her engineer's chances—but she was afraid that simply leaving, *abandoning* B'Elanna, would give the wrong impression.

"What's happening, Mr. Chakotay?" she asked as the turbolift doors slid open at the bridge.

"Nothing."

"Didn't you just call me to the bridge?"

"Yes, Captain. It's what happened an hour ago that I think you need to see."

Tuvok took up the tale. "We have spent considerable time using every means available to track the Fury wormhole. It has been, I must admit, an unsatisfactory experience. The supernova left high residual radiation levels: the sector's current temperature is still several hundred degrees, broadcast as electromagnetic radiation in the infrared and radiowave portion of the spectrum. This temperature dissipates the energy signature left behind by the wormhole."

"Give me the short version, Mr. Tuvok."

"The Furies' attempt to create an artificial wormhole

large enough to transport their entire planet was largely successful."

Janeway was silent for a long time. "Then we failed," she said at last, mastering her emotions so completely that Tuvok was impressed.

"Not exactly," said Chakotay. "I don't know what B'Elanna and Redbay did down there, but the Furies didn't jump to the Alpha Quadrant."

"Tuvok just said—"

"I said the effort was *largely* successful, Captain. They did, in fact, jump . . . *away* from the Alpha Quadrant."

Janeway looked back and forth between her senior officers. "Do we know where they jumped to?"

"No, Captain," said Chakotay. "We cannot narrow down the trail smaller than about a ninety-degree spread. They could have gone in any direction within that spread."

"All right, where *might* they have gone? Which direction?"

"They might have jumped into the Gamma Quadrant, or they might have jumped completely outside the galaxy."

"Mr. Tuvok, what are the odds that the Furies will jump anywhere near a star system?"

"I have insufficient data to make even a plausible conjecture, Captain."

She thought about a planet of twenty-seven billion condemned to wander for eternity, lost between the stars. Twenty-seven billion souls whose only crime was attempting to eradicate or enslave every living being in her home quadrant.

"They must have had some provision for supporting their population away from a star," she mused; "they were planning a blind jump into *our* quadrant, after all."

"That would be logical."

Janeway leaned her head back, closing her eyes, not caring who saw her in such a state of exhaustion. "We didn't have to kill twenty-seven billion people. That counts for something, doesn't it?"

She hadn't expected an answer; she got one anyway, from Tuvok. "It counts for much, Captain."

"Have we merely unleashed the same horror on the Gamma Quadrant?" Janeway opened her eyes; the entire rest of the bridge crew was silent, staring at her. She looked from one to the other, pausing at last on Chakotay's inscrutible face.

"I don't think so," he said. "They were utterly peaceful to everyone except the ones they called Unclean: us, in the Alpha Quadrant." The commander paused, pressing his lips together. "I think the rest of the galaxy is safe . . . unless somehow the Furies make it back to a planet in our own quadrant."

"Tuvok?" asked the captain.

"Insufficient data to estimate the odds," said the Vulcan.

Janeway shuddered. Eventually, when the dust settled, the Furies would take stock. They would not lose interest in their holy war; they would begin building the same technology all over again, as soon as they found a star to suck dry for the energy to jump across the galaxy to hurl themselves again upon what they *knew* was theirs.

All over again; it would happen all over again, and again and again, until finally—somebody *did* kill them all. Or until they succeeded.

Somebody, someday; but not Katherine Janeway, not this day. "Still . . . it's—it's quite something to think about. What we did."

"We defended ourselves!" exploded Paris.

"We defended our civilization," corrected Tuvok.

"Aren't you the ones who preach about Infinite Diversity in Infinite Combinations? They simply wanted to retake what had once been theirs."

"What they held by force and terror."

Chakotay sat back, simply observing; he allowed Paris and Tuvok to carry the point. But the captain held her own.

"Yes, a slave revolt. For thousands of years, they nursed their hatred and determination to retake heaven, which their god gave them, they believed. What will they do now? I think they'll figure out pretty quickly that they went in the opposite direction and can never get back. Then what? What violent race have we unleashed upon another part of the galaxy, driven into permanent exile? Will they set up a Fury empire in the Gamma Quadrant? Will they start enslaving the races in the Magellanic Clouds?

"I would rather we had stopped them completely and killed every last one of the twenty-seven billion. *That* guilt I could live with, or die with, as the case may be."

Chakotay spoke out. "I feel no guilt whatsoever, Captain. We did what a warrior must do. We took the best victory condition offered."

"Is your spirit guide okay with this?"

"I will find out tonight."

"Take me with you. Please."

Chakotay inclined his head in the affirmative.

"Captain," said a hesitant Ensign Kim, "I didn't want to interrupt. But I just monitored a log entry by the EMH program."

"Yes?"

"The doctor just pronounced Lieutenant Redbay dead. He thinks Lieutenant Torres is going to make it."

Janeway rose and crossed to the young ensign. She put her hand on his shoulder. "You care very much about her, don't you? I think Chell can use some watchstanding experience . . . why don't you go down to sickbay."

Kim stood without a word and hurriedly walked to the turbolift.

CHAPTER 31

Two days after the supernova, the radiation level had dropped substantially in the sector that once had belonged to the Furies, the first true terrorists of the galaxy. The *U.S.S. Voyager* remained in the sector; Captain Kathryn Janeway had ordered them to maintain orbit around the remnants of the Fury sun until Lieutenant B'Elanna Torres regained consciousness. Janeway wanted to know what happened, what Torres and the strange Lieutenant Redbay from the *Enterprise* had done, before the captain decided whether it was safe to leave. That meant Torres had to wake up.

Twelve hours later, B'Elanna sighed. It was a good sign but not spectacular; she had emitted sounds before. But the sigh was followed by weak sobbing, and that *was* exciting: it was the first actual emotion she had shown since she was beamed aboard.

The captain took B'Elanna's mummy-wrapped hand, while Kes gently touched the patient's brow. Tucked as she had been, the lieutenant had mostly shielded her face from the intense, searing heat. The rest of her body would take weeks to heal fully, even with the most advanced skin repligrafting techniques in the Delta Quadrant.

B'Elanna opened her eyes and began to scream. When the doctor moved to restrain her, she bit his hand hard enough to sever his thumb—had he been flesh and blood. Fortunately, B'Elanna did not break her teeth on the holographic forcefield.

They held her and talked her back for another half hour before she was coherent enough for Janeway to debrief her. Haltingly, B'Elanna Torres told of finding the aiming mechanism at the very last moment and sabotaging it.

"It's a damned good thing you thought of that," said the captain. "None of the other gremlins you pulled did a thing: the beam still fired, created the wormhole, and the planet still passed through it to . . . to anybody's guess where."

"I saved us?"

"You saved us, Lieutenant."

"Are the Furies gone?"

Janeway smiled, an oddly down-turning expression that simultaneously expressed warmth, reassurance, and deep sadness. "They're gone. They were sent into the middle of nowhere; I doubt they'll ever find their way back to our galaxy, and definitely not to the Alpha Quadrant. Not ever."

"We fished you out of the exploding supernova," said Kes. "You were really badly burned and more than fifteen bones were broken! But you're going to be all right."

"And . . . Redbay?"

Janeway answered quickly before any awkward pauses. "He didn't make it, Torres. I'm sorry."

The doctor leaned close. "You survived in part because you're half-Klingon, Lieutenant. Lieutenant Redbay was a human, and his body couldn't take the strain."

She stared at the doctor as if he'd grown a second head. She did not seem pleased. Then B'Elanna closed her eyes and tilted her head. *So once again, my face is rubbed in it,* she thought; *either I'm flying off the handle because I'm an angry young Klingon; or I survive a supernova because I have a tough Klingon hide! Can't I ever just be ME?*

But she knew the answer almost before she asked the question: she was who she was, and part of who she was was a bumpy-headed, thick-skinned, warrior-hearted Klingon. She could no longer deny it. And now it had saved her life!

Later, when the doctor had moved on to other patients, and Janeway had left, Kes returned to B'Elanna's side. Ocampan eyes met the Klingon face; Kes bit her lip and finally asked a question that had built inside her like an overinflated balloon. "You said you were hit by the Furies' terror beam . . . what was it like? That kind of fear. I've never . . ." Kes paused, admitting her grievous fault. "I've never even imagined that kind of emotion!" she blurted.

B'Elanna said nothing.

"Is it different from just being afraid? I have to know . . . I have to know there was a reason why all the races of the Alpha Quadrant would rather be slaves and give up freedom than face that weapon. It has to be something more than just being afraid of death or pain."

"I don't remember," said Lieutenant Torres. "Selective amnesia. The doctor said it might happen."

Kes lowered her brows, puzzled. "But you remember everything else!"

"*I said,*" hissed Torres, "I—don't—*REMEMBER.*" Cold, defiant, Klingon eyes burned into the Ocampan face. Kes understood, and she dropped the subject.

STAR TREK®
INVASION!

A Word from Our Authors

Of Ships and Men
  Diane Carey.. 287

Our *STAR TREK* Memories (or How Can a TV Show Be So Important?)
  Kristine Kathryn Rusch............................ 293

A *STAR TREK* Appreciation
  L. A. Graf... 299

STAR TREK: Shaken, but Not Stirred (and with a Twist)
  Dafydd ab Hugh.. 303

A Word from the Editor
  John Ordover.. 307

Diane Carey is the author of eleven *STAR TREK* novels and novelizations—*Dreadnought, Battlestations, Final Frontier, Best Destiny, The Great Starship Race, First Frontier, Ghost Ship, Descent, The Search, The Way of the Warrior, Station Rage,* and *INVASION! Book One: First Strike.* As the only *STAR TREK* author who actually sails the Tall Ships, she has a unique perspective on sea captains—and on space captains as well.

Of Ships and Men

"THAT'S WHAT SETS YOU APART FROM THE REST OF US, JIM. You look at these alien people with nine eyes and no arms, and you see the fact that they just want a home and safety. You look at aliens in terms of how they're like us, while everybody else sees how they're different."

I'm not sure whether Dr. McCoy said this to Jim Kirk in *First Strike,* or I said it to him myself during a misty moment at the schooner's wheel, but I'm sure one of us did.

Star Trek as a TV show, or shall we say as fourth-wall theater, gave us a glimpse into a future we wouldn't mind living. While most science fiction of the 1960s and much of it now shows us a glum, dismal, postholocaust future where people wear rags and are reduced to ratlike behavior, *STAR TREK* gave us a clean, bright future with crisp military panache melded into the dynamism of individuality.

Jim Kirk was the individual who set the design, and without him there would be no *STAR TREK* today, but not because he was perfect or charismatic, though he was certainly the latter. Jim Kirk provided a magnetic compass for us because he was charismatic and yet deeply flawed. Yes, as classical heroic drama has always shown us, the hero's imperfections and how he handles them are the real barometers of heroism. Perfection is easy. With perfection we don't need drama to provide exemplars in life, and in fact we don't even need heroes.

But life isn't perfect. Neither are any of my captains, and I've sailed with several. As many of you know, I work as a deckhand and helmsman aboard several Tall Ships, including the tough old 125' Baltic trader topsail schooner *Alexandria* out of Alexandria, Virginia, the pilot schooner *William H. Albury* out of Man-o'-War Cay in the Bahamas, the 1883 Portuguese fisherman barkentine *Gazela* of Philadelphia, which is the oldest and largest working square-rigger on Earth, and the breathtakingly fast Baltimore clipper *Pride of Baltimore II*. I mention these ships because they are all a piece of the *Enterprise* to me. She is their legacy.

My captains range from a former Chesapeake Bay tug captain to a former CIA mercenary. Yeah, really. I've never had a female captain yet, but I've worked under many female first and second mates and bosuns, some of whom had their captain's licenses, so I also feel quite comfortable watching Captain Janeway at work. There are some people under whose command I won't go to sea—but I'd go with her.

She's not perfect either. If I ever run into a captain who seems to be perfect, I ain't signing on that ship.

Why not? Because I'm not perfect; neither are any of my shipmates, and for that matter neither are any of my ships. A "perfect" captain just couldn't function on the real sea, with a real crew and real trouble, and that means life or death to those of us who man the sheets and halyards.

My work on ships is certainly one of the reasons *STAR TREK* is so comfortable for me, though I do write in other genres and media. I seem to keep coming back to *STAR TREK* no matter how far I wander—whether my continual returns are like springtime or the flu season is a matter of personal taste, but I leave that to the readers. Surely it bears an eerie resemblance to going back out to sea—no matter how taxing, wet, crowded, hot, cold, or scary the last voyage was, I keep signing back on.

Yes, that's what I mean—it's not always fun, but it's always a challenge, and that's what fuels me. I have yet to tire of watching my captains try to sort out a gripping situation, wrestling with their own flaws and the flaws of the amalgamated crews, usually a gaggle of persons from all walks of life and any dozen given philosophies. I watch my captains trying to figure out which person has which best ability, and which duty that person just shouldn't be assigned to—and all this very often in the midst of notable danger, whether during Hurricane Andrew or piloting upstream on the swollen Mississippi.

Or trying to pull the starship out of a gravity well or to survive a battle of monumental odds. Yes, I watch my starship captains the same way. I've watched Jim Kirk for the better part of my life, and he's a bundle of extremes, both noble and petty, and even nobility can be a fault in some situations. What sets him apart is his determination to work through those faults. I never tire of examining that kind of person, and *STAR TREK* has continually given us a vehicle with which to hold that mirror up to ourselves and take a close look.

To date I've written more Jim Kirk books than any other author. I've spent more hours watching him over and over again and working with him than anyone. With so many thousands of words to write about him, I've had to examine his personality very closely and find out just what about him makes me keep watching, so I can make you keep watching.

What I discovered during the writing of *First Strike* was Jim Kirk's relentless plumbing for the commonality between people and peoples. He'd stare into alien eyes, if he could find them, and sift out the ways he and that alien were alike. That's where he'd start—from the point of familiarity. Everyone who met him—crewmates, aliens, enemies—felt instantly as if they'd known him for years. They might not like him or agree with him, but they always knew where he stood, because he would chip out that common element and work from there.

Most science fiction concentrates on the differences. Kirk and his crew had the idea that there would be, had to be, something in common even with the oddest creature, and all we had to do was find that thing, that common desire, goal, passion, no matter how small.

Jim Kirk looked at women much the same way—the ultimate alien, of course. He saw not only face or hair or figure, or how different women were from one another, but how much they were the same. He saw not females, but femininity. His attitude changed when, in the episode "Metamorphosis," he found out the Companion was female, just as it changed during "Devil in the Dark" when he found out the Horta was a mother protecting her young.

William Shatner knew that also, instinctively if not professionally. If we pay attention to the way the professional science-fiction writers wrote the original *STAR TREK* and the way Shatner played it, we discover that Jim Kirk wasn't a hound after all. He was an appreciator. He appreciated women for the poetic loveliness he saw in all of them, human or otherwise, and he appreciated aliens for the relationship that could be built out of a vacuum.

That's what set the original *STAR TREK* apart from other science fiction and sets the pace for us now—it went out of its way to show how individuals, ever separate unto ourselves, are more like than unlike. That is also what real captains have to do—bring together crewmen who may never have seen each other before, and by the time the ship leaves the dock make us all have a common goal. Usually it's something quite humble, like making the next port on schedule. Occasionally, survival itself is at stake. But sea and space are great equalizers—keep the water out, the people in, and get to the next port.

Whatever happens between is just the pub story we'll tell.

So be careful whose command you sign under. Make sure your captain has flaws and a good stout temper. Your chances of surviving are better, and you might even have a great adventure between those dockside sighs of relief.

       Fair weather,

Diane Carey

       Diane Carey

Kristine Kathryn Rusch and Dean Wesley Smith are the authors of the *STAR TREK* novels *The Big Game* (as Sandy Schofield), *The Escape, The Long Night, Rings of Tautee,* the novelization of *Star Trek: Klingon* and *INVASION! Book Two: The Soldiers of Fear.* They are also, respectively, the editors of *The Magazine of Fantasy and Science Fiction* and *Pulphouse Magazine.* Below, Kristine tells us a bit of what *STAR TREK* has meant to both of them over the years. That both their middle names are the first names of *Star Trek* characters is strictly coincidental.

Our
STAR TREK Memories
(Or How Can a TV Show
Be So Important?)

When my husband, Dean Wesley Smith, and I met, I was twenty-five and he was thirty-five. We lived in separate parts of the country, and we both wrote science fiction. I was an admitted *STAR TREK* fan who had never been to any of the conventions because I was too broke to attend. Dean, who never speaks of the things he likes, was a closet Trekker whose love for the series turned out to be a big surprise to his friends. The night *Star Trek: The Next Generation* premiered, I watched in my apartment, and he watched it in his, and it wasn't until the next day that I discovered he loved *STAR TREK* as much as I did.

At that point, we had been seeing each other for nearly a year.

So, when John Ordover, our editor at Pocket Books, asked us to write an essay about how *STAR TREK* had influenced us for the last book of the *INVASION!* series, we knew we immediately had a problem. Because when *STAR TREK* premiered, I was six. Dean was sixteen. I was in grade school. He was in high school. I saw two episodes during the show's entire first run (I couldn't stay up that late). He saw them all when they aired. And so on.

Dean and I run into these generational things all the time, especially concerning the sixties. While I was learning to walk, Dean was learning to duck and cover in preparation for a nuclear attack. While I was riding my bicycle after school, he was worried about being sent to Vietnam. When I experienced my first kiss, he had broken off his second engagement.

Even though we have a lot in common now, our ages prevented us from having a lot in common then.

So . . . how did *STAR TREK* influence us? Well, it influenced us differently.

Dean grew up in Boise, Idaho, then a fairly small city on the scale of things. It had an air force base and it was near several nuclear bases. It was, in nuclear parlance, a first-strike area.

During his years in grade school, Dean learned how to protect himself in a nuclear attack. Instead of fire drills, his school held duck-and-cover drills. The children hid under their desks, covered their heads, and waited for a teacher to whistle an all-clear. This, somehow, would save them from a nuclear explosion. People built bomb shelters in their backyards. And most public places had a visibly displayed yellow-and-black sign that showed where to hide if the sirens went off, warning of an attack.

By the time he was ten, it seemed clear that the world wouldn't last the decade. By the time he got into high school, that prediction came true on a personal level. Many boys his age went to Vietnam, and most never came back. High-school graduation meant, for many, the draft, and years of service in a war few believed in. Dean spent the first twenty-four years of his life thinking that (1) the world would end and/or (2) he would die in a police action so controversial Congress never voted it into war.

But this was just a backdrop. On the surface, Dean was a regular guy. I went to his high-school reunion. The folks who didn't know him well thought he was handsome (and he was; I saw pictures), smart, and shy (and he wasn't; I heard stories). He made the newspaper fairly regularly as part of the golf team, and he spent most days after school in the winter skiing at nearby Bogus Basin.

Except on Fridays. On Fridays, Dean W. Smith, handsome high-school student, stayed home.

To watch *STAR TREK*.

He watched it because it was science fiction and, unbeknownst to all but his closest friends, he was an avid science-fiction fan. But if *STAR TREK* had been bad science fiction, he might have dated on some of those Friday nights. Some of the episodes were bad, but more were good. But it wasn't the quality that held him.

It was the hope.

The hope existed in science-fiction novels. Man lived beyond 1970 in Robert Heinlein's books and Arthur C. Clarke's. But not on television. Television brought us the grim visions of Rod Serling and the *Outer Limits*. Television showed us the world ending, not thriving.

STAR TREK showed us a world in which the human race somehow survived the nightmares of the mid-twentieth century, and developed a culture that went to the stars in peace and exploration. Hope, for a generation that didn't have any.

The possibility that the world wouldn't end, that wars like Vietnam would become anathema to the human race. The idea that human beings of all races, all nationalities, and all credos, could get along.

The belief that we had a future after all.

It was that vision that kept Dean home on Fridays. And made him first in line to all the movies. And made him stay home for the premier of *Star Trek: The Next Generation* in the off-chance his new girlfriend (me) hated that *STAR TREK* stuff.

Well, the new girlfriend loved that *Star Trek* stuff. The first short story I ever wrote was *STAR TREK* fan fic about Jim Kirk coming to Superior, Wisconsin, and saving a lonely fifteen-year-old from—

Never mind. You get the idea. I was twelve at the time. Fifteen seemed awfully sophisticated back then.

STAR TREK didn't have the wider implications for me in those days. I simply loved the series. It came on every day after school (about four o'clock). My best friend, Toni, told me about the show, and we started watching it together. We even wrote a *STAR TREK* novel in Mrs. Anderson's English class (except for the week we took off to read *The Exorcist*, which we kept hidden in our English text). We were going to finish over the summer, but during the summer Toni moved away, and I was left to watch *STAR TREK* alone.

By the time I was fourteen, *STAR TREK* was cool. All my friends watched it. We all discussed it. And during those discussions, I learned to read the credits on TV shows. When my new best friend, Mindy Walgren, heard that my favorite *STAR TREK* episode was "City on the Edge of Forever," she loaned me a short-story collection by Harlan Ellison, the guy who had written that marvelous episode. Harlan's short stories led me to his essays, and his essays led me to some of the best writers working in the field at that time.

A television program opened a whole new world for me. The world of science fiction. The world of short stories. The world of essays. Television, instead of turning me away from books, led me to books. It expanded my horizons instead of limiting them.

I will be forever grateful.

I love to write *STAR TREK* novels because I like to play in the *STAR TREK* universe. I've played in it since Mrs. Anderson's English class twenty-four years ago. But I don't write the books solely because of that. I also write them for people, like me, who go from television to books. In *STAR TREK* novels, some of the best writers in the SF field get to play with SF ideas too big for the television screen. Like Jerry Oltion's planet rescue in *Twilight's End* or Peter David's wonderful spin on time travel in *Imzadi*.

Dean plays with big ideas in our *STAR TREK* novels (the commuting-through-time idea in *The Escape* was his; and so were the Jibetians in *The Long Night*). But he brings something else to our books.

He brings the hope. Because he's never forgotten how badly it's needed.

You see, sometimes ten years is a long time. When I graduated from high school, Vietnam was a name from a (seemingly) distant past. The kids in my class went to college or into the workforce. No one died (except in car wrecks). We never ducked or covered. Those yellow-and-black signs were dust-covered oddities in old buildings. We knew we'd live to see our grandchildren. We knew the world wasn't going to end.

We had hope and we didn't even realize it.

Which isn't to say *STAR TREK* became irrelevant. It didn't. But we took different things out of it. We talked about the show's racial unity. We liked the way women held positions of power. We liked the strange new worlds because we believed we'd visit them someday.

That there would be a future was a given. We simply had to decide how to live it.

How important was *STAR TREK* in creating that attitude?

Let's be real for a moment. We are talking television, after all. Television is entertainment. Entertainment is a way to kill a few hours. Nothing more.

Right?

Maybe. Maybe not.

You see, I believe we create the futures we can envision. If we can see only death and destruction ahead, then that's what's going to happen. But *STAR TREK* and science-fiction novels gave us a future, a real future, a future to envision.

It touched me at twelve. It touched Dean at sixteen.

And it touched countless others in his generation and mine. His needed the hope. Mine needed the goals.

How important is *STAR TREK?*

Important enough.

Kristene Kathryn Rusch

Some people require little introduction; L. A. Graf is, or are, one or more of those people. So without further ado...

A STAR TREK Appreciation

Captain's Log, Earthdate 012696. On a routine trip through the wormhole, the *Defiant* apparently encountered an editorial anomaly of unkown origin. As a consequence, the crew has been transported off the ship and thrown into a strange world of eerie black on white....

Dr. Bashir craned a look at the monstrous column of print towering over their heads. "Does Paramount know we're here?"

"Let's hope so, Doctor." Sisko tugged at a nearby comma, making a face when it came loose in his hand and left only a poorly constructed sentence behind. "If not, *Deep Space Nine* is going to be the first Federation space station ever commanded by a Ferengi."

Kira banged her fist against one square of black text, then grunted with annoyance when even the dots on the tops of the i's failed to move. "Whatever this is, it's awfully dense."

"Looks like nine-point to me," O'Brien volunteered, from where he'd crawled underneath a paragraph to examine its basic structure.

"Dax..." Sisko ducked beneath a dangling particle to shoot a keen look at his science officer. "Can you identify the typeface?"

Dax nodded, stepping into the plain white border to scan one cleanly justified margin. As the results scrolled across her tricorder's little screen, she glanced up at the others with a smile. "It's all right, Benjamin—we're in a *STAR TREK* novel."

"Am I on the cover?" Bashir asked eagerly. Dax flicked the question mark at him with a sigh.

"Well, what are we doing here?" Kira wanted to know.

She stooped to catch the question mark as it tumbled past, turning it over in her hands in the hopes of finding something useful about it. "We're supposed to be back on *Deep Space Nine*, protecting Federation space from the Dominion, and the Cardassians, and the Klingons."

"Not to mention *Xena: Warrior Princess*." Bashir ducked to avoid a rain of displaced apostrophes and commas from farther up the page. "Chief, what are you doing?"

"Scouting our surroundings," O'Brien called down from above. Scrambling for better footing on the end of a run-on sentence, he squinted at the bold title overshadowing the first few paragraphs of text. "According to this, we're in an appreciation of *STAR TREK*, written by somebody named L. A. Graf."

"L. A. Graf?" Dax maneuvered around a closing parenthesis to look up at him. "Isn't she the only Trill *STAR TREK* author?"

"Not exactly, old man." Sisko plucked a period from within the author's name and tossed it in his palm as though weighing it for a curveball pitch. "Although she is a bimodal entity, consisting of award-winning science-fiction author Julia Ecklar and university scientist Karen Rose Cercone. You're just not familiar with them because *INVASION! Book Three: Time's Enemy* is their first *STAR TREK: Deep Space Nine* novel." He lobbed the period at the edge of the page, grinning when it bounced neatly back at him. "All their previous *STAR TREK* books were about *The original series*."

O'Brien slid off the bottom of the column with a thoughtful grunt. "So why did they decide to write about us now?"

"Because we're the best-looking crew *STAR TREK*'s ever had?" Bashir suggested with a puckish grin.

Dax bounced an apostrophe off the top of her head. "No," she countered. "They like us because they feel we've continued in the spirit of the classic *STAR TREK* series by focusing on cultural conflicts and sociological problems in addition to exciting action/adventure."

"They seem to like our nifty new starship, too," O'Brien

admitted, scrubbing his hands against the legs of his trousers to wipe off the printer's ink. "They use it a lot in their story."

"Also, L. A. Graf has always celebrated the diversity that *STAR TREK* represents." Sisko replaced the period with a respectful smile, and leaned back against the edge of a paragraph. "They highlight the fact that *STAR TREK* has depicted women and minorities in positions of responsibility since the 1960s."

"They were particularly impressed by *STAR TREK*'s courage in introducing a character of Middle Eastern descent in the early 1990s," Bashir picked up as he used a hyphen to boost himself onto the second page. "If you think about it, that was as progressive as casting a Russian as part of the *Enterprise*'s crew back in the 1960s."

Dax took the hand he offered her and stepped across to join him as she passed her tricorder over the new words piling up below them. "According to this, L. A. Graf says that their own optimistic views of the future were strongly influenced by watching *STAR TREK*. They hope that the fact that *STAR TREK* has remained so popular through the decades means that people haven't given up hope that the world can be a better place in the future."

"But that's all about a TV series." Kira took the low route through a subversive comment and came in near the bottom of the page, at the bottom line of their discussion. "How does that relate to writing novels? All this black and white is so . . . so . . ." She pawed through the words close at hand, looking for something appropriate, until Bashir suggested, "One-dimensional?"

"Precisely!"

"Well, actually, that's not true." Frowning at her in disapproval, O'Brien lifted the previous comment out of Kira's hands and fitted it neatly back into place. "Written *STAR TREK* fiction can go places the television and movies can't. There's no special-effects budget, no one-hour time limit. *STAR TREK* novels can blow up entire planets, create enormous space battles, and introduce complicated and bizarre alien societies without worrying about makeup restrictions."

"Besides . . ." Bashir crouched beside Dax to give Sisko a hand across the page break, tearing the sleeve of his uniform on the underside of a quotation. "I like having thoughts as well as actions. For example—" He planted his hands on his hips and looked around the page. "—right now, I'm thinking that Odo really should be here. L. A. Graf always gives him the funniest lines, after all."

Just then, the constable's name ran into a glossy blob and dripped down the available white space. As he recongealed into his former self, Odo remarked dryly, "I am here, Doctor. I was just blending with the native inhabitants of this place in an effort to find some means of escape." He looked smugly at the humanoids surrounding him. "Which I did."

"Did you find a secret passage?" O'Brien asked eagerly.

"Or find a phaser so we can blast our way out?" Kira threw in.

"Whatever it is," Dax sighed, closing her tricorder, "I hope it's quick. I'm getting hungry."

Bashir tossed her a grin from behind a line of dialogue. "And I'd hate to have to eat my words."

This time it was Sisko who silenced the doctor with a scowl and a brandished exclamation point. "Would you all just let the constable tell us?"

"There's no need now, Captain." Odo peered at the widening scene break beneath his feet, and the two ominous words quickly closing on them from below. "I'm afraid we're already almost there."

"Really?" Sisko followed the constable's gaze. "How will we know when we've reached it?"

"We'll know. . . . Here it comes. . . ."

THE END

L. A. Graf

Julia Ecklar   Karen Rose Cercone

302

Dafydd ab Hugh—not a pseudonym, really!—is the author of *Star Trek: Deep Space Nine #5: Fallen Heroes* (the one where everybody dies), *Star Trek: The Next Generation #33: Balance of Power* (where there's a big auction and nobody dies), and *INVASION! Book Four: The Final Fury* (the one you've just finished reading); he also cowrote all four *Doom* books, turning the bloodthirsty computer game phenomenon into an award-winning literary event (Green Slime Award from BuboniCon for "most awful novel of 1995"). But he has a life outside media series books, you know. I mean, like, he's also written many other books, including two (2) fantasies (*Heroing* and *Warriorwards*), two SFs masquerading as fantasies (*Arthur War Lord* and *Far Beyond the Wave*), three non-SF young-adult thrillers about floods and teen serial killers (*Swept Away, Swept Away II: The Mountain,* and *Swept Away III: The Pit*) (you find them in the YA section of your bookstore), and, of course, a hard SF book with rivets, *The Pandora Point* (in press). The dude usually writes a book a week in between hanging out on GEnie, arguing with weenies.

STAR TREK: Shaken, but Not Stirred (and with a Twist)

So, it's not like thirty years ago, dude; and there's like, you know, a dozen sci-fi shows on the tube now—rilly. (Forgive him, Caesar; for he is a Southern Californian and thinks the customs and traditions of his native speech are laws of English.) There are or were paranoid detective shows about alien conspiracies, silly shows about Space Marines who can't even get a haircut, shows about humans fleeing (a) cyborgs, (b) aliens, (c) the remnants of our own evil culture; there are or were shows about alien cops, alien pops, and pets from a peculiar planet; there are or were so many time-travel shows that you haven't time to watch them; there are or were—dude, I don't have the patience, man. You know the list; you probably watched them all . . . I did—some only once.

But none invaded the American psyche as *STAR TREK* did—the sometimes campy, sometimes brilliant chronicle of Kirk and Spock and the crochety, old dude who was a doctor, not an antediluvian ark-builder. So, like, why not? Why didn't *Space: $19.99* or *Space: Behind and Between* take off and grab America by the—ah—by the lapels and shake us into submission?

I can't tell you for certain; I'm not Howard Rosenberg, and nobody pays me three hundred Gs a year (or, these days, should I like say three hundred *K?*) to tell you why TV shows are cool or suck. But one thing even I notice: of all that litany of sci-fi shows, past and present, even marching off into the distant future . . . *only one* showed us a human race driven to explore space *by our natures,* not our failures.

In *STAR TREK*, we *weren't* chased away from Earth by metallic cyborgs with red dots in the middle of their foreheads; we *weren't* blown out of orbit, riding our own moon, by the explosion of a backyard barbecue; we *didn't* get lost in the starry deep; we *weren't* invaded; we *didn't* have to take in a refugee alien population; we *didn't* stubbornly rebuild a space station that big, bad aliens had destroyed four previous times.

Earth *wasn't* destroyed to make way for a hyperspace bypass, the empire *didn't* strike back, we *didn't* become unstuck in time, and bug-eyed monsters *haven't* infiltrated the FBI. In *STAR TREK*, we set out deliberately to explore the galaxy—you know, like the whole strange new worlds, new life, and new civilizations rap, dude.

Don't misunderstand: a lot of the other sci-fi shows were cool; they didn't all suck. In fact, I enjoyed watching most of them. Well ... let's say some of them. But only *STAR TREK* actually embedded itself into American culture, making the *Starship Enterprise* as instantly recognizable as the dude with the red cape and the big, red S (or the yellow dude with spiky hair and a skateboard). And (coincidence?) only *STAR TREK* was about humans with a future—humans needing to reach out to the stars, not because Earth was closed to us, but because it's in our natures to demand to know what's over the next mountain range, what's across the ocean, what's past the last planet in the solar system ... we're monkey-boys, all of us, and we're driven by a mechanism so deep it must be evolutionary to monkey around with stuff we find.

I don't know why no other show has tried to tap into the potential of the human need for exploration, excitement, and (as Freeman Dyson says) "disturbing the universe." Maybe the rest of TV Land thinks that theme is already "owned" by *STAR TREK;* or worse ... maybe the guys who produce shows where the human race is on its last legs really, honest-to-God, believe humans—let's be honest, Americans—don't even have a future ... and don't *deserve* one.

If they really think that, then they should make depressing police procedurals or produce a gaudy talk show, with its endless parade of whining weirdos for whom America is dead. If a person has no vision or hope for the future or doesn't believe in the greatness of the human race; if a person can't see any damned good coming from science and technology; if he thinks There Are Some Things Man Was Not Meant to Know—then he has no damned business calling himself a *science-fiction* writer. Stay outta my field, you sniveling creeps!

I'll just take Kirk and Picard, Janeway and especially Sisko instead; they've read their Heinlein and Asimov—they know there's a brave new universe out there, full of such people as . . . as *STAR TREK* is made of. Remember Bob Browning: "A man's reach should exceed his grasp." Is there any other show where men and women constantly reach far out past yesterday's grasp? Not even, dude. So let's, like, you know, give *STAR TREK* credit for being—in that sense—the only *real* science-fiction show that's ever been on TV.

A Word from the Editor

First of all, a hearty thanks to all our writers: Diane Carey and her writing partner and husband Greg Brodeur, who took a small notion and turned it into *INVASION!*; Dean Wesley Smith and Kristine Kathryn Rusch, who took many frantic 7:00 A.M. (Pacific Time) phone calls; Julia Ecklar and Karen Rose Cercone, otherwise known as L. A. Graf, who took their normally excellent work to a higher (and longer!) plane for this series; and Dafydd ab Hugh, for constant good humor under stress and for extraordinary professionalism.

But a project the size and complexity of *INVASION!* would be impossible without tremendous effort from a number of people whose names didn't make it to the book covers. I would like to thank Paula Block of Viacom Consumer Products for helping to develop this series, and for pulling double duty with Thom Parham in the final stages; Terry McGarry for her exemplary copyediting; Carol Greenburg and Terry Erdmann for sharp-eyed continuity editing; Kathleen Stahl, Penny Haynes, Donna O'Neill, and Joann Foster of Pocket for working the magic that makes a manuscript into a real, honest-to-God book; Keith Birdsong for a top-notch painting that made a great poster and four top-notch covers; Matt Galemmo for designing said poster and covers; Greg Cox for the great cover copy; Scott Shannon for his active support throughout this project; John Perrella for Xeroxing above and beyond the call of duty; Tyya Turner for keeping track of it all; and Kevin Ryan for saying, "Cool idea! Go for it!"

Thanks, guys!

**It is the Day of Reckoning
It is the Day of Judgement
It is...**

STAR TREK®
THE DAY OF HONOR

A Four-Part Klingon™ Saga
That Spans the Generations

Coming Summer 1997
from Pocket Books

JOIN
THE OFFICIAL
STAR TREK™
FAN CLUB

For only $19.95 (Canadian $22.95-U.S. Dollars)* you receive *a year's subscription* to the *Star Trek Communicator* magazine including a bimonthly merchandise insert, and an *exclusive membership kit!*

Send check or money order to:

Official *Star Trek* Fan Club
P.O. Box 111000
Aurora, CO 80042

or call 1-800-TRUE-FAN (1-800-878-3326)
to use your VISA/MasterCard!
*Price may be subject to change

1252.01

STAR TREK
DEEP SPACE NINE

24" X 36" CUT AWAY POSTER,
7 COLORS WITH 2 METALLIC INKS & A GLOSS AND MATTE VARNISH, PRINTED ON ACID FREE ARCHIVAL QUALITY
65# COVER WEIGHT STOCK INCLUDES OVER 90 TECHNICAL CALLOUTS, AND HISTORY OF THE SPACE STATION.
U.S.S. DEFIANT EXTERIOR, HEAD SHOTS OF MAIN CHARACTERS, INCREDIBLE GRAPHIC OF WORMHOLE.

STAR TREK™
U.S.S. ENTERPRISE™ NCC-1701

24" X 36" CUT AWAY POSTER,
6 COLORS WITH A SPECIAL METALLIC INK & A GLOSS AND MATTE VARNISH, PRINTED ON ACID FREE ARCHIVAL
QUALITY 100# TEXT WEIGHT STOCK INCLUDES OVER 100 TECHNICAL CALLOUTS,
HISTORY OF THE ENTERPRISE CAPTAINS & THE HISTORY OF THE ENTERPRISE SHIPS.

ALSO AVAILABLE:
LIMITED EDITION SIGNED AND NUMBERED BY ARTISTS.
LITHOGRAPHIC PRINTS ON 80# COVER STOCK (DS9 ON 100 # STOCK) WITH OFFICIAL LICENSED CERTIFICATE OF
AUTHENTICITY. QT. AVAILABLE 2,500

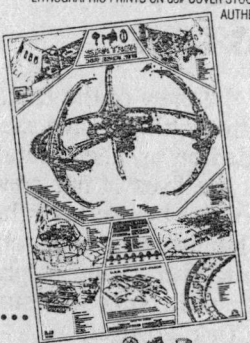
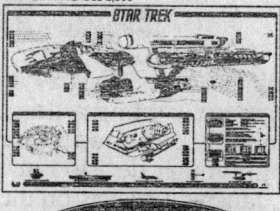
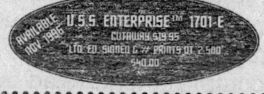

AVAILABLE NOV 1996 — U.S.S. ENTERPRISE™ 1701-E
COMING $19.95
LTD. ED. SIGNED C/# PRINTS QT. 2,500
$40.00

SciPubTech

Deep Space Nine Poster
Poster Qt. ___ @ $19.95 each _____
Limited Edition Poster
Poster Qt. ___ @ $40.00 each _____

U.S.S. Enterprise NCC-1701-E Poster
Poster Qt. ___ @ $19.95 each _____
Limited Edition Poster
Poster Qt. ___ @ $40.00 each _____

U.S.S. Enterprise NCC-1701 Poster
Poster Qt. ___ @ $14.95 each _____
Limited Edition Poster
Poster Qt. ___ @ $30.00 each _____
$4 Shipping U.S. Each _____
$10 Shipping Foreign Each _____
Michigan Residents Add 6% Tax _____
TOTAL _____

METHOD OF PAYMENT (U.S. FUNDS ONLY)
☐ Check ☐ Money Order ☐ MasterCard ☐ Visa
Account # __ __ __ __ - __ __ __ __ - __ __ __ __ - __ __ __ __

Card Expiration Date ___/___(Mo./Yr.)
Your Day Time Phone (___) - _____

Your Signature _____

SHIP TO ADDRESS:
NAME: _____
ADDRESS: _____
CITY: _____ STATE: _____
POSTAL CODE: _____ COUNTRY: _____

Mail, Phone, or Fax Orders to:
SciPubTech • 15318 Mack Avenue • Grosse Pointe Park • Michigan 48230
Phone 313.884.6882 Fax 313.885.7426 Web Site http://www.scipubtech.com

TM & © 1996 Paramount Pictures. All rights reserved. STAR TREK and Related Marks are Trademarks of Paramount Pictures.
SciPubTech Authorized User.

ST5196

SIMON & SCHUSTER AUDIO

Simon & Schuster   A Viacom Company

A DAZZLING AUDIO PRODUCTION ENHANCED WITH SOUND EFFECTS AND AN ORIGINAL SCORE!

STAR TREK VOYAGER
MOSAIC
JERI TAYLOR

Captain Kathryn Janeway and the crew of the U.S.S. *Voyager* are fighting a desperate battle to save their ship and their comrades stranded on an alien planet. Facing a tough decision about the lives of her crew, Capt. Janeway reflects on the toughest episodes in her life, from Starfleet Academy to her first command, and the tragic secret that drives her to ever-greater heights of accomplishment. Read by Kate Mulgrew, who stars as Janeway on television's *Star Trek: Voyager*.

☐ **MOSAIC**
by Jeri Taylor
Read by Kate Mulgrew
ISBN: 0-671-57400-0
3 Hours/2 Cassettes
$18.00/$24.00 Can.

Simon & Schuster Mail Order
200 Old Tappen Rd., Old Tappan, N.J. 07675

Please send me the tape I have checked above. I am enclosing $_____ (please add $0.75 to cover the postage and handling for each order. Please add appropriate sales tax). Send check or money order—no cash or C.O.D.'s please. Allow up to six weeks for delivery. For purchase over $10.00 you may use VISA: card number, expiration date and customer signature must be included.

Name _____
Address _____
City _____ State/Zip _____
VISA Card # _____ Exp.Date _____
Signature _____ 1364